KT-385-419

Ken Follett was only twenty-seven when he wrote the award-winning novel *Eye of the Needle,* which became an international bestseller. He has since written several equally successful novels including, most recently, *Whiteout.* He is also the author of the non-fiction bestseller, *On Wings of Eagles.* He lives with his family in London and Hertfordshire.

Visit the Ken Follett web site at http://www.ken-follett.com

Also by Ken Follett

THE MODIGLIANI SCANDAL

PAPER MONEY

TRIPLE

THE KEY TO REBECCA

THE MAN FROM ST PETERSBURG

LIE DOWN WITH LIONS

THE PILLARS OF THE EARTH

NIGHT OVER WATER

A DANGEROUS FORTUNE

A PLACE CALLED FREEDOM

THE THIRD TWIN

THE HAMMER OF EDEN

CODE TO ZERO

JACKDAWS

HORNET FLIGHT

Non-fiction

ON WINGS OF EAGLES

KEN FOLLETT

EYE OF THE NEEDLE
&
WHITEOUT

PAN BOOKS

Eye of the Needle first published 1978 by Arbor House, New York.
First published in Great Britain 1978 by Futura as *Storm Island.*
First published by Pan Books 1998.
Whiteout first published 2004 by Macmillan.
First published in paperback 2005 by Pan Books.

This omnibus first published 2007 by Pan Books
an imprint of Pan Macmillan, a division of Macmillan Publishers limited
Pan Macmillan, 20 New Wharf Road, London N1 9RR
Basingstoke and Oxford
Associated companies throughout the world
www.panmacmillan.com

ISBN 978-0-330-45205-2

Eye of the Needle copyright © Ken Follett 1978
Whiteout copyright © Ken Follett 2004

The right of Ken Follett to be identified as the
author of this work has been asserted by him in accordance
with the Copyright, Designs and Patents Act 1988.

All rights reserved. No part of this publication may be
reproduced, stored in or introduced into a retrieval system, or
transmitted, in any form, or by any means (electronic, mechanical,
photocopying, recording or otherwise) without the prior written
permission of the publisher. Any person who does any unauthorized
act in relation to this publication may be liable to criminal
prosecution and civil claims for damages.

3 5 7 9 8 6 4

A CIP catalogue record for this book is available from
the British Library.

Printed and bound in the UK by
CPI Mackays, Chatham ME5 8TD

This book is sold subject to the condition that it shall not,
by way of trade or otherwise, be lent, re-sold, hired out,
or otherwise circulated without the publisher's prior consent
in any form of binding or cover other than that in which
it is published and without a similar condition including this
condition being imposed on the subsequent purchaser.

EYE OF THE NEEDLE

The Germans were almost completely deceived – only Hitler guessed right, and he hesitated to back his hunch . . .

A. J. P. Taylor
English History 1914–1945

PREFACE

Early in 1944 German Intelligence was piecing together evidence of a huge army in south-eastern England. Reconnaissance planes brought back photographs of barracks and airfields and fleets of ships in the Wash; General George S. Patton was seen in his unmistakable pink jodhpurs walking his white bulldog; there were bursts of wireless activity, signals between regiments, in the area; confirming signs were reported by German spies in Britain.

There was no army, of course. The ships were rubber-and-timber fakes, the barracks no more real than a movie set; Patton did not have a single man under his command; the radio signals were meaningless; the spies were double agents.

The object was to fool the enemy into preparing for an invasion via the Pas de Calais, so that on D-Day the Normandy assault would have the advantage of surprise.

It was a huge, near-impossible deception. Literally thousands of people were involved in perpetrating the trick. It would have been a miracle if none of Hitler's spies ever got to know about it.

Were there any spies? At the time people thought

they were surrounded by what were then called Fifth Columnists. After the war a myth grew up that MI5 had rounded up the lot by Christmas 1939. The truth seems to be that there were very few: MI5 did capture nearly all of them.

But it only needs one . . .

We know that the Germans saw the signs they were meant to see in East Anglia. We also know that they suspected a trick. And we know that they tried very hard to discover the truth.

That much is history, and I have discovered no facts that aren't already in history books. What follows is fiction.

Still and all, I think something like this must have happened . . .

Camberley, Surrey
June 1977

*My thanks to Malcolm Hulke for
invaluable help, generously given.*

Part One

CHAPTER ONE

IT WAS the coldest winter for forty-five years. Villages in the English countryside were cut off by the snow, and the Thames froze over. One day in January the Glasgow to London train arrived at Euston twenty-four hours late. The snow and the blackout combined to make motoring perilous: road accidents doubled, and people told jokes about how it was more risky to drive an Austin Seven along Piccadilly at night than to take a tank across the Siegfried Line.

Then, when the spring came, it was glorious. Barrage balloons floated majestically in bright blue skies, and soldiers on leave flirted with girls in sleeveless dresses on the streets of London.

The city did not look much like the capital of a nation at war. There were signs, of course; and Henry Faber, cycling from Waterloo Station toward Highgate, noted them: piles of sandbags outside important public buildings, Anderson shelters in suburban gardens, propaganda posters about evacuation and Air Raid Precautions. Faber watched such things – he was considerably more observant than the average railway clerk. He saw crowds of children in the parks, and concluded that evacuation had been a failure. He marked the number of motor cars on the road, despite petrol rationing; and he read about the new models announced by the motor manufacturers. He knew the significance of night-shift workers pouring into factories where, only months previously, there had been hardly enough work for the day shift. Most of all he monitored the movement of troops around Britain's railway network: all the paperwork passed through his office. One could learn a lot from that paperwork. Today, for example, he had rubber-stamped a batch of forms which led him to believe that a new Expeditionary Force was being gathered. He was fairly sure that it would have a complement of about 100,000 men, and that it was for Finland.

There were signs, yes; but there was something jokey about it all. Radio shows satirised the red tape of wartime regulations, there was community singing in the air-raid shelters, and fashionable women carried their gas masks in couturier-designed containers. They talked about the Bore War. It was at once larger-than-life and trivial, like a moving-picture show. All the air-raid warnings, without exception, had been false alarms.

Faber had a different point of view – but then, he was a different kind of person.

He steered his cycle into Archway Road and leaned forward a little to take the uphill slope, his long legs pumping as tirelessly as the pistons of a railway engine. He was very fit for his age, which was thirty-nine, although he lied about it: he lied about most things, as a safety precaution.

4

He began to perspire as he climbed the hill into Highgate. The building in which he lived was one of the highest in London, which was why he chose to live there. It was a Victorian brick house at one end of a terrace of six. The houses were high, narrow and dark, like the minds of the men for whom they had been built. Each had three storeys plus a basement with a servants' entrance – the English middle class of the nineteenth century insisted on a servants' entrance, even if they had no servants. Faber was a cynic about the English.

Number six had been owned by Mr Harold Garden, of Garden's Tea And Coffee, a small company which went broke in the Slump. Having lived by the principle that insolvency is a mortal sin, the bankrupt Mr Garden had no option but to die. The house was all he bequeathed to his widow, who was then obliged to take in lodgers. She enjoyed being a landlady, although the etiquette of her social circle demanded that she pretend to be a little ashamed of it. Faber had a room on the top floor with a dormer window. He lived there from Monday to Friday, and told Mrs Garden that he spent weekends with his mother in Erith. In fact he had another landlady in Blackheath who called him Mr Baker and believed he was a travelling salesman for a stationery manufacturer and spent all week on the road.

He wheeled his cycle up the garden path under the disapproving frown of the tall front-room windows. He put it in the shed and padlocked it to the lawn-mower – it was against the law to leave a vehicle unlocked. The

5

seed potatoes in boxes all around the shed were sprouting. Mrs Garden had turned her flower beds over to vegetables for the war effort.

Faber entered the house, hung his hat on the hall-stand, washed his hands and went in to tea.

Three of the other lodgers were already eating: a pimply boy from Yorkshire who was trying to get into the Army; a confectionery salesman with receding sandy hair; and a retired naval officer who, Faber was convinced, was a degenerate. Faber nodded to them and sat down.

The salesman was telling a joke. 'So the Squadron-Leader says, "You're back early!" and the pilot turns round and says, "Yes, I dropped my leaflets in bundles, wasn't that right?" so the Squadron-Leader says, "Good God! You might've hurt somebody!"'

The naval officer cackled and Faber smiled. Mrs Garden came in with a teapot. 'Good evening, Mr Faber. We started without you – I hope you don't mind.'

Faber spread margarine thinly on a slice of whole-meal bread, and momentarily yearned for a fat sausage. 'Your seed potatoes are ready to plant,' he told her.

Faber hurried through his tea. The others were arguing over whether Chamberlain should be sacked and replaced by Churchill. Mrs Garden kept voicing opinions then looking at Faber for a reaction. She was a blowsy woman, a little overweight. About Faber's age, she wore the clothes of a woman of thirty, and he guessed she wanted another husband. He kept out of the discussion.

Mrs Garden turned on the radio. It hummed for a while, then an announcer said: 'This is the BBC Home Service. *It's That Man Again*!'

Faber had heard the show. It regularly featured a German spy called Funf. He excused himself and went up to his room.

Mrs Garden was left alone after *It's That Man Again*: the naval officer went to the pub with the salesman, and the boy from Yorkshire, who was religious, went to a prayer meeting. She sat in the parlour with a small glass of gin, looking at the blackout curtains and thinking about Mr Faber. She wished he wouldn't spend so much time in his room. She needed company, and he was the kind of company she needed.

Such thoughts made her feel guilty. To assuage the guilt she thought of Mr Garden. Her memories were familiar but blurred, like an old print of a movie with worn sprocket-holes and an indistinct soundtrack; so that, although she could easily remember what it was like to have him here in the room with her, it was difficult to imagine his face, or the clothes he might be wearing, or the comment he would make on the day's war news. He had been a small, dapper man, successful in business when he was lucky and unsuccessful when he was not, undemonstrative in public and insatiably affectionate in bed. She had loved him a lot. There would be many women in her position if this war ever got going properly. She poured another drink.

Mr Faber was a quiet one – that was the trouble. He didn't seem to have any vices. He didn't smoke, she had never smelled drink on his breath, and he spent every evening in his room, listening to classical music on his radio. He read a lot of newspapers and went for long walks. She suspected he was quite clever, despite his humble job: his contributions to the conversation in the dining-room were always a shade more thoughtful than anyone else's. He surely could get a better job if he tried. He seemed not to give himself the chance he deserved.

It was the same with his appearance. He was a fine figure of a man: tall, quite heavy around the neck and shoulders, not a bit fat, with long legs. And he had a strong face, with a high forehead and a long jaw and bright blue eyes; not pretty, like a film star, but the kind of face that appealed to a woman. Except for the mouth – that was small and thin, and she could imagine him being cruel. Mr Garden had been incapable of cruelty.

And yet at first sight he was not the kind of man a woman would look at twice. The trousers of his old worn suit were never pressed – she would have done that for him, and gladly, but he never asked – and he always wore a shabby raincoat and a flat docker's cap. He had no moustache, and his hair was trimmed short every fortnight. It was as if he wanted to look like a nonentity.

He needed a woman, there was no doubt of that. She wondered for a moment whether he might be what people called effeminate, but she dismissed the idea quickly. He needed a wife to smarten him up and give him ambition. She needed a man to keep her company and for – well, love.

Yet he never made a move. Sometimes she could scream with frustration. She was sure she was attractive. She looked in a mirror as she poured another gin. She had a nice face, and fair curly hair, and there was something for a man to get hold of ... She giggled at that thought. She must be getting tiddly.

She sipped her drink and considered whether *she* ought to make the first move. Mr Faber was obviously shy – chronically shy. He wasn't sexless – she could tell by the look in his eyes on the two occasions he had seen her in her nightdress. Perhaps she could overcome his shyness by being brazen. What did she have to lose? She tried imagining the worst, just to see what it felt like. Suppose he rejected her. Well, it would be embarrassing – even humiliating. It would be a blow to her pride. But nobody else need know it had happened. He would just have to leave.

The thought of rejection had put her off the whole idea. She got to her feet slowly, thinking: I'm just not the brazen type. It was bedtime. If she had one more gin in bed she would be able to sleep. She took the bottle upstairs.

Her bedroom was below Mr Faber's, and she could hear violin music from his radio as she undressed. She put on a new nightdress – pink, with an embroidered neckline, and no one to see it! – and made her last drink. She wondered what Mr Faber looked like undressed. He would have a flat stomach, and hairs on his nipples, and you would be able to see his ribs, because he was slim. He probably had a small bottom. She giggled again, thinking: I'm a disgrace.

She took her drink to bed and picked up her book, but it was too much effort to focus on the print. Besides, she was bored with vicarious romance. Stories about dangerous love affairs were fine when you yourself had a perfectly safe love affair with your husband, but a woman needed more than Barbara Cartland. She sipped her gin, and wished Mr Faber would turn the radio off. It was like trying to sleep at a tea-dance!

She could, of course, ask him to turn it off. She looked at her bedside clock: it was past ten. She could put on her dressing-gown, which matched the night-dress, and just comb her hair a little, then step into her slippers – quite dainty, with a pattern of roses – and just pop up the stairs to the next landing, and just, well, tap on his door. He would open it, perhaps wearing his trousers and singlet, and then he would *look* at her the way he had *looked* when he saw her in her nightdress on the way to the bathroom . . .

'Silly old fool,' she said to herself aloud. 'You're just making excuses to go up there.'

And then she wondered why she needed excuses. She was a mature adult, and it was her house, and in ten years she had not met another man who was just right for her, and what the *hell*, she needed to feel someone strong and hard and hairy on top of her, squeezing her breasts and panting in her ear and parting her thighs with his broad flat hands, for tomorrow the gas bombs might come over from Germany and they would all die choking and gasping and poisoned and she would have lost her last chance.

So she drained her glass, and got out of bed, and put on her dressing-gown, and just combed her hair a little, and stepped into her slippers, and picked up her bunch of keys in case he had locked the door and couldn't hear her knock above the sound of the radio.

There was nobody on the landing. She found the stairs in the darkness. She intended to step over the stair that creaked, but she stumbled on the loose carpet and trod on it heavily; but it seemed that nobody heard, so she went on up and tapped on the door at the top. She tried it gently. It was locked.

The radio was turned down, and Mr Faber called out: 'Yes?'

He was well-spoken: not cockney, or foreign – not anything, really, just a pleasantly neutral voice.

She said: 'Can I have a word with you?'

He seemed to hesitate, then he said: 'I'm undressed.'

'So am I,' she giggled, and she opened the door with her duplicate key. He was standing in front of the radio with some kind of screwdriver in his hand. He wore his trousers and *no* singlet. His face was white and he looked scared to death.

She stepped inside and closed the door behind her, not knowing what to say. Suddenly she remembered a line from an American film, and she said: 'Would you buy a lonely girl a drink?' It was silly, really, because she knew he had no drink in his room, and she certainly wasn't dressed to go out; but it sounded vampish.

It seemed to have the desired effect. Without speaking, he came slowly toward her. He *did* have hair on his nipples. She took a step forward, and then his arms went around her, and she closed her eyes and turned up her face, and he kissed her, and she moved slightly in his arms, and then there was a terrible, awful, unbearable *sharp* pain in her back and she opened her mouth to scream.

He had heard her stumble on the stairs. If she'd waited another minute he would have had the radio transmitter back in its case and the code books in the drawer and there would have been no need for her to die. But before he could conceal the evidence he had heard her key in the lock, and when she opened the door the stiletto had been in his hand.

Because she moved slightly in his arms, Faber missed her heart with the first jab of the weapon, and he had to thrust his fingers down her throat to stop her crying out. He jabbed again, but she moved again and the blade struck a rib and merely slashed her superficially. Then the blood was spurting and he knew it would not be a clean kill, it never was when you missed with the first stroke.

She was wriggling too much to be killed with a jab now. Keeping his fingers in her mouth, he gripped her jaw with his thumb and pushed her back against the door. Her head hit the woodwork with a loud bump, and he wished he had not turned the radio down, but how could he have expected this?

He hesitated before killing her, because it would be much better if she died on the bed – better for the cover-up which was already taking shape in his mind – but he could not be sure of getting her that far in silence. He tightened his hold on her jaw, kept her head still by jamming it against the door, and brought the stiletto around in a wide slashing arc that ripped away most of her throat, for the stiletto was not a slashing knife and the throat was not Faber's favoured target.

He jumped back to avoid the first horrible gush of blood, then stepped forward again to catch her before she hit the floor. He dragged her to the bed, trying not to look at her neck, and laid her down.

He had killed before, so he expected the reaction: it always came as soon as he felt safe. He went over to the sink in the corner of the room and waited for it. He could see his face in the little shaving mirror. He was white, and his eyes were staring. He looked at himself and thought: *Killer*. Then he threw up.

When that was over he felt better. He could go to work now. He knew what he had to do: the details had come to him even while he was killing her.

He washed his face, brushed his teeth, and cleaned the washbasin. Then he sat down at the table beside his radio. He looked at his notebook, found his place, and began tapping the key. It was a long message, about the mustering of an army for Finland, and he had been half way through when he was interrupted. It was written down in cipher on the pad. When he had completed it he signed off with: 'Regards to Willi.'

The transmitter packed away neatly into a specially designed suitcase. Faber put the rest of his possessions

13

into a second case. He took off his trousers and sponged the bloodstains, then washed himself all over.

At last he looked at the corpse.

He was able to be cold about her now. It was wartime; they were enemies: if he had not killed her, she would have caused his death. She had been a threat, and all he felt now was relief that the threat had been nullified. She should not have frightened him.

Nevertheless, his last task was distasteful. He opened her robe and lifted her nightdress, pulling it up around her waist. She was wearing knickers. He tore them, so that the hair of her pubis was visible. Poor woman: she had wanted only to seduce him. But he could not have got her out of the room without her seeing the transmitter; and the British propaganda had made these people alert for spies – ridiculously so: if the Abwehr had as many agents as the newspapers made out then the British would have lost the war already.

He stepped back and looked at her with his head on one side. There was something wrong. He tried to think like a sex maniac. If I were crazed with lust for a woman like Una Garden, and I killed her just so that I could have my way with her, what would I then do?

Of course: that kind of lunatic would want to look at her breasts. Faber leaned over the body, gripped the neckline of the nightdress, and ripped it to the waist. Her large breasts sagged sideways.

The police doctor would soon discover that she had not been raped, but Faber did not think that mattered. He had taken a criminology course at Heidelberg, and he knew that many sexual assaults were not consummated. Besides, he could not have carried the deception that far, not even for the Fatherland. He was not in the SS. Some of *them* would queue up to rape the corpse . . . He put the thought out of his mind.

He washed his hands again and got dressed. It was almost midnight. He would wait an hour before leaving: it would be safer later.

He sat down to think about how he had gone wrong.

There was no question that he had made a mistake. If his cover were perfect, he would be totally secure. If he were totally secure no one could discover his secret. Mrs Garden had discovered his secret – or rather, she would have if she had lived a few seconds longer – therefore he had not been totally secure, therefore his cover was not perfect, therefore he had made a mistake.

He should have put a bolt on the door. Better to be thought chronically shy than to have landladies with duplicate keys sneaking in at night in their bedwear.

That was the surface error. The deep flaw was that he was too eligible to be a bachelor. He thought this with irritation, not conceit. He knew that he was a pleasant, attractive man, and that there was no apparent reason why he should be single. He turned his mind to thinking up a cover that would explain this without inviting advances from the Mrs Gardens of this world.

He ought to be able to find inspiration in his real personality. Why *was* he single? He stirred uneasily: he did not like mirrors. The answer was simple. He was

15

single because of his profession. If there were deeper reasons, he did not want to know them.

He would have to spend tonight in the open. Highgate Wood would do. In the morning he would take his suitcases to a railway station left-luggage office, then tomorrow evening he would go to his room in Blackheath.

He would shift to his second identity. He had little fear of being caught by the police. The commercial traveller who occupied the room at Blackheath on weekends looked rather different from the railway clerk who had killed his landlady. The Blackheath persona was expansive, vulgar and flashy. He wore loud ties, bought rounds of drinks, and combed his hair differently. The police would circulate a description of a shabby little pervert who would not say boo to a goose until he was inflamed with lust, and no one would look twice at the handsome salesman in the striped suit who was obviously the type that was more or less permanently inflamed with lust and did not have to kill women to get them to show him their breasts.

He would have to set up another identity – he always kept at least two. He needed a new job, fresh papers – passport, identity card, ration book, birth certificate. It was all so *risky*. Damn Mrs Garden. Why couldn't she have drunk herself to sleep as usual?

It was one o'clock. Faber took a last look around the room. He was not concerned about leaving clues – his fingerprints were obviously all over the house, and there would be no doubt in anyone's mind about who was the murderer. Nor did he feel any sentiment about leaving the place that had been his home for two years: he had never thought of it as home. He had never thought of anywhere as home.

He would always think of this as the place where he had learned to put a bolt on a door.

He turned out the light, picked up his cases, and crept down the stairs and out of the door into the night.

CHAPTER TWO

HENRY II was a remarkable king. In an age when the term 'flying visit' had not yet been coined, he flitted between England and France with such rapidity that he was credited with magical powers; a rumour which, understandably, he did nothing to suppress. In 1173 – either the June or the September, depending upon which secondary source one favours – he arrived in England and left for France again so quickly that no contemporary writer ever found out about it. Later historians discovered the record of his expenditure in the Pipe Rolls. At the time his kingdom was under attack by his sons at its northern and southern extremes – the Scottish border and the South of France. But what, precisely, was the purpose of his visit? Whom did he see? Why was it secret, when the myth of his magical speed was worth an army? What did he accomplish?

This was the problem that taxed Percival Godliman in the summer of 1940, when Hitler's armies swept across the French cornfields like a scythe, and the British poured out of the Dunkirk bottleneck in bloody disarray.

Professor Godliman knew more about the Middle

Ages than any man alive. His book on the Black Death had upended every convention of medievalism; it had also been a bestseller and published as a Penguin. With that behind him he had turned to a slightly earlier and even more intractable period.

At 12.30 on a splendid June day in London, a secretary found Godliman hunched over an illuminated manuscript, laboriously translating its medieval Latin, making notes in his own even less legible handwriting. The secretary, who was planning to eat her lunch in the garden of Gordon Square, did not like the manuscript room because it smelled dead. You needed so many keys to get in there, it might as well have been a tomb.

Godliman stood at a lectern, perched on one leg like a bird, his face lit bleakly by a spotlight above: he might have been the ghost of the monk who wrote the book, standing a cold vigil over his precious chronicle. The girl cleared her throat and waited for him to notice her. She saw a short man in his fifties, with round shoulders and weak eyesight, wearing a tweed suit. She knew he could be perfectly sensible once you dragged him out of the Middle Ages. She coughed again and said: 'Professor Godliman?'

He looked up, and when he saw her he smiled, and then he did not look like a ghost, more like someone's dotty father. 'Hello!' he said, in an astonished tone, as if he had just met his next-door neighbour in the middle of the Sahara Desert.

'You asked me to remind you that you have lunch at the Savoy with Colonel Terry.'

'Oh, yes.' He took his watch out of his waistcoat

pocket and peered at it. 'If I'm going to walk it, I'd better leave now.'

She nodded. 'I brought your gas mask.'

'You are thoughtful!' He smiled again, and she decided he looked quite nice. He took the mask from her and said: 'Do I need my coat?'

'You didn't wear one this morning. It's quite warm. Shall I lock up after you?'

'Thank you, thank you.' He jammed his notebook into his jacket pocket and went out.

The secretary looked around, shivered, and followed him.

Colonel Andrew Terry was a red-faced Scot, pauper-thin from a lifetime of heavy smoking, with sparse dark-blond hair thickly brilliantined. Godliman found him at a corner table in the Savoy Grill, wearing civilian clothes. There were three cigarette stubs in the ashtray. He stood up to shake hands.

Godliman said: 'Morning, Uncle Andrew.' Terry was his mother's baby brother.

'How are you, Percy?'

'I'm writing a book about the Plantagenets.' Godliman sat down.

'Are your manuscripts still in London? I'm surprised.'

'Why?'

Terry lit another cigarette. 'Move them to the country in case of bombing.'

'Should I?'

'Half the National Gallery has been shoved into a bloody big hole in the ground somewhere up in Wales. Young Kenneth Clark is quicker off the mark than you. Might be sensible to take yourself off out of it too, while you're about it. I don't suppose you've many students left.'

'That's true.' Godliman took a menu from a waiter and said: 'I don't want a drink.'

Terry did not look at his menu. 'Seriously, Percy, why are you still in Town?'

Godliman's eyes seemed to clear, like the image on a screen when the projector is focused, as if he had to think for the first time since he walked in. 'It's all right for children to leave, and national institutions like Bertrand Russell. But for me – well, it's a bit like running away and letting other people fight for you. I realize that's not a strictly logical argument. It's a matter of sentiment, not logic.'

Terry smiled the smile of one whose expectations have been fulfilled. But he dropped the subject and looked at the menu. After a moment he said: 'Good God. *Le Lord Woolton Pie.*'

Godliman grinned. 'I'm sure it's still just potatoes and vegetables.'

When they had ordered, Terry said: 'What do you think of our new Prime Minister?'

'The man's an ass. But then, Hitler's a fool, and look how well he's doing. You?'

'We can live with Winston. At least he's bellicose.'

Godliman raised his eyebrows. '"We?" Are you back in the game?'

21

'I never really left it, you know.'

'But you said—'

'Percy. Can't you think of a department whose staff all say they don't work for the Army?'

'Well, I'm damned. All this time . . .'

Their first course came, and they started a bottle of white Bordeaux. Godliman ate potted salmon and looked pensive.

Eventually Terry said: 'Thinking about the last lot?'

Godliman nodded. 'Young days, you know. Terrible time.' But his tone was wistful.

'This war isn't the same at all. My chaps don't go behind enemy lines and count bivouacs like you did. Well, they do, but that side of things is much less important this time. Nowadays we just listen to the wireless.'

'Don't they broadcast in code?'

Terry shrugged. 'Codes can be broken. Candidly, we get to know just about everything we need these days.'

Godliman glanced around, but there was no one within earshot, and it was not for him to tell Terry that careless talk costs lives.

Terry went on: 'In fact my job is to make sure *they* don't have the information they need about *us*.'

They both had chicken pie to follow. There was no beef on the menu. Godliman fell silent, but Terry talked on.

'Canaris is a funny chap, you know. Admiral Wilhelm Canaris, head of the Abwehr. I met him before this lot started. Likes England. My guess is he's none too fond of Hitler. Anyway, we know he's been told to mount a major intelligence operation against us, in preparation for the invasion – but he's not doing much. We arrested their best man in England the day after war broke out. He's in Wandsworth prison now. Useless people, Canaris's spies. Old ladies in boarding-houses, mad Fascists, petty criminals—'

Godliman said: 'Look here, old boy, this is too much.' He trembled slightly with a mixture of anger and incomprehension. 'All this stuff is secret. I don't want to know!'

Terry was unperturbed. 'Would you like something else?' he offered. 'I'm having chocolate ice-cream.'

Godliman stood up. 'I don't think so. I'm going to go back to my work, if you don't mind.'

Terry looked up at him coolly. 'The world can wait for your reappraisal of the Plantagenets, Percy. There's a war on, dear boy. I want you to work for me.'

Godliman stared down at him for a long moment. 'What on earth would I do?'

Terry smiled wolfishly. 'Catch spies.'

Walking back to the college, Godliman felt depressed despite the weather. He would accept Colonel Terry's offer: no doubt about that. His country was at war; it was a just war; and if he was too old to fight, he was still young enough to help.

But the thought of leaving his work – and for how many years? – depressed him. He loved history, and he had been totally absorbed in medieval England since the death of his wife ten years ago. He liked the unravelling of mysteries, the discovery of faint clues, the resolution of contradictions, the unmasking of lies and propaganda and myth. His new book would be the best on its subject written in the last hundred years, and there would not be one to equal it for another century. It had ruled his life for so long that the thought of abandoning it was almost unreal, as difficult to digest as the discovery that one is an orphan and no relation at all to the people one has always called Mother and Father.

An air-raid warning stridently interrupted his thoughts. He contemplated ignoring it: so many people did now, and he was only ten minutes' walk from the college. But he had no real reason to return to his study – he knew he would do no more work today. So he hurried into a Tube station and joined the solid mass of Londoners crowding down the staircases and on to the grimy platform. He stood close to the wall, staring at a Bovril poster, and thought: But it's not just the things I'm leaving behind.

Going back into the game depressed him, too. There were some things he liked about it: the importance of *little* things, the value of simply being clever, the meticulousness, the guesswork. But he hated the blackmail and the treachery, the deceit, the desperation, and the way one always stabbed the enemy in the back.

The platform was becoming more crowded. Godliman sat down while there was still room, and found himself leaning against a man in bus-driver's uniform. The man smiled and said: 'Oh to be in England, now that summer's here. Know who said that?'

'Now that April's there,' Godliman corrected him. 'It was Browning.'

'I heard it was Adolf Hitler,' the driver said. A woman next to him squealed with laughter, and he turned his attention to her. 'Did you hear what the evacuee said to the farmer's wife?'

Godliman tuned out and remembered an April when he had longed for England, crouching on a high branch of a plane tree, peering through a cold mist across a French valley behind the German lines. He could see nothing but vague dark shapes, even through his telescope, and he was about to slide down and walk a mile or so farther when three German soldiers came from nowhere to sit around the base of the tree and smoke. After a while they took out cards and began to play, and young Percival Godliman realized they had found a way of skiving off and were here for the day. He stayed in the tree, hardly moving, until he began to shiver and his muscles knotted with cramp and his bladder felt as if it would burst. Then he took out his revolver and shot the three of them, one after another, through the tops of their close-cropped heads. And three people, laughing and cursing and gambling their pay, had simply ceased to exist. It was the first time he killed, and all he could think was: Just because I had to pee.

Godliman shifted on the cold concrete of the station platform and let the memory fade away. There was a warm wind from the tunnel and a train came in. The people who got off found spaces and settled to wait. Godliman listened to the voices.

'Did you hear Churchill on the wireless? We was listening in at the Duke of Wellington. Old Jack Thornton cried. Silly old bugger . . .'

'From what I can gather Kathy's boy's in a stately home and got his own footman! My Alfie milks the cow . . .'

'Haven't had fillet steak on the menu for so long I've forgotton the bally taste . . . wine committee saw the war coming and bought in twenty thousand dozen, thank God . . .'

'Yes, a quiet wedding, but what's the point in waiting when you don't know what the next day's going to bring?'

'They call it Spring, Ma, he says to me, and they have one down here every year . . .'

'She's pregnant again, you know . . . yes, thirteen years since the last . . . I thought I'd found out what was causing it!'

'No, Peter never came back from Dunkirk . . .'

The bus driver offered him a cigarette. Godliman refused, and took out his pipe. Someone started to sing.

> *A blackout warden passing yelled*
> *'Ma, pull down that blind—*
> *Just look at what you're showing,' and we*
> *Shouted 'Never mind.' Oh!*
> *Knees up Mother Brown . . .*

The song spread through the crowd until everyone was singing. Godliman joined in, knowing that this was a nation losing a war and singing to hide its fear, as a man will whistle past the graveyard at night; knowing that the sudden affection he felt for London and Londoners was an ephemeral sentiment, akin to mob hysteria; mistrusting the voice inside him which said 'This, this is what the war is about, this is what makes it worth fighting'; knowing but not caring, because for the first time in so many years he was feeling the sheer physical thrill of comradeship and he liked it.

When the all-clear sounded they went singing up the staircases and into the street, and Godliman found a phone box and called Colonel Terry to ask how soon he could start.

CHAPTER THREE

T HE SMALL country church was old and very beautiful. A dry-stone wall enclosed a graveyard where wild flowers grew. The church itself had been there – well, bits of it had – the last time Britain was invaded, almost a millennium ago. The north wall of the nave, several feet thick and pierced with only two tiny windows, could remember that last invasion; it had been built when churches were places of physical as well as spiritual sanctuary, and the little round-headed windows were better for shooting arrows out of than for letting the Lord's sunshine in. Indeed, the Local Defence Volunteers had detailed plans for using the church if and when the current bunch of European thugs crossed the Channel.

But no jackboots sounded in the tiled choir in this August of 1940; not yet. The sun glowed through stained-glass windows which had survived Cromwell's iconoclasts and Henry VIII's greed, and the roof resounded to the notes of an organ which had yet to yield to woodworm and dry rot.

It was a lovely wedding. Lucy wore white, of course; and her five sisters were bridesmaids in apricot dresses. David wore the Mess uniform of a Flying Officer in the

Royal Air Force, all crisp and new for it was the first time he had put it on. They sang Psalm 23, The Lord's My Shepherd, to the tune *Crimond*.

Lucy's father looked proud, as a man will on the day his eldest and most beautiful daughter marries a fine boy in a uniform. He was a farmer, but it was a long time since he had sat on a tractor: he rented out his arable land and used the rent to raise racehorses, although this winter of course his pasture would go under the plough and potatoes would be planted. Although he was really more gentleman than farmer, he nevertheless had the open-air skin, the deep chest, and the big stubby hands of agricultural people. Most of the men on that side of the church bore him a resemblance: barrel-chested men, with weathered red faces, those not in tail coats favouring tweed suits and stout shoes.

The bridesmaids had something of that look, too; they were country girls. But the bride was like her mother. Her hair was a dark, dark red, long and thick, shining and glorious, and she had wide-apart amber eyes set in an oval face; and when she looked at the vicar with that clear, direct gaze and said 'I will' in that firm, clear voice, the vicar was startled and thought, 'By God she means it!' which was an odd thought for a vicar to have in the middle of a wedding.

The family on the other side of the nave had a certain look about them, too. David's father was a lawyer: his permanent frown was a professional affectation, and concealed a sunny nature. (He had been a Major in the Army in the last war, and thought all this

business about the RAF and war in the air was a fad
which would soon pass.) But nobody looked like him,
not even his son who stood now at the altar promising
to love his wife until death, which might not be far
away, God forbid. No, they all looked like David's
mother, who sat beside her husband now, with almost-
black hair, dark skin and long, slender limbs.

David was the tallest of the lot. He had broken high-
jump records last year at Cambridge University. He was
rather too good-looking for a man – his face would
have been feminine were it not for the dark, ineradic-
able shadow of a heavy beard. He shaved twice a day.
He had long eyelashes, and he looked intelligent, as he
was, and sensitive, which he was not.

It was idyllic: two happy, handsome people, children
of solid, comfortably off, backbone-of-England type
families, getting married in a country church in the
finest summer weather Britain can offer.

When they were pronounced man and wife both
mothers were dry-eyed, and both the fathers cried.

Kissing the bride was a barbarous custom, Lucy thought
as yet another middle-aged pair of champagne-wet lips
smeared her cheek. It was probably descended from
even more barbarous customs in the Dark Ages, when
every man in the tribe was allowed to – well, anyway, it
was time we got properly civilized and dropped the
whole business.

She had known she would not like this part of the

wedding. She liked champagne, but she was not crazy about chicken drumsticks or dollops of caviar on squares of cold toast, and as for the speeches and the photographs and the honeymoon jokes, well . . . But it could have been worse. If it had been peacetime Father would have hired the Albert Hall.

So far nine people had said, 'May all your troubles be little ones,' and one person, with scarcely more originality, had said, 'I want to see more than a fence running around your garden.' Lucy had shaken count-less hands and pretended not to hear remarks like, 'I wouldn't mind being in David's pyjamas tonight.' David had made a speech in which he thanked Lucy's parents for giving him their daughter, as if she were an inani-mate object to be gift-wrapped in white satin and presented to the most deserving applicant. Lucy's father had been crass enough to say that he was not losing a daughter but gaining a son. It was all hopelessly gaga, but one did it for one's parents.

A distant uncle loomed up from the direction of the bar, swaying slightly, and Lucy repressed a shudder. She introduced him to her husband. 'David, this is Uncle Norman.'

Uncle Norman pumped David's bony hand. 'Well, m'boy, when do you take up your commission?'

'Tomorrow, sir.'

'What, no honeymoon?'

'Just twenty-four hours.'

'But you've only just finished your training, so I gather.'

'Yes, but I could fly before, you know. I learned at Cambridge. Besides, with all this going on they can't spare pilots. I expect I shall be in the air tomorrow.'

Lucy said quietly: 'David, don't,' but she was ignored.

'What'll you fly?' Uncle Norman asked with school-boy enthusiasm.

'Spitfire. I saw her yesterday. She's a lovely kite.' David had consciously adopted all the RAF slang, kites and crates and the drink and bandits at two o'clock. 'She's got eight guns, she does three hundred and fifty knots, and she'll turn around in a shoebox.'

'Marvellous, marvellous. You boys are certainly knocking the stuffing out of the Luftwaffe, what?'

'We got sixty yesterday for eleven of our own,' David said, as proudly as if he had shot them all down himself. 'The day before, when they had a go at Yorkshire, we sent the bally lot back to Norway with their tails between their legs – and we didn't lose a single kite!'

Uncle Norman gripped David's shoulder with tipsy fervour. 'Never,' he quoted pompously, 'was so much owed by so many to so few. Churchill said that the other day.'

David tried a modest grin. 'He must have been talking about the mess bills.'

Lucy hated the way they trivialized bloodshed and destruction. She said: 'David, we should go and change now.'

They went in separate cars to Lucy's home. Her mother helped her out of the wedding dress and said: 'Now, my dear, I don't quite know what you're expecting tonight, but you ought to know—'

'Oh, mother, don't be embarrassing,' Lucy interrupted. 'You're about ten years too late to tell me the facts of life. This *is* 1940, you know!'

Her mother coloured slightly. 'Very well, dear,' she said mildly. 'But if there is anything you want to talk about, later on . . .'

It occurred to Lucy that to say things like this cost her mother considerable effort, and she regretted her sharp reply. 'Thank you,' she said. She touched her mother's hand. 'I will.'

'I'll leave you to it, then. Call me if you want anything.' She kissed Lucy's cheek and went out.

Lucy sat at the dressing-table in her slip and began to brush her hair. She knew exactly what to expect tonight. She felt a faint glow of pleasure as she remembered.

It was a well-planned seduction, although at the time it did not occur to Lucy that David might have plotted every move beforehand.

It happened in June, a year after they had met at the Glad Rag Ball. They were seeing each other every week by this time, and David had spent part of the Easter vacation with Lucy's people. Mother and Father approved of him: he was handsome, clever and gentlemanly, and he came from precisely the same stratum of society as they did. Father thought he was a shade too opinionated, but Mother said the landed gentry had been saying that about undergraduates for six hundred years, and *she* thought David would be kind to his wife, which was the most important thing in the long run. So in June Lucy went to David's family home for a weekend.

The place was a Victorian copy of an eighteenth-century grange, a square-shaped house with nine bed-rooms and a terrace with a vista. What impressed Lucy about it was the realization that the people who planted the garden must have known they would be long dead before it reached maturity. The atmosphere was very easy, and the two of them drank beer on the terrace in the afternoon sunshine. That was when David told her that he had been accepted for officer training in the RAF, along with four pals from the university flying club. He wanted to be a fighter pilot.

'I can fly all right,' he said, 'and they'll need people once this war gets going – they say it'll be won and lost in the air, this time.'

'Aren't you afraid?' she said quietly.

'Not a bit,' he said. Then he covered his eyes with his hand and said: 'Yes, I am.'

She thought he was very brave, and held his hand.

A little later they put on swimming costumes and went down to the lake. The water was clear and cool, but the sun was still strong and the air was warm. They splashed about gleefully, as if they knew this was the end of their childhood.

'Are you a good swimmer?' he asked her.

'Better than you!'

'All right. Race you to the island.'

She shaded her eyes to look into the sun. She held the pose for a minute, pretending she did not know how desirable she was in her wet swimsuit with her arms raised and her shoulders back. The island was a small patch of bushes and trees about three hundred yards away, in the centre of the lake.

She dropped her hands, shouted 'Go!', and struck out in a fast crawl.

David won, of course, with his long arms and legs. Lucy found herself in difficulty when she was still fifty yards from the island. She switched to breaststroke, but she was too exhausted even for that, and she had to roll over on to her back and float. David, who was already sitting on the bank blowing like a walrus, slipped back into the water and swam to meet her. He got behind her, held her beneath the arms in the correct lifesaving position, and pulled her slowly to the shore. His hands were just below her breasts.

'I'm enjoying this,' he said, and she giggled despite her breathlessness.

A few moments later he said: 'I suppose I might as well tell you.'

'What?' she panted.

'The lake is only four feet deep.'

'You rogue!' She wriggled out of his arms, spluttering and laughing, and found her footing.

He took her hand and led her out of the water and through the trees. He pointed to an old wooden rowing-boat, rotting upside-down beneath a hawthorn. 'When I was a boy I used to row out here in that, with one of Papa's pipes, a box of matches, and a pinch of tobacco in a twist of paper. This is where I used to smoke it.'

They were in a clearing, completely surrounded by

bushes. The turf underfoot was clean and springy. Lucy flopped on the ground.

'We'll swim back slowly,' David said.

'Let's not even talk about it just yet,' she replied.

He sat beside her and kissed her, then pushed her gently backwards until she was lying down. He stroked her hip and kissed her throat, and soon she stopped shivering. When he laid his hand gently, nervously, on the soft mound between her legs, she arched upwards, willing him to press harder. She pulled his face to hers and kissed him open-mouthed and wetly. His hands went to the straps of her swimsuit, and he pulled them down over her shoulders. She said: 'No.'

He buried his face between her breasts. 'Lucy, please.'

'No.'

He looked at her. 'It might be my last chance.'

She rolled away from him and stood up. Then, because of the war, and because of the pleading look on his flushed young face, and because of the glow inside her which would not go away, she took off her costume with one swift movement, and removed her swimming-cap so that her dark red hair shook out over her shoulders, and knelt in front of him, taking his face in her hands and guiding his lips to her breast.

She lost her virginity painlessly, enthusiastically, and only a little too quickly.

The spice of guilt made the memory more pleasant, not less. If it had been a well-planned seduction then she had been a willing, not to say eager, victim, especially at the end.

She began to dress in her going-away outfit. She had startled him a couple of times, that afternoon on the island: once when she wanted him to kiss her breasts, and again when she had guided him inside her with her hands. Apparently such things did not happen in the books he read. Like most of her friends, Lucy read D. H. Lawrence for information about sex. She believed in his choreography and mistrusted the noises-off: the things his people did to one another sounded nice, but not that nice; she was not expecting trumpets and thunderstorms and the clash of cymbals at her sexual awakening.

David was a little more ignorant than she; but he was gentle, and he took pleasure in her pleasure, and she was sure that was the important thing.

They had done it only once since the first time. Exactly a week before their wedding they had made love again, and it caused their first row.

This time it was at her parents' house, in the morning after everyone else had left. He came to her room in his dressing-gown and got into bed with her. She almost changed her mind about Lawrence's trumpets and cymbals. David got out of bed immediately afterwards.

'Don't go,' she said.

'Somebody might come in.'

'I'll chance it. Come back to bed.' She was warm and drowsy and comfortable, and she wanted him beside her.

He put on his dressing-gown. 'It makes me nervous.'

'You weren't nervous five minutes ago.' She reached for him. 'Lie with me. I want to get to know your body.'

37

'My God, you're brazen.'

She looked at him to see whether he was joking, and when she realized he was not, she became angry. '*Just* what the *hell* does *that* mean?'

'You're just not . . . ladylike!'

'What a *stupid* thing to say—'

'You act like a – a – tart.'

She flounced out of bed, naked and furious, her lovely breasts heaving with rage. 'Just how much do you know about tarts?'

'Nothing!'

'How much do you know about women?'

'I know how a virgin is supposed to behave!'

'I am . . . I was . . . until I met you . . .' She sat on the edge of the bed and burst into tears.

That was the end of the quarrel, of course. David put his arms around her and said: 'I'm sorry, sorry, sorry. You're the first one for me, too, and I don't know what to expect, and I feel confused . . . I mean, nobody tells you anything about this, do they?'

She snuffled and shook her head in agreement, and it occurred to her that what was *really* unnerving him was the knowledge that in eight days' time he had to take off in a flimsy aircraft and fight for his life above the clouds; so she forgave him, and he dried her tears, and they got back into bed and held each other tightly for courage.

Lucy told her friend Joanna about the row, saying it was over a dress David thought to be brazen. Joanna said that couples always quarrelled before the wedding, usually the night before: it was the last chance to test the strength of their love.

She was just about ready. She examined herself in a full-length mirror. Her suit was faintly military, with square shoulders and epaulettes, but the blouse beneath it was feminine, for balance. Her hair fell in sausage curls beneath a natty pill-box hat. It would not have been right to go away gorgeously dressed, not this year; but she felt she had achieved the kind of briskly practical, yet attractive, look which was rapidly becoming fashionable.

David was waiting for her in the hall. He kissed her and said: 'You look wonderful, Mrs Rose.'

They were driven back to the reception to say goodbye to everyone, before leaving to spend the night in London, at Claridge's; then David would drive on to Biggin Hill and Lucy would come home again. She was going to live with her parents: she had the use of a cottage for when David was on leave.

There was another half-hour of handshakes and kisses, then they went out to the car. Some of David's cousins had got at his open-top MG. There were tin cans and an old boot tied to the bumpers with string, the running-boards were awash with confetti, and 'Just Married' was scrawled all over the paintwork in bright red lipstick.

They drove away, smiling and waving, the guests filling the street behind them. A mile down the road they stopped and cleaned up the car.

It was dusk when they got going again. David's

headlights were fitted with blackout masks, but he drove very fast just the same. Lucy felt very happy.

David said: 'There's a bottle of bubbly in the glove box.'

Lucy opened the compartment and found the champagne and two glasses carefully wrapped in tissue paper. It was still quite cold. The cork came out with a loud pop and shot off into the night. David lit a cigarette while Lucy poured the wine.

'We're going to be late for supper,' he said.

'Who cares?' She handed him a glass.

She was too tired to drink, really. She became sleepy. The car seemed to be going terribly fast. She let David have most of the champagne. He began to whistle *St Louis Blues*.

Driving through England in the blackout was a weird experience. One missed lights which one hadn't realized were there before the war: lights in cottage porches and farmhouse windows, lights on cathedral spires and inn signs, and – most of all – the luminous glow, low in the distant sky, of the thousand lights of a nearby town. Even if one had been able to see, there were no signposts to look at: they had been removed to confuse the German parachutists who were expected any day. (Just a few days ago in the Midlands farmers had found parachutes, radios and maps; but since there were no footprints leading away from the objects, it had been concluded that no men had landed, and the whole thing was a feeble Nazi attempt to panic the population.) Anyway, David knew the way to London.

They climbed a long hill. The little sports car took it

nimbly. Lucy gazed through half-closed eyes at the blackness ahead. The downside of the hill was steep and winding. Lucy heard the distant roar of an approaching lorry.

The MG's tyres squealed as David raced around the bends. 'I think you're going too fast,' Lucy said mildly.

The back of the car skidded on a left-hander. David changed down, afraid to brake in case he skidded again. On either side, the hedgerows were dimly picked out by the shaded headlights. There was a sharp right-hand bend, and David lost the back again. The curve seemed to go on and on forever. The little car slid sideways and turned through 180 degrees, so that it was going backwards; then continued to turn in the same direction.

Lucy screamed: 'David!'

The moon came out suddenly, and they saw the lorry. It was struggling up the hill at a snail's pace, with thick smoke, made silvery by the moonlight, pouring from its snout-shaped bonnet. Lucy glimpsed the driver's face, even his cloth cap and his moustache; his mouth was open in terror as he stood on his brakes.

The car was travelling forward again now. There was just room to pass the lorry if David could regain control of the car. He heaved the steering wheel over and touched the accelerator. It was a mistake.

The car and the lorry collided head-on.

CHAPTER FOUR

FOREIGNERS HAVE spies: Britain has Military
Intelligence. As if that were not euphemism
enough, it is abbreviated to MI. In 1940, MI was part of
the War Office. It was spreading like couch grass at the
time – not surprisingly – and its different sections were
known by numbers: MI9 ran the escape routes from
prisoner-of-war camps through Occupied Europe to
neutral countries; MI8 monitored enemy wireless
traffic, and was of more value than six regiments; MI6
sent agents into France.

It was MI5 that Professor Percival Godliman joined
in the autumn of 1940. He turned up at the War Office
in Whitehall on a cold September morning after a
night spent putting out fires all over the East End:
the Blitz was at its height and he was an Auxiliary
Fireman.

Military Intelligence was run by soldiers in peacetime, when – in Godliman's opinion – espionage made
no difference to anything anyhow; but now, he found,
it was populated by amateurs, and he was delighted to
discover that he knew half the people in MI5. On his
first day he met a barrister who was a member of his
club, an art historian with whom he had been to

college, an archivist from his own university, and his favourite writer of detective stories.

He was shown into Colonel Terry's office at ten a.m. Terry had been there for several hours: there were two empty cigarette packets in the waste-paper bin.

Godliman said: 'Should I call you "Sir" now?'

'There's not much bull around here, Percy. "Uncle Andrew" will do fine. Sit down.'

All the same, there was a briskness about Terry which had not been present when they had lunch at the Savoy. Godliman noticed that he did not smile, and his attention kept wandering to a pile of unread signals on the desk.

Terry looked at his watch and said: 'I'm going to put you in the picture, briefly – finish the lecture I started over lunch.'

Godliman smiled. 'This time I won't get up on my high horse.'

Terry lit another cigarette.

Canaris's spies in Britain were useless people (Terry resumed, as if their conversation had been interrupted five minutes rather than three months ago). Dorothy O'Grady was typical: we caught her cutting military telephone wires on the Isle of Wight. She was writing letters to Portugal in the kind of secret ink you buy in joke shops.

A new wave of spies began in September. Their task was to reconnoitre Britain in preparation for the invasion: to map beaches suitable for landings, fields and roads which could be used by troop-carrying gliders, tank traps and road blocks and barbed-wire obstacles.

They seem to have been badly selected, hastily mustered, inadequately trained and poorly equipped. Typical were the four who came over on the night of 2–3 September: Meier, Kieboom, Pons and Waldberg. Kieboom and Pons landed at dawn near Hythe, and were arrested by Private Tollervey of the Somerset Light Infantry, who came upon them in the sand-dunes tucking in to a dirty great *wurst*.

Waldberg actually managed to send a signal to Hamburg:

ARRIVED SAFELY. DOCUMENT DESTROYED. ENGLISH PATROL 200 METRES FROM COAST. BEACH WITH BROWN NETS AND RAILWAY SLEEPERS AT A DISTANCE OF 50 METRES. NO MINES. FEW SOLDIERS. UNFINISHED BLOCK-HOUSE. NEW ROAD. WALDBERG.

Clearly he did not know where he was, nor did he even have a code name. The quality of his briefing is indicated by the fact that he knew nothing of English licensing laws: he went into a pub at nine o'clock in the morning and asked for a quart of cider.

(Godliman laughed at this, and Terry said: 'Wait – it gets funnier.')

The landlord told Waldberg to come back at ten. He could spend the hour looking at the village church, he suggested. Amazingly, Waldberg was back at ten sharp, whereupon two policemen on bicycles arrested him.

('It's like a script for *It's That Man Again*,' said Godliman.)

Meier was found a few hours later. Eleven more

agents were picked up over the next few weeks, most of them within hours of landing on British soil. Almost all of them were destined for the scaffold.

('*Almost* all?' said Godliman. Terry said: 'Yes. A couple have been handed over to our section B-1(a). I'll come back to that in a minute.')

Others landed in Eire. One was Ernst Weber-Drohl, a well-known acrobat who had two illegitimate children in Ireland – he had toured music-halls there as 'The World's Strongest Man'. He was arrested by the Garda Siochania, fined three pounds, and turned over to B-1(a).

Another was Hermann Goetz, who parachuted into Ulster instead of Eire by mistake, was robbed by the IRA, swam the Boyne in his fur underwear, and eventually swallowed his suicide pill. He had a torch marked 'Made in Dresden'.

('If it's so easy to pick these bunglers up,' Terry said, 'why are we taking on brainy types like yourself to catch them? Two reasons. One: we've got no way of knowing how many we *haven't* picked up. Two: it's what we do with the ones we don't hang that matters. This is where B-1(a) comes in. But to explain that I have to go back to 1936.')

Alfred George Owens was an electrical engineer with a company that had a few government contracts. He visited Germany several times during the thirties, and voluntarily gave to the Admiralty odd bits of technical information he picked up there. Eventually Naval Intelligence passed him on to MI6 who began to develop him as an agent. The Abwehr recruited him at about the same time, as MI6 discovered when they intercepted a letter from him to a known German cover address. Clearly he was a man totally without loyalty: he just wanted to be a spy. We called him 'Snow'; the Germans called him 'Johnny'.

In January 1939 Snow got a letter containing (i) instructions for the use of a wireless transmitter and (ii) a ticket for the cloakroom at Victoria Station.

He was arrested the day after war broke out, and he and his transmitter (which he had picked up, in a suitcase, when he presented the cloakroom ticket) were locked up in Wandsworth Prison. He continued to communicate with Hamburg, but now all the messages were written by section B-1(a) of MI5.

The Abwehr put him in touch with two more German agents in England, whom we immediately nabbed. They also gave him a code and detailed wireless procedure, all of which was invaluable.

Snow was followed by Charlie, Rainbow, Summer, Biscuit, and eventually a small army of enemy spies, all in regular contact with Canaris, all apparently trusted by him, and all totally controlled by the British counter-intelligence apparatus.

At that point MI5 began dimly to glimpse an awesome and tantalizing prospect: with a bit of luck, *they could control and manipulate the entire German espionage network in Britain.*

'Turning agents into double agents instead of hanging them has two crucial advantages,' Terry wound up. 'Since the enemy thinks his spies are still active, he doesn't try to replace them with others who may not get caught. And, since *we* are supplying the information the spies tell their controllers, we can deceive the enemy and mislead his strategists.'

'It can't be that easy,' said Godliman.

'Certainly not.' Terry opened a window to let out the fug of cigarette and pipe smoke. 'To work, the system has to be very nearly total. If there is any substantial number of genuine agents here, their information will contradict that of the double agents and the Abwehr will smell a rat.'

'It sounds tremendously exciting,' Godliman said. His pipe had gone out.

Terry smiled for the first time that morning. 'The people here will tell you it's hard work – long hours, high tension, frustration – but yes, of course it's exciting.' He looked at his watch. 'Now I want you to meet a very bright young member of my staff. Let me walk you to his office.'

They went out of the room, up some stairs, and along several corridors. 'His name is Frederick Bloggs, and he gets annoyed if you make jokes about it,' Terry continued. 'We pinched him from Scotland Yard – he was an inspector with Special Branch. If you need arms and legs, use his. You'll rank above him, but I shouldn't make too much of that – we don't, here. I suppose I hardly need to say that to you.'

They entered a small, bare room which looked out on to a blank wall. There was no carpet. A photograph of a pretty girl hung on the wall, and there was a pair of handcuffs on the hat-stand.

Terry said: 'Frederick Bloggs, Percival Godliman. I'll leave you to it.'

The man behind the desk was blond, stocky and short – he must have been only just tall enough to get into the police force, Godliman thought. His tie was an eyesore, but he had a pleasant, open face and an attractive grin. His handshake was firm.

He said: 'Tell you what, Percy – I was just going to nip home for lunch – why don't you come along? The wife makes a lovely sausage and chips.' He had a broad cockney accent.

Sausage and chips was not Godliman's favourite meal, but he went along. They walked to Trafalgar Square and caught a bus to Hoxton. Bloggs said: 'I married a wonderful girl, but she can't cook for nuts. I have sausage and chips every day.'

East London was still smoking from the previous night's air raid. They passed groups of firemen and volunteers digging through rubble, playing hoses over dying fires, and clearing debris from the streets. They saw an old man carry a precious radio out of a half-ruined house.

Godliman made conversation. 'So we're to catch spies together.'

'We'll have a go, Perce.'

Bloggs's home was a three-bedroom semi in a street of exactly similar houses. The tiny front gardens were all being used to grow vegetables. Mrs Bloggs was the pretty girl in the photograph on the office wall. She looked tired. Bloggs said: 'She drives an ambulance during the raids, don't you, love?' He was proud of her. Her name was Christine.

She said: 'Every morning when I come home I wonder if the house will still be here.'

'Notice it's the house she's worried about, not me,' Bloggs said.

Godliman picked up a medal in a presentation case from the mantelpiece. 'How did you get this?'

Christine answered. 'He took a shotgun off a villain who was robbing a post office.'

'You're quite a pair,' Godliman said.

'You married, Percy?' Bloggs asked.

'I'm a widower.'

'Sorry.'

'My wife died of tuberculosis in 1930. We never had any children.'

'We're not having any yet,' Bloggs said. 'Not while the world's in this state.'

Christine said: 'Oh, Fred, he's not interested in that!' She went out to the kitchen.

They sat around a square table in the centre of the room to eat. Bloggs was touched by this couple and the domestic scene, and found himself thinking of his Eleanor. That was unusual: he had been immune to sentiment for some years. Perhaps the nerves were coming alive again, at last. War did funny things.

Christine's cooking was truly awful. The sausages were burned. Bloggs drowned his meal in tomato ketchup, and Godliman cheerfully followed suit.

When they got back to Whitehall Bloggs showed Godliman the file on unidentified enemy agents still thought to be operating in Britain.

There were three sources of information about such

people. The first was the immigration records of the Home Office. Passport control had long been an arm of Military Intelligence, and there was a list – going back to the last war – of aliens who had entered the country but had not left or been accounted for in other ways, such as death or naturalization. At the outbreak of war they had all gone before tribunals which classified them in three groups. At first only 'A' class aliens were interned; but by July of 1940, after some scaremongering by Fleet Street, the 'B' and 'C' classes were taken out of circulation. There was a small number of immigrants who could not be located, and it was a fair assumption that some of them were spies.

Their papers were in Bloggs's file.

The second source was wireless transmissions. Section C of MI8 scanned the airwaves nightly, recorded everything they did not know for certain to be ours, and passed it to the Government Code and Cypher School. This outfit, which had recently been moved from London's Berkeley Street to a country house at Bletchley Park, was not a school at all but a collection of chess champions, musicians, mathematicians and crossword-puzzle enthusiasts dedicated to the belief that if a man could invent a code a man could crack it. Signals originating in the UK which could not be accounted for by any of the Services were assumed to be messages from spies.

The decoded messages were in Bloggs's file.

Finally there were the double agents; but their value was largely hoped-for rather than actual. Messages to them from the Abwehr had warned of several incoming agents, and had given away one resident spy – Mrs Matilda Krafft of Bournemouth, who had sent money to Snow by post and was subsequently incarcerated in Holloway prison. But the doubles had not been able to reveal the identity or location of the kind of quietly effective professional spies who are most valuable to a secret intelligence service. No one doubted that there were such people. There were clues: someone, for example, had brought Snow's transmitter over from Germany and deposited it in the cloakroom at Victoria Station for him to collect. But either the Abwehr or the spies themselves were too cautious to be caught by the doubles.

However, the clues were in Bloggs's file.

Other sources were being developed: the boffins were working to improve methods of triangulation (the directional pin-pointing of radio transmitters); and MI6 were trying to rebuild the networks of agents in Europe which had sunk beneath the tidal wave of Hitler's armies.

What little information there was, was in Bloggs's file.

'It can be infuriating at times,' he told Godliman. 'Look at this.'

He took from the file a long radio intercept about British plans for an expeditionary force for Finland. 'This was picked up early in the year. The information is impeccable. They were trying to get a fix on him when he broke off in the middle, for no apparent reason – perhaps he was interrupted. He resumed a few minutes later, but he was off the air again before our boys had a chance to plug in.'

Godliman said: 'What's this – "Regards to Willi"?'

'Now, that's important,' said Bloggs. He was getting enthusiastic. 'Here's a scrap of another message, quite recent. Look – "Regards to Willi". This time there was a reply. He's addressed as "Die Nadel".'

'The Needle.'

'This bloke's a pro. Look at his messages: terse, economical, but detailed and completely unambiguous.'

Godliman studied the fragment of the second message. 'It appears to be about the effects of the bombing.'

'He's obviously toured the East End. A pro, a pro.'

'What else do we know about Die Nadel?'

Bloggs's expression of youthful eagerness collapsed comically. 'That's it, I'm afraid.'

'His code name is Die Nadel, he signs off "Regards to Willi", and he has good information – and that's it?'

''Fraid so.'

Godliman sat on the edge of the desk and stared out of the window. On the wall of the opposite building, underneath an ornate windowsill, he could see the nest of a house-marten. 'On that basis, what chance have we of catching him?'

Bloggs shrugged. 'On that basis, none at all.'

CHAPTER FIVE

I T IS for places like this that the word 'bleak' has been invented.

The island is a J-shaped lump of rock rising sullenly out of the North Sea. It lies on the map like the top half of a broken walking-stick; parallel with the equator but a long, long way north; its curved handle toward Aberdeen, its broken, jagged stump pointing threateningly at distant Denmark. It is ten miles long.

Around most of its coast the cliffs rise out of the cold sea without the courtesy of a beach. Angered by this rudeness the waves pound on the rock in impotent rage; a ten-thousand-year fit of bad temper which the island ignores with impunity.

In the cup of the J the sea is calmer, for there it has provided itself with a more pleasant reception. Its tides have thrown into that cup so much sand and seaweed, driftwood and pebbles and seashells, that there is now, between the foot of the cliff and the water's edge, a crescent of something closely resembling dry land, a more-or-less beach.

Each summer the vegetation at the top of the cliff drops a handful of seeds on to the beach, the way a rich man throws loose change to beggars. If the winter is mild and the spring comes early, a few of the seeds take feeble root; but they are never healthy enough to flower themselves and spread their own seeds, so the beach exists from year to year on handouts.

On the land itself, the proper land, held out of the sea's reach by the cliffs, green things do grow and multiply. The vegetation is mostly coarse grass, only just good enough to nourish the few bony sheep, but tough enough to bind the topsoil to the island's bedrock. There are some bushes, all thorny, which provide homes for rabbits; and a brave stand of conifers on the leeward slope of the hill at the eastern end.

The higher land is ruled by heather. Every few years the man – yes, there is a man here – the man sets fire to the heather, and then the grass will grow and the sheep can graze here too; but after a couple of years the heather comes back, God knows from where, and drives the sheep away until the man burns it again.

The rabbits are here because they were born here; the sheep are here because they were brought here; and the man is here to look after the sheep; but the birds are here because they like it. There are hundreds of thousands of them: long-legged rock pipits whistling *peep peep peep* as they soar and *pe-pe-pe-pe* as they dive like a Spitfire coming at a Messerschmitt out of the sun; corncrakes, which the man rarely sees, but he knows they are there because their bark keeps him awake at night; ravens and carrion crows and kittiwakes and *countless* gulls; and a pair of golden eagles which the man shoots at when he sees them, for he *knows* – regardless of what naturalists and experts from Edinburgh may tell him – that they *do* prey upon live lambs and not just the carcases of those already dead.

The island's most constant visitor is the wind. It comes mostly from the north-east, from *really* cold places where there are fiords and glaciers and icebergs; often bringing with it unwelcome gifts of snow and driving rain and cold, cold mist; sometimes arriving empty-handed, just to howl and whoop and raise hell, tearing up bushes and bending trees and whipping the intemperate ocean into fresh paroxysms of foam-flecked rage. It is tireless, this wind; and that is its mistake. If it came occasionally it could take the island by surprise and do some real damage; but because it is almost always here, the island has learned to live with it. The plants put down deep roots, and the rabbits hide far inside the thickets, and the trees grow up with their backs ready-bent for the flogging, and the birds nest on sheltered ledges, and the man's house is sturdy and squat, built with a craftsmanship that knows this wind of old.

This house is made of big grey stones and grey slates, the colour of the sea. It has small windows and close-fitting doors and a chimney in its pine end. It stands at the top of the hill at the eastern end of the island, close to the splintered stub of the broken walking-stick. It crowns the hill, defying the wind and the rain, not out of bravado but so that the man can see the sheep.

There is another house, very similar, ten miles away at the opposite end of the island near the more-or-less beach; but nobody lives there. There was once another man. He thought he knew better than the island; he thought he could grow oats and potatoes and keep a few cows. He battled for three years with the wind and the cold and the soil before he admitted he was wrong. When he had gone, nobody wanted his home.

This is a hard place. Only hard things survive here: hard rock, coarse grass, tough sheep, savage birds, sturdy houses and strong men. Hard things and cold things, and cruel and bitter and pointed things, rugged and slow-moving and determined things; things as cold and hard and ruthless as the island itself.

It is for places like this that the word 'bleak' has been invented.

'It's called Storm Island,' said Alfred Rose. 'I think you're going to like it.'

David and Lucy Rose sat in the prow of the fishing-boat and looked across the choppy water. It was a fine November day, cold and breezy yet clear and dry. A weak sun sparkled off the wavelets.

'I bought it in 1926,' Papa Rose continued, 'when we thought there was going to be a revolution and we'd need somewhere to hide from the working class. It's just the place for a convalescence.'

Lucy thought he was being suspiciously hearty, but she had to admit it looked lovely: all windblown and natural and fresh. And it made sense, this move. They had to get away from their parents and make a new start at being married; and there was no point in moving to a city to be bombed, when neither of them was really well enough to help; and then David's father

had revealed that he owned an island off the coast of
Scotland, and it seemed too good to be true.

'I own the sheep, too,' Papa Rose said. 'Shearers
come over from the mainland each spring, and the
wool brings in just about enough money to pay Tom
McAvity's wages. Old Tom's the shepherd.'

'How old is he?' Lucy asked.

'Good Lord, he must be – oh, seventy?'

'I suppose he's eccentric.' The boat turned into the
bay, and Lucy could see two small figures on the jetty:
a man and a dog.

'Eccentric? No more than you'd be if you'd lived
alone for twenty years. He talks to his dog.'

Lucy turned to the skipper of the small boat. 'How
often do you call?'

'Once a fortnight, missus. I bring Tom's shopping,
which isna much, and his mail, which is even less. You
just give me your list, every other Monday, and if it can
be bought in Aberdeen I'll bring it.'

He cut the motor and threw a rope to Tom. The dog
barked and ran around in circles, beside himself with
excitement. Lucy put one foot on the gunwale and
sprang out on to the jetty.

Tom took her hand. He had a face of leather and a
huge briar pipe with a lid. He was shorter than she, but
wide, and he looked ridiculously healthy. He wore the
hairiest tweed jacket she had ever seen, with a knitted
sweater that must have been made by an elderly sister
somewhere, plus a checked cap and army boots. His
nose was huge, red and veined. 'Pleased to meet you,'
he said politely, as if she was his ninth visitor today

instead of the first human face he had seen in fourteen days.

'Here y'are, Tom,' said the skipper. He handed two cardboard boxes out of the boat. 'No eggs this time, but here's a letter from Devon.'

'It'll be from ma niece.'

Lucy thought: That explains the sweater.

David was still in the boat. The skipper stood behind him and said: 'Are you ready?'

Tom and Papa Rose leaned into the boat to assist, and the three of them lifted David in his wheelchair on to the jetty.

'If I don't go now I'll have to wait a fortnight for the next bus,' Papa Rose said with a smile. 'The house has been done up quite nicely, you'll see. All your stuff is in there. Tom will show you where everything is.' He kissed Lucy, squeezed David's shoulder, and shook Tom's hand. 'Have a few months of rest and together-ness, get completely fit, then come back: there are important war jobs for both of you.'

They would not be going back, Lucy knew; not before the end of the war: but she had not told anyone about that yet.

Papa got back into the boat. It wheeled away in a tight circle. Lucy waved until it disappeared around the headland.

Tom pushed the wheelchair, so Lucy took his groceries. Between the landward end of the jetty and the cliff top was a long, steep, narrow ramp rising high above the beach like a bridge. Lucy would have had trouble getting the wheelchair to the top, but Tom managed without apparent exertion.

The cottage was perfect.

It was small and grey, and sheltered from the wind by a little rise in the ground. All the woodwork was freshly painted, and a wild rose bush grew beside the doorstep. Curls of smoke rose from the chimney to be whipped away by the breeze. The tiny windows looked over the bay.

Lucy said: 'I love it!'

The interior had been cleaned and aired and painted, and there were thick rugs on the stone floors. It had four rooms: downstairs, a modernized kitchen and a living-room with a stone fireplace; upstairs, two bedrooms. One end of the house had been carefully remodelled to take modern plumbing, with a bathroom above and a kitchen extension below.

Their clothes were in the wardrobes. There were towels in the bathroom and food in the kitchen.

Tom said: 'There's something in the barn I've to show you.'

It was a shed, not a barn. It lay hidden behind the cottage, and inside it was a gleaming new jeep.

'Mr Rose says it's been specially adapted for young Mr Rose to drive,' Tom said. 'It's got automatic gears, and the throttle and brake are operated by hand. That's what he said.' He seemed to be repeating the words parrot-fashion, as if he had very little idea of what gears, brakes and throttles might be.

Lucy said: 'Isn't that super, David?'

'Top-hole. But where shall I go in it?'

Tom said: 'You're always welcome to visit me and share a pipe and a drop of whisky. I've been looking forward to having neighbours again.'

'Thank you,' said Lucy.

'This here's the generator,' Tom said, turning around and pointing. 'I've got one just the same. You put the fuel in here. It delivers alternating current.'

David said: 'That's unusual – small generators are usually direct current.'

'Aye. I don't really know the difference, but they tell me this is safer.'

'True. A shock from this would throw you across the room, but direct current would kill you.'

They went back to the cottage. Tom said: 'Well, you'll want to settle in, and I've sheep to tend, so I'll say good-day. Oh! I ought to tell you: in an emergency, I can contact the mainland by wireless radio.'

David was surprised. 'You've got a radio transmitter?'

'Aye,' Tom said proudly. 'I'm an enemy aircraft spotter in the Royal Observer Corps.'

'Ever spotted any?' David asked.

Lucy flashed her disapproval of the sarcasm in David's voice, but Tom seemed not to notice. 'Not yet,' he replied.

David said: 'Jolly good show.'

When Tom had gone Lucy said: 'He only wants to do his bit.'

'There are lots of us who *want* to do our bit,' David said bitterly. And that, Lucy reflected, was the trouble.

She dropped the subject, and wheeled her crippled husband into their new home.

When Lucy had been asked to visit the hospital psychologist, she had immediately assumed that David had brain damage. It was not so. 'All that's wrong with his head is a nasty bruise on the left temple,' the psychologist said. She went on: 'However, the loss of both his legs brings about a trauma, and there's no telling how it will affect his state of mind. Did he want very much to be a pilot?'

Lucy pondered. 'He was afraid, but I think he wanted it very badly, all the same.'

'Well, he'll need all the reassurance and support that you can give him. And patience, too: one thing we can predict is that he will be resentful and ill-tempered for a while. He needs love and rest.'

However, during their first few months on the island he seemed to want neither. He did not make love to her, perhaps because he was waiting until his injuries were fully healed. But he did not rest, either. He threw himself into the business of sheep farming, tearing about the island in his jeep with the wheelchair in the back. He built fences along the more treacherous cliffs, shot at the eagles, helped Tom train a new dog when Betsy began to go blind, and burned-off the heather; and in the spring he was out every night delivering lambs. One day he felled a great old pine tree near Tom's cottage, and spent a fortnight stripping it,

61

hewing it into manageable logs, and carting them back to the house for firewood. He relished really hard manual labour. He learned to strap himself tightly to the chair to keep his body anchored while he wielded an axe or a mallet. He carved a pair of Indian clubs and exercised with them for hours when Tom could find nothing more for him to do. The muscles of his arms and back became grotesque, like those of men who win body-building contests.

He refused point-blank to wash dishes, cook food or clean the house.

Lucy was not unhappy. She had been afraid he might sit by the fire all day and brood over his bad luck. The way he worked was faintly worrying because it was so obsessive, but at least he was not vegetating.

She told him about the baby at Christmas.

In the morning she gave him a petrol-driven saw, and he gave her a bolt of silk. Tom came over for dinner, and they ate a wild goose he had shot. David drove the shepherd home after tea, and when he came back Lucy opened a bottle of brandy.

Then she said: 'I have another present for you, but you can't open it until May.'

He laughed. 'What on earth are you talking about? How much of that brandy did you drink while I was out?'

'I'm having a baby.'

He stared at her, and all the laughter went out of his face. 'Good God, that's all we bloody well need.'

'David!'

'Well, for God's sake . . . When the hell did it happen?'

'That's not too difficult to figure out, is it?' she said bitterly. 'It must have been a week before the wedding. It's a miracle it survived the crash.'

'Have you seen a doctor?'

'Huh – when?'

'So how do you know for sure?'

'Oh, David, don't be so boring. I know for sure because my periods have stopped and my nipples hurt and I throw up in the mornings and my waist is four inches bigger than it used to be. If you ever *looked* at me *you* would know for sure.'

'All right.'

'What's the matter with you? You're supposed to be thrilled!'

'Oh, sure. Perhaps we'll have a son, and then I can take him for walks and play football with him, and he'll grow up wanting to be like his father the war hero, a legless fucking joke!'

'Oh, David, David,' she whispered. She knelt in front of his wheelchair. 'David, don't think like that. He will respect you. He'll look up to you because you put your life together again, and because you can do the work of two men from your wheelchair, and because you carried your disability with courage and cheerfulness.'

'Don't be so damned condescending,' he snapped. 'You sound like a sanctimonious priest.'

She stood up. 'Well, don't act as if it's my fault. Men can take precautions too, you know.'

'You can't take precautions against invisible lorries in the blackout!'

That was a silly, feeble excuse, and they both knew it, so Lucy said nothing. The whole idea of Christmas seemed utterly trite now: the bits of coloured paper on the walls, and the tree in the corner, and the remains of a goose in the kitchen waiting to be thrown away – none of it had anything to do with her life. She began to wonder what she was doing on this bleak island with a man who seemed not to love her, having a baby he didn't want. Why shouldn't she – why not – well, she could ... Then she realized she had nowhere else to go, nothing else to do with her life, nobody else to *be* other than Mrs David Rose.

Eventually David said: 'Well, I'm going to bed.' He wheeled himself to the hall and dragged himself out of the chair and up the stairs backwards. She heard him scrape across the floor, heard the bed creak as he hauled himself on to it, heard his clothes hit the corner of the room as he undressed, then heard the final groaning of the springs as he lay down and pulled the blankets up over his pyjamas.

And still she would not cry.

She looked at the brandy bottle and thought: If I drink all of this now, and have a bath, perhaps I won't be pregnant in the morning.

She thought about it for a long time, until she came to the conclusion that life without David and the island and the baby would be even worse because it would be empty.

So she did not cry, and she did not drink the brandy,

and she did not leave the island; but instead she went upstairs and got into bed, and lay awake beside her sleeping husband, listening to the wind and trying not to think, until the gulls began to call, and a grey rainy dawn crept over the North Sea and filled the little bedroom with a cold, cheerless, silver light, and then at last she went to sleep.

A kind of peace settled over her in the spring, as if all threats were postponed until after the baby was born. When the February snow had thawed she planted flowers and vegetables in the patch of ground between the kitchen door and the barn, not really believing they would grow. She cleaned the house thoroughly and told David that if he wanted it done again before August he would have to do it himself. She wrote to her mother and did a lot of knitting and ordered nappies by post. They suggested she go home to have the baby, but she knew that if she went she would never come back. She went for long walks over the moors, with a bird book under her arm, until her own weight became too much for her to carry very far. She kept the bottle of brandy in a cupboard David never used, and whenever she felt depressed she went to look at it and remind herself of what she had almost lost.

Three weeks before the baby was due, she got the boat into Aberdeen. David and Tom waved from the jetty. The sea was so rough that both she and the skipper were terrified she might give birth before they reached the mainland. She went into hospital in Aberdeen, and four weeks later brought the baby home on the same boat.

David knew none of it. He probably thought that women gave birth as easily as ewes. He was oblivious to the pain of contractions, and that awful, impossible stretching, and the soreness afterwards, and the bossy, know-all nurses who didn't want you to *touch* your baby because you weren't brisk and efficient and trained and *sterile* like they were; he just saw you go away pregnant and come back with a beautiful, white-wrapped, healthy baby boy and said: 'We'll call him Jonathan.'

They added Alfred for David's father, and Malcolm for Lucy's, and Thomas for old Tom, but they called the boy Jo, because he was too tiny for Jonathan, let alone Jonathan Alfred Malcolm Thomas Rose. David learned to give him his bottle and burp him and change his nappy, and he even dandled him in his lap occasionally, but his interest was distant, uninvolved. He had a problem-solving approach, like the nurses; it was not for him as it was for Lucy. Tom was closer to the baby than David. Lucy would not let him smoke in the room where the baby was, and the old boy would put his great briar pipe with the lid in his pocket for hours and gurgle at little Jo, or watch him kick his feet, or help Lucy bath him. Lucy suggested mildly that he might be neglecting the sheep. Tom said they did not need him to watch them feed – he would rather watch Jo feed. He carved a rattle out of driftwood and filled it with small round pebbles, and was overjoyed when Jo grabbed it and shook it, first time, without having to be shown how.

And still David and Lucy did not make love.

First there had been his injuries, and then she had been pregnant, and then she had been recovering from childbirth; but now the reasons had run out.

One night she said: 'I'm back to normal, now.'

'How do you mean?'

'After the baby. My body is normal. I've healed.'

'Oh, I see. That's good.' And he turned away.

She made sure to go up to bed with him so that he could watch her undress, but he always turned his back.

As they lay there, dozing off, she would move so that her hand, or her thigh, or her breast, brushed against him, a casual but unmistakable invitation. There was no response.

She believed firmly that there was nothing wrong with her. She wasn't a nymphomaniac: she didn't simply want sex, she wanted sex with David. She was sure that, even if there had been another man under seventy on the island, she would not have been tempted. She wasn't a sex-starved tart, she was a love-starved wife.

The crunch came on one of those nights when they lay on their backs, side by side, both wide awake, listening to the wind outside and the small sounds of Jo from the next room. It seemed to Lucy that it was time he either did it or came right out and said why not; and that he was going to avoid the issue until she forced it; and that she might as well force it now as live in miserable incomprehension any longer.

So she brushed her arm across his thighs and opened her mouth to speak – and almost cried out with shock to discover that he had an erection. So he could do it!

And he wanted to, or why else – And her hand closed triumphantly around the evidence of his desire, and she shifted closer to him, and sighed: 'David—'

He said: 'Oh, for God's sake!' He gripped her wrist and thrust her hand away from him and turned on to his side.

But this time she was not going to accept his rebuff in modest silence. She said: 'David, why not?'

'Jesus, Christ!' He threw the blankets off, swung himself to the floor, grabbed the eiderdown with one hand, and dragged himself to the door.

Lucy sat up in bed and screamed at him: 'Why not?'

Jo began to cry.

David pulled up the empty legs of his cut-off pyjama trousers, pointed to the pursed white skin of his stumps, and said: 'That's why not! That's why not!'

He slithered downstairs to sleep on the sofa, and Lucy went into the next bedroom to comfort Jo.

It took a long time to lull him back to sleep, probably because she herself was so much in need of comfort. The baby tasted the tears on her cheeks, and she wondered if he had any inkling of their meaning: wouldn't tears be one of the first things a baby came to understand? She could not bring herself to sing to him, nor could she with any sincerity murmur that everything was all right; so she held him tight and rocked him, and when *he* had soothed *her* with his warmth and his clinging, he went to sleep in her arms.

She put him back in the cot and stood looking at him for a while. There was no point in going back to bed. She could hear David's deep-sleep snoring from the living-room – he had to take powerful pills, otherwise the old pain kept him awake. Lucy needed to get right away from him, where she could neither see nor hear him, where he couldn't find her for a few hours even if he wanted to. She put on trousers and a sweater, a heavy coat and boots, and crept downstairs and out into the night.

There was a swirling mist, damp and bitterly cold, the kind the island specialized in. She put up the collar of her coat, thought about going back inside for a scarf, and decided not to. She squelched along the muddy path, welcoming the bite of the fog in her throat, the small discomfort of the weather taking her mind off the larger hurt inside her.

She reached the cliff top and walked gingerly down the steep, narrow ramp, placing her feet carefully on the slippery boards. At the bottom she jumped off on to the sand and walked to the edge of the sea.

The wind and the water were carrying on their perpetual quarrel, the wind swooping down to tease the waves and the sea hissing and spitting as it crashed against the land, the two of them doomed to bicker forever because neither could be calm while the other was there, but neither had any place else to go.

Lucy walked along the hard sand, letting the noise and the weather fill her head, until the beach ended in a sharp point where the water met the cliff, when she turned and walked back. She paced the shore all night. Toward dawn a thought came to her, unbidden: It is his way of being strong.

As it was, the thought was not much help, holding its

meaning in a tightly clenched fist. But she worked on it for a while, and the fist opened to reveal what looked like a small pearl of wisdom nestling in its palm: for perhaps David's coldness to her was of one piece with his chopping down trees, and undressing himself, and driving the jeep, and throwing the Indian clubs, and coming to live on a cold cruel island in the North Sea...

What was it he had said? '... his father the war hero, a legless joke...' He had something to prove, something that would sound trite if it were put into words; something he could have done as a fighter pilot, but now had to do with trees and fences and Indian clubs and a wheelchair. They wouldn't let him take the test, and he wanted to be able to say: 'I could have passed it anyway, just *look* how I can suffer.'

It was cruelly, hopelessly, screamingly unjust: he had had the courage, and he had suffered the wounds, but he could take no pride in it. If a Messerschmitt had taken his legs the wheelchair would have been like a medal, a badge of courage. But now, all his life, he would have to say: 'It was during the war – but no, I never saw any action, this was a car crash, I did my training and I was going to fight, the very next day, I had seen my kite, she was a beauty, and I *would* have been brave, I know...'

Yes, it was his way of being strong. And perhaps she could be strong, too. She might find ways of patching up the wreck of her life so that it would sail again. David had once been good and kind and loving, and she might now learn to wait patiently while he battled to become the complete man he used to be. She could find new hopes, new things to live for. Other women had found the strength to cope with bereavement, and bombed-out houses, and husbands in prisoner-of-war camps.

She picked up a pebble, drew back her arm, and threw it out to sea with all her might. She did not see or hear it land: it might have gone on forever, circling the earth like a satellite in a space story.

She shouted: 'I can be strong, too!'

Then she turned around and started up the ramp to the cottage. It was almost time for Jo's first feed.

CHAPTER SIX

I T LOOKED like a mansion; and, up to a point, that was what it was: a large house, in its own grounds, in the leafy town of Wohldorf just outside North Hamburg. It might have been the home of a mine owner, or a successful importer, or an industrialist. It was in fact owned by the Abwehr.

It owed its fate to the weather – not here, but two hundred miles south-east in Berlin, where atmospheric conditions were unsuitable for wireless communication with England.

It was a mansion only down to ground level. Below that were two huge concrete shelters and several million Reichsmarks worth of radio equipment. The electronics system had been put together by one Major Werner Trautmann, and he did a good job. Each hall had twenty neat little soundproofed listening posts, occupied by radio operators who could recognize a spy by the way he tapped out his message, as easily as you can recognize your mother's handwriting on an envelope.

The receiving equipment was built with quality in mind, for the transmitters that were sending the messages had been designed for compactness rather than power. Most of them were the little suitcase sets called Klamotten which had been developed by Telefunken for Admiral Wilhelm Canaris, the head of the Abwehr.

On this night the airwaves were relatively quiet, so everyone knew when Die Nadel came through. The message was taken by one of the older operators. He tapped out an acknowledgement, transcribed the signal quickly, tore the sheet off his notepad and went to the phone. He read the message over the direct line to Abwehr headquarters at Sophien Terrace in Hamburg, then he came back to his booth for a smoke.

He offered a cigarette to the youngster in the next booth, and the two of them stood together for a few minutes, leaning against the wall and smoking.

The youngster said: 'Anything?'

The older man shrugged. 'There's always *something* when he calls. But not much, this time. The Luftwaffe missed St Paul's Cathedral again.'

'No reply for him?'

'We don't think he waits for replies. He's an independent bastard, that one. Always was. I trained him in wireless, you know: and once I'd finished he thought he knew it better than me.'

The youngster was awestruck. 'You've *met* Die Nadel?'

'Oh, yes,' said the old-timer, flicking ash.

'What's he like?'

'As a drinking companion, he's about as much fun as a dead fish. I think he likes women, on the quiet, but as for sinking a few steins with the boys – forget it. All the same, he's the best agent we've got.'

'Really?'

'Definitely. Some say the best spy ever. There's a story that he spent five years working his way up in the NKVD in Russia, and ended up one of Stalin's most trusted aides ... I don't know whether it's true, but it's the kind of thing he'd do. A real pro. And the Führer knows it.'

'Hitler knows him?'

The older man nodded. 'At one time he wanted to see all Die Nadel's signals. I don't know if he still does. Not that it would make any difference to Die Nadel. Nothing impresses that man. You know something? He looks at everybody the same way: as if he's figuring out how he'll kill you if you make a wrong move.'

'I'm glad I didn't have to train him.'

'He learned quickly, I'll give him that.'

'Good pupil?'

'The best. He worked at it twenty-four hours a day, then when he'd mastered it, he wouldn't give me a good morning. It takes him all his time to remember to salute Canaris.'

'*Ach du meine Scheisse.*'

'Oh, yes. Didn't you know – he always signs off "Regards to Willi". That's how much he cares about rank.'

'No. Regards to Willi? *Ach du meine Scheisse.*'

They finished their cigarettes, dropped them on the floor, and trod them out. Then the older man picked up the stubs and pocketed them, because smoking was not really permitted in the dugout. The radios were still quiet.

'Yes, he won't use his code name,' the older man went on. 'Von Braun gave it to him, and he's never liked it. He's never liked Von Braun either. Do you remember the time – no, it was before you joined us – Braun told Nadel to go to the airfield in Farnborough, Kent. The message came back, quick as a flash: "There is no airfield at Farnborough, Kent. There is one at Farnborough, Hampshire. Fortunately the Luftwaffe's geography is better than yours, you cunt." Just like that.'

'I suppose it's understandable. When we make mistakes we put their lives at risk.'

The older man frowned. He was the one who delivered such judgements, and he did not like his audience to weigh in with opinions of its own. 'Perhaps,' he said grudgingly.

The youngster reverted to his original wide-eyed role. 'Why doesn't he like his code name?'

'He says it has a meaning, and a code word with a meaning can give a man away. Von Braun wouldn't listen.'

'A meaning? The Needle? What does it mean?'

But at that moment the old-timer's radio chirped, and he returned quickly to his station; so the youngster never did find out.

Part Two

CHAPTER SEVEN

THE MESSAGE annoyed Faber, because it forced him to face issues which he had been avoiding.

Hamburg had made damn sure the message reached him. He had given his call-sign, and instead of the usual 'Acknowledge – proceed' they had sent back 'Make rendezvous one'.

He acknowledged the order, transmitted his report, and packed the wireless set back into its suitcase. Then he wheeled his bicycle out of Erith Marshes – his cover was that of a bird-watcher – and he got on the road to Blackheath. As he cycled back to his cramped two-room flatlet, he wondered whether to obey the order.

He had two reasons for disobedience: one professional, one personal.

The professional reason was that 'rendezvous one' was an old code, set up by Canaris back in 1937. It meant he was to go to the doorway of a certain shop between Leicester Square and Piccadilly Circus to meet another agent. The agents would recognize each other by the fact that they both carried a Bible. Then there was a patter:

'What is today's chapter?'

'One Kings thirteen.'

Then, if they were certain they were not being followed, they would agree that the chapter was 'most inspiring'. Otherwise one would say: 'I'm afraid I haven't read it yet.'

The shop doorway might not be there any more, but it was not that which troubled Faber. He thought Canaris had probably given the code to most of the bumbling amateurs who had crossed the Channel in 1940 and landed in the arms of MI5. Faber knew they had been caught because the hangings had been publicized, no doubt to reassure the public that something was being done about Fifth Columnists. They would certainly have given away secrets before they died, so the British now probably knew the old rendezvous code. If they had picked up the message from Hamburg, that shop doorway must by now be swarming with well-spoken young Englishmen carrying Bibles and practising saying 'Most inspiring' in a German accent.

The Abwehr had thrown professionalism to the wind, back in those heady days when the invasion seemed so close. Faber had not trusted Hamburg since. He would not tell them where he lived, he refused to communicate with their other agents in Britain, he varied the frequency he used for transmission without caring whether he trod all over someone else's signal.

If he had always obeyed his masters, he would not have survived so long.

At Woolwich Faber was joined by a mass of other cyclists, many of them women, as the workers came streaming out of the munitions factory at the end of the day shift. Their cheerful weariness reminded Faber of his personal reason for disobedience: he thought his side was losing the war.

They certainly were not winning. The Russians and the Americans had joined in, Africa was lost, the Italians had collapsed; the Allies must invade France this year, 1944.

Faber did not want to risk his life to no purpose.

He arrived home and put his bicycle away. While he was washing his face it dawned on him that, against all logic, he *wanted* to make the rendezvous.

It was a foolish risk, taken in a lost cause, but he was itching to get to it. And the simple reason was that he was unspeakably bored. The routine transmissions, the bird-watching, the bicycle, the boarding-house teas: it was four years since he had experienced anything remotely like action. He seemed to be in no danger whatsoever, and that made him jumpy, because he imagined invisible perils. He was happiest when every so often he could identify a threat and take steps to neutralize it.

Yes, he would make the rendezvous. But not in the way they expected.

There were still crowds in the West End of London, despite the war; Faber wondered whether it was the same in Berlin. He bought a Bible at Hatchard's bookshop in Piccadilly, and stuffed it into his inside coat pocket, out of sight. It was a mild, damp day, with intermittent drizzle, and Faber was carrying an umbrella.

This rendezvous was timed for either between nine and ten o'clock in the morning or between five and six in the afternoon, and the arrangement was that one went there every day until the other party turned up. If no contact was made for five successive days one went there on alternate days for a fortnight. After that one gave up.

Faber got to Leicester Square at ten past nine. The contact was there, in the tobacconist's doorway, with a blackbound Bible under his arm, pretending to shelter from the rain. Faber spotted him out of the corner of his eye and hurried past, head down. The man was youngish, with a blond moustache and a well-fed look. He wore a black double-breasted showerproof coat, and he was reading the *Daily Express* and chewing gum. He was not familiar.

When Faber walked by the second time on the opposite side of the street, he spotted the tail. A short, stocky man wearing the trench coat and trilby hat beloved of English plain-clothes policemen was standing just inside the foyer of an office building, looking through the glass doors across the street to the spy in the doorway.

There were two possibilities. If the agent did not know he had been rumbled, Faber had only to get him away from the rendezvous and lose the tail. However, the alternative was that the agent had been captured and the man in the doorway was a substitute, in which case neither he nor the tail must be allowed to see Faber's face.

82

Faber assumed the worst, then thought of a way to deal with it.

There was a telephone kiosk in the Square. Faber went inside and memorized the number. Then he found I Kings 13 in the Bible, tore out the page, and scribbled in the margin: 'Go to the phone box in the Square.'

He walked around the back streets behind the National Gallery until he found a small boy, aged about ten or eleven, sitting on a doorstep throwing stones at puddles.

Faber said: 'Do you know the tobacconist in the Square?'

The boy said: 'Yerst.'

'Do you like chewing-gum?'

'Yerst.'

Faber gave him the page torn from the Bible. 'There's a man in the doorway of the tobacconist's. If you give him this he'll give you some gum.'

'All right,' the boy said. He stood up. 'Is this geezer a Yank?'

Faber said: 'Yerst.'

The boy ran off. Faber followed him. As the boy approached the agent, Faber ducked into the doorway of the building opposite. The tail was still there, peering through the glass. Faber stood just outside the door, blocking the tail's view of the scene across the street, and opened his umbrella. He pretended to be struggling with it. He saw the agent give something to the boy and walk off. He ended his charade with the umbrella, and walked in the direction opposite to the way the agent had gone. He looked back over his shoulder to see the tail run into the street, looking for the vanished agent.

Faber stopped at the nearest call box and dialled the number of the kiosk in the Square. It took a few minutes to get through. At last a deep voice said: 'Hello?'

Faber said: 'What is today's chapter?'

'One Kings thirteen.'

'Most inspiring.'

'Yes, isn't it.'

The fool has no idea of the trouble he's in, Faber thought. Aloud he said: 'Well?'

'I must see you.'

'That is impossible.'

'But I must!' There was a note in the voice which Faber thought close to despair. 'The message comes from the very top – do you understand?'

Faber pretended to waver. 'All right, then. I will meet you in one week's time under the arch at Euston Station at nine a.m.'

'Can't you make it sooner?'

Faber hung up and stepped outside. Walking quickly, he rounded two corners and came within sight of the phone box in the Square. He saw the agent walking in the direction of Piccadilly. There was no sign of the tail. Faber followed the agent.

The man went into Piccadilly Circus underground station and bought a ticket to Stockwell. Faber immediately realized he could get there by a more direct route. He came out of the station, walked quickly to Leicester

Square, and got on a Northern Line train. The agent would have to change trains at Waterloo, whereas Faber's train was direct; so Faber would reach Stockwell first, or at the worst they would arrive on the same train.

In fact Faber had to wait outside the station at Stockwell for twenty-five minutes before the agent emerged. Faber followed him again. He went into a café.

There was absolutely nowhere nearby where a man could plausibly stand still for any length of time: no shop windows to gaze into, no benches to sit on or parks to walk around, no bus stops or taxi ranks or public buildings. It was a dreary, blank suburb. Faber had to walk up and down the street, always looking as if he were going somewhere, carrying on until he was just out of sight of the café then returning on the opposite side, while the agent sat in the warm, steamy café drinking tea and eating hot toast.

He came out after half an hour. Faber tailed him through a succession of residential streets. The agent knew where he was going, but was in no hurry: he walked like a man who is going home with nothing to do for the rest of the day. He did not look back, and Faber thought: Another amateur.

At last he went into a house – one of the poor, anonymous, inconspicuous lodging-houses used by spies everywhere. It had a dormer window in the roof: that would be the agent's room, high up for better wireless reception.

Faber walked past, scanning the opposite side of the

street. Yes – there. A movement behind an upstairs window, a glimpse of a jacket and tie, a watching face withdrawn: the opposition was here too. The agent must have gone to the rendezvous yesterday and allowed himself to be followed home by MI5 – unless, of course, he *was* MI5.

Faber turned the corner and walked down the next parallel street, counting the houses. Almost directly behind the place the agent had entered there was the bomb-damaged shell of what had been a pair of semi-detached houses. Good.

As he walked back to the station he felt a buzz of excitement. His step was springier, his heart beat a shade faster, and he looked around him with bright-eyed interest. It was good. The game was on.

He dressed in black that night: a woollen hat, a roll-neck sweater under a short leather flying jacket, trousers tucked into socks, rubber-soled shoes; all black. He would be almost invisible, for London, too, was blacked out.

He cycled through the quiet streets with dimmed lights, keeping off main roads. It was after midnight, and he saw no one. He left the bike a quarter of a mile away from his destination, padlocking it to the fence in a pub yard.

He went, not to the agent's house, but to the bombed-out shell in the next street. He picked his way carefully across the rubble in the front garden, entered the gaping doorway, and went through the house to the back. It was very dark. A thick screen of low cloud hid the moon and stars. Faber had to walk slowly with his hands in front of him.

He reached the end of the garden, jumped over the fence, and crossed the next two gardens. In one of the houses a dog barked for a minute.

The garden of the lodging-house was unkempt. Faber walked into a blackberry bush and stumbled. The thorns scratched his face. He ducked under a line of washing – there was enough light for him to see that.

He found the kitchen window and took from his pocket a small tool with a scoop-shaped blade. The putty around the glass was old and brittle, and already flaking away in places. After twenty minutes' silent work he took the pane out of the frame and laid it gently on the grass. He shone a torch through the empty hole to make sure there were no noisy obstacles in his way, then climbed in.

The darkened house smelled of boiled fish and disinfectant. Faber unlocked the back door – a precaution for fast escape – before entering the hall. He flashed his pencil torch on and off quickly, once. In that instant of light he took in a tiled hallway, a kidney table he must circumvent, a row of coats on hooks and a staircase, to the right, carpeted.

He climbed the stairs silently.

He was halfway across the landing to the second flight when he saw the light under the door. A split-second later there was an asthmatic cough and the sound of a toilet flushing. Faber reached the door in two strides and froze against the wall.

Light flooded the landing as the door opened. Faber slipped his stiletto out of his sleeve. The old man came out of the toilet and crossed the landing, leaving the light on. At his bedroom door he grunted, turned, and came back.

He must see me, Faber thought. He tightened his grip on the handle of his knife. The old man's half-open eyes were directed to the floor. He looked up as he reached for the light cord, and Faber almost killed him then – but the man fumbled for the switch, and Faber realized he was so sleepy he was practically sleepwalking.

The light died, the old man shuffled back to bed, and Faber breathed again.

There was only one door at the top of the second flight of stairs. Faber tried it gently. It was locked.

He took another tool from the pocket of his jacket. The noise of the cistern filling covered the sound of Faber picking the lock. He opened the door and listened.

He could hear deep, regular breathing. He stepped inside. The sound came from the opposite corner of the room. He could see nothing. He crossed the pitch-black room very slowly, feeling the air in front of him at each step, until he was beside the bed.

He had the torch in his left hand, the stiletto loose in his sleeve, and his right hand free. He switched on the torch and grabbed the sleeping man's throat in a strangling grip.

The agent's eyes snapped open, full of fear, but he could make no sound. Faber straddled the bed and sat on him. Then he whispered: 'One Kings thirteen,' and relaxed his grip.

'You!' the agent said. He peered into the torchlight, trying to see Faber's face. He rubbed his neck where Faber's hand had squeezed.

Faber hissed: 'Be still!' He shone the torch into the agent's eyes, and with his right hand drew the stiletto.

'Aren't you going to let me get up?'

'I prefer you in bed where you can do no more damage.'

'Damage? More damage?'

'You were watched in Leicester Square, you let me follow you here, and they are observing this house. Should I trust you to do anything?'

'My God, I'm sorry.'

'Why did they send you?'

'The message had to be delivered personally. The orders come from the Führer himself.' The agent stopped.

'Well? What orders?'

'I . . . have to be sure it is you.'

'How can you be sure?'

'I must see your face.'

Faber hesitated, then shone the torch at himself briefly. 'Satisfied?'

'Die Nadel,' the man breathed.

'And who are you?'

'Major Friedrich Kaldor, at your service, sir.'

'Then I should call you "Sir".'

'Oh, no, sir. You've been promoted twice in your absence. You are now a lieutenant-colonel.'

'Have they nothing better to do in Hamburg?'

'Aren't you pleased?'

'I should be pleased to go back and put Major von Braun on latrine duty.'

'May I get up, sir?'

'Certainly not. What if Major Kaldor is languishing in Wandsworth gaol, and you are a substitute, just waiting to give some kind of signal to your watching friends in the house opposite?'

'Very well.'

'So – what are these orders from Hitler himself?'

'Well, sir, the Reich believes there will be an invasion of France this year.'

'Brilliant, brilliant. Go on.'

'They believe that General Patton is massing the First United States Army Group in the part of England known as East Anglia. If that army is the invasion force, then it follows that they will attack via the Pas de Calais.'

'That makes sense. But I have seen no sign of this army of Patton's.'

'There is some doubt in the highest circles in Berlin. The Führer's astrologer—'

'What?'

'Yes, sir, he has an astrologer, who tells him to defend Normandy.'

'My God. Are things that bad there?'

'He gets plenty of earthbound advice, too. I person-ally believe he uses the astrologer as an excuse when he thinks the generals are wrong but he cannot fault their arguments.'

Faber sighed. He had been afraid of news like this. 'Go on.'

'Your assignment is to assess the strength of FUSAG: numbers of troops, artillery, air support—'

'I know how to measure armies, thank you.'

'Of course.' He paused. 'I am instructed to emphasize the importance of the mission, sir.'

'And you have done so. Tell me: are things that bad in Berlin?'

The agent hesitated, and said: 'No, sir. Morale is high, output of munitions increases every month, the people spit at the bombers of the RAF—'

'Never mind,' Faber interrupted him. 'I can get the propaganda from my radio.'

The younger man was silent.

Faber said: 'Do you have anything else to tell me? Officially, I mean.'

'Yes. For the duration of the assignment you have a special bolthole.'

'They *do* think it's important,' Faber said.

'You rendezvous with a U-boat in the North Sea, ten miles due east of a town called Aberdeen. Just call them in on your normal radio frequency and they will surface. As soon as you or I have told Hamburg that the orders have been passed from me to you, the route will be open. The boat will be there every Friday and Monday at six p.m. and will wait until six a.m.'

'Aberdeen is a big town. Do you have an exact map reference?'

'Yes.' The agent recited the numbers, and Faber memorized them.

'Is that everything, Major?'

'Yes, sir.'

'What do you plan to do about the gentlemen from MI5 in the house across the road?'

The agent shrugged. 'I shall have to give them the slip.'

Faber thought: It's no good. 'What are your orders for action after you have seen me? Do you have a bolthole?'

'No. I am to go to a place called Weymouth and steal a boat in which to return to France.'

That was no plan at all. So, Faber thought: Canaris knew how it would be. Very well.

He said: 'And if you are caught by the British, and tortured?'

'I have a suicide pill.'

'And you will use it?'

'Most certainly.'

Faber looked at him. 'I think you might,' he said. He placed his left hand on the agent's chest and put his weight on it, as if he were about to get off the bed. That way he was able to feel exactly where the rib cage ended and the soft belly began. He thrust the point of the stiletto in just under the ribs and stabbed upward to the heart.

The agent's eyes widened for a terror-stricken instant. A cry came to his throat but did not escape. His body convulsed. Faber pushed the stiletto an inch farther in. The eyes closed and the body went limp.

Faber said: 'You saw my face.'

CHAPTER EIGHT

'I THINK we've lost control of it,' said Percival Godliman.

Frederick Bloggs nodded agreement, and added: 'It's my fault.'

The boy looked weary, Godliman thought. He had had that look for almost a year, ever since the night they dragged the crushed remains of his wife from underneath the rubble of their bombed house in Hoxton.

'I'm not interested in apportioning blame,' Godliman said briskly. 'The fact is that something happened in Leicester Square those few seconds when you lost sight of Blondie.'

'Do you think the contact was made?'

'Possibly.'

'When we picked him up again back in Stockwell, I thought he had simply given up for the day.'

'If that were the case he would have made the rendezvous again yesterday and today.' Godliman was making patterns with matchsticks on his desk, an aid to thinking he had developed into a habit. 'Still no movement at the house?'

'Nothing. He's been in there for forty-eight hours.' Bloggs repeated: 'It's my fault.'

'Don't be a bore, old chap,' Godliman said. 'It was my decision to let him run, so that he would lead us to someone else; and I still think it was the right move.'

Bloggs sat motionless, his expression blank, his hands in the pockets of his raincoat. 'If the contact has been made, we shouldn't delay picking Blondie up and finding out what his mission was.'

'That way we lose whatever chance we have of following Blondie to somebody really dangerous.'

'Your decision.'

Godliman had made a church with his matches. He stared at it for a moment, then took a halfpenny from his pocket and tossed it. 'Tails,' he observed. 'Give him another twenty-four hours.'

The landlord was a middle-aged Irish Republican from Lisdoonvarna, County Clare, who harboured a secret hope that the Germans would win the war and thus free the Emerald Isle from English oppression forever. He limped arthritically around the old house, collecting his weekly rents, thinking how much he would be worth if those rents were allowed to rise to their true market value. He was not a rich man – he owned only two houses, this and the smaller one in which he lived. He was permanently bad-tempered.

On the first floor he tapped on the door of the old man. This tenant was always pleased to see him. He was probably pleased to see anybody. He said: 'Hello, Mr Riley, would you like a cup of tea?'

'No time today.'

'Oh, well.' The old man handed over the money. 'I expect you've seen the kitchen window.'

'No, I didn't go in there.'

'Oh! Well, there's a pane of glass out. I patched it over with blackout curtain, but of course there is a draught.'

'Who smashed it?' the landlord asked.

'Funny thing, it ain't broke. Just lying there on the grass. I expect the old putty just gave way. I'll mend it myself, if you can get hold of a bit of putty.'

You old fool, the landlord thought. Aloud he said: 'I don't suppose it occurred to you that you might have been burgled?'

The old man looked astonished. 'I never thought of that.'

'Nobody's missing any valuables?'

'Nobody's said so to me.'

The landlord went to the door. 'All right, I'll have a look when I go down.'

The old man followed him out. 'I don't think the new bloke is in, upstairs,' he said. 'I haven't heard a sound for a couple of days.'

The landlord was sniffing. 'Has he been cooking in his room?'

'I wouldn't know, Mr Riley.'

The two of them went up the stairs. The old man said: 'He's very quiet, if he is in there.'

'Whatever he's cooking, he'll have to stop. It smells bloody awful.'

The landlord knocked on the door. There was no answer. He opened it and went in, and the old man followed him.

'Well, well, well,' the old sergeant said heartily. 'I think you've got a dead one.'

He stood in the doorway, surveying the room. 'You touched anything, Paddy?'

'No,' the landlord replied. 'And the name's Mr Riley.'

The policeman ignored this. 'Not long dead, though. I've smelled worse.' His survey took in the old chest of drawers, the suitcase on the low table, the faded square of carpet, the dirty curtains on the dormer window, and the rumpled bed in the corner. There were no signs of a struggle.

He went over to the bed. The young man's face was peaceful, his hands clasped over his chest. 'I'd say heart attack, if he wasn't so young.' There was no empty sleeping-pill bottle to indicate suicide. He picked up the leather wallet on top of the chest and looked through its contents. There was an identity card and a ration book, and a fairly thick wad of notes. 'Papers in order and he ain't been robbed.'

'He's only been here a week or so,' the landlord ventured. 'I don't know much about him at all. He came from North Wales to work in a factory.'

The sergeant observed: 'If he was as healthy as he looked he'd be in the Army.' He opened the suitcase on the table. 'Bloody hell, what's this lot?'

The landlord and the old man had edged their way into the room now. The landlord said: 'It's a radio' at the same time as the old man said: 'He's bleeding.'

'Don't touch that body!' the sergeant said.

'He's had a knife in the guts,' the old man persisted.

The sergeant gingerly lifted one of the dead hands from the chest to reveal a small patch of dried blood. 'He *was* bleeding,' he said. 'Where's the nearest phone?'

'Five doors down,' the landlord told him.

'Lock this room and stay out until I get back.'

The sergeant left the house and knocked at the door of the neighbour with the phone. A woman opened it. 'Good morning, madam. May I use your telephone?'

'Come in.' She showed him the phone, on a stand in the hall. 'What's happened – anything exciting?'

'A tenant died in a lodging-house just up the road,' he told her as he dialled.

'Murdered?' she asked, wide-eyed.

'I leave that to the experts. Hello? Superintendent Jones, please. This is Canter.' He looked at the woman. 'Might I ask you just to pop in the kitchen while I talk to my governor?'

She went, disappointed.

'Hello, Super. This body's got a knife wound and a suitcase radio.'

'What's the address again, Sarge?'

Sergeant Canter told him.

'Yes, that's the one they've been watching. This is an MI5 job, Sarge. Go to number forty-two and tell the surveillance team what you've found. I'll get on to their chief. Off you go.'

Canter thanked the woman and crossed the road. He was quite thrilled: this was only his second murder in 31 years as a Metropolitan Policeman, and it turned out to involve espionage! He might make Inspector yet.

He knocked on the door of number forty-two. It opened, and two men stood there.

Sergeant Canter said: 'Are you the secret agents from MI5?'

Bloggs arrived at the same time as a Special Branch man, Detective-Inspector Harris, whom he had known in his Scotland Yard days. Canter showed them the body.

They stood still for a moment, looking at the peaceful young face with its blond moustache.

Harris said: 'Who is he?'

'Codename Blondie,' Bloggs told him. 'We think he came in by parachute a couple of weeks ago. We picked up a radio message to another agent arranging a rendezvous. We knew the code, so we were able to watch the rendezvous. We hoped Blondie would lead us to the resident agent, who would be a much more dangerous specimen.'

'So what happened here?'

'Buggered if I know.'

Harris looked at the wound in the agent's chest. 'Stiletto?'

'Something like that. A very neat job. Under the ribs and straight up into the heart. Quick.'

'There are worse ways to die.'

Sergeant Canter said: 'Would you like to see the method of entry?'

He led them downstairs to the kitchen. They looked at the window-frame and the unbroken pane of glass lying on the lawn.

Canter said: 'Also, the lock on the bedroom door had been picked.'

They sat down at the kitchen table, and Canter made tea. Bloggs said: 'It happened the night after I lost him in Leicester Square. I fouled it all up.'

Harris said: 'Nobody's perfect.'

They drank their tea in silence for a while. Harris said: 'How are things with you, anyway? You don't drop in at the Yard.'

'Busy.'

'How's Christine?'

'Killed in the bombing.'

Harris's eyes widened. 'You poor bastard.'

'You all right?'

'Lost my brother in North Africa. Did you ever meet Johnny?'

'No.'

'He was a lad. Drink? You've never seen anything like it. Spent so much on booze, he could never afford to get married – which is just as well, the way things turned out.'

'Most people have lost somebody.'

'If you're on your own, come round our place for dinner on Sunday.'

'Thanks, I work Sundays now.'

Harris nodded. 'Well, whenever you feel like it.'

A detective-constable poked his head around the door and addressed Harris. 'Can we start bagging-up the evidence, guv?'

Harris looked at Bloggs.

'I've finished,' Bloggs said.

'All right, son, carry on,' Harris told him.

Bloggs said: 'Suppose he made contact after I lost him, and arranged for the resident agent to come here. The resident may have suspected a trap – that would explain why he came in through the window and picked the lock.'

'It makes him a devilish suspicious bastard,' Harris observed.

'That might be why we've never caught him. Anyway, he gets into Blondie's room and wakes him up. Now he knows it isn't a trap, right?'

'Right.'

'So why does he kill Blondie?'

'Maybe they quarrelled.'

'There were no signs of a struggle.'

Harris frowned into his empty cup. 'Perhaps he twigged that Blondie was being watched, and he was afraid we'd pick the boy up and make him spill the beans.'

Bloggs said: 'That makes him a ruthless bastard.'

'That might be why we've never caught him.'

'Come in. Sit down. I've just had a call from MI6. Canaris has been fired.'

Bloggs went in, sat down, and said: 'Is that good news or bad?'

'Very bad,' said Godliman. 'It's happened at the worst possible moment.'

'Do I get told why?'

Godliman looked at him through narrow eyes, then said: 'I think you need to know. At this moment we have forty double-agents broadcasting to Hamburg false information about Allied plans for the invasion of France.'

Bloggs whistled. 'I didn't know it was quite that big. I suppose the doubles say we're going in at Cherbourg, but really it will be Calais, or vice versa.'

'Something like that. Apparently I don't need to know the details. Anyway they haven't told me. However, the whole thing is in danger. We knew Canaris; we knew we had him fooled; we could have gone on fooling him. A new broom may mistrust his predecessor's agents. There's more: we've had some defections from the other side, people who could have betrayed the Abwehr's people over here if they hadn't been betrayed already. It's another reason for the Germans to begin to suspect our doubles.

'Then there's the possibility of a leak. Literally thousands of people now know about the double-cross system. There are doubles in Iceland, Canada, and Ceylon. We ran a double-cross in the Middle East.

'And we made a bad mistake last year by repatriating a German called Erich Carl. We later learned he was an Abwehr agent – a real one – and that while he was in internment on the Isle of Man he may have learned about two doubles called Mutt and Jeff, and possibly a third called Tate.

'So we're skating on thin ice. If one decent Abwehr agent in Britain gets to know about Fortitude – that's the codename for the deception plan – the whole strategy will be endangered. Not to mince words, we could lose the fucking war.'

Bloggs suppressed a smile: he could remember a time when Professor Godliman did not know the meaning of such words.

The professor went on: 'The Twenty Committee has made it quite clear that they expect me to make sure there aren't any decent Abwehr agents in Britain.'

'Last week we would have been quite confident that there weren't,' Bloggs said.

'Now we know there's at least one.'

'And we let him slip through our fingers.'

'So now we have to find him again.'

'I don't know,' Bloggs said gloomily. 'We don't know what part of the country he's operating from, we haven't the faintest idea what he looks like. He's too crafty to be pinpointed by triangulation while he's transmitting – otherwise we would have nabbed him long ago. We don't even know his codename. So where do we start?'

'Unsolved crimes,' said Godliman. 'Look: a spy is bound to break the law. He forges papers, he steals petrol and ammunition, he evades checkpoints, he enters restricted areas, he takes photographs, and when people rumble him he kills them. The police are bound to get to know of some of these crimes, if the spy has been operating for any length of time. If we go through the unsolved crimes files since the war, we'll find traces.'

'Don't you realize that *most* crimes are unsolved?' Bloggs said incredulously. 'The files would fill the Albert Hall!'

Godliman shrugged. 'So, we narrow it down to London, and we start with murders.'

They found what they were looking for on the very first day of their search.

It happened to be Godliman who came across it, and at first he did not realize its significance.

It was the file on the murder of a Mrs Una Garden in Highgate in 1940. Her throat had been cut and she had been sexually molested, although not raped. She had been found in the bedroom of her lodger, with a considerable amount of alcohol in her bloodstream. The picture was fairly clear: she had had a tryst with the lodger, he had wanted to go farther than she was prepared to let him, they had quarrelled, he had killed her, and the murder had neutralized his libido. But the police had never found the lodger.

Godliman had been about to pass over the file: spies did not get involved in sexual assaults. But he was a meticulous man with records, so he read every word, and consequently discovered that the unfortunate Mrs Garden had received stiletto wounds in her back, as well as the fatal wound to her throat.

Godliman and Bloggs were on opposite sides of a wooden table in the records room at Old Scotland Yard. Godliman tossed the file across the table and said: 'I think this is it.'

Bloggs glanced through it and said: 'The stiletto.'

They signed for the file and walked the short distance to the War Office. When they returned to Godliman's room, there was a decoded signal on his desk. He read it casually, then thumped the table in excitement. 'It's him!'

Bloggs read: 'Orders received. Regards to Willi.'

'Remember him?' Godliman said. 'Die Nadel?'

'Yes,' Bloggs said hesitantly. 'The Needle. But there's not much information here.'

'Think, think! A stilletto is like a needle. It's the same man: the murder of Mrs Garden, all those signals in 1940 that we couldn't trace, the rendezvous with Blondie . . .'

'Possibly.' Bloggs looked thoughtful.

'I can prove it,' Godliman said. 'Remember the transmission about Finland that you showed me the first day I came here? The one which was interrupted?'

'Yes.' Bloggs went to the file to find it.

'If my memory serves me well, the date of that transmission is the same as the date of this murder . . . and I'll bet the time of death coincides with the interruption.'

Bloggs looked at the signal in the file. 'Right both times.'

'There!'

'He's been operating in London for at least five

years, and it's taken us until now to get on to him,' Bloggs reflected. 'He won't be easy to catch.'

Godliman suddenly looked wolfish. 'He may be clever, but he's not as clever as me,' he said tightly. 'I'm going to nail him to the fucking wall.'

Bloggs laughed out loud. 'My God, you've changed, Professor.'

Godliman said: 'Do you realize that's the first time you've laughed for a year?'

CHAPTER NINE

T HE SUPPLY boat rounded the headland and chugged into the bay at Storm Island under a blue sky. There were two women in it: one was the skipper's wife – he had been called up and now she ran the business – and the other was Lucy's mother.

Mother got out of the boat, wearing a utility suit – a mannish jacket and an above-the-knee skirt. Lucy hugged her mightily.

'Mother! What a surprise!'

'But I wrote to you.'

The letter was with the mail on the boat – Mother had forgotten that the post only came once a fortnight on Storm Island.

'Is this my grandson? Isn't he a big boy?'

Little Jo, almost three years old, turned bashful and hid behind Lucy's skirt. He was dark-haired, pretty, and tall for his age.

Mother said: 'Isn't he like his father!'

'Yes,' Lucy said. Her assent held a note of disapproval. 'You must be freezing – come up to the house. Where *did* you get that skirt?'

They picked up the groceries and began to walk up the ramp to the cliff top. Mother chattered as they went. 'It's the fashion, dear. It saves on material. But it isn't as cold as this on the mainland. Such a wind! I suppose it's all right to leave my case on the jetty – nobody to steal it! Jane is engaged to an American soldier – a white one, thank God. He comes from a place called Milwaukee, and he doesn't chew gum. Isn't that nice? I've only got four more daughters to marry off now. Your father is a Captain in the Home Guard, did I tell you? He's up half the night patrolling the common waiting for German parachutists. Uncle Stephen's warehouse was bombed – I don't know *what* he'll do, it's an Act of War or something—'

'Don't rush, Mother, you've got fourteen days to tell me the news.' Lucy laughed.

They reached the cottage. Mother said: 'Isn't this *lovely*?' They went in. 'I think this is just lovely.'

Lucy parked Mother at the kitchen table and made tea. 'Tom will get your case up. He'll be here for his lunch shortly.'

'The shepherd?'

'Yes.'

'Does he find things for David to do, then?'

Lucy laughed. 'It's the other way around. I'm sure he'll tell you all about it himself. You haven't told me why you're here.'

'My dear, it's about time I saw you. I know we're not supposed to make unnecessary journeys, but once in four years isn't extravagant, is it?'

They heard the jeep outside, and a moment later David wheeled himself in. He kissed his mother-in-law and introduced Tom.

Lucy said: 'Tom, you can earn your lunch today by bringing Mother's case up, as she carried your groceries.'

David was warming his hands at the stove. 'It's raw today.'

Mother said: 'You're really taking sheep-farming seriously, then?'

'The flock is double what it was three years ago,' David told her. 'My father never farmed this island seriously. I've fenced six miles of the cliff top, improved the grazing, and introduced modern breeding methods. Not only do we have more sheep, but each animal gives us more meat and wool.'

Mother said tentatively: 'I suppose Tom does the physical work and you give the orders.'

David laughed. 'Equal partners, Mother.'

They had hearts for lunch, and both men ate mountains of potatoes. Mother commented favourably on Jo's table manners. Afterwards David lit a cigarette and Tom stuffed his pipe.

Mother said: 'What I really want to know is when you're going to give me more grandchildren.' She smiled brightly.

There was a long silence.

'Well, I think it's wonderful, the way David copes,' said Mother.

Lucy said: 'Yes,' and again there was that note of disapproval.

They were walking along the cliff top. The wind had

dropped on the third day of Mother's visit, and it was mild enough to go out. They took Jo, dressed in a fisherman's sweater and a fur coat. They had stopped at the top of a rise to watch David, Tom and the dog herding sheep. Lucy could see in Mother's face an internal struggle as concern vied with discretion. She decided to save her mother the effort of asking.

'He doesn't love me,' she said.

Mother looked quickly to make sure Jo was out of earshot. 'I'm sure it's not that bad, dear. Different men show their love in diff—'

'Mother, we haven't been man and wife – properly – since we were married.'

'But . . .?' She indicated Jo with a nod.

'That was a week before the wedding.'

'Oh! Oh, dear.' She was shocked. 'Is it, you know, the accident?'

'Yes, but not in the way you mean. It's nothing physical. He just . . . won't.' Lucy was crying quietly, the tears trickling down her wind-browned cheeks.

'Have you talked about it?'

'I've tried. Mother, what shall I do?'

'Perhaps with time—'

'It's been almost four years!'

There was a pause. They began to walk on across the heather, into the weak afternoon sun. Jo chased gulls. Mother said: 'I almost left your father, once.'

It was Lucy's turn to be shocked. 'When?'

'It was soon after Jane was born. We weren't so well-off in those days, you know – Father was still working for his father, and there was a slump. I was expecting for the third time in three years, and it seemed that a life of having babies and making ends meet stretched out in front of me with nothing to relieve the monotony. Then I discovered he was seeing an old flame of his – Brenda Simmonds, you never knew her, she went to Basingstoke. Suddenly I asked myself what I was doing it for, and I couldn't think of a sensible answer.'

Lucy had dim, patchy memories of those days: her grandfather with a white moustache; her father, a more slender edition; extended-family meals in the great farmhouse kitchen; a lot of laughter and sunshine and animals. Even then her parents' marriage had seemed to represent solid contentment, happy permanence. She said: 'Why didn't you? Leave, I mean.'

'Oh, people just didn't, in those days. There wasn't all this divorce, and a woman couldn't get a job.'

'Women work at all sorts of things now.'

'They did in the last war, but everything changed afterwards with a bit of unemployment. I expect it will be the same this time. Men get their way, you know, generally speaking.'

'And you're glad you stayed.' It was not a question.

'People my age shouldn't make pronouncements about Life. But *my* life has been a matter of making-do, and the same goes for most of the women I know. Steadfastness always looks like a sacrifice, but usually it isn't. Anyway, I'm not going to give you advice. You wouldn't take it, and if you did you'd blame your problems on me, I expect.'

'Oh, Mother.' Lucy smiled.

Mother said: 'Shall we turn round? I think we've gone far enough for one day.'

In the kitchen one evening Lucy said to David: 'I'd like Mother to stay another two weeks, if she will.'

Mother was upstairs putting Jo to bed, telling him a story.

David said: 'Isn't a fortnight long enough for you to dissect my personality?'

'Don't be silly, David.'

He wheeled himself over to her chair. 'Are you telling me you don't talk about me?'

'Of course we talk about you – you're my husband.'

'What do you say to her, then?'

'Why are you so worried?' Lucy said, not without malice. 'What are you so ashamed of?'

'Damn you, I've nothing to be ashamed of. No one wants his personal life talked about by a pair of gossiping women.'

'We don't gossip about you.'

'What do you say?'

'Aren't you touchy!'

'Answer my question.'

'I say I want to leave you, and she tries to talk me out of it.'

He spun around and wheeled away. 'Tell her not to bother for my sake.'

She called: 'Do you mean that?'

He stopped. 'I don't need anybody, do you understand? I can manage alone. I'm self-sufficient.'

'And what about me?' she said quietly. 'Perhaps I need somebody.'

'What for?'

'To love me.'

Mother came in, and sensed the atmosphere. 'He's fast asleep,' she said. 'Dropped off before Cinderella got to the ball. I think I'll pack a few things, not to leave it all until tomorrow.' She went out again.

'Do you think it will ever change, David?' Lucy asked.

'I don't know what you mean.'

'Will we ever be . . . the way we were, before the wedding?'

'My legs won't grow back, if that's what you mean.'

'Oh, God, don't you know that doesn't bother me? I just want to be loved.'

David shrugged. 'That's your problem.' He went out before she started to cry.

Mother did not stay the second fortnight. Lucy walked with her down to the jetty the next day. It was raining hard, and they both wore mackintoshes. They stood in silence waiting for the boat, watching the rain pit the sea with tiny craters. Mother held Jo in her arms.

'Things will change, in time, you know,' she said. 'Four years is nothing in a marriage.'

Lucy said: 'I don't think he'll change, but there's not much I can do other than give it a chance. There's Jo, and the war, and David's disability – how can I leave?'

The boat arrived, and Lucy exchanged her mother for three boxes of groceries and five letters. The water was choppy. Mother sat in the boat's tiny cabin. They waved her around the headland. Lucy felt very lonely.

Jo began to cry. 'I don't want Gran to go away!'

'Nor do I,' said Lucy.

CHAPTER TEN

GODLIMAN AND Bloggs walked side by side along the pavement of a bomb-damaged London shopping street. They were a mismatched pair: the stooped, bird-like professor, with pebble-lensed spectacles and a pipe, not looking where he was going, taking short, scurrying steps; and the flatfooted youngster, blond and purposeful, in his detective's raincoat and melodramatic hat: a cartoon looking for a caption.

Godliman was saying: 'I think Die Nadel is well-connected.'

'Why?'

'The only way he could be so insubordinate with impunity. It's this "Regards to Willi" line. It must refer to Canaris.'

'You think he was pals with Canaris.'

'He's pals with somebody – perhaps someone more powerful than Canaris was.'

'I have the feeling this is leading somewhere.'

'People who are well-connected generally make those connections at school, or university, or staff college. Look at that.'

114

They were outside a shop which had a huge empty space where once there had been a plate-glass window. A rough sign, hand-painted and nailed to the window-frame, said: 'Even more open than usual.'

Bloggs laughed, and said: 'I saw one outside a bombed police station: "Be good. We are still open."'

'It's become a minor art form.'

They walked on. Bloggs said: 'So, what if Die Nadel did go to school with someone high in the Wermacht?'

'People always have their pictures taken at school. Midwinter down in the basement at Kensington – that house where MI6 used to be before the war – he's got a collection of thousands of photographs of German officers: school photos, binges in the Mess, passing-out parades, shaking hands with Adolf, newspaper pictures – everything.'

'I see,' Bloggs said. 'So if you're right, and Die Nadel has been through Germany's equivalent of Eton and Sandhurst, we've probably got a picture of him.'

'Almost certainly. Spies are notoriously camera-shy, but they don't become spies until they're well into adulthood. It will be a youthful Die Nadel that we find in Midwinter's files.'

They skirted a huge crater outside a barber's. The shop was intact, but the traditional red-and-white striped pole lay in shards on the pavement. The sign in the window said: 'We've had a close shave – come and get one yourself.'

Bloggs said: 'How will we recognize him? No one has ever seen him.'

'Yes, they have. At Mrs Garden's boarding-house in Highgate they know him quite well.'

The Victorian house stood on a hill overlooking London. It was built of red brick, and Bloggs thought it looked angry at the damage Hitler was doing to its city. It was high up; a good place from which to broadcast. Die Nadel would have lived on the top floor. Bloggs wondered what secrets the spy had transmitted to Hamburg from this place in the dark days of 1940. Map references for aircraft factories and steelworks, details of coastal defences, political gossip, gas masks and Anderson shelters and sandbags, British morale, bomb damage reports, 'Well done, boys, you got Christine Bloggs at last – ' Shut up.

The door was opened by an elderly man in a black jacket and striped trousers.

'Good morning. I'm Inspector Bloggs, from Scotland Yard. I'd like a word with the householder, please.'

Bloggs saw fear leap to the man's eyes, then a young woman appeared in the doorway and said: 'Come in, please.'

The tiled hall smelled of wax polish. Bloggs hung his hat and coat on a stand. The old man disappeared into the depths of the house, and the woman led Bloggs into a lounge. It was expensively furnished in a rich, old-fashioned way. There were bottles of whisky, gin and sherry on a trolley: all the bottles were unopened. The woman sat down on a floral armchair and crossed her legs.

Bloggs said: 'Why is the old man frightened of the police?'

'My father-in-law is a German Jew. He came here in 1935 to escape Hitler, and in 1940 you put him in a concentration camp. His wife killed herself at the prospect. He has just been released from the Isle of Man. He had a letter from the King, apologizing for the inconvenience to which he had been put.'

Bloggs said: 'We don't have concentration camps.'

'We invented them. In South Africa. Didn't you know? We go on about our history, but we forget bits. We're so good at blinding ourselves to unpleasant facts.'

'Perhaps it's just as well.'

'What?'

'In 1939 we blinded ourselves to the unpleasant fact that we couldn't win a war with Germany – and look what happened.'

'That's what my father-in-law says. He's not as cynical as I. What can we do to assist Scotland Yard?'

Bloggs had been enjoying the exchange, and now it was with reluctance that he turned his attention to work. 'It's about a murder that took place here four years ago.'

'So long!'

'Some new evidence may have come to light.'

'I know about it, of course. The previous owner was killed by a tenant. My husband bought the house from her executor – she had no heirs.'

'I want to trace the other people who were tenants at that time.'

'Yes.' The woman's hostility had gone, now, and her intelligent face showed the effort of recollection. 'When

we arrived there were three who had been here before
the murder: a retired naval officer, a salesman, and a
young boy from Yorkshire. The boy joined the Army –
he still writes to us. The salesman was called up, and he
died at sea. I know because two of his five wives got in
touch with us! And the Commander is still here.'

'Still here!' That was a piece of luck. 'I'd like to see
him, please.'

'Surely.' She stood up. 'He's aged a lot. I'll take you
to his room.'

They went up the carpeted stairs to the first floor.
She said: 'While you're talking to him, I'll look up the
last letter from the boy in the Army.' She knocked on
the door. It was more than Bloggs's landlady would
have done, he thought wryly.

A voice called: 'It's open,' and Bloggs went in.

The Commander sat in a chair by the window with a
blanket over his knees. He wore a blazer, a collar and a
tie, and spectacles. His hair was thin, his moustache
grey, his skin loose and wrinkled over a face that might
once have been strong. The room was the home of a
man living on memories: there were paintings of sailing
ships, a sextant and a telescope, and a photograph of
himself as a boy aboard HMS *Winchester*.

'Look at this,' he said without turning around. 'Tell
me why that chap isn't in the Navy.'

Bloggs crossed to the window. A horse-drawn baker's
van was at the kerb outside the house, the elderly horse
dipping into its nosebag while the deliveries were made.
That 'chap' was a woman with short blonde hair in

trousers. She had a magnificent bust. Bloggs laughed. 'It's a woman in trousers,' he said.

'Bless my soul, so it is!' The Commander turned around. 'Can't tell, these days, you know. Women in trousers!'

Bloggs introduced himself. 'We've reopened the case of a murder committed here in 1940. I believe you lived here at the same time as the main suspect, one Henry Faber.'

'Indeed! What can I do to help?'

'How well do you remember Faber?'

'Perfectly. Tall chap, dark hair, well-spoken, quiet. Rather shabby clothes – if you were the kind who judges by appearances, you might well mistake him. I didn't dislike him – wouldn't have minded getting to know him better, but he didn't want that. I suppose he was about your age.'

Bloggs suppressed a smile: he was used to people assuming he must be older simply because he was a detective.

The Commander added: 'I'm sure he didn't do it, you know. I know a bit about character – you can't command a ship without learning – and if that man was a sex maniac, I'm Hermann Goering.'

Bloggs suddenly connected the blonde in trousers with the mistake about his age, and the conclusion depressed him. He said: 'You know, you should always ask to see a policeman's warrant card.'

The Commander was slightly taken aback. 'All right, then, let's have it.'

Bloggs opened his wallet and folded it to display the picture of Christine. 'Here.'

The Commander studied it for a moment, then said: 'A very good likeness.'

Bloggs sighed. The old man was very nearly blind.

He stood up. 'That's all, for now,' he said. 'Thank you.'

'Any time. Whatever I can do to help. I'm not much value to England these days – you've got to be pretty useless to get invalided out of the Home Guard, you know.'

'Goodbye.' Bloggs went out.

The woman was in the hall downstairs. She handed Bloggs a letter. 'The address is a Forces box number,' she said. 'No doubt you'll be able to find out where he is.'

'You knew the Commander would be no use,' Bloggs said.

'I guessed not. But a visitor makes his day.' She opened the door.

On impulse, Bloggs said: 'Will you have dinner with me?'

A shadow crossed her face. 'My husband is still on the Isle of Man.'

'I'm sorry – I thought—'

'It's all right. I'm flattered.'

'I wanted to convince you we're not the Gestapo.'

'I know you're not. A woman alone just gets bitter.'

Bloggs said: 'I lost my wife in the bombing.'

'Then you know how it makes you hate.'

'Yes,' said Bloggs. 'It makes you hate.' He went down the steps. The door closed behind him. It had started to rain.

It had been raining then. Bloggs was late. He had been going over some new material with Godliman. Now he was hurrying, so that he would have half an hour with Christine before she went out to drive her ambulance. It was dark, and the raid had already started. The things Christine saw at night were so awful she had stopped talking about them.

Bloggs was proud of her, proud. The people she worked with said she was better than two men: she hurtled through blacked-out London, driving like a veteran, taking corners on two wheels, whistling and cracking jokes as the city turned to flame around her. Fearless, they called her. Bloggs knew better: she was terrified, but she would not let it show. He knew because he saw her eyes in the morning, when he got up and she went to bed; when her guard was down and it was over for a few hours. He knew it was not fearlessness but courage, and he was proud.

It was raining harder when he got off the bus. He pulled down his hat and put up his collar. At a kiosk he bought cigarettes for Christine: she had started smoking recently, like a lot of women. The shopkeeper would let him have only five, because of the shortage. He put them in a Woolworth's bakelite cigarette case.

A policeman stopped him and asked for his identity

card: another two minutes wasted. An ambulance passed him, similar to the one Christine drove; a requisitioned fruit lorry, painted grey.

He began to get nervous as he approached home. The explosions were sounding closer, and he could hear the aircraft clearly. The East End was in for another bruising tonight: he would sleep in the Morrison shelter. There was a big one, terribly close, and he quickened his step. He would eat his supper in the shelter, too.

He turned into his own street, saw the ambulances and the fire engines, and broke into a run.

The bomb had landed on his side of the street, around the middle. It must be close to his own home. Jesus in heaven, not us, no—

There had been a direct hit on the roof, and the house was literally flattened. He raced up to the crowd of people, neighbours and firemen and volunteers. 'Is my wife all right? Is she out? IS SHE IN THERE?'

A fireman looked at him with compassion. 'Nobody's come out of there, mate.'

Rescuers were picking over the rubble. Suddenly one of them shouted: 'Over here!' Then he said: 'Bugger me, it's Fearless Bloggs!'

Frederick dashed to where the man stood. Christine was underneath a huge chunk of brickwork. Her face was visible: the eyes were closed.

The rescuer called: 'Lifting gear, boys, sharp's the word.'

Christine moaned and stirred.

Bloggs said: 'She's alive!' He knelt down beside her

and got his hands under the edge of the lump of rubble.

The rescuer said: 'You won't shift that, son.'

The brickwork lifted.

The rescuer said: 'Strewth, you'll kill yourself,' and bent down to help.

When it was two feet off the ground they got their shoulders under it. The weight was off Christine now. A third man joined in, and a fourth. They all straightened up together.

Bloggs said: 'I'll lift her out.'

He crawled under the sloping roof of brick and cradled his wife in his arms.

Someone shouted: 'Fuck me it's slipping!'

Bloggs scurried out from under with Christine held tightly to his chest. As soon as he was clear the rescuers let go of the rubble and jumped away. It fell back to earth with a sickening thud; and when Bloggs realized that *that* had landed on Christine, he knew she was going to die.

He carried her to the ambulance, and it took off immediately. She opened her eyes again once, before she died, and said: 'You'll have to win the war without me, kiddo.'

More than a year later, as he walked downhill from Highgate into the bowl of London, with the rain on his face mingling with the tears again, he thought the woman in the spy's house had said a mighty truth: it makes you hate.

*

In war boys become men, and men become soldiers, and soldiers get promoted; and this is why Billy Parkin, aged 18, who should have been an apprentice in his father's tannery at Scarborough, was believed by the Army to be twenty-one, made up to sergeant, and given the job of leading his advance squad through a hot, dry forest toward a dusty whitewashed Italian village.

The Italians had surrendered but the Germans had not, and it was the Germans who were defending Italy against the combined British-American invasion. The Allies were going to Rome, and for Sergeant Parkin's squad it was a long walk.

They came out of the forest at the top of a hill, and lay flat on their bellies to look down on the village. Parkin got out his binoculars and said: 'What wouldn't I fookin give for a fookin cup of fookin tea.' He had taken to drinking, and cigarettes, and women, and his language was like that of soldiers everywhere. He no longer went to prayer meetings.

Some of these villages were defended and some were not. Parkin recognized that as sound tactics: you didn't know which were undefended, so you approached them all cautiously, and caution cost time.

The downside of the hill held little cover – just a few bushes – and the village began at its foot. There were a few white houses, a river with a wooden bridge, then more houses around a little piazza with a town hall and a clock tower. There was a clear line-of-sight from the tower to the bridge: if the enemy were here at all, he would be in the town hall. A few figures worked in the surrounding fields: God knew who they were. They might be genuine peasants, or any one of a host of factions: fascisti, mafia, corsos, partigianos, communisti . . . or even Germans. You didn't know whose side they would be on until the shooting started.

Parkin said: 'All right, Corporal.'

Corporal Watkins disappeared back into the forest and emerged, five minutes later, on the dirt road into the village, wearing a civilian hat and a filthy old blanket over his uniform. He stumbled, rather than walked, and over his shoulder was a bundle that could have been anything from a bag of onions to a dead rabbit. He reached the near edge of the village and vanished into the darkness of a low cottage.

After a moment he came out. Standing close to the wall, where he could not be seen from the village, he looked toward the soldiers on the hilltop and waved: one, two, three.

The squad scrambled down the hillside into the village.

Watkins said: 'All the houses empty, Sarge.'

Parkin nodded. It meant nothing.

They moved through the houses to the edge of the river. Parkin said: 'Your turn, Smiler. Swim the Mississippi here.'

Private 'Smiler' Hudson put his equipment in a neat pile, took off his helmet, boots and tunic, and slid into the narrow stream. He emerged on the far side, climbed the bank, and disappeared among the houses. This time there was a longer wait: more area to check. Finally Hudson walked back across the wooden bridge. 'If they're 'ere, they're 'iding,' he said.

He retrieved his gear and the squad crossed the bridge into the village. They kept to the sides of the street as they walked toward the piazza. A bird flew off a roof and startled Parkin. Some of the men kicked open a few doors as they passed. There was nobody.

They stood at the edge of the piazza. Parkin nodded at the town hall. 'Did you go inside the place, Smiler?'

'Yes, sir.'

'Looks like the village is ours, then.'

'Yes, sir.'

Parkin stepped forward to cross the piazza, and then the storm broke. There was a crash of rifles, and bullets hailed all around them. Someone screamed. Parkin was running, dodging, ducking. Watkins, in front of him, shouted with pain and clutched his leg: Parkin picked him up bodily. A bullet clanged off his tin hat. He raced for the nearest house, charged the door, and fell inside.

The shooting stopped. Parkin risked a peep outside. One man lay wounded in the piazza: Hudson. Rough justice. Hudson moved, and a solitary shot rang out. Then he was still. Parkin said: 'Fookin bastards.'

Watkins was doing something to his leg, cursing. Parkin said: 'Bullet still in there?'

Watkins yelled: 'Ouch!' then grinned and held something up. 'Not any more.'

Parkin looked outside again. 'They're in the clock tower,' he said. 'You wouldn't think there was room. Can't be many of them.'

'They can shoot, though.'

'Yes. They've got us pinned.' Parkin frowned. 'Got any fireworks?'

'Aye.'

'Let's have a look.' Parkin opened Watkins's pack and took out the dynamite. 'Here. Fix me a ten-second fuse.'

The others were in the house across the street. Parkin called out: 'Hey!'

A face appeared at the door. 'Sarge?'

'I'm going to throw a tomato. When I shout, give me covering fire.'

'Right.'

Parkin lit a cigarette. Watkins handed him a bundle of dynamite. Parkin shouted: 'Fire!' He lit the fuse with the cigarette, stepped into the street, drew back his arm, and threw the bomb at the clock tower. He ducked back into the house, the fire of his own men ringing in his ears. A bullet shaved the woodwork, and he caught a splinter under his chin. He heard the dynamite explode.

Before he could look, someone across the street shouted: 'Bull's-eye!'

Parkin stepped outside. The ancient clock tower had crumbled. A chime sounded incongruously as dust settled over the ruins.

Watkins said: 'You ever play cricket? That was a bloody good shot.'

Parkin walked to the centre of the piazza. There seemed to be enough human spare parts to make about three Germans. He said: 'The tower was pretty unsteady anyway. It would probably have fallen down if we'd all sneezed at it in unison.' He turned away. 'Another day, another dollar.' It was a phrase the Yanks used.

'Sarge? Radio.' It was the R/T operator.

Parkin walked back and took the handset from him. 'Sergeant Parkin.'

'Major Roberts. You're discharged from active duty as of now, Sergeant.'

'Why?' Parkin's first thought was that they had discovered his true age.

'The brass want you in London. Don't ask me why because I don't know. Leave your corporal in charge and make your way back to base. A car will meet you on the road.'

'Yes, sir.'

'The orders also say that on no account are you to risk your life. Got that?'

Parkin grinned, thinking of the clock tower and the dynamite. 'Got it.'

'All right. On your way. You lucky sod.'

Everyone had called him a boy, but they had known him before he joined the Army, Bloggs thought. There was no doubt he was a man now. He walked with confidence and grace, looked about him sharply, and was respectful without being ill-at-ease in the company of superior officers. Bloggs knew that he was lying about his age, not because of his looks or manner, but because of the small signs that appeared whenever age was mentioned – signs which Bloggs, an experienced interrogator, picked up out of habit.

He had been amused when they told him they wanted him to look at pictures. Now, in his third day in

Mr Midwinter's dusty Kensington vault, the amusement had gone and tedium had set in. What irritated him most was the no-smoking rule.

It was even more boring for Bloggs, who had to sit and watch him.

At one point Parkin said: 'You wouldn't call me back from Italy to help in a four-year-old murder case that could wait until after the war. Also, these pictures are mostly of German officers. If this case is something I should keep mum about, you'd better tell me.'

'It's something you should keep mum about,' said Bloggs.

Parkin went back to his pictures.

They were all old, mostly browned and fading. Many were out of books, magazines and newspapers. Sometimes Parkin picked up a magnifying glass Mr Midwinter had thoughtfully provided, to peer more closely at a tiny face in a group; and each time this happened Bloggs's heart raced, only to slow down when Parkin put the glass to one side and picked up the next photograph.

They went to a nearby pub for lunch. The ale was weak, like most wartime beer, but Bloggs still thought it wise to restrict young Parkin to two pints – on his own he would have sunk a gallon.

'Mr Faber was the quiet sort,' Parkin said. 'You wouldn't think he had it in him. Mind you, the landlady wasn't bad looking. And she wanted it. Looking back, I think I could have had her myself if I'd known how to go about it. There, I was, only – eighteen.'

They ate bread and cheese, and Parkin swallowed a

dozen pickled onions. When they went back, they stopped outside the house while Parkin smoked another cigarette.

'Mind you,' he said, 'he was a biggish chap, good-looking, well-spoken. We all thought he was nothing much because his clothes were poor, and he rode a bike, and he'd no money. I suppose it could have been a subtle kind of disguise.' His eyebrows were raised in a question.

'It could have been,' Bloggs said.

That afternoon Parkin found not one but three pictures of Faber.

One of them was only nine years old.

And Mr Midwinter had the negative.

Henrik Rudolph Hans von Muller-Guder ('Let's just call him Faber,' said Godliman with a laugh) was born on 26 May 1900 at a village called Oln in West Prussia. His father's family had been substantial landowners in the area for generations. His father was the second son; so was Henrik. All the second sons were Army officers. His mother, the daughter of a senior official of the Second Reich, was born and raised to be an aristocrat's wife, and that was what she was.

At the age of thirteen he went to the Karlsruhe cadet school in Baden; two years later he was transferred to the more prestigious Gross-Lichterfelde, near Berlin. Both places were hard, disciplinarian institutions where the minds of the pupils were improved with canes and cold baths and bad food. However, Henrik learned to speak English and French and studied history, and passed the Reifeprüfung with the highest mark recorded since the turn of the century. There were only three other points of note in his school career: one bitter winter he rebelled against authority to the extent of sneaking out of the school at night and walking 150 miles to his aunt's house; he broke the arm of his wrestling instructor during a practice bout; and he was flogged for insurbordination.

He served briefly as an ensign-cadet in the neutral zone of Friedrichsfeld, near Wesel, in 1920; did token officer training at the War School at Metz in 1921, and was commissioned Second Lieutenant in 1922.

('What was the phrase you used?' Godliman asked Bloggs. 'The German equivalent of Eton and Sandhurst.')

Over the next few years he did short tours of duty in half a dozen places, in the manner of one who is being groomed for the general staff. He continued to distinguish himself as an athlete, specializing in longer-distance running. He made no close friendships, never married, and refused to join the National Socialist party. His promotion to lieutenant was somewhat delayed by a vague incident involving the pregnancy of the daughter of a lieutenant-colonel in the Defence Ministry, but eventually came about in 1928. His habit of talking to superior officers as if they were equals came to be accepted as pardonable in one who was both a rising young officer and a Prussian aristocrat.

In the late twenties Admiral Wilhelm Canaris became friendly with Henrik's Uncle Otto, his father's elder brother, and spent several holidays at the family estate at Oln. In 1931 Adolf Hitler, not yet Chancellor of Germany, was a guest there.

In 1933 Henrik was promoted Captain, and went to Berlin for unspecified duties. This is the date of the last photograph.

About then, according to published information, he seems to have ceased to exist.

'We can conjecture the rest,' said Percival Godliman. 'The Abwehr trains him in wireless transmission, codes, map-making, burglary, blackmail, sabotage and silent killing. He comes to London in about 1937 with plenty of time to set himself up with a solid cover – perhaps two. His loner instincts are honed sharp by the spying game. When war breaks out, he considers himself licensed to kill.' He looked at the photograph on his desk. 'He's a handsome fellow.'

It was a picture of the running team of the 10th Hanoverian Jaeger Battalion. Faber was in the middle, holding a cup. He had a high forehead, with cropped hair; a long chin; and a small mouth decorated with a narrow moustache.

Godliman passed the picture to Billy Parkin. 'Has he changed much?'

'He looks a lot older, but that might be his ... bearing.' He studied the photograph thoughtfully. 'His hair is longer now, and the moustache has gone.' He passed the picture back across the desk. 'But it's him, all right.'

'There are two more items in the file, both of them conjectural,' Godliman said. 'First, they say he may have gone into Intelligence in 1933 – that's the routine assumption when an officer's record just stops for no apparent reason. The second item is a rumour, unconfirmed by any reliable source, that he spent some years as a confidential advisor to Stalin, using the name Vasily Zankov.'

'That's incredible,' Bloggs said. 'I don't believe that.'

Godliman shrugged. '*Somebody* persuaded Stalin to execute the cream of his officer corps during the years Hitler rose to power.'

Bloggs shook his head, and changed the subject. 'Where do we go from here?'

Godliman considered. 'Let's have Sergeant Parkin transferred to us. He's the only man we know who has actually seen Die Nadel. Besides, he knows too much for us to risk him in the front line: he could get captured and interrogated, and give the game away. Next, make a first-class print of this photo, and have the hair thickened and the moustache obliterated by a re-touch artist. Then we can distribute copies.'

'Do we want to start a hue and cry?' Bloggs said doubtfully.

'No. For now, let's tread softly. If we put the thing in the newspapers he'll get to hear of it, and vanish. Just send the photo to police forces for the time being.'

'Is that all?'

'I think so. Unless you've got other ideas.'

Parkin cleared his throat. 'Sir?'

'Yes.'

'I really would prefer to go back to my unit. I'm not really the administrative type, if you know what I mean.'

'You're not being offered a choice, Sergeant. At this stage of the conflict, one Italian village more or less makes no difference – but this man Faber could lose us the war. As the Americans say, I'm not kidding.'

CHAPTER ELEVEN

FABER HAD gone fishing.

He was stretched out on the deck of a thirty-foot boat, enjoying the spring sunshine, moving along the canal at about three knots. One lazy hand held the tiller, the other rested on a rod which trailed its line in the water behind the boat.

He hadn't caught a thing all day.

As well as fishing, he was bird-watching – both out of interest (he was actually getting to know quite a lot about the damn birds) and as an excuse for carrying binoculars. Earlier today he had seen a kingfisher's nest.

The people at the boatyard in Norwich had been delighted to rent him the vessel for a fortnight. Business was bad: they had only two boats nowadays, and one of them had not been used since Dunkirk. Faber had haggled over the price, just for the sake of form. In the end they had thrown in a locker of tinned food.

He had bought bait in a shop nearby; the fishing tackle he had brought from London. They had observed that he had nice weather for it, and wished him good fishing. Nobody even asked to see his identity card.

So far, so good.

The difficult bit was to come. For assessing the strength of an army was difficult. First you had to find it.

In peacetime the Army would put up its own road signs to help you. Now they had taken down, not only their own but everyone else's road signs.

The simple solution would be to get in a car and follow the first military vehicle you saw until it stopped. However, Faber had no car; it was nearly impossible for a civilian to hire one; and even if you got one you couldn't get petrol for it. Besides, a civilian driving around the countryside following Army lorries and looking at Army camps was liable to be arrested.

Hence the boat.

Some years ago, before it had become illegal to sell maps, Faber had discovered that Britain had thousands of miles of inland waterways. The original network of rivers had been augmented during the nineteenth century by a spider-web of canals. In some areas there was almost as much waterway as there was road. Norfolk was one of these areas.

The boat had many advantages. On a road, a man was going somewhere: on a river he was just sailing. Sleeping in a parked car was conspicuous: sleeping in a moored boat was natural. The waterway was lonely. And who ever heard of a canal-block?

There were disadvantages. Airfields and barracks had to be near roads, but they were located without reference to access by water. Faber had to explore the countryside at night, leaving his moored boat and tramping the hillsides by moonlight, exhausting forty-mile round trips during which he could easily miss what he was looking for because of the darkness or because he simply did not have enough time to check every square mile of land.

When he returned, a couple of hours after dawn, he would sleep until midday then move on, stopping occasionally to climb a nearby hill and check the outlook. At locks, isolated farmhouses and riverside pubs he would talk to people, hoping for hints of a military presence. So far there had been none.

He was beginning to wonder whether he was in the right area. He had tried to put himself in General Patton's place, thinking: If I were planning to invade France east of the Seine from a base in eastern England, where would I locate that base? Norfolk was obvious: a vast expanse of lonely countryside, plenty of flat ground for aircraft, close to the sea for rapid departure. And the Wash was a natural place to gather a fleet of ships. However, his guesswork might be wrong for reasons unknown to him. Soon he would have to consider a rapid move across country to a new area: perhaps the Fens.

A lock appeared ahead of him, and he trimmed his sails to slow his pace. He glided gently into the lock and bumped softly against the gates. The lock-keeper's house was on the bank. Faber cupped his hands around his mouth and hallooed. Then he settled down to wait. He had learned that lock-keepers were a breed that could not be hurried. Moreover, it was tea-time, and at tea-time they could hardly be moved at all.

A woman came to the door of the house and beckoned. Faber waved back, then jumped on to the bank, tied up the boat, and went into the house. The lock-keeper was in his shirt-sleeves at the kitchen table. He said: 'Not in a hurry, are you?'

Faber smiled. 'Not at all.'

'Pour him a cup of tea, Mavis.'

'No, really,' Faber said politely.

'It's all right, we've just made a pot.'

'Thank you.' Faber sat down. The little kitchen was airy and clean, and his tea came in a pretty china cup.

'Fishing holiday?' the lock-keeper asked.

'Fishing and bird-watching,' Faber answered. 'I'm thinking of tying-up quite soon and spending a couple of days on land.'

'Oh, aye. Well, best keep to the far side of the canal, then. Restricted area this side.'

'Really? I didn't know there was Army land hereabouts.'

'Aye, it starts about half a mile from here. As to whether it's Army, I wouldn't know. They don't tell me.'

'Well, I suppose we don't need to know,' Faber said.

'Aye. Drink up, then, and I'll see you through the lock. Thanks for letting me finish my tea.'

They left the house, and Faber got into the boat and untied it. The gates behind him closed slowly, and then the keeper opened the sluices. The boat gradually sank with the level of the water in the lock, then the keeper opened the front gates.

Faber made sail and moved out. The lock-keeper waved.

He stopped again about four miles away and moored the boat to a stout tree on the bank. While he waited for night to fall he made a meal of tinned sausage-meat, dry biscuits, and bottled water. He dressed in his black clothes, put into a shoulder-bag his binoculars, camera, and copy of *Rare Birds of East Anglia*, pocketed his compass and picked up his torch. He was ready.

He doused the hurricane lamp, locked the cabin door, and jumped on to the bank. Consulting his compass by torchlight, he entered the belt of woodland alongside the canal.

He walked due south from his boat for about half a mile until he hit the fence. It was six feet high, chicken-wire, with coiled barbed wire on top. He backtracked into the wood and climbed a tall tree.

There was scattered cloud above. The moon showed through fitfully. Beyond the fence was open land, a gentle rise. Faber had done this sort of thing before, at Biggin Hill, Aldershot, and a host of military areas all over Southern England. There were two levels of security: a mobile patrol around the perimeter fence, and stationary sentries at the installations.

Both could be evaded by patience and caution.

Faber came down the tree and returned to the fence. He concealed himself behind a bush and settled down to wait.

He had to know when the mobile patrol passed this point. If they did not come until dawn, he would simply return the following night. If he was lucky, they would pass shortly. From the apparent size of the area under guard he guessed they would only make one complete tour of the fence each night.

He was lucky. Soon after ten o'clock he heard the tramp of feet, and three men marched by on the inside of the fence.

Five minutes later Faber crossed the fence.

He walked due south: when all directions are equal, a straight line is best. He did not use his flashlight. He kept close to hedges and trees when he could, and avoided high ground where he might be silhouetted against a sudden flash of moonlight. The sparse countryside was an abstract in black, grey and silver. The ground underfoot was a little soggy, as if there might be marshes nearby. A fox ran across a field in front of him, as fast as a greyhound, as graceful as a cat.

It was 11.30 p.m. when he came across the first indications of military activity – and very odd indications they were.

The moon came out and he saw, perhaps a quarter of a mile ahead, several rows of one-storey buildings laid out with the unmistakable precision of an Army barracks. He dropped to the ground immediately, but he was already doubting the reality of what he apparently saw; for there were no lights and no noise.

He lay still for ten minutes, to give explanations a chance to emerge, but nothing happened except that a badger lumbered into view, saw him, and made off.

Faber crawled forward.

As he got closer he realized that the barracks were

not just unoccupied, but unfinished. Most of them were little more than a roof supported by cornerposts. Some had one wall.

A sudden sound stopped him: a man's laugh. He lay still and watched. A match flared briefly and died, leaving two glowing red spots in one of the unfinished huts: guards.

Faber touched the stiletto in his sleeve, then began to crawl again, making for the side of the camp away from the sentries.

The half-built huts had no floors and no foundations. There were no construction vehicles around, no wheelbarrows, concrete mixers, shovels or piles of bricks. A mud track led away from the camp across the fields, but spring grass was growing in the ruts: it had not been used much lately.

It was as if someone had decided to billet ten thousand men here, then changed his mind a few weeks after building started.

Yet there was something about the place that did not quite fit that explanation.

Faber walked around softly, alert lest the sentries should take it into their heads to make a patrol. There was a group of military vehicles in the centre of the camp. They were old and rusting, and had been degutted – none had an engine or any interior components. But if one was going to cannibalize obsolete vehicles, why not take the shells for scrap?

Those huts which did have a wall were on the outermost rows, and their walls faced out. It was like a movie set, not a building site.

Faber decided he had learned all he could from this place. He walked to the east edge of the camp, then dropped to his hands and knees and crawled away until he was out of sight behind a hedge. Half a mile farther on, near the top of a rise, he looked back. Now it looked exactly like a barracks again.

The glimmer of an idea formed in his mind. He gave it time.

The land was still relatively flat, relieved only by gentle folds. There were patches of woodland and marshy scrub which Faber took advantage of. Once he had to detour around a lake, its surface a silver mirror under the moon. He heard the hoot of an owl, and looked in that direction to see a tumbledown barn in the distance.

Five miles on, he saw the airfield.

There were more planes here than he thought were possessed by the entire Royal Air Force. There were Pathfinders to drop flares, Lancasters and American B-17S for softening-up bombing, Hurricanes and Spitfires and Mosquitoes for reconnaissance and strafing: enough planes for an invasion.

Without exception their undercarriages had sunk into the soft earth, and they were up to their bellies in mud.

Once again there were no lights and no noise.

Faber followed the same procedure, crawling flat toward the planes until he located the guards. In the middle of the airfield was a small tent. The faint glow of a lamp shone through the canvas. Two men, perhaps three.

As Faber approached the planes they seemed to become flatter, as if they had all been squashed.

He reached the nearest and touched it in amazement. It was a piece of half-inch plywood, cut out in the outline of a Spitfire, painted with camouflage, and roped to the ground.

Every other plane was the same.

There were more than a thousand of them.

Faber got to his feet, watching the tent from the corner of his eye, ready to drop to the ground at the slightest sign of movement. He walked all around the phoney airfield, looking at the phoney fighters and bombers, connecting them with the movie-set barracks, reeling at the implications of what he had found.

He knew that if he continued to explore he would find more airfields like this, more half-built barracks. If he went to the Wash he would find a fleet of plywood destroyers and troop ships.

It was a vast, meticulous, costly, outrageous trick.

Of course, it could not possibly fool an onlooker for very long. But it was not designed to deceive observers on the ground.

It was meant to be seen from the air.

Even a low-flying reconnaissance plane equipped with the latest cameras and fast film would come back with pictures which indisputably showed an enormous concentration of men and machines.

No wonder the general staff were anticipating an invasion east of the Seine.

There would be other elements to the deception, he guessed. The British would refer to FUSAG in signals, using codes they knew to be broken. There would be phoney espionage reports channelled through the Spanish diplomatic bag to Hamburg. The possibilities were endless.

The British had had four years to arm themselves for this invasion. Most of the German army was fighting Russia. Once the Allies got a toehold on French soil, they would be unstoppable. The Germans' only chance was to catch them on the beaches and annihilate them as they came off the troop ships.

If they were waiting in the wrong place, they would lose that one chance.

The whole strategy was immediately clear. It was simple, and it was devastating.

Faber had to tell Hamburg.

He wondered whether they would believe him.

War strategy was rarely altered on the word of one man. His own standing was particularly high, but was it that high?

He needed to get proof, and then take it to Berlin.

He needed photographs.

He would take pictures of this gigantic dummy army, then he would go to Scotland and meet the U-boat, and he would deliver the pictures personally to the Führer. He could do no more.

For photography he needed light. He would have to wait until dawn. There had been a ruined barn a little way back: he could spend the rest of the night there.

He checked his compass and set off. The barn was farther than he thought, and the walk took him an hour. It was an old wooden building with holes in the roof. The rats had long ago deserted it for lack of food, but there were bats in the hayloft.

Faber lay down on some planks, but he could not sleep for the knowledge that he was now personally capable of altering the course of the greatest war in history.

Dawn was due at 05.21. At 04.20 Faber left the barn.

Although he had not slept, the two hours of immobility had rested his body and calmed his mind, and he was now in fine spirits. The cloud was clearing with a west wind, so although the moon had set there was starlight.

His timing was good. The sky was growing perceptibly brighter as he came in sight of the 'airfield'.

The sentries were still in their tent. With luck, they would be sleeping: Faber knew from his own experience of such duties that it was hardest to stay awake during the last few hours.

And if they did come out, he would just have to kill them.

He selected his position and loaded the Leica with a 36-frame roll of 35mm fast Agfa film. He hoped the film's light-sensitive chemicals had not spoiled, for it had been stored in his suitcase since before the war: you couldn't buy film in Britain nowadays. It should be all right, for he had kept it in a light-proof bag away from any heat.

When the red rim of the sun edged over the horizon he began shooting. He took a series of shots from different vantage points and various distances, finishing with a close-up of one dummy plane: the pictures would show both the illusion and the reality.

As he took the last he saw movement from the corner of his eye. He dropped flat and crawled under a plywood Mosquito. A soldier emerged from the tent, walked a few paces, and urinated on the ground. The man stretched and yawned, then lit a cigarette. He looked around the airfield, shivered, and returned to the tent.

Faber got up and ran.

A quarter of a mile away he looked back. The airfield was out of sight. He headed west, toward the barracks.

This would be more than an ordinary espionage coup. Hitler had had a life of being the only one in step. The man who brought the proof that, yet again, the Führer was right and all the experts were wrong, could look for more than a pat on the back. Faber knew that already Hitler rated him the Abwehr's best agent: this triumph would probably get him Canaris's job.

If he made it.

He increased his pace, jogging twenty yards, walking the next twenty, and jogging again, so that he reached the barracks by 06.30. It was bright daylight now, and he could not approach close, because these sentries were not in a tent, but in one of the wall-less huts, with a clear view all around them. He lay down by the hedge and took his pictures from a distance. Ordinary prints would just show a barracks, but big enlargements ought to reveal the details of the deception.

When he headed back toward the boat he had exposed thirty frames. Again he hurried, for he was now terribly conspicuous, a black-clad man carrying a canvas bag of equipment, jogging across the open fields of a restricted area.

He reached the fence an hour later, having seen nothing but wild geese. As he climbed over the wire, he felt a great release of tension. Inside the fence the balance of suspicion had been against him; outside it was in his favour. He could revert to his bird-watching, fishing, sailing role. The period of greatest risk was over.

He strolled through the belt of woodland, catching his breath and letting the strain of the night's work seep away. He would sail a few miles on, he decided, before mooring again to catch a few hours' sleep.

He reached the canal. It was over. The boat looked pretty in the morning sunshine. As soon as he was under way he would make some tea, then—

A man in uniform stepped out of the cabin of the boat and said: 'Well, well. And who might you be?'

Faber stood stock still, letting the icy calm and the old instincts come into play. The intruder wore the uniform of a captain in the Home Guard. He had some kind of handgun in a holster with a buttoned flap. He was tall and rangy, but he looked to be in his late fifties. White hair showed under his cap. He made no move to draw his gun. Faber took all this in as he said: 'You are on my boat, so I think it is I who should ask who you are.'

'Captain Stephen Langham, Home Guard.'

'James Baker.' Faber stayed on the bank. A captain did not patrol alone.

'And what are you doing?'

'I'm on holiday.'

'Where have you been?'

'Bird-watching.'

'Since before dawn? Cover him, Watson.'

A youngish man in denim uniform appeared on Faber's left, carrying a shotgun. Faber looked around. There was another man to his right and a fourth behind him.

The captain called: 'Which direction did he come from, Corporal?'

The reply came from the top of an oak tree. 'From the restricted area, sir.'

Faber was calculating odds. Four to one – until the corporal came down from the tree. They had only two guns: the shotgun and the captain's pistol. And they were amateurs. The boat would help, too.

He said: 'Restricted area? All I saw was a bit of fence. Look, do you mind pointing that blunderbuss away? It might go off.'

The captain said: 'Nobody goes bird-watching in the dark.'

'If you set up your hide under cover of darkness, you're concealed by the time the birds wake up. It's the accepted way to do it. Now look, the Home Guard is jolly patriotic and keen and all that, but let's not take it too far, what? Don't you just have to check my papers and file a report?'

The captain was looking a shade doubtful. 'What's in that canvas bag?'

'Binoculars, a camera, and a reference book.' Faber's hands went to the bag.

'No, you don't,' the captain said. 'Look inside it, Watson.'

There it was: the amateur's error.

Watson said: 'Hands up.'

Faber raised his hands above his head, his right hand close to the left sleeve of his jacket. Faber choreographed the next few seconds: there must be no gunfire.

Watson came up on Faber's left side, pointing the shotgun at him, and opened the flap of Faber's canvas bag. Faber drew the stiletto from his sleeve, moved inside Watson's guard, and plunged the knife downward into Watson's neck up to the hilt. Faber's other hand twisted the shotgun out of the young man's grasp.

The other two soldiers on the bank moved toward him, and the corporal began to crash down through the branches of the oak.

Faber tugged the stiletto out of Watson's neck as the man collapsed to the ground. The captain was fumbling at the flap of his holster. Faber leaped into the well of the boat. It rocked, sending the captain staggering. Faber struck at him with the knife, but the man was too far away for an accurate thrust. The point caught in the lapel of his uniform jacket, then jerked up, slashing his chin. His hand came away from the holster to clutch the wound.

Faber whipped around to face the bank. One of the soldiers jumped. Faber stepped forward and held his right arm out rigidly. The leaping soldier impaled himself on the eight-inch needle.

The impact knocked Faber off his feet, and he lost his grip on the stiletto. The soldier fell on top of the weapon. Faber got to his knees: there was no time to retrieve the stiletto, for the captain was opening his holster. Faber jumped at him, his hands going for the officer's face. The gun came out. Faber's thumbs gouged at the captain's eyes, and he screamed in pain and tried to push Faber's arms aside.

There was a thud as the fourth guardsman landed in the well of the boat. Faber turned from the captain, who would now be unable to see to fire his pistol even if he could get the safety off. The fourth man held a policeman's truncheon. He brought it down hard. Faber shifted to the right, so that the blow missed his head and caught his left shoulder. His left arm momentarily became paralysed. He chopped the man's neck with the side of his right hand, a powerful, accurate blow. Amazingly, the man survived it, and brought his truncheon up for a second swipe. Faber closed in. The feeling returned to his left arm, and it began to hurt mightily. He took the soldier's face in both his hands, pushed, twisted, and pushed again. There was a sharp crack as the man's neck broke. At the same instant the truncheon landed again, this time on Faber's head. He reeled away, dazed.

The captain bumped into him, still staggering. Faber pushed him. His cap went flying as he stumbled backward over the gunwale and fell into the canal with a huge splash.

The corporal jumped the last six feet from the oak tree on to the ground. Faber retrieved his stiletto from the impaled guard and leaped to the bank. Watson was still alive, but it would not be for long: blood was pumping out of the wound in his neck.

Faber and the corporal faced each other. The corporal had a gun.

He was utterly terrified. In the few seconds it had taken him to climb down the oak tree, this stranger had killed three of his mates and thrown the fourth into the canal. Horror shone from his eyes like torchlight.

Faber looked at the gun. It was *old* – it looked like a museum piece. If the corporal had any confidence in it, he would have fired it already.

The corporal took a step forward, and Faber noticed that he favoured his right leg – perhaps he had hurt it coming out of the tree. Faber stepped sideways, forcing the corporal to put his weight on the weak leg as he swung to keep his gun on target. Faber got the toe of his shoe under a stone and kicked upward. The corporal's eyes flicked to the stone, and Faber moved.

The corporal pulled the trigger, and nothing happened. The old gun had jammed. Even if it had fired, he would have missed Faber: his eyes were on the stone, he stumbled on the weak leg, and Faber had moved.

Faber killed him with the neck stab.

Only the captain was left.

Faber looked, to see the man clambering out of the water on the far bank. He found a stone and threw it.

151

It hit the captain's head, but the man heaved himself on to dry land and began to run.

Faber ran to the bank, dived in, swam a few strokes, and came up on the far side. The captain was a hundred yards away and running; but he was old. Faber gave chase. He gained steadily until he could hear the man's agonized, ragged breathing. The captain slowed, then collapsed into a bush.

Faber came up to him and turned him over.

The captain said: 'You're a . . . devil.'

'You saw my face,' Faber said, and killed him.

CHAPTER TWELVE

THE JU-52 trimotor transport plane with swastikas on the wings bumped to a halt on the rain-wet runway at Rastenburg in the East Prussian forest. A small man with big features – a large nose, a wide mouth, big ears – disembarked and walked quickly across the tarmac to a waiting Mercedes car.

As the car drove through the gloomy, damp forest, Field Marshal Erwin Rommel took off his cap and rubbed a nervous hand along his receding hairline. In a few weeks' time, he knew, another man would travel this route with a bomb in his briefcase – a bomb destined for the Führer himself. Meanwhile the fight must go on, so that the new leader of Germany – who might even be Rommel himself – could negotiate with the Allies from a strong position.

At the end of a ten-mile drive the car arrived at the Wolfsschanze, the Wolves' Lair, headquarters now for Hitler and the increasingly tight, neurotic circle of generals who surrounded him.

There was a steady drizzle, and raindrops dripped from the tall conifers in the compound. At the gate to Hitler's personal quarters, Rommel put on his cap and got out of the car. Oberführer Rattenhuber, the chief of the SS bodyguard, wordlessly held out his hand to receive Rommel's pistol.

The conference was to be held in the underground bunker, a cold, damp, airless shelter lined with concrete. Rommel went down the steps and entered. There were a dozen or so there already, waiting for the noon meeting: Himmler, Goering, von Ribbentrop, Keitel. Rommel nodded greetings and sat on a hard chair to wait.

They all stood when Hitler entered. He wore a grey tunic and black trousers, and he was becoming more and more stooped, Rommel observed. He walked straight to the far end of the bunker, where a large wall map of north-western Europe was tacked to the concrete. He looked tired and irritable. He spoke without preamble.

'There will be an Allied invasion of Europe. It will come this year. It will be launched from Britain, with English and American troops. They will land in France. We will destroy them at the high-water mark. On this there is no room for discussion.'

He looked around, as if daring his staff to contradict him. There was silence. Rommel shivered: the bunker was as cold as death.

'The question is: where will they land? Von Roenne – your report.'

Colonel Alexis von Roenne, who had taken over, effectively, from Canaris, got to his feet. A mere captain at the outbreak of war, he had distinguished himself with a superb report on the weaknesses of the French army – a report which had been called a decisive factor in the German victory. He had become chief of the army intelligence bureau in 1942, and that bureau had absorbed the Abwehr on the fall of Canaris. Rommel had heard that he was proud and outspoken, but able.

Roenne said: 'Our information is extensive, but by no means complete. The Allies' codename for the invasion is Overlord. Troop concentrations in Britain are as follows.' He picked up a pointer and crossed the room to the wall map. 'First: along the south coast. Second: here in the district known as East Anglia. Third: in Scotland. The East Anglian concentration is *by far* the greatest. We conclude that the invasion will be three-pronged. First: a diversionary attack on Normandy. Second: the main thrust, across the Straits of Dover to the Calais coast. Third: a flanking invasion from Scotland across the North Sea to Norway. All intelligence sources support this prognosis.' He sat down.

Hitler said: 'Comments?'

Rommel, who was Commander of Army Group B, which controlled the north coast of France, said: 'I can report one confirming sign: the Pas de Calais has received by far the greatest tonnage of bombs.'

Goering said: 'What intelligence sources support your prognosis, von Roenne?'

Roenne stood up again. 'There are three: air reconnaissance, monitoring of enemy wireless signals, and the reports of agents.' He sat down.

Hitler crossed his hands protectively in front of his genitals, a nervous habit which was a sign that he was about to make a speech. 'I shall now tell you,' he began, 'how I would be thinking if I were Winston Churchill. Two choices confront me: east of the Seine, or west of the Seine. East has one advantage: it is nearer. But in modern warfare there are only two distances – *within* fighter range and *outside* fighter range. *Both* of these choices are within fighter range. Therefore distance is not a consideration.

'West has a great port – Cherbourg – but east has none. And most important – east is more heavily fortified than west. The enemy too has air reconnaissance.

'So, I would choose west. And what would I do then? I would try to make the Germans think the opposite! I would send two bombers to the Pas de Calais for every one to Normandy. I would try to knock out every bridge over the Seine. I would put out misleading wireless signals, send false intelligence reports, dispose my troops in a misleading fashion. I would deceive fools like Rommel and von Roenne. I would hope to deceive the Führer himself!'

Goering spoke first after a lengthy silence. 'My Führer, I believe you flatter Churchill by crediting him with ingenuity equal to your own.'

There was a noticeable easing of tension in the uncomfortable bunker. Goering had said exactly the right thing, managing to voice his disagreement in the form of a compliment. The others followed him, each stating the case a little more strongly: the Allies would choose the shorter sea crossing for speed; the closer coast would allow the covering fighter aircraft to refuel and return in shorter time; the south-east was a better launch pad, with more estuaries and harbours; it was unlikely that all the intelligence reports would be unanimously wrong.

Hitler listened for half an hour, then held up his hand for silence. He picked up a yellowing sheaf of papers from the table and waved them. 'In 1941,' he said, 'I issued my directive *Construction of Coastal Defences*, in which I forecast that the decisive landing of the Allies would come at the protruding parts of Normandy and Brittany, where the excellent harbours would make ideal beachheads. That was what my intuition told me then, and that is what it tells me now!' A fleck of foam appeared on the Führer's lower lip.

Von Roenne spoke up. (He has more courage than I, Rommel thought.) 'My Führer, our investigations continue, quite naturally, and there is one particular line of inquiry which you should know about. I have in recent weeks sent an emissary to England to contact the agent known as Die Nadel.'

Hitler's eyes gleamed. 'Ah! I know the man. Carry on.'

'Die Nadel's orders are to assess the strength of the First United States Army Group under General Patton in East Anglia. If he finds that this has been exaggerated, we must surely reconsider our prognosis. If, however, he reports that the army is as strong as we presently believe, there can be little doubt that Calais is the target.'

Goering looked at von Roenne. 'Who is this Nadel?'

Hitler answered the question. 'The only decent agent Canaris ever recruited – because he recruited

him at my behest,' he said. 'I know his family – a pillar
of the Reich. Strong, loyal, upright Germans. And Die
Nadel – a brilliant man, brilliant! I see all his reports.
He has been in London since before the English started
the war. Earlier than that, in Russia—'

Von Roenne interrupted: 'My Führer—'

Hitler glared at him, but he seemed to realize that
the spy chief had been right to stop him. 'Well?'

Von Roenne said tentatively: 'Then you will accept
Die Nadel's report?'

Hitler nodded. 'That man will discover the truth.'

Part Three

Part Three

CHAPTER THIRTEEN

FABER LEANED against a tree, shivering, and threw up.

Then he considered whether he should bury the five dead men.

It would take between thirty and sixty minutes, he estimated, depending on how well he concealed the bodies. During that time he might be caught.

He had to weigh that risk against the precious hours he might gain by delaying the discovery of the deaths. The five men would be missed very soon: there would be a search under way by around nine o'clock. Assuming they were on a regular patrol, their route would be known. The searchers' first move would be to send a runner to cover the route. If the bodies were left as they were, he would see them and raise the alarm. Otherwise, he would report back and a full-scale search would be mounted, with bloodhounds and policemen beating the bushes. It might take them all day to discover the corpses. By that time Faber could be in London. It was important for him to be out of the area before they knew they were looking for a murderer. He decided to risk the additional hour.

He swam back across the canal with the elderly

captain across his shoulder. He dumped him uncer-emoniously behind a bush. He retrieved the two bodies from the well of the boat and piled them on top of the captain. Then he added Watson and the corporal to the heap.

He had no spade, and he needed a big grave. He found a patch of loose earth a few yards into the wood. The ground there was slightly hollowed, to give him an advantage. He got a saucepan from the boat's tiny galley and began to dig.

For a couple of feet there was just leaf-mould, and the going was easy. Then he got down to clay, and digging became extremely difficult. In half an hour he had added only another eighteen inches of depth to the hole. It would have to do.

He carried the bodies to the hole one by one and threw them in. Then he took off his muddy, blood-stained clothes and dropped them on top. He covered the grave with loose earth and a layer of foliage ripped from nearby bushes and trees. It should be good enough to pass that first, superficial inspection.

He kicked earth over the patch of ground near the bank where the life-blood of Watson had poured out. There was blood in the boat, too, where the impaled soldier had lain. Faber found a rag and swabbed-down the deck.

Then he put on clean clothes, made sail, and moved off.

He did not fish or watch birds: this was no time for pleasant embellishments to his cover. Instead he piled-on the sail, putting as much distance as possible between himself and the grave. He had to get off the water and into some faster transport as soon as possible. He reflected, as he sailed, on the relative merits of catching a train or stealing a car. A car was faster, if one could be found to steal; but the search for it might start quite soon, regardless of whether the theft was connected with the missing Home Guard patrol. Finding a railway station might take a long time, but it seemed safer: if he were careful he could escape suspicion for most of the day.

He wondered what to do about the boat. Ideally he would scuttle it, but he might be seen doing so. If he left it in a harbour somewhere, or simply moored at the canalside, the police would connect it with the murders that much sooner; and that would tell them in which direction he was moving. He postponed the decision.

Unfortunately, he was not sure where he was. His map of England's waterways gave every bridge, harbour and lock; but it did not show railway lines. He calculated he was within an hour or two's walk of half a dozen villages, but a village did not necessarily mean a station.

In the end luck solved two problems at once: the canal went under a railway bridge.

He took his compass, the film from the camera, his wallet and his stiletto. All his other possessions would go down with the boat.

The towpath on both sides was shaded with trees, and there were no roads nearby. He furled the sails, dismantled the base of the mast, and laid the pole on the deck. Then he removed the bung-hole stopper from the keel and stepped on to the bank, holding the rope.

Gradually filling with water, the boat drifted under the bridge. Faber hauled on the rope to hold the vessel in position directly under the brick arch as it sank. The after-deck went under first, the prow followed, and finally the water of the canal closed over the roof of the cabin. There were a few bubbles, then nothing. The outline of the boat was hidden from a casual glance by the shadow of the bridge. Faber threw the rope in.

The railway line ran north-east to south-west. Faber climbed the embankment and walked south-west, which was the direction in which London lay. It was a two-line track, probably a rural branch line. There would be few trains, but they would stop at all stations.

The sun grew stronger as he walked, and the exertion made him hot. When he had buried his blood-stained black clothes he had put on a double-breasted blazer and heavy flannel trousers. Now he took off the blazer and slung it over his shoulder.

After forty minutes he heard a distant chuff-chuff-chuff, and hid in a bush beside the line. An old steam engine went slowly by, heading north-west, puffing great clouds of smoke and hauling a train of coal trucks. If one came by in the opposite direction, he could jump it. Should he? It would save him a long walk. On the other hand, he would get conspicuously dirty, and he might have trouble disembarking without being seen. No, it was safer to walk.

The line ran straight as an arrow across the flat countryside. Faber passed a farmer, ploughing a field with a tractor. There was no way to avoid being seen.

The farmer waved to him without stopping in his work. He was too far away to get a good sight of Faber's face.

He had walked about ten miles when he saw a station ahead. It was half a mile away, and all he could see was the rise of the platforms and a cluster of signals. He left the line and cut across the fields, keeping close to borders of trees, until he met a road.

Within a few minutes he entered the village. There was nothing to tell him its name. Now that the threat of invasion was a memory, signposts and place-names were being re-erected, but this village had not got around to it.

There was a Post Office, a Corn Store, and a pub called The Bull. A woman with a pram gave him a friendly 'Good morning!' as he passed the War Memorial. The little station basked sleepily in the spring sunshine. Faber went in.

A timetable was pasted to a notice-board. Faber stood in front of it. From behind the little ticket window a voice said: 'I shouldn't take any notice of that, if I were you. It's the biggest work of fiction since *The Forsyte Saga.*'

Faber had known the timetable would be out-of-date, but he had needed to establish whether the trains went to London. They did. He said: 'Any idea what time the next train leaves for Liverpool Street?'

The clerk laughed sarcastically. 'Some time today, if you're lucky.'

'I'll buy a ticket anyway. Single, please.'

'Five-and-fourpence. They say the Italian trains run on time,' the clerk said.

'Not any more,' Faber remarked. 'Anyway, I'd rather have bad trains and our politics.'

The man shot him a nervous look. 'You're right, of course. Do you want to wait in The Bull? You'll hear the train – or, if not, I'll send for you.'

Faber did not want more people to see his face. 'No, thanks, I'd only spend money.' He took his ticket and went on to the platform.

The clerk followed him a few minutes later, and sat on the bench beside him in the sunshine. He said: 'You in a hurry?'

Faber shook his head. 'I've written today off. I got up late, I quarrelled with the boss, and the lorry that gave me a lift broke down.'

'One of those days. Ah, well.' The clerk looked at his watch. 'She went up on time this morning, and what goes up must come down, they say. You might be lucky.' He went back into his office.

Faber was lucky. The train came twenty minutes later. It was crowded with farmers, families, business-men and soldiers. Faber found a space on the floor close to a window. As the train lumbered away, he picked up a discarded two-day-old newspaper, bor-rowed a pencil, and started to do the crossword. He was proud of his ability to do crosswords in English: it was the acid test of fluency in a foreign language. After a while the motion of the train lulled him into a shallow sleep, and he dreamed.

*

It was a familiar dream, the dream of his arrival in London.

He had crossed from France, carrying a Belgian passport which said he was Jan van Gelder, a representative for Philips (which would explain his suitcase radio if the Customs opened it). His English then was fluent but not colloquial. The Customs had not bothered him: he was an ally. He had caught the train to London. In those days there had been plenty of empty seats in the carriages, and you could get a meal. Faber had dined on roast beef and Yorkshire pudding. It amused him. He had talked with a history student from Cardiff about the European political situation. The dream was like the reality until the train stopped at Waterloo. Then it turned into a nightmare.

The trouble started at the ticket barrier. Like all dreams it had its own weird illogicality. The document they queried was not his forged passport but his perfectly legitimate railway ticket. The collector said: 'This is an Abwehr ticket.'

'No, it is not,' said Faber, speaking with a ludicrously thick German accent. What had happened to his dainty English consonants? They would not come. 'I have it in Dover gekauft.' Damn, that did it.

But the ticket collector, who had turned into a London policeman complete with helmet, seemed to ignore the sudden lapse into German. He smiled politely and said: 'I'd better just check your Klamotte, sir.'

The station was crowded with people. Faber thought that if he could get into the crowd he might escape. He dropped the suitcase radio and fled, pushing his way through the crowd. Suddenly he realized he had left his trousers on the train, and there were swastikas on his socks. He would have to buy trousers at the very first shop, before people noticed the trouserless running man with Nazi hose – then someone in the crowd said: 'I've seen your face before,' and tripped him, and he fell with a bump and landed on the floor of the railway carriage where he had gone to sleep.

He blinked, yawned, and looked around him. He had a headache. For a moment he was filled with relief that it was all a dream, then he was amused by the ridiculousness of the symbolism – swastika socks, for God's sake!

A man in overalls beside him said: 'You had a good sleep.'

Faber looked up sharply. He was always afraid of talking in his sleep and giving himself away. He said: 'I had an unpleasant dream.' The man made no comment.

It was getting dark. He *had* slept for a long time. The carriage light came on suddenly, a single blue bulb, and someone drew the blinds. People's faces turned into pale, featureless ovals. The workman became talkative again. 'You missed the excitement,' he told Faber.

Faber frowned. 'What happened?' It was impossible he should have slept through some kind of police check.

'One of them Yank trains passed us. It was going about ten miles an hour, nigger driving it, ringing its bell, with a bloody great cow-catcher on the front! Talk about the Wild West.'

Faber smiled and thought back to the dream. In fact his arrival in London had been without incident. He had checked into an hotel at first, still using his Belgian cover. Within a week he had visited several country churchyards, taken the names of men his age from the gravestones, and applied for three duplicate birth certificates. Then he took lodgings and found humble work, using forged references from a non-existent Manchester firm. He had even got on to the electoral register in Highgate before the war. He voted Conservative. When rationing came in, the ration books were issued via householders to every person who had slept in the house on a particular night. Faber contrived to spend part of that night in each of three different houses, and so obtained papers for each of his personae. He burned the Belgian passport – in the unlikely event he should need a passport, he could get three British ones.

The train stopped, and from the noise outside the passengers guessed they had arrived. When Faber got out he realized how hungry and thirsty he was. His last meal had been sausage-meat, dry biscuits and bottled water, the day before. He went through the ticket barrier and found the station buffet. It was full of people, mostly soldiers, sleeping or trying to sleep at the tables. Faber asked for a cheese sandwich and a cup of tea.

'The food is reserved for servicemen,' said the woman behind the counter.

'Just the tea, then.'

'Got a cup?'

Faber was surprised. 'No, I haven't.'

'Neither have we, chum.'

Faber left in disgust. He contemplated going into the Great Eastern Hotel for dinner, but that would take time. He found a pub and drank two pints of weak beer, then bought a bag of chips at a fish-and-chip shop and ate them from the newspaper wrapping, standing on the pavement. They made him feel surprisingly full.

Now he had to find a chemist's shop and break in.

He wanted to develop his film, to make sure the pictures came out. He was not going to risk returning to Germany with a roll of spoiled, useless film. If the pictures were no good he would have to steal more film and go back. The thought was unbearable.

It would have to be a small independent shop, not a branch of a chain which would process film centrally. It must be in an area where the local people could afford cameras (or could have afforded them before the war). The part of East London in which Liverpool Street Station stood was no good. He decided to head toward Bloomsbury.

The moonlit streets were quiet. There had been no sirens so far tonight. Two Military Policemen stopped him in Chancery Lane and asked for his identity card. Faber pretended to be slightly drunk, and the MPs did not ask what he was doing out of doors.

He found the shop he was looking for at the north end of Southampton Row. There was a Kodak sign in the window. Surprisingly, the shop was open. He went in.

A stooped, irritable man with thinning hair and glasses stood behind the counter, wearing a white coat. He said: 'We're only open for doctors' prescriptions.'

'That's all right. I just want to ask whether you develop photographs.'

'Yes, if you come back tomorrow—'

'Do you do them on the premises?' Faber asked. 'I need them quickly, you see.'

'Yes, if you come back tomorrow—'

'Could I have the prints the same day? My brother's on leave, and he wants to take some back—'

'Twenty-four hours is the best we can do. Come back tomorrow.'

'Thank you, I will,' Faber lied. On his way out he noticed that the shop was due to close in ten minutes. He crossed the road and stood in the shadows, waiting.

Promptly at nine o'clock the pharmacist came out, locking the shop behind him, and walked off down the road. Faber went in the opposite direction and turned two corners.

There seemed to be no access to the back of the shop. That was something of a blow: Faber did not want to break in the front way, in case the unlocked door was noticed by a patrolling policeman while he was in there. He walked along the parallel street, looking for a way through. Apparently there was none. Yet there had to be a well of some kind at the back, for the two

KEN FOLLETT

streets were too far apart for the buildings to be joined
back-to-back.

Finally he came across a large old house with a
nameplate marking it as a Hall of Residence for a
nearby college. The front door was unlocked. Faber
went in and walked quickly through to a communal
kitchen. A lone girl sat at a table, drinking coffee and
reading a book. Faber muttered: 'College blackout
check.' She nodded and returned to her text. Faber
went out of the back door.

He crossed a yard, bumping into a cluster of garbage
cans on the way, and found a door to a lane. In seconds
he was at the rear of the chemist's shop. This entrance
was obviously never used. He clambered over some
tyres and a discarded mattress, and threw his shoulder
at the door. The rotten wood gave easily, and Faber was
inside.

He found the darkroom and shut himself in. The
light switch operated a dim red lamp in the ceiling.
The place was quite well-equipped, with neatly labelled
bottles of developing fluid, an enlarger, and even a
dryer for prints.

Faber worked quickly but carefully, getting the temperature of the tanks exactly right, agitating the fluids
to develop the film evenly, timing the processes by the
hands of a large electric clock on the wall.

The negatives were perfect.

He let them dry, then fed them through the enlarger
and made one complete set of ten-by-eight prints. He
felt a sense of elation as he saw the images gradually

appear in the bath of developer – God, he had done a good job!

There was now a major decision to be made.

The problem had been in his mind all day, and now that the pictures had come out he was forced to confront it.

What if he did not make it home?

The journey ahead of him was, to say the least, hazardous. He was confident of his own ability to make the rendezvous in spite of travel restrictions and coastal security; but he could not guarantee that the U-boat would be there; or that it would get back across the North Sea. Indeed, he might walk out of here and get run over by a bus.

The possibility that, having discovered the greatest secret of the war, he might die and his secret die with him, was too awful to contemplate.

He had to have a fall-back stratagem; a second method of ensuring that the evidence of the Allied deception reached the Abwehr. And that meant writing to Hamburg.

There was, of course, no postal service between England and Germany. Mail had to go via a neutral country. All such mail was sure to be censored. He could write in code, but there was no point: he had to send the pictures, for it was the evidence that counted.

There was a route, but it was an old one. At the Portuguese Embassy in London there was an official, sympathetic to Germany for political reasons and because he was well bribed, who would pass messages via the diplomatic bag to the German Embassy in Lisbon. The route had been opened early in 1939, and Faber had never used it except for one routine test communication Canaris had asked for.

It would have to do.

Faber felt irrationally angry. He *hated* to place his faith in others. This route might no longer be open, or it might be insecure; in which case the British could discover that he had found out their secret.

It was a fundamental rule of espionage that the opposition must not know which of their secrets you have found out; for if they do, the value of your discoveries is nullified. However, in this case that was not so; for what could the British do with their knowledge? They still had the problem of conquering France.

Faber's mind was clear. The balance of argument indisputably favoured entrusting his secret to the Portuguese Embassy contact.

Against all his instincts, he sat down to write a letter.

CHAPTER FOURTEEN

FREDERICK BLOGGS had spent an unpleasant afternoon in the countryside.

When five worried wives had contacted their local police station to say their husbands had not come home, a rural constable had exercised his limited powers of deduction and concluded that a whole patrol of the Home Guard had gone missing. He was fairly sure they had simply got lost – they were all deaf, daft or senile, otherwise they would have been in the Army – but all the same he notified his Constabulary head-quarters, just to cover himself. The operations-room sergeant who took the message realized at once that the missing men had been patrolling a particularly sensitive military area, and he notified his inspector, who notified Scotland Yard, who sent a Special Branch man down there and notified M15, who sent Bloggs.

The Special Branch man was Harris, who had been on the Stockwell murder. He and Bloggs met on the train, which was one of the Wild West locomotives lent to Britain by the Americans because of the shortage of trains. Harris repeated his invitation to Sunday dinner, and Bloggs told him again that he worked most Sundays.

When they got off the train they borrowed bicycles to ride along the canal towpath until they met up with the search party. Harris, ten years older than Bloggs and four stone heavier, found the ride a strain.

They met a section of the search party under a railway bridge. Harris welcomed the opportunity to get off the bicycle. 'What have you found?' he said. 'Bodies?'

'No, a boat,' said a policeman. 'Who are you?'

They introduced themselves. A constable stripped to his underwear was diving down to examine the vessel. He came up with a bung in his hand.

Bloggs looked at Harris. 'Deliberately scuttled?'

'Looks like it.' Harris turned to the diver. 'Notice anything else?'

'She hasn't been down there for long, she's in good condition, and the mast has been taken down, not broken.'

Harris said: 'That's a lot of information from a minute under water.'

'I'm a weekend sailor,' the diver said.

Harris and Bloggs mounted their cycles and moved on.

When they met up with the main party, the bodies had been found.

'Murdered, all five,' said the uniformed inspector in charge. 'Captain Langham, Corporal Lee, and Privates Watson, Dayton and Forbes. Dayton's neck was broken, the rest were killed with some kind of knife. Langham's body had been in the canal. All found together in a shallow grave. Bloody murder.' He was quite shaken.

Harris looked closely at the five bodies, laid out in a line. 'I've seen wounds like this before, Fred,' he said.

Bloggs looked closely. 'Jesus Christ, it's him.'

Harris nodded. 'Stiletto.'

The inspector said in astonishment: 'You know who did it?'

'We can guess,' Harris said. 'We think he's killed twice before. If it's the same man, we know *who* he is but not *where* he is.'

The inspector's eyes narrowed. 'What with the restricted area so close, and Special Branch and MI5 arriving on the scene so quick, is there anything else I need to know about this case?'

Harris answered: 'Just that you keep very quiet until your Chief Constable has talked to our people.'

''Nuff said.'

Bloggs asked. 'Anything else found, Inspector?'

'We're still combing the area, in ever-widening circles; but nothing so far. There were some clothes in the grave.' He pointed.

Bloggs touched them gingerly: black trousers, a black sweater, a short black leather jacket, RAF-style.

Harris said: 'Clothes for night work.'

'To fit a big man,' Bloggs added.

'How tall is your man?'

'Over six foot.'

The inspector said: 'Did you pass the men who found the sunken boat?'

'Yes.' Bloggs frowned. 'Where's the nearest lock?'

'Four miles upstream.'

'If our man was in a boat, the lock-keeper must have seen him, mustn't he?'

'Must have,' the inspector agreed.

Bloggs said: 'We'd better talk to him.' He returned to his cycle.

'Not another four miles,' Harris complained.

Bloggs said: 'Work off some of those Sunday dinners.'

The four-mile ride took them most of an hour, because the towpath was made for horses, not wheels, and it was uneven, muddy, and mined with loose boulders and tree roots. Harris was sweating and cursing by the time they reached the lock.

The lock-keeper was sitting outside his little house, smoking a pipe and enjoying the mild air of afternoon. He was a middle-aged man of slow speech and slower movements. He regarded the two cyclists with faint amusement.

Bloggs spoke, because Harris was out of breath. 'We're police officers,' he said.

'Is that so?' said the lock-keeper. 'What's the excitement?' He looked as excited as a cat in front of a fire.

Bloggs took the photograph of Die Nadel out of his wallet and gave it to the man. 'Have you ever seen him?'

The lock-keeper put the picture on his lap while he held a fresh match to his pipe. Then he studied the photograph for a while, and handed it back.

'Well?' Harris said.

'Aye.' The lock-keeper nodded slowly. 'He was here about this time yesterday. Came in for a cup of tea.

Nice enough chap. What's he done, shown a light after blackout?'

Bloggs sat down heavily. 'That clinches it,' he said.

Harris thought aloud. 'He moors the boat downstream from here, and goes into the restricted area after dark.' He spoke quietly, so that the lock-keeper should not hear. 'When he comes back, the Home Guard has his boat staked out. He deals with them, sails a bit farther to the railway, scuttles his boat and . . . hops a train?'

Bloggs said to the lock-keeper: 'The railway line that crosses the canal a few miles downstream – where does it go?'

'London.'

Bloggs said: 'Oh, shit.'

Bloggs got back to the War Office in Whitehall at midnight. Godliman and Parkin were there, waiting for him. Bloggs said: 'It's him, all right,' and told them the story.

Parkin was excited, Godliman just looked tense. When Bloggs had finished, Godliman said: 'So now he's back in London, and we're looking for a needle in a haystack again.' He was playing with matches, forming a picture with them on his desk. 'Do you know, every time I look at that photograph I get the feeling I've actually *met* the damn fellow.'

'Well, think!' Bloggs said. 'Where?'

Godliman shook his head in frustration. 'It must have been only once, and somewhere strange. It's like a face I've seen in a lecture audience, or in the background at a cocktail party. A fleeting glimpse, a casual encounter – when I remember it probably won't do us any good.'

Parkin said: 'What's in that area?'

'I don't know, which means it's probably highly important,' Godliman said.

There was a silence. Parkin lit a cigarette with one of Godliman's matches. Bloggs looked up. 'We could print a million copies of his picture – give one to every policeman, ARP warden, member of the Home Guard, serviceman, railway porter; paste them up on hoardings and publish them in the papers . . .'

Godliman shook his head. 'Too risky. What if he's already talked to Hamburg about whatever he's seen? If we make a public fuss about the man they'll know that his information is good. We'd only be lending credence to him.'

'We've got to do something.'

'Surely. We will circulate his picture to police officers. We'll give his description to the press, and say he's just a straightforward murderer. We can give the details of the Highgate and Stockwell murders, without saying that security is involved.'

Parkin said: 'What you're saying is, we can fight with one hand tied behind our back.'

'For now, anyway.'

'I'll start the ball rolling with the Yard,' Bloggs said. He picked up the phone.

Godliman looked at his watch. 'There's not much

more we can do tonight, but I don't feel like going home. I shan't sleep.'

Parkin stood up. 'In that case I'm going to find a kettle and make some tea.' He went out.

The matches on Godliman's desk made a picture of a horse and carriage. He took away one of the horse's legs and lit his pipe with it. 'Have you got a girl, Fred?' he asked conversationally.

'No.'

'Not since—?'

'No.'

Godliman puffed at his pipe. 'There has to be an end to grief, you know.'

Bloggs made no reply.

Godliman said: 'Look, perhaps I shouldn't talk to you like a Dutch uncle. But I know how you feel – I've been through it myself. The only difference was that I didn't have anyone to blame.'

'You didn't remarry,' Bloggs said, not looking at Godliman.

'No. And I don't want you to make the same mistake. When you reach middle age, living alone can be very depressing.'

'Did I ever tell you, they called her Fearless Bloggs.'

'Yes, you did.'

Bloggs looked at Godliman at last. 'Tell me, where in the world will I find another girl like that?'

'Does she have to be a hero?'

'After Christine – yes.'

'England is full of heroes, Fred.'

At that moment Colonel Terry walked in.

Godliman said: 'Ah, Uncle Andrew—'

Terry interrupted: 'Don't get up. This is important. Listen carefully, because I have to give it to you fast. Bloggs, you need to know this, too. Whoever killed those five Home Guard has learned our most vital secret.

'Number one: our invasion force for Europe will land at Normandy. Number two: the Germans believe it will land at Calais. Number three: one of the most vital aspects of the deception is a very large phoney army, called the First United States Army Group, located in the restricted area those men were patrolling. That area contains dummy barracks, cardboard aircraft, rubber tanks – a huge toy army which looks real to the observers in the reconnaissance planes we've been letting through.'

Bloggs said: 'How come you're so sure the spy found out?'

Terry went to the door. 'Come in, Rodriguez.'

A tall, handsome man with jet-black hair and a long nose entered the room and nodded politely to Godliman and Bloggs. Terry said: 'Senhor Rodriguez is our man at the Portuguese Embassy. Tell them what happened, Rodriguez.'

The man stood by the door, holding his hat. 'A taxi came to the Embassy at about eleven o'clock. The passenger did not get out, but the driver came to the door with an envelope addressed to Francisco. The doorman called me, as he has been instructed to do, and I took possession of the envelope. I was in time to take the number of the cab.'

'I'm having the cabbie traced,' Terry said. 'All right, Rodriguez, you'd better get back. And thank you.'

The tall Portuguese left the room. Terry handed to Godliman a large yellow envelope, addressed to Manuel Francisco. Godliman opened it – it had already been unsealed – and withdrew a second envelope marked with a meaningless series of letters: presumably a code.

Within the inner envelope were several sheets of paper covered with handwriting and a set of ten-by-eight photographs. Godliman examined the letter. 'It looks like a very basic code,' he said.

'You don't need to read it,' Terry said impatiently. 'Look at the photographs.'

Godliman did so. There were about thirty of them, and he looked at each one before speaking. He handed them to Bloggs and said: 'This is a catastrophe.'

Bloggs glanced through the pictures then put them down.

Godliman said: 'This is only his back-up. He's still got the negatives, *and he's going somewhere with them.*'

The three men sat still in the little office, like a tableau. The only illumination came from a spotlight on Godliman's desk. With the cream walls, the blacked-out window, the spare furniture and the worn Civil Service carpet, they might have been anywhere in the world.

Terry said: 'I'm going to have to tell Churchill.'

The phone rang, and the Colonel picked it up. 'Yes. Good. Bring him here right away, please – but before you do, ask him where he dropped the passenger. What? Really? Thank you, get here fast.' He hung up. 'The taxi dropped our man at University College Hospital.'

Bloggs said: 'Perhaps he was injured in the fight with the Home Guard.'

Terry said: 'Where is that hospital?'

'About five minutes' walk from Euston Station,' Godliman said. 'Trains from Euston go to Holyhead, Liverpool, Glasgow . . . all places from which you can catch a ferry to Ireland.'

'Liverpool to Belfast,' Bloggs said. 'Then a car to the border and across into Eire, and a U-boat on the Atlantic coast. He wouldn't risk Holyhead-to-Dublin because of the passport control, and there would be no point in going beyond Liverpool to Glasgow.'

Godliman said: 'Fred, you'd better go to the station and show the picture of Faber around, see if anyone noticed him getting on a train. I'll phone the station and warn them you're coming, and at the same time find out which trains have left since about ten-thirty.'

Bloggs picked up his hat and coat. 'I'm on my way.'

Godliman lifted the phone. 'Yes, we're on our way.'

There were still plenty of people at Euston Station. Although in normal times the station closed around midnight, wartime delays were such that the last train often had not left before the earliest milk train of the morning arrived. The station concourse was a mass of kitbags and sleeping bodies.

Bloggs showed the picture to three railway policemen. None of them recognized the face. He tried ten women porters: nothing. He went to every ticket barrier. One of the guards said: 'We look at tickets, not faces.' He tried half a dozen passengers without result. Finally he went into the ticket office and showed the picture to each of the clerks.

A very fat, bald clerk with ill-fitting false teeth recognized the face. 'I play a game,' he told Bloggs. 'I try to spot something about a passenger that tells me why he's catching a train. Like, he might have a black tie for a funeral, or muddy boots means he's a farmer going home, or there might be a college scarf, or a white mark on a woman's finger where she's took off her wedding ring . . . know what I mean? This is a dull job – not that I'm complaining—'

'What did you notice about this chap?' Bloggs interrupted him.

'Nothing. That was it, see – I couldn't make him out at all. Almost like he was trying to be inconspicuous, know what I mean?'

'I know what you mean.' Bloggs paused. 'Now, I want you to think very carefully. Where was he going – can you remember?'

'Yes,' said the fat clerk. 'Inverness.'

'That doesn't mean he's going there,' said Godliman. 'He's a professional – he knows we can ask questions at railway stations. I expect he automatically buys a ticket for the wrong destination.' He looked at his watch. 'He must have caught the eleven forty-five. That train is now pulling into Stafford. I checked with the railway, they checked with the signalman,' he added by way of explanation. 'They're going to stop the train this side of Crewe. I've got a plane standing by to fly you two to Stoke-on-Trent.

'Parkin, you'll board the train where it's stopped, outside Crewe. You'll be dressed as a ticket inspector, and you'll look at every ticket – and every face – on that train. When you've spotted Faber, just stay close to him.

'Bloggs, you'll be waiting at the ticket barrier at Crewe, just in case Faber decides to hop off there. But he won't. You'll get on the train, and be first off at Liverpool, and waiting at the ticket barrier for Parkin and Faber to come off. Half the local constabulary will be there to back you up.'

'That's all very well if he doesn't recognize me,' Parkin said. 'What if he remembers my face from Highgate?'

Godliman opened a desk drawer, took out a pistol, and gave it to Parkin. 'If he recognizes you, shoot the bastard.'

Parkin pocketed the weapon without comment.

Godliman said: 'I want both of you to be quite clear on the importance of all this. If we don't catch this man, the invasion of Europe will have to be postponed – possibly for a year. In that year the balance of war could turn against us. The time may never be this right again.'

Bloggs said: 'Do we get told how long it is to D-Day?'

'All I know is that it's a matter of weeks.'

Parkin was thinking. 'It'll be June, then.'

Bloggs said: 'Shit.'

Godliman said: 'No comment.'

The phone rang and Godliman picked it up. After a moment he looked up. 'Your car's here.'

Bloggs and Parkin stood up.

Godliman said: 'Wait a minute.'

They stood by the door, looking at the professor. He was saying: 'Yes, sir. Certainly. I will. Goodbye, sir.'

Bloggs could not think of anyone Godliman called Sir. He said: 'Who was that?'

Godliman said: 'Churchill.'

'What did he have to say?' Parkin asked, awestruck.

Godliman said: 'He wishes you both good luck and Godspeed.'

CHAPTER FIFTEEN

T HE CARRIAGE was pitch dark. Faber thought of the jokes people made: 'Take your hand off my knee. No, not you, you.' The British would make jokes out of anything. Their railways were now worse than ever, but nobody complained any more because it was in a good cause. Faber preferred the dark: it was anonymous.

There had been singing, earlier on. Three sailors in the corridor had started it, and the whole carriage had joined in. They had been through *Be Like The Kettle And Sing, There'll Always Be An England* (followed by *Glasgow Belongs To Me* and *Land Of My Fathers* for ethnic balance), and appropriately, *Don't Get Around Much Any More.*

There had been an air-raid warning, and the train slowed to thirty miles an hour. They were all supposed to lie on the floor, but of course there was no room. An anonymous female voice had said: 'Oh, God, I'm frightened,' and a male voice, equally anonymous except that it was Cockney, had said: 'You're in the safest place, girl – they can't 'it a movin' target.' Then everyone laughed and nobody was scared any more. Someone opened a suitcase and passed around a packet of dried-egg sandwiches.

One of the sailors wanted to play cards.

'How can we play cards in the dark?'

'Feel the edges. All Harry's cards are marked.'

The train stopped unaccountably at about 4 a.m. A cultured voice – the dried-egg sandwich supplier, Faber thought – said: 'My guess is we're outside Crewe.'

'Knowing the railways, we could be anywhere from Bolton to Bournemouth,' said the Cockney.

The train jerked and moved off, and everyone cheered. Where, Faber wondered, was the caricature Englishman, with his icy reserve and his stiff upper lip? Not here.

A few minutes later a voice in the corridor said: 'Tickets, please.' Faber noted the Yorkshire accent: they were in the north now. He fumbled in his pockets for his ticket.

He had the corner seat, near the door, so he could see into the corridor. The inspector was shining a torch on to the tickets. Faber saw the man's silhouette in the reflected light. It looked vaguely familiar.

He settled back in his seat to wait. He remembered the nightmare: 'This is an Abwehr ticket' – and smiled in the dark.

Then he frowned. The train stops unaccountably; shortly afterwards a ticket inspection begins; the inspector's face is vaguely familiar ... It might be nothing, but Faber stayed alive by worrying about things that *might* be nothing. He looked in the corridor again, but the man had entered a compartment.

The train stopped briefly – the station was Crewe, according to informed opinion in Faber's compartment – and moved off again.

Faber got another look at the inspector's face, and now he remembered. The boarding house in Highgate! The boy from Yorkshire who wanted to get into the Army!

Faber watched him carefully. His torch flashed across the face of every passenger. He was not just looking at the tickets.

No, Faber told himself, don't jump to conclusions. How could they possibly have got on to him? They could not have found out which train he was on, got hold of one of the few people in the world who knew what he looked like, and got the man on the train dressed as a ticket inspector in so short a time. It was unbelievable.

Parkin, that was his name. Billy Parkin. Somehow he looked a lot older now. He was coming closer.

It must be a look-alike – perhaps an elder brother. This had to be a coincidence.

Parkin entered the compartment next to Faber's. There was no time left.

Faber assumed the worst and prepared to deal with it.

He got up, left the compartment, and went along the corridor, picking his way over suitcases and kitbags and bodies, to the lavatory. It was vacant. He went in and locked the door.

He was only buying time – ticket inspectors did not fail to check the toilets. He sat on the seat and wondered how to get out of this. The train had speeded up, and was travelling too fast for him to jump off.

Besides, someone would see him go, and if they were really searching for him they would stop the train.

'All tickets, please.'

Parkin was getting close again.

Faber had an idea. The coupling between the carriages was a tiny space like an air-lock, enclosed by a bellows-like cover between the cars of the train, shut off at both ends by doors because of the noise and draughts. He left the lavatory, fought his way to the end of the carriage, opened the door, and stepped into the connecting passage. He closed the door behind him.

It was freezing cold, and the noise was terrific. Faber sat on the floor and curled up, pretending to sleep. Only a dead man could sleep here, but people did strange things on trains these days. He tried not to shiver.

The door opened behind him. 'Tickets, please.'

He ignored it. He heard the door close.

'Wake up, Sleeping Beauty.' The voice was unmistakable.

Faber pretended to stir, then got to his feet, keeping his back to Parkin. When he turned the stiletto was in his hand. He pushed Parkin up against the door, held the point of the knife at his throat, and said: 'Be still or I'll kill you.'

With his left hand he took Parkin's torch, and shone it into the young man's face. Parkin did not look as frightened as he ought to be.

Faber said: 'Well, well. Billy Parkin, who wanted to

191

join the Army, and ended up on the railways. Still, it's a uniform.'

Parkin said: 'You.'

'You know damn well it's me, little Billy Parkin. You were looking for me. Why?' He was doing his best to sound vicious.

'I don't know why I should be looking for you – I'm not a policeman.'

Faber jerked the knife melodramatically. 'Stop lying to me.'

'Honest, Mr Faber. Let me go – I promise I won't tell anyone I've seen you.'

Faber began to have doubts. Either Parkin was telling the truth, or he was overacting as much as Faber himself.

Parkin's body shifted, his right arm moving in the darkness. Faber grabbed the wrist in an iron grip. Parkin struggled for an instant, but Faber let the needle point of the stiletto sink a fraction of an inch into Parkin's throat, and the man was still. Faber found the pocket Parkin had been reaching for, and pulled out a gun.

'Ticket inspectors do not go armed,' he said. 'Who are you with, Parkin?'

'We all carry guns now – there's a lot of crime on trains because of the dark.'

Parkin was lying courageously and persistently. Faber decided that threats were not enough to loosen his tongue.

His movement was sudden, swift and accurate. The blade of the stiletto leaped in his fist. Its point entered a measured half-inch into Parkin's left eye and came out again.

Faber's hand covered Parkin's mouth. The muffled scream of agony was drowned by the noise of the train. Parkin's hands went to his ruined eye.

Faber pressed his advantage. 'Save yourself the other eye, Parkin. Who are you with?'

'Military Intelligence, oh God, please don't do it again.'

'Who? Menzies? Masterman?'

'Oh, God, it's Godliman, Percy Godliman.'

'Godliman!' Faber knew the name, but this was no time to search his memory for details. 'What have they got?'

'A picture – I picked you out from the files.'

'What picture? *What picture?*'

'A racing team – running – with a cup – the Army—'

Faber remembered. Christ, where had they got hold of that? It was his nightmare: *they had a picture.* People would know his face. His *face.*

He moved the knife closer to Parkin's right eye. 'How did you know where I was?'

'Don't do it, please – agent in the Portuguese Embassy intercepted your letter – took the cab's number – inquiries at Euston – please, not the other eye—' He covered both his eyes with his hands.

'What's the plan? Where is the trap?'

'Glasgow. They're waiting for you at Glasgow. The train will be emptied there.'

Faber lowered the knife to the level of Parkin's belly.

To distract him, he said: 'How many men?' Then he pushed hard, inward and upward to the heart.

Parkin's one eye stared in horror, and he did not die. It was the drawback to Faber's favoured method of killing. Normally the shock of the knife was enough to stop the heart. But if the heart was strong it did not always work – after all, surgeons sometimes stuck a hypodermic needle directly into the heart to inject adrenalin. If the heart continued to pump, the motion would work a hole around the blade, from which the blood would leak. It was just as fatal, but longer.

At last Parkin's body went limp. Faber held him against the wall for a moment, thinking. There had been something – a flicker of courage, the ghost of a smile – before the man died. It meant something. Such things always did.

He let the body fall to the floor, then arranged it in a sleeping position, with the wounds hidden from view. He kicked the railway cap into a corner. He cleaned his stiletto on Parkin's trousers, and wiped the ocular liquid from his hands. It had been a messy business.

He put the knife away in his sleeve and opened the door to the carriage. He made his way back to his compartment in the dark.

As he sat down the Cockney said: 'You took your time – is there a queue?'

Faber said: 'It must have been something I ate.'

'Probably a dried-egg sandwich.' The Cockney laughed.

Faber was thinking about Godliman. He knew the name – he could even put a vague face to it: a middle-aged, bespectacled face, with a pipe and an absent, professorial air. That was it – he was a professor.

It was coming back. In his first couple of years in London Faber had had little to do. The war had not yet started, and most people believed it would not come. (Faber was not among the optimists.) He had been able to do a little useful work – mostly checking and revising the Abwehr's out-of-date maps, plus general reports based on his own observations and his reading of the newspapers – but not much. To fill in time, to improve his English, and to flesh out his cover, he had gone sightseeing.

His purpose in visiting Canterbury Cathedral had been innocent, although he did buy an aerial view of the town and the cathedral which he sent back for the Luftwaffe – not that it did much good: they spent most of 1942 missing it. Faber had taken a whole day to see the building: reading the ancient initials carved in walls, distinguishing the different architectural styles, reading the guidebook line by line as he walked slowly around.

He had been in the south ambulatory of the choir, looking at the blind arcading, when he became conscious of another absorbed figure by his side; an older man. 'Fascinating, isn't it?' the man said; and Faber asked him what he meant.

'The one pointed arch in an arcade of round ones. No reason for it – that section obviously hasn't been rebuilt. For some reason, somebody just altered that one. I wonder why.'

Faber saw what he meant. The choir was Romanesque, the nave Gothic; yet here in the choir was a solitary Gothic arch. 'Perhaps,' he said, 'the monks demanded to see what the pointed arches would look like, and the architect did this to show them.'

The older man stared at him. 'What a splendid conjecture! Of course that's the reason. Are you an historian?'

Faber laughed. 'No, just a clerk and an occasional reader of history books.'

'People get doctorates for inspired guesses like that!'

'Are you? An historian, I mean.'

'Yes, for my sins.' He stuck out his hand. 'Percy Godliman.'

Was it possible, Faber thought as the train rattled on through Lancashire, that that unimpressive figure in a tweed suit could be the man who had discovered his identity? Spies generally claimed they were civil servants, or something equally vague; not historians – that lie could be too easily found out. Yet it was rumoured that Military Intelligence had been bolstered by a number of academics. Faber had imagined them to be young, fit, aggressive and bellicose as well as clever. Godliman was clever, but none of the rest. Unless he had changed.

Faber had seen him once again, although he had not spoken to him on the second occasion. After the brief encounter in the cathedral Faber had seen a notice advertising a public lecture on Henry II to be given by Professor Godliman at his college. He had gone along, out of curiosity. The talk had been erudite, lively and convincing. Godliman was still a faintly comic figure, prancing about behind the lectern, getting enthusiastic about his subject; but it was clear his mind was as sharp as a knife.

So that was the man who had discovered what Die Nadel looked like.

Jesus Christ, an *amateur*.

Well, he would make amateur mistakes. Sending Billy Parkin had been one: Faber had recognized the boy. Godliman should have sent someone Faber did not know. Parkin had a better chance of recognizing Faber, but no chance at all of surviving the encounter. A professional would have known that.

The train shuddered to a halt, and a muffled voice outside announced that this was Liverpool. Faber cursed under his breath: he should have been spending the time working out his next move, not remembering Percival Godliman.

They were waiting at Glasgow, Parkin had said before he died. Why Glasgow? Their inquiries at Euston would have told them he was going to Inverness. And if they suspected Inverness to be a red herring, they would have speculated that he was coming here, to Liverpool, for this was the nearest link point for an Irish ferry.

Faber hated snap decisions.

He had to get off the train, whatever.

He stood up, opened the door, stepped out, and headed for the ticket barrier.

He thought of something else. What was it that had flashed in Billy Parkin's eyes before he died? Not hatred, not fear, not pain – although all those had been present. It was more like . . . triumph.

Faber looked up, past the ticket collector, and understood.

Waiting on the other side, dressed in a hat and raincoat, was the blond young tail from Leicester Square.

Parkin, dying in agony and humiliation and betrayal, had deceived Faber at the last. The trap was here.

The man in the raincoat had not yet noticed Faber in the crowd. Faber turned and stepped back on to the train. Once inside, he pulled aside the blind and looked out. The tail was searching the faces in the crowd. He had not noticed the man who got back on the train.

Faber watched while the passengers filtered through the gate until the platform was empty. The blond man spoke urgently to the ticket collector, who shook his head in negation. The man seemed to insist. After a moment he waved to someone out of sight. A police officer emerged from the shadows and spoke to the collector. The platform guard joined the group, followed by a man in a civilian suit who was presumably a more senior railway official.

The engine driver and his fireman left the locomotive and went over to the barrier. There was more waving of arms and shaking of heads.

Finally the railwaymen shrugged, turned away, or rolled their eyes upward, all telegraphing surrender. The blond and the police officer summoned other policemen, and they moved determinedly on to the platform.

They were going to search the train.

All the railway officials, including the engine crew,

had disappeared in the opposite direction, no doubt to seek tea and sandwiches while the lunatics tried to search a jampacked train. That gave Faber an idea.

He opened the door and jumped out of the wrong side of the train, the side opposite the platform. Concealed from the police by the carriages, he ran along the tracks, stumbling on the sleepers and slipping on the gravel, toward the engine.

It had to be bad news, of course. From the moment he realized Billy Parkin was not going to saunter off that train, Frederick Bloggs knew that Die Nadel had slipped through their fingers again. As the uniformed police moved on to the train in pairs, two men to search each carriage, Bloggs thought of several possible explanations of Parkin's non-appearance; and all the explanations were depressing.

He turned up his coat collar and paced the draughty platform. He wanted very badly to catch Die Nadel: not just for the sake of the invasion – although that was reason enough, God knew – but for Percy Godliman, and for the five Home Guard, and for Christine.

He looked at his watch: four o'clock. Soon it would be day. Bloggs had been up all night, and he had not eaten since breakfast yesterday, but until now he had kept going on adrenalin. The failure of the trap – he was quite sure it *had* failed – drained him of energy. Hunger and fatigue caught up with him. He had to make a conscious effort not to daydream about hot food and a warm bed.

'Sir!' A policeman was leaning out of a carriage and waving at him. 'Sir!'

Bloggs walked toward him, then broke into a run. 'What have you found?'

'It might be your man Parkin.'

Bloggs climbed into the carriage. 'What do you mean, might be?'

'You'd better have a look.' The policeman opened the communicating door between the carriages and shone his torch inside.

It was Parkin; Bloggs could tell by the ticket-inspector's uniform. He was curled up on the floor. Bloggs took the policeman's torch, knelt down beside Parkin, and turned him over.

He saw Parkin's face, looked quickly away, and said: 'Oh, dear God.'

'I take it this is Parkin?' the policeman said.

Bloggs nodded. He got up, very slowly, without looking again at the body. 'We'll interview everybody in this carriage and the next,' he said. 'Anyone who saw or heard anything unusual will be detained for further questioning. Not that it will do us any good: the murderer must have jumped off the train before it got here.'

Bloggs went back out on to the platform. All the searchers had completed their tasks and were gathered in a group. He detailed six of them to help with the interviewing.

The police inspector said: 'Your villain's hopped it, then.'

'Almost certainly,' Bloggs agreed. 'You've looked in every toilet, and the guard's van?'

'Yes, and on top of the train and under it, and in the engine and the coal tender.'

A passenger got off the train and approached Bloggs and the inspector. He was a small man with a bad chest, and he wheezed badly. He said: 'Excuse me.'

'Yes, sir,' the inspector said.

The passenger said: 'I was wondering, are you looking for somebody?'

'Why do you ask?'

'Well, if you are, I was wondering, would he be a tall chap?'

The inspector said: 'Why do you ask?'

Bloggs interrupted impatiently. 'Yes, a tall man. Come on, spit it out.'

'Well, it's just that a tall chap got out the wrong side of the train.'

'When?'

'A minute or two after the train pulled into the station. He got on, like, then he got off, on the wrong side. Jumped down on to the track. Only he had no luggage, you see, which was another odd thing, and I just thought—'

The inspector said: 'Balls.'

'He must have spotted the trap,' Bloggs said. 'But how? He doesn't know my face, and your men were out of sight.'

'Something made him suspicious.'

'So he crossed the line to the next platform and went out that way. Wouldn't he have been seen?'

The inspector shrugged. 'Not too many people about, this late. And if he was seen he could just say he was too impatient to queue at the ticket barrier.'

'Didn't you have the other ticket barriers covered?'

'I didn't think of it.'

'Nor did I.'

'Well, we can search the surrounding area, and later on we can check various places in the city, and of course we'll watch the ferry—'

'Yes, please do,' Bloggs said.

But somehow he knew Faber would not be found.

It was more than an hour before the train started to move. Faber had cramp in his left calf and dust in his nose. He heard the footplatemen climb back into their cab, and caught snatches of conversation about a body being found on the train. There was a metallic rattle as the fireman shovelled coal, then the hiss of steam, a clanking of pistons, a jerk and a sigh of smoke as the train moved off. Gratefully, Faber shifted his position and indulged in a smothered sneeze. Then he felt better.

He was at the back of the coal tender, buried deep in the coal, where it would take a man with a shovel ten minutes' hard work to expose him. As he had hoped, the police search of the tender had consisted of one good long look and no more.

He wondered whether he could risk emerging now. It must be getting light: would he be visible from a bridge over the line? He thought not. His skin was now quite black, and in a moving train in the pale light of dawn he would just be a dark blur on a dark background. Yes, he would chance it. Slowly and carefully, he dug his way out of his grave of coal.

He breathed the cool air deeply. The coal was shovelled out of the tender via a small hole in the front end. Later, perhaps, the fireman would have to enter the tender, when the pile of fuel got lower. Faber was safe for now.

As the light strengthened he looked himself over. He was covered from head to toe in coal dust, like a miner coming up from the pit. Somehow he had to wash and change his clothes.

He chanced a peep over the side of the tender. The train was still in the suburbs, passing factories and warehouses and rows of grimy little houses. He had to think about his next move.

His original plan had been to get off the train at Glasgow and there catch another train to Dundee and up the east coast to Aberdeen. It was still possible for him to disembark at Glasgow. He could not get off at the station, of course, but he might jump off either just before or just after. However, there were risks in that. The train was sure to stop at intermediate stations between Liverpool and Glasgow, and at those stops Faber might be spotted. No, he had to get off the train soon and find other means of transport.

The ideal spot would be a lonely stretch of track just outside a city or village. It had to be lonely, for he must not be seen leaping from the coal tender; but it had to be fairly near houses so that he could steal clothes and a car. And it needed to be an uphill stretch of track, so that the train would be travelling slowly enough for him to jump.

Right now its speed was about forty miles an hour. Faber lay back on the coal to wait. He could not keep a permanent watch on the country through which he was passing, for fear of being seen. He decided he would look out whenever the train slowed down. Otherwise he would lie still.

After a few minutes he caught himself dropping off to sleep, despite the discomfort of his bed. He shifted his position and reclined on his elbows, so that if he did sleep he would fall and be wakened by the impact.

The train was gathering speed. Between London and Liverpool it had seemed to be stationary more than moving; now it steamed through the country at a fine pace. To complete his discomfort, it started to rain; a cold, steady drizzle that soaked right through his clothes and seemed to turn to ice on his skin. There was another reason for getting off the train: he could die of exposure before they reached Glasgow!

After half an hour at high speed he was contemplating killing the footplate crew and stopping the train himself. A signal box saved their lives. The train slowed suddenly as brakes were applied. It decelerated in stages: Faber guessed the track was marked with descending speed limits. He looked out. They were in the countryside again. He could see the reason for the slowdown – they were approaching a track junction, and the signals were against them.

Faber stayed in the tender while the train stood still. After five minutes it started up again. Faber scrambled up the side of the tender, perched on the edge for a moment, and jumped.

He landed on the embankment and lay, face down, in the overgrown weeds. When the train was out of earshot he got to his feet. The only sign of civilization nearby was the signal box, a two-storey wooden structure with large windows in the control room at the top, an outside staircase, and a door at ground-floor level. On the far side was a cinder track leading away.

Faber walked in a wide circle to approach the place from the back, where there were no windows. He entered a ground-floor door and found what he had been expecting: a toilet, a washbasin and a coat hanging on a peg.

He took off his soaking wet clothes, washed his hands and face, and rubbed himself vigorously all over with a grubby towel. The little cylindrical film can containing the negatives was still taped securely to his chest. He put his clothes back on, but substituted the signalman's overcoat for his own sopping wet jacket.

Now all he needed was transport. The signalman must have got here somehow. Faber went outside and found a bicycle padlocked to a rail on the other side of the little building. He snapped the little lock with the blade of his stiletto. Moving in a straight line away from the blank rear wall of the signal box, he wheeled the cycle until he was out of sight of the building. Then he cut across until he reached the cinder track, climbed on the cycle, and rode away.

CHAPTER SIXTEEN

PERCIVAL GODLIMAN had brought a little camp bed from his home. He lay on it in his office, dressed in trousers and shirt, trying in vain to sleep. He had not suffered insomnia for almost forty years, since he took his final exams at university. He would gladly swap the anxieties of those days for the worries which kept him awake now.

He had been a different man then, he knew; not just younger, but also a lot less . . . abstracted. He had been outgoing, aggressive, ambitious: he planned to go into politics. He was not studious then – he had reason to be anxious about the exams.

His two mismatched enthusiasms in those days had been debating and ballroom dancing. He had spoken with distinction at the Oxford Union and had been pictured in *The Tatler* waltzing with debutantes. He was no great womanizer: he wanted sex with a woman he loved, not because he believed in any high-minded principle to that effect, but because that was the way he felt about it.

And so he had been a virgin until he met Eleanor, who was not one of the debutantes, but a brilliant graduate mathematician with grace and warmth and a father dying of lung disease after forty years as a collier. The young Percival had taken her to meet his people. His father was Lord Lieutenant of the county, and the house had seemed a mansion to Eleanor, but she had been natural and charming and not in the least awe-struck; and when Percy's mother had been disgracefully condescending to her at one point she had reacted with merciless wit, for which he loved her all the more.

He had taken his master's degree, then after the Great War he taught in a public school and stood in three by-elections. They were both disappointed when they discovered they could not have children; but they loved each other totally, and they were happy, and her death was the most appalling tragedy Godliman ever knew. It had ended his interest in the real world, and he had retreated into the Middle Ages.

It had drawn him and Bloggs together, this common bereavement. The war had brought Godliman back to life; revived in him those characteristics of dash and aggression and fervour which had made him a great speaker and teacher and the hope of the Liberal Party. He wished for something in Bloggs's life to rescue him from an existence of bitterness and introversion.

While he was in Godliman's thoughts, Bloggs phoned from Liverpool to say that Die Nadel had slipped through the net, and Parkin had been killed.

Godliman, sitting on the edge of the camp bed to speak on the phone, closed his eyes in despair. 'I should have put you on the train,' he murmured.

'Thanks!' Bloggs said.

'Only because he doesn't know your face.'

'I think he may,' Bloggs argued. 'We suspect he spotted the trap, and mine was the only face visible to him as he got off the train.'

'But where could he have seen you? Oh! No, surely . . . not Leicester Square?'

'I don't see how, but then . . . we always seem to underestimate him.'

'I wish he were on our side,' Godliman muttered. 'Have you got the ferry covered?'

'Yes.'

'He won't use it, of course – too obvious. He's more likely to steal a boat. On the other hand, he may still be heading for Inverness.'

'I've alerted the police up there.'

'Good. But look, I don't think we can make any assumptions about his destination. Let's keep an open mind.'

'Agreed.'

Godliman stood, picked up the phone, and began to pace the carpet. 'Also, don't assume it was he who got off the train on the wrong side. Work on the premise that he got off before, at, or after Liverpool.' Godliman's brain was in gear again, sorting permutations and possibilities. 'Let me talk to the Chief Superintendent.'

'He's here.'

There was a pause, then a new voice said: 'Chief Superintendent Anthony speaking.'

Godliman said: 'Do you agree with me that our man has got off this train somewhere in your area?'

'That seems likely, yes.'

'Good. Now the first thing he needs is transport – so I want you to get details of every car, boat, bicycle or donkey stolen within a hundred miles of Liverpool during the next twenty-four hours. Keep me informed, but give the information to Bloggs and work closely with him in following-up the leads.'

'Yes, sir.'

'Keep an eye on other crimes that might be committed by a fugitive – theft of food or clothing, unexplained assaults, identity card irregularities, and so on.'

'Right.'

'Now, Mr Anthony, you realize this man is more than just a mass murderer?'

'I assume so, sir, from the fact of your involvement. However, I don't know the details.'

'Nor shall you. Suffice it to say that this is a matter of national security so grave that the Prime Minister is in hourly contact with this office.'

'I understand. Uh, Mr Bloggs would like a word, sir.'

Bloggs came back on. 'Have you remembered how you know his face?'

'Oh, yes – but it's of no value, as I forecast. I met him by chance at Canterbury Cathedral, and we had a conversation about the architecture. All it tells us is that he's clever – he made some rather perceptive remarks, as I recall.'

'We knew he was clever.'

'Only too well.'

*

Chief Superintendent Anthony was a burly member of the middle class with a carefully softened Liverpool accent. He did not know whether to be peeved at the way MI5 ordered him about or thrilled at the chance to save England on his own manor.

Bloggs knew of the man's inner struggle – he met this sort of thing all the time when working with local police forces – and he knew how to tip the balance in his own favour. He said: 'I'm grateful for your helpfulness, Chief Superintendent. These things don't go unnoticed in Whitehall.'

'Only doing our duty,' Anthony said. He was not sure whether he was supposed to call Bloggs 'Sir'.

'Still, there's a big difference between reluctant assistance and willing help.'

'Yes. Well, it'll likely be a few hours before we pick up this man's scent again. Do you want to catch forty winks?'

'Yes,' Bloggs said gratefully. 'If you've got a chair in a corner somewhere . . .'

'Stay here,' Anthony said, indicating his office. 'I'll be down in the operations room. I'll wake you as soon as we've got something. Make yourself comfortable.'

Anthony went out, and Bloggs moved to an easy chair and sat back with his eyes closed. Immediately, he saw Godliman's face, as if projected on to the backs of his eyelids like a film, saying: 'There has to be an end to bereavement . . . I don't want you to make the same mistake.' Bloggs realized suddenly that he did not want the war to end, for that would make him face issues like the one Godliman had raised. The war made life simple, for he knew why he hated the enemy and he knew what he was supposed to do about it. Afterwards . . . the thought of another woman seemed disloyal, not just to Christine but, in some obscure way, to England.

He yawned and slumped farther into his seat, his thinking becoming woolly as sleep crept up on him. If Christine had died before the war, he would have felt very differently about remarrying. He had always been fond of her and respected her, of course; but after she took that ambulance job respect had turned to awe-struck admiration, and fondness turned to love. Then they had something special, something they knew other lovers did not share. Now, more than a year later, it would be easy for Bloggs to find another woman he could respect and be fond of, but he knew that would never be enough for him. An ordinary marriage, an ordinary woman, would always remind him that once he had possessed the ideal.

He stirred in his chair, trying to shake off imponder-ables so that he could sleep. England was full of heroes, Godliman had said. If Die Nadel got away England would be full of slaves. First things first . . .

Someone shook him. He was in a very deep sleep, dreaming that he was in a room with Die Nadel but could not pick him out because Die Nadel had blinded him with the stiletto. When he awoke he still thought he was blind because he could not see who was shaking him, until he realized he simply had his eyes closed. He opened them to see the large uniformed figure of Superintendent Anthony above him.

Bloggs raised himself to a more upright position and rubbed his eyes. 'Got something?' he asked.

'Lots of things,' Anthony said. 'Question is, which of 'em counts? Here's your breakfast.' He put a cup of tea and a biscuit on the desk and went to sit on the other side of it.

Bloggs left his easy chair and pulled a hard chair up to the desk. He sipped the tea. It was weak and very sweet. 'Let's get to it,' he said.

Anthony handed him a sheaf of five or six slips of paper.

Bloggs said: 'Don't tell me these are the only crimes in your area—'

'Of course not,' Anthony said. 'We're not interested in drunkenness, domestic disputes, blackout violations, traffic offences, or crimes for which arrests have already been made.'

'Sorry,' Bloggs said. 'I'm still waking up. Give me a chance to read these.'

There were three house burglaries. In two of them, valuables had been taken – jewellery in one case, furs in another. Bloggs said: 'He might steal valuables just to throw us off the scent. Mark these on the map, will you? They may show some pattern.' He handed the two slips back to Anthony. The third burglary had only just been reported, and no details were available. Anthony marked the location on the map.

A Food Office in Manchester had been robbed of

hundreds of ration books. Bloggs said: 'He doesn't need ration books – he needs food.' He set that one aside. There was a bicycle theft just outside Preston and a rape in Birkenhead. 'I don't think he's a rapist, but mark it anyway,' Bloggs told Anthony.

The bicycle theft and the third of the house burglaries were close together. Bloggs said: 'The signal box that the bike was stolen from – is that on the main line?'

'Yes, I think so,' Anthony said.

'Suppose Faber was hiding on that train and somehow we missed him. Would the signal box be the first place at which the train stopped after it left Liverpool?'

'It might be.'

Bloggs looked at the sheet of paper. 'An overcoat was stolen and a wet jacket left in its place.'

Anthony shrugged. 'Could mean anything.'

'No cars stolen?' Bloggs said sceptically.

'Nor boats, nor donkeys,' Anthony replied. 'We don't get many car thefts these days. Cars are easy to come by – it's petrol people steal.'

'I felt sure he'd steal a car in Liverpool,' Bloggs said. He thumped his knee in frustration. 'A bicycle isn't much use to him, surely.'

'I think we should follow it up, anyway,' Anthony pressed. 'It's our best lead.'

'All right. But meanwhile, double-check the burglaries to see whether food or clothing was pinched – the losers might not have noticed at first. Show Faber's picture to the rape victim, too. And keep checking all crimes. Can you fix me transport to Preston?'

'I'll get you a car,' Anthony said.

'How long will it take to get details of this third burglary?'

'They're probably interviewing at this minute,' Anthony said. 'By the time you reach the signal box I should have the complete picture.'

'Don't let them drag their feet.' Bloggs reached for his coat. 'I'll check with you the minute I get there.'

'Anthony? This is Bloggs. I'm at the signal box.'

'Don't waste any time there. The third burglary was your man.'

'Sure?'

'Unless there are two buggers running around threatening people with stiletto knives.'

'Who?'

'Two old ladies living alone in a little cottage.'

'Oh, God. Dead?'

'Not unless they died of excitement.'

'Eh?'

'Get over there. You'll see what I mean.'

'I'm on my way.'

It was the kind of cottage which is always inhabited by two elderly ladies living alone. It was small and square and old, and around the door grew a wild rose bush fertilized by thousands of pots of used tea leaves. Rows of vegetables sprouted tidily in a little front garden with a trimmed hedge. There were pink-and-white curtains at the leaded windows, and the gate creaked. The front door had been painted painstakingly by an amateur, and its knocker was made from a horse brass.

Bloggs's knock was answered by an octogenarian with a shotgun.

He said: 'Good morning. I'm from the police.'

'No, you're not,' she said. 'They've been already. Now get going before I blow your head off.'

Bloggs regarded her. She was less than five feet tall, with thick white hair in a bun and a pale, wrinkled face. Her hands were matchstick-thin, but her grasp on the shotgun was firm. The pocket of her apron was full of clothes-pegs. Bloggs looked down at her feet, and saw that she was wearing a man's working boots. He said: 'The police you saw this morning were local. I'm from Scotland Yard.'

'How do I know that?' she said.

Bloggs turned and called to his police driver. The constable got out of the car and came to the gate. Bloggs said to the old lady: 'Is the uniform enough to convince you?'

'All right,' she said, and stood aside for him to enter.

He stepped down into a low-ceilinged room with a tiled floor. The room was crammed with heavy, old furniture, and every surface was decorated with ornaments of china and glass. A small coal fire burned in the grate. The place smelled of lavender and cats.

A second old lady got out of a chair. She was like the first, but about twice as wide. Two cats spilled from her lap as she rose. She said: 'Hello, I'm Emma Parton, my sister is Jessie. Don't take any notice of that shotgun

– it's not loaded, thank God. Jessie loves drama. Will you sit down? You look so young to be a policeman. I'm surprised Scotland Yard is interested in our little rob-bery. Have you come from London this morning? Make the boy a cup of tea, Jessie.'

Bloggs sat down. 'If we're right about the identity of the burglar, he's a fugitive from justice,' he said.

'I told you!' Jessie said. 'We might have been done in – slaughtered, in cold blood!'

'Don't be silly,' Emma said. She turned to Bloggs. 'He was such a nice man.'

'Tell me what happened,' Bloggs said.

'Well, I'd gone out the back,' Emma began. 'I was in the hen coop, hoping for some eggs. Jessie was in the kitchen—'

'He surprised me,' Jessie interrupted. 'I didn't have time to go for me gun.'

'You see too many cowboy films,' Emma admonished her.

'They're better than your love films – all tears and kisses—'

Bloggs took the picture of Faber from his wallet. 'Is this the man?'

Jessie scrutinized it. 'That's him.'

'Aren't you clever?' Emma marvelled.

'If we were clever we'd have caught him by now,' Bloggs said. 'What did he do?'

Jessie said: 'He held a knife to my throat and said: "One false move and I'll slit your gizzard." And he meant it.'

'Oh, Jessie, you told me he said: "I won't harm you if you do as I say."'

'Words to that effect, Emma!'

Bloggs said: 'What did he want?'

'Food, a bath, dry clothes and a car. Well, we gave him the eggs, of course. We found some clothes that belonged to Jessie's late husband Norman—'

'Would you describe them?'

'Yes. A blue donkey jacket, blue overalls, a check shirt. And he took poor Norman's car. I don't know how we'll be able to go to the pictures without it. That's our only vice, you know – the pictures.'

'What sort of car?'

'A Morris. Norman bought it in 1924. It's served us well, that little car.'

Jessie said: 'He didn't get his hot bath, though!'

'Well,' Emma said, 'I had to explain to him that two ladies living alone can hardly have a man taking a bath in their kitchen . . .' She blushed.

Jessie said: 'You'd rather have your throat slit than see a man in his combinations, wouldn't you, you silly fool.'

Bloggs said: 'What did he say when you refused?'

'He laughed,' Emma said. 'But I think he understood our position.'

Bloggs could not help but smile. 'I think you're very brave,' he said.

'I don't know about that, I'm sure.'

'So he left here in a 1924 Morris, wearing overalls and a blue jacket. What time was that?'

'About half-past nine.'

Bloggs absently stroked a marmalade cat. It blinked and purred. 'Was there much petrol in the car?'

'A couple of gallons – but he took our coupons.'

A thought struck Bloggs. 'How do you ladies qualify for a petrol ration?'

'Agricultural purposes,' Emma said defensively. She blushed.

Jessie snorted. 'And we're isolated, and we're elderly. Of course we qualify.'

'We always go to the corn stores at the same time as the pictures,' Emma added. 'We don't waste petrol.'

Bloggs smiled and held up a hand. 'All right, don't worry – rationing isn't my department anyway. How fast does the car go?'

Emma said: 'We never exceed thirty miles per hour.'

Bloggs looked at his watch. 'Even at that speed he could be seventy-five miles away by now.' He stood up. 'I must phone the details to Liverpool. You don't have a telephone, do you?'

'No.'

'What kind of Morris is it?'

'A Cowley. Norman used to call it a Bullnose.'

'Colour?'

'Grey.'

'Registration number?'

'MLN 29.'

Bloggs wrote it all down.

Emma said: 'Will we ever get our car back, do you think?'

'I expect so – but it may not be in very good

condition. When someone is driving a stolen car he generally doesn't take good care of it.' He walked to the door.

'I hope you catch him,' Emma called.

Jessie saw him out. She was still clutching the shotgun. At the door she caught Bloggs's sleeve and said in a stage whisper: 'Tell me – what is he? Escaped convict? Murderer? Rapist?'

Bloggs looked down at her. Her small green eyes were bright with excitement. She would believe anything he chose to tell her. He bent his head to speak quietly in her ear. 'Don't tell a soul,' he murmured, 'but he's a German spy.'

CHAPTER SEVENTEEN

FABER CROSSED the Sark Bridge and entered Scotland shortly after midday. He passed the Sark Toll Bar House, a low building with a signboard announcing that it was the first house in Scotland and a tablet above the door bearing some legend about marriages which he could not read. A quarter of a mile farther on he understood, when he entered the village of Gretna: he knew this was a place runaways came to get married.

The roads were still damp from the early rain, but the sun was drying them rapidly. Signposts and name-boards had been re-erected since the relaxation of invasion precautions, and Faber sped through a series of small lowland villages: Kirkpatrick, Kirtlebridge, Ecclefechan. The open countryside was pleasant, the green moors sparkling in the sunshine.

He had stopped for petrol in Carlisle. The pump attendant, a middle-aged woman in an oily apron, had not asked any awkward questions. Faber had filled the tank and the spare can fixed to the offside running-board.

He was very pleased with the little two-seater. It would still do fifty miles an hour, despite its age. The

four-cylinder, 1548cc side-valve engine worked smoothly
and tirelessly as he climbed and descended the Scottish
hills. The leather-upholstered bench seat was comfortable. He squeezed the bulb horn to warn a straying
sheep of his approach.

He went through the little market town of Lockerbie,
crossed the River Annan by the picturesque Johnstone
Bridge, and began the ascent to Beattock Summit. He
found himself using the three-speed gearbox more and
more.

He had decided not to take the most direct route to
Aberdeen, via Edinburgh and the coast road. Much of
Scotland's east coast, either side of the Firth of Forth,
was a restricted area. Visitors were prohibited from a
ten-mile-wide strip of land. Of course, the authorities
could not seriously police such a long border. Nevertheless, Faber was less likely to be stopped and questioned
while he stayed outside the security zone.

He would have to enter it eventually – later rather
than sooner – and he turned his mind to the story he
would tell if he were interrogated. Private motoring for
pleasure had virtually ceased in the last couple of years
because of the ever-stricter petrol rationing, and people
who had cars for essential journeys were liable to be
prosecuted for going a few yards off their necessary
route for personal reasons. Faber had read of a famous
impresario gaoled for using petrol supplied for agricultural purposes to take several actors from a theatre to
the Savoy Hotel. Endless propaganda told people that
a Lancaster bomber needed 2,000 gallons to get to the
Ruhr. Nothing would please Faber more than to waste

petrol which might otherwise be used to bomb his homeland, in normal circumstances; but to be stopped now, with the information he had taped to his chest, and arrested for a rationing violation would be an unbearable irony.

It was difficult. Most traffic was military, but he had no military papers. He could not claim to be delivering essential supplies because he had nothing in the car to deliver. He frowned. Who travelled, these days? Sailors on leave, officials, rare holidaymakers, skilled workmen . . . That was it. He would be an engineer, a specialist in some esoteric field like high-temperature gearbox oils, going to solve a manufacturing problem in a factory at Inverness. If he were asked which factory, he would say it was classified. (His fictitious destination had to be a long way from the real one so that he would never be questioned by someone who knew for certain there were no such factory.) He doubted whether consulting engineers ever wore overalls like the ones he had stolen from the elderly sisters – but anything was possible in wartime.

Having figured all that out, he felt he was reasonably safe from any random spot checks. The danger of being stopped by someone who was looking specifically for Henry Faber, fugitive spy, was another problem. They had that picture—

They knew his face. His face!

—and before long they would have a description of the car in which he was travelling. He did not think they would set up roadblocks, as they had no way of guessing where he was headed; but he was sure that every policeman in the land would be on the lookout for the grey Morris Cowley Bullnose, registration number MLN 29.

If he were spotted in the open country, he would not be captured immediately, for country policemen had bicycles, not cars. But the policeman would telephone his headquarters, and cars would be after Faber within minutes. If he saw a policeman, he decided, he would have to ditch this car, steal another, and divert from his planned route. However, in the sparsely populated Scottish lowlands there was a good chance he could get all the way to Aberdeen without passing a country policeman. The towns would be different. There, the danger of being chased by a police car was very great. He would be unlikely to escape: his car was old and relatively slow, and the police were generally good drivers. His best chance would be to get out of the vehicle and hope to lose himself in crowds or back streets. He contemplated ditching the car and stealing another each time he was forced to enter a major town. The problem there was that he would be leaving a trail a mile wide for MI5 to follow. Perhaps the best solution was a compromise: he would drive into the towns but try to use only the back streets. He looked at his watch. He would reach Glasgow around dusk, and thereafter he would benefit from the darkness.

Well, it was not satisfactory, but the only way to be totally safe was not to be a spy.

As he topped the one-thousand-feet-high Beattock Summit, it began to rain. Faber stopped the car and got out to raise the canvas roof. The air was oppressively warm. Faber looked up. The sky had clouded over very quickly. Thunder and lightning were promised.

As he drove on he discovered some of the little car's shortcomings. Wind and rain leaked in through several flaws in the canvas roof, and the small wiper sweeping the top half of the horizontally divided windscreen provided only a tunnel-like view of the road ahead. As the terrain became progressively more hilly, the engine note began to sound faintly ragged. It was hardly surprising: the twenty-year-old car was being pushed hard.

The shower ended. The threatened storm had not arrived, but the sky remained dark and the atmosphere forbidding.

Faber passed through Crawford, nestling in green hills; Abington, a church and a Post Office on the west bank of the River Clyde; and Lesmahagow, on the edge of a heathery moor.

Half an hour later he reached the outskirts of Glasgow. As soon as he entered the built-up area, he turned north off the main road, hoping to circumvent the city. He followed a succession of minor roads, crossing the major arteries into the city's east side, until he reached Cumbernauld Road, where he turned east again and sped out of the city.

It had been quicker than he expected. His luck was holding.

He was on the A80 road, passing factories, mines and farms. More Scots place-names drifted in and out of his consciousness: Millerston, Stepps, Muirhead, Mollinsburn, Condorrat.

His luck ran out between Cumbernauld and Stirling.

He was accelerating along a straight stretch of road, slightly downhill, with open fields on either side. As the speedometer needle touched forty-five there was a sudden, very loud noise from the engine; a heavy rattle, like the sound of a large chain pulling over a cog. He slowed to thirty, but the noise did not get perceptively quieter. Clearly some large and important piece of the mechanism had failed. Faber listened carefully. It was either a cracked ball-bearing in the transmission, or a hole in a big end. Certainly it was nothing so simple as a blocked carburettor or a dirty sparking-plug; nothing that could be repaired outside a workshop.

He pulled up and looked under the bonnet. There seemed to be a lot of oil everywhere, but otherwise he could see no clues. He got back behind the wheel and drove off. There was a definite loss of power, but the car would still go.

Three miles farther on, steam began to billow out of the radiator. Faber realized that the car would soon stop altogether. He looked for a place to dump it.

He found a mud track leading off the main road, presumably to a farm. One hundred yards from the road, the track curved behind a blackberry bush. Faber parked the car close to the bush and killed the engine. The hiss of escaping steam gradually subsided. He got out and locked the door. He felt a twinge of regret for Emma and Jessie, who would find it very difficult to get their car repaired before the end of the war.

He walked back to the main road. From there, the car could not be seen. It might be a day or even two before the abandoned vehicle aroused suspicion. By then, Faber thought, I may be in Berlin.

He began to walk. Sooner or later he would hit a town where he could steal another vehicle. He was doing well enough: it was less than twenty-four hours since he had left London, and he still had a whole day before the U-boat arrived at the rendezvous at six p.m. tomorrow.

The sun had set long ago, and now darkness fell suddenly. Faber could hardly see. Fortunately there was a painted white line down the middle of the road – a safety innovation made necessary by the blackout – and he was just about able to follow it. Because of the night silence he would hear an oncoming car in plenty of time.

In fact only one car passed him. He heard its deep-throated engine in the distance, and went off the road a few yards to lie out of sight until it had gone. It was a large car, a Vauxhall Ten, Faber guessed, and it was travelling at speed. He let it go by, then got up and resumed walking. Twenty minutes later he saw it again, parked by the roadside. He would have taken a detour across the field if he had noticed the car in time, but its light were off and its engine silent, and he almost bumped into it in the darkness.

Before he could consider what to do, a torch shone up toward him from under the car's bonnet, and a voice said: 'I say, is anybody there?'

Faber moved into the beam and said: 'Having trouble?'

'I'll say.'

The torch was pointed down, and as Faber moved closer he could see, by the reflected light, the moustached face of a middle-aged man in a double-breasted coat. In his other hand the man held, rather uncertainly, a large spanner; seeming unsure of what to do with it.

Faber looked at the engine. 'What's wrong?'

'Loss of power,' the man said, pronouncing it 'Lorse of par'. 'One moment she was going like a top, the next she started to hobble. I'm afraid I'm not much of a mechanic.' He shone the torch at Faber again. 'Are you?' he finished hopefully.

'Not exactly,' Faber said, 'but I know a disconnected lead when I see one.' He took the torch from the man, reached down into the engine, and plugged the stray lead back on to the cylinder head. 'Try her now.'

The man got into the car and started the engine. 'Perfect!' he shouted over the noise. 'You're a genius! Hop in.'

It crossed Faber's mind that this might be an elaborate MI5 trap, but he dismissed the thought: in the unlikely event they knew where he was, why should they tread softly? They could as easily send twenty policemen and a couple of armoured cars to pick him up.

He got in.

The driver pulled away and moved rapidly up through the gears until the car was travelling at a good speed. Faber made himself comfortable. The driver said: 'By the way, I'm Richard Porter.'

Faber thought quickly of the identity card in his wallet. 'James Baker.'

'How do you do. I must have passed you on the road back there – didn't see you.'

Faber realized the man was apologizing for not picking him up – everyone picked up hitch-hikers since the petrol shortage. 'It's okay,' Faber said. 'I was probably off the road, behind a bush, answering a call of nature. I did hear a car.'

'Have you come far?' Porter offered a cigar.

'It's good of you, but I don't smoke,' Faber said. 'Yes, I've come from London.'

'Hitch-hiked all the way?'

'No, my car broke down in Edinburgh. Apparently it requires a spare part which isn't in stock, so I had to leave it at the garage.'

'Hard luck. Well, I'm going to Aberdeen, so I can drop you anywhere along the way.'

Faber thought fast. This was a piece of good fortune. He closed his eyes and pictured the map of Scotland. 'That's marvellous,' he said. 'I'm going to Banff, so Aberdeen would be a great help. But I was planning to take the high road, because I didn't get myself a pass – is Aberdeen a Restricted Area?'

'Only the harbour,' Porter said. 'Anyway, you neen't worry about that sort of thing while you're in my car – I'm a JP and a member of the Watch Committee. How's that?'

Faber smiled in the darkness. It was his lucky day. 'Thank you,' he said. He decided to change the subject of the conversation. 'Is that a full-time job? Being a magistrate, I mean.'

Porter put a match to his cigar and puffed smoke.

'Not really. I'm semi-retired, y'know. Used to be a solicitor, until they discovered my weak heart.'

'Ah.' Faber tried to put some sympathy into his voice.

'Hope you don't mind the smoke?' Porter waved the fat cigar.

'Not a bit.'

'What takes you to Banff?'

'I'm an engineer. There's a problem in a factory . . . actually, the job is sort of classified.'

Porter held up his hand. 'Don't say another word. I understand.'

There was silence for a while. The car flashed through several towns. Porter obviously knew the road very well, to drive so fast in the blackout. The big car gobbled up the miles. Its smooth progress was soporific. Faber smothered a yawn.

'Damn, you must be tired,' Porter said. 'Silly of me. Don't be too polite to have a nap.'

'Thank you,' said Faber. 'I will.' He closed his eyes.

The motion of the car was like the rocking of a train, and Faber had his arrival nightmare again, only this time it was slightly different. Instead of dining on the train and talking politics with a fellow passenger, he was obliged for some unknown reason to travel in the coal tender, sitting on his suitcase radio with his back against the hard iron side of the truck. When the train arrived at Waterloo, everyone – including the disembarking passengers – was carrying a little duplicated photograph of Faber in the running team; and they were all looking at each other and comparing the faces they saw with the face in the picture. At the ticket barrier the collector took his shoulder and said: 'You're the man in the photo, aren't you?' Faber found himself dumb. All he could do was stare at the photograph and remember the way he had run to win that cup. God, how he had run: he had peaked a shade too early, started his final burst a quarter of a mile sooner than he had planned, and for the last 500 metres he wanted to die – and now perhaps he would die, because of that photograph in the ticket collector's hand ... The collector was saying: 'Wake up! Wake up!' and suddenly Faber was back in Richard Porter's Vauxhall Ten, and it was Porter who was telling him to wake up.

His right hand was half way to his left sleeve, where the stiletto was sheathed, in the split-second before he remembered that as far as Porter was concerned James Baker was an innocent hitch-hiker. Then his hand dropped and he relaxed.

'You wake up like a soldier,' Porter said with amusement. 'This is Aberdeen.'

Faber noted that 'soldier' had been pronounced 'sol-juh', and recalled that Porter was a magistrate and a member of the police authority. He looked at the man in the dull light of early day: Porter had a red face and a waxed moustache, and his camel-coloured overcoat looked expensive. He was wealthy and powerful in this town, Faber guessed. If he were to disappear he would be missed almost immediately. Faber decided not to kill him.

Faber said: 'Good morning.'

He looked out of the window at the granite city.

They were moving slowly along the main street with shops on either side. There were several early workers about, all moving purposefully in the same direction: fishermen, Faber reckoned. It seemed a cold, windy place.

Porter said: 'Would you like to have a shave and a bit of breakfast before you continue your journey? You're welcome to come to my place.'

'You're very kind—'

'Not at all. If it weren't for you I should still be on the A80 at Stirling, waiting for a garage to open.'

'—but I won't, thank you. I want to get on with the journey.'

Porter did not insist, and Faber suspected that he was relieved not to have his offer taken up. The man said: 'In that case, I'll drop you at George Street – that's the start of the A96, and it's a straight road to Banff.' A moment later he stopped the car at a corner. 'Here you are.'

Faber opened the door. 'Thanks for the lift.'

'A pleasure.' Porter offered a handshake. 'Good luck!'

Faber got out and closed the door, and the car pulled away. He had nothing to fear from Porter, he thought; the man would go home and sleep all day, and by the time he realized he had helped a fugitive, it would be too late to do anything about it.

He watched the Vauxhall out of sight, then crossed the road and entered the promisingly named Market Street. Shortly he found himself in the docks and, following his nose, arrived at the fish market. He felt safely anonymous in the bustling, noisy, smelly market, where everyone was dressed in working clothes as he was. Wet fish and cheerful profanities flew through the air. Faber found it hard to understand the clipped, guttural accents. At a stall he bought hot, strong tea in a chipped half-pint mug and a large bread roll with a doorstep of white cheese.

He sat on a barrel to eat and drink. This evening would be the time to steal a boat. It was galling, to have to wait all day; and it left him with the problem of concealing himself for the next twelve hours; but he was too close now to take risks, and stealing a boat in broad daylight was much more risky than at the twilit end of the day.

He finished his breakfast and stood up. It would be a couple of hours before the rest of the city came to life. He would use the time to pick out a good hiding-place.

He made a circuit of the docks and the tidal harbour. The security was perfunctory, and he spotted several places where he could slip past the checkpoints. He worked his way around to the sandy beach, and set off along the two-mile esplanade. At its far end, a couple of pleasure yachts were moored at the mouth of the River Don. They would have suited Faber's purpose very well, but they would have no fuel.

A thick ceiling of cloud hid the sunrise. The air became very warm and thundery again. A few determined holidaymakers emerged from the seafront hotels and sat stubbornly on the beach, waiting for sunshine. Faber doubted they would get it today.

The beach might be the place to hide. The police would check the railway station and the bus depot, but they would not mount a full-scale search of the city. They might check a few hotels and guest-houses. It was unlikely they would approach everyone on the beach. He decided to spend the day in a deck-chair.

He bought a newspaper from a stall and hired a chair. He removed his shirt and put it back on over his overalls. He left his jacket off.

He would see a policeman, if one came, well before he reached the spot where Faber sat. There would be plenty of time to leave the beach and vanish into the streets.

He began to read the paper. There was a new Allied offensive in Italy, the newspaper rejoiced. Faber was sceptical. Anzio had been a shambles. The paper was badly printed and there were no photographs. He read that the police were searching for one Henry Faber, who had murdered two people in London with a stiletto . . .

A woman in a bathing suit walked by, looking hard at Faber. His heart missed a beat. Then he realized she was being flirtatious. For an instant he was tempted to speak to her. It had been so long . . . He shook himself mentally. Patience, patience. Tomorrow he would be home.

She was a small fishing boat, fifty or sixty feet long and broad in the beam, with an inboard motor. The aerial told of a powerful radio. Most of the deck was taken up with hatches to the small hold below. The cabin was aft, and only large enough to hold two men, standing, plus the dashboard and controls. The hull was clinker-built and newly caulked, and the paintwork looked fresh.

Two other boats in the harbour would have done as well, but Faber had stood on the quay and watched the crew of this one tie her up and refuel before they left for their homes.

He gave them a few minutes to get well away, then walked around the edge of the harbour and jumped on to the boat. She was called *Marie II*.

He found the wheel chained up. He sat on the floor of the little cabin, out of sight, and spent ten minutes picking the lock. Darkness was coming early because of the cloud layer which still blanketed the sky.

When he had freed the wheel he raised the small anchor, then sprang back on to the quay and untied the ropes. He returned to the cabin, primed the diesel engine, and pulled the starter. The motor coughed and died. He tried again. This time it roared to life. He began to manoeuvre out of the mooring.

He got clear of the other craft at the quayside and found the main channel out of the harbour, marked by buoys. He guessed that only boats of much deeper draught really needed to stick to the channel, but he saw no harm in being overcautious.

Once outside the harbour, he felt a stiff breeze, and hoped it was not a sign that the weather was about to break. The sea was surprisingly rough, and the stout little boat lifted high on the waves. Faber opened the throttle wide, consulted the dashboard compass, and set a course. He found some charts in a locker below the wheel. They looked old and little-used: no doubt the boat's skipper knew the local waters too well to need charts. Faber checked the map reference he had memorized that night in Stockwell, set a more exact course, and engaged the wheel-clamp.

The cabin windows were obscured by water. Faber could not tell whether it was rain or spray. The wind was slicing off the tops of the waves now. He poked his head out of the cabin door for a moment, and got his face thoroughly wet.

He switched on the radio. It hummed for a moment, then crackled. He moved the frequency control, wandering the airwaves, and picked up a few garbled messages. The set was working perfectly. He tuned to the U-boat's frequency, then switched off – it was too soon to make contact.

The waves increased in size as he progressed into deeper waters. Now the boat reared up like a bucking horse with each wave, then teetered momentarily at the top before plunging sickeningly down into the next trough. Faber stared blindly out of the cabin windows. Night had fallen, and he could see nothing at all. He felt faintly seasick.

Each time he convinced himself that the waves could not possibly get bigger, a new monster taller than the rest lifted the vessel toward the sky. They started to come closer together, so that the boat was always lying with its stern pointed either up at the sky or down at the sea bed. In a particularly deep trough the little boat was suddenly illuminated, as clearly as if it were day, by a flash of lightning. Faber saw a grey-green mountain of water descend on the prow and wash over the deck and the cabin where he stood. He could not tell whether the terrible crack which sounded a second afterwards was the thunderclap or the noise of the timbers of the boat breaking up. Frantically he searched the little cabin for a life jacket. There was none.

The lightning came repeatedly then. Faber held the locked wheel and braced his back against the cabin wall to stay upright. There was no point in operating the controls now – the boat would go where the sea threw it.

He kept telling himself that the boat must be built to withstand such sudden summer gales. He could not convince himself. Experienced fishermen probably would have seen the signs of such a storm, and refrained from leaving shore, knowing their vessel could not survive such weather.

He had no idea where he was, now. He might be almost back in Aberdeen, or he might be at his rendez-vous. He sat on the cabin floor and switched on the radio. The wild rocking and shuddering made it diffi-cult to operate the set. When it warmed up he experi-mented with the dials, and could pick up nothing. He turned the volume to maximum: still no sound.

The aerial must have been broken off its fixing on the cabin roof.

He switched to Transmit and repeated the simple message 'Come in, please,' several times; then left the set on Receive. He had little hope of his signal getting through.

He killed the engine to conserve fuel. He was going to have to ride out the storm – if he could – then find a way to repair or replace the aerial. He might need his fuel.

The boat slid terrifyingly sideways down the next big wave, and Faber realized he needed the engine power to ensure the vessel met waves head-on. He pulled the starter, but nothing happened. He tried several times, then gave up, cursing his foolishness for switching off.

The boat rolled so far on to its side that Faber fell and cracked his head on the wheel. He lay dazed on the cabin floor, expecting the vessel to turn turtle at any minute. Another wave crashed on the cabin, and this time the glass in the windows shattered. Suddenly Faber was under water. Certain the boat was sinking, he struggled to his feet, and broke surface. All the windows were out, but the vessel was still floating. He kicked open the cabin door, and the water gushed out. He clutched the wheel to prevent himself being washed into the sea.

Incredibly, the storm continued to get worse. One of Faber's last coherent thoughts was that these waters probably did not see such a storm more than once in a century. Then all his concentration and will were focused on the problem of keeping hold of the wheel. He should have tied himself to it, but now he did not dare to let go long enough to find a piece of rope. He lost all sense of up and down as the boat pitched and rolled on waves like cliffs. Gale force winds and thousands of gallons of water strained to pull him from his place. His feet slipped continually on the wet floor and walls, and the muscles of his arms burned with pain. He sucked air when he found his head above water, but otherwise held his breath. Many times he came close to blacking out. He vaguely realized that the flat roof of the cabin had disappeared.

He got brief, nightmarish glimpses of the sea whenever the lightning flashed. He was always surprised to see where the wave was: ahead, below, rearing up beside him, or completely out of sight. He discovered with a shock that he could not feel his hands, and looked down to see that they were still locked to the wheel, frozen in a grip like rigor mortis. There was a continuous roar in his ears, the wind indistinguishable from the thunder and the sea.

The power of intelligent thought slipped slowly away from him. In something that was less than a hallucination but more than a daydream, he saw the girl who had stared at him on the beach. She walked endlessly toward him over the bucking deck of the fishing boat, her swimsuit clinging to her body, always getting closer but never reaching him. He knew that, when she came within touching distance, he would take his dead hands from the wheel and reach for her, but he kept saying 'Not yet, not yet,' as she walked and smiled and swayed her hips. He was tempted to leave the wheel and close the gap himself, but something at the back of his mind told him that if he moved he would never reach her, so he waited and watched and smiled back at her from time to time, and even when he closed his eyes he could see her still.

He was slipping in and out of consciousness now.

His mind would drift away, the sea and the boat disappearing first, then the girl fading, until he would jerk awake to find that, incredibly, he was still standing, still holding the wheel, still alive; then for a while he would will himself to stay conscious, but eventually exhaustion would take over again.

In one of his last clear moments he noticed that the waves were moving in one direction, carrying the boat with them. Lightning flashed again, and he saw to one side a huge dark mass, an impossibly high wave – no, it was not a wave, it was a cliff . . . The realization that he was close to land was swamped by the fear of being hurled against the cliff and smashed. Stupidly, he pulled the starter, then hastily returned his hand to the wheel; but it would no longer grip.

A new wave lifted the boat and threw it down like a discarded toy. As he fell through the air, still clutching the wheel with one hand, Faber saw a pointed rock like a stiletto sticking up out of the trough of the wave. It seemed certain to impale the boat. But the hull of the little craft scraped the edge of the rock and was carried past.

The mountainous waves were breaking now. The next one was too much for the vessel's timbers. The boat hit the trough with a solid impact, and the sound of the hull splitting cracked the night like an explosion. Faber knew the boat was finished.

The water retreated, and Faber realized that the hull had broken because it had hit land. He stared in dumb astonishment as a new flash of lightning revealed a beach. The sea lifted the ruined boat off the sand as water crashed over the deck again, knocking Faber to the floor. But he had seen everything with daylight clarity in that moment. The beach was narrow, and the waves were breaking right up to the cliff. But there was a jetty, over to his right, and a bridge of some kind leading from the jetty to the cliff top. He knew that if he left the boat for the beach, the next wave would kill him with tons of water or break his head like an egg against the cliff. But if he could reach the jetty in between waves, he might scramble far enough up the bridge to be out of reach of the water.

He might survive yet.

The next wave split the deck open as if the seasoned wood were no stronger than a banana skin. The boat collapsed under Faber, and he found himself sucked backward by the receding surf. He scrambled upright, his legs like jelly beneath him, and broke into a run, splashing through the shallows toward the jetty. Running those few yards was the hardest thing he had ever done. He *wanted* to stumble, so that he could rest in the water and die; but he stayed upright, just as he had when he won the 5,000 metres race, until he crashed into one of the pillars of the jetty. He reached up and grabbed the boards with his hands, willing them to come back to life for a few seconds; and lifted himself until his chin was over the edge; then he swung his legs up and rolled over.

The wave came as he got to his knees. He threw himself forward. The wave carried him a few yards then flung him brutally against the wooden planking. He swallowed water and saw stars. When the weight lifted from his back he summoned the will to move. It would not come. He felt himself being dragged inexorably back. A sudden rage possessed him. He would not be beaten, not now! He screamed his hatred of the storm and the sea and the British and Percival Godliman, and suddenly he was on his feet and running, running, away from the sea and up the ramp, running with his eyes shut and his mouth open and madness in his heart, daring his lungs to burst and his bones to break; remembering, dimly, that he had called on this madness once before and almost died; running with no sense of destination, but knowing he would not stop until he lost his mind.

The ramp was long and steep. A strong man might have run all the way to the top, if he were in training and rested. An Olympic athlete, if he were tired, might have got half way. The average forty-year-old man would have managed a yard or two.

Faber made it to the top.

A yard from the end of the ramp he had a slight heart attack and lost consciousness, but his legs pumped twice more before he hit the sodden turf.

He never knew how long he lay there. When he opened his eyes the storm still raged, but day had broken, and he could see, a few yards away from him, a small cottage which looked inhabited.

He got to his knees and began the long crawl to the front door.

CHAPTER EIGHTEEN

THE *U-505* wheeled in a tedious circle, her powerful diesels chugging slowly as she nosed through the depths like a grey, toothless shark. Lieutenant-Commander Werner Heer, her master, was drinking ersatz coffee and trying not to smoke any more cigarettes. It had been a long day and a long night. He disliked his assignment, for he was a fighting man and there was no fighting to be done; and he disliked the quiet Abwehr officer with sly blue eyes who was an unwelcome guest aboard the submarine.

The Intelligence man, Major Wohl, sat opposite the captain. The man never looked tired, damn him. Those blue eyes looked around, taking things in, but the expression in them never changed. His uniform never got rumpled, despite the rigours of underwater life; and he lit a new cigarette every twenty minutes, on the dot, and smoked it to a quarter-inch stub. Heer would have stopped smoking, just so that he could enforce regulations and prevent Wohl from enjoying tobacco, but Heer himself was too much of an addict.

Heer never liked Intelligence people, because he always had the feeling they were gathering intelligence on him. Nor did he like working with Abwehr. His vessel was made for battle, not for skulking around the British coast waiting to pick up secret agents. It seemed to him plain madness to put at risk a costly piece of fighting machinery, not to mention its skilled crew, for the sake of one man who might even fail to appear.

He emptied his cup and made a face. 'Damn coffee,' he said. 'It tastes vile.'

Wohl's expressionless gaze rested on him for a moment then moved away. He said nothing.

Heer shifted restlessly in his seat. On the bridge of a ship he would have paced up and down, but men on submarines learn to avoid unnecessary movement. He said: 'Your man won't come in this weather, you know.'

Wohl looked at his watch. 'We will wait until six a.m.,' he said calmly.

It was not an order, for Wohl could not give orders to Heer; but the bald statement of fact was still an insult to a superior officer. Heer said: 'Damn you, I'm the master of this vessel!'

'We will both follow our orders,' Wohl said. 'As you know, they originate from a very high authority indeed.'

Heer controlled his anger. The young whipper-snapper was right, of course. Heer would follow his orders. When they returned to port he would report Wohl for insubordination. Not that it would do much good: fifteen years in the Navy had taught Heer that headquarters people were a law unto themselves.

He said: 'If your man is fool enough to venture out tonight, he is certainly not seaman enough to survive.'

Wohl's only reply was the same blank gaze.

Heer called to the radio operator. 'Weissman?'

'Nothing, sir.'

Wohl said: 'I have an unpleasant feeling that the murmurs we heard a few hours ago were from him.'

'If they were, he was a long way from the rendezvous, sir,' the radio operator volunteered. 'To me it sounded more like lightning.'

Heer added: 'If it was not him, it was not him. If it was him, he is now drowned.' His tone was smug.

'You don't know the man,' Wohl said, and this time there was a trace of emotion in his voice.

Heer subsided into silence. The engine note altered slightly, and he thought he could distinguish a faint rattle. If it increased on the journey home he would have it looked at in port. He might do that anyway, just to avoid another voyage with the unspeakable Major Wohl.

A seaman looked in. 'Coffee, sir?'

Heer shook his head. 'If I drink any more I'll be pissing coffee.'

Wohl said: 'I will, please.' He took out a cigarette.

That made Heer look at his watch. It was ten past six. The subtle Major Wohl had delayed his six o'clock cigarette to keep the U-boat there a few extra minutes. Heer said: 'Set a course for home.'

'One moment,' Wohl said. 'I think we should take a look on the surface before we leave.'

'Don't be a fool,' Heer said. He knew he was on safe ground now. 'Do you realize what kind of storm is raging up there? We would not be able to open the hatch, and the periscope will show us nothing that is more than a few yards away.'

'How can you tell what the storm is like from this depth?'

'Experience,' Heer told him.

'Then at least send a signal to base, telling them that our man has not made contact. They may order us to stay here.'

Heer gave an exasperated sigh. 'It's not possible to make radio contact from this depth, not with base,' he said.

Wohl's calm was shattered at last. 'Commander Heer, I strongly recommend you surface and radio home before leaving this rendezvous. The man we are to pick up has information vital to the future of the Reich. The Führer himself is waiting for his report!'

Heer looked at him. 'Thank you for letting me have your opinion, Major,' he said. He turned away. 'Full ahead both!' he barked.

The sound of the twin diesels rose to a roar, and the U-boat began to pick up speed.

Part Four

CHAPTER NINETEEN

WHEN LUCY woke up, the storm that had broken the evening before was still raging. She leaned over the edge of the bed, moving cautiously so that she would not disturb David, and picked up her wristwatch from the door. It was just after six. The wind was howling around the roof. David could sleep on: little work would be done today.

She wondered whether they had lost any slates off the roof during the night. She would need to check the loft. The job would have to wait until David was out, otherwise he would be angry that she had not asked him to do it.

She slipped out of bed. It was very cold. The warm weather of the last few days had been a phoney summer, the build-up to the storm. Now it was as cold as November. She pulled the flannel nightdress off over her head and quickly got into her underwear, trousers and sweater. David stirred. She looked at him: he turned over, but did not wake.

She crossed the tiny landing and looked into Jo's room. The three-year-old had graduated from a cot to a bed, and he often fell out during the night without waking. This morning he was on his bed, lying asleep on his back with his mouth wide open. Lucy smiled. He looked adorable when he was asleep.

She went quietly downstairs, wondering briefly why she had woken up so early. Perhaps Jo had made a noise, or maybe it was the storm.

She knelt in front of the fireplace, pushing back the sleeves of her sweater, and began to make the fire. As she swept out the grate she whistled a tune she had heard on the radio, *Is You Is Or Is You Ain't My Baby?* She raked the cold ashes, using the biggest lumps to form the base for today's fire. Dried bracken provided the tinder and wood and then coal went on top. Sometimes she just used wood, but coal was better in this weather. She held a page of newspaper across the fireplace for a few minutes to create an updraught in the chimney. When she removed it the wood was burning and the coal glowing red. She folded the paper and placed it under the coal scuttle for use tomorrow.

The blaze would soon warm the little house, but a hot cup of tea would help meanwhile. Lucy went into the kitchen and put the kettle on the electric cooker. She put two cups on a tray, then found David's cigarettes and an ashtray. She made the tea, filled the cups, and carried the tray through the hall to the stairs.

She had one foot on the lowest stair when she heard the tapping. She stopped, frowned, decided it was the wind rattling something, and took another step. The sound came again. It was like someone knocking on the front door.

That was ridiculous, of course. There was no one to

knock on the front door – only Tom, and he always came to the kitchen door and never knocked.

The tapping came again.

Just to assuage her curiosity, she came down the stairs and, balancing the tea tray on one hand, opened the front door.

She dropped the tray in shock. The man fell into the hall, knocking her over. Lucy screamed.

She was frightened only for a moment. The stranger lay prone beside her on the hall floor, plainly incapable of attacking anyone. His clothes were soaking wet, and his hands and face were stone-white with cold.

Lucy got to her feet. David slid down the stairs on his bottom, saying: 'What is it? What is it?'

'Him,' Lucy said, and pointed.

David arrived at the foot of the stairs, clad in pyjamas, and hauled himself into his wheelchair. 'I don't see what there is to scream about,' he said. He wheeled himself closer and peered at the man on the floor.

'I'm sorry. He startled me.' She bent over and, taking the man by his upper arms, dragged him into the living-room. David followed. Lucy laid the man in front of the fire.

David stared pensively at the unconscious body. 'Where the devil did he come from?' he wondered.

'He must be a shipwrecked sailor.'

'Of course.'

But he was wearing the clothes of a workman, not a sailor, Lucy noticed. She studied him. He was quite a

big man, longer than the six-foot hearth-rug, and heavy
around the neck and shoulders. His face was strong
and fine-boned, with a high forehead and a long jaw.
He might be handsome, she thought, if he were not
such a ghastly colour.

The stranger stirred and opened his eyes. At first he
looked terribly frightened, like a little boy waking in
strange surroundings; but, very quickly, his expression
became relaxed, and he looked about him sharply, his
gaze resting briefly on Lucy, David, the window, the
door, and the fire.

Lucy said: 'We must get him out of these clothes.
Fetch a pair of pyjamas and a robe, David.'

David wheeled himself out, and Lucy knelt beside
the stranger. She took off his boots and socks first.
There almost seemed to be a hint of amusement in his
eyes as he watched her. But when she reached for his
jacket he crossed his arms protectively over his chest.

'You'll die of pneumonia if you keep these clothes
on,' she said in her best bedside manner. 'Let me take
them off.'

The stranger said: 'I really don't think we know each
other well enough – after all, we haven't been
introduced.'

It was the first time he had spoken. His voice was so
confident, his words so formal, that the contrast with
his terrible appearance made Lucy laugh out loud.
'You're shy?' she said.

'I just think a man should preserve an air of mystery.'
He was grinning broadly, but his smile collapsed suddenly and his eyes closed in pain.

David came back in with clean nightclothes over his arm. 'You two seem to be getting on remarkably well already,' he said.

'You'll have to undress him,' Lucy said. 'He won't let me.'

David's look was unreadable.

The stranger said: 'I'll manage on my own, thanks – if it's not too awfully ungracious of me.'

'Suit yourself,' David said. He dumped the clothes on a chair and wheeled out.

'I'll make some more tea,' Lucy said as she followed. She closed the living-room door behind her.

In the kitchen, David was already filling the kettle, a lighted cigarette dangling from his lips. Lucy quickly cleared up the broken china in the hall then joined him.

David said: 'Five minutes ago I wasn't at all sure the chap was alive – and now he's dressing himself.'

Lucy busied herself with a teapot. 'Perhaps he was shamming.'

'The prospect of being undressed by you certainly brought about a rapid recovery.'

'I can't believe anyone could be that shy.'

'Your own deficiency in that area may lead you to underestimate its power in others.'

Lucy rattled cups. 'You don't usually get all bitter and twisted until after breakfast. Besides, how can an area be powerful?'

'Semantics is always your last line of defence.' David doused the butt of his cigarette in a pool of water in the sink.

Lucy poured boiling water into the teapot. 'Let's not quarrel today – we've got something more interesting to do, for a change.' She picked up the tray and walked into the living-room.

The stranger was buttoning his pyjama jacket. He turned his back to her as she walked in. She put the tray down and poured tea. When she turned back he was wearing David's robe.

'You're very kind,' he said. His gaze was direct.

He really didn't seem the shy type, Lucy thought. However, he was some years older than she – about forty, she guessed. That might account for it. He was looking less of a castaway every minute.

'Sit close to the fire,' she told him. She handed him a cup of tea.

'I'm not sure I can manage the saucer,' he said. 'My fingers aren't functioning.' He took the cup from her stiff-handed, holding it between both palms, and carried it carefully to his lips.

David came in and offered him a cigarette. He declined.

The stranger emptied the cup. 'Where am I?' he asked.

David said: 'This place is called Storm Island.'

The man showed a trace of relief. 'I thought I might have been blown back to the mainland.'

David spread his hands to the fire to warm his fingers. 'You were probably swept into the bay,' he said. 'Things usually are. That's how the beach was formed.'

Jo came in, bleary-eyed, trailing a one-armed panda

as big as himself. When he saw the stranger he ran to Lucy and hid his face.

'I've frightened your little girl,' the man smiled.

'He's a boy. I must cut his hair.' Lucy lifted Jo on to her lap.

'I'm sorry.' The stranger's eyes closed again, and he swayed in his seat.

Lucy stood up, dumping Jo on the sofa. 'We must put the poor man to bed, David.'

'Just a minute,' David said. He wheeled himself closer to the man. 'Might there be any other survivors?' he asked.

The man's face looked up. 'I was alone,' he muttered. He was very nearly all in.

'David—' Lucy began.

'One more question: Did you notify the coastguard of your route?'

'What does it matter?' Lucy said.

'It matters because, if he did, there may be men out there risking their lives looking for him, and we can let them know he's safe.'

The man said slowly: 'I . . . did . . . not.'

'That's enough,' Lucy told David. She knelt in front of the man. 'Can you make it upstairs?'

He nodded and got slowly to his feet.

Lucy looped his arm over her shoulders and began to walk him out. 'I'll put him in Jo's bed,' she said.

They took the stairs one at a time, pausing on each. When they reached the top, the little colour that the fire had restored to the man's face had drained away again. Lucy led him into the smaller bedroom. He collapsed on to the bed.

Lucy arranged the blankets over him, tucked him in, and left the room, closing the door quietly.

Relief washed over Faber in a tidal wave. For the last few minutes, the effort of self-control had been super-human. He felt limp, defeated and ill.

After the front door had opened, he had allowed himself to collapse for a while. The danger had come when the beautiful girl had started to undress him, and he had remembered the can of film taped to his chest. Dealing with that had restored his alertness for a while. He had also been afraid they might call for an ambu-lance, but that had not been mentioned: perhaps the island was too small to have a hospital. At least he was not on the mainland – there, it would have been impossible to prevent the reporting of the shipwreck. However, the trend of the husband's questions had indicated that no report would be made immediately.

Faber had no energy to speculate about perils farther in the future. He seemed to be safe for the time being, and that was as far as he could go. In the meantime he was warm and dry and alive, and the bed was soft.

He turned over, reconnoitring the room: door, window, chimney. The habit of caution survived every-thing but death itself. The walls were pink, as if the couple had hoped for a baby girl. There was a train set and a great many picture books on the floor. It was a safe, domestic place; a home. He was a wolf in a sheep fold, but a lame wolf.

He closed his eyes. Despite his exhaustion, he had to

force himself to relax, muscle by muscle. Gradually his
head emptied of thought, and he slept.

Lucy tasted the porridge, and added another pinch of
salt. They had got to like it the way Tom made it, the
Scots way, without sugar. She would never go back to
making sweet porridge, even when sugar became plen-
tiful and unrationed again. It was funny how you got
used to things when you had to: brown bread and
margarine and salt porridge.

She ladled it out and the family sat down to breakfast. Jo had lots of milk to cool his. David ate vast
quantities these days, without getting fat: it was the
outdoor life. She looked at his hands, on the table.
They were rough, and permanently brown, the hands
of a manual worker. She had noticed the stranger's
hands. His fingers were long, the skin white under the
blood and the bruising. He was unused to the abrasive
work of crewing a boat.

Lucy said: 'You won't get much done today. The
storm looks like staying.'

'Makes no difference,' David grunted. 'Sheep still
have to be cared for, whatever the weather.'

'Where will you be?'

'Tom's end. I'll go up there in the jeep.'

Jo said: 'Can I come?'

'Not today,' Lucy told him. 'It's too wet and cold.'

'But I don't like the man.'

Lucy smiled. 'Don't be silly. He won't do us any
harm. He's almost too ill to move.'

'Who is he?'

'We don't know his name. He's been shipwrecked, and we have to look after him until he's well enough to go back to the mainland. He's a very nice man.'

'Is he my uncle?'

'Just a stranger, Jo. Eat up.'

Jo looked disappointed. He had met an uncle once. In his mind uncles were people who gave out candy, which he liked, and money, which he had no use for.

David finished his breakfast and put on his mackintosh. It was a tent-shaped garment, with sleeves and a hole for his head, and it covered most of his wheelchair as well as him. He put a sou'wester on his head and tied it under his chin. He kissed Jo and said goodbye to Lucy.

A minute or two later she heard the jeep start up. She went to the window to watch David drive off into the rain. The rear wheels of the vehicle slithered about in the mud. He would have to take care.

She turned to Jo. He said: 'This is a dog.' He was making a picture on the tablecloth with porridge and milk.

Lucy slapped his hand, saying: 'What a horrid mess!' The boy's face took on a grim, sulky look, and Lucy thought how much he resembled his father. They had the same dark skin and nearly black hair, and they both had a way of withdrawing when they were cross. But Jo laughed a lot – he had inherited something from Lucy's side of the family, thank God.

Jo mistook her contemplative stare for anger, and said: 'I'm sorry.'

She washed him at the kitchen sink, then cleared away the breakfast things, thinking about the stranger upstairs. Now that the immediate crisis was past, and she knew the man was not going to die, she was consumed with curiosity about him. Who was he? Where was he from? What had he been doing in the storm? Did he have a family? Why did he have workman's clothes, a clerk's hands, and a Home Counties accent? It was rather exciting.

It occurred to her that, if she had lived anywhere else, she would not have accepted his sudden appearance so readily. He might, she supposed, be a deserter, or a criminal, or even an escaped prisoner-of-war. But one forgot, living on the island, that other human beings could be threatening instead of companionable. It was so nice to see a new face that to harbour suspicions seemed ungrateful. Maybe – unpleasant thought – she more than most people was ready to welcome an attractive man . . . She pushed the thought out of her mind.

Silly, silly. He was so tired and ill that he could not possibly threaten anyone. Even on the mainland, who could have refused to take him in, bedraggled and unconscious? When he felt better they could question him, and if his account of how he got here was less than plausible, they could radio the mainland from Tom's cottage.

When she had washed up she crept upstairs to peep at him. He slept facing the door, and when she looked in his eyes opened instantly. Again there was that initial, split-second flash of fear.

'It's all right,' Lucy whispered. 'Just making sure you're okay.'

He closed his eyes without speaking.

She went downstairs again. She dressed herself and Jo in oilskins and wellington boots, and they went out. The rain was still coming down in torrents and the wind was terrific. She glanced up at the roof: they had lost some slates. Leaning into the wind, she headed for the cliff top.

She held Jo's hand tightly – he might quite easily be blown away. Two minutes later she was wishing she had stayed indoors. Rain came in under her raincoat collar and over the tops of her boots, and she was soaked. Jo must be too, but now that they were wet they might as well stay wet for a few minutes more. Lucy wanted to go to the beach.

However, when they reached the top of the ramp she realized it was impossible. The narrow wooden walkway was slippery with rain, and in this wind she might lose her balance and fall off, to plunge sixty feet to the beach below. She had to content herself with looking.

It was quite a sight.

Vast waves, each the size of a small house, were rolling in rapidly, close on each other's heels. Crossing the beach the wave would rise even higher, its crest curling in a question mark, then throw itself against the foot of the cliff in a rage. Spray rose over the cliff top in sheets, causing Lucy to step back hurriedly and Jo to squeal with delight. Lucy could hear her son's laughter only because he had jumped into her arms, and his mouth was now close to her ear: the noise of the wind and the sea drowned more distant sounds.

There was something terribly thrilling in watching the elements spit and sway and roar in fury, in standing fractionally too close to the cliff edge, feeling threatened and safe at the same time, shivering with cold and yet perspiring in fear. It was thrilling, and there were few thrills in Lucy's life.

She was about to go back, mindful of Jo's health, when she saw the boat.

It was not a boat any more, of course; that was what was so shocking about it. All that was left were the huge timbers of the deck and the keel. They were scattered on the rocks below the cliffs like a dropped handful of matches. It had been a *big* boat, Lucy realized. One man might have piloted it alone, but not easily. And the damage the sea had wrought on man's craftsmanship was awesome. It was hard to spot two bits of wood still joined together.

How, in Heaven's name, had the stranger come out of it alive?

She shuddered when she thought of what those waves and those rocks might have done to a human body. Jo caught her sudden change of mood, and said into her ear: 'Go home, now.' She turned quickly away from the sea and hurried back along the muddy path to the cottage.

Back inside, they took off their wet coats, hats and boots, and hung them in the kitchen to dry. Lucy went upstairs and looked in on the stranger again. This time he did not open his eyes. He seemed to be sleeping very peacefully, yet she had a feeling that he had awakened and recognized her tread on the stairs, and closed his eyes again before she opened the door.

She ran a hot bath. She and the boy were soaked to the skin. She undressed Jo and put him in the tub, then – on impulse – took off her own clothes and got in with him. The heat was blissful. She closed her eyes and relaxed. This was good, too: to be in a house, feeling warm, while the storm beat impotently at the strong stone walls.

Life had turned interesting, all of a sudden. In one night there had come a storm, a shipwreck and a mystery man; this after three years of tedium. She hoped the stranger would wake up soon, so that she could find out all about him.

It was time she started cooking lunch for the men. She had some breast of lamb to make a stew. She got out of the bath and towelled herself gently. Jo was playing with his bath toy, a much-chewed rubber cat. Lucy looked at herself in the mirror, examining the stretch-marks on her belly left by pregnancy. They were fading, slowly, but they would never completely disappear. An all-over suntan would help, though. She smiled to herself, thinking: Fat chance of that! Besides, who was interested in her tummy? Nobody but herself.

Jo said: 'Can I stay in a minute more?' It was a phrase he used, 'a minute more', and it could mean anything up to half a day.

Lucy said: 'Just while I get dressed.' She hung the towel on a rail and moved toward the door.

The stranger stood in the doorway, looking at her.

They stared at each other. It was odd – Lucy thought later – that she felt not a bit afraid. It was the way he looked at her: there was no threat in his expression, no lewdness, no smirk, no lust. He was not looking at her pubis, or even her breasts, but at her face – into her eyes. She gazed back, a little shocked but not embarrassed, with just a tiny part of her mind wondering why she did not squeal, cover herself with her hands, and slam the door on him.

Something did come into his eyes, at last – perhaps she was imagining it, but she saw admiration, and a faint twinkle of honest humour, and a trace of sadness – and then the spell was broken, and he turned away and went back into his bedroom, closing the door. A moment later Lucy heard the springs creak as his weight settled on the bed.

And for no good reason at all she felt dreadfully guilty.

CHAPTER TWENTY

BY THIS time Percival Godliman had pulled out all the stops.

Every policeman in the UK had a copy of the photograph of Faber, and about half of them were engaged full-time in the search. In the cities they were checking hotels and guest-houses, railway stations and bus terminals, cafés and shopping centres; and the bridges, arches, and bombed lots where the derelict hang out. In the country they were looking in barns and silos, empty cottages and ruined castles, thickets and clearings and cornfields. They were showing the photograph to ticket clerks, petrol station staff, ferry hands and toll collectors. All the passenger ports and airfields were covered, with the picture pinned behind a board at every Passport Control desk.

The police thought they were looking for a straight-forward murderer.

The cop on the street knew that the man in the picture had killed two people with a knife in London. Senior officers knew a bit more: that one of the murders had been a sexual assault, another apparently motive-less, and a third – which their men were not to know of – was an unexplained but bloody attack on a soldier on the Euston-to-Liverpool train. Only chief constables, and a few officers at Scotland Yard, realized that the soldier had been on temporary attachment to MI5 and that all the murders were connected with Security.

The newspapers, too, thought it was just an ordinary murder hunt. The day after Godliman had released details, most of the papers had carried the story in their later editions – the first editions, bound for Scotland, Ulster and North Wales, had missed it, so they had carried a shortened version a day later. The Stockwell victim had been identified as a labourer, and given a false name and a vague London background. Godliman's press release had connected that murder with the death of Mrs Una Garden in 1940, but had been vague about the nature of the link. The murder weapon was said to be a stiletto.

The two Liverpool newspapers heard very quickly of the body on the train, and both wondered whether the London knife murderer was responsible. Both made enquiries with the Liverpool police. The editors of both papers received phone calls from the Chief Constable. Neither paper carried the story.

A total of one hundred and fifty-seven tall dark men were arrested on suspicion of being Faber. All but twenty-nine of them were able to prove that they could not possibly have committed the murders. Interviewers from MI5 talked to the twenty-nine. Twenty-seven called in parents, relatives and neighbours who affirmed that they had been born in Britain and had been living there during the twenties, when Faber had been in Germany.

The last two were brought to London and interviewed again, this time by Godliman. Both were bachelors, living alone, with no surviving relatives, leading a transient existence.

The first was a well-dressed, confident man who claimed implausibly that his way of life was to travel the country taking odd jobs as a manual labourer. Godliman explained that he was looking for a German spy, and that he – unlike the police – had the power to incarcerate anyone for the duration of the war, and no questions asked. Furthermore, he went on, he was not in the least interested in capturing ordinary criminals, and any information given him here at the War Office was strictly confidential, and would go no further.

The prisoner promptly confessed to being a confidence trickster and gave the addresses of nineteen elderly ladies whom he had cheated out of their old jewellery during the past three weeks. Godliman turned him over to the police.

He felt no obligation to be honest with a professional liar.

The last suspect also cracked under Godliman's treatment. His secret was that he was not a bachelor at all, not by a long way. He had a wife in Brighton. And in Solihull, Birmingham. And in Colchester, Newbury and Exeter. All five were able to produce marriage certificates later that day. The bigamist went to gaol to await trial.

Godliman slept in his office while the hunt went on.

*

Bristol, Temple Meads, railway station:

'Good morning, Miss. Would you look at this, please?'

'Hey, girls – the bobby's going to show us his snaps!'

'Now, don't muck about, just tell me if you've seen him.'

'Ooh, ain't he handsome! I wish I had!'

'You wouldn't if you knew what he'd done. Would you all take a look, please?'

'Never seen him.'

'Me neither.'

'Not me.'

'No.'

'When you catch him, ask him if he wants to meet a nice young Bristol girl.'

'You girls – I don't know ... Just because they give you a pair of trousers and a porter's job, you think you're supposed to act like men ...'

The Woolwich Ferry:

'Filthy day, Constable.'

'Morning, Captain. I expect it's worse on the high seas.'

'Can I help you? Or are you just crossing the river?'

'I want you to look at a face, Captain.'

'Let me put my specs on. Oh, don't worry, I can see to guide the ship. It's close things I need the glasses for, Now then ...'

'Ring any bells?'

'Sorry, Constable. Means nothing to me.'

'Well, let me know if you see him.'

'Certainly.'

'Bon voyage.'

Number thirty-five Leak Street, London E1:

'Sergeant Riley – what a nice surprise!'

'Never mind the lip, Mabel. Who've you got here?'

'All respectable guests, Sergeant; you know me.'

'I know you, all right. That's why I'm here. Would any of your nice respectable guests happen to be on the trot?'

'Since when have you been recruiting for the Army?'

'I'm not, Mabel, I'm looking for a villain, and if he's here, he's probably told you he's on the trot.'

'Look, Jack – if I tell you there's nobody here I don't know, will you go away and stop pestering me?'

'Why should I trust you?'

'Because of 1936.'

'You were better looking then, Mabel.'

'So were you, Jack.'

'You win ... Take a butcher's at this. If chummy comes in here, send word, okay?'

'Promise.'

'Don't waste any time about it, either.'

'All right!'

'Mabel ... he knifed a woman your age. I'm just marking your cards.'

'I know. Thanks.'

'Ta-ta.'
'Take care, Jacko.'

Bill's Café, on the A30 near Bagshot:
    'Tea, please, Bill. Two sugars.'
    'Good morning, Constable Pearson. Filthy day.'
    'What's on that plate, Bill – pebbles from Portsmouth?'
    'Buttered buns, as well you know.'
    'Oh! I'll have two, then. Thanks . . . Now then, lads! Anyone who wants his lorry checked from top to bottom can leave right away . . . That's better. Take a look at this picture, please.'
    'What are you after him for, Constable – cycling without lights?'
    'Never mind the jokes, Harry – pass the picture round. Anybody given a lift to that bloke?'
    'Not me.'
    'No.'
    'Sorry, Constable.'
    'Never clapped eyes on him.'
    'Thank you, lads. If you see him, report it. Cheerio.'
    'Constable?'
    'Yes, Bill?'
    'You haven't paid for the buns.'
    'I'm confiscating them as evidence. Cheerio.'

Smethwick's Garage, Carlisle:
    'Morning, Missus. When you've got a minute . . .'
    'Be right with you, officer. Just let me attend to this

gentleman . . . Twelve and sixpence, please, sir. Thank you. Goodbye . . .'

'How's business?'

'Terrible, as usual. What can I do for you?'

'Can we go in the office for a minute?'

'Aye, come on . . . Now, then.'

'Take a look at this picture and tell me whether you've served that man with petrol recently.'

'Well, it shouldn't be too difficult. It's not as if we get hordes of customers passing through . . . ooh! D'you know, I think I have served him!'

'When?'

'Day before yesterday, in the morning.'

'How sure are you?'

'Well . . . he was older than the picture, but I'm pretty sure.'

'What was he driving?'

'A grey car. I'm no good on makes, this is my husband's business really, but he's in the Navy now.'

'Well, what did it look like? Sports car? Limousine?'

'It was the old sort, with a canvas roof that comes up. A two-seater. Sporty. It had a spare petrol tank bolted to the running-board, and I filled that, too.'

'Do you remember what he was wearing?'

'Not really. Working clothes, I think.'

'A tall man?'

'Yes, taller than you.'

'By the heck, I think it's him! Have you got a telephone . . .?'

*

William Duncan was twenty-five years old, five-feet-ten, weighed a trim 150 pounds, and was in first-class health. His open-air life and total lack of interest in tobacco, drink, late nights and loose living kept him that way. Yet he was not in the Armed Services.

He had seemed to be a normal child, if a little backward, until the age of eight, when his mind simply stopped developing. There had been no trauma that anyone knew about, no physical damage to account for sudden breakdown. Indeed, it was some years before anyone noticed that there was anything wrong, for at the age of ten he was no more than a little backward, and at twelve he was just dim-witted; but by fifteen he was obviously simple, and by eighteen he was known as Daft Willie.

His parents both belonged to an obscure Fundamentalist religious group whose members were not allowed to marry outside the Church (which may or may not have had something to do with Willie's daftness). They prayed for him, of course; but they also took him to a specialist in Stirling. The doctor, an elderly man, did several tests and then told them, over the tops of his gold-rimmed half-glasses, that the boy had a mental age of eight and his mind would grow no older, ever. They continued to pray for him, but they suspected that the Lord had sent this to try them, so they made sure that Willie was Saved and looked forward to the day when they would meet him again in the Glory and he would be healed. Meanwhile, he needed a job.

An eight-year-old can herd cows, but herding cows is nevertheless a job, so Daft Willie became a cowherd.

271

And it was while herding cows that he saw the car for the first time.

He assumed there were lovers in it.

Willie knew about lovers. That is to say, he knew that lovers existed, and that they did unmentionable things to one another in dark places like copses and cinemas and cars; and that one did not speak of them. So he hurried the cows quickly past the bush beside which was parked the 1924 Morris Cowley Bullnose two-seater (he knew about cars, too, like any eight-year-old) and tried very hard not to look inside it in case he should behold sin.

He took his little herd into the cowshed for milking, went by a roundabout route to his home, ate supper, read a chapter from Leviticus to his father – aloud, painstakingly – then went to bed to dream about lovers.

The car was still there on the evening of the next day.

For all his innocence, Willie knew that lovers did not do whatever it was that they did to one another for twenty-four hours at a stretch.

This time he went right up to the car and looked inside. It was empty. The ground beneath the engine was black and sticky with oil. Willie devised a new explanation: the car had broken down and had been abandoned by its driver. It did not occur to him to wonder why it had been semi-concealed in a bush.

When he arrived at the cowshed he told the farmer what he had seen. 'There's a broken-down car on the path up by the main road.'

The farmer was a big man with heavy sand-coloured eyebrows which drew together when he was thinking. 'Was there nobody about?'

'No – and it was there yesterday.'

'Why did you not tell me yesterday, then?'

Willie blushed. 'I thought it was maybe . . . lovers.'

'Och!' 'The farmer realized that Willie was not being coy, but was genuinely embarrassed. He patted the boy's shoulder. 'Well, away home and leave it to me to deal with.'

After the milking the farmer went to look for himself. It did occur to him to wonder why the car was semi-concealed. He had heard about the London stiletto murderer; and while he did not jump to the conclusion that the car had been abandoned by the killer, all the same he thought there might be a connection between the car and some crime or other. So after supper he sent his eldest son into the village on horseback to telephone the police in Stirling.

The police arrived before his son got back from the phone. There were at least a dozen of them, every one apparently a non-stop tea drinker. The farmer and his wife were up half the night looking after them.

Daft Willie was summoned to tell his story again, repeating that he had first seen the car the previous evening, blushing again when he explained that he had assumed it contained lovers.

All in all, it was the most exciting night of the war.

*

That evening Percival Godliman, facing his fourth consecutive night in the office, went home to bathe, change, and pack a suitcase.

He had a service flat in a block in Chelsea. It was small, though plenty big enough for a single man, and it was clean and tidy except for the study, which the cleaner was not allowed to enter and in consequence was littered with books and papers. The furniture was all pre-war, of course, but it was rather well-chosen, and the flat had a comfortable air. There were leather club chairs and a gramophone in the living-room, and the kitchen was full of hardly used labour-saving devices.

While his bath was filling he smoked a cigarette – he had taken to them lately, a pipe was so much fuss – and looked at his most valuable possession, a grimly fantastic medieval scene which was probably by Hieronymous Bosch. It was a family heirloom and Godliman had never sold it, even when he needed the money, because he liked it.

In the bath he thought about Barbara Dickens and her son, Peter. He had not told anyone about her, not even Bloggs, although he had been about to mention her during their conversation about remarrying, but Colonel Terry had interrupted. She was a widow: her husband had been killed in action at the very beginning of the war. Godliman did not know how old she was, but she looked about forty, which was young for the mother of a twenty-two-year-old boy. She worked on translations of intercepted enemy signals, and she was bright, amusing, and very attractive. She was also rich. Godliman had taken her to dinner, three times, before the present crisis blew up. He thought she was in love with him.

She had contrived a meeting between Godliman and her son Peter, who was a captain. Godliman liked the boy. But he knew something which neither Barbara nor her son was aware of: Peter was going to Normandy.

Which was all the more reason to catch Die Nadel.

He got out of the bath and took a long, careful shave, thinking: Am I in love with her? He was not sure what love ought to feel like in middle age. Not, surely, the burning passion of youth. Affection, admiration, tenderness, and a trace of uncertain lust? If they amounted to love, he loved her.

And he needed to share his life, now. For years he had wanted only solitude and his research. Now the camaraderie of Military Intelligence was sucking him in: the parties, the all-night sessions when something big broke, the spirit of dedicated amateurism, the frantic pleasure-seeking of people to whom death is always close and never predictable – all these had infected him. It would vanish after the war, he knew; but other things would remain: the need to talk to someone close about his disappointment and his triumphs, the need to touch someone else at night, the need to say: 'There! Look at that! Isn't it fine?'

War was gruelling and oppressive and frustrating and uncomfortable, but one had friends. If peace brought back loneliness, Godliman thought he would be unhappy.

Right now the feel of clean underwear and a crisply ironed shirt was the height of luxury. He put more fresh clothes in a case, then sat down to enjoy a glass of whisky before returning to the office. The military chauffeur in the commandeered Daimler outside could wait a little longer.

He was filling a pipe when the phone rang. He put down the pipe and lit a cigarette instead.

His phone was connected to the War Office switchboard. The telephonist told him that a Chief Superintendent Dalkeith was calling from Stirling.

He waited for the click of the connection, and said: 'Godliman speaking.'

'We've found your Morris Cowley,' Dalkeith said without preamble.

'Where?'

'On the A80 just south of Stirling.'

'Empty?'

'Aye, broken down. It's been there at least twenty-four hours. It was driven a few yards off the main road and hidden in a bush. A half-witted farm boy found it.'

'Is there a bus stop or railway station within walking distance of the spot?'

'No.'

Godliman grunted. 'So it's likely our man had to walk or hitch-hike after leaving the car.'

'Aye.'

'In that case, will you ask around—'

'We're already trying to find out whether anyone local saw him or gave him a lift.'

'Good. Let me know . . . Meanwhile, I'll pass the news to the Yard. Thank you, Dalkeith.'

'We'll keep in touch. Goodbye, sir.'

Godliman put the phone on the hook and went into his study. He sat down with an atlas open to the road map of northern Britain. London, Liverpool, Carlisle, Stirling . . . Faber was heading for north-east Scotland.

Godliman wondered whether he should reconsider the theory that Faber was trying to get out. The best way out was west, via neutral Eire. Scotland's east coast, however, was the scene of military activity of various kinds. Was it possible that Faber had the nerve to continue his reconnaissance, knowing that MI5 was on his tail? It was possible, Godliman decided – he knew Faber had a lot of guts – but nevertheless unlikely. Nothing the man might discover in Scotland could be as important as the information he already had.

Therefore Faber was getting out via the east coast. Godliman ran over the methods of escape which were open to the spy: a light plane, landing on a lonely moor; a one-man voyage across the North Sea in a stolen vessel; a rendezvous with a U-boat off the coast; a passage in a merchant ship via a neutral country to the Baltic, disembarking in Sweden and crossing the border to occupied Norway . . . there were many ways.

The Yard must be told of the latest development. They would ask all Scots police forces to try to find someone who had picked up a hitch-hiker outside Stirling. Godliman returned to the living-room to phone, but the instrument rang before he got there. He picked it up.

'Godliman speaking.'

'A Mr Richard Porter is calling from Aberdeen.'

'Oh!' Godliman had been expecting Bloggs to check in from Carlisle. 'Put him on, please. Hello? Godliman speaking.'

'Ah, Richard Porter here. I'm on the local Watch Committee up here.'

'Yes, what can I do for you?'

'Well, actually, old boy, it's terribly embarrassing.'

Godliman controlled his impatience. 'Go on.'

'This chappie you're looking for – knife murders and so on. Well, I'm pretty sure I gave the bally fellow a lift in my own car.'

Godliman gripped the receiver more tightly. 'When?'

'Night before last. My car broke down on the A80 just outside Stirling. Middle of the bally night. Along comes this chappie, on foot, and mends it, just like that. So naturally—'

'Where did you drop him?'

'Right here in Aberdeen. Said he was going on to Banff. Thing is, I slept most of yesterday, so it wasn't until this afternoon—'

'Don't reproach yourself, Mr Porter. Thank you for calling.'

'Well, goodbye.'

Godliman jiggled the receiver and the War Office telephonist came back on the line.

Godliman said: 'Get Mr Bloggs for me, would you? He's in Carlisle.'

'He's holding on for you right now, sir.'

'Good!'

'Hello, Percy. What news?'

'We're on his trail again, Fred. He abandoned the Morris just outside Stirling and hitched a lift to Aberdeen.'

'Aberdeen!'

'He must be trying to get out through the east door.'

'When did he reach Aberdeen?'

'Probably early yesterday morning.'

'In that case he won't have had time to get out, unless he was very quick indeed. They're having the worst storm in living memory up here. It started last night and it's still going on. No ships are going out and it's certainly too rough to land a plane.'

'Good! Get up there as fast as you can. I'll start the local police moving in the meantime. Call me when you reach Aberdeen.'

'I'm on my way.'

'Fred?'

'Yes?'

'We'll catch the bastard yet.'

Fred was still laughing as Godliman hung up.

CHAPTER TWENTY-ONE

WHEN FABER woke up it was almost dark. Through the bedroom window he could see the last streaks of grey being inked out of the sky by the encroaching night. The storm had not eased: rain drummed on the roof and overflowed from a gutter, and the wind howled and gusted tirelessly.

He switched on the little lamp beside the bed. The effort tired him, and he slumped back on to the pillow. It frightened him, to be this weak. Those who believe that Might is Right must always be mighty, and Faber was sufficiently self-aware to know the implications of his own ethics. Fear was never far from the surface of his emotions: perhaps that was why he had survived so long. He was chronically incapable of feeling safe. He understood, in that vague way in which we understand the most fundamental things about ourselves, that his insecurity was the reason he chose the profession of spy: it was the only walk of life which permitted him instantly to kill anyone who posed him the slightest threat. The fear of being weak was part of the syndrome which included his obsessive independence, his insecurity, and his contempt for his military superiors.

He lay on the child's bed in the pink-walled bedroom

and inventoried his body. He seemed to be bruised just about everywhere, but apparently nothing was broken. He did not feel feverish: his constitution had withstood bronchial infection despite the night on the boat. There was just the weakness. He suspected it was more than exhaustion. He remembered a moment, as he had reached the top of the ramp, when he had thought he was going to die; and he wondered whether he had inflicted upon himself some permanent damage with that last mindbending uphill dash.

He checked his possessions, too. The can of photographic negatives was still taped to his chest, the stiletto was strapped to his left arm, and his papers and money were in the jacket pocket of his borrowed pyjamas.

He pushed the blankets aside and swung himself into a sitting position with his feet on the floor. A moment of dizziness came and went. He stood up. It was important not to permit oneself the psychological attitudes of the invalid. He put on the dressing-gown and went into the bathroom.

When he returned his own clothes were at the foot of the bed, clean and pressed: underwear, overalls, and shirt. Suddenly he remembered getting up some time during the morning and seeing the woman naked in the bathroom: it had been an odd scene, and he was not sure what it meant. She was very beautiful, he recalled.

He dressed slowly. He would have liked a shave, but he decided to ask his host's permission before borrowing the blade on the bathroom shelf: some men were as possessive of their razors as they were of their wives.

However, he did take the liberty of using the child's plastic comb he found in the top drawer of the chest.

He looked into the mirror without pride. He had no conceit. He knew that some women found him attractive, and others did not; and he assumed this was so for most men. Of course, he had had more women than most men, but he attributed this to his appetite, not to his looks. His reflection told him he was presentable, and that was all he needed to know.

Satisfied, he left the bedroom and went slowly down the stairs. Again he felt a wave of weakness; again he willed himself to overcome it, gripping the banister rail and placing one foot deliberately before the other until he reached the ground floor.

He paused outside the living-room door and, hearing no noise, went on to the kitchen. He knocked and went in. The young couple were at the table, finishing supper.

The woman stood up when he entered. 'You got up!' she said. 'Are you sure you should?'

Faber permitted himself to be led to a chair. 'Thank you,' he said. 'You really mustn't encourage me to pretend to be ill.'

'I don't think you realize what a terrible experience you've been through,' she said. 'Do you feel like food?'

'I'm imposing on you—'

'Not at all. Don't be silly. I kept some soup hot for you.'

Faber said: 'You're so kind, and I don't even know your names.'

'David and Lucy Rose.' She ladled soup into a bowl

and placed it on the table in front of him. 'Cut some bread, David, would you?'

'I'm Henry Baker.' Faber did not know why he had said that: he had no papers in that name. Henry Faber was the man the police were hunting, so he should have used his James Baker identity; but somehow he wanted this woman to call him Henry, the nearest English equivalent of his real name, Henrik. Perhaps it did not matter – he could always say his name was James but he had always been called Henry.

He took a sip of the soup, and suddenly he was ravenously hungry. He ate it all quickly, then the bread. When he had finished, Lucy laughed. She looked lovely when she laughed: her mouth opened wide, showing lots of even white teeth, and her eyes crinkled merrily at the corners.

'More?' she offered.

'Thank you very much.'

'I can see it doing you good. The colour is coming back to your cheeks.'

Faber realized he felt physically better. He ate his second helping more slowly, out of courtesy rather than repletion.

David said: 'How did you happen to be out in this storm?' It was the first time he had spoken.

Lucy said: 'Don't badger him, David.'

'It's all right,' Faber said. 'I was foolish, that's all. This is the first fishing holiday I've been able to have since before the war, and I just refused to let the weather spoil it. Are you a fisherman?'

David shook his head. 'Sheep farmer.'

'Do you have many employees?'

'Just one, old Tom.'

'I suppose there are other sheep farms on the island.'

'No. We live at this end, Tom lives at the other end, and in between there's nothing but sheep.'

Faber nodded slowly. This was good – very good. A woman, a cripple, a child and an old man could not constitute an obstacle. And he was feeling much stronger already.

Faber said: 'How do you contact the mainland?'

'There's a boat once a fortnight. It's due this Monday, but it won't come if the storm keeps up. There's a radio transmitter in Tom's cottage, but we can only use that in emergencies. If I thought people might be searching for you, or if you needed urgent medical help, I should use it. But as things are I don't feel it's necessary. There's little point: nobody can come to fetch you off the island until the storm clears, and when that happens the boat will come anyway.'

'Of course.' Faber concealed his delight. The problem of how to contact the U-boat on Monday had been nagging at the back of his mind. He had seen an ordinary wireless set in the Roses' living-room, and he would, in a pinch, have been able to rig up a transmitter from that. But the fact that Tom had a proper radio made everything so much easier.

Faber said: 'What does Tom need a transmitter for?'

'He's a member of the Royal Observer Corps. Aberdeen was bombed in July 1940. There was no air-raid warning. Consequently there were fifty casualties. That was when they recruited Tom. It's a good thing his hearing is better than his eyesight.'

'I suppose the bombers come from Norway.'

'I suppose so.'

Lucy stood up. 'Let's go into the other room.'

The two men followed her. Faber felt no weakness, no dizziness. He held the living-room door for David, who wheeled himself close to the fire. Lucy offered Faber brandy. He declined. She poured for her husband and herself.

Faber sat back and studied the couple. Lucy's looks were really quite striking: she had an oval face, wide-set eyes of an unusual, cat-like amber colour, and a lot of rich, dark-red hair. Under the mannish fisherman's sweater and baggy trousers there was the suggestion of a very fine, fullish figure. If she were to curl her hair and put on silk stockings and a cocktail dress she might be very glamorous. David was also good-looking – almost pretty, except for the shadow of a very dark beard. His hair was nearly black and his skin looked Mediterranean. He would have been tall, if he had had legs in proportion to his arms. Faber suspected that those arms might be powerful, muscled from years of pushing the wheels of the chair to get from A to B.

Yes, they were an attractive couple – but there was something badly wrong between them. Faber was no expert on marriage, but his training in interrogation techniques had taught him to read the silent language of the body – to know, from small gestures, when someone was frightened, confident, hiding something, or lying. Lucy and David rarely looked at one another, and never touched. They spoke to him more than to each other. They circled one another, like turkeys trying to keep in front of them a few square feet of vacant portable territory. The tension between them was enormous. They were like Churchill and Stalin, obliged temporarily to fight side by side, fiercely suppressing a deeper enmity. Faber wondered what awful trauma lay at the back of their hatred.

This cosy little house must be an emotional pressure-cooker, despite its rugs and its bright paintwork, its floral armchairs and blazing fires and framed water-colours. To live alone, with only an old man and a child for company, with this thing between them . . . it reminded him of a play he had seen in London, by an American called Tennessee something.

Abruptly, David swallowed his drink and said: 'I must turn in. My back's playing up.'

Faber got to his feet and said: 'I'm sorry – I've been keeping you up.'

David waved him down. 'Not at all. You've been asleep all day – you won't want to go back to bed right away. Besides, Lucy would like to chat, I'm sure. It's just that I mistreat my back – backs were designed to share the load with the legs, you know.'

Lucy said: 'You'd better take two pills tonight, then.' She took a bottle from the top shelf of the bookcase, shook out two tablets, and gave them to her husband.

He swallowed them dry. 'I'll say goodnight.' He wheeled himself out.

'Goodnight, David.'

'Goodnight, Mr Rose.'

After a moment Faber heard David dragging himself up the stairs, and wondered just how he did it.

Lucy spoke, as if to cover the sound of David. 'Where do you live, Mr Baker?'

'Please call me Henry. I live in London.'

'I haven't been to London for years. There's probably not much of it left.'

'It's changed, but not as much as you might think. When were you last there?'

'Nineteen-forty.' She poured herself another brandy. 'Since we came here, I've only been off the island once, and that was to have the baby. One can't travel much these days, can one?'

'What made you come here?'

'Um.' She sat down, sipped her drink, and looked into the fire.

'Perhaps I shouldn't—'

'It's all right. We had an accident the day we got married. That's how David lost his legs. He'd been training as a fighter pilot . . . we both wanted to run away, I think. I believe it was a mistake, but it seemed like a good idea at the time.'

'It has allowed his resentment to incubate.'

She shot him a sharp look. 'You're a perceptive man.'

'It's obvious.' He spoke very quietly. 'You don't deserve such unhappiness.'

She blinked several times. 'You see too much.'

'It's not difficult. Why do you continue, if it's not working?'

'I don't know what to tell you. Do you want clichés? The vows of marriage, the child, the war . . . If there's another answer, I can't find words for it.'

'Guilt,' Faber said. 'But you're thinking of leaving him, aren't you?'

She stared at him, slowly shaking her head with incredulity. 'How do you know so much?'

'You've lost the art of dissembling in four years on this island. Besides, these things are so much simpler from the outside.'

'Have you ever been married?'

'No. That's what I mean.'

'Why not? I think you ought to be.'

It was Faber's turn to look pensively into the fire. Why not, indeed? His stock answer – to himself – was his profession. But he could not tell her that, and anyway it was too glib. He said suddenly: 'I don't trust myself to love anyone that much.' The words had come out without forethought, and he wondered whether they were true. A moment later he wondered how Lucy had got past his guard, when he had thought he was disarming her.

Neither of them spoke for a while. The fire was dying. A few stray raindrops found their way down the chimney and hissed in the cooling coals. The storm showed no sign of letting up. Faber found himself thinking of the last woman he had had. What was her name? Gertrude. It was seven years ago, but he could picture her now, in the flickering fire: a round German face, fair hair, green eyes, beautiful breasts, much-too-wide hips, fat legs, bad feet; the conversational style of an express train, a wild, inexhaustible enthusiasm for sex . . . She had flattered him, admiring his mind (she said) and adoring his body (she had no need to tell him). She wrote lyrics for popular songs, and read them to him in a poor basement flat in Berlin: it was not a lucrative profession. He visualized her in that untidy bedroom, lying naked, urging him to do more bizarre and erotic things with her: to hurt her, to touch himself, to lie completely still while she made love to him . . . He shook his head slightly to brush away the memories. He had not thought like that in all the years he had been celibate. Such visions were disturbing. He looked at Lucy.

'You were far away,' she said with a smile.

'Memories,' he said. 'This talk of love . . .'

'I shouldn't burden you.'

'You're not.'

'Good memories?'

'Very good. And yours? You were thinking, too.'

She smiled again. 'I was in the future, not the past.'

'What do you see there?'

She seemed about to answer, then changed her mind. It happened twice. There were signs of tension about her eyes.

'I see you finding another man,' Faber said. As he spoke he was thinking: Why am I doing this? 'He is a weaker man than David, and less handsome; but it is for his weakness that you love him. He is clever, but not rich; compassionate without being sentimental; tender, caring, loving. He—'

The brandy glass in her hand shattered under the

pressure of her grip. The fragments fell into her lap and on to the carpet, and she ignored them. Faber crossed to her chair and knelt in front of her. Her thumb was bleeding. He took her hand.

'You've hurt yourself.'

She looked at him. She was crying.

'I'm sorry,' he said.

The cut was superficial. She took a handkerchief from her trousers pocket and staunched the blood. Faber released her hand and began to pick up the pieces of broken glass, wishing he had kissed her when he had the chance. He put the shards on the chimney-breast.

'I didn't mean to upset you,' he said.

She took away the handkerchief and looked at her thumb. It was still bleeding.

'A little bandage,' he suggested.

'In the kitchen.'

He found a roll of bandage, a pair of scissors, and a safety pin. He filled a small bowl with hot water and returned to the living-room.

In his absence she had somehow obliterated the evidence of tears on her face. She sat passively, limp, while he bathed her thumb in the hot water, dried it, and fixed a small strip of bandage over the cut. She looked all the time at his face, not at his hands; but her expression was unreadable.

He finished the job and stood back abruptly. This was silly: he had taken the thing too far. It was time to disengage. He said: 'I think I'd better go to bed.'

She nodded.

'I'm sorry—'

'Stop apologizing,' she told him. 'It doesn't suit you.'

Her tone was harsh. He guessed that she, too, felt the thing had got out of hand.

'Are you staying up?' he asked.

She shook her head.

'Well . . .' He walked to the door and held it for her.

She avoided his eyes as she passed him. He followed her through the hall and up the stairs. As he watched her climb, he could not help imagining her in other clothes, her hips swaying gently underneath some silky material, long legs clad in stockings instead of worsted grey trousers, high-heeled dress shoes instead of worn felt slippers.

At the top of the stairs, on the tiny landing, she turned and whispered: 'Goodnight.'

He said: 'Goodnight, Lucy.'

She looked at him for a moment. He reached for her hand, but she foresaw his intention and turned quickly away, entering her bedroom and closing the door without a backward look, leaving him standing there with his hand out and his mouth open, wondering what was in her mind and – more to the point – what was in his.

CHAPTER TWENTY-TWO

BLOGGS DROVE dangerously fast through the night in a commandeered Sunbeam Talbot with a souped-up engine. The hilly, winding Scottish roads were slick with rain and, in a few low places, two or three inches deep in water. The rain drove across the windscreen in sheets. On the more exposed hilltops the gale-force winds threatened to blow the car off the road and into the soggy turf alongside. For mile after mile, Bloggs sat forward in the seat, peering through the small area of glass that was cleared by the wiper, straining his eyes to make out the shape of the road in front as the headlights battled with the obscuring rain. Just north of Edinburgh he ran over three rabbits, feeling the sickening bump as the tyres squashed their small furry bodies. He did not slow the car, but for a while afterwards he wondered whether rabbits normally came out at night.

The strain gave him a headache, and his sitting position made his back hurt. He also felt hungry. He opened the window for a cold breeze to keep him awake, but so much water came in that he was forced to close it again immediately. He thought about Die Nadel, or Faber or whatever he was calling himself now:

a smiling young man in running-shorts holding a trophy. Well, Faber was winning this race. He was forty-eight hours ahead and he had the advantage that only he knew the route that had to be followed. Bloggs would have enjoyed a contest with that man, if the stakes had not been so high, so bloody high.

He wondered what he would do if he ever came face to face with the man. I'd shoot the bugger out of hand, he thought, before he killed me. Faber was a pro, and you couldn't mess with that type. Most spies were amateurs: frustrated revolutionaries of the left or right, people who wanted the imaginary glamour of espionage, greedy men or lovesick women, or blackmail victims. The few professionals were very dangerous indeed, because they knew that the professionals they were up against were not merciful men.

Dawn was still an hour or two away when Bloggs drove into Aberdeen. Never in his life had he been so grateful for street lights, dimmed and masked though they were. He had no idea where the police station was, and there was no one on the streets to give him directions, so he drove around the town until he saw the familiar blue lamp (also dimmed).

He parked the car and dashed through the rain into the building. He was expected. Godliman had been on the phone, and Godliman was now very senior indeed. Bloggs was shown into the office of Alan Kincaid, a Detective-Chief-Inspector in his middle fifties. There were three other officers in the room: Bloggs shook their hands and instantly forgot their names.

Kincaid said: 'You made bloody good time from Carlisle.'

'Nearly killed myself doing it,' Bloggs replied. He sat down. 'If you can rustle up a sandwich . . .'

'Of course.' Kincaid leaned his head out of the door and shouted something. 'It'll be here in two shakes,' he told Bloggs.

The office had off-white walls, a plank floor, and plain hard furniture: a desk, a few chairs and a filing cabinet. It was totally unrelieved: no pictures, no ornaments, no personal touches of any kind. There was a tray of dirty cups on the floor, and the air was thick with smoke. It smelled like somewhere men had been working all night.

Kincaid had a small moustache, thin grey hair, and spectacles. A big, intelligent-looking man in shirtsleeves and braces, he was the kind of policeman that – Bloggs thought – made up the backbone of the British police force. He spoke with a local accent, a sign that, like Bloggs, he had come up through the ranks – though from his age it was clear that his rise had been slower than Bloggs's.

Bloggs said: 'How much do you know of what this is all about?'

'Not much,' Kincaid said. 'But your governor, Godliman, did say that the London murders are the least of this man's crimes. We also know which department you're with, so we can put two and two together and conclude that Faber is a very dangerous spy.'

'That's about it,' Bloggs said.

Kincaid nodded.

'What have you done so far?' Bloggs asked.

Kincaid put his feet on his desk. 'He arrived here two days ago, yes?'

'Yes.'

'That was when we started looking for him. We had the pictures – I assume every force in the country got them.'

'Yes.'

'We checked the hotels and lodging houses, the station and the bus depot. We did it quite thoroughly, although at the time we didn't know he had come here. Needless to say, we had no results. We're checking again, of course; but my opinion is that he probably left Aberdeen immediately.'

A woman police constable came in with a cup of tea and a very thick cheese sandwich. Bloggs thanked her and set about the sandwich greedily.

Kincaid went on: 'We had a man at the railway station before the first train left in the morning. Ditto for the bus depot. So, if he left the town, either he stole a car or he hitched a ride. We've had no stolen cars reported.'

'Damn,' Bloggs said through a mouthful of whole-meal bread. He swallowed. 'That makes it about as difficult as it can be to trace him.'

'No doubt that's why he chose to hitch-hike.'

'He might have gone by sea.'

'Of the boats that left the harbour that day, none was big enough to stow away on. Since then, of course, nothing's gone out because of the storm.'

'Stolen boats?'

'None reported.'

Bloggs shrugged. 'If there's no prospect of going out, the owners might not come to the harbour – in which case the theft of a boat might go unnoticed until the storm ends.'

One of the officers in the room said: 'We missed that one, Chief.'

'We did,' Kincaid said.

Bloggs said: 'Perhaps the harbourmaster could look around all the regular moorings—'

'I'm with you,' Kincaid said. He was already dialling. After a moment he spoke into the phone. 'Captain Douglas? Kincaid. Aye, I know civilized people sleep at this hour. You haven't heard the worst – I want you to take a walk in the rain. Aye, you heard me right . . .'

The other policemen started to laugh.

Kincaid put his hand over the mouthpiece and said: 'You know what they say about seamen's language? It's true.' He spoke into the phone again. 'Go round all the regular moorings and make a note of any vessels not in their usual spot. Ignoring those you know to be legitimately out of port, give me the names and addresses – and phone numbers if you have them – of the owners. Aye. Aye, I know . . . I'll make it a double. All right, a bottle. And a good morning to you too, old friend.' He hung up.

Bloggs smiled. 'Salty?'

'If I did what he suggested I do with my truncheon, I'd never be able to sit down again.' Kincaid became serious. 'It'll take him about half an hour, then we'll need a couple of hours to check all the addresses.

It's worth doing, although I still think he hitched a ride.'

'So do I,' Bloggs said.

The door opened, and a middle-aged man in civilian clothes walked in. Kincaid and his officers stood up, and Bloggs followed suit.

Kincaid said: 'Good morning, sir. This is Mr Bloggs. Mr Bloggs, Richard Porter.'

They shook hands. Porter had a red face and a carefully cultivated moustache. He wore a double-breasted, camel-coloured overcoat. He said: 'How do you do. I'm the blighter that gave your chappie a lift to Aberdeen. Most embarrassing.' He had no local accent.

Bloggs said: 'How do you do.' On first acquaintance Porter seemed to be exactly the kind of silly ass who would give a spy a lift half across the country. However, Bloggs knew the type: the air of empty-headed heartiness might well mask a shrewd mind. He asked: 'What made you realize that the man you'd picked up was the . . . the stiletto murderer?'

'I heard about the abandoned Morris. I picked him up at that very spot.'

'You've seen the picture?'

'Yes. Of course, I didn't get a good look at the chappie, because it was dark for most of the journey. But I saw enough of him, in the light of the torch when we were under the bonnet, and afterwards when we entered Aberdeen – it was dawn by then. If I'd only seen the picture, I'd say it *could* have been him. Given the spot at which I picked him up, so near to where the Morris was found, I say it *was* him.'

'I agree,' Bloggs said. He thought for a moment, wondering what useful information he could get out of this man. 'How did Faber impress you?' he asked eventually.

Porter said promptly: 'He struck me as exhausted, nervous and determined, in that order. Also, he was no Scotsman.'

'How would you describe his accent?'

'Neutral. No trace of the Hun in his voice . . . except perhaps in retrospect, and that might be my imagination. The accent – minor public school, Home Counties. Jarred with his clothes, if you know what I mean. He was wearing overalls. Another thing I didn't remark until afterwards.'

Kincaid interrupted to offer tea. Everyone accepted. The policeman went to the door.

Bloggs had decided that Porter was less foolish than he looked. 'What did you talk about?'

'Oh, nothing much.'

'But you were together for hours—'

'He slept most of the way. He mended the car – it was only a disconnected lead, but I'm afraid I'm hopeless with machines – then he told me his own car had broken down in Edinburgh, and he was going to Banff. Said he didn't really want to go through Aberdeen, as he didn't have a Restricted Area Pass. I'm afraid I . . . I told him not to worry about that. Said I'd vouch for him if we were stopped. Makes one feel such a bloody fool, you know – but I felt I owed him a favour. He had got me out of a bit of a hole, y'know.'

Kincaid said: 'Nobody's blaming you, sir.'

Bloggs was, but he did not say so. Instead he said: 'There are very few people who have met Faber and can tell us what he's like. Can you think hard and tell me what kind of a man you took him to be?'

'He woke up like a soldier,' Porter said. 'He was courteous, and seemed intelligent. Firm handshake. I take notice of handshakes.'

'Anything else? Think very hard.'

'Something else about when he woke up . . .' Porter's florid face creased up in a frown. 'His right hand went to his left forearm, like this.' He demonstrated.

'That's something,' Bloggs said. 'That'll be where he keeps the knife. A sleeve-sheath.'

'Nothing else, I'm afraid.'

'And he said he was going to Banff. That means he's not.'

'Really?'

'Spies always lie, on principle. I'll bet you told him where you were going before he told you where he was going.'

'I believe I did.' Porter nodded thoughtfully. 'Well, well.'

'Either Aberdeen was his destination, or he went south after you dropped him. Since he said he was going north, he probably didn't go north.'

Kincaid said: 'That kind of second-guessing could get out of hand.'

'Sometimes it does,' Bloggs grinned. 'Did you tell him that you're a magistrate?'

'Yes.'

'That's why he didn't kill you.'

'What? Good Lord! What do you mean?'

'He knew you'd be missed.'

'Good Lord!' Porter repeated. He had gone slightly pale. The idea that he might actually have been killed clearly had not occurred to him.

The door opened again. The man who walked in said: 'I've got your information, and I hope it was fucken worth it.'

Bloggs grinned. This was, undoubtedly, the harbourmaster: a short man with cropped white hair, smoking a large pipe and wearing a blazer with brass buttons.

Kincaid said: 'Come in, Captain. How did you get so wet? You shouldn't go out in the rain.'

'Fuck off,' the Captain said. Bloggs was not sure how much of his anger was real: very little of it, to judge by the delighted expressions on the other faces in the room.

Porter said: 'Morning, Captain.'

'Good morning, Your Worship,' the Captain said.

Kincaid said: 'What have you got?'

The Captain took off his cap and shook drops of rain from its crown. 'The *Marie II* has gone missing,' he said. 'I saw her come in on the afternoon the storm began. I didn't see her go out, but I know she shouldn't have sailed again that day. However, it seems she did.'

'Who owns her?'

'Tam Halfpenny. I telephoned him. He left her in her mooring that day and hasn't seen her since.'

Bloggs said: 'What kind of vessel is she?'

'A small fishing boat, sixty feet and broad in the beam. Stout little craft. Inboard motor. No particular style – the fishermen round here don't follow the pattern book when they build boats.'

'Let me ask you a very important question,' Bloggs said. 'Could that boat have survived the storm?'

The Captain paused in the act of putting a match to his pipe. After a moment he said: 'With a very skilful sailor at the helm – maybe. Maybe not.'

'How far might he have got before the storm broke?'

'Not far – a few miles. The *Marie II* was not tied up until evening.'

Bloggs stood up, walked around his chair, and sat down again. 'So where is he now?'

'At the bottom of the sea, in all probability, the bloody fool.' The Captain's statement was not without relish.

Bloggs could take no satisfaction in the likelihood that Faber was dead. It was too inconclusive. The discontent spread to his body, and he felt restless, itchy, and frustrated. He scratched his chin: he needed a shave. 'I'll believe it when I see it,' he said.

'You won't.'

'Save your lugubrious guesswork,' Bloggs said sharply. 'I want information, not pessimism.' The other men in the room suddenly remembered that, despite his youth, he was the senior officer there. 'Let's rehearse the possibilities. One: he left Aberdeen by land and someone else stole the *Marie II*. In that case he has probably reached his destination by now, but he won't have left the country because of the storm. We already have all the other police forces looking for him, and that's all we can do about number one.

'Two: he's still in Aberdeen. Again, we have this possibility covered: we're still looking for him.

'Three: he left Aberdeen by sea. I think we're agreed this is the strongest option. Let's break it down. Three A: he transferred to another vessel – probably a U-boat – before the storm broke. We don't think he had time, but he might've. Three B: he found shelter somewhere, or was shipwrecked somewhere – mainland or island. Three C: he died.

'If he caught a U-boat, we've had it. We've lost. There's nothing more we can do. So let's forget that one. If he found shelter, or was shipwrecked, we'll find evidence sooner or later – either the *Marie II*, or bits of it. We can search the coastline right away and survey the sea as soon as the weather clears sufficiently for us to get a plane up. If he's gone to the bottom of the ocean we may still find bits of the boat floating.

'So we have three courses of action to take. We continue the searches already going on; we mount a new search of the coastline, working north and south from Aberdeen; and we prepare for an air-sea search the minute the weather improves.'

Bloggs had begun to pace up and down as he spoke, thinking on his feet. He stopped now, and looked around. 'Comments, queries and suggestions?'

The late hour had got to all of them. Bloggs's sudden access of energy jerked them out of a creeping lethargy. One leaned forward, rubbing his hands; another tied his shoelaces; a third put his jacket on. They wanted to go to work. There were no questions.

'All right,' said Bloggs. 'Let's win the war.'

CHAPTER TWENTY-THREE

FABER WAS awake. His body probably needed sleep, despite the fact that he had spent the day in bed; but his mind was hyperactive, turning over possibilities, sketching scenarios, thinking about women and about home.

Now that he was so close to getting out, his memories of home became quite painfully sweet. He thought of quite silly things, like sausages fat enough to eat in slices, and motor cars on the right-hand side of the road, and *really* tall trees, and most of all his own language – words with guts and precision, hard consonants and pure vowels and the verb at the end of the sentence where it ought to be, finality and meaning in the same climactic terminal.

Thoughts of climaxes brought Gertrude to mind again: her face beneath his, make-up washed away by his kisses, eyes closing tight in pleasure then opening again to look with delight into his, mouth stretched wide in a permanent gasp, saying '*Ja, Liebling, ja . . .*'

It was silly. He had led the life of a monk for seven years, but she had no reason to do the same. She would have had a dozen men since Faber. She might even be dead, bombed by the RAF or murdered by the maniacs because her nose was half an inch too long or run over by a motor car in the blackout. Anyway, she would hardly remember him. He would probably never see her again. But she was a symbol.

He did not normally permit himself the indulgence of sentiment. There was in his nature a very cold streak, and he cultivated it because it protected him. Now, however, he was within an inch of success, and he felt free, not to relax his vigilance, but to fantasize a little.

The storm was his safeguard while it continued. He would simply contact the U-boat with Tom's radio on Monday, and its captain would send a dinghy into the bay as soon as the weather cleared. However, if the storm ended before Monday, there was a slight complication: the supply boat. David and Lucy would naturally expect him to take the boat back to the mainland.

Lucy came into his thoughts in vivid, full-colour visions which he could not quite control. He saw her striking amber eyes watching him as he made a bandage for her thumb; her outline walking up the stairs in front of him clad in shapeless man's clothing; her heavy breasts, perfectly round, as she stood naked in the bathroom: and as the visions developed from memory into fantasy she leaned over the bandage and kissed his mouth, turned back on the stairs and took him in her arms, stepped out of the bathroom and placed his hands on her breasts.

He turned restlessly in the little bed, cursing the imagination which sent him dreams the like of which he had not suffered since his schooldays. At that time, before he had experienced the reality of sex, he had constructed elaborate sexual scenarios featuring the older women with whom he came into daily contact: the starchy Matron; Professor Nagel's dark, thin, intellectual wife; the shopkeeper in the village who wore red lipstick and talked to her husband with contempt. Sometimes he put all three of them into one orgiastic fantasy. When at the age of fifteen he had seduced a housemaid's daughter in the twilight of a West Prussian forest, he abandoned the imaginary orgies because they were so much better than the disappointing real thing. Young Henrik had been greatly puzzled by this: where was the blinding ecstasy, the sensation of soaring through the air like a bird, the mystical fusion of two bodies into one? The fantasies became painful, reminding him of his failure to make them real. Later, of course, the reality improved, and Henrik formed the view that ecstasy comes not from a man's pleasure in a woman, but from their pleasure in each other. He had voiced that opinion to his elder brother, who seemed to think it banal, a truism rather than a discovery; and before long Henrik saw it that way too.

He became a good lover, eventually. He found sex interesting, as well as physically pleasant. He was never a great seducer, for the thrill of conquest was not what he wanted. But he was expert at giving and receiving sexual gratification, without the expert's illusion that technique is all. For some women he was a highly desirable man, and the fact that he did not know this only served to make him even more attractive.

He tried to remember how many women he had had: Anna, Gretchen, Ingrid, the American girl, those two whores in Stuttgart ... he could not recall them all, but there could not have been more than about twenty.

None of them, he thought, had been quite as beautiful as Lucy. He gave an exasperated sigh: he had let this woman get to him, just because he was close to home and had been so careful for so long. He was annoyed with himself. It was undisciplined: one should not relax until the assignment was over, and this was not over, not quite.

There was the problem of the supply boat. Several solutions came to mind: perhaps the most promising was to incapacitate the island's inhabitants, meet the boat himself, and send the boatman away with a cock-and-bull story. He could say he was visiting them, had come out on another boat; that he was a relative, or a bird-watcher ... anything. It was too small a problem to engage his full attention at present. Later, when and if the weather improved, he would work something out.

He had no serious problems. A lonely island, miles off the coast, with four inhabitants – it was an ideal hideout. From now on, leaving Britain was going to be as easy as breaking out of a baby's playpen. When he thought of the situations he had already come through, the people he had killed – the five Home Guard men, the Yorkshire lad on the train, the Abwehr messenger – he considered himself now to be sitting pretty.

An old man, a cripple, a woman and a child ... Killing them would be so simple.

*

Lucy, too, lay awake. She was listening. There was a lot to hear. The weather was an orchestra, rain drumming on the roof, wind fluting in the eaves of the cottage, sea performing glissandi with the beach. The old house talked, too, creaking in its joints as it suffered the buffeting of the storm. Within the room there were more sounds: David's slow, regular breathing, threatening but never quite achieving a snore as he slept deeply under the influence of the double dose of soporific; and the quicker, shallow breaths of Jo, sprawled comfortably across a camp bed beside the far wall.

The noise is keeping me awake, Lucy thought; then immediately: Who am I trying to fool? Her wakefulness was caused by Henry, who had looked at her naked body, and had touched her hands gently as he bandaged her thumb, and who now lay in bed in the next room, probably fast asleep.

He had not told her much about himself, she realized: only that he was unmarried. She did not know where he had been born – his accent gave no clue. He had not even hinted at what he did for a living, though she imagined he must be a professional man, perhaps a dentist or a soldier. He was not dull enough to be a solicitor, too intelligent to be a journalist, and doctors could never keep their profession secret for longer than five minutes. He was not rich enough to be a barrister, too self-effacing to be an actor. She would bet on the Army.

Did he live alone, she wondered? Or with his mother? Or a woman? What did he wear when he wasn't fishing? She would like to see him in a dark blue suit, double-breasted, with a white handkerchief in the top pocket. Did he have a motor car? Yes, he would; something rather unusual, and quite new. He probably drove very fast.

That thought brought back memories of David's two-seater, and she closed her eyes tightly to shut out the nightmare images. Think of something else, think of something *else*.

She thought of Henry again, and realized an odd thing: she wanted to make love to him.

It was a peculiar wish; the kind of wish that, in her scheme of things, afflicted men but not women. A woman might meet a man briefly and find him attractive, want to get to know him better, even begin to fall in love with him; but she did not feel an immediate physical desire, not unless she was . . . abnormal.

She told herself that this was ridiculous; that what she needed was to make love with her husband, not to copulate with the first eligible man who came along. She told herself she was not that kind.

All the same, it was pleasant to speculate. David and Jo were fast asleep: there was nothing to stop her getting out of bed, crossing the landing, entering his room, sliding into bed next to him . . .

Nothing to stop her, except character, good breeding, and a respectable upbringing.

If she were going to do it with anybody, she would do it with someone like Henry. He would be kind, and gentle, and considerate; he would not despise her for offering herself like a Soho streetwalker.

She turned over in the bed, smiling at her own foolishness: for how could she possibly know whether he would despise her? She had known him only for a day, and he had spent most of that day asleep.

Still, it would be nice to have him look at her again, his expression of admiration tinged with some kind of amusement. It would be nice to feel his hands, to touch his body, to squeeze against the warmth of his skin.

She realized that her body was responding to the images in her mind. She felt the urge to touch herself, and resisted it, as she had done for four years. At least I haven't dried up, like an old crone, she thought.

She moved her legs, and sighed as a warm sensation spread through her loins. This was getting unreasonable. It was time to go to sleep. There was just no way she would make love to Henry, or to anyone else, tonight.

With that thought she got out of bed and went to the door.

Faber heard a footfall on the landing, and he reacted automatically.

His mind cleared instantly of the idle, lascivious thoughts with which it had been occupied. He swung his legs to the floor and slid out from under the bedclothes in a single, fluid movement; then silently crossed the room to stand beside the window in the darkest corner, the stiletto knife in his hand.

He heard the door open, heard the intruder step inside, heard the door close again. At that point he started to think, for an assassin would have left the door open for a quick getaway, and it occurred to him that there were a hundred reasons why it was impossible that an assassin should have found him here.

He ignored the thought, for he had survived this long by catering for the one-in-a-thousand chance. The wind dropped momentarily, and he heard an indrawn breath, a faint gasp, from beside his bed, enabling him to locate the intruder's exact position. He sprang.

He had her on the bed, face down, with his knife at her throat and his knee in the small of her back, before he realized that the intruder was a woman. A split-second later he guessed her identity. He eased his grip, reached out to the bedside table, and switched on the light.

Her face was pale in the dim glow of the lamp.

Faber sheathed the knife before she could see it. He took his weight off her body. 'I'm awfully sorry,' he said.

She turned on to her back and looked up at him as he straddled her. She began to giggle.

Faber added: 'I thought you were a burglar.'

'And where would a burglar come from?' she laughed. The colour rushed back to her cheeks in a blush.

She was wearing a very loose, old-fashioned flannel nightgown which covered her from her throat to her ankles. Her dark-red hair spread across Faber's pillow in disarray. Her eyes seemed very large, and her lips were moist.

'You are remarkably beautiful,' Faber said quietly.

She closed her eyes.

Faber bent over her and kissed her mouth. Her lips parted immediately, and she returned his kiss hungrily. With his fingertips he stroked her shoulders, her neck and her ears. She moved beneath him.

He wanted to kiss her for a long time, to explore her mouth and savour the intimacy; but he realized that she had no time for tenderness. She reached inside his pyjama trousers and squeezed. She moaned softly and began to breathe hard.

Still kissing her, Faber reached for the light and killed it. He pulled away from her and took off his pyjama jacket. Quickly, so that she would not wonder what he was doing, he tugged at the can stuck to his chest, ignoring the sting as the sticky tape was jerked away from his skin. He slid the photographs under the bed. He also unbuttoned the sheath on his left forearm and dropped that.

He pushed the skirt of her nightdress up to her waist. She wore nothing underneath.

'Quickly,' she said. 'Quickly.'

Faber lowered his body to hers.

Lucy did not feel the least bit guilty afterwards. She just felt content, satisfied, replete. She had had what she wanted, and she was glad. She lay still, eyes closed, stroking the bristly hair at the back of Henry's neck, enjoying the rough tickling sensation on her hands.

After a while she said: 'I was in such a rush . . .'

'It's not over yet,' he murmured.

She frowned in the dark. 'Didn't you . . . ?'

'No, I didn't. You hardly did.'

She smiled. 'I beg to differ.'

He turned on the light and looked at her. 'We'll see.'

He slipped down the bed, his torso between her thighs, and kissed her belly. His tongue flicked in and out of her navel. It was quite nice. Then his head went lower. Surely, she thought, he doesn't want to kiss me *there*. He did. And he did more than kiss. His lips pulled at the soft folds of her skin. She was paralysed by shock as his tongue began to probe in the crevices and then, as he parted her lips with his fingers, to thrust deep inside her.

Finally his restless tongue found a tiny, sensitive place, so small she had not known it existed, so sensitive that his touch was almost painful at first. She forgot her shock as she was overwhelmed by the most piercing sensation she had ever experienced. Unable to restrain herself, she moved her hips up and down, faster and faster, rubbing her slippery flesh over his mouth, his chin, his nose, his forehead; totally absorbed in her own pleasure. The thrill built and built, like feedback in a microphone, feeding upon itself, until she felt utterly possessed by joy and opened her mouth to scream, whereupon Henry clapped his hand over her face to quiet her; but she screamed in her throat as the climax went on and on, ending in something that felt like an explosion and left her so drained that she thought she would never get up.

Her mind seemed to go blank for a while. She knew

vaguely that Henry still lay between her legs, his bristly
cheek against the soft inside of her thigh, his lips
moving gently, affectionately.

Eventually she said: 'Now I *know* what Lawrence
means.'

He lifted his head. 'I don't understand.'

She sighed. 'I didn't realize it could be like that. It
was lovely.'

'*Was?*'

'Oh, God, I've no more energy . . .'

He changed position, kneeling astride her chest, and
she realized what he wanted her to do, and for the
second time she was frozen by shock: it was just too *big*
. . . but suddenly she *wanted* to do it, she *needed* to take
him into her mouth; so she lifted her head, and her
lips closed around him, and he gave a soft groan.

He held her head in his hands, moving it to and fro,
moaning quietly. She looked at his face. He was staring
wild-eyed at her, drinking in the sight of what she was
doing. She wondered what she would do when he . . .
came . . . and she decided she didn't care, because
everything else had been so good with him that she
knew she would enjoy even that.

But it was not to be. When she thought he was on
the point of losing control he stopped, moved away, lay
on top of her, and entered her again. This time it was
very slow and relaxed, like the rhythm of the sea on the
beach; until he put his hands under her hips and
grasped the globes of her bottom, and she looked at his
face and knew that now, now he was ready to shed his
self-control and lose himself in her. That excited her

313

more than anything, so that when at last he arched his back, his face screwed up into a mask of pain, and groaned deep in his chest, she wrapped her legs around his waist and abandoned herself to ecstasy; and then, after so long, she heard the trumpets and thunderstorms and the clash of cymbals that Lawrence had promised.

They were quiet for a long time. Lucy felt warm, as if she were glowing; she had never felt so warm in all her time on the island. When their breathing subsided she could hear the storm outside. Henry was heavy on top of her, but she did not want him to move: she liked his weight, and the faint tang of perspiration from his white skin. From time to time he moved his head to brush his lips against her cheek.

He was the perfect man to have an affair with. He knew more about her body than she did. His own body was very beautiful: broad and muscular at the shoulders, narrow at the waist and hips, with long, strong, hairy legs. She thought he had some scars: she was not sure. Strong, gentle and handsome: perfect. Yet she knew she would never fall in love with him, never want to run away with him and marry him. Deep inside him, she sensed, there was something very cold and hard, some part of him that was committed elsewhere, a readiness to abandon commonplace emotions for some higher duty. He would never belong to any woman, for he had some other ultimate loyalty – like a painter's art, a businessman's greed, a patriot's country, a socialist's revolution. She would have to hold him at arm's length, and use him cautiously, like an addictive drug.

Not that she would have time to get hooked: he would be gone in little more than a day.

She stirred at last, and immediately he rolled off her and on to his back. She lifted herself on one elbow and looked at his naked body. Yes, he did have scars: a long one on his chest, and a small mark like a star – it might have been a burn – on his hip. She rubbed his chest with the palm of her hand.

'It's not very ladylike,' she said, 'but I want to say thank you.'

He reached out to touch her cheek, and smiled. 'You're very ladylike.'

'You don't know what you've done. You've—'

He put a finger over her lips. 'I know what I've done.'

She bit his finger, then put his hand on her breast. He felt for her nipple. She said: 'Please do it again.'

'I don't think I can,' he said.

But he did.

She left him a couple of hours after dawn. There was a small noise from the other bedroom, and she seemed suddenly to remember that she had a husband and a son in the house. Faber wanted to tell her that it didn't matter, that neither he nor she had the least reason to care what the husband knew or thought; but he held his tongue and let her go. She kissed him once more, very wetly; then she stood up, smoothed her rumpled nightgown over her body, and tiptoed out. He watched her fondly.

She's quite something, he thought. He lay on his back and looked at the ceiling. She was quite naive, and very inexperienced, but all the same she had been very good. I could fall in love with her, he thought.

He got up and retrieved the film can and the knife in its sheath from under the bed. He wondered whether to keep them on his person. He might want to make love to her in the day . . . He decided to wear the knife – he would feel undressed without it – and leave the can somewhere. He put it on top of the chest-of-drawers and covered it with his papers and his wallet. He knew that he was breaking all the rules; but this was sure to be his last assignment, and he felt entitled to enjoy a woman. It would hardly matter if someone saw the pictures – what could they do?

He lay down on the bed, then got up again. Years of training would not let him take risks. He put the can and his papers into the pocket of his jacket. Now he could relax.

He heard the child's voice, then Lucy's tread as she went down the stairs, and then David dragging himself to the bathroom. He would have to get up and have breakfast with the household. He did not want to sleep now, anyway.

He stood at the rain-streaked window, watching the weather rage, until he heard the bathroom door open. Then he put on his pyjama jacket and went in to shave. He used David's razor, without permission.

It did not seem to matter now.

CHAPTER TWENTY-FOUR

E RWIN ROMMEL knew from the start that he was
going to quarrel with Heinz Guderian.

General Guderian was exactly the kind of aristocratic
Prussian officer Rommel hated. He had known him for
some time. They had both, in their early days, commanded the Goslar Jaeger Battalion, and they had met
again during the Polish campaign. When Rommel left
Africa he had recommended Guderian to succeed him,
knowing the battle was lost: the manoeuvre was a failure
because at that time Guderian had been out of favour
with Hitler and the recommendation was rejected out
of hand.

The General was, Rommel felt, the kind of man who
put a silk handkerchief on his knee to protect the
crease in his trousers as he sat drinking in the Herren-
klub. He was an officer because his father had been an
officer and his grandfather had been rich. Rommel,
the schoolteacher's son who had risen from Lieutenant-
Colonel to Field Marshal in only four years, despised
the military caste of which he had never been a
member.

Now he stared across the table at the General, who
was sipping brandy appropriated from the French

Rothschilds. Guderian and his sidekick, General von Geyr, had come to Rommel's headquarters at La Roche Guyon in Northern France to tell him how to deploy his troops. Rommel's reactions to such visits ranged from impatience to fury. In his view the General Staff were there to provide reliable intelligence and regular supplies, and he knew from his experience in Africa that they were incompetent at both tasks.

Guderian had a cropped, fair moustache, and the corners of his eyes were heavily wrinkled so that he always appeared to be grinning at you. He was tall and handsome, which did nothing to endear him to the short, ugly, balding Rommel. He seemed relaxed, and any German general who could relax at this stage of the war was surely a fool. The meal they had just finished – local veal and wine from farther south – was no excuse.

Rommel looked out of the window and watched the rain dripping from the lime trees into the courtyard while he waited for Guderian to begin the discussion. When eventually he spoke, it was clear the General had been thinking about the best way to make his point, and had decided to approach it sideways.

'In Turkey,' he began, 'the British 9th and 10th armies, with the Turkish army, are grouping at the border with Greece. In Yugoslavia, the partisans are also concentrating. The French in Algeria are preparing to invade the Riviera. The Russians appear to be mounting an amphibious invasion of Sweden. In Italy, the Allies are ready to march on Rome.

'There are smaller signals: a general kidnapped in

Crete; an Intelligence officer murdered at Lyon; a radar post attacked at Rhodes; an aircraft sabotaged with abrasive grease and destroyed at Athens; a commando raid on Sagvaag; an explosion in the oxygen factory at Boulogne-sur-Seine; a train derailed in the Ardennes; a petrol dump fired at Boussens . . . I could go on.

'The picture is clear. In occupied territories, there is ever-increasing sabotage and treachery; on our borders, everywhere we see preparations for invasion. None of us doubts that there will be a major Allied offensive this summer; and we can be equally sure that all this skirmishing is intended to confuse us about where the attack will come.'

The General paused. The lecture, delivered in schoolmaster style, was irritating Rommel, and he took the opportunity to interrupt. 'This is why we have a General Staff: to digest such information, produce appreciations of enemy activity, and forecast his future moves.'

Guderian smiled indulgently. 'We must also be aware of the limitations of such crystal-gazing. You have your ideas about where the attack will come, I'm sure: we all do. Our strategy must take into account the possibility that our guesses are wrong.'

Rommel now saw where the General's roundabout argument was leading, and he suppressed the urge to shout his disagreement before the conclusion was stated.

'You have four armoured divisions under your command,' Guderian continued. 'The 2nd Panzers at Amiens; the 116th at Rouen; the 21st at Caen; and the

2nd SS at Toulouse. General von Geyr has already proposed to you that these should be grouped well back from the coast, all together, ready for fast retaliation at any point. Indeed, this stratagem is a principle of OKW policy. Nevertheless, you have not only resisted von Geyr's suggestion, but have in fact moved the 21st right up to the Atlantic coast.'

'And the other three must be moved to the coast as soon as possible,' Rommel burst out. 'When will you people learn? *The Allies rule the air.* Once the invasion is launched there will be no further major movements of armour. Mobile operations are no longer possible. If your precious panzers are in Paris when the Allies land on the coast, they will *stay* in Paris – pinned down by the RAF – until the Allies march along the Boulevard St Michel. I *know* – they've done it to me. Twice!' He paused to draw breath. 'To group our armour as a mobile reserve is to render it useless. There will be no counter-attack. The invasion must be met on the beaches, when it is most vulnerable, and pushed back into the sea.'

The flush receded from his face as he began to expound his own defensive strategy. 'I have created underwater obstacles, strengthened the Atlantic Wall, laid minefields, and driven stakes into every meadow that might be used to land airplanes behind our lines. All my troops are engaged in digging defences whenever they're not actually training.

'My armoured divisions must be moved to the coast. The OKW reserve should be redeployed in France. The 9th and 10th SS divisions have to be brought back from the Eastern Front. Our whole strategy must be to prevent the Allies from securing a beachhead, for once they achieve that, the battle is lost . . . perhaps even the war.'

Guderian leaned forward, his eyes narrowing in that infuriating half-grin. 'You want us to defend the European coastline from Tromso in Norway all around the Iberian Peninsula to Rome. From where shall we get the armies?'

'That question should have been asked in 1938,' Rommel muttered.

There was an embarrassed silence after this remark, which was all the more shocking coming from the notoriously apolitical Rommel.

Von Geyr broke the spell. 'Where do *you* believe the attack will come, Field-Marshal?'

Rommel considered. 'Until recently I was convinced of the Pas de Calais theory. However, last time I was with the Führer I was impressed by his arguments in favour of Normandy. I am also impressed by his instinct, and its record of accuracy. Therefore I believe our panzers should be deployed primarily along the Normandy coast, with perhaps one division at the mouth of the Somme – this last supported by forces outside my group.'

Guderian shook his head solemnly. 'No, no, no. It's far too risky.'

'I'm prepared to take this argument to Hitler himself,' Rommel threatened.

'Then that's what you must do,' Guderian said resignedly, 'for I shan't assent to your plan, unless . . .'

'Well?' Rommel was surprised that the General's position might be qualified.

Guderian shifted in his seat, reluctant to give a concession to so obdurate an antagonist as Rommel. 'You may know that the Führer is waiting for a report from an unusually effective agent in England.'

'I remember,' Rommel nodded. 'Die Nadel.'

'Yes. He has been assigned to assess the strength of the First United States Army Group under Patton's command in the eastern part of England. If he finds – as I am certain he will – that that army is large, strong, and ready to move, then I shall continue to oppose you. However, if he finds that FUSAG is a bluff – a small army masquerading as an invasion force – then I shall concede that you are right, and you shall have your panzers. Will you accept that compromise?'

Rommel bowed his large head in assent. 'It all depends on Die Nadel, then.'

'It all depends on Die Nadel.'

Part Five

CHAPTER TWENTY-FIVE

THE COTTAGE was terribly small, Lucy realized quite suddenly. As she went about her morning chores – lighting the stove, making porridge, tidying up, dressing Jo – the walls seemed to press in on her claustrophobically. After all, it was only four rooms, linked by a little passage with a staircase; you couldn't move without bumping into someone else. If you stood still and listened you could hear what everyone was doing: Henry running water into the wash-basin, David sliding down the stairs, Jo chastising his teddy-bear in the living-room. Lucy would have liked some time on her own before meeting people: time to let the events of the night settle into her memory, recede from the forefront of her thoughts, so that she could act normally without a conscious effort.

She guessed she was not going to be good at deception. It did not come naturally to her. She had no experience of it. She tried to think of another occasion in her life when she had deceived someone close to her, and she could not. It was not that she lived by very high principles – the *thought* of lying did not trouble her. It was just that she had never had reason for dishonesty. Does that mean, she wondered, that I've led a sheltered life?

David and Jo sat down at the kitchen table and began to eat. David was silent, Jo talked non-stop just for the pleasure of making words. Lucy did not want food.

'Aren't you eating?' David said casually.

'I've had some.' There – her first lie. It wasn't so bad.

The storm made the claustrophobia worse. The rain was so heavy that Lucy could hardly see the barn from the kitchen window. One felt even more shut-in when to open a door or window was a major operation. The low, steel-grey sky and the wisps of mist created a permanent twilight. In the garden, the rain ran in rivers between the rows of potato plants, and the herb patch was a shallow pond. The sparrow's nest under the outhouse roof had been washed away, and the birds flitted in and out of the eaves, panicking.

Lucy heard Henry coming down the stairs, and she felt better. For some reason, she was quite sure that he was very good at deception.

'Good morning!' Faber said heartily. David, sitting at the table in his wheelchair, looked up and smiled. Lucy busied herself at the stove. There was guilt written all over her face. Faber groaned inwardly, but David did not seem to notice her expression. Faber began to think that David was an oaf.

Lucy said: 'Sit down and have some breakfast, Henry.'

'Thank you very much.'

David said: 'Can't offer to take you to church, I'm

afraid. Hymn-singing on the wireless is the best we can do.'

Faber realized it was Sunday. 'Are you churchgoing people?'

'No,' David said. 'You?'

'No.'

'Sunday is much the same as any other day for farmers,' David continued. 'I'll be driving over to the other end of the island to see my shepherd. You could come, if you feel up to it.'

'I'd like to,' Faber told him. It would give him a chance to reconnoitre. He would need to know the way to the cottage with the transmitter. 'Would you like me to drive you?'

David looked at him sharply. 'I can manage quite well.' There was a strained moment of silence. 'In this weather, the road is just a memory. We'll be a lot safer with me at the wheel.'

'Of course.' Faber began to eat.

'It makes no difference to me,' David persisted. 'I don't want you to come if you think it would be too much—'

'Really, I'd be glad to.'

'Did you sleep all right? It didn't occur to me you might still be tired. I hope Lucy didn't keep you up late.'

Faber willed himself not to look at Lucy. Out of the corner of his eye he could see that she was blushing to the roots of her hair. 'I slept all day yesterday,' he said, trying to fix David's eyes with his own.

It was no use. David was looking at his wife. She

turned her back. The trace of a frown creased his forehead, and then just for a moment, his jaw dropped open in a classic expression of surprise.

Faber was mildly annoyed. David would be hostile now, and antagonism was half way to suspicion. It was not dangerous, but it might be tiresome.

The husband recovered his composure quickly. He pushed his chair away from the table and wheeled himself to the back door. 'I'll get the jeep out of the barn,' he muttered. He took an oilskin off a hook and put it over his head, then opened the door and rolled out.

In the few moments the door was open, the storm blew into the little kitchen, leaving the floor wet and the people cold. When it shut, Lucy shivered and began to mop the water from the tiles.

Faber reached out and touched her arm.

'Don't,' she said, jerking her head toward Jo in warning.

'You're being silly,' Faber told her.

'I think he knows,' she said.

'But, if you reflect for a minute, you don't really care whether he knows or not, do you?'

She considered. 'I'm not supposed to.'

Faber shrugged. The jeep's horn sounded impatiently outside. Lucy handed him an oilskin and a pair of wellington boots.

'Don't talk about me,' she said.

Faber put on the waterproof clothes and went to the front door. Lucy followed him, closing the kitchen door on Jo.

With his hand on the latch, Faber turned and kissed her.

She kissed him back, forcefully, then turned and went into the kitchen.

Faber dashed through the rain, across a sea of mud, and jumped into the jeep beside David. He pulled away immediately.

The vehicle had been specially adapted for the legless man to drive. It had a hand throttle, automatic gearshift, and a handle on the rim of the wheel to enable the driver to steer one-handed. The folded-up wheelchair slid into a special compartment behind the driver's seat. There was a shotgun in a rack above the windscreen.

David drove competently. He had been right about the road: it was no more than a strip of heath worn bare by the jeep's tyres. The rain pooled in the deep ruts. The car slithered about in the mud. David seemed to enjoy it. There was a cigarette between his lips, and he wore an incongruous air of bravado. Perhaps this was his substitute for flying.

'What do you do when you're not fishing?' he said around the cigarette.

'Civil servant,' Faber told him.

'What sort of work?'

'Finance. I'm just a cog in the machine.'

'Treasury, eh?'

'Mainly.'

Even that asinine answer did not stop David's questioning. 'Interesting work?' he persisted.

'Fairly.' Faber summoned up the energy to invent a

story. 'I know a bit about how much a given piece of engineering ought to cost, and I spend most of my time making sure the taxpayer isn't being overcharged.'

'Any particular sort of engineering?'

'Everything from paper clips to aircraft engines.'

'Ah, well. We all contribute to the war effort in our own way.'

It was a snide remark, and David would naturally have no idea why Faber did not resent it. 'I'm too old to fight,' Faber said mildly.

'Were you in the first lot?'

'Too young.'

'A lucky escape.'

'Doubtless.'

The track ran quite close to the cliff edge, but David did not slow down. It crossed Faber's mind that he might want to kill them both. He reached for a grab handle.

'Am I going too fast for you?' David asked.

'You seem to know the road,' Faber replied.

'You looked frightened,' David said.

Faber ignored that, and David slowed down a little, apparently satisfied that he had made some kind of point.

The island was fairly flat, and bare, Faber observed. The ground rose and fell slightly, but as yet he had seen no hills. The vegetation was mostly grass, with some ferns and bushes, but few trees: there was little protection from the weather. David Rose's sheep must be hardy, he thought.

'Are you married?' David asked suddenly.

'No.'

'Wise man.'

'Oh, I don't know.'

'I'll bet you put yourself about a bit up in London,' David leered.

Faber had never liked the nudging, contemptuous way some men talked about women. He said sharply: 'I should think you're extremely fortunate to have Lucy.'

'Oh, would you.'

'Yes.'

'Nothing like variety, though, eh?'

Faber thought: What the devil is he getting at? He said: 'I haven't had the chance to discover the merits of monogamy.'

'Quite.'

Faber thought: *He* doesn't know what he's getting at, either. He decided to say no more, since everything he said was fuel to the fire.

'I must say, you don't *look* like a Government account-ant. Where's the rolled umbrella and the bowler hat?'

Faber tried a thin smile.

'And you seem quite fit for a pen-pusher.'

'I ride a bicycle.'

'You must be quite tough, to have survived that wreck.'

'Thank you.'

'You don't *look* too old to be in the Army, either.'

Faber turned his gaze on David. 'What are you driving at, David?' he asked calmly.

'We're there,' David said.

Faber looked out of the windscreen and saw a

cottage very similar to Lucy's, with stone walls, a slate roof, and small windows. It stood at the top of a hill, the only hill Faber had seen on the island, and not much of a hill at that. The house had a squat, resilient look about it. Climbing up to it, the jeep skirted a small stand of pine and fir trees. Faber wondered why the cottage had not been built in the shelter of the trees.

Beside the house was a hawthorn tree in bedraggled blossom. David stopped the car. Faber watched him unfold the wheelchair and ease himself out of the driving seat into the chair: he would have resented an offer of help.

They entered the house by a plank door with no lock. They were greeted in the hall by a black-and-white collie, a small, broad-headed dog who wagged his tail but did not bark. The layout of the cottage was identical with that of Lucy's, but the atmosphere was different: this place was bare, cheerless, and none too clean.

David led the way into the kitchen. The shepherd sat by an old-fashioned wood-burning kitchen range, warming his hands. He stood up.

David said: 'Henry, this is Tom McAvity.'

'Pleased to meet you,' Tom said formally.

Faber shook his hand. He was a short man, and broad, with a face like an old tan suitcase. He was wearing a cloth cap and smoking a very large briar pipe with a lid. His grip was firm, and the skin of his hand felt like sandpaper. He had a very big nose. Faber had to concentrate hard to understand what he was saying: his Scots accent was very broad.

'I hope I'm not going to be in the way,' Faber said. 'I only came along for the ride.'

David wheeled himself up to the table. 'I don't suppose we'll do much this morning, Tom – just take a look around.'

'Aye. We'll have some tay before we go, though.'

Tom poured strong tea into three mugs, and added a shot of whisky to each. The three men sat and sipped it in silence, David smoking a cigarette and Tom drawing gently at his pipe, and Faber felt certain that the other two spent a great deal of time together in this way, smoking and warming their hands and saying nothing.

When they had finished their tea Tom put the mugs in the shallow stone sink and they went out in the jeep. Faber sat in the back. David drove slowly this time, and the dog, which was called Bob, loped alongside, keeping pace without apparent effort. It was obvious that David knew the terrain very well, for he steered confidently across the open grassland without once getting bogged down in swampy ground. The sheep looked very sorry for themselves. With their fleeces sopping wet, they huddled in hollows, or close to bramble bushes, or on the leeward slopes, too dispirited to graze. Even the lambs were subdued, hiding beneath their mothers.

Faber was watching the dog when it stopped, listened for a moment, and then raced off at a tangent.

Tom had been watching, too. 'Bob's found something,' he said.

The jeep followed the dog for a quarter of a mile. When they stopped Faber could hear the sea: they were close to the island's northern edge. The dog was standing at the brink of a small gully. When the men got out of the car they could hear what the dog had heard: the bleating of a sheep in distress. They went to the edge of the gully and looked down.

The animal lay on its side about twenty feet down, balanced precariously on the steeply sloping bank. It held one foreleg at an awkward angle. Tom went down to it, treading cautiously, and examined the leg.

'Mutton tonight,' he called.

David got the gun from the jeep and slid it down to him. Tom put the sheep out of its misery.

'Do you want to rope it up?' David called.

'Aye – unless Henry wants to come and give me a hand.'

'Surely,' Faber said. He picked his way down to where Tom stood. They took a leg each and dragged the dead animal back up the slope. Faber's oilskin caught on a thorny bush, and he almost fell before he tugged the material free with a loud ripping sound.

They threw the sheep into the jeep and drove on. Faber felt very wet, and he realized he had torn away most of the back of the oilskin. 'I'm afraid I've ruined this garment,' he said.

'All in a good cause,' Tom told him.

Soon they returned to Tom's cottage. Faber took off

the oilskin and his wet donkey jacket, and Tom put the jacket over the stove to dry. Then each went to the outhouse – Tom's cottage did not have the modern plumbing that had been added to Lucy's – and Tom made more tea.

'She's the first we've lost this year,' David said.

'Aye.'

'We'll fence the gully this summer.'

'Aye.'

Faber sensed a change in the atmosphere: it was not the same as it had been two or three hours earlier. They sat, drinking and smoking as before, but David seemed restless. Twice Faber caught the man staring at him, deep in thought.

Eventually David said: 'We'll leave you to butcher the ewe, Tom.'

'Aye.'

David and Faber left. Tom did not get up, but the dog saw them to the door.

Before starting the jeep David took the shotgun from its rack above the windscreen, reloaded it, and put it back.

On the way home he underwent another change of mood and became chatty. 'I used to fly Spitfires, you know. Lovely kites. Four guns in each wing – American Brownings, they were, firing one thousand two hundred and sixty rounds a minute. The Jerries prefer cannon, of course – their Me 109s only have two machine guns. A cannon does more damage, but our Brownings are faster, and more accurate.'

'Really?' Faber said politely.

'They put cannon in the Hurricanes later, but it was the Spitfire that won the Battle of Britain.'

Faber found his boastfulness irritating. He said: 'How many enemy aircraft did you shoot down?'

'I lost my legs while I was training,' David said.

Faber stole a glance at his face: it was a mask of repressed fury.

David said: 'No, I haven't killed a single German, yet.'

It was an unmistakable signal. Faber suddenly became very alert. He had no idea what David might have deduced or discovered, but there could be no doubt that the man knew something was up. Faber turned slightly sideways to face David, braced himself with his foot against the transmission tunnel on the floor, and rested his right hand lightly on his left forearm. He waited for David's next move.

'Are you interested in aircraft?' David asked.

'No.' Faber's voice was flat.

'It's become a national pastime, I gather – aircraft spotting. Like bird-watching. People buy books on aircraft identification. Spend whole afternoons on their backs, looking at the sky through telescopes. I thought you might be an enthusiast.'

'Why?'

'Pardon?'

'What made you think I might be an enthusiast?'

'Oh, I don't know.' David stopped the jeep to light a cigarette. They were at the island's mid-point, five miles from Tom's cottage with another five miles to go to

Lucy's. David dropped the match on the floor. 'Perhaps it was the photographs that fell out of your jacket pocket—'

As he spoke, he tossed the lighted cigarette at Faber's face, and reached for the gun above the windscreen.

CHAPTER TWENTY-SIX

SID CRIPPS looked out of the window and cursed under his breath. The meadow was full of American tanks – at least eighty of them. He realized there was a war on, and all that, but if only they'd asked him he would have offered them another field, where the grass was not so lush. By now the caterpillar tracks would have chewed up his best grazing.

He pulled on his boots and went out. There were some Yank soldiers in the field, and he wondered whether they had noticed the bull. When he got to the stile he stopped and scratched his head. There was something very funny going on.

The tanks had *not* chewed up his grass. They had left no tracks. But the American soldiers were *making* tank tracks with a tool something like a harrow.

While Sid was trying to figure it all out, the bull noticed the tanks. It stared at them for a while, then pawed the ground and lumbered into a run. It was going to charge a tank.

'Daft bugger, you'll break your head,' Sid muttered.

The soldiers were watching the bull, too. They seemed to think it was funny.

The bull ran full-tilt into the tank, its horns pierc-

338

ing the armour-plated side of the vehicle. Sid hoped fervently that British tanks were stronger than the American ones.

There was a loud hissing noise as the bull worked its horns free. The tank collapsed like a deflated balloon. The American soldiers fell about laughing.

Sid Cripps scratched his head again. It was all very strange.

Percival Godliman walked quickly across Parliament Square, carrying an umbrella. He wore a dark striped suit under his raincoat, and his black shoes were highly polished – at least, they had been until he stepped out into the rain – for it was not every day, come to that it was not every year, that he had a private audience with Churchill.

A career soldier would have been nervous at going with such bad news to see the supreme commander of the nation's armed forces. Godliman was not nervous, for a distinguished historian has nothing to fear from soldiers and politicians, not unless his view of history is a good deal more radical than Godliman's was. Not nervous, then; but he was worried.

He was thinking about the effort, the forethought, the care, the money and the manpower that had gone into the creation of the totally phoney First United States Army Group stationed in East Anglia: the four hundred landing ships, made of canvas and scaffolding floated on oil drums, which thronged the harbours and estuaries; the carefully manufactured inflatable dummies of tanks, artillery, trucks, half-tracks and even ammunition dumps; the complaints planted in the correspondence columns of the local newspapers about the decline in moral standards since the arrival of thousands of American troops in the area; the phoney oil dock at Dover, designed by Britain's most distinguished architect and built – out of cardboard and old sewage pipes – by craftsmen borrowed from film studios; the carefully faked reports transmitted to Hamburg by German agents who had been 'turned' by the XX Committee; and the incessant radio chatter, broadcast solely for the benefit of the German listening posts, consisting of messages compiled by professional writers of fiction, and including such gems as 'I/5th Queen's Royal Regiment report a number of civilian women, presumably unauthorized, in the baggage train. What are we going to do with them – take them to Calais?'

A lot had been achieved. The signs were that the Germans had fallen for it. And now the whole elaborate deception had been placed in jeopardy because of one spy – a spy Godliman had failed to catch.

His short, birdlike paces measured the Westminster pavement to the small doorway at No 2, Great George Street. The armed guard standing beside the wall of sandbags examined his pass and waved him in. He crossed the lobby and went down the stairs to Churchill's underground headquarters.

It was like going below decks on a battleship. Protected from bombs by a four-foot-thick ceiling of reinforced concrete, the command post featured steel bulkhead doors and roof props of ancient timber. As

Godliman entered the map room a cluster of youngish people with solemn faces emerged from the conference room beyond. An aide followed them a moment later, and spotted Godliman.

'You're very punctual, sir,' the aide said. 'He's ready for you.'

Godliman stepped into the small, comfortable conference room. There were rugs on the floor and a portrait of the King on the wall. An electric fan stirred the tobacco smoke in the air. Churchill sat at the head of an old, mirror-smooth table in the centre of which was a statuette of a faun – the emblem of Churchill's own deception outfit, the London Controlling Section.

Godliman decided not to salute.

Churchill said: 'Sit down, Professor.'

Godliman suddenly realized that Churchill was not a big man – but he *sat* like a big man: shoulders hunched, elbows on the arms of his chair, chin lowered, legs apart. Instead of the famous siren suit he was wearing a solicitor's black-and-stripes – short black jacket and striped grey trousers – with a spotted blue bow tie and a brilliant-white shirt. Despite his stocky frame and his paunch, the hand holding the fountain pen was delicate, thin-fingered. His complexion was baby-pink. The other hand held a cigar, and on the table beside the papers stood a glass containing what looked like whisky.

He was making notes in the margin of a typewritten report, and as he scribbled he muttered occasionally. Godliman was not in the least awed by the great man. As a peacetime statesman Churchill had been, in Godliman's view, a disaster. However, the man had the qualities of a great warrior chieftain, and Godliman respected him for that. (Years later, Churchill modestly denied having been the British lion, saying that he had merely been privileged to give the roar: Godliman thought that assessment was just about right.)

He looked up abruptly and said: 'I suppose there's no doubt this damned spy has discovered what we're up to?'

'None whatsoever, sir,' Godliman said.

'You think he's got away?'

'We chased him to Aberdeen. It's almost certain that he left there two nights ago in a stolen boat – presumably for a rendezvous in the North Sea. However, he can't have been far out of port when the storm blew up. He may have met the U-boat before the storm hit, but it's unlikely. In all probability he drowned. I'm sorry we can't offer more definite information.'

'So am I,' Churchill said. Suddenly he seemed angry, though not with Godliman. He got out of his chair and went over to the clock on the wall, staring as if mesmerized at the inscription *Victoria RI, Ministry of Works, 1889.* Then, as if he had forgotten that Godliman was there, he began to pace up and down alongside the table, muttering to himself. Godliman was able to make out the words, and what he heard astonished him. The great man was mumbling: 'This stocky figure, with a slight stoop, striding up and down, suddenly unconscious of any presence beyond his own thoughts . . .' It was as if Churchill were acting out a Hollywood screenplay which he wrote as he went along.

The performance ended as abruptly as it had begun,

and if the man knew he had been behaving eccentric-
ally, he gave no sign of it. He sat down, handed
Godliman a sheet of paper, and said: 'This is the
German order of battle as of last week.'

Godliman read:

Russian front:	122	*infantry divisions*
	25	*panzer divisions*
	17	*miscellaneous divisions*
Italy & Balkans:	37	*infantry divisions*
	9	*panzer divisions*
	4	*miscellaneous divisions*
Western front:	64	*infantry divisions*
	12	*panzer divisions*
	12	*miscellaneous divisions*
Germany:	3	*infantry divisions*
	1	*panzer division*
	4	*miscellaneous divisions*

Churchill said: 'Of those twelve panzer divisions in
the west, only *one* is actually on the Normandy coast.
The great SS divisions, *Das Reich* and *Adolf Hitler*, are at
Toulouse and Brussels respectively and show no signs
of moving. What does all this tell you, Professor?'

'Our deception and cover plans seem to have been
successful,' Godliman answered.

'Totally!' Churchill barked. 'They are confused and
uncertain, and their best guesses about our intentions
are wildly wrong. And yet!' He paused for effect. 'And
yet, despite all that, General Walter Bedell Smith – Ike's
Chief of Staff – tells me that . . .' He picked up another

piece of paper from the table and read it aloud. 'Our chances of holding the beachhead, particularly after the Germans get their buildup, are only fifty-fifty.'

He put his cigar down, and his voice became quite soft. 'It will be June the fifth – possibly the sixth or the seventh. The tides are right ... it has been decided. The build-up of troops in the West Country has already begun. The convoys are even now making their way along the country roads of England. It has taken the total military and industrial might of the whole English-speaking world – the greatest civilization since the Roman Empire – four years to win this fifty-fifty chance. If this spy gets out, we lose even that.'

He stared at Godliman for a moment, then he picked up his pen with a frail white hand. 'Don't bring me probabilities, Professor,' he said. 'Bring me the body of Die Nadel.'

He looked down and began to write. After a moment Percival Godliman got up and quietly left the room.

CHAPTER TWENTY-SEVEN

CIGARETTE TOBACCO burns at eight hundred degrees centigrade. However, the coal at the end of the cigarette is normally surrounded by a thin layer of ash. To cause a burn, the cigarette has to be pressed against the skin for the better part of a second: a glancing touch will hardly be felt. This applies even to the eyes, for blinking is the fastest involuntary reaction of the human body. Only amateurs throw cigarettes. Professionals – there are just a few people in the world for whom hand-to-hand fighting is a professional skill – ignore them.

Faber ignored the lighted cigarette that David Rose threw at him. He did right, for the cigarette glanced off his forehead and fell to the metal floor of the jeep. Then he made a grab for David's gun, and this was an error. He should have drawn his stiletto and stabbed David: for although David *might* have shot him first, he had never before pointed a gun at a human being, let alone killed somebody; so he would almost certainly have hesitated, and in that moment Faber could have killed him.

The mistake cost dear.

David had both hands on the midsection of the gun

– left hand on the barrel, right hand around the breech – and had pulled the weapon about six inches from its rack when Faber got a one-handed grip on the muzzle. David tugged the gun toward himself, but for a moment Faber's grasp held, and the gun pointed at the windscreen.

Faber was a strong man, but David was exceptionally strong. His shoulders, arms and wrists had moved his body and his wheelchair for four years, and the muscles had become abnormally developed. Furthermore, he had both hands on the gun in front of him, and Faber was holding on with one hand at an awkward angle. David tugged again, more determinedly this time, and the muzzle slipped from Faber's grasp.

At that instant, with the shotgun pointed at his belly and David's finger curling around the trigger, Faber felt very close to death.

He jerked upwards, catapulting himself out of his seat. His head hit the canvas roof of the jeep as the gun exploded with a crash that numbed the ears and produced a physical pain behind the eyes. The window by the passenger seat shattered into innumerable small pieces and the rain blew in through the empty frame. Faber twisted his body and fell back, not on to his own seat, but across David. He got both hands to David's throat and squeezed with his thumbs.

David tried to bring the gun around between their bodies to fire the other barrel, but the weapon was too big. Faber looked into his eyes, and saw . . . what was it? Exhilaration! Of course – at last the man had a chance to fight for his country. Then his expression changed as his body felt the lack of oxygen and he began to fight for breath.

David released his grip on the gun and brought both elbows back as far as he could, then punched Faber's lower ribs with a powerful double jab.

The pain was excruciating, and Faber screwed up his face in anguish, but he held his grip on David's throat. He knew he could withstand David's punches longer than David could hold his breath.

David must have had the same thought. He crossed his forearms between their bodies and pushed Faber away; then, when the gap was a few inches wide, he brought his hands up in an upward-and-outward blow against Faber's arms, breaking the stranglehold. He bunched his right fist and swung downwards with a mighty but unscientific punch which landed on Faber's cheekbone and brought water to his eyes.

Faber replied with a series of body jabs; David continued to bruise his face. They were too close together to do real damage to each other in a short time, but David's greater strength began to tell.

Grimly, Faber realized that David had shrewdly picked the time and place for the fight: he had had the advantages of surprise, the gun, and the confined space in which his muscle counted for much and Faber's better balance and greater manoeuvrability counted for little.

Faber shifted his weight slightly and his hip came into contact with the gearshift, throwing the transmission into forward. The engine was still running, and the car jerked, putting him off balance. David took the opportunity to release a long straight left which – more by luck than judgement – caught Faber full on the chin and threw him clear across the cab of the jeep. His head cracked against the A-post, he slumped with his shoulder on the door handle, the door opened, and he fell out of the car in a backward somersault to land on his face in the mud.

For a moment he was too dazed to move. When he opened his eyes he could see nothing but flashes of blue lightning against a misty red background. He heard the engine of the jeep racing. He shook his head, desperately trying to clear the fireworks from his vision, and struggled on to his hands and knees. The sound of the jeep receded and came closer again. He turned his head toward the noise, and as the colours in front of his eyes dissolved and disappeared, he saw the vehicle bearing down on him at high speed.

David was going to run him over.

With the front bumper less than a yard from his face he hurled himself sideways. He felt a blast of wind. A fender struck his outflung foot as the jeep roared past, its heavy-gauge tyres tearing up the spongy turf and spitting mud. He rolled over twice in the wet grass, then got to one knee. His foot hurt. He watched the jeep turn in a tight circle and come for him again.

He could see David's face through the windscreen. The young man was leaning forward, hunched over the steering wheel, his lips drawn back over his teeth in a savage, almost maniacal grin. He seemed to be imagining himself in the cockpit of a Spitfire, coming down out of the sun at an enemy plane with all eight Browning machine-guns blazing 1,260 rounds per minute.

Faber moved toward the cliff edge. The jeep gathered speed. Faber knew that, for a moment, he was incapable of running. He looked over the cliff: it was a rocky, almost vertical slope to the angry sea a hundred feet below. The jeep was coming straight down the cliff's edge toward him. Frantically, Faber looked up and down for a ledge, or even a foothold. There was none.

The jeep was four or five yards away, travelling at something like forty miles per hour. Its wheels were less than two feet from the cliff's edge. Faber dropped flat and swung his legs out into space, supporting his weight on his forearms as he hung on the brink.

The wheels passed him within inches. A few yards farther on, one tyre actually slipped over the edge. For a moment Faber thought the whole vehicle would slide over and fall into the sea below, but the other three wheels dragged the jeep to safety.

The ground under Faber's arms shifted. The vibration of the jeep's passing had loosened the earth. He felt himself slip a fraction. One hundred feet below, a raging sea boiled among the rocks. Faber stretched one arm to its farthest extent and dug his fingers deep into the soft ground. He felt a nail tear, and ignored it. He repeated the process with his other arm. With two hands anchored in the earth he pulled himself upward. It was agonizingly slow, but eventually his head drew level with his hands, his hips reached firm ground, and he was able to swivel around and roll away from the edge.

The jeep was turning again. Faber ran toward it. His foot was painful, but not broken. David accelerated for another pass. Faber turned and ran at right angles to the jeep's direction, forcing David to turn the wheel and consequently slow down.

Faber could not keep this up much longer. He was certain to tire before David. This had to be the last pass.

He ran faster. David steered an interception course, headed for a point in front of Faber. Faber doubled back, and the jeep zigzagged. It was now quite close. Faber broke into a sprint, his course compelling David to drive in a tight circle. The jeep was getting slower and Faber was getting closer. There were only a few yards between them when David realized what Faber was up to. He steered away, but it was too late. Faber raced to the jeep's side and threw himself upwards, landing face down on top of the canvas roof.

He lay there for a few seconds, catching his breath. His injured foot felt as if it was being held in a fire, and his lungs ached painfully.

The jeep was still moving. Faber drew the stiletto from its sheath under his sleeve and cut a long, jagged tear in the canvas roof. The material flapped downwards and Faber found himself staring at the back of David's head.

David looked up and back. A look of utter astonishment crossed his face. Faber drew back his arm for a knife thrust.

David jammed the throttle open and heaved the wheel around. The jeep leaped forward and lifted on two wheels as it screeched around in a tight curve. Faber struggled to stay on. The jeep, gathering speed still, crashed down on to four wheels then lifted again. It teetered precariously for a few yards, then the wheels slipped on the sodden ground and the vehicle toppled on to its side with a grinding crash.

Faber was thrown several yards and landed awkwardly. The breath was knocked out of him by the impact. It was several seconds before he could move.

The jeep's crazy course had taken it perilously close to the cliff once more.

Faber saw his knife in the grass a few yards away. He picked it up, then turned to the jeep.

Somehow, David had got himself and his wheelchair out through the ripped roof, and he was now sitting in the chair and pushing himself away along the cliff edge. Faber had to acknowledge his courage.

All the same, he had to die.

Faber ran after him. David must have heard the footsteps, for just before Faber caught up the chair stopped dead and spun around; and Faber glimpsed a heavy spanner in David's hand.

Faber crashed into the wheelchair, overturning it. His last thought was that both men and the chair might end up in the sea below – then the spanner hit the back of his head and he blacked out.

When he came to, the wheelchair lay beside him, but David was nowhere to be seen. He stood up and looked around in dazed puzzlement.

'Here! '

The voice came from over the cliff. David must have been flung from the chair and slid over the edge. Faber crawled to the cliff and looked over.

David had one hand around the stem of a bush which grew just under the lip of the cliff. The other hand was jammed into a small crevice in the rock. He hung suspended, just as Faber had a few minutes earlier. His bravado had gone, and there was naked terror in his eyes.

'Pull me up, for God's sake,' he shouted hoarsely.

Faber leaned closer. 'How did you know about the pictures?' he said.

'Help me, please!'

'Tell me about the pictures.'

'Oh, God.' David made a mighty effort to concentrate. 'When you went to Tom's outhouse you left your jacket drying in the kitchen. Tom went upstairs for more whisky, and I went through your pockets. I found the negatives.'

'And that was evidence enough for you to try to kill me?' Faber said wonderingly.

'That, and what you did with my wife in my house. No Englishman would behave like that.'

Faber could not help laughing. 'Where are the negatives now?'

'In my pocket.'

'Give them to me, and I'll pull you up.'

'You'll have to take them – I can't let go.'

Faber lay flat on his stomach and reached down, under David's oilskin, to the breast pocket of his jacket. He gave a sigh of satisfaction as his fingers touched the film can and withdrew it. He looked at the films: they all seemed to be there. He put the can in the pocket of his jacket, buttoned the flap, and reached down to David again.

He took hold of the bush David was clinging to and uprooted it with a savage jerk.

David screamed: 'No!' He scrabbled desperately for grip as his other hand slipped inexorably out of the crack in the rock.

'It's not fair!' he screamed. Then his hand came away from the crevice.

He seemed to hang in mid-air: then he dropped, faster and faster, bouncing twice against the cliff on his way down, until he hit the water with a huge splash.

Faber watched for a while to make sure he did not come up again. 'Not fair?' he murmured to himself. 'Not fair? Don't you know there's a war on?'

He looked down at the sea for some minutes. Once he thought he saw a flash of yellow oilskin on the surface, but it was gone before he could focus on it. There was just the sea and the rocks.

Suddenly he felt terribly tired. His injuries penetrated his consciousness one by one: the damaged foot, the bump on his head, the bruises all over his face. David Rose had been a fool, a braggart and a poor husband, and he had died screaming for mercy; but he had been a brave man too, and he had died for his country – he had got his wish.

Faber wondered whether his own death would be as good.

At last he turned away from the cliff edge and walked back toward the overturned jeep.

CHAPTER TWENTY-EIGHT

PERCIVAL GODLIMAN felt refreshed, determined, even inspired.

When he reflected on it, this made him uncomfortable. Pep-talks are for the rank-and-file, and intellectuals believe themselves immune from inspirational speeches. Yet, although he knew that the great man's performance had been carefully scripted, the crescendos and diminuendos of the speech predetermined like a symphony, nevertheless it had worked on him, as effectively as if he had been the captain of the school cricket team hearing last-minute exhortations from the games master.

He got back to his office itching to do *something*.

He dropped his brolly in the umbrella-stand, hung up his wet raincoat, and looked at himself in the mirror on the inside of the cupboard door. Without doubt something had happened to his face since he became one of England's spycatchers. The other day he had come across a photograph of himself taken in 1937, with a group of students at a seminar in Oxford. In those days he actually looked older than he did now: pale skin, wispy hair, the patchy shave and ill-fitting clothes of a retired man. The wispy hair had gone: he was now bald except for a monkish fringe. His clothes were those of a business executive, not a teacher. It seemed to him – he might, he supposed, have been imagining it – that the set of his jaw was firmer, his eyes were brighter, and he took more care shaving.

He sat down behind his desk and lit a cigarette. *That* innovation was not welcome: he had developed a cough, tried to give it up, and discovered that he had become addicted. But almost everybody smoked in wartime Britain, even some of the women. Well, they were doing men's jobs – they were entitled to masculine vices. The smoke caught in Godliman's throat, making him cough. He put the cigarette out in the tin-lid he used for an ashtray (crockery was scarce).

The trouble with being inspired to perform the impossible, he reflected, was that the inspiration gave you no clues to the practical means. He recalled his college thesis, about the travels of an obscure medieval monk called Thomas of the Tree. Godliman had set himself the minor but difficult task of plotting the monk's itinerary over a five-year period. There had been a baffling gap of eight months when he had been either in Paris or Canterbury, but Godliman had been unable to determine which, and this had threatened the value of the whole project. The records he was using simply did not contain the information. If the monk's stay had gone unrecorded, then there was no way to find out where he had been, and that was that. With the optimism of youth, young Godliman had refused to believe that the information was just not there, and he had worked on the assumption that *somewhere* there had to be a record of how Thomas had spent those months – despite the well-known fact that almost everything that happened in the Middle Ages went unrecorded. If Thomas was not in Paris or Canterbury he must have been in transit between the two, Godliman had argued; and then he had found shipping records in an Amsterdam museum which showed that Thomas had boarded a vessel bound for Dover which got blown off course and was eventually wrecked on the Irish coast. This model piece of historical research had got Godliman his professorship.

He might try applying that kind of thinking to the problem of what had happened to Faber.

It was most likely that Faber had drowned. If he had not, then he was probably in Germany by now. Neither of those possibilities presented any course of action that Godliman could follow, so they should be discounted. He must assume that Faber was alive and had reached land somewhere.

He left his office and went down one flight of stairs to the map room. His uncle, Colonel Terry, was there, standing in front of the map of Europe with a cigarette between his lips, thinking. Godliman realized that this was a familiar sight in the War Office these days: senior men gazing entranced at maps, silently making their own computations of whether the war would be won or lost. He guessed it was because all the plans had been made, the vast machine had been set in motion, and for those who made the big decisions there was nothing to do but wait and see if they had been right.

Terry saw him come in, and said: 'How did you get on with the great man?'

'He was drinking whisky,' Godliman said.

'He drinks all day, but it never seems to make any difference to him,' Terry said. 'What did he say?'

'He wants Die Nadel's head on a platter.' Godliman crossed the room to the wall map of Great Britain and put a finger on Aberdeen. 'If you were sending a U-boat in to pick up a fugitive spy, what would you think was the nearest the sub could safely come to the coast?'

Terry stood beside him and looked at the map. 'I wouldn't want to come closer than the three-mile limit. But for preference, I'd stop ten miles out.'

'Right.' Godliman drew two pencil lines parallel to the coast, three miles and ten miles out respectively. 'Now, if you were an amateur sailor setting out from Aberdeen in a smallish fishing boat, how far would you go before you began to get nervous?'

'You mean, what's a reasonable distance to travel in such a boat?'

'Indeed.'

Terry shrugged. 'Ask the Navy. I'd say fifteen or twenty miles.'

'I agree.' Godliman drew an arc of twenty miles radius with its centre on Aberdeen. 'Now: if Faber is alive, he's either back on the mainland or somewhere within this space.' He indicated the area bounded by the parallel lines and the arc.

'There's no land in that area.'

'Have we got a bigger map?'

Terry pulled open a drawer and got out a large-scale

map of Scotland. He spread it on top of the chest. Godliman copied the pencil marks from the smaller map on to the larger.

There was still no land within the area.

'But look,' Godliman said. Just to the east of the ten-mile limit was a long, narrow island.

Terry peered closer. 'Storm Island,' he read. 'How apt.'

Godliman snapped his fingers. 'I'll bet that's where he is.'

'Can you send someone there?'

'When the storm clears. Bloggs is up there: I'll get a plane laid on for him. He can take off the minute the weather improves.' He went to the door.

'Good luck!' Terry called after him.

Godliman ran up the stairs to the next floor and entered his office. He picked up the phone. 'Get Mr Bloggs in Aberdeen, please.'

While he waited he doodled on his blotter, drawing the island. It was shaped like the top half of a walking-stick, with the crook at the western end. It must have been about ten miles long, and perhaps a mile wide. He wondered what sort of place it was: was it a barren lump of rock, or a thriving community of crofters? If Faber was there he might still be able to contact his U-boat: Bloggs would have to get to the island before the submarine. It would be difficult.

'I have Mr Bloggs,' the switchboard girl said.

'Fred?'

'Hello, Percy.'

'I think he's on an island called Storm Island.'

'No, he's not,' Bloggs said. 'We've just arrested him.'

The stiletto was nine inches long, with an engraved handle and a stubby little crosspiece. Its needle-like point was extremely sharp. Bloggs thought it looked like a highly efficient killing instrument. It had recently been polished.

Bloggs and Detective-Chief-Inspector Kincaid stood looking at it, neither man wanting to touch it.

'He was trying to catch a bus to Edinburgh,' Kincaid said. 'A PC spotted him at the ticket office and asked for his identification. He dropped his suitcase and ran away. A woman bus-conductor hit him over the head with her ticket machine. He took ten minutes to come around.'

'Let's have a look at him,' Bloggs said.

They went down the corridor to the cells. 'This one,' Kincaid said.

Bloggs looked through the judas. The man sat on a stool in the far corner of the cell with his back against the wall. His legs were crossed, his eyes closed, his hands in his pockets. 'He's been in cells before,' Bloggs remarked. The man was tall, with a long, handsome face and dark hair. It could have been the man in the photograph, but it was hard to be certain.

'Want to go in?' Kincaid asked.

'In a minute. What was in his suitcase, apart from the stiletto?'

'The tools of a burglar's trade. Quite a lot of money

in small notes. A pistol and some ammunition. Black clothes and crepe-soled shoes. Two hundred Lucky Strike cigarettes.'

'No photographs?'

Kincaid shook his head.

'Balls,' Bloggs said feelingly.

'Papers identify him as Peter Fredericks, of Wembley, Middlesex. Says he's an unemployed toolmaker looking for work.'

'Toolmaker?' Bloggs said sceptically. 'There hasn't been an unemployed toolmaker in Britain in the last four years. You'd think a spy would know that. Still . . .'

Kincaid asked: 'Shall I start the questioning, or will you?'

'You.'

Kincaid opened the door and Bloggs followed him in. The man in the corner opened his eyes incuriously. He did not alter his position.

Kincaid sat at a small, plain table. Bloggs leaned against the wall.

Kincaid said: 'What's your real name?'

'Peter Fredericks.'

'What are you doing so far from home?'

'Looking for work.'

'Why aren't you in the Army?'

'Weak heart.'

'Where have you been for the last few days?'

'Here, in Aberdeen. Before that Dundee, before that Perth.'

'When did you arrive in Aberdeen?'

'The day before yesterday.'

Kincaid glanced at Bloggs, who nodded. Kincaid said: 'Your story is silly. Toolmakers don't need to look for work. The country hasn't got enough of them. You'd better tell the truth.'

'I'm telling the truth.'

Bloggs took all the loose change out of his pocket and tied it up in his handkerchief. He stood watching, saying nothing, swinging the little bundle in his right hand.

'Where are the photographs?' Kincaid said.

The man's expression did not change. 'I don't know what you're talking about.'

Kincaid shrugged, and looked at Bloggs.

Bloggs said: 'On your feet.'

'Pardon?' the man said.

'On your FEET!' Bloggs bawled.

The man stood up casually.

'Forward!'

He took two steps up to the table.

'Name?'

'Peter Fredericks.'

Bloggs came off the wall and hit the man with the weighted handkerchief. The blow caught him accurately on the bridge of the nose, and he cried out. His hands went to his face.

'Stand to attention!' Bloggs shouted. 'Name!'

The man stood upright, let his hands fall to his sides, and whispered: 'Peter Fredericks.'

Bloggs hit him again in exactly the same place. This time he went down on one knee, and his eyes watered.

'Where are the photographs?' Bloggs screamed.

The man shook his head dumbly.

Bloggs pulled him to his feet, kneed him in the groin, and punched his stomach. 'What did you do with the negatives?'

The man fell to the floor and threw up. Bloggs kicked his face. There was a sharp crack, as if something had broken. 'What about the U-boat? Where is the rendezvous? What is the signal?'

Kincaid grabbed Bloggs from behind. 'That's enough, Bloggs,' he said. 'This is my station, and I can only turn a blind eye for so long, you know.'

Bloggs rounded on him. 'We're not dealing with a case of petty housebreaking, Kincaid – this man is jeopardizing the whole war effort.' He wagged a finger under the detective's nose. 'Just remember: I'm MI5, and I'll do what I fucking well like in your station. If the prisoner dies, I'll take responsibility.' He turned back to the man on the floor.

The man was staring at Bloggs and Kincaid. His face, covered with blood, showed an expression of incredulity. 'What are you talking about?' he said weakly. 'What is this?'

Bloggs hauled him to his feet again. 'You are Henrik Rudolph Hans von Muller-Guder, born at Oln on 26 May 1900; also known as Henry Faber; a lieutenant-colonel in German Intelligence. Within three months you will be hanged for espionage, unless you turn out to be more useful to us dead than alive. You'd better start making yourself useful, Colonel Muller-Guder.'

'No,' the man said. 'No, no! I'm a thief, not a spy. Please!' He cowered away from Bloggs's upraised fist. 'I can prove it.'

Bloggs hit him again, and Kincaid intervened for the second time. 'Wait,' the detective said. 'All right, Fredericks – if that's your name – prove you're a thief.'

'I done three houses in Jubilee Crescent last week,' the man gasped. 'I took about five hundred quid from one and some jewellery from the next one – diamond rings and some pearls – and I never got nothing from the other one because of the dog ... you must know I'm telling the truth, they must have reported it, didn't they? Oh, Jesus—'

Kincaid looked at Bloggs. 'All those burglaries took place.'

'He could have read about them in the newspapers.'

'The third one wasn't reported.'

'Perhaps he did them – he could still be a spy. Spies can steal.'

'But this was last week – your man was in London, wasn't he?'

Bloggs was silent for a moment. Then he said: 'Well, fuck it,' and walked out.

Peter Fredericks looked up at Kincaid through a mask of blood. 'Who's he, the bleedin' Gestapo?' he said.

Kincaid stared at him thoughtfully. 'Be glad you're not really the man he's looking for.'

*

'Well?' Godliman said into the phone.

'False alarm.' Bloggs's voice was scratchy and distorted over the long-distance line. 'A small-time housebreaker who happens to carry a stiletto and look like Faber.'

'Back to square one,' Godliman said. 'Damn.'

'You said something about an island.'

'Yes. Storm Island – it's about ten miles off the coast, due east of Aberdeen. You'll find it on a large-scale map.'

'What makes you sure he's there?'

'I'm not sure; not at all. We still have to cover every other possibility – other towns, the coast, everything. But if he did steal that boat, the . . . ?'

'*Marie II.*'

'Yes. If he did steal it, his rendezvous was probably in the area of this island; and if I'm right about *that*, then he's either drowned or shipwrecked on the island.'

'Okay, that makes sense.'

'What's the weather like up there?'

'No change.'

'Could you reach the island in a big ship?'

Bloggs grunted. 'I suppose you can ride any storm if your ship's big enough. But this island won't have much of a dock, will it?'

'You'd better find out. However, I expect you're right. Now listen: there's an RAF fighter base near Edinburgh. By the time you get there, I'll have an amphibious plane standing by. You take off the minute the storm begins to clear. Have the local coastguard ready to move at a moment's notice, too – I'm not sure who'll get there first.'

'Mm.' Bloggs sounded dubious. 'If the U-boat is also waiting for the storm to clear, it will get there first.'

'You're right.' Godliman lit a cigarette, fumbling for inspiration. 'Well, we can get a Navy corvette to circle the island and listen for Faber's radio signal. When the storm clears it can land a boat on the island. Yes, that's a good idea.'

'What about some fighters?'

'Yes. Although like you, they'll have to wait until the weather breaks.'

'It can't go on much longer.'

'What do the Scottish meteorologists say?'

'Another day of it, at least.'

'Damn.'

'It doesn't make much difference,' Bloggs said. 'All the time we're grounded he's bottled up.'

'If he's there at all.'

'Yes.'

'All right,' Godliman said. 'We'll have a corvette, the coastguard, some fighters and an amphibian.'

'And me.'

'You'd better get on your way. Call me from Rosyth. Take care.'

'Cheerio.'

Godliman hung up. His cigarette, neglected in the ashtray, had burned down to a tiny stub. He lit another, then picked up the phone again and began organizing.

CHAPTER TWENTY-NINE

LYING ON its side, the jeep looked powerful but helpless, like a wounded elephant. The engine had stalled. Faber gave it a hefty push and it toppled majestically on to all four wheels. It had survived the fight relatively undamaged. The canvas roof was destroyed, of course: the rip Faber's knife had made had become a long tear running from one side to the other. The offside front wing, which had ploughed into the earth and stopped the vehicle, was crumpled. The headlight on that side had smashed. The window on the same side had been broken by the shot from the gun. The windscreen was miraculously intact.

Faber climbed into the driving seat, put the gearshift into neutral, and tried the starter. It kicked over and died. He tried again, and the engine fired. He sighed with relief: he could not have faced a long walk just then.

He sat in the car for a while, inventorying his wounds. He touched his right ankle gingerly: it was swelling massively. Perhaps he had cracked a bone. It was as well that the jeep was designed to be driven by a man with no legs, for Faber could not have pressed a brake pedal. The lump on the back of his head felt huge, the size of a golf ball; and when he touched it his hand came away sticky with blood. He examined his face in the driving mirror. It was a mass of small cuts and big bruises, like the face of the loser at the end of a boxing match.

He had abandoned his oilskin back at the cottage, so his jacket and overalls were soggy with rain and smeared with mud. He needed to get warm and dry very soon.

He gripped the steering wheel, and a burning pain shot through his hand: he had forgotten the torn fingernail. He looked at it. It was the nastiest of his injuries. He would have to drive one-handed.

He pulled away slowly and found what he guessed was the road. There was no danger of getting lost on this island – all he had to do was follow the cliff-edge until he came to Lucy's cottage.

He needed to invent a lie to explain to Lucy what had become of her husband. He might, of course, tell her the truth: there was nothing she could do about it. However, if she became awkward he might have to kill her; and there had grown within him an aversion to killing Lucy. Driving slowly along the cliff-top through the pouring rain and howling wind, he marvelled at this new thing inside him, this scruple. It was the first time he had ever felt reluctance to kill. It was not that he was amoral: quite the contrary. He had made up his mind that the killing he did was on the same moral level as death on the battlefield, and his emotions followed his intellect. He always had the physical reaction, the vomiting, after he killed, but that was some thing incomprehensible which he ignored.

So why did he not want to kill Lucy?

The feeling was on a par with the affection which drove him to send the Luftwaffe erroneous directions to St Paul's Cathedral: a compulsion to protect a thing of beauty. She was a remarkable creation, as full of loveliness and subtlety as a work of art. Faber could live with himself as a killer, but not as an iconoclast. It was, he recognized as soon as the thought occurred to him, a peculiar way to be. But then, spies were peculiar people.

He thought of some of the spies who had been recruited by the Abwehr at the same time as he: Otto, the Nordic giant who made delicate paper sculptures in the Japanese fashion and hated women; Friedrich, the sly little mathematical genius who jumped at shadows and went into a five-day depression if he lost a game of chess; Helmut, who liked to read books about slavery in America and had soon joined the SS . . . all different, all peculiar. If they had anything more specific in common, he did not know what it was.

He seemed to be driving more and more slowly, and the rain and mist became more impenetrable. He began to worry about the cliff-edge on his left-hand side. He felt very hot, but suffered spasms of shivering. He realized he had been speaking aloud about Otto and Friedrich and Helmut; and he recognized the signs of delirium. He made an effort to think of nothing but the problem of keeping the jeep on a straight course.

The noise of the wind took on some kind of rhythm, becoming hypnotic. Once he found himself stationary, staring out over the sea, and had no idea how long he had stopped.

It seemed hours later that Lucy's cottage came into view. He steered toward it, thinking: I must remember to put the brake on before I hit the wall. There was a figure standing in the doorway, looking at him through the rain. He had to stay in control of himself long enough to tell her the lie. He had to remember, had to remember . . .

It was late afternoon by the time the jeep came back. Lucy was worried about what had happened to the men, and at the same time angry with them for not coming home for the lunch she had prepared. As the day waned she had spent more and more time at the windows, looking out for them.

When the jeep came down the slight slope to the cottage, it was clear something was wrong. It was moving terribly slowly, weaving all over the track, and there was only one person in it. It came closer, and she saw that the front was dented and the headlamp smashed.

'Oh, God,' she murmured.

The vehicle shuddered to a halt in front of the cottage, and she saw that the figure inside was Henry. He made no move to get out. Lucy ran out into the rain and opened the driver's door.

Henry sat there with his head back and his eyes half-closed. His hand was on the brake. His face was bloody and bruised.

Lucy said: 'What happened? *What happened?*'

Henry's hand slipped off the brake, and the jeep moved forward. Lucy leaned across him and slipped the gearshift into neutral.

Henry said: 'Left David at Tom's cottage . . . had crash on way back . . .' The words seemed to cost him a great effort.

Now that she knew what had happened, Lucy's panic subsided. 'Come inside,' she said sharply. The urgency in her voice got through to Henry. He turned toward her, put his foot on the running board to step down, and promptly fell to the ground. Lucy saw that his ankle was swollen like a balloon.

She got her hands under his shoulders and pulled him upright, saying: 'Put your weight on the other foot and lean on me.' She got his right arm around her neck and half-carried him inside.

Jo watched wide-eyed as she helped Henry into the living-room and got him on to the sofa. He lay back with his eyes shut. His clothes were soaked and muddy.

Lucy said: 'Jo, go upstairs and get your pyjamas on, please.'

'But I haven't had my story. Is *he* dead?'

'He's not dead, but he's had a car crash, and you can't have a story tonight. Go on.'

The child made a complaining sound, and Lucy looked threateningly at him. He went.

Lucy got the big scissors out of her sewing basket

and cut Henry's clothes away: first the jacket, then the overalls, then the shirt. She frowned in puzzlement when she saw the knife in its sheath strapped to his left forearm: she guessed it was a special implement for cleaning fish, or something. When she tried to take it off, Henry pushed her hand away. She shrugged, and turned her attention to his boots. The left one came off easily, and its sock; but he cried out in pain when she touched the right.

'It must come off,' she told him. 'You'll have to be brave.'

A funny kind of smile came over his face, then, and he nodded assent. She cut the laces, took the shoe gently but firmly in both hands, and pulled it off. This time he made no sound. She cut the elastic in the sock and pulled that off too.

Jo came in and said: 'He's in his pants!'

'His clothes are all wet.' She kissed the boy goodnight. 'Put yourself to bed, darling. I'll tuck you up later.'

'Kiss teddy, then.'

'Goodnight, teddy.'

Jo went out. Lucy looked back to Henry. His eyes were open, and he was smiling. He said: 'Kiss Henry, then.'

She leaned over him and kissed his battered face. Then, carefully, she cut away his underpants.

The heat from the fire would quickly dry his naked skin. She went into the kitchen and filled a bowl with warm water and a little antiseptic to bathe his wounds.

She found a roll of cotton wool and returned to the living-room.

'This is the second time you've turned up on the doorstep half dead,' she said as she set about her task.

'The usual signal,' Henry said.

'What?'

'Waiting at Calais for a phantom army.'

'Henry, what are you talking about?'

'Every Friday and Monday.'

She realized he was delirious. 'Don't try to talk,' she said. She lifted his head slightly to clean away the dried blood from around the bump.

Suddenly he sat upright, looked fiercely at her, and said: 'What day is it? What day is it?'

'It's Sunday, relax.'

'Okay.'

He was quiet after that, and he let her remove the knife. She bathed his face, bandaged his finger where he had lost the nail, and put a dressing on his ankle. When she had finished she stood looking at him for a while. He seemed to be sleeping. She touched the long scar on his chest, and the star-shaped mark on his hip. The star was a birthmark, she decided.

She went through his pockets before throwing the lacerated clothes away. There wasn't much: some money, his papers, a leather wallet and a film can. She put them all in a little pile on the mantelpiece beside his fish knife. He would have to have some of David's clothes.

She left him and went upstairs to see Jo. The boy was

asleep, lying on his teddy bear, with his arms outflung. She kissed his soft cheek and tucked him in. She went outside and put the jeep in the barn.

She made herself a drink in the kitchen then sat watching Henry, wishing he would wake up and make love to her again.

It was almost midnight when he awoke. He opened his eyes, and his face showed the series of expressions which were now familiar to her: first the fear, then the wary survey of the room, then the relaxation. On impulse, she asked him: 'What are you afraid of, Henry?'

'I don't know what you mean.'

'You always look frightened when you wake up.'

'I don't know.' He shrugged, and the movement seemed to hurt. 'God, I'm battered.'

'Do you want to tell me what happened?'

'Yes, if you'll give me a small amount of brandy.'

She got the brandy out of the cupboard. 'You can have some of David's clothes.'

'In a minute . . . unless you're embarrassed.'

She handed him the glass, smiling. 'I'm afraid I'm enjoying it.'

'What happened to my clothes?'

'I had to cut them off you. I've thrown them away.'

'Not my papers, I hope.' He smiled, but there was some other emotion just below the surface.

'On the mantelpiece.' She pointed. 'I suppose that knife is for cleaning fish, or something.'

His right hand went to his left forearm, where the sheath had been. 'Something like that,' he said. He seemed uneasy for a moment, then relaxed with an effort and sipped his drink. 'That's good.'

After a moment she said: 'Well?'

'What?'

'How did you manage to lose my husband and crash my jeep?'

'David decided to stay over at Tom's for the night. Some of the sheep got into trouble in a place they called the Gully—'

'I know it.'

'—and six or seven of them were injured. They're all in Tom's kitchen, being bandaged up and making a frightful row. Anyway, David suggested I came back to tell you he would be staying. I don't really know how I managed to crash. The car is unfamiliar, there's no real road, I hit something and went into a skid, and the jeep ended up on its side. The details . . .' he shrugged.

'You must have been going quite fast – you were in an awful mess when you got here.'

'I suppose I rattled around inside the jeep a bit. Banged my head, twisted my ankle . . .'

'Lost a fingernail, bashed your face, and almost caught pneumonia. You must be accident-prone.'

He swung his legs to the floor, stood up, and went to the mantelpiece.

Lucy said: 'Your powers of recuperation are incredible.'

He was strapping the knife to his arm. 'We fishermen are very healthy. What about those clothes?'

She got up and stood close to him. 'What do you need clothes for? It's bedtime.'

He drew her to him, pressing her against his naked body, and kissed her hard. She stroked his thighs.

After a while he broke away from her. He picked up his things from the mantelpiece, took her hand, then, hobbling, he led her upstairs to bed.

CHAPTER THIRTY

T HE WIDE, white autobahn snaked through the
Bavarian valley up into the mountains. In the
leather rear seat of the staff Mercedes, Field Marshal
Gerd von Rundstedt was still and weary. Aged sixty-
nine, he knew he was too fond of champagne and not
fond enough of Hitler. His thin, lugubrious face
reflected a career longer and more erratic than that of
any of Hitler's other officers: he had been dismissed in
disgrace more times than he could remember, but the
Führer always asked him to come back.

As the car passed through the sixteenth-century
village of Berchtesgaden, he wondered why he always
returned to his command when Hitler forgave him.
Money meant nothing to him: he had already achieved
the highest possible rank; decorations were valueless in
the Third Reich; and he believed that it was not possible
to win honour in this war.

It was Rundstedt who had first called Hitler 'the
Bohemian corporal'. The little man knew nothing of
the German military tradition, nor – despite his flashes
of inspiration – of military strategy. If he had, he would
not have started this war, for it was unwinnable. Rundstedt was Germany's finest soldier, and he had proved

it in Poland, France and Russia; but he had no hope of victory.

All the same, he would have nothing to do with the small group of generals who – he knew – were plotting to overthrow Hitler. He turned a blind eye to them, but the *Fahneneid*, the blood oath of the German warrior, was too strong within him to permit him to join the conspiracy. And that, he supposed, was why he continued to serve the Reich. Right or wrong, his country was in danger, and he had no option but to protect it. I'm like an old cavalry horse, he thought: if I stayed at home I should feel ashamed.

He commanded five armies on the Western front, now. A million and a half men were under him. They were not as strong as they might be – some divisions were little better than rest homes for invalids from the Russian front, there was a shortage of armour, and there were many non-German conscripts among the other ranks – but Rundstedt could still keep the Allies out of France if he deployed his forces shrewdly.

It was that deployment that he must now discuss with Hitler.

The car climbed the Kehlsteinstrasse until the road ended at a vast bronze door in the side of the Kehlstein Mountain. An SS guard touched a button, the door hummed open, and the car entered a long marble tunnel lit by bronze lanterns. At the far end of the tunnel the driver stopped the car, and Rundstedt walked to the elevator and sat in one of its leather seats for the four-hundred-foot ascent to the Adlerhorst, the Eagle's Nest.

In the anteroom Rattenhuber took his pistol and left him to wait. He stared unappreciatively at Hitler's porcelain and went over in his mind the words he would say.

A few moments later the blond bodyguard returned to usher him into the conference room.

The place made him think of an eighteenth-century palace. The walls were covered with oil paintings and tapestries, and there was a bust of Wagner and a huge clock with a bronze eagle on its top. The view from the side window was truly remarkable: one could see the hills of Salzburg and the peak of the Untersberg, the mountain where the body of the Emperor Frederick Barbarossa waited, according to legend, to rise from the grave and save the Fatherland. Inside the room, seated in the peculiarly rustic chairs, were Hitler and just three of his staff: Admiral Theodor Krancke, the naval commander in the west; General Alfred Jodl, chief of staff; and Admiral Karl Jesko von Puttkamer, Hitler's aide-de-camp.

Rundstedt saluted and was motioned to a chair. A footman brought a plate of caviar sandwiches and a glass of champagne. Hitler stood at the large window, looking out, with his hands clasped behind his back. Without turning, he said abruptly: 'Rundstedt has changed his mind. He now agrees with Rommel that the Allies will invade Normandy. This is what my instinct has all along told me. Krancke, however, still favours Calais. Rundstedt, tell Krancke how you arrived at your conclusion.'

Rundstedt swallowed a mouthful and coughed into

his hand. Damn, Hitler had no manners: didn't even give a chap a chance to catch his breath. 'There are two things: one new piece of information and one new line of reasoning,' Rundstedt began. 'First, the information. The latest summaries of Allied bombing in France show without doubt that their principal aim is to destroy every bridge across the River Seine. Now, if they land at Calais the Seine is irrelevant to the battle; but if they land in Normandy all our reserves have to cross the Seine to reach the zone of conflict.

'Second, the reasoning. I have given some thought to how I would invade France if I were commanding the Allied forces. My conclusion is that the first goal must be to establish a bridgehead through which men and supplies can be funnelled at speed. The initial thrust must therefore come in the region of a large and roomy harbour. The natural choice is Cherbourg.

'Both the bombing pattern and the strategic requirements point to Normandy,' he finished. He picked up his glass and emptied it, and the footman came forward to refill it.

Jodl said: 'All our intelligence points to Calais—'

'And we have just executed the head of the Abwehr as a traitor,' Hitler interrupted. 'Krancke, are you convinced?'

'My Führer, I am not,' the Admiral said. 'I, too, have considered how I would conduct the invasion if I were on the other side – but I have brought into the reasoning a number of factors of a nautical nature of which Rundstedt may not have been aware. I believe they will attack under cover of darkness, by moonlight, at full tide to sail over Rommel's underwater obstacles, and away from cliffs, rocky waters and strong currents. Normandy? Never.'

Hitler shook his head in disgusted disagreement. Jodl said: 'There is another small piece of information which I find significant. The Guards Armoured Division has been transferred from the north of England to Hove, on the south-east coast, to join the First United States Army Group under General Patton. We learned this from wireless surveillance – there was a baggage mix-up en route, one unit had another's silver cutlery, and the fools have been quarrelling about it over the radio. This is a crack British division, very blue-blooded, commanded by General Sir Allan Henry Shafto Adair. I feel sure they will not be far from the centre of the battle when it comes.'

Hitler's hands moved nervously, and his face twitched in an agony of indecision. 'Generals!' he barked at them. 'Either I get conflicting advice, or no advice at all! I have to tell you everything – everything!'

With characteristic boldness, Rundstedt plunged on. 'My Führer, you have four superb panzer divisions doing nothing here in Germany. If I am right, they will never get to Normandy in time to repel the invasion. I beg you, order them to France and put them under Rommel's command. If we are wrong, and the invasion begins at Calais, they will still be close enough to enter the battle at an early stage.'

'I don't know – I don't know!' Hitler's eyes widened, and Rundstedt wondered if he had pushed too hard – again.

Puttkamer spoke for the first time. 'My Führer, today is Sunday.'

'Well?'

'Tomorrow night the U-boat may pick up the spy, Die Nadel.'

'Ah, yes! Someone I can trust.'

'Of course, he can report by radio at any time. However, there may be some reason for him to avoid the radio; in which case he would bring his information personally. Given this possibility, you may like to consider postponing your decision for twenty-four hours, in case he does contact us, one way or the other, today or tomorrow.'

Rundstedt said: 'There isn't time to postpone decisions. Both air attacks and sabotage activities have increased dramatically. The invasion may come any day.'

'I disagree,' Krancke said. 'The weather conditions will not be right until early June.'

'That is not very far away!'

'Enough!' Hitler shouted. 'I have made up my mind. My panzers stay in Germany – for now. On Tuesday, when we have heard from Die Nadel, I will reconsider the disposition of these forces. If his information favours Normandy – as I believe it will – I will move the panzers.'

Rundstedt said softly: 'And if he does not report?'

'If he does not report, I shall reconsider just the same.'

Rundstedt bowed assent. 'With your permission, I shall return to my command.'

'Very well.'

Rundstedt got to his feet, saluted and went out. In the copper-lined elevator, falling four hundred feet to the underground garage, he felt his stomach turn over, and wondered whether the sensation was caused by the speed of descent or by the thought that the destiny of his country lay in the hands of a single, lonely spy.

Part Six

CHAPTER THIRTY-ONE

LUCY WOKE up slowly. She rose gradually, languidly, from the warm void of deep sleep, up through layers of unconsciousness, perceiving the world piece by isolated piece: first the warm, hard male body beside her; then the strangeness of the little bed; the noise of the storm outside, as angry and tireless as yesterday and the day before; the faint smell of the man's skin; her arm across his chest, her leg thrown across his as if to keep him there, her breasts pressed against his side; the light of day beating against her eyelids; the regular, light breathing that blew softly across her face; and then, all at once like the solution to a puzzle, the realization that she was flagrantly and adulterously lying with a man she had met only forty-eight hours before, and that they were naked in bed in her husband's house.

She opened her eyes and saw Jo.

He was standing beside the bed in his rumpled pyjamas, hair tousled, a battered rag doll under his arm, sucking his thumb and staring wide-eyed at his mummy and the strange man cuddling each other in his, Jo's, bed. Lucy could not read his expression, for at this time of day he stared wide-eyed at most things, as if all the world was new and marvellous every morning. She stared back at him in silence, not knowing what to say.

Then Henry's deep voice said: 'Good morning.'

Jo took his thumb out of his mouth, said: 'Good morning,' turned around and went out of the bedroom.

Lucy said: 'Damn, damn, damn.'

Henry slid down in the bed until his face was level with hers, and kissed her. His hand went between her thighs and held her possessively.

She pushed him away. 'For God's sake, stop.'

'Why?'

'Jo's seen us!'

'So what?'

'He can talk, you know. Sooner or later he'll say something to David. What am I going to do?'

'Do nothing. So David finds out. Does it matter?'

'Of course it matters.'

'I don't see why. He has wronged you, and this is the consequence. You shouldn't feel guilty.'

Lucy suddenly realized that Henry simply had no conception of the complex tangle of loyalties and obligations that constituted a marriage. She said: 'It's not *that* simple.'

She got out of bed and crossed the landing to her own bedroom. She slipped into knickers, trousers and a sweater, then remembered she had destroyed all Henry's clothes and had to lend him some of David's. She found underwear and socks, a knitted shirt and a V-necked pullover, and finally – right at the bottom of a trunk – one pair of trousers that were not cut off at the knee and sewn up. All the while Jo watched her in silence.

She took the clothes into the other bedroom. Henry had gone into the bathroom to shave. She called through the door: 'Your clothes are on the bed.'

She went downstairs, lit the stove in the kitchen, and put a saucepan of water on to heat. She decided to have boiled eggs for breakfast. She washed Jo's face at the kitchen sink, combed his hair, and dressed him quickly. 'You're very quiet this morning,' she said brightly. He made no reply.

Henry came down and sat at the table, as naturally as if he had been doing it every morning for years. Lucy felt very weird, seeing him there in David's clothes, handing him a breakfast egg, putting a rack of toast on the table in front of him.

Jo said suddenly: 'Is my daddy dead?'

Henry gave the boy a queer look and said nothing.

Lucy said: 'Don't be silly. He's at Tom's house.'

Jo ignored her and spoke to Henry. 'You've got my daddy's clothes, *and* you've got my mummy. Are you going to be my daddy now?'

Lucy muttered: 'Out of the mouth of babes and sucklings . . .'

Henry said: 'Didn't you see my clothes last night?'

Jo nodded.

'Well, then, you know why I had to borrow some of your daddy's clothes. I'll give them back to him when I get some more of my own.'

'Will you give my mummy back?'

'Of course.'

389

Lucy said: 'Eat your egg, Jo.'

The child tucked into his breakfast, apparently satisfied. Lucy was gazing out of the kitchen window. 'The boat won't come today,' she said.

'Are you glad?' Henry asked her.

She looked at him. 'I don't know.'

Lucy did not feel hungry. She drank a cup of tea while Jo and Henry ate. Afterwards, Jo went upstairs to play and Henry cleared the table. As he stacked crockery in the sink he said: 'Are you afraid David will hurt you, physically?'

She shook her head in negation.

'You should forget him,' Henry went on. 'You were planning to leave him anyway. Why should it concern you whether he finds out or not?'

'He's my *husband*,' she said. 'That counts for something. The kind of husband he's been ... all that ... doesn't give me the right to humiliate him.'

'I think it gives you the right not to care whether he's humiliated or not.'

'It's not a question that can be settled logically. It's just the way I *feel*.'

He made a giving-up gesture with his arms. 'I'd better drive over to Tom's and find out whether your *husband* wants to come back. Where are my boots?'

'In the living-room. I'll get you a jacket.' She went upstairs and got David's old hacking jacket out of the wardrobe. It was a fine grey-green tweed, very elegant with a nipped-in waist and slanted pocket flaps. Lucy had put leather patches on the elbows to preserve it: you couldn't buy clothes like this any more. She took it down to the living-room, where Henry was putting his boots on. He had laced the left one, and was gingerly inserting his injured right foot into the other. Lucy knelt to help him.

'The swelling has gone down,' she said.

'The damn thing still hurts.'

They got the boot on, but left it untied and took the lace out. Henry stood up experimentally.

'It's okay,' he said.

Lucy helped him into the jacket. It was a little tight across the shoulders. 'We haven't got another oilskin,' she said.

'Then I'll get wet.' He pulled her to him and kissed her roughly. She put her arms around him and held tightly for a moment.

'Drive more carefully today,' she said.

He smiled and nodded, kissed her again – briefly this time – and went out. She watched him limp across to the barn, and stood at the window while he started the jeep and drove away, up the slight rise and out of sight. When he had gone she felt relieved, but somehow empty.

She began to put the house straight, making beds and washing dishes, cleaning and tidying; but she could summon up no enthusiasm for the task. She was restless. She worried at the problem of what to do with her life, following old arguments around in familiar circles, unable to put her mind to anything else. She found the cottage claustrophobic instead of snug. There was a big world out there somewhere, a world of war and heroism, full of colour and passion and people, millions of people; she wanted to be out there in the midst of it, to meet new minds and see cities and hear music. She turned on the radio: a futile gesture, for the news broadcast made her feel more isolated, not less. There was a battle report from Italy, the rationing regulations had been eased a little, the London stiletto murderer was still at large, Roosevelt had made a speech. Sandy Macpherson began to play a theatre organ, and Lucy switched off. None of it touched her, for she did not live in that world.

She wanted to scream.

She had to get out of the house, despite the weather. It would be only a symbolic escape, for the stone walls of the cottage were not what imprisoned her; but the symbol was better than nothing. She collected Jo from upstairs, separating him with some difficulty from a regiment of toy soldiers, and wrapped him up in waterproof clothing.

'Why are we going out?' he asked.

'To see if the boat comes.'

'You said it won't come today.'

'Just in case.'

They put bright yellow sou'westers on their heads, lacing them under their chins, and stepped outside the door.

The wind was like a physical blow, unbalancing Lucy so that she staggered. In seconds her face was as wet as if she had dipped it in a bowl, and the ends of hair protruding from under her hat lay limp and clinging on her cheeks and the shoulders of her oilskin. Jo screamed with delight and jumped in a puddle.

They walked along the cliff-top to the head of the bay, and looked down at the huge North Sea rollers hurling themselves to destruction against the cliffs and on the beach. The storm had uprooted underwater vegetation from God-only-knew what depth and flung it in heaps on the sand and rocks. Mother and son became absorbed in the ceaselessly shifting patterns of the waves. They had done this before: the sea had a hypnotic effect on both of them, and Lucy was never quite sure, afterwards, how long they had spent silently watching.

The spell was broken this time by something she saw. At first there was only a flash of colour in the trough of a wave, so fleeting that she was not certain what colour it had been, so small and far away that she immediately doubted whether she had seen it at all. She looked for it, but did not see it again, and her gaze drifted back to the bay and the little jetty, on which flotsam gathered in drifts only to be swept away by the next big wave. After the storm, on the first fine day, she and Jo would go beachcombing to see what treasures the sea had disgorged, and come back with oddly coloured rocks, bits of wood of mystifying origin, huge seashells and twisted fragments of rusted metal.

She saw the flash of colour again, much nearer, and this time it stayed within sight for a few seconds. It was bright yellow, the colour of all their oilskins. She peered at it through the sheets of rain, but could not identify its shape before it disappeared again. But the current was bringing it closer, as it brought everything to the bay, depositing its rubbish on the sand like a man emptying his trouser pockets on to a table.

It *was* an oilskin: she could see that when the sea lifted it on the crest of a wave and showed it to her for the third and final time. Henry had come back without his, yesterday, but how had it got into the sea? The wave broke over the jetty and flung the object on the wet wooden boards of the ramp, and Lucy realized it was not Henry's oilskin, for the owner was still inside it. Her gasp of horror was whipped away by the wind so that not even she could hear it. Who was he? Where had he come from? Another shipwreck?

It occurred to her that he might still be alive. She must go and see. She bent and shouted in Jo's ear: 'Stay here – keep still – don't move.' Then she ran down the ramp.

Half way down she heard footsteps behind her: Jo was following. The ramp was narrow and slippery, quite dangerous. She stopped, turned, and scooped the child up in her arms, saying: 'You naughty boy, I told you to wait!' She looked from the body below to the safety of the clifftop, dithered for a moment in painful indecision, discerned that the sea would wash the body away at any moment, and proceeded downward, carrying Jo.

A smaller wave covered the body, and when the water receded Lucy was close enough to see that it was a man, and that it had been in the sea long enough for the water to swell and distort the features. That meant he was dead. She could therefore do nothing for him, and she was not going to risk her life and her son's to preserve a corpse. She was about to turn back when something about the bloated face struck her as familiar. She stared at it, uncomprehending, trying to fit the features to something in her memory; and then, quite abruptly, she saw the face for what it was, and sheer, paralysing terror gripped her, and it seemed that her heart stopped, and she whispered: 'No, David, no!'

Oblivious now to the danger she walked forward. Another lesser wave broke around her knees, filling her wellington boots with foamy salt water, but she did not notice. Jo twisted in her arms to face forward, but she screamed 'Don't look!' in his ear and pushed his face into her shoulder. He began to cry.

She knelt beside the body and touched the horrible face with her hand. It was David. There was no doubt. He was dead, and had been for some time. Moved by some deep instinct to make absolutely certain, she lifted the skirt of the oilskin and looked at the stumps of his legs.

It was impossible to take in the fact of the death. She had, in a way, been wishing him dead; but her feelings about him were confused by guilt and the fear of being found out in infidelity. Grief, horror, liberation, relief: they fluttered in her mind like birds, none of them willing to settle.

She would have stayed there, motionless, but the next wave was a big one. Its force knocked her flying, and she took a great gulp of sea water. Somehow she managed to keep Jo in her grasp and stay on the ramp;

and when the surf settled she got to her feet and ran up out of the greedy reach of the ocean.

She walked all the way to the cliff-top without looking back. When she came within sight of the cottage, she saw the jeep standing outside. Henry was back.

Still carrying Jo, she broke into a stumbling run, desperate to share her hurt with Henry, to feel his arms around her and have him comfort her. Her breath came in ragged sobs, and tears mixed invisibly with the rain on her face. She went to the back of the cottage, burst into the kitchen, and dumped Jo urgently on the floor.

Henry said: 'David decided to stay over at Tom's another day.'

She stared at him, her mind an incredulous blank; and then, in a flash of intuition, she understood everything.

Henry had killed David.

The conclusion came first, like a punch in the stomach, winding her; the reasons followed a split-second later. The shipwreck, the odd-shaped knife he was so attached to, the crashed jeep, the news bulletin about the London stiletto murderer: suddenly everything fitted together, a box of jigsaw pieces thrown in the air and landing, improbably, fully assembled.

'Don't look so surprised,' Henry said with a smile. 'They've got a lot of work to do over there, and I didn't encourage him to come back.'

Tom. She had to go to Tom. He would know what to do; he would protect her and Jo until the police came; he had a dog and a gun.

Her fear was interrupted by a shaft of sadness, of sorrow for the Henry she had believed in, had almost loved; for clearly he did not exist – she had imagined him. Instead of a warm, strong, affectionate man, she saw in front of her a monster who sat and smiled and calmly gave her invented messages from the husband he had murdered.

She suppressed a shudder. Taking Jo's hand, she walked out of the kitchen, along the hall, and out of the front door. She got into the jeep, sat Jo beside her, and started the engine.

But Henry was there, resting his foot casually on the running-board, and holding David's shotgun, saying: 'Where are you going?'

Her heart sank. If she drove away now he might shoot – what instinct had warned him to take the gun into the house this time? – and while she herself might chance it, she could not endanger Jo. She said: 'Just putting the jeep away.'

'You need Jo's help for that?'

'He likes the ride. Don't cross-examine me!'

Henry shrugged, and stepped back.

She looked at him for a moment, wearing David's hacking jacket and holding David's gun so casually, and wondered whether he really would shoot her if she simply drove away. Then she recalled the vein of ice she had sensed within him right from the start, and knew that that ultimate commitment, that ruthlessness, would permit him to do anything.

With an awful feeling of weariness, she surrendered. She threw the jeep into reverse and backed into the barn. She switched off, got out, and walked with Jo back into the cottage. She had no idea what she would say to Henry, what she would do in his presence, how she would hide her knowledge – if, indeed she had not already betrayed it.

She had no plans.

But she had left the barn door open.

CHAPTER THIRTY-TWO

'THAT'S THE place, Number One,' the captain said, and lowered his telescope.

The first lieutenant peered out through the rain and the spray. 'Not quite the ideal holiday resort, what, sir? Jolly stark, I should say.'

'Indeed.' The captain was an old-fashioned naval officer with a grizzled beard who had been at sea during the first war with Germany. However, he had learned to overlook his first lieutenant's foppish conversational style, for the boy had turned out – against all expectations – to be a perfectly good sailor.

The 'boy', who was past thirty and an old salt by this war's standards, had no idea of the magnanimity from which he benefited. He held on to a rail and braced himself as the corvette mounted the steep side of a wave, righted itself at the crest, and dived into the trough 'Now that we're here, sir, what do we do?'

'Circle the island.'

'Very good, sir.'

'And keep our eyes open for a U-boat.'

'We're not likely to get one anywhere near the surface in this weather – and if we did, we couldn't see it unless it came within spitting distance.'

'The storm will blow itself out tonight – tomorrow at the latest.' The captain began stuffing tobacco into a pipe.

'Do you think so?'

'I'm sure.'

'Nautical instinct, I suppose?'

The captain grunted. 'That, and the weather forecast.'

The corvette rounded a headland, and they saw a small bay with a jetty. Above it, on the cliff top, was a little cottage standing small and square, hunched against the wind.

The captain pointed. 'We'll land a party there as soon as we can.'

The first lieutenant nodded. 'All the same . . .'

'Well?'

'Each circuit of the island will take us about an hour, I should say.'

'So?'

'So, unless we're jolly lucky and happen to be in exactly the right place at exactly the right time . . .'

'The U-boat will surface, take on its passenger, and submerge again without us even seeing the ripples,' the captain finished.

'Yes.'

The captain lit his pipe with an expertise which spoke of long experience of lighting pipes in heavy seas. He puffed a few times, then inhaled a lungful of smoke. 'Ours not to reason why,' he said, and blew smoke through his nostrils.

'A rather unfortunate quotation, sir.'

'Why?'

'It refers to the notorious charge of the Light Brigade.'

'Good God! I never knew that.' The captain puffed contentedly. 'What it must be to be educated.'

There was another little cottage at the eastern end of the island. The captain scrutinized it through his telescope, and observed that it had a large, professional-looking radio aerial. 'Sparks!' he called. 'See if you can raise that cottage. Try the Royal Observer Corps's frequency.'

'Aye, aye, sir.'

When the cottage had passed out of sight, the radio operator called: 'No response, sir.'

'All right, Sparks,' the captain said. 'It wasn't important.'

The crew of the coastguard cutter sat below decks in Aberdeen Harbour, playing pontoon for halfpennies and musing on the feeble-mindedness which seemed invariably to accompany high rank.

'Twist,' said Jack Smith, who was more Scots than his name.

Albert 'Slim' Parish, a fat Londoner far from home, dealt him a jack.

'Bust,' Smith said.

Slim raked in his stake. 'A penny-ha'penny,' he said in mock wonder. 'I only hope I live to spend it.'

Smith rubbed condensation off the inside of a porthole and peered out at the boats bobbing up and down in the harbour. 'The way the skipper's panicking,' he observed, 'you'd think we were going to bloody Berlin, not Storm Island.'

'Didn't you know? We're the spearhead of the Allied invasion.' Slim turned over a ten, dealt himself a king, and said: 'Pay twenty-ones.'

Smith said: 'What is this guy, anyway – a deserter? If you ask me, it's a job for the military police, not us.'

Slim shuffled the pack. 'I'll tell you what he is: an escaped prisoner-of-war.'

There was a chorus of disbelieving jeers.

'All right, don't listen to me. But when we pick him up, just take note of his accent.' He put the cards down. 'Listen: what boats go to Storm Island?'

'Only the grocer,' someone said.

'So, if he's a deserter, the only way he can get back to the mainland is on the grocer's boat. So, the Military Police just have to wait for Charlie's regular trip to the island, and pick the deserter up when he steps off the boat at this end. There's no reason for us to be sitting here, waiting to weigh anchor and shoot over there at the speed of light the minute the weather clears, unless . . .' He paused melodramatically. 'Unless he's got some other means of getting off the island.'

'Like what?'

'A U-boat.'

'Bollocks,' Smith said contemptuously. The others merely laughed.

Slim dealt another hand. Smith won this time, but everyone else lost. 'I'm a shilling up,' Slim said. 'I think

I'll retire to that nice little cottage in Devon. We won't catch him, of course.'

'The deserter?'

'The prisoner-of-war.'

'Why not?'

Slim tapped his head. 'Use your noddle. When the storm clears, we'll be here and the U-boat will be at the bottom of the bay in the island. So who'll get there first? The Jerries.'

'So why are we doing it?' Smith said.

'Because the people who are giving the orders are not as sharp as yours truly, Albert Parish. You may laugh!' He dealt another hand. 'Place your bets. You'll see I'm right. What's that, Smithie, a penny? Gorblimey, don't go mad. I tell you what, I'll give odds of five to one we come back from Storm Island empty-handed. Any takers? What if I say ten to one? Eh? Ten to one?'

'No takers,' said Smith. 'Deal the cards.'

Slim dealt the cards.

Squadron-Leader Peterkin Blenkinsop (he had tried to shorten Peterkin to Peter, but somehow the men always found out) stood ramrod-straight in front of the map and addressed the room. 'We fly in formations of three,' he began. 'The first three will take off as soon as weather permits. Our target—' he touched the map with a pointer. '—is here. Storm Island. On arrival, we will circle for twenty minutes at low altitudes, looking for U-boats. After twenty minutes, we return to base.'

He paused. 'Those of you with a logical turn of mind will by now have deduced that, to achieve continuous cover, the second formation of three aircraft must take off precisely twenty minutes after the first, and so on. Any questions?'

Flying-Officer Longman said: 'Sir?'

'Longman?'

'What do we do if we see this U-boat?'

'Strafe it, of course. Drop a few grenades. Cause trouble.'

'But we're flying fighters, sir – there's not much we can do to stop a U-boat. That's a job for battleships, isn't it?'

Blenkinsop sighed. 'As usual, those of you who can think of better ways to win the war are invited to write directly to Mr Winston Churchill, number ten Downing Street, London South-West-One. Now, are there any questions, as opposed to fat-headed criticisms?'

There were no questions.

The later years of the war had produced a different kind of RAF officer, Bloggs mused. He sat on a soft chair in the scramble room, close to the fire, listening to the rain drumming on the tin roof, and intermittently dozing. The Battle of Britain pilots had seemed incorrigibly cheerful, with their undergraduate slang, their perpetual drinking, their tirelessness, and their cavalier disregard of the flaming death they faced every day. That schoolboy heroism had not been enough to carry them through subsequent years, as the war dragged on in places far from home, and the emphasis shifted from the dashing individuality of aerial dogfighting to the mechanical drudgery of bombing missions. They still drank and talked in jargon, but they appeared older, harder, more cynical: there was nothing in them now of *Tom Brown's Schooldays*. Bloggs recalled what he had done to that poor common-or-garden housebreaker in the police cells at Aberdeen, and he thought: It's happened to us all.

They were very quiet. They sat all around him: some dozing, like himself; others reading books or playing board games. A bespectacled navigator in a corner was learning Russian.

As Bloggs surveyed the room with half-closed eyes, another pilot came in, and he thought immediately that this one had not been aged by the war. He had a wide grin and a fresh face that looked as if it hardly needed shaving more than once a week. He wore his jacket open and carried his helmet. He made a beeline for Bloggs.

'Detective-Inspector Bloggs?'

'That's me.'

'Jolly good show. I'm your pilot. Charles Calder.'

'Fine.' Bloggs shook hands.

'The kite's all ready, and the engine's as sweet as a bird. She's an amphibian, I suppose you know.'

'Yes.'

'Jolly good show. We'll land on the sea, taxi in to about ten yards from the shore, and put you off in a dinghy.'

'Then you wait for me to come back.'

'Indeed. Well, all we need now is the weather.'

'Yes. Look, Charles, I've been chasing this bloke all over the country for six days and nights, so I'm catching up on my sleep while I've got the chance. You won't mind.'

'Of course not!' The pilot sat down and produced a thick book from under his jacket. 'Catching up on my education,' he said. '*War and Peace.*'

Bloggs said: 'Jolly good show,' and closed his eyes.

Percival Godliman and his uncle, Colonel Terry, sat side by side in the map room, drinking coffee and tapping the ash of their cigarettes into a fire bucket on the floor between them. Godliman was repeating himself.

'I can't think of anything more we can do,' he said.

'So you said.'

'The corvette is already there, and the fighters are only a few minutes away, so the sub will come under fire as soon as she shows herself above the surface.'

'If she's seen.'

'The corvette will land a party as soon as possible. Bloggs will be there soon after that, and the coastguard will bring up the rear.'

'And none of them can be sure to get there in time.'

'I know,' Godliman said wearily. 'We've done all we can, but is it enough?'

Terry lit another cigarette. 'What about the inhabitants of the island?'

'Oh, yes. There are only two houses there. There's a

sheep farmer and his wife in one – they have a young child – and an old shepherd lives in the other. The shepherd's got a radio – Royal Observer Corps – but we can't raise him: he probably keeps the set switched to Transmit. He's old.'

'The farmer sounds promising,' Terry said. 'If he's a bright fellow he might stop your spy.'

Godliman shook his head. 'The poor chap's in a wheelchair.'

'Dear God, we don't get any luck, do we?'

'No,' said Godliman. 'Die Nadel gets all the luck there is.'

CHAPTER THIRTY-THREE

Lucy WAS becoming quite calm. The feeling crept over her gradually, like the icy spread of an anaesthetic, deadening her emotions and sharpening her wits. The times when she was momentarily paralysed by the thought that she was sharing a house with a murderer became fewer, and she was possessed by a cool-headed watchfulness that surprised her.

As she went about the household chores, sweeping around Henry as he sat in the living-room reading a novel, she wondered how much he had noticed of the change in her feelings. He was very observant: he did not miss much, and there had been a definite wariness, if not outright suspicion, in that confrontation over the jeep. He must have known she was shaken by something. On the other hand, she had been upset before he left, because Jo had discovered them in bed together: he might think that that was all that had been wrong.

She had the strangest feeling that he knew exactly what was in her mind, but he preferred to pretend that everything was all right.

She hung her laundry on a clothes-horse in the kitchen to dry. 'I'm sorry about this,' she said, 'but I can't wait forever for the rain to stop.'

He looked uninterestedly at the clothes and said: 'That's all right.' He went back into the living-room.

Scattered among the wet garments was a complete set of clean, dry clothes for Lucy.

For lunch she made a vegetable pie using an austerity recipe. She called Jo and Henry to the table and served up.

David's gun was propped in a corner of the kitchen. Lucy said: 'I don't like having a loaded gun in the house, Henry.'

'I'll take it outside after lunch,' he said. 'The pie is good.'

'I don't like it,' Jo said.

Lucy picked up the gun and put it on top of the Welsh dresser. 'I suppose it's all right as long as it's out of Jo's reach.'

Jo said: 'When I grow up I'm going to shoot Germans.'

'This afternoon I want you to have a sleep,' Lucy told him. She went into the living-room and took one of David's sleeping pills from the bottle in the cupboard. Two of the pills were a heavy dose for a 160-pound man, she reasoned, therefore one quarter of one pill should be just enough to make a 50-pound boy sleep in the afternoon. She put the pill on her chopping-block and halved it, then halved it again. She put a quarter on a spoon, crushed it with the back of another spoon, and stirred the powder into a small glass of milk. She gave the glass to Jo and said: 'I want you to drink every last drop.'

Henry watched the whole thing without comment.

After lunch she settled Jo on the sofa with a pile of books. He could not read, of course; but he had heard the stories read aloud so many times that he knew them by heart, and he could turn the pages of the books, looking at the pictures and reciting from memory the words on the page.

'Would you like some coffee?' she asked Henry.

'Real coffee?' he said, surprised.

'I've got a little hoard.'

'Yes, please!'

He watched her making it. She wondered if he was afraid she might try to give him sleeping pills, too. She could hear Jo's voice from the next room:

'What I said was, "Is anybody at home?"' called out Pooh very loudly.

'No!' said a voice . . .

– and he laughed heartily, as he always did at that joke. Oh, God, Lucy thought: don't let Jo be hurt.

She poured the coffee and sat opposite Henry. He reached across the table and held her hand. They sat in silence, sipping coffee and listening to the rain and Jo's voice.

'How long does getting thin take?' asked Pooh anxiously.

'About a week, I should think.'

'But I can't stay here for a week!'

He began to sound sleepy, and then he stopped. Lucy went and covered him with a blanket. She picked up the book, which had slipped from his fingers to the floor. It had been hers when she was a child, and she, too, knew the stories by heart. The flyleaf was inscribed in her mother's copperplate: 'To Lucy, aged four, with love from Mother and Father.' She put the book on the sideboard.

She went back into the kitchen. 'He's asleep.'

'And . . . ?'

She held out her hand. Henry took it. She tugged gently. He stood up. She led him upstairs and into the bedroom. She closed the door, then pulled her sweater off over her head.

For a moment he stood still, looking at her breasts. Then he began to undress.

As she got into the bed, she thought: Give me strength. This was the part that she dreaded, the part she was not sure she could manage: pretending to enjoy his body, when really all she could feel was fear, loathing, and guilt.

He got into bed and embraced her.

In a little while she found she did not have to pretend after all.

For a few seconds she lay in the crook of his arm, wondering how it was that a man could kill so coldly and love so warmly.

But what she said was: 'Would you like a cup of tea?'

He grinned. 'No, thank you.'

'Well, I would.' She extricated herself and got up. When he moved, she put her hand on his flat belly and said: 'No, you stay there. I'll bring the tea up. I haven't finished with you.'

He grinned again. 'You're really making up for your four wasted years.'

As soon as she was outside the room the smile dropped from her face like a mask. Her heart pounded in her chest as she went quickly, naked, down the stairs. In the kitchen she banged the kettle on the stove and rattled some china for realism. Then she began to put on the clothes she had left hidden in the wet laundry. Her hands were shaking so much that she could hardly button the trousers.

She heard the bed creak upstairs, and she stood frozen to the spot, listening, thinking: Stay there! Stay there! But he was only shifting his position.

She was ready. She went into the living-room. Jo was in a deep sleep, grinding his teeth. Dear God, don't let him wake up, Lucy prayed. She picked him up. He muttered in his sleep, something about Christopher Robin, and Lucy closed her eyes tightly and *willed* him to be quiet.

She wrapped the blanket around him securely. She went back into the kitchen and reached up to the top of the Welsh dresser for the gun. It slipped from her grasp and fell to the shelf, smashing a plate and two cups. The crash was deafening. She stood rooted to the spot.

'What happened?' Henry called from upstairs.

'I dropped a cup,' she shouted. She could not suppress the tremor in her voice.

The bed creaked again, and there was a footfall on the floor above her. But it was now too late for her to turn back. She picked up the gun, opened the back door, and, clutching Jo to her, ran across to the barn.

On the way she had a moment of panic: had she left the keys in the jeep? Surely she had: she always did.

She slipped in the wet mud and fell to her knees. She burst into tears. For a second she was tempted to stay there, and let him catch her and kill her as he had killed her husband; then she remembered the child in her arms, and she got up and ran on.

She entered the barn and opened the passenger door of the jeep. She put Jo on the seat. He slipped sideways. Lucy sobbed: 'Oh, God!' She pulled Jo upright, and this time he stayed that way. She ran around to the other side of the jeep and got in, dropping the gun on to the floor between her legs.

She turned the starter.

It coughed and died.

'Please, *please*!'

She turned it again.

The engine roared into life.

Henry came out of the back door at a run.

Lucy raced the engine and threw the gearshift into forward. The jeep leaped out of the barn. She rammed the throttle open.

The wheels spun in the mud for a second, then bit again. The jeep gathered speed with agonizing languor. She steered away from Henry. He chased the vehicle, barefoot in the mud.

She realized he was gaining on her.

She pushed the hand-throttle with all her might, almost snapping the thin lever. She wanted to scream with frustration. Henry was only a yard or so away, almost level with her, running like an athlete, his arms going like pistons, his bare feet pounding the turf, his cheeks blowing, his naked chest heaving.

The engine screamed, and there was a jerk as the automatic transmission changed up, then a new surge of power.

Lucy looked sideways again. Henry seemed to see that he had almost lost her. He flung himself forward through the air in a dive. He got a grip on the door handle with his left hand, and brought the right hand across. Pulled by the jeep, he ran alongside for a few paces, his feet hardly touching the ground. Lucy stared at his face, so close to hers: it was red with effort, twisted in pain; the cords of his powerful neck bulged with the strain.

Suddenly she knew what she had to do.

She took her hand off the wheel, reached through the open window, and poked him viciously in the eye with a long-nailed forefinger.

He let go and fell away, his hands covering his face.

The distance between him and the jeep increased rapidly.

Lucy realized she was crying like a baby.

Two miles from her cottage she saw the wheelchair.

It stood on the cliff top like a memorial, its metal frame and big rubber tyres impervious to the incessant rain. Lucy approached it from a slight dip, and saw its black outline framed by the slate-grey sky and the boiling sea. It had a wounded look, like the hole left by an uprooted tree or a house with broken windows; as if its passenger had been wrenched from it.

She recalled the first time she had seen it, in the hospital. It had stood beside David's bed, new and shiny, and he had swung himself into it expertly and swished up and down the ward, showing off. 'She's light as a feather – made of aircraft alloy,' he had said with brittle enthusiasm, and sped off between the rows of beds. He had stopped at the far end of the ward with his back to her, and after a minute she went up behind him and saw that he was weeping. She had knelt in front of him and held his hands, saying nothing.

It was the last time she had been able to comfort him.

There on the cliff-top, the rain and the salt wind would soon blemish the alloy, and eventually it would rust and crumble, its rubber perished, its leather seat rotted away.

Lucy drove past without slowing.

Three miles farther on, when she was half way between the two cottages, she ran out of petrol.

She fought down the panic and tried to think rationally as the jeep shuddered to a halt.

People walked at four miles an hour, she remembered reading somewhere. Henry was athletic, but he had hurt his ankle, and even though it seemed to have healed rapidly, the running he had done after the jeep must have hurt it. Therefore she must be a good hour ahead of him.

(She had no doubt he *would* come after her: he knew as well as she did that there was a wireless transmitter in Tom's cottage.)

She had plenty of time. In the back of the jeep was a half-gallon can of fuel for just such occasions as this. She got out of the car, fumbled the can out of the back, and opened the petrol cap.

Then she thought again, and the inspiration that came to her surprised her by its fiendishness.

She replaced the petrol cap and went to the front of the car. She checked that the ignition was off and opened the bonnet. She was no mechanic, but she could identify the distributor cap and trace the leads to the engine. She lodged the petrol can securely beside the wheel arch and took off its cap.

There was a plug spanner in the tool kit. She took out a plug, checked again that the ignition was off, and put the plug in the mouth of the petrol can, securing it there with tape. Then she closed the bonnet.

When Henry came along he was certain to try to start the jeep. He would switch on, the starter motor would turn, the plug would spark and the half-gallon of petrol would explode.

She was not sure how much damage it would do, but she could be certain it would be no help.

An hour later she was regretting her cleverness.

Trudging through the mud, soaked to the skin, with the sleeping child a dead weight over her shoulder, she wanted nothing more than to lie down and die. The booby-trap seemed, on reflection, dubious and risky: petrol would burn, not explode; if there was not enough air in the mouth of the can it might not even ignite; worst of all, Henry might suspect a trap, look under the bonnet, dismantle the bomb, pour the petrol into the tank and drive after her.

She contemplated stopping for a rest, but decided that if she sat down she might never get up again.

She should have been in sight of Tom's house by now. She could not possibly have got lost – even if she had not walked this path a dozen times before, the whole island just was not big enough to get lost on.

She recognized a thicket where she and Jo had once seen a fox. She must be about a mile from the shepherd's home. She could have seen it, but for the rain.

She shifted Jo to the other shoulder, switched the shotgun from one hand to the other, and forced herself to continue putting one foot in front of the other.

When at last the cottage became visible through the sheeting rain she could have cried with relief. She was nearer than she thought – perhaps a quarter of a mile.

Suddenly Jo seemed lighter, and although the last stretch was uphill – the only hill on the island – she seemed to cover it in no time at all.

'Tom!' she called as she approached the front door, 'Tom, oh, Tom!'

She heard the answering bark of Bob.

She went in by the front door. 'Tom, quickly!' Bob dodged excitedly about her ankles, barking furiously. Tom could not be far away – he was probably in the outhouse. Lucy went upstairs and laid Jo on Tom's bed.

The wireless was in the bedroom, a complex-looking construction of wires and dials and knobs. There was something that looked like a Morse key: she touched it experimentally, and it gave a beep. A thought came to her from the depths of her memory – something from a schoolgirl thriller – the Morse code for SOS. She touched the key again: three short, three long, three short.

Where was Tom?

She heard a noise, and rushed to the window.

The jeep was making its way up the hill to the house.

Henry had found the booby-trap, and used the petrol to fill the tank.

Where was Tom?

She rushed out of the bedroom, intending to go and bang on the outhouse door. At the head of the stairs she paused. Bob was standing in the open doorway of the other bedroom, the empty one.

'Come here, Bob,' she said. The dog stood his ground, barking. She went to him and bent to pick him up.

Then she saw Tom.

He lay on his back, on the bare floorboards of the vacant bedroom, his eyes staring sightlessly at the ceiling, his cap upside-down on the floor behind his head. His jacket was open, and there was a small spot of blood on the shirt underneath. Close to his hand was a crate of whisky, and Lucy found herself thinking wildly, irrelevantly: I didn't know he drank that much.

She felt his pulse.

He was dead.

Think, *think*!

Yesterday Henry had returned to Lucy's cottage

battered, as if he had been in a fight. That must have been when he killed David. Today he had come here, to Tom's cottage, 'to fetch David' he had said. But he had known David was not there. So why had he made the journey?

Obviously, to kill Tom.

What drove him? What purpose burned inside him so fiercely that he would get in a car, drive ten miles, stick a knife into an old man, and drive back as calm and quiet and composed as if he had been out to take the air? Lucy shuddered.

Now she was on her own.

She took hold of the dog by its collar and dragged it away from the body of its master. On impulse, she returned and buttoned the jacket over the small stiletto wound which had killed the shepherd. Then she closed the door on the corpse. She said to the dog: 'He's dead, but I need you.'

She returned to the front bedroom and looked out of the window.

The jeep drew up in front of the house and stopped; and Henry got out.

CHAPTER THIRTY-FOUR

Lucy's distress call was heard by the corvette.

'Captain, sir,' said Sparks, 'I just picked up an SOS from the island.'

The captain frowned. 'Nothing we can do until we can land a boat,' he said. 'Did they say anything else?'

'Not a thing, sir. It wasn't even repeated.'

The captain thought a little more. 'Nothing we can do,' he said again. 'Send a signal to the mainland, reporting it. And keep listening.'

'Aye, aye, sir.'

It was also picked up by an M18 listening post on top of a Scottish mountain. The R/T operator, a young man with abdominal wounds who had been invalided out of the RAF and had only six months to live, was trying to pick up German Navy signals from Norway, and he ignored the SOS. However, he went off duty five minutes later, and he mentioned it casually to his Commanding Officer.

'It was only broadcast once,' he said. 'Probably a

fishing vessel off the Scottish coast – there might well be the odd small ship in trouble, in this weather.'

'Leave it with me,' the CO said. 'I'll give the Navy a buzz. And I suppose I'd better inform Whitehall. Protocol, y'know.'

'Thank you, sir.'

At the Royal Observer Corps station there was something of a panic. Of course, SOS was not the signal an observer was *supposed* to give when he sighted enemy aircraft, but they knew that Tom was old, and who could say what he might send if he got excited? So the air-raid sirens were sounded, and all other posts were alerted, and anti-aircraft guns were rolled out all over the east coast of Scotland, and the radio operator tried frantically to raise Tom.

No German bombers came, of course; and the War Office wanted to know why a full alert had been sounded when there was nothing in the sky but a few bedraggled geese?

So they were told.

The Coastguard heard it, too.

They would have responded to it, if it had been on the correct frequency, and if they had been able to establish the position of the transmitter, and if that position had been within reasonable distance of the coast.

As it was they guessed, from the fact that the signal

421

came over on the Observer Corps frequency, that it originated from Old Tom; and they were already doing all they could about *that* situation, whatever the hell that situation was.

When the news reached the below-deck card game on the cutter in the harbour at Aberdeen, Slim dealt another hand of pontoon and said: 'I'll tell you what's happened. Old Tom's caught the prisoner-of-war and he's sitting on his head waiting for the Army to arrive and take the bugger away.'

'Bollocks,' said Smith, and there was general agreement with that sentiment.

And the *U-505* heard it.

She was still more than thirty nautical miles away from Storm Island, but Weissman was roaming the dial to see what he could pick up – and hoping, improbably, to hear Glenn Miller records from the American Forces Network in Britain – and his tuner happened to be on the right wavelength at the right time. He passed the information to Lieutenant-Commander Heer, adding: 'It was not on our man's frequency.'

Major Wohl, who was still around and as irritating as ever, said: 'Then it means nothing.'

Heer did not miss the opportunity to correct him. 'It means *something*,' he said. 'It means that there may be some activity on the surface when we go up.'

'But this is unlikely to trouble us.'

'Most unlikely,' Heer agreed.

'Then it is meaningless.'

'It is *probably* meaningless.'

They argued about it all the way to the island.

So it was that within the space of five minutes the Navy, the Royal Observer Corps, M18 and the Coastguard all phoned Godliman to tell him about the SOS. And Godliman phoned Bloggs.

Bloggs had finally fallen into a deep sleep in front of the fire in the scramble room. The shrill ring of the telephone startled him, and he leaped to his feet, thinking that the planes were about to take off.

A pilot picked it up, said 'Yes' into it twice, and handed it to Bloggs. 'A Mr Godliman for you.'

Bloggs said: 'Hello, Percy.'

'Fred, somebody on the island just broadcast an SOS.'

Bloggs shook his head to clear the last remaining clouds of sleep. 'Who?'

'We don't know. There was just the one signal, not repeated, and they don't seem to be receiving at all.'

'Still, there's not much doubt now.'

'No. Everything ready up there?'

'All except the weather.'

'Good luck.'

'Thanks.'

Bloggs hung up and turned to the young pilot who was still reading *War and Peace*. 'Good news,' he told him. 'The bastard's definitely on the island.'

'Jolly good show,' said the pilot.

CHAPTER THIRTY-FIVE

H ENRY CLOSED the door of the jeep and began walking quite slowly toward the house. He was wearing David's hacking jacket again. There was mud all over his trousers, where he had fallen, and his hair was plastered wetly against his skull. He was limping slightly on his right foot.

Lucy backed away from the window and ran out of the bedroom and down the stairs. The shotgun was on the floor in the hall, where she had dropped it. She picked it up. Suddenly it felt very heavy. She had never actually fired a gun, and she had no idea how to check whether this one was loaded. She could figure it out, given time; but there was no time.

She took a deep breath and flung open the front door. 'Stop!' she shouted. Her voice was pitched higher than she had intended, and it sounded shrill and hysterical.

Henry smiled pleasantly and kept on walking.

Lucy pointed the gun at him, holding the barrel with her left hand and the breech with her right. Her finger was on the trigger. 'I'll kill you!' she yelled.

'Don't be silly, Lucy,' he said mildly. 'How could you hurt me? After all the things we've done together? Haven't we loved each other, a little . . . ?'

It was true. She had told herself she could not fall in love with him, and that was true too; but she *had* felt *something* for him, and if it was not love, it was something very like.

'You knew about me this afternoon,' he said, and now he was thirty yards away, 'but it made no difference to you then, did it?'

That was true. For a moment, she saw in her mind's eye a vivid picture of herself sitting astride him, holding his sensitive hands to her breasts, and then she realized what he was doing—

'We can work something out, Lucy, we can still have each other—'

– and she pulled the trigger.

There was an ear-splitting crash, and the weapon jumped in her hands like a live thing, its butt bruising her hip with the recoil. She almost dropped it in shock. She had never imagined that firing a gun would feel like that. She was quite deaf for a moment.

The shot went high over Henry's head, but all the same he ducked, turned, and ran zig-zagging back to the jeep. Lucy was tempted to fire again, but she stopped herself just in time, realizing that if he knew both barrels had been emptied there would be nothing to stop him turning and coming back.

He flung open the door of the jeep, leaped in, and shot off down the hill.

Lucy knew he would be back.

Suddenly she felt happy, almost gay. She had won the first round – she had driven him off – and she was a woman!

But he would be back.

Still, she had the upper hand. She was indoors, and she had the gun. And she had time to prepare.

Prepare. She must be ready for him. Next time he would be more subtle. He would surely try to creep up on her.

She hoped he would wait until dark, for that would give her time.

First she had to reload the gun.

She went into the kitchen. Tom kept everything in his kitchen – food, coal, tools, stores – and he had a gun like David's. She knew the two firearms were the same, for David had examined Tom's then sent away for one exactly like it. The two men had enjoyed long discussions about weaponry.

She found Tom's gun and a box of ammunition. She put the two guns and the box on the kitchen table.

Machines were simple, she was convinced: it was apprehension, not stupidity, which made women fumble when faced with a piece of engineering.

She fiddled with David's gun, keeping the barrel pointed away from herself, until it came open at the breech. Then she worked out what she had done to open it, and practised doing it again a couple of times.

It was incredibly simple.

She loaded both guns. Then, to make sure she had done everything correctly, she pointed Tom's gun at the kitchen wall and pulled the trigger.

There was a shower of plaster, Bob barked like a maniac, and she bruised her hip and deafened herself again. But she was armed.

She must remember to pull the triggers gently so as not to jerk the gun and spoil her aim. Men probably got taught that kind of thing in the Army.

What to do next? She should make it difficult for Henry to get into the house.

Neither of the doors had locks, of course: if a house was burgled on this island, one would know that the culprit lived in the other house. Lucy rummaged in Tom's tool box and found a shiny, sharp-bladed axe. She stood on the stairs and began to hack away at the bannister.

The work made her arms ache, but in five minutes she had six short lengths of stout, seasoned oak. She found a hammer and some nails, and fixed the oak bars across the front and back doors, three bars to each door, four nails to each bar. When it was done her wrists were agony and the hammer felt as heavy as lead, but she was not finished.

She got another handful of the shiny, four-inch nails, and went around every window in the house, nailing them shut. She realized, with a sense of discovery, why men always put nails in their mouths: it was because you needed both hands for the work and if you put them in your pocket they stuck into your skin.

By the time she had finished it was dark. She left the lights off.

He could still get into the house, of course; but he could not get in quietly. He would have to break something and give himself away – and then she would be ready with the guns.

She went upstairs, carrying both guns, to check on

Jo. He was still asleep, wrapped in his blanket, on Tom's bed. Lucy struck a match to look at his face. The sleeping pill must have really knocked him out, but he was an average sort of colour, his temperature seemed normal, and he was breathing easily. 'Just stay that way, little boy,' Lucy whispered. The sudden access of tenderness left her feeling more savage toward Henry.

She patrolled the house restlessly for a while, peering through the windows into the darkness, the dog following her everywhere. She took to carrying just one of the guns, leaving the other at the head of the stairs; but she hooked the axe into the belt of her trousers.

She remembered the radio, and tapped out her SOS several more times. She had no idea whether anybody was listening, or even whether the radio was working. She knew no more Morse, so she could not broadcast anything else.

It occurred to her that Tom probably did not know Morse code. Surely he must have a book somewhere? If only she could tell someone what was happening here! She searched the house, using dozens of matches, feeling terrified every time she lit one within sight of a downstairs window; but she found nothing.

All right, perhaps he *did* know Morse.

On the other hand, why should he need it? He only had to tell the mainland that there were enemy aircraft approaching, and there was no reason why that information shouldn't go over the air . . . what was the phrase David had used? . . . *en clair*.

She went back to the bedroom and looked again at

the wireless set. To one side of the main cabinet, hidden from her previous cursory glance, was a microphone.

If she could talk to them, they could talk to her.

The sound of another human voice – a normal, sane, mainland voice – suddenly seemed the most desirable thing in the world.

She picked up the microphone and began to experiment with the switches.

Bob growled softly.

She put the mike down and reached out her hand toward the dog in the darkness. 'What is it, Bob?'

He growled again. She could feel his ears standing stiffly upright. She was terribly afraid: the confidence won by confronting Henry with the gun, by learning how to reload, by barricading the doors and nailing down the windows . . . all evaporated at one growl from an alert dog.

'Downstairs,' she whispered. 'Quietly.'

She held his collar and let him lead her down the stairs. In the darkness she felt for the bannister, forgetting that she had chopped it up for barricades, and she almost overbalanced. She regained her equilibrium and sucked at a splinter in her finger.

The dog hesitated in the hall, then growled more loudly and tugged her toward the kitchen. She picked him up and held his muzzle shut to silence him. Then she crept through the doorway.

She looked in the direction of the window, but there was nothing in front of her eyes other than velvet blackness.

She listened. The window creaked: at first almost inaudibly, then louder. He was trying to get in. Bob rumbled threateningly, deep in his throat, but seemed to understand the sudden squeeze she gave his muzzle.

The night became quieter. Lucy realized the storm was easing, almost imperceptibly. Henry seemed to have given up on the kitchen window. She moved to the living-room.

She heard the same creak of old wood resisting pressure. Now Henry seemed more determined: there were three muffled bumps, as if he were tapping the window-frame with the cushioned heel of his hand.

Lucy put the dog down and hefted the shotgun. It might almost have been imagination, but she could just make out the window as a square of grey in the blank darkness. If he got the window open, she would fire immediately.

There was a much harder bang. Bob lost control and gave a loud bark. She heard a scuffling noise outside.

Then came the voice.

'Lucy?'

She bit her lip.

'Lucy?'

He was using the voice he used in bed: deep, soft, and intimate.

'Lucy, can you hear me? Don't be afraid. I don't want to hurt you. Talk to me, please.'

She had to fight the urge to pull both triggers there and then, just to silence that awful sound and repress the memories it brought to her unwilling consciousness.

'Lucy, my darling . . .' She thought she heard a muffled sob. 'Lucy, he attacked me – I had to kill him . . . I killed for my country, you shouldn't hate me for that.'

She could not understand that. It sounded mad. Could he be insane, and have hidden it for two intimate days? He had seemed saner than most people – and yet he had murdered before . . . unless he was a victim of injustice . . . Damn. She was softening up, and that must be exactly what he wanted.

She had an idea.

'Lucy, just speak to me . . .'

His voice faded as she tip-toed into the kitchen. Bob would warn her if Henry did anything more than talk. She fumbled in Tom's tool-box and found a pair of pliers. She went to the kitchen window and found with her fingertips the heads of the three nails she had hammered there. Carefully, as quietly as possible, she drew them out. The job demanded all her strength.

When they were out she went back into the living-room to listen.

' . . . don't obstruct me, and I'll leave you . . .'

As silently as she could she lifted the kitchen window open. She crept into the living-room, picked the dog up, and returned yet again to the kitchen.

' . . . hurt you, last thing in the world . . .'

She stroked the dog once or twice, and murmured: 'I wouldn't do this if I didn't have to, boy.' Then she pushed him out of the window.

She closed it rapidly, found a nail, and hammered it in at a new spot with three sharp blows.

She dropped the hammer, picked up the gun, and ran into the front room to stand close to the window, pressing herself up against the wall.

' . . . give you one last chance – ah!'

There was a rush of small feet; a blood-curdling bark Lucy had never heard from a sheepdog before; a scuffling sound; and the noise of a big man falling. She could hear Henry's breathing, gasping, grunting; then another flurry of canine paws; a shout of pain; a curse in a foreign language; another bark. She wished she could see what was happening.

The noises became muffled and more distant, then suddenly ceased. Lucy waited, pressed against the wall next to the window, straining her ears. She wanted to go and check on Jo, wanted to try the radio again, wanted to cough; but she did not dare to move. Bloodthirsty visions of what Bob might have done to Henry passed in and out of her mind, and she yearned to hear the dog snuffling at the door.

She looked at the window. Then she *realized* she was looking at the window: she could see, not just a square patch of faintly lighter grey, but the wooden crosspiece of the frame. It was still night, but only just: she knew that if she looked outside the sky would be faintly diffused with a just-perceptible light, instead of being impenetrably black. Dawn would come at any minute. Then she would be able to see the furniture in the room, and Henry would no longer be able to surprise her in the darkness—

There was a crash of breaking glass inches away from her face. She jumped. She felt a small sharp pain in her cheek, touched the spot, and knew that she had been cut by a flying shard. She hefted the shotgun, waiting for Henry to come through the window; but nothing happened. It was not until a minute or two had passed that she wondered what had broken the window.

She peered at the floor. Among the pieces of broken glass was a large dark shape. She found she could see it better if she looked to one side of it rather than directly at it. When she did that, she was able to make out the familiar shape of the dog.

She closed her eyes, then looked away. She was unable to feel any emotion at all at the death of the faithful sheepdog. Her heart had been numbed by all the danger and death that had gone before: first David, then Tom, then the endless screaming tension of the all-night siege . . . All she felt was hunger. All day yesterday she had been too nervous to eat, which meant it was thirty-six hours since her last meal. Now, incongruously, ridiculously, she found herself longing for a cheese sandwich.

Something else was coming through the window.

She saw it out of the corner of her eye, then turned her head to look directly at it.

It was Henry's hand.

She stared at it, mesmerized: a long-fingered hand, without rings, white under the dirt, with cared-for nails and a band-aid around the tip of the index finger; a hand that had touched her intimately, had played her body like a harp, and thrust a knife into the heart of an old shepherd.

The hand broke away a piece of glass, then another,

enlarging the hole in the pane. Then it reached right through, up to the elbow, and fumbled along the windowsill, searching for a catch to unfasten.

Trying to be utterly silent, with painful slowness, Lucy shifted the gun to her left hand, and with her right took the axe from her belt, lifted it high above her head, and brought it down with all her might on Henry's hand.

He must have sensed it, or heard the rush of wind, or seen a blur of ghostly movement behind the window; for he moved sharply a split-second before the blow landed.

The axe thudded into the wood of the windowsill, sticking there. For a fraction of an instant Lucy thought she had missed: then, from outside, there came a scream of pain and loss, and she saw beside the axe blade, lying on the varnished wood like caterpillars, two severed fingers.

She heard the sound of feet running away.

Lucy threw up.

The exhaustion hit her then, closely followed by a surge of self-pity. She had suffered enough, surely to God, had she not? There were policemen and soldiers in the world to deal with situations like this – nobody could expect an ordinary housewife and mother to keep a killer at bay indefinitely. Who could blame her if she gave up now? Who could honestly say they would have done better, lasted longer, stayed brave and resolute and resourceful for another minute?

She was finished. *They* would have to take over: the outside world, the policemen and soldiers, whoever was at the other end of that radio link. She could do no more.

She tore her eyes away from the grotesque objects on the windowsill and went wearily up the stairs. She picked up the second gun and took both weapons into the bedroom with her.

Jo was still asleep, bless him. He had hardly moved all night, utterly oblivious to the apocalypse going on around him. She could tell, somehow, that he was not sleeping so deeply now: something about the look on his face and the way he breathed let her know that he would wake soon and want his breakfast.

She longed for that simple life, now: getting up in the morning, making breakfast, dressing Jo, doing simple, tedious, *safe* household chores like washing and cleaning and cutting herbs from the garden and making pots of tea. It seemed incredible that she had been so dissatisfied with David's lovelessness, the long boring evenings, the endless bleak landscape of turf and heather and rain.

It would never come back, that life.

She had wanted excitement, cities, music, people, ideas. Now the desire for those things had left her, and she could not understand how she had ever wanted them. Peace was all a human being ought to ask for, it seemed to her.

She sat in front of the radio and studied its switches and dials. She would do this one thing, then she would rest. She made a tremendous effort and forced herself to think analytically for a little longer. There were not *so* many possible combinations of switch and dial. She

found a knob with two settings, turned it, and tapped
the Morse key. There was no sound. Perhaps that meant
the microphone was now in circuit.

She pulled it to her and spoke into it. 'Hello, hello,
is there anybody there? Hello?'

There was a switch which had 'Transmit' above it
and 'Receive' below. It was turned to 'Transmit'. If the
world was to talk back to her, obviously she had to
throw the switch to 'Receive'.

She said: 'Hello, is anybody listening?' and threw the
switch to 'Receive'.

Nothing.

Then: 'Come in, Storm Island, receiving you loud
and clear.'

It was a man's voice. He sounded young and strong,
capable and confident and reassuring and alive and
normal.

'Come in, Storm Island, we've been trying to raise
you all night . . . where the devil have you *been?*'

Lucy switched to 'Transmit', tried to speak, and
burst into tears.

CHAPTER THIRTY-SIX

PERCIVAL GODLIMAN had a headache from too many cigarettes and too little sleep. He had taken a little whisky to help him through the long, worried night in his office, and that had been a mistake. Everything oppressed him: the weather, his office, his job, the war. For the first time since he had become a spycatcher he found himself longing for dusty libraries, illegible manuscripts, and medieval Latin.

Colonel Terry walked in with two cups of tea on a tray. 'Nobody around here sleeps,' he said cheerfully. He sat down. 'Ship's biscuit?' He offered Godliman a plate.

Godliman refused the biscuit and drank the tea. It gave him a temporary lift.

'I just had a call from the man with the fat cigar,' Terry said. 'He's keeping the night vigil with us.'

'I can't imagine why,' Godliman said sourly.

'He's worried.'

The phone rang.

'Godliman.'

'I have the Royal Observer Corps in Aberdeen for you, sir.'

'Yes.'

A new voice came on, the voice of a young man. 'Royal Observer Corps, Aberdeen, here, sir.'

'Yes.'

'Is that Mr Godliman?'

'*Yes.*' Dear God, these military types took their time.

'We've raised Storm Island at last, sir.'

'Thank God!'

'It's not our regular observer. In fact it's a woman.'

'What did she say?'

'Nothing, yet, sir.'

'What do you *mean*?' Godliman fought down the angry impatience that rose inside him.

'She's just . . . well, crying, sir.'

'Oh.' Godliman hesitated. 'Can you connect me to her?'

'Yes. Hold on.' There was a pause punctuated by several clicks and a hum. Then Godliman heard the sound of a woman weeping.

He said: 'Hello, can you hear me?'

The weeping went on.

The young man came back on the line to say: 'She won't be able to hear you until she switches to "Receive", sir – ah, she's done it. Go ahead.'

Godliman said: 'Hello, young lady. When I've finished speaking I'll say "Over", then you switch to "Transmit" to speak to me and *you* say "Over" when *you* have finished. Do you understand? Over.'

The woman's voice came on. 'Oh, thank God for somebody sane. Yes, I understand. Over.'

'Now, then,' Godliman said gently, 'tell me what's been happening there. Over.'

'A man was shipwrecked here two – no, three days ago. I think he's the stiletto murderer from London. He killed my husband and our shepherd, and now he's outside the house, and I've got my little boy here . . . I've nailed the windows shut, and fired at him with a shotgun, and barred the doors, and set the dog on him but he killed the dog, and I hit him with the axe when he tried to get in through the window and *I can't do it any more so please come and save me* . . . Over.'

Godliman put his hand over the phone. His face was white. 'You poor woman,' he breathed. But when he spoke to her, he was brisk. 'You must hold on a little longer,' he began. 'There are sailors and coastguards and policemen and all sorts of people on their way to you, but they can't land until the storm ends. Now, there's something I want you to do, and I can't tell you why you must do it because the wrong people may be listening to us, but I can tell you that it is *absolutely essential*. Are you hearing me clearly? Over.'

'Yes, go on. Over.'

'You must destroy your radio. Over.'

'Oh, no, please . . . must I?'

'Yes,' Godliman said, then he realized she was still transmitting.

'I don't . . . I can't . . .' Then there was a scream.

Godliman said: 'Hello, Aberdeen, what's happening?'

The young man came on. 'The set's still transmitting, sir, but she's not speaking. We can't hear anything.'

'She screamed.'

'Yes, we got that.'

'Damn.' Godliman thought for a minute. 'What's the weather like up there?'

'It's raining, sir.' The young man sounded puzzled.

'I'm not making conversation, lad,' Godliman snapped. 'Is there any sign of the storm letting up?'

'It has eased a little in the last few minutes, sir.'

'Good. Get back to me the instant that woman comes back on air.'

'Very good, sir.'

Godliman said to Terry: 'God only knows what that girl's going through up there.' He jiggled the cradle of the phone.

The Colonel crossed his legs. 'If only she would smash up the radio, then . . .'

'Then we don't care if he kills her?'

'You said it.'

Godliman spoke into the phone. 'Get me Bloggs at Rosyth.'

Bloggs woke up with a start, and listened. Outside, it was dawn. Everyone in the scramble hut was listening, too. They could hear nothing. That was what they were listening to: the silence.

The rain had stopped drumming on the tin roof.

Bloggs went to the window. The sky was grey with a band of white on the eastern horizon. The wind had dropped suddenly, and the rain had become a light drizzle.

The pilots started putting on jackets and helmets, lacing boots, lighting last cigarettes.

A klaxon sounded, and a voice boomed out over the airfield: 'Scramble! Scramble!'

The phone rang. The pilots ignored it and piled out through the door. Bloggs picked it up. 'Yes?'

'Percy here, Fred. We just contacted the island. He's killed the two men. The woman's holding him off at the moment, but she won't last much longer.'

Bloggs said: 'The rain has stopped. We're taking off now.'

'Make it fast, Fred. Goodbye.'

Bloggs hung up and looked around for his pilot. Charles Calder had fallen asleep over *War and Peace*. Bloggs shook him roughly. 'Wake up, you dozy bastard, wake up!'

He opened his eyes.

Bloggs could have hit him. 'Wake up, come on, we're going, the storm's ended!'

The pilot jumped to his feet. 'Jolly good show,' he said.

He ran out of the door and Bloggs followed him.

The lifeboat dropped into the water with a crack like a pistol and a wide, V-shaped splash. The sea was far from calm, but here in the partial shelter of the bay there was no risk to a stout boat in the hands of experienced sailors.

The captain said: 'Carry on, Number One.'

The first lieutenant was standing at the rail with three ratings. He wore a pistol in a waterproof holster. He said: 'Let's go, chaps.'

The four men scrambled down the ladders and into the boat. The first mate sat in the stern and the three sailors broke out the oars and began to row.

For a few moments the captain watched their steady progress toward the jetty. Then he returned to the bridge and gave orders for the corvette to continue circling the island.

The shrill ringing of a bell broke up the card game on the cutter.

Slim said: 'I thought something was different. We aren't going up and down so much. Almost motionless, really. Makes me quite seasick.'

Nobody was listening: the crew were hurrying to their stations, some of them fastening life-jackets as they went.

The engines fired with a roar, and the vessel began to tremble faintly but perceptibly.

Up on deck, Smith stood in the prow, enjoying the fresh air and the spray on his face after a day and a night below.

As the cutter left the harbour Slim joined him.

'Here we go again,' Slim said.

'I knew the bell was going to ring then,' Smith said. 'You know why?'

'Tell me.'

'Know what I had in my hand? Ace and a king.'

'Banker's pontoon,' said Slim. 'Well I never.'

*

Lieutenant-Commander Werner Heer looked at his watch and said: 'Thirty minutes.'

Major Wohl nodded impassively. 'What is the weather like?' he asked.

'The storm has ended,' Heer said reluctantly. He would have preferred to keep that information to himself.

'Then we should surface.'

'If your man were there, he would send us a signal.'

'The war is not won by hypothesis, Captain,' said Wohl. 'I firmly suggest that we surface.'

There had been a blazing row, while the U-boat was in dock, between Heer's superior officer and Wohl's; and Wohl's had won. Heer was still captain of the ship, but he had been told in no uncertain terms that he had better have a damned good reason next time he ignored one of Major Wohl's firm suggestions.

'We will surface at six o'clock exactly,' he said.

Wohl nodded again and looked away.

CHAPTER THIRTY-SEVEN

T HE SOUND of breaking glass, then an explosion like an incendiary bomb:

Whooomph!

Lucy dropped the microphone. Something was happening downstairs. She picked up a shotgun and ran down.

The living-room was ablaze. The fire centred on a broken jar on the floor. Henry had made some kind of bomb with the petrol from the jeep. The flames were spreading hungrily across Tom's threadbare carpet and licking up over the loose covers of his ancient three-piece suite. A feather-filled cushion caught, and the fire reached up toward the ceiling.

Lucy picked up the cushion and flung it through the broken window, singeing her hand. She tore her coat off and threw it on the carpet, stamping on it. She picked it up again and draped it over the floral settee. She was winning—

There was another crash of glass.

It came from upstairs.

Lucy screamed: 'Jo!'

She dropped the coat and raced up the stairs and into the front bedroom.

Henry was sitting on the bed with Jo on his lap. The child was awake, sucking his thumb, wearing his wide-eyed morning look. Henry was stroking his tousled hair.

Henry said: 'Throw the gun on the bed, Lucy.'

Her shoulders sagged in defeat, and she did as he said. 'You climbed the wall and got through the window,' she said dully.

Henry dumped Jo off his lap. 'Go to Mummy.'

Jo ran to her and she lifted him up.

Henry picked up both guns and went to the radio. He was holding his right hand under his left armpit, and there was a great red bloodstain on his jacket. He sat down. 'You hurt me,' he said. Then he turned his attention to the transmitter.

Suddenly it spoke. 'Come in, Storm Island.'

Henry picked up the microphone. 'Hello?'

'Just a minute.'

There was a pause, then another voice came on. Lucy recognized it as the man in London who had told her to destroy the radio. He would be disappointed in her. It said: 'Hello, this is Godliman again. Can you hear me? Over.'

Henry said: 'Yes, I can hear you, Professor. Seen any good cathedrals lately?'

'Is that . . .'

'Yes.' Henry smiled. 'How do you do.' Then the smile left his face abruptly, as if playtime was over, and he turned the frequency dial of the radio.

Lucy turned and left the room. It was over, and she had lost. She walked listlessly down the stairs and into the kitchen. There was nothing for her to do but wait for him to kill her. She could not run away – she did not have the energy, and he obviously knew it.

She looked out of the window. The storm had ended. The howling gale had dropped to a stiff breeze, there was no rain, and the eastern sky was bright with the promise of sunshine. The sea—

She frowned, and looked again.

Yes, it *was* a submarine.

Destroy the radio, the Professor had said.

Last night Henry had cursed in a foreign language.

'*I did it for my country,*' he had said.

And, in his delirium: *Waiting at Calais for a phantom army.*

Destroy the radio.

Why would a man take a wallet of photographic negatives on a fishing trip?

She had known all along he was not insane.

The submarine was a German U-boat, Henry was an enemy agent, and he was at this very second trying to contact the vessel by radio.

Destroy the radio.

She knew what she had to do. She had no right to give up, now that she understood; for it was not only her life that was at stake. She had to do this one last thing for David and for all the other young men who had died in the war.

She knew what she had to do. She was not afraid of the pain – it would be *very* painful, she knew, and might well kill her – but she had known the pain of childbirth, and it could not be worse than that.

She knew what she had to do. She would have liked to put Jo somewhere else, where he could not see it; but there was no time for that, for Henry would find his frequency at any second, and then it might be too late.

She knew what she had to do. She had to destroy the radio, but the radio was upstairs with Henry, and he had both the guns and he *would* kill her.

She knew what she had to do.

She placed one of Tom's kitchen chairs in the centre of the room, stood on it, reached up and unscrewed the light bulb.

She got off the chair, went to the door, and threw the switch.

'Are you changing the bulb?' Jo said.

Lucy climbed on the chair, hesitated for a moment, then thrust three fingers into the live socket.

There was a bang, an instant of agony, and then unconsciousness.

Faber heard the bang. He had found the right frequency on the transmitter, had thrown the switch to 'Transmit', and had picked up the microphone. He was about to speak when the noise came. Immediately afterwards the lights on the dials of the wireless set went out.

His face suffused with anger. She had short-circuited the electricity supply to the whole house. He had not credited her with that much ingenuity.

He should have killed her before. What the hell was wrong with him? He had never hesitated, not ever, until he met this woman.

He picked up one of the guns and went downstairs.

The child was crying. Lucy lay in the kitchen doorway, out cold. Faber took in the empty light socket with the chair beneath it. He frowned in amazement.

She had done it with her *hand.*

Faber said: 'Jesus Christ Almighty.'

Lucy's eyes opened. She hurt all over.

Henry was standing over her with the gun in his hands. He said: 'Why did you use your hand? Why not a screwdriver?'

She said: 'I didn't know you could do it with a screwdriver.'

He shook his head in incredulity. 'You are a truly astonishing woman,' he said. He lifted the gun, aimed it at her, and lowered it again. '*Damn* you!'

His gaze went to the window, and he started.

'You saw it,' he said.

She nodded.

He stood tense for a moment, then he went to the door. Finding it nailed shut, he smashed the window with the butt of his gun and climbed out.

Lucy got to her feet. Jo threw his arms around her legs. She did not feel strong enough to pick him up. She staggered to the window and looked out.

Henry was running toward the cliff. The U-boat was still there, perhaps half a mile offshore. Henry reached the cliff edge and crawled over. He was going to try to swim to the submarine.

Lucy had to stop him.

Dear God, no more, she prayed.

She climbed through the window, blotting out the cries of her son, and ran after Henry.

When she reached the cliff edge she lay down and looked over. He was about half way between her and the sea. He looked up and saw her, froze for a moment, and then began to move faster, dangerously fast.

Her first thought was to climb down after him. But what would she do then? Even if she caught him, she could not stop him.

The ground beneath her shifted slightly. She scrambled back, afraid it would give way and throw her down the cliff.

That gave her an idea.

She thumped on the rocky ground with both fists. It seemed to shake a little more, and a crack appeared. She got one hand over the edge and thrust the other into the crack. A piece of earthy chalk the size of a watermelon came away in her hands.

She looked over the edge and sighted Henry.

She took careful aim and dropped the stone.

It seemed to fall very slowly. He saw it coming, and covered his head with his arm. It looked as if it would miss him.

The rock passed within a couple of inches of his head, and hit his left shoulder. He was holding on with his left hand. He seemed to loosen his grip. He balanced precariously for a moment. The right hand, the injured one, scrabbled for a hold. Then he appeared to lean out, away from the face of the rock, arms windmilling, until his feet slipped from their narrow ledge and he was suddenly in mid-air, suspended; and finally he dropped like a stone to the rocks below.

He made no sound.

He landed on a flat rock that jutted above the surface of the water. The noise his body made hitting the rock was sickening. He lay there on his back like a broken doll, arms outflung, head at an impossible angle.

Something vile seeped out from inside him on to the stone, and Lucy turned away.

She had killed him.

Everything happened at once, then.

There was a roaring sound from the sky and three aircraft with RAF circles on their wings flew out of the clouds and dipped low over the U-boat, their guns blazing.

Four sailors came up the hill toward the house at a jog-trot, one of them shouting 'Left-right-left-right-left-right.'

Another plane landed on the sea, a dinghy emerged, and a man in a life-jacket began to row toward the cliff.

A small ship came around the headland and steamed aggressively toward the U-boat.

The U-boat submerged.

The dinghy bumped into the rocks at the foot of the cliff, and the man got out and examined the body of Henry.

A boat she recognized as the coastguard cutter appeared.

One of the sailors came up to her and said: 'Are you all right, love? Only there's a little girl in the cottage crying for her mummy.'

'It's a boy,' Lucy said. 'I must cut his hair.' And for no reason at all she smiled.

Bloggs steered the dinghy toward the body at the foot of the cliff. The boat bumped against the rock, and he scrambled out and on to the flat surface.

It was Die Nadel.

He was very dead. His skull had smashed like a glass goblet when he hit the rock. Looking more closely, Bloggs could see that the man had been somewhat battered even before the fall: his right hand was mutilated and there was something wrong with his ankle.

Bloggs searched the body. The stiletto was where he had guessed it might be: in a sheath strapped to the left forearm. In the inside pocket of the expensive-looking, bloodstained jacket, Bloggs found a wallet, papers, money, and a little film can containing twenty-four 35mm photographic negatives. He held them up to the strengthening light: they were the negatives of the prints found in the envelopes Faber had sent to the Portuguese Embassy.

The sailors on the cliff top threw down a rope. Bloggs put Faber's possessions into his own pockets, then tied the rope around the corpse. They hauled it up, then sent the rope down for Bloggs.

When he got to the top one of the sailors said: 'You left his brains on the rock, but never mind.'

The sub-lieutenant introduced himself, and they walked across to the little cottage on top of the hill.

'We haven't touched anything, for fear of destroying evidence,' the senior sailor said.

'Don't worry too much,' Bloggs told him. 'There won't be a prosecution.'

They had to enter the house through the broken kitchen window. The woman was sitting at a table, with the child on her lap. Bloggs smiled at her. He could not think of anything to say.

He looked quickly around the little cottage. It was a battlefield. He saw the nailed-up windows, the barred doors, the remains of the fire, the dog with its throat cut, the shotguns, the broken bannister, and the axe embedded in the windowsill beside two severed fingers.

He thought: What kind of woman is she?

He set the sailors to work: one to tidy the house and unbar the doors and windows; another to mend the blown fuse; a third to make tea.

He sat down in front of the woman and looked at her. She was dressed in ill-fitting, mannish clothes; her hair was wet; her face was dirty. Despite all that she was remarkably beautiful, with lovely amber eyes in an oval face.

Bloggs smiled at the child and spoke very gently to the woman. 'What you've done is enormously important to the war,' he said. 'One of these days I'll explain just how important it is. But for now, I have to ask you two questions. Is that, okay?'

Her eyes focused on him, and after a moment she nodded.

'Did the man Faber succeed in contacting the U-boat by radio?'

The woman just looked blank.

Bloggs found a toffee in his trousers pocket. 'Can I give the boy a sweet?' he asked. 'He looks hungry.'

'Thank you,' she said.

'Now: did Faber contact the U-boat?'

'His name was Henry Baker,' she said.

'Ah. Well, did he?'

'No. I short-circuited the electricity.'

'That was smart,' Bloggs said. 'How did you do it?' She pointed at the empty light socket above them.

'Screwdriver, eh?'

'No.' She smiled thinly. 'I wasn't that smart. Fingers.'

He gave her a look of horror. The thought of deliberately . . . He shook himself. It was ghastly. He put it out of his mind. 'Right. Do you think anyone on the U-boat could have seen him coming down the cliff?'

The effort of concentration showed on her face. 'Nobody came out of the hatch,' she said. 'Could they have seen him through their periscope?'

'No,' he said confidently. 'This is good news. It means they don't know he's been captured and . . . neutralized. Anyway . . .' He changed the subject hastily. 'You've been through as much as men on the front line are expected to suffer. We're going to get you and the boy to a hospital on the mainland.'

'Yes,' she said.

Bloggs addressed the senior sailor. 'Is there any form of transport around?'

'Yes – a jeep down in that little stand of trees.'

'Good. Will you drive these two over to the jetty and get them on to your boat?'

'Surely.'

'Treat them gently.'

'Of course.'

Bloggs turned to the woman again. He felt an overwhelming surge of affection and admiration for her. She looked frail and helpless, now: but he knew she was brave and strong as well as beautiful. Impulsively, he took her hand. 'When you've been in hospital a day or two, you'll begin to feel terribly depressed. That's a sign you're getting better. I won't be far away, and the doctors will tell me. I'll want to talk to you some more. But not before you feel like it. Okay?'

At last she smiled at him, and it felt like the warmth of a fire. 'You're kind,' she said.

She stood up and carried her child out of the house.

'Kind?' Bloggs muttered to himself. 'God's truth, what a woman.'

He went upstairs to the radio and tuned it to the Royal Observer Corps frequency.

'Storm Island calling, over.'

'Come in, Storm Island.'

'Patch me through to London.'

'Hold on.' There was a long pause, then a familiar voice. 'Godliman.'

'Percy. We caught the . . . smuggler. He's dead.'

'Marvellous, marvellous.' There was triumph in God-liman's voice. 'Did he manage to contact his partner?'

'Almost certainly not.'

'Well done, well done!'

'Don't congratulate me,' Bloggs said. 'By the time I got here it was all over bar the tidying up.'

'Who killed him, then?'

'The woman.'

'Well, I'm damned. What's she like?'

Bloggs grinned. 'She's a hero, Percy.'

Godliman laughed aloud. 'I think I know what you mean.'

CHAPTER THIRTY-EIGHT

H ITLER STOOD at the panoramic window, looking out at the mountains. He wore his dove-grey uniform, and he looked tired and depressed. He had called his physician during the night.

Admiral Puttkamer saluted and said: 'Good morning, my Führer.'

Hitler turned and peered closely at his aide-de-camp. Those beady eyes never failed to unnerve Puttkamer. Hitler said: 'Was Die Nadel picked up?'

'No.' There was some trouble at the rendezvous – the English police were chasing smugglers. It appears Die Nadel was not there, anyway. He sent a wireless message a few minutes ago.' He proffered a sheet of paper.

Hitler took it from him, put on his spectacles, and began to read:

YOUR RENDEZVOUS INSECURE YOU CUNTS I AM
WOUNDED AND TRANSMITTING LEFT HANDED
FIRST UNITED STATES ARMY GROUP ASSEMBLED
EAST ANGLIA UNDER PATTON ORDER OF BATTLE
AS FOLLOWS TWENTYONE INFANTRY DIVISIONS
FIVE ARMOURED DIVISIONS APPROXIMATELY FIVE
THOUSAND AIRCRAFT PLUS REQUISITE TROOP

SHIPS IN THE WASH FUSAG WILL ATTACK CALAIS
JUNE FIFTEENTH REGARDS TO WILLI

Hitler handed the message back to Puttkamer and sighed. 'So it's Calais after all.'

'Can we be sure of this man?' the aide asked.

'Absolutely.' Hitler turned and walked across the room to a chair. His movements were stiff, and he seemed in pain. 'He is a loyal German. I know his family.'

'But your instinct . . .'

'Ach . . . I said I would trust this man's report, and so I shall.' He made a gesture of dismissal. 'Tell Rommel and Rundstedt they can't have their panzers. And send in that damned doctor.'

Puttkamer saluted again and went out to relay the orders.

Epilogue

CHAPTER THIRTY-NINE

WHEN GERMANY defeated England in the quarter-final of the 1970 World Cup soccer tournament Grandpa was furious.

He sat in front of the colour television set and muttered through his beard at the screen. 'Cunning!' he told the assorted experts who were now dissecting the game. 'Cunning and stealth! That's the way to defeat the Hun!'

He would not be mollified until his grandchildren arrived. Jo's white Jaguar drew up on the drive of the modest three-bedroom house, and little David rushed in to sit on Grandpa's lap and pull his beard. The rest of the family followed more sedately: Rebecca, David's little sister; then Jo's wife Ann; then Jo himself, prosperous-looking in a suede jacket. Grandma came out of the kitchen to greet them.

Jo said: 'Did you watch the football, Pop?'

'Terrible,' Grandpa said. 'We were rubbish.' Since he retired from the Force and had more leisure time, he had taken an interest in sport.

Jo scratched his moustache. 'The Germans were better,' he said. 'They play good football. We can't win it every time.'

'Don't talk to me about bloody Germans,' Grandpa said.

Jo grinned. 'I do a lot of business with Germany.'

Grandma's voice came from the kitchen. 'Don't start him off, Jo!' She pretended to be going deaf, but there was not much she missed.

'I know,' Grandpa said. 'Forgive and forget, and drive round in a bloody Audi.'

'Good cars.'

'Cunning and stealth, that's the way to defeat the Hun,' Grandpa repeated. He addressed the grandson on his lap, who was not really his grandson, since Jo was not his son. 'That's the way we beat them in the war, Davy – we tricked them.'

'How did you trick them?' David asked, with the child's assumption that his forebears did everything in history.

'Well, see, we made them think—' Grandpa's voice became low and conspiratorial, and the child giggled in anticipation. 'We made them think we were going to attack Calais—'

'That's in France, not Germany.'

'Yes, but the Germans were all over France, then. The Froggies didn't defend themselves as well as we did.'

Jo said: 'Nothing to do with the fact that we're an island, of course.'

Ann shushed him. 'Let Grandpa tell his war stories.'

'Anyway,' Grandpa continued, 'we made them think we were going to attack Calais, so they put all their tanks and soldiers there.' He used a cushion to represent France, an ashtray for the Germans, and a penknife for the Allies. '*But* we attacked Normandy, and there was nobody there but old Rommel and a few pop-guns! Cunning and stealth, see?'

'Didn't they find out about the trick?' David asked.

'They *nearly* did. In fact, there was one spy who found out. Now not many people know that, but I know because I was a spycatcher in the war.'

'What happened to the spy?'

'We killed him before he could tell.'

'Did you kill him, Grandpa?'

'No – Grandma did.'

David's eyes widened. '*Grandma* killed him?'

Grandma came in carrying a teapot, and said: 'Fred Bloggs, are you frightening the children?'

'Why shouldn't they know?' he groused. 'She's got a medal, you know. She won't tell me where she keeps it because she doesn't like me showing it to visitors.'

Grandma was pouring tea. 'It's all over now, and best forgotten, just as Jo says. Anyway, not much good came out of it.' She handed a cup and saucer to Grandpa.

He took her arm and held her there. '*Some* good came out of it,' he said. His voice was suddenly quite gentle, all the elderly grumpiness gone. 'I met a hero, and married her.'

They looked at each other for a moment. Her beautiful hair was pepper-and-salt now, and she wore it in a bun. She was heavier than she used to be. For years her clothes had always been fashionable and glamorous, but she no longer had the figure for haute couture.

But her eyes were still the same: large and amber, and remarkably beautiful.

Those eyes looked back at him, now, and they both were very still, remembering the way it had been.

Then David jumped off his grandpa's lap and knocked the cup of tea to the floor, and the spell was broken.

WHITEOUT

CHRISTMAS EVE

1 a.m.

Two tired men looked at Antonia Gallo with resentment and hostility in their eyes. They wanted to go home, but she would not let them. And they knew she was right, which made it worse.

All three were in the personnel department of Oxenford Medical. Antonia, always called Toni, was facilities director, and her main responsibility was security. Oxenford was a small pharmaceuticals outfit – a boutique company, in stock-market jargon – that did research on viruses that could kill. Security was deadly serious.

Toni had organized a spot check of supplies, and had found that two doses of an experimental drug were missing. That was bad enough: the drug, an antiviral agent, was top secret, its formula priceless. It might have been stolen for sale to a rival company. But another, more frightening possibility had brought the look of grim anxiety to Toni's freckled face, and drawn dark circles under her green eyes. A thief might have stolen the drug for personal use. And there was only one reason for that: someone had become infected by one of the lethal viruses used in Oxenford's laboratories.

The labs were located in a vast nineteenth-century

house built as a Scottish holiday home for a Victorian millionaire. It was nicknamed the Kremlin, because of the double row of fencing, the razor wire, the uniformed guards, and the state-of-the-art electronic security. But it looked more like a church, with pointed arches and a tower and rows of gargoyles along the roof.

The personnel office had been one of the grander bedrooms. It still had Gothic windows and linenfold panelling, but now there were filing cabinets instead of wardrobes, and desks with computers and phones where once there had been dressing tables crowded with crystal bottles and silver-backed brushes.

Toni and the two men were working the phones, calling everyone who had a pass to the top-security laboratory. There were four biosafety levels. At the highest, BSL4, the scientists worked in space suits, handling viruses for which there was no vaccine or antidote. Because it was the most secure location in the building, samples of the experimental drug were stored there.

Not everyone was allowed into BSL4. Biohazard training was compulsory, even for the maintenance men who went in to service air filters and repair autoclaves. Toni herself had undergone the training, so that she could enter the lab to check on security.

Only twenty-seven of the company's eighty staff had access. However, many had already departed for the Christmas vacation, and Monday had turned into Tuesday while the three people responsible doggedly tracked them down.

Toni got through to a resort in Barbados called Le Club Beach and, after much insistence, persuaded the assistant manager to go looking for a young laboratory technician called Jenny Crawford.

As Toni waited, she glanced at her reflection in the window. She was holding up well, considering the late hour. Her chocolate-brown chalk-stripe suit still looked businesslike, her thick hair was tidy, her face did not betray fatigue. Her father had been Spanish, but she had her Scottish mother's pale skin and red-blonde hair. She was tall and looked fit. Not bad, she thought, for thirty-eight years old.

'It must be the middle of the night back there!' Jenny said when at last she came to the phone.

'We've discovered a discrepancy in the BSL4 log,' Toni explained.

Jenny was a little drunk. 'That's happened before,' she said carelessly. 'But no one's ever made, like, a great big drama over it.'

'That's because I wasn't working here,' Toni said crisply. 'When was the last time you entered BSL4?'

'Tuesday, I think. Won't the computer tell you that?'

It would, but Toni wanted to know whether Jenny's story would match the computer record. 'And when was the last time you accessed the vault?' The vault was a locked refrigerator within BSL4.

Jenny's tone was becoming surly. 'I really don't remember, but it will be on video.' The touchpad combination lock on the vault activated a security camera that rolled the entire time the door was open.

'Do you recall the last time you used Madoba-2?' This was the virus the scientists were working on right now.

Jenny was shocked. 'Bloody hell, is that what's gone missing?'

'No, it's not. All the same—'

'I don't think I've ever handled an actual virus. I mostly work in the tissue-culture lab.'

That agreed with the information Toni had. 'Have you noticed any of your colleagues behaving in a way that was strange, or out of character, in the last few weeks?'

'This is like the sodding Gestapo,' Jenny said.

'Be that as it may, have you—'

'No, I have not.'

'Just one more question. Is your temperature normal?'

'Fuck me, are you saying I might have Madoba-2?'

'Have you got a cold or fever?'

'No!'

'Then you're all right. You left the country eleven days ago – by now you would have flu-like symptoms if anything were wrong. Thank you, Jenny. It's probably just an error in the log, but we have to make sure.'

'Well, you've spoiled my night.' Jenny hung up.

'Shame,' Toni said to the dead phone. She cradled the receiver and said: 'Jenny Crawford checks out. A cow, but straight.'

The laboratory director was Howard McAlpine. His bushy grey beard grew high on his cheekbones, so that the skin around his eyes looked like a pink mask. He was meticulous without being prissy, and Toni normally enjoyed working with him, but now he was bad-tempered. He leaned back in his chair and clasped his hands behind his head. 'The overwhelming likelihood is that the material unaccounted for was used perfectly legitimately by someone who simply forgot to make entries in the log.' His tone of voice was testy: he had said this twice before.

'I hope you're right,' Toni said non-comittally. She got up and went to the window. The personnel office overlooked the extension that housed the BSL4 laboratory. The new building seemed similar to the rest of the Kremlin, with barley-sugar chimneys and a clock tower, so that it would be difficult for an outsider to guess, from a distance, where in the complex the high-security lab was located. But its arched windows were opaque, the carved oak doors could not be opened, and closed-circuit television cameras gazed one-eyed from the monstrous heads of the gargoyles. It was a concrete blockhouse in Victorian disguise. The new building was on three levels. The labs were on the ground floor. As well as research space and storage, there was an intensive-care medical isolation facility for anyone who became infected with a dangerous virus. It had never been used. On the floor above was the air-handling equipment. Below, elaborate machinery sterilized all waste coming from the building. Nothing left the place alive, except human beings.

'We've learned a lot from this exercise,' Toni said in a placatory tone. She was in a delicate position, she thought anxiously. The two men were senior to her in rank and age – both were in their fifties. Although she had no right to give them orders, she had insisted they treat the discrepancy as a crisis. They both liked her, but she was stretching their goodwill to the limit. Still she felt she had to push it. At stake were public safety, the company's reputation, and her career. 'In future we must always have live phone numbers for everyone who has access to BSL4, wherever in the world they might be, so that we can reach them quickly in emergency. And we need to audit the log more than once a year.'

McAlpine grunted. As lab director he was responsible for the log, and the real reason for his mood was that he should have discovered the discrepancy himself. Toni's efficiency made him look bad.

She turned to the other man, who was the director of human resources. 'How far down your list are we, James?'

James Elliot looked up from his computer screen. He dressed like a stockbroker, in a pinstriped suit and spotted tie, as if to distinguish himself from the tweedy scientists. He seemed to regard the safety rules as tiresome bureaucracy, perhaps because he never worked hands-on with viruses. Toni found him pompous and silly. 'We've spoken to all but one of the twenty-seven staff that have access to BSL4,' he said. He spoke with exaggerated precision, like a tired teacher explaining something to the dullest pupil in the class. 'All of them told the truth about when they last entered the lab and opened the vault. None has noticed a colleague behaving strangely. And no one has a fever.'

'Who's the missing one?'

'Michael Ross, a lab technician.'

'I know Michael,' Toni said. He was a shy, clever man about ten years younger than Toni. 'In fact I've been to his home. He lives in a cottage about fifteen miles from here.'

'He's worked for the company for eight years without a blemish on his record.'

McAlpine ran his finger down a printout and said: 'He last entered the lab three Sundays ago, for a routine check on the animals.'

'What's he been doing since?'

'Holiday.'

'For how long – three weeks?'

Elliot put in: 'He was due back today.' He looked at his watch. 'Yesterday, I should say. Monday morning. But he didn't show up.'

'Did he call in sick?'

'No.'

Toni raised her eyebrows. 'And we can't reach him?'

'No answer from his home phone or his mobile.'

'Doesn't that strike you as odd?'

'That a single young man should extend his vacation without forewarning his employer? About as odd as rain in Glen Coe.'

Toni turned back to McAlpine. 'But you say Michael has a good record.'

The lab director looked worried. 'He's very conscientious. It's surprising that he should take unauthorized leave.'

Toni asked: 'Who was with Michael when he last entered the lab?' She knew he must have been accompanied, for there was a two-person rule in BSL4: because of the danger, no one could work there alone.

McAlpine consulted his list. 'Dr Ansari, a biochemist.'

'I don't think I know him.'

'Her. It's a woman. Monica.'

Toni picked up the phone. 'What's her number?'

Monica Ansari spoke with an Edinburgh accent and sounded as if she had been fast asleep. 'Howard McAlpine called me earlier, you know.'

'I'm sorry to trouble you again.'

'Has something happened?'

'It's about Michael Ross. We can't track him down.

I believe you were in BSL4 with him two weeks ago last Sunday.'

'Yes. Just a minute, let me put the light on.' There was a pause. 'God, is that the time?'

Toni pressed on. 'Michael went on holiday the next day.'

'He told me he was going to see his mother in Devon.'

That rang a bell. Toni recalled the reason she had gone to Michael Ross's house. About six months ago she had mentioned, in a casual conversation in the canteen, how much she liked Rembrandt's pictures of old women, with every crease and wrinkle lovingly detailed. You could tell, she had said, how much Rembrandt must have loved his mother. Michael had lit up with enthusiasm and revealed that he had copies of several Rembrandt etchings, cut out of magazines and auction-house catalogues. She had gone home with him after work to see the pictures, all of old women, tastefully framed and covering one wall of his small living room. She had worried that he was going to ask her for a date – she liked him, but not *that* way – but, to her relief, he genuinely wanted only to show off his collection. He was, she had concluded, a mother's boy.

'That's helpful,' Toni said to Monica. 'Just hold on.' She turned to James Elliot. 'Do we have his mother's contact details on file?'

Elliot moved his mouse and clicked. 'She's listed as next of kin.' He picked up the phone.

Toni spoke to Monica again. 'Did Michael seem his normal self that afternoon?'

'Totally.'

'Did you enter BSL4 together?'

'Yes. Then we went to separate changing rooms, of course.'

'When you entered the lab itself, was he already there?'

'Yes, he changed quicker than I did.'

'Did you work alongside him?'

'No. I was in a side lab, dealing with tissue cultures. He was checking on the animals.'

'Did you leave together?'

'He went a few minutes before I did.'

'It sounds to me as if he could have accessed the vault without your knowing about it.'

'Easily.'

'What's your impression of Michael?'

'He's all right . . . inoffensive, I suppose.'

'Yeah, that's a good word for him. Do you know if he has a girlfriend?'

'I don't think so.'

'Do you find him attractive?'

'Nice-looking, but not sexy.'

Toni smiled. 'Exactly. Anything odd about him, in your experience?'

'No.'

Toni sensed a hesitation, and remained silent, giving the other woman time. Beside her, Elliot was speaking to someone, asking for Michael Ross or his mother.

After a moment, Monica said: 'I mean, the fact that someone lives alone doesn't make them a nutcase, does it?'

Beside Toni, Elliot was saying into the phone: 'How very strange. I'm sorry to have troubled you so late at night.'

Toni's curiosity was pricked by what she could hear of

Elliot's conversation. She ended her call, saying: 'Thanks again, Monica. I hope you get back to sleep all right.'

'My husband's a family doctor,' she said. 'We're used to phone calls in the middle of the night.'

Toni hung up. 'Michael Ross had plenty of time to open the vault,' she said. 'And he lives alone.' She looked at Elliot. 'Did you reach his mother's house?'

'It's an old folks' home,' Elliot said. He looked frightened. 'And Mrs Ross died last winter.'

'Oh, shit,' said Toni.

3 a.m.

Powerful security lights lit up the towers and gables of the Kremlin. The temperature was five below zero, but the sky was clear and there was no snow. The building faced a Victorian garden, with mature trees and shrubs. A three-quarter moon shed a grey light on naked nymphs sporting in dry fountains while stone dragons stood guard.

The silence was shattered by the roar of engines as two vans drove out of the garage. Both were marked with the international biohazard symbol, four broken black circles on a vivid yellow background. The guard at the gatehouse had the barrier up already. They drove out and turned south, going dangerously fast.

Toni Gallo was at the wheel of the lead vehicle, driving as if it were her Porsche, using the full width of the road, racing the engine, powering through bends. She feared she was too late. In the van with Toni were three men trained in decontamination. The second vehicle was a mobile isolation unit with a paramedic at the wheel and a doctor, Ruth Solomons, in the passenger seat.

Toni was afraid she might be wrong, but terrified she might be right.

She had activated a red alert on the basis of nothing

but suspicion. The drug might have been used legitimately by a scientist who just forgot to make the appropriate entry in the log, as Howard McAlpine believed. Michael Ross might simply have extended his holiday without permission; and the story about his mother might have been no more than a misunderstanding. In that case, someone was sure to say that Toni had overreacted – like a typical hysterical woman, James Elliot would add. She might find Michael Ross safely asleep in bed with his phone turned off, and she winced to think what she would then say to her boss, Stanley Oxenford, in the morning.

But it would be much worse if she turned out to be right.

An employee was absent without leave; he had lied about where he was going; and samples of the new drug were missing from the vault. Had Michael Ross done something that put him at risk of catching a lethal infection? The drug was still in the trial stage, and was not effective against all viruses, but he would have figured it was better than nothing. Whatever he was up to, he had wanted to make sure no one called at his house for a couple of weeks; and so he had pretended he was going to Devon, to visit a mother who was no longer alive.

Monica Ansari had said: 'The fact that someone lives alone doesn't make them a nutcase, does it?' It was one of those statements that meant the opposite of what it said. The biochemist had sensed something odd about Michael even though, as a rational scientist, she hesitated to rely on mere intuition.

Toni believed that intuition should never be ignored.

She could hardly bear to think of the consequences if the Madoba-2 virus had somehow escaped. It was highly infectious, spreading fast through coughs and sneezes. And it was fatal. A shudder of dread went through her, and she pushed down on the accelerator pedal.

The road was deserted and it took only twenty minutes to reach Michael Ross's isolated home. The entrance was not clearly marked, but Toni remembered it. She turned into a short drive that led to a low stone cottage behind a garden wall. The place was dark. Toni stopped the van next to a Volkswagen Golf, presumably Michael's. She sounded her horn long and loud.

Nothing happened. No lights came on, no one opened a door or window. Toni turned off the engine. Silence.

If Michael had gone away, why was his car here?

'Bunny suits, please, gentlemen,' she said.

They all climbed into orange space suits, including the medical team from the second van. It was an awkward business. The suit was made of a heavy plastic that did not easily yield or fold. It closed with an airtight zip. They helped each other attach the gloves to the wrists with duct tape. Finally they worked the plastic feet of the suits into rubber overboots.

The suits were completely sealed. The wearer breathed through a HEPA filter – a High Efficiency Particulate Air filter – with an electric fan powered by a battery pack worn on the suit belt. The filter would keep out any breathable particles that might carry germs or viruses. It also took out all but the strongest smells. The fan made a constant shushing noise that some people found oppressive. A headset in the helmet enabled them to speak to one another and to the switchboard at the Kremlin over a scrambled radio channel.

When they were ready, Toni looked again at the house. Should someone glance out of a window now, and see seven people in orange space suits, he would think UFO aliens were real.

If there was someone in there, he was not looking out of any windows.

'I'll go first,' Toni said.

She went up to the front door, walking stiffly in the clumsy plastic suit. She rang the bell and banged the knocker. After a few moments, she went around the building to the back. There was a neat garden with a wooden shed. She found the back door unlocked, and stepped inside. She remembered standing in the kitchen while Michael made tea. She walked quickly through the house, turning on lights. The Rembrandts were still on the living-room wall. The place was clean, tidy and empty.

She spoke to the others over the headset. 'No one home.' She could hear the dejected tone of her own voice.

Why had he left his house unlocked? Perhaps he was never coming back.

This was a blow. If Michael had been here, the mystery could have been solved quickly. Now there would have to be a search. He might be anywhere in the world. There was no knowing how long it would take to find him. She thought with dread of the nerve-racking days, or even weeks, of anxiety.

She went back out into the garden. To be thorough, she tried the door of the garden shed. It, too, was unlocked. When she opened it, she caught the trace of a smell, unpleasant but vaguely familiar. It must be very strong, she realized, to penetrate the suit's filter. Blood, she thought. The shed smelled like a slaughterhouse. She murmured: 'Oh my God.'

Ruth Solomons, the doctor, heard her and said: 'What is it?'

'Just a minute.' The inside of the little wooden building was black: there were no windows. She fumbled in the dark and found a switch. When the light came on, she cried out in shock.

The others all spoke at once, asking what was wrong.

'Come quickly!' she said. 'To the garden shed. Ruth first.'

Michael Ross lay on the floor, face up. He was bleeding from every orifice: eyes, nose, mouth, ears. Blood pooled around him on the plank floor. Toni did not need the doctor to tell her that Michael was suffering from a massive multiple haemorrhage – a classic symptom of Madoba-2 and similar infections. He was very dangerous, his body an unexploded bomb full of the deadly virus. But he was alive. His chest went up and down, and a weak bubbling sound came from his mouth. She bent down, kneeling in the sticky puddle of fresh blood, and looked closely at him. 'Michael!' she said, shouting to be heard through the plastic of her helmet. 'It's Toni Gallo from the lab!'

There was a flicker of intelligence in his bloody eyes. He opened his mouth and mumbled something.

'What?' she shouted. She leaned closer.

'No cure,' he said. Then he vomited. A jet of black fluid exploded from his mouth, splashing Toni's faceplate. She jerked back and cried out in alarm, even though she knew she was protected by the suit.

She was pushed aside, and Ruth Solomons bent over Michael.

'The pulse is very weak,' the doctor said over the headset. She opened Michael's mouth and used her gloved fingers to clear some of the blood and vomit from his throat. 'I need a laryngoscope – fast!' Seconds later, a paramedic rushed in with the implement. Ruth pushed it into Michael's mouth, clearing his throat so that he could breathe more easily. 'Bring the isolation stretcher, quick as you can.' She opened her medical case and took out a syringe already loaded – with morphine and a blood coagulant, Toni assumed. Ruth pushed the needle into Michael's neck and depressed the plunger. When she pulled the syringe out, Michael bled copiously from the small hole.

Toni was swamped by a wave of grief. She thought of Michael walking around the Kremlin, sitting in his house drinking tea, talking animatedly about etchings; and the sight of this desperately damaged body became all the more painful and tragic.

'Okay,' Ruth said. 'Let's get him out of here.'

Two paramedics picked Michael up and carried him out to a gurney enclosed in a transparent plastic tent. They slid the patient through a porthole in one end of the tent, then sealed it. They wheeled the gurney across Michael's garden.

Before getting into the ambulance, they had to decontaminate themselves and the stretcher. One of Toni's team had already got out a shallow plastic tub like a children's paddling pool. Now Dr Solomons and the paramedics took it in turns to stand in the tub and be sprayed with a powerful disinfectant that destroyed any virus by oxidizing its protein.

Toni watched, aware that every second's delay made it less likely that Michael would survive, knowing that the decontamination procedure had to be followed rigorously to prevent other deaths. She felt distraught that a deadly virus had escaped from her laboratory. It had never occurred before in the history of Oxenford Medical. The fact that she had been right to make such a fuss about the missing drugs, and her colleagues had been wrong to play it down, was small consolation. Her job was to prevent this happening, and she had failed. Would poor Michael die in consequence? Would others die?

The paramedics loaded the stretcher into the ambulance. Dr Solomons jumped into the back with the patient. They slammed the doors and roared off into the night.

Toni said: 'Let me know what happens, Ruth. You can phone me on this headset.'

Ruth's voice was already weakening with distance. 'He's gone into a coma,' she said. She added something else, but she was out of range, and her words became indistinguishable, then faded away altogether.

Toni shook herself to get rid of her gloomy torpor. There was work to be done. 'Let's clean up,' she said.

One of the men took a roll of yellow tape that read 'Biohazard – do not cross line' and began to run it around the entire property, house and shed and garden, and around Michael's car. Luckily there were no other houses near enough to worry about. If Michael had lived in a block of flats with communal air vents, it would already have been too late for decontamination.

The others got out rolls of garbage bags, plastic garden sprayers already filled with disinfectant, boxes of cleaning cloths, and large white plastic drums. Every surface had to be sprayed and wiped down. Hard objects and precious possessions such as jewellery would be sealed in the drums and taken to the Kremlin to be sterilized by high-pressure steam in an autoclave. Everything else would be double-bagged and destroyed in the medical incinerator underneath the BSL4 lab.

Toni got one of the men to help her wipe Michael's black vomit off her suit and spray her. She had to repress an urge to tear the defiled suit off her body.

While the men cleaned up, she looked around, searching for clues as to why this had happened. As she had feared, Michael had stolen the experimental drug because he knew or suspected he had been infected with Madoba-2. But what had he done to expose himself to the virus?

In the shed there was a glass case with an air extractor, rather like an improvised biosafety cabinet. She had hardly looked at it before, because she was concentrating on Michael, but now she saw that there was a dead rabbit in the case. It looked as if it had died of the illness that had infected Michael. Had it come from the laboratory?

Beside it was a water bowl labelled 'Joe'. That was significant. Laboratory staff rarely named the creatures they worked with. They were kind to the subjects of their experiments, but they did not allow themselves to become attached to animals that were going to be killed. However,

Michael had given this creature an identity, and treated it as a pet. Did he feel guilty about his work?

She stepped outside. A police patrol car was drawing up alongside the biohazard van. Toni had been expecting them. In accordance with the Critical Incident Response Plan that Toni herself had devised, the security guards at the Kremlin had automatically phoned regional police headquarters at Inverburn to notify them of a Red Alert. Now they were coming to find out how real the crisis was.

Toni had been a police officer herself, all her working life, until two years ago. For most of her career, she had been a golden girl – promoted rapidly, shown off to the media as the new style of modern cop, and tipped to be Scotland's first woman chief constable. Then she had clashed with her boss over a hot-button issue, racism in the force. He maintained that police racism was not institutionalized. She said that officers routinely concealed racist incidents, and that amounted to institutionalization. The row had been leaked to a newspaper, she had refused to deny what she believed, and she had been forced to resign.

At the time she had been living with Frank Hackett, another detective. They had been together eight years, although they had never married. When she fell out of favour, he left her. It still hurt.

Two young officers got out of the patrol car, a man and a woman. Toni knew most local police of her own generation, and some of the older ones remembered her late father, Sergeant Antonio Gallo, inevitably called Spanish Tony. However, she did not recognize these two. Over the headset, she said: 'Jonathan, the police have arrived. Would you please decontaminate and talk to them? Just say we have confirmed the escape of a virus from the lab. They'll call Jim Kincaid, and I'll brief him when he gets here.'

Superintendent Kincaid was responsible for what they called CBRN – chemical, biological, radiological, and nuclear incidents. He had worked with Toni on her plan. The two of them would implement a careful, low-key response to this incident.

By the time Kincaid arrived, she would like to have some information to give him about Michael Ross. She went into the house. Michael had turned the second bedroom into his study. On a side table were three framed photographs of his mother: as a slim teenager in a tight sweater; as a happy parent, holding a baby that looked like Michael; and in her sixties, with a fat black-and-white cat in her lap.

Toni sat at his desk and read his emails, operating the computer keyboard clumsily with her rubber-gloved hands. He had ordered a book called *Animal Ethics* from Amazon. He had also enquired about university courses in moral philosophy. She checked his Internet browser, and found he had recently visited animal-rights websites. Clearly, he had become troubled about the morality of his work. But it seemed no one at Oxenford Medical had realized that he was unhappy.

Toni sympathized with him. Every time she saw a beagle or a hamster lying in a cage, deliberately made ill by a disease the scientists were studying, she felt a tug of pity. But then she remembered her father's death. He had suffered a brain tumour in his fifties, and he had died bewildered, humiliated and in pain. His condition might one day be curable thanks to research on monkey brains. Animal research was a sad necessity, in her opinion.

Michael kept his papers in a cardboard filing box, neatly labelled: Bills, Guarantees, Bank Statements, Instruction Manuals. Under Memberships, Toni found an acknowledgement of his subscription to an organization called Animals Are Free. The picture was becoming clear.

The work calmed her distress. She had always been good at detective procedures. Being forced out of the police had been a bitter blow. It felt good to use her old skills, and know that she still had the talent.

She found Michael's address book and his appointments diary in a drawer. The diary showed nothing for the last two weeks. As she was opening the address book, a blue flash caught her eye through the window, and she looked out to see a grey Volvo saloon with a police light on its roof. That would be Jim Kincaid.

She went outside and got one of the team to decontaminate her. Then she took off her helmet to talk to the Superintendent. However, the man in the Volvo was not Jim. When his face caught the moonlight, Toni saw that it was Superintendent Frank Hackett – her ex. Her heart sank. Although he was the one who had left, he always acted as if he had been the injured party.

She resolved to be calm, friendly and businesslike.

He got out of the car and came towards her. She said: 'Please don't cross the line – I'll come out.' She realized right away she had made an error of tact. He was the police officer and she was the civilian – he would feel that he should be giving orders to her, not the other way around.

The frown that crossed his face showed her that he had felt the slight. Trying to be more friendly, she said: 'How are you, Frank?'

'What's going on here?'

'A technician from the lab appears to have caught a virus. We've just taken him away in an isolation ambulance. Now we're decontaminating his house. Where's Jim Kincaid?'

'He's on holiday.'

'Where?' Toni hoped Jim might be reached and brought back for this emergency.

'Portugal. He and his wife have a wee timeshare.'

A pity, Toni thought. Kincaid knew about biohazards, but Frank did not.

Reading her mind, Frank said: 'Don't worry.' He had in his hand a photocopied document an inch thick. 'I've got the protocol here.' It was the plan Toni had agreed with Kincaid. Frank had obviously been reading it while waiting. 'My first duty is to secure the area.' He looked around.

Toni had already secured the area, but she said nothing. Frank needed to assert himself.

He called out to the two uniformed officers in the patrol car. 'You two! Move that car to the entrance of the driveway, and don't let anyone by without asking me.'

'Good idea,' Toni said, though in truth it made no difference to anything.

Frank was referring to the document. 'Then we have to make sure no one leaves the scene.'

Toni nodded. 'There's no one here but my team, all in biohazard suits.'

'I don't like this protocol – it puts civilians in charge of a crime scene.'

'What makes you think this is a crime scene?'

'Samples of a drug were stolen.'

'Not from here.'

Frank let that pass. 'How did your man catch the virus, anyway? You all wear those suits in the laboratory, don't you?'

'The local health board must figure that out,' Toni said, prevaricating. 'There's no point in speculation.'

'Were there any animals here when you arrived?'

Toni hesitated.

That was enough for Frank, who was a good detective because he did not miss much. 'So an animal got out of the lab and infected the technician when he wasn't wearing a suit?'

'I don't know what happened, and I don't want half-baked theories circulating. Could we concentrate for now on public safety?'

'Aye. But you're not just worried about the public. You want to protect the company and your precious Professor Oxenford.'

Toni wondered why he said 'precious' – but before she could react she heard a chime from her helmet. 'I'm getting a phone call,' she said to Frank. 'Sorry.' She took the headset out of the helmet and put it on. The chime came again, then there was a hiss as the connection was made, and she heard the voice of a security guard on the switchboard at the Kremlin. 'Doctor Solomons is calling Ms Gallo.'

Toni said: 'Hello?'

The doctor came on the line. 'Michael died, Toni.'

Toni closed her eyes. 'Oh, Ruth, I'm so sorry.'

'He would have died even if we'd got to him twenty-four hours earlier. I'm almost certain he had Madoba-2.'

Toni's voice was choked by grief. 'We did all we could.'

'Have you any idea how it happened?'

Toni did not want to say much in front of Frank. 'He was troubled about cruelty to animals. And I think he may have been unbalanced by the death of his mother, a year ago.'

'Poor boy.'

'Ruth, I've got the police here. I'll talk to you later.'

'Okay.' The connection was broken. Toni took off the headset.

Frank said: 'So he died.'

'His name was Michael Ross, and he appears to have contracted a virus called Madoba-2.'

'What kind of animal was it?'

On the spur of the moment, Toni decided to set a little trap for Frank. 'A hamster,' she said. 'Named Fluffy.'

'Could others have become infected?'

'That's the number one question. Michael lived here alone; he had no family and few friends. Anyone who visited him before he got sick would be safe, unless they did something highly intimate, like sharing a hypodermic needle. Anyone who came here when he was showing symptoms would surely have called a doctor. So there's a good chance he has not passed the virus on.' Toni was playing it down. If she had been talking to Kincaid, she would have been more candid, for she could have trusted him not to start a scare. But Frank was different. She finished: 'But obviously our first priority must be to contact everyone who might have met Michael in the last sixteen days. I've found his address book.'

Frank tried a different tack. 'I heard you say he was troubled about cruelty to animals. Did he belong to a group?'

'Yes – Animals Are Free.'

'How do you know?'

'I've been checking his personal stuff.'

'That's a job for the police.'

'I agree. But you can't go into the house.'

'I could put on a suit.'

'It's not just the suit, it's the biohazard training that you have to undergo before you're allowed to wear one.'

Frank was becoming angry again. 'Then bring the stuff out here to me.'

'Why don't I get one of my team to fax all his papers to you? We could also upload the entire hard disk of his computer.'

'I want the originals! What are you hiding in there?'

'Nothing, I promise you. But everything in the house has to be decontaminated, either with disinfectant or by high-pressure steam. Both processes destroy papers and might well damage a computer.'

'I'm going to get this protocol changed. I wonder whether the chief constable knows what Kincaid has let you get away with.'

Toni felt weary. It was the middle of the night, she had a major crisis to deal with, and she was being forced to pussyfoot around the feelings of a resentful former lover. 'Oh, Frank, for God's sake – you might be right, but this is what we've got, so could we try to forget the past and work as a team?'

'Your idea of teamwork is everyone doing what you say.'

She laughed. 'Fair enough. What do you think should be our next move?'

'I'll inform the health board. They're the lead agency, according to the protocol. Once they've tracked down their designated biohazard consultant, he'll want to convene a meeting here first thing in the morning. Meanwhile, we should start contacting everyone who might have seen Michael Ross. I'll get a couple of detectives phoning every number in that address book. I suggest you question every employee at the Kremlin. It would be useful to have that done by the time we meet with the health board.'

'All right.' Toni hesitated. She had something she had to ask Frank. His best friend was Carl Osborne, a local television reporter who valued sensation more than accuracy. If Carl got hold of this story he would start a riot.

She knew that the way to get something from Frank was to be matter-of-fact, not appearing either assertive or needy. 'There's a paragraph in the protocol I've got to mention,' she began. 'It says that no statements should be made to the press without first being discussed by the main interested parties, including the police, the health board and the company.'

'No problem.'

'The reason I mention it is that this doesn't need to become a major public scare. The chances are that no one is in danger.'

'Good.'

'We don't want to hold anything back, but the publicity should be calm and measured. No one needs to panic.'

Frank grinned. 'You're frightened of tabloid stories about killer hamsters roaming the Highlands.'

'You owe me, Frank. I hope you remember.'

His face darkened. 'I *owe* you?'

She lowered her voice, although there was no one nearby. 'You remember Farmer Johnny Kirk.' Kirk had been a big-time cocaine importer. Born in the rough Glasgow neighbourhood of Garscube Road, he had never seen a farm in his life, but got the nickname from the oversize green rubber boots he wore to ease the pain of the corns on his feet. Frank had put together a case against Farmer Johnny. During the trial, by accident, Toni had come across evidence that would have helped the defence. She had told Frank, but Frank had not informed the court. Johnny was as guilty as sin, and Frank had got a conviction – but, if the truth ever came out, Frank's career would be over.

Now Frank said angrily: 'Are you threatening to bring that up again if I don't do what you want?'

'No, just reminding you of a time when you needed me to keep quiet about something, and I did.'

His attitude changed again. He had been frightened, for a moment, but now he was his old arrogant self. 'We all bend the rules from time to time. That's life.'

'Yes. And I'm asking you not to leak this story to your friend Carl Osborne, or anyone else in the media.'

Frank grinned. 'Why, Toni,' he said in a tone of mock indignation, 'I never do things like that.'

7 a.m.

Kit Oxenford woke early, feeling eager and anxious at the same time. It was a strange sensation.

Today he was going to rob Oxenford Medical.

The idea filled him with excitement. It would be the greatest prank ever. It would be written up in books with titles like *The Perfect Crime*. Even better, it would be revenge on his father. The company would be destroyed, and Stanley Oxenford would be ruined financially. The fact that the old man would never know who had done this to him somehow made it better. It would be a secret gratification that Kit could hug to himself for the rest of his life.

But he was anxious, too. This was unusual. By nature, he was not a worrier. Whatever trouble he was in, he could generally talk his way out. He rarely planned anything.

He had planned today. Perhaps that was his problem.

He lay in bed with his eyes closed, thinking of the obstacles he had to overcome.

First, there was the physical security around the Kremlin: the double row of fencing, the razor wire, the lights, the intruder alarms. Those alarms were protected by tamper switches, shock sensors, and end-of-line circuitry that would detect a short circuit. The alarms were directly connected to regional police headquarters at Inverburn via a phone line that was continuously checked by the system to verify that it was operational.

None of that would protect the place against Kit and his collaborators.

Then there were the guards, watching important areas on closed-circuit television cameras, patrolling the premises hourly. Their TV monitors were fitted with high-security biased switches that would detect equipment substitution, for example if the feed from a camera were replaced by a signal from a videotape player.

Kit had thought of a way around that.

Finally there was the elaborate scheme of access control: the plastic credit-card passes, each bearing a photo of the authorized user plus details of the user's fingerprint embedded in a chip.

Defeating this system would be complicated, but Kit knew how to do it.

His degree was in computer science, and he had been top of his class, but he had an even more important advantage. He had designed the software that controlled the entire security set-up at the Kremlin. It was his baby. He had done a terrific job for his ungrateful father, and the system was virtually impenetrable to an outsider, but Kit knew its secrets.

At around midnight tonight, he would walk into the holy of holies, the BSL4 laboratory, the most secure location in Scotland. With him would be his client, a quietly menacing Londoner called Nigel Buchanan, and two collaborators. Once there, Kit would open the refrigerated vault with a simple four-digit code. Then Nigel would steal samples of Stanley Oxenford's precious new antiviral drug.

They would not keep the samples long. Nigel had a strict deadline. He had to hand over the samples by ten o'clock tomorrow morning, Christmas Day. Kit did not know the reason for the deadline. He did not know who the customer was, either, but he could guess. It had to be one of the pharmaceutical multinationals. Having a sample to analyse would save years of research. The company would be able to make its own version of the drug, instead of paying Oxenford millions in licensing fees.

It was dishonest, of course, but men found excuses for dishonesty when the stakes were high. Kit could picture the company's distinguished chairman, with his silver hair and pinstriped suit, saying hypocritically: 'Can you assure me categorically that no employee of our organization broke any laws in obtaining this sample?'

The best part of Kit's plan, he felt, was that the intrusion would go unnoticed until long after he and Nigel had left the Kremlin. Today, Tuesday, was Christmas Eve. Tomorrow and the next day were holidays. At the earliest, the alarm might be sounded on Friday, when one or two eager-beaver scientists would show up for work; but there was a good chance the theft would not be spotted then or at the weekend, giving Kit and the gang until Monday of next week to cover their tracks. It was more than they needed.

So why was he frightened? The face of Toni Gallo, his father's security chief, came into his mind. She was a freckled redhead, very attractive in a muscular sort of way, though too formidable a personality for Kit's taste. Was she the reason for his fear? Once before he had underestimated her – with disastrous results.

But his plan was brilliant. 'Brilliant,' he said aloud, trying to convince himself.

'What is?' said a female voice beside him.

He grunted in surprise. He had forgotten that he was not alone. He opened his eyes. The apartment was pitch dark.

'What's brilliant?' she repeated.

'The way you dance,' he said, improvising. He had met her in a club last night.

'You're not bad yourself,' she said in a strong Glasgow accent. 'Nifty footwork.'

He racked his brains for her name. 'Maureen,' he said. She must be Catholic, with a name like that. He rolled over and put his arm around her, trying to remember what she looked like. She felt nicely rounded. He liked girls not too thin. She moved towards him willingly. Blonde or brunette? he wondered. It might be interestingly kinky to have sex with a girl not knowing what she looked like. He was reaching for her breasts when he remembered what he had to do today, and his amorousness evaporated. 'What's the time?' he said.

'Time for a wee shag,' Maureen said eagerly.

Kit rolled away from her. The digital clock on the hi-fi said 07:10. 'Got to get up,' he said. 'Busy day.' He wanted to be at his father's house in time for lunch. He was going there ostensibly for the Christmas holiday, actually to steal something he needed for tonight's robbery.

'How can you be busy on Christmas Eve?'

'Maybe I'm Santa Claus.' He sat on the edge of the bed and switched on the light.

Maureen was disappointed. 'Well, this wee elf is going to have a lie in, if that's all right with Santa,' she said grumpily.

He glanced at her, but she had pulled the duvet over her head. He still did not know what she looked like.

He walked naked to the kitchen and started making coffee.

His loft was divided into two big spaces. There was a living room, with open kitchen, and a bedroom beyond. The living room was full of electronic gear: a big flat-screen television, an elaborate sound system, and a stack of computers and accessories connected by a jungle of cables. Kit had always enjoyed picking the locks of other people's computer defences. The only way to become an expert in software security was to be a hacker first.

While he was working for his father, designing and installing protection for the BSL4 laboratory, he had pulled off one of his best scams. With the help of Ronnie Sutherland, then head of security for Oxenford Medical, he had devised a way of skimming money from the company. He had rigged the accounting software so that, in summing a series of suppliers' invoices, the computer simply added one per cent to the total, then transferred the one per cent to Ronnie's bank account in a transaction that did not appear on any report. The scam relied on no one checking the computer's arithmetic – and no one had, until one day Toni Gallo had seen Ronnie's wife parking a new Mercedes coupé outside Marks & Spencer's in Inverburn.

Kit had been astonished and frightened by the dogged persistence with which Toni had investigated. There was a discrepancy, and she had to have the explanation. She just never gave up. Worse, when she figured out what was going on, nothing in the world would prevent her from telling the boss, Kit's father. He had pleaded with her not to bring anguish to an old man. He had tried to convince her that Stanley Oxenford in his rage would fire her, not Kit. Finally he had rested a hand lightly on her hip, given her his best naughty-boy grin, and said in a come-to-bed voice: 'You and I should be friends, not enemies.' None of it had worked.

Kit had not found employment since being fired by his father. Unfortunately, he had continued to gamble. Ronnie had introduced him to an illegal casino where he was able to get credit, doubtless because his father was a famous millionaire scientist. He tried not to think of how much money he now owed: the figure made him sick with fear and self-disgust, and he just wanted to throw himself off the Forth Bridge. But his reward for tonight's work would pay off the entire sum and give him a fresh start.

He took his coffee into the bathroom and looked at himself in the mirror. At one time he had been in the British team for the Winter Olympics, and he had spent every weekend either skiing or training. Then he had been as lean and fit as a greyhound. Now he saw a little softness in his outline. 'You're putting on weight,' he said. But he still had thick brown hair that flopped adorably over his forehead. His face looked strained. He tried his Hugh Grant expression, head down bashfully, looking up out of the corners of his blue eyes with a winning smile. Yes, he could still do it. Toni Gallo might be immune, but Maureen had fallen for it only last night.

While shaving he turned on the bathroom TV and got

a local news programme. The British Prime Minister had arrived in his Scottish constituency for Christmas. Glasgow Rangers had paid nine million pounds for a striker called Giovanni Santangelo. 'There's a good old Scots name,' Kit said to himself. The weather was going to continue cold but clear. A fierce blizzard in the Norwegian Sea was drifting south, but was expected to pass to the west of Scotland. Then came a local news story that froze Kit's blood.

He heard the familiar voice of Carl Osborne, a Scottish television celebrity with a reputation for lurid reports. Glancing at the screen, Kit saw the very building he was planning to rob tonight. Osborne was broadcasting from outside the gates of Oxenford Medical. It was still dark, but powerful security lights illuminated the ornate Victorian architecture. 'What the hell is this?' Kit said worriedly.

Osborne said: 'Scientists experiment with some of the most dangerous viruses in the world right here in Scotland, in the building behind me, dubbed "Frankenstein's Castle" by local people.'

Kit had never heard anyone call it 'Frankenstein's Castle'. Osborne was making that up. Its nickname was the Kremlin.

'But today, in what seems to some observers to be Nature's retribution for Mankind's meddling, a young technician died of one of these viruses.'

Kit put down his razor. This would be woundingly bad publicity for Oxenford Medical, he realized immediately. Normally, he would have gloated at his father's trouble, but today he was more worried about the effect of such publicity on his own plans.

'Michael Ross, thirty-one, was struck down by a virus called Ebola, after the African village where it germinated. This agonizing affliction causes painful, suppurating boils all over the victim's body.'

Kit was pretty sure Osborne was getting the facts wrong, but his audience would not know. This was tabloid television. But would the death of Michael Ross jeopardize Kit's planned robbery?

'Oxenford Medical has always claimed its research poses no threat to local people or the surrounding countryside, but the death of Michael Ross throws that claim into serious doubt.'

Osborne was wearing a bulky anorak and a woolly hat, and he looked as if he had not slept much last night. Someone had woken him up in the early hours of the morning with a tip-off, Kit guessed.

'Ross may have been bitten by an animal he stole from the laboratory here and took to his home a few miles away,' Osborne went on.

'Oh, no,' said Kit. This was getting worse and worse. Surely he was not going to be forced to abandon his grand scheme? It would be too much to bear.

'Did Michael Ross work alone, or was he part of a larger group that may attempt to free more plague-carrying animals from Oxenford Medical's secret laboratories? Do we face the prospect of innocent-seeming dogs and rabbits roaming free over the Scottish landscape, spreading the lethal virus wherever they go? No one here is prepared to say.'

Whatever they might or might not say, Kit knew what the people at the Kremlin were doing: upgrading their security as fast as they could. Toni Gallo would be there already, tightening up procedures, checking alarms and cameras, briefing the security guards. It was the worst possible news for Kit. He was enraged. 'Why do I have such bad luck?' he said aloud.

'Be that as it may,' said Carl Osborne, 'Michael Ross appears to have died for love of a hamster named Fluffy.' His tone was so tragic that Kit half expected the reporter to wipe a tear from his eye, but Osborne stopped short of that.

The studio anchor, an attractive blonde with carved hair, now said: 'Carl, has Oxenford Medical made any comment at all on this extraordinary incident?'

'Yes.' Carl looked at a notebook. 'They say they are saddened and distressed by the death of Michael Ross, but the indications are that nobody else will be affected by the virus. Nevertheless, they would like to speak to anyone who has seen Ross in the past sixteen days.'

'Presumably, people who have been in contact with him may have picked up the virus.'

'Yes, and perhaps infected others. So the company's statement that no one else is affected seems more like a pious hope than a scientific prediction.'

'A very worrying story,' the anchor said to camera. 'Carl Osborne with that report. And now football.'

In a fury, Kit stabbed at the remote control, trying to turn off the television, but he was too agitated, and kept pressing the wrong buttons. In the end he grabbed the lead and yanked the plug out of its socket. He was tempted to throw the set through the window. This was a catastrophe.

Osborne's doomsday forecast about the virus spreading

might not be true, but the one sure consequence was that security at the Kremlin would be watertight. Tonight was the worst possible time to try to rob the place. Kit would have to call it off. He was a gambler: if he had a good hand, he was willing to bet the farm, but he knew that when the cards were against him it was best to fold.

At least I won't have to spend Christmas with my father, he thought sourly.

Maybe they could do the job some other time, when the excitement had died down, and security had returned to its normal level. Perhaps the customer could be persuaded to postpone his deadline. Kit shuddered when he thought of his enormous debt remaining unpaid. But there was no point in going ahead when failure was so likely.

He left the bathroom. The clock on the hi-fi said 07:28. It was early to telephone, but this was urgent. He picked up the handset and dialled.

The call was answered immediately. A man's voice said simply: 'Yes?'

'This is Kit. Is he in?'

'What do you want?'

'I need to speak to him. It's important.'

'He's not up yet.'

'Shit.' Kit did not want to leave a message. And, on reflection, he did not want Maureen to hear what he had to say. 'Tell him I'm coming round,' he said. He hung up without waiting for a reply.

7:30 a.m.

Toni Gallo thought she would be out of work by lunchtime.

She looked around her office. She had not been here long. She had only just begun to make the place her own. On the desk was a photograph of her with her mother and her sister, Bella, taken a few years ago when Mother was in good health. Beside it was her battered old dictionary – she had never been able to spell. Just last week she had hung on the wall a picture of herself in her police constable's uniform, taken seventeen years ago, looking young and eager.

She could hardly believe she had already lost this job.

She now knew what Michael Ross had done. He had devised a clever and elaborate way of getting around all her security precautions. He had found the weaknesses and exploited them. There was no one to blame but herself.

She had not known this two hours ago, when she had phoned Stanley Oxenford, chairman and majority shareholder in Oxenford Medical.

She had been dreading the call. She had to give him the worst possible news, and take the blame. She steeled herself for his disappointment, indignation, or perhaps rage.

He had said: 'Are you all right?'

She almost cried. She had not anticipated that his first

thought would be for her welfare. She did not deserve such kindness. 'I'm fine,' she had said. 'We all put on bunny suits before we went into the house.'

'But you must be exhausted.'

'I snatched an hour's sleep.'

'Good,' Stanley said, and briskly moved on. 'I know Michael Ross. Quiet chap, about thirty, been with us for a few years – an experienced technician. How the hell did this happen?'

'I found a dead rabbit in his garden shed. I think he brought home a laboratory animal and it bit him.'

'I doubt it,' Stanley said crisply. 'More likely he cut himself with a contaminated knife. Even experienced people may get careless. The rabbit is probably a normal pet that starved after Michael fell ill.'

Toni wished she could pretend to believe that, but she had to give her boss the facts. 'The rabbit was in an improvised biosafety cabinet,' she argued.

'I still doubt it. Michael can't have been working alone, in BSL4. Even if his buddy wasn't looking, there are television cameras in every room – he couldn't have stolen a rabbit without being seen on the monitors. Then he had to pass several security guards on the way out – they would have noticed if he had been carrying a rabbit. Finally, the scientists working in the lab the following morning would have realized immediately that an animal was missing. They might not be able to tell the difference between one rabbit and another, but they certainly know how many there are in the experiment.'

Early though it was, his brain had fired up like the V12 engine in his Ferrari, Toni thought. But he was wrong. 'I put all those security barriers in place,' she said. 'And I'm telling you that no system is perfect.'

'You're right, of course.' If you gave him good arguments, he could back down alarmingly fast. 'I presume we have video footage of the last time Michael was in BSL4?'

'Next thing on my checklist.'

'I'll be there at about eight. Have some answers for me then, please.'

'One more thing. As soon as the staff begin arriving, rumours will spread. May I tell people that you'll be making an announcement?'

'Good point. I'll speak to everyone in the Great Hall at, say, nine thirty.' The grand entrance hall of the old house was the biggest room in the building, always used for large meetings.

Toni had then summoned Susan Mackintosh, one of the security guards, a pretty girl in her twenties with a boyish haircut and a pierced eyebrow. Susan immediately noticed the picture on the wall. 'You look good in a uniform,' she said.

'Thanks. I realize you're due to go off duty, but I need a woman for this job.'

Susan raised an eyebrow flirtatiously. 'I know the feeling.'

Toni recalled the company Christmas party, last Friday. Susan had dressed like John Travolta in the movie *Grease*, with slicked hair, drainpipe jeans, and the kind of crêpe-soled shoes known in Glasgow as brothel creepers. She had asked Toni to dance. Toni had smiled warmly and said: 'I don't think so.' A little later, after a few more drinks, Susan had asked her if she slept with men. 'Not as much as I'd like,' Toni had said.

Toni was flattered that someone so young and pretty was attracted to her, but she pretended not to notice. 'I need you to stop all employees as they arrive. Set up a desk in the Great Hall, and don't let them go to their offices or labs until you've spoken to them.'

'What should I say?'

'Tell them there's been a virus security breach, and Professor Oxenford is going to give them a full briefing this morning. Be calm and reassuring, but don't go into detail – best leave that to Stanley.'

'Okay.'

'Then ask them when they last saw Michael Ross. Some will have been asked that question over the phone last night, but only those certified for BSL4, and it does no harm to double check. If anyone has seen him since he left here on Sunday two weeks ago, tell me immediately.'

'Okay.'

Toni had a delicate question to ask, and she hesitated, then just came out with it. 'Do you think Michael was gay?'

'Not actively.'

'Are you sure?'

'Inverburn is a small town. There are two gay pubs, a club, a couple of restaurants, a church . . . I know all those places and I've never seen him in any of them.'

'Okay. I hope you don't mind my assuming you'd know, just because . . .'

'It's all right.' Susan smiled and gave Toni a direct look. 'You'll have to work harder than that to offend me.'

'Thanks.'

That was almost two hours ago. Toni had spent most of the time since then viewing video footage of Michael Ross on his last visit to BSL4. She now had the answers Stanley wanted. She was going to tell him what had happened, and then he would probably ask for her resignation.

She recalled her first meeting with Stanley. She had been at the lowest point of her entire life. She was pretending to be a freelance security consultant, but she had no clients. Her partner of eight years, Frank, had left her. And her mother was becoming senile. Toni had felt like Job after he was forsaken by God.

Stanley had summoned her to his office and offered her a short-term contract. He had invented a drug so valuable that he feared he might be the target of industrial espionage. He wanted her to check. She had not told him it was her first real assignment.

After combing the premises for listening devices, she had looked for signs that key employees were living above their means. No one was spying on Oxenford Medical, as it turned out – but, to her dismay, she had discovered that Stanley's son, Kit, was stealing from the company.

She had been shocked. Kit had struck her as charming and untrustworthy; but what kind of man robs his own father? 'The old bugger can afford it, he's got plenty,' Kit had said carelessly; and Toni knew, from her years with the police, that there was nothing profound about wickedness – criminals were just shallow, greedy people with inadequate excuses.

Kit had tried to persuade her to hush it up. He promised never to do it again if Toni would keep quiet this time. She had been tempted: she did not want to tell a recently bereaved man that his son was no good. But to keep quiet would have been dishonest.

So, in the end, and with great trepidation, she had told Stanley everything.

She would never forget the look on his face. He had gone pale, grimaced, and said: 'Aah,' as if feeling a sudden internal pain. In that moment, as he struggled to master his profound emotion, she saw both his strength and his sensitivity, and she felt strongly drawn to him.

Telling him the truth had been the right decision. Her integrity had been rewarded. Stanley had fired Kit and given Toni a full-time job. For that, she would always owe him her iron loyalty. She was fiercely determined to repay his trust.

And life had improved. Stanley quickly promoted her from head of security to facilities director and gave her a raise. She bought a red Porsche.

When she mentioned, one day, that she had played squash for the national police team, Stanley challenged her to a game on the company court. She beat him, but only just, and they began to play every week. He was very fit, and had a longer reach, but she was twenty years younger, with hair-trigger reflexes. He took a game from her now and again, when her concentration slipped, but in the end she usually won.

And she got to know him better. He played a shrewd game, taking risks that often paid off. He was competitive, but good-humoured about losing. Her quick mind was a match for his brain, and she enjoyed the cut and thrust. The more she got to know him, the better she liked him.

Until, one day, she realized that she did not just like him. It was more than that.

Now she felt that the worst part of losing this job would be not seeing him any longer.

She was about to head down to the Great Hall, to meet him on his way in, when her phone rang.

A woman's voice with a southern English accent said: 'This is Odette.'

'Hi!' Toni was pleased. Odette Cressy was a detective with the Metropolitan Police in London. They had met on a course at Hendon five years ago. They were the same age. Odette was single and, since Toni had split up with Frank, they had been on holiday together twice. Had they not lived so far apart, they would have been best friends. As it was, they spoke on the phone every couple of weeks.

Odette said: 'It's about your virus victim.'

'Why would you be interested?' Odette was on the anti-terrorist team, Toni knew. 'I suppose I shouldn't ask.'

'Correct. I'll just say that the name Madoba-2 rang an alarm bell here, and leave you to work it out.'

Toni frowned. As a former cop, she could guess what was going on. Odette had intelligence indicating that some group was interested in Madoba-2. A suspect might have mentioned it under interrogation, or the virus had come up in a bugged conversation, or someone whose phone lines were being monitored had typed the name into a computer search engine. Now, any time a quantity of the virus went astray, the anti-terrorist unit would suspect that it had been stolen by fanatics. 'I don't think Michael Ross was a terrorist,' Toni said. 'I think he just became attached to a particular laboratory animal.'

'What about his friends?'

'I found his address book, and the Inverburn police are checking the names right now.'

'Did you keep a copy?'

It was on her desk. 'I can fax it to you right away.'

'Thanks – it will save me time.' Odette recited a number and Toni wrote it down. 'How are you getting on with your handsome boss?'

Toni had not told anyone how she felt about Stanley, but Odette was telepathic. 'I don't believe in sex at work, you know that. Anyway, his wife died recently—'

'Eighteen months ago, as I recall.'

'Which is not long after nearly forty years of marriage. And he's devoted to his children and grandchildren, who would probably hate anyone who tried to replace his late wife.'

'You know the good thing about sex with an older man? He's so worried about not being young and vigorous that he works twice as hard to please you.'

'I'm going to have to take your word for that.'

'And what else? Oh, yes, I almost forgot, ha ha, he's rich. Listen, all I'm going to say is this: if you decide you don't want him, I'll have him. Meanwhile, let me know personally if you find out anything new about Michael Ross.'

'Of course.' Toni hung up and glanced out of the window. Stanley Oxenford's dark-blue Ferrari F50 was pulling into the chairman's parking space. She put the copy of Michael's address book into the fax machine and dialled Odette's number.

Then, feeling like a criminal about to be sentenced, she went to meet her boss.

8 a.m.

The Great Hall was like the nave of a church. It had tall arched windows that let in shafts of sunlight to make patterns on the flagstone floor. The room was spanned by the mighty timbers of an open hammer-beam roof. In the middle of this graced space, incongruously, was a modern oval reception desk with high counters. A uniformed security guard sat on a stool inside the oval.

Stanley Oxenford came through the grand entrance. He was a tall man of sixty with thick grey hair and blue eyes. He did not look the part of a scientist – no bald dome, no stoop, no spectacles. Toni thought he was more like the kind of actor who plays the general in a movie about the Second World War. He dressed well without seeming stuffy. Today he wore a soft grey tweed suit with a waistcoat, a light-blue shirt and – out of respect for the dead, perhaps – a black knitted tie.

Susan Mackintosh had placed a trestle table near the front door. She spoke to Stanley as he came in. He replied briefly then turned to Toni. 'This is a good idea – buttonholing everyone as they arrive and asking when they last saw Michael.'

'Thank you.' I've done one thing right, at least, Toni thought.

Stanley went on: 'What about staff who are on holiday?'

'Personnel will phone them all this morning.'

'Good. Have you found out what happened?'

'Yes. I was right and you were wrong. It was the rabbit.'

Despite the tragic circumstances, he smiled. He liked people to challenge him, especially attractive women. 'How do you know?'

'From the video footage. Would you like to see it?'

'Yes.'

They walked along a wide corridor with oak linenfold panelling, then turned down a side passage to the Central Monitoring Station, normally called the control room. This was the security centre. It had once been the billiards room, but the windows had been bricked up for security, and the ceiling had been lowered to create a hiding place for a snake's nest of cabling. One wall was a bank of television monitors showing key areas of the site, including every room within BSL4. On a long desk were touch screens controlling alarms. Thousands of electronic check points monitored temperature, humidity, and air-management systems in all the laboratories – if you held a door open too long an alarm would sound. A guard in a neat uniform sat at a work station that gave access to the central security computer.

Stanley said in a surprised tone: 'This place has been tidied up since last I was here.'

When Toni had taken over security the control room had been a mess, littered with dirty coffee cups, old newspapers, broken biros, and half-empty Tupperware lunch boxes. Now it was clean and tidy, with nothing on the desk except the file the guard was reading. She was pleased Stanley had noticed.

He glanced into the adjacent equipment room, once the gun room, now full of support devices, including the central processing unit for the phone system. It was brightly lit. A thousand cables were clearly labelled with nonremovable, easy-to-read tags, to minimize downtime in case of technical failure. Stanley nodded approval.

This was all to the good, Toni felt; but Stanley already knew she was an efficient organizer. The most important part of her job was making sure nothing dangerous escaped from the BSL4 lab – and in that she had failed.

There were times when she did not know what Stanley was thinking, and this was one. Was he grieving for Michael Ross, fearful for the future of his company, or furious about the security breach? Would he turn his wrath on her, or the dead Michael, or Howard McAlpine? When Toni showed him what Michael had done, would Stanley praise her for having figured it out so quickly, or fire her for letting it happen?

They sat side by side in front of a monitor, and Toni tapped the keyboard to bring up the pictures she wanted him to see. The computer's vast memory stored images for twenty-eight days before erasing them. She was intimately familiar with the program and navigated it with ease.

Sitting beside Stanley, she was absurdly reminded of going to the pictures with a boyfriend at the age of fourteen, and allowing him to put his hand up her sweater. The memory embarrassed her, and she felt her neck redden. She hoped Stanley would not notice.

On the monitor, she showed him Michael arriving at the main gate and presenting his pass. 'The date and time are on the bottom of the screen,' she said. 'It was fourteen twenty-seven on the eighth of December.' She tapped the keyboard, and the screen showed a green Volkswagen Golf pulling into a parking space. A slight man got out and took a duffel bag from the back of the car. 'Watch that bag,' Toni said.

'Why?'

'There's a rabbit in it.'

'How did he manage that?'

'I guess it's tranquillized, and probably wrapped up tightly. Remember, he's been dealing with laboratory animals for years. He knows how to keep them calm.'

The next shot showed Michael presenting his pass again at Reception. A pretty Pakistani woman of about forty came into the Great Hall. 'That's Monica Ansari,' said Stanley.

'She was his buddy. She needed to do some work on tissue cultures, and he was performing the routine weekend check on the animals.'

They walked along the corridor Toni and Stanley had taken, but went past the turning for the control room and continued to the door at the end. It looked like all the other doors in the building, with four recessed panels and a brass knob, but it was made of steel. On the wall beside the door was the yellow-and-black warning of the international biohazard symbol.

Dr Ansari waved a plastic pass in front of a remote card reader, then pressed the forefinger of her left hand to a small screen. There was a pause, while the computer checked that her fingerprint matched the information on the microchip embedded in the smart card. This ensured that lost or stolen cards could not be used by unauthorized persons. While she waited, she glanced up at the television camera and gave a mock salute. Then the door opened and she stepped through. Michael followed.

Another camera showed them in a small lobby. A row of dials on the wall monitored the air pressure in the lab. The farther you went inside BSL4, the lower the air pressure. This downward gradient ensured that any leakage of air was inward, not outward. From the lobby they went to separate men's and women's changing rooms. 'This is when he took the rabbit out of the bag,' Toni said. 'If his buddy that day had been a man, the plan wouldn't have worked. But he had Monica and, of course, there are no cameras in the changing rooms.'

'But damn it, you can't put security cameras in changing rooms,' Stanley said. 'No one would work here.'

'Absolutely,' said Toni. 'We'll have to think of something else. Watch this.'

The next shot came from a camera inside the lab. It showed conventional rabbit racks housed in a clear plastic isolation cover. Toni froze the picture. 'Could you explain to me what the scientists are doing in this lab, exactly?'

'Of course. Our new drug is effective against many viruses, but not all. In this experiment it was being tested against Madoba-2, a variant of the Ebola virus that causes a lethal haemorrhagic fever in both rabbits and humans. Two groups of rabbits were challenged with the virus.'

'Challenged?'

'Sorry – it's the word we use. It means they were infected. Then one group was injected with the drug.'

'What did you find?'

'The drug doesn't defeat Madoba-2 in rabbits. We're a bit disappointed. Almost certainly, it won't cure this type of virus in humans either.'

'But you didn't know that sixteen days ago.'

'Correct.'

'In that case, I think I understand what Michael was trying to do.' She touched the keyboard to unfreeze the picture. A figure stepped into shot wearing a light-blue plastic space suit with a clear helmet. He stopped by the door to push his feet into rubber overboots. Then he reached up and grabbed a curly yellow air hose hanging from the ceiling. He connected it to an inlet on his belt. As air was pumped in, the suit inflated, until he looked like the Michelin Man.

'This is Michael,' Toni said. 'He changed faster than Monica, so at the moment he's in there alone.'

'It shouldn't happen, but it does,' Stanley said. 'The two-person rule is observed, but not minute-by-minute. *Merda.*' Stanley often cursed in Italian, having learned a ripe vocabulary from his wife. Toni, who spoke Spanish, usually understood.

On screen Michael went up to the rabbit rack, moving with deliberate slowness in the awkward costume. His back was to the camera and, for a few moments, the pumped-up suit shielded what he was doing. Then he stepped away and dropped something on a stainless-steel laboratory bench.

'Notice anything?' Toni said.

'No.'

'Nor did the security guards who were watching the monitors.' Toni was defending her staff. If Stanley had not seen what happened, he could hardly blame the guards for missing it too. 'But look again.' She went back a couple of minutes and froze the frame as Michael stepped into shot. 'One rabbit in that top right-hand cage.'

'I see.'

'Look harder at Michael. He's got something under his arm.'

'Yes – wrapped in blue plastic suit fabric.'

She ran the footage forward, stopping again as Michael moved away from the rabbit rack. 'How many rabbits in the top right-hand cage?'

'Two, damn it.' Stanley looked perplexed. 'I thought your theory was that Michael took a rabbit out of the lab. You've shown him bringing one in!'

'A substitute. Otherwise the scientists would have noticed one was missing.'

'Then what's his motivation? In order to save one rabbit, he has to condemn another to death!'

'In so far as he was rational at all, I imagine he felt there was something special about the rabbit he saved.'

'For God's sake, one rabbit is the same as another.'

'Not to Michael, I suspect.'

Stanley nodded. 'You're right. Who knows how his mind was working at this point?'

Toni ran the video footage forward. 'He did his chores as usual, checking the food and water in the cages, making sure the animals were still alive, ticking his tasks on a checklist. Monica came in, but she went to a side laboratory to work on her tissue cultures, so she could not see him. He went next door, to the larger lab, to take care of the macaque monkeys. Then he came back. Now watch.'

Michael disconnected his air hose, as was normal when moving from one room to another within the lab – the suit contained three or four minutes' worth of fresh air, and when it began to run out the faceplate would fog, warning the wearer. He stepped into a small room containing the vault, a locked refrigerator used for storing live samples of viruses. Being the most secure location in the entire building, it also held all stocks of the priceless antiviral drug. He tapped a combination of digits on its keypad. A security camera inside the refrigerator showed him selecting two doses of the drug, already measured and loaded into disposable syringes.

'The small dose for the rabbit and the large one, presumably, for himself,' Toni said. 'Like you, he expected the drug to work against Madoba-2. He planned to cure the rabbit and immunize himself.'

'The guards could have seen him taking the drug from the vault.'

'But they wouldn't find that suspicious. He's authorized to handle these materials.'

'They might have noticed that he didn't write anything in the log.'

'They might have, but remember that one guard is watching thirty-seven screens, and he's not trained in laboratory practice.'

Stanley grunted.

Toni said: 'Michael must have figured that the

discrepancy wouldn't be noticed until the annual audit, and even then it would be put down to clerical error. He didn't know I was planning a spot check.'

On the television screen, Michael closed the vault and returned to the rabbit lab, reconnecting his air hose. 'He's finished his chores,' Toni explained. 'Now he returns to the rabbit racks.' Once again, Michael's back concealed what he was doing from the camera. 'Here's where he takes his favourite rabbit out of its cage. I think he slips it into its own miniature suit, probably made from parts of an old worn-out one.'

Michael turned his left side to the camera. As he walked to the exit, he seemed to have something under his right arm, but it was hard to tell.

Leaving BSL4, everyone had to pass through a chemical shower that decontaminated the suit, then take a regular shower before dressing. 'The suit would have protected the rabbit in the chemical shower,' Toni said. 'My guess is that he then dumped the rabbit suit in the incinerator. The water shower would not have harmed the animal. In the dressing room he put the rabbit in the duffel bag. As he exited the building, the guards saw him carrying the same bag he came in with, and suspected nothing.'

Stanley sat back in his seat. 'Well, I'm damned,' he said. 'I would have sworn it was impossible.'

'He took the rabbit home. I think it may have bitten him when he injected it with the drug. He injected himself and thought he was safe. But he was wrong.'

Stanley looked sad. 'Poor boy,' he said. 'Poor, foolish boy.'

'Now you know everything I know,' Toni said. She watched him, waiting for the verdict. Was this phase of her life over? Would she be out of work for Christmas?

He gave her a level look. 'There's one obvious security precaution we could have taken that would have prevented this.'

'I know,' she said. 'A bag search for everyone entering and leaving BSL4.'

'Exactly.'

'I've instituted it from this morning.'

'Thereby closing the stable door after the horse has bolted.'

'I'm sorry,' she said. He wanted her to quit, she felt sure. 'You pay me to stop this kind of thing happening. I've failed. I expect you'd like me to tender my resignation.'

He looked irritated. 'If I want to fire you, you'll know soon enough.'

She stared at him. Had she been reprieved?

His expression softened. 'All right, you're a conscientious person and you feel guilty, even though neither you nor anyone else could have anticipated what happened.'

'I could have instituted the bag check.'

'I probably would have vetoed it, on the grounds that it would upset staff.'

'Oh.'

'So I'll tell you this once. Since you came, our security has been tighter than ever before. You're damn good, and I aim to keep you. So, please, no more self-pity.'

She suddenly felt weak with relief. 'Thank you,' she said.

'Now, we've got a busy day ahead – let's get on with it.'
He went out.

She closed her eyes in relief. She had been forgiven.
Thank you, she thought.

8:30 a.m.

Miranda Oxenford ordered a cappuccino Viennoise, with a pyramid of whipped cream on top. At the last moment she asked for a piece of carrot cake as well. She stuffed her change into the pocket of her skirt and carried her breakfast to the table where her thin sister, Olga, was seated with a double espresso and a cigarette. The place was bedecked with paper chains, and a Christmas tree twinkled over the panini toaster, but someone with a nice sense of irony had put the Beach Boys on the music system, and they were singing 'Surfin' USA'.

Miranda often ran into Olga first thing in the morning at this coffee bar in Sauchiehall Street, in the centre of Glasgow. They worked nearby: Miranda was managing director of a recruitment agency specializing in IT personnel, and Olga was an advocate. They both liked to take five minutes to gather their thoughts before going into their offices.

They did not look like sisters, Miranda thought, catching a glimpse of her reflection in a mirror. She was short, with curly blonde hair, and her figure was, well, cuddly. Olga was tall like Daddy, but she had the same black eyebrows as their late mother, who had been Italian by birth and was always called Mamma Marta. Olga was dressed for work in a dark-grey suit and sharply pointed shoes. She could have played the part of Cruella De Vil. She probably terrified juries.

Miranda took off her coat and scarf. She wore a pleated skirt and a sweater embroidered with small flowers. She dressed to charm, not to intimidate. As she sat down, Olga said: 'You're working on Christmas Eve?'

'Just for an hour,' Miranda replied. 'To make sure nothing's left undone over the holiday.'

'Same here.'

'Have you heard the news? A technician at the Kremlin died of a virus.'

'Oh, God, that's going to blight our Christmas.'

Olga could seem heartless, but she was not really so, Miranda thought. 'It was on the radio. I haven't spoken to Daddy yet, but it seems the poor boy became fond of a lab hamster and took it home.'

'What did he do, have sex with it?'

'It probably bit him. He lived alone, so nobody called for help. At least that means he probably didn't pass the virus to anyone else. All the same, it's awful for Daddy. He won't show it, but he's sure to feel responsible.'

'He should have gone in for a less hazardous branch of science – something like atomic-weapons research.'

Miranda smiled. She was especially pleased to see Olga today. She was glad of the chance of a quiet word. The whole family was about to gather at Steepfall, their father's house, for Christmas. She was bringing her fiancé, Ned Hanley, and she wanted to make sure Olga would be nice to him. But she approached the subject in a roundabout way. 'I hope this doesn't spoil the holiday. I've been looking forward to it so much. You know Kit's coming?'

'I'm deeply sensible of the honour our little brother is doing us.'

'He wasn't going to come, but I talked him round.'

'Daddy will be pleased.' Olga spoke with a touch of sarcasm.

'He will, actually,' Miranda said reproachfully. 'You know it broke his heart to fire Kit.'

'I know I've never seen him so angry. I thought he would kill someone.'

'Then he cried.'

'I didn't see that.'

'Nor did I. Lori told me.' Lori was Stanley's housekeeper. 'But now he wants to forgive and forget.'

Olga stubbed her cigarette. 'I know. Daddy's magnanimity is boundless. Does Kit have a job yet?'

'No.'

'Can't you find him something? It's your field, and he's good.'

'Things are quiet – and people know he was sacked by his father.'

'Has he stopped gambling?'

'He must have. He promised Daddy he would. And he's got no money.'

'Daddy paid his debts, didn't he?'

'I don't think we're supposed to know.'

'Come on, Mandy.' Olga was using Miranda's childhood name. 'How much?'

'You should ask Daddy – or Kit.'

'Was it ten thousand pounds?'

Miranda looked away.

'More than that? Twenty?'

Miranda whispered: 'Fifty.'

'Good God! That little bastard pissed away fifty grand of our inheritance? Wait till I see him.'

'Anyway, enough of Kit. You're going to get to know Ned much better this Christmas. I want you to treat him as one of the family.'

'Ned should *be* one of the family by now. When are you getting married? You're too old for a long engagement. You've both been married before – it's not as if you have to save up for your trousseau.'

This was not the response Miranda was hoping for. She wanted Olga to feel warm towards Ned. 'Oh, you know what Ned's like,' she said defensively. 'He's lost in his own world.' Ned was editor of the *Glasgow Review of Books*, a respected cultural-political journal, but he was not practical.

'I don't know how you stand it. I can't abide vacillation.'

The conversation was not going the way Miranda wanted. 'Believe me, it's a blessed relief after Jasper.' Miranda's first husband had been a bully and a tyrant. Ned was the opposite, and that was one of the reasons she loved him. 'Ned will never be organized enough to boss me around – half the time he can't remember what day it is.'

'Still, you managed perfectly well without a man for five years.'

'I did, and I was proud of myself, especially when the economy turned down and they stopped paying me those big bonuses.'

'So why do you want another man?'

'Well, you know . . .'

'Sex? Oh, please. Haven't you heard of vibrators?'

Miranda giggled. 'It's not the same.'

'Indeed it's not. A vibrator is bigger and harder and more reliable and, when you've done with it, you can put it back in the bedside table and forget about it.'

Miranda began to feel attacked, as often happened when she talked to her sister. 'Ned's very good with Tom,' she said. Tom was her eleven-year-old son. 'Jasper hardly ever spoke to Tom, except to give him orders. Ned takes an interest in him, asks him questions, and listens to the answers.'

'Speaking of stepchildren, how does Tom get along with Sophie?' Ned's daughter by his first marriage was fourteen.

'She's coming to Steepfall too – I'm picking her up later this morning. Tom looks at Sophie the way the Greeks regarded the gods, as supernatural beings who are dangerous unless pacified by constant sacrifices. He's always trying to give her sweets. She'd rather have cigarettes. She's as thin as a stick and prepared to die to stay that way.' Miranda looked pointedly at Olga's pack of Marlboro Lights.

'We all have our weaknesses,' said Olga. 'Have some more carrot cake.'

Miranda put down her fork and took a sip of coffee. 'Sophie can be difficult, but it's not her fault. Her mother resents me, and the child is bound to pick up that attitude.'

'I bet Ned leaves you to deal with the problem.'

'I don't mind.'

'Now that he's living in your flat, does he pay you rent?'

'He can't afford it. That magazine pays peanuts. And

he's still carrying the mortgage on the house his ex lives in. He's not comfortable about being financially dependent, believe you me.'

'I can't think why he wouldn't be comfortable. He can have a bonk whenever he feels like it, he's got you to look after his difficult daughter, and he's living rent-free.'

Miranda was hurt. 'That's a bit harsh.'

'You shouldn't have let him move in without committing to a date for the wedding.'

The same thought had occurred to Miranda, but she was not going to admit it. 'He just thinks everyone needs more time to get used to the idea of his remarriage.'

'Who's "everyone", then?'

'Well, Sophie, for a start.'

'And she reflects her mother's attitudes, you've already admitted. So what you're saying is that Ned won't marry you until his ex gives permission.'

'Olga, please take off your advocate's wig when you're talking to me.'

'Someone's got to tell you these things.'

'You oversimplify everything. I know it's your job, but I'm your sister, not a hostile witness.'

'I'm sorry I spoke.'

'I'm glad you spoke, because this is just the kind of thing I *don't* want you to say to Ned. He's the man I love, and I want to marry him, so I'm asking you to be nice to him over Christmas.'

'I'll do my best,' Olga said lightly.

Miranda wanted her sister to understand how important this was. 'I need him to feel that he and I can build a new family together, for ourselves and the two children. I'm asking you to help me convince him we can do that.'

'All right. Okay.'

'If this holiday goes well, I think he'll agree to a date for the wedding.'

Olga touched Miranda's hand. 'I get the message. I know how much it means to you. I'll be good.'

Miranda had made her point. Satisfied, she turned her mind to another area of friction. 'I hope things go all right between Daddy and Kit.'

'So do I, but there's not much we can do about it.'

'Kit called me a few days ago. For some reason, he's dead keen to sleep in the guest cottage at Steepfall.'

Olga bridled. 'Why should he have the cottage all to himself? That means you and Ned and Hugo and I will all have to squeeze into two poky bedrooms in the old house!'

Miranda had expected Olga to resist this. 'I know it's unreasonable, but I said it was okay by me. It was difficult enough to persuade him to come – I didn't want to put an obstacle in the way.'

'He's a selfish little bastard. What reason did he give you?'

'I didn't question him.'

'Well, I will.' Olga took her mobile phone from her briefcase and pressed a number.

'Don't make an issue of this,' Miranda pleaded.

'I just want to ask him the question.' Speaking into the phone, she said: 'Kit – what's this about you sleeping in the cottage? Don't you think it's a bit . . .' She paused. 'Oh. Why not? I see . . . but why don't you—' She stopped abruptly, as if he had hung up on her.

Miranda thought, sadly, that she knew what Kit had said. 'What is it?'

Olga put the phone back into her bag. 'We don't need to argue about the cottage. He's changed his mind. He's not coming to Steepfall after all.'

9 a.m.

Oxenford Medical was under siege. Reporters, photographers, and television crews massed outside the entrance gates, harassing employees as they arrived for work, crowding around their cars and bicycles, shoving cameras and microphones in their faces, shouting questions. The security guards were trying desperately to separate the media people from the normal traffic, to prevent accidents, but were getting no cooperation from the journalists. To make matters worse, a group of animal-rights protestors had seized the opportunity for some publicity, and were holding a demonstration at the gates, waving banners and singing protest songs. The cameramen were filming the demonstration, having little else to shoot. Toni Gallo watched, feeling angry and helpless.

She was in Stanley Oxenford's office, a large corner room that had been the master bedroom of the house. Stanley worked with the old and the new mingled around him: his computer work station stood on a scratched wooden table he had had for thirty years, and on a side table was an optical microscope from the sixties that he still liked to use from time to time. The microscope was now surrounded by Christmas cards, one of them from Toni.

On the wall, a Victorian engraving of the periodic table of the elements hung beside a photograph of a striking black-haired girl in a wedding dress – his late wife, Marta.

Stanley mentioned his wife often. 'As cold as a church, Marta used to say . . . When Marta was alive we went to Italy every other year . . . Marta loved irises.' But he had spoken of his feelings about her only once. Toni had said how beautiful Marta looked in the photograph. 'The pain fades, but it doesn't go away,' Stanley had said. 'I believe I'll grieve for her every day for the rest of my life.' It had made Toni wonder whether anyone would ever love her the way Stanley had loved Marta.

Now Stanley stood beside Toni at the window, their shoulders not quite touching. They watched with dismay as more Volvos and Subarus parked on the grass verge, and the crowd became noisier and more aggressive.

'I'm so sorry about this,' Toni said miserably.

'Not your fault.'

'I know you said no more self-pity, but I let a rabbit get through my security cordon, then my bastard ex-partner leaked the story to Carl Osborne, the television reporter.'

'I gather you don't get on with your ex.'

She had never talked candidly to Stanley about this, but Frank had now intruded into her working life, and she welcomed the chance to explain. 'I honestly don't know why Frank hates me. I never rejected him. He left me – and he did it at a moment when I really needed help and support. You'd think he'd punished me enough for whatever I did wrong. But now this.'

'I can understand it. You're a standing reproach to him.

Every time he sees you, he's reminded of how weak and cowardly he was when you needed him.'

Toni had never thought about Frank in quite that way, and now his behaviour made a kind of sense. She felt a warm surge of gratitude. Careful not to show too much emotion, she said: 'That's perceptive.'

He shrugged. 'We never forgive those we've wronged.'

Toni smiled at the paradox. Stanley was clever about people as well as viruses.

He put a hand on her shoulder lightly, a gesture of reassurance – or was it something more? He rarely made physical contact with his employees. She had felt his touch exactly three times in the year she had known him. He had shaken her hand when he gave her the initial contract, when he took her on the staff, and when he promoted her. At the Christmas party, he had danced with his secretary, Dorothy, a heavy woman with a maternally efficient manner, like an attentive mother duck. He had not danced with anyone else. Toni had wanted to ask him, but she was afraid of making her feelings obvious. Afterwards she had wished she were more brash, like Susan Mackintosh.

'Frank may not have leaked the story merely to spite you,' Stanley said. 'I suspect he would have done it anyway. I imagine Osborne will show his gratitude by reporting favourably on the Inverburn police in general and Superintendent Frank Hackett in particular.'

His hand warmed her skin through the silk of her blouse. Was this a casual gesture, made without thought? She suffered the familiar frustration of not knowing what was in his mind. She wondered if he could feel her bra strap. She hoped he could not tell how much she enjoyed being touched by him.

She was not sure he was right about Frank and Carl Osborne. 'It's generous of you to look at it that way,' she said. All the same, she resolved that somehow she would make sure the company did not suffer from what Frank had done.

There was a knock at the door and Cynthia Creighton, the company's public-relations officer, came in. Stanley took his hand off Toni's shoulder quickly.

Cynthia was a thin woman of fifty in a tweed skirt and knitted stockings. She was a sincere do-gooder. Toni had once made Stanley laugh by saying Cynthia was the kind of person who made her own muesli. Normally hesitant in manner, she was now on the edge of hysteria. Her hair was dishevelled, she was breathing hard, and she talked too fast. 'Those people *shoved* me,' she said. 'They're animals! Where are the police?'

'A patrol car is on its way,' Toni said. 'They should be here in ten or fifteen minutes.'

'They should arrest the lot of them.'

Toni realized, with a sinking feeling, that Cynthia was not capable of dealing with this crisis. Her main job was to dispense a small charity budget, giving grants to school football teams and sponsored walkers, ensuring that the name of Oxenford Medical appeared frequently in the *Inverburn Courier* in stories that had nothing to do with viruses or experiments on animals. It was important work, Toni knew, for readers believed the local press, whereas they were sceptical of national newspapers. Consequently, Cynthia's low-key publicity immunized the company against the virulent Fleet Street scare stories that could blight any scientific enterprise. But Cynthia had never dealt with the jackal pack that was the British press in full cry, and she was too distressed to make good decisions.

Stanley was thinking the same thing. 'Cynthia, I want you to work with Toni on this,' he said. 'She has experience of the media from her time with the police.'

Cynthia looked relieved and grateful. 'Have you?'

'I did a year in the press office – although I never dealt with anything this bad.'

'What do you think we should do?'

'Well.' Toni did not feel she was qualified to take charge, but this was an emergency, and it seemed she was the best candidate available. She went back to first principles. 'There's a simple rule for dealing with the media.' It might be too simple for this situation, she thought, but she did not say so. 'One, decide what your message is. Two, make sure it's true, so that you'll never have to go back on it. Three, keep saying it over and over again.'

'Hmm.' Stanley looked sceptical, but he did not seem to have a better suggestion.

Cynthia said: 'Don't you think we should apologize?'

'No,' Toni said quickly. 'It will be interpreted as confirmation that we've been careless. That's not true. Nobody's perfect, but our security is top notch.'

Stanley said: 'Is that our message?'

'I don't think so. Too defensive.' Toni thought for a moment. 'We should start by saying that we're doing work here which is vital for the future of the human race. No, that's too apocalyptic. We're doing medical research that will save lives – that's better. And it has its hazards, but our security is as tight as mortal beings can make it. One thing certain is that many people will die unnecessarily if we *stop*.'

'I like that,' said Stanley.

'Is it true?'

'No question. Every year a new virus comes out of China and kills thousands. Our drug will save their lives.'

Toni nodded. 'That's perfect. Simple and telling.'

Stanley was still worried. 'How will we get the message across?'

'I think you should call a press conference in a couple of hours' time. By midday the newsdesks will be looking for a fresh angle on the story, so they'll be glad to get something more from us. And most of these people outside will leave once that's happened. They'll know that further developments are unlikely, and they want to go home for Christmas like everyone else.'

'I hope you're right,' Stanley said. 'Cynthia, will you make the arrangements, please?'

Cynthia had not yet recovered her composure. 'But what should I do?'

Toni took over. 'We'll hold the press conference in the Great Hall. It's the only room big enough, and the chairs are already being set out for Professor Oxenford's address to the staff at half-past nine. The first thing you should do is alert the people outside. It will give them something to tell their editors, and might calm them down a bit. Then phone the Press Association and Reuters and ask them to put it on the wire, to inform any of the media who aren't already here.'

'Right,' Cynthia said uncertainly. 'Right.' She turned to

go. Toni made a mental note to check on her as soon as possible.

As Cynthia left, Dorothy buzzed Stanley and said: 'Laurence Mahoney from the United States Embassy in London is on line one.'

'I remember him,' Toni said. 'He was here a few months ago. I showed him around.' The US military was financing much of Oxenford Medical's research. The Department of Defense was keenly interested in Stanley's new antiviral drug, which promised to be a powerful counter to biological warfare. Stanley had needed to raise money for the prolonged testing process, and the American government had been eager to invest. Mahoney kept an eye on things on behalf of the Defense Department.

'Just a minute, Dorothy.' Stanley did not pick up the phone. He said to Toni: 'Mahoney is more important to us than all the British media put together. I don't want to talk to him cold. I need to know what line he's taking, so that I can think about how to handle him.'

'Do you want me to stall him?'

'Feel him out.'

Toni picked up the handset and touched a button. 'Hello, Larry, this is Toni Gallo, we met in September. How are you?'

Mahoney was a peevish press officer with a whiney voice that made Toni think of Donald Duck. 'I'm worried,' he said.

'Tell me why.'

'I was hoping to speak to Professor Oxenford,' he answered with an edge to his voice.

'And he's keen to talk to you at the first opportunity,'

Toni said as sincerely as she could manage. 'Right now he's with the laboratory director.' In fact he was sitting on the edge of his desk, watching her, with an expression on his face that might have been either fond or merely interested. She caught his eye and he looked away. 'He'll call you as soon as he has the complete picture – which will certainly be before midday.'

'How the hell did you let something like this happen?'

'The young man sneaked a rabbit out of the laboratory in his duffel bag. We've already instituted a compulsory bag search at the entrance to BSL4 to make sure it can't happen again.'

'My concern is bad publicity for the American government. We don't want to be blamed for unleashing deadly viruses on the population of Scotland.'

'There's no danger of that,' Toni said with her fingers crossed.

'Have any of the local reports played up the fact that this research is American-financed?'

'No.'

'They'll pick it up sooner or later.'

'We should certainly be prepared to answer questions about that.'

'The most damaging angle for us – and therefore for you – is the one that says the research is done here because Americans think it's too dangerous to be done in the United States.'

'Thanks for the warning. I think we have a very convincing response to that. After all, the drug was invented right here in Scotland by Professor Oxenford, so it's natural it should be tested here.'

'I just don't want to get into a situation where the only way to prove our goodwill is to transfer the research to Fort Detrick.'

Toni was shocked into silence. Fort Detrick, in the town of Frederick, Maryland, housed the US Army Medical Research Institute of Infectious Diseases. How could the research be transferred there? It would mean the end of the Kremlin. After a long pause, she said: 'We're not in that situation, not by a million miles.' She wished she could think of a more devastating put-down.

'I sure hope not. Have Stanley call me.'

'Thank you, Larry.' She hung up and said to Stanley: 'They can't transfer your research to Fort Detrick, can they?'

He went pale. 'There's certainly no provision in the contract to that effect,' he said. 'But they are the government of the most powerful country in the world, and they can do anything they want. What would I do – sue them? I'd be in court for the rest of my life, even if I could afford it.'

Toni was rocked by seeing Stanley appear vulnerable. He was always the calm, reassuring one who knew how to solve the problem. Now he just looked daunted. She would have liked to give him a comforting hug. 'Would they do it?'

'I'm sure the microbiologists at Fort Detrick would prefer to be doing this research themselves, if they had the choice.'

'Where would that leave you?'

'Bankrupt.'

'What?' Toni was appalled.

'I've invested everything in the new laboratory,' Stanley said grimly. 'I have a personal overdraft of a million pounds. Our contract with the Department of Defense would cover the cost of the lab over four years. But if they pull the rug now, I've got no way of paying the debts – either the company's or my own.'

Toni could hardly take it in. How could Stanley's entire future – and her own – be threatened so suddenly? 'But the new drug is worth millions.'

'It will be, eventually. I'm sure of the science – that's why I was happy to borrow so much money. But I didn't foresee that the project might be destroyed by mere publicity.'

She touched his arm. 'And all because a stupid television personality needs a scare story,' she said. 'I can hardly believe it.'

Stanley patted the hand she had rested on his arm, then removed it and stood up. 'No point in whining. We've just got to manage our way out of this.'

'Yes. You're due to speak to the staff. Are you ready?'

'Yes.' They walked out of his office together. 'It will be good practice for the press later.'

As they passed Dorothy's desk, she held up a hand to stop them. 'One moment, please,' she said into the phone. She touched a button and spoke to Stanley. 'It's the First Minister of Scotland,' she said. 'Personally,' she added, evidently impressed. 'He wants a word.'

Stanley said to Toni: 'Go down to the hall and hold them. I'll be as quick as I can.' He went back into his office.

9:30 a.m.

Kit Oxenford waited more than an hour for Harry McGarry.

McGarry, known as Harry Mac, had been born in Govan, a working-class district of Glasgow. He was raised in a tenement near Ibrox Park, the home of the city's Protestant football team, Rangers. With his profits from drugs, illegal gambling, theft, and prostitution he had moved – only a mile geographically, but a long way socially – across the Paisley Road to Dumbreck. Now he lived in a large new-built house with a pool.

The place was decorated like an expensive hotel, with reproduction furniture and framed prints on the wall, but no personal touches: no family photographs, no ornaments, no flowers, no pets. Kit waited nervously in the spacious hall, staring at the striped yellow wallpaper and the spindly legs of the occasional tables, watched by a fat bodyguard in a cheap black suit.

Harry Mac's empire covered Scotland and the north of England. He worked with his daughter, Diana, always called Daisy. The nickname was ironic: she was a violent, sadistic thug.

Harry owned the illegal casino where Kit played.

Licensed casinos in Britain suffered under all kinds of petty laws that limited their profits: no house percentage, no table fee, no tipping, no drinking at the tables, and you had to be a member for twenty-four hours before you could play. Harry ignored the laws. Kit liked the louche atmosphere of an illegitimate game.

Most gamblers were stupid, Kit believed; and the people who ran casinos were not much brighter. An intelligent player should always win. In blackjack there was a correct way to play every possible hand – a system called Basic – and he knew it backwards. Then, he improved his chances by keeping track of the cards that were dealt from the six-pack deck. Starting with zero, he added one point for every low card – twos, threes, fours, fives and sixes – and took away one point for every high card – tens, jacks, queens, kings and aces. (He ignored sevens, eights and nines.) When the number in his head was positive, the remaining deck contained more high cards than low, so he had a better-than-average chance of drawing a ten. A negative number gave a high probability of drawing a low card. Knowing the odds told him when to bet heavily.

But Kit had suffered a run of bad luck and, when the debt reached fifty thousand pounds, Harry had asked for his money.

Kit had gone to his father and begged to be rescued. It was humiliating, of course. When Stanley had fired him, Kit had accused his father bitterly of not caring about him. Now he was admitting the truth: his father did love him, and would do almost anything for him, and Kit knew that perfectly well. His pretence had collapsed ignominiously. But it was worth it. Stanley had paid.

Kit had promised he would never gamble again, and meant it, but the temptation had been too strong. It was madness; it was a disease; it was shameful and humiliating; but it was the most exciting thing in the world, and he could not resist.

Next time his debt reached fifty thousand he had gone back to his father, but this time Stanley put his foot down. 'I haven't got the money,' he had said. 'I could borrow it, perhaps, but what's the point? You'd lose it and come back for more until we both were broke.' Kit had accused him of heartlessness and greed, called him Shylock and Scrooge and fucking Fagin, and sworn never to speak to him again. The words had hurt – he could always hurt his father, he knew that – but Stanley had not changed his mind.

At that point, Kit should have left the country.

He dreamed of going to Italy to live in his mother's home town of Lucca. The family had visited several times during his childhood, before the grandparents died. It was a pretty walled town, ancient and peaceful, with little squares where you could drink espresso in the shade. He knew some Italian – Mamma Marta had spoken her native tongue to all of them when they were small. He could rent a room in one of the tall old houses and get a job helping people with their computer problems, easy work. He thought he could be happy, living like that.

But, instead, he had tried to win back what he owed.

His debt went up to a quarter of a million.

For that much money, Harry Mac would pursue him to the North Pole. He thought about killing himself, and eyed tall buildings in central Glasgow, wondering if he could get up on the roofs in order to throw himself to his death.

Three weeks ago, he had been summoned to this house. He had felt sick with fear. He was sure they were going to beat him up. When he was shown into the drawing room, with its yellow silk couches, he wondered how they would prevent the blood spoiling the upholstery. 'There's a gentleman here wants to ask you a question,' Harry had said. Kit could not imagine what question any of Harry's friends would want to ask him, unless it was *Where's the fucking money?*

The gentleman was Nigel Buchanan, a quiet type in his forties wearing expensive casual clothes: a cashmere jacket, dark slacks, and an open-necked shirt. Speaking in a soft London accent, he said: 'Can you get me inside the Level Four laboratory at Oxenford Medical?'

There had been two other people in the yellow drawing room at the time. One was Daisy, a muscular girl of about twenty-five with a broken nose, bad skin, and a ring through her lower lip. She was wearing leather gloves. The other was Elton, a handsome black man about the same age as Daisy, apparently a sidekick of Nigel's.

Kit was so relieved at not being beaten up that he would have agreed to anything.

Nigel offered him a fee of three hundred thousand pounds for the night's work.

Kit could hardly believe his luck. It would be enough to pay his debts and more. He could leave the country. He could go to Lucca and realize his dream. He felt overjoyed. His problems were solved at a stroke.

Later, Harry had talked about Nigel in reverent tones. A professional thief, Nigel stole only to order for a prearranged price. 'He's the greatest,' Harry said. 'You're after a painting by Michelangelo? No problem. A nuclear warhead? He'll get it for you – if you can afford it Remember Shergar, the racehorse that was kidnapped? That was Nigel.' He added: 'He lives in Liechtenstein,' as if Liechtenstein were a more exotic place of residence than Mars.

Kit had spent the next three weeks planning the theft of the antiviral drug. He felt the occasional twinge of remorse as he refined the scheme to rob his father, but mostly he felt a delirious glee at the thought of revenge on the Daddy who had fired him then refused to rescue him from gangsters. It would be a nasty poke in the eye for Toni Gallo, too.

Nigel had gone over the details with him meticulously, questioning everything. Occasionally he would consult with Elton, who was in charge of equipment, especially cars. Kit got the impression that Elton was a valued technical expert who had worked with Nigel before. Daisy was to join them on the raid, ostensibly to provide extra muscle if necessary – though Kit suspected her real purpose was to take £250,000 from him as soon as the fee was in his hands.

Kit had suggested they rendezvous at a disused airfield near the Kremlin. Nigel looked at Elton. 'That's cool,' Elton said. He spoke with a broad London accent: 'We could meet the buyer there after – he might want to fly in.'

In the end, Nigel had pronounced the plan brilliant, and Kit had glowed with pleasure.

Now, today, Kit had to tell Harry the whole deal was off. He felt wretched: disappointed, depressed, and scared.

At last he was summoned to Harry's presence. Nervous, he followed the bodyguard through the laundry at the back of the house to the pool pavilion. It was built to look like an Edwardian orangery, with glazed tiles in sombre colours, the pool itself an unpleasant shade of dark green. Some interior decorator had proposed this, Kit guessed, and Harry had said yes without looking at the plans.

Harry was a stocky man of fifty with the grey skin of a lifelong smoker. He sat at a wrought-iron table, dressed in a purple towelling robe, drinking dark coffee from a small china cup and reading the *Sun*. The newspaper was open at the horoscope. Daisy was in the water, swimming laps tirelessly. Kit was startled to see that she seemed to be naked except for diver's gloves. She always wore gloves.

'I don't need to see you, laddie,' Harry said. 'I don't want to see you. I don't know anything about you or what you're doing tonight. And I've never met anyone called Nigel Buchanan. Are you catching my drift?' He did not offer Kit a cup of coffee.

The air was hot and humid. Kit was wearing his best suit, a midnight-blue mohair, with a white shirt open at the neck. It seemed an effort to breathe, and his skin felt uncomfortably damp under his clothes. He realized he had broken some rule of criminal etiquette by contacting Harry on the day of the robbery, but he had no alternative. 'I had to talk to you,' Kit said. 'Haven't you seen the news?'

'What if I have?'

Kit suppressed a surge of irritation. Men such as Harry could never bring themselves to admit to not knowing something, however trivial. 'There's a big flap on at Oxenford Medical,' Kit said. 'A technician died of a virus.'

'What do you want me to do, send flowers?'

'They'll be tightening security. This is the worst possible time to rob the place. It's difficult enough anyway. They have a state-of-the-art alarm system. And the woman in charge is as tough as a rubber steak.'

'What a whinger you are.'

Kit had not been asked to sit down, so he leaned on the back of a chair, feeling awkward. 'We have to call it off.'

'Let me explain something to you.' Harry took a cigarette from a packet on the table and lit it with a gold lighter. Then he coughed, an old smoker's cough from the depths of his lungs. When the spasm had passed, he spat into the pool and drank some coffee. Then he resumed. 'For one thing, I've said it's going to happen. Now you may not realize this, being so well brought up, but when a man says something's going to happen, and then it doesn't, people think he's a wanker.'

'Yes, but—'

'Don't even dream of interrupting me.'

Kit shut up.

'For another thing, Nigel Buchanan's no drugged-up schoolboy wanting to rob Woolworth's in Govan Cross. He's a legend and, more important than that, he's connected with some highly respected people in London. When you're dealing with folk like that, even more you don't want to look like a wanker.'

He paused, as if daring Kit to argue. Kit said nothing. How had he got himself involved with these people? He had walked into the wolves' cave, and now he stood paralysed, waiting to be torn to pieces.

'And for a third thing, you owe me a quarter of a million pounds. No one has ever owed me that much money for so long and still been able to walk without crutches. I trust I'm making myself clear.'

Kit nodded silently. He was so scared he felt he might throw up.

'So don't tell me we have to call it off.' Harry picked up the *Sun* as if the conversation were over.

Kit forced himself to speak. 'I meant postpone it, not call it off,' he managed. 'We can do it another day, when the fuss has died down.'

Harry did not look up. 'Ten a.m. on Christmas Day, Nigel said. And I want my money.'

'There's no point in doing it if we're going to get caught!' Kit said desperately. Harry did not respond. 'Everyone can wait a little longer, can't they?' It was like talking to the wall. 'Better late than never.'

Harry glanced towards the pool and made a beckoning gesture. Daisy must have been keeping an eye on him, for she immediately climbed out of the pool. She did not take off the gloves. She had powerful shoulders and arms. Her shallow breasts hardly moved as she walked. Kit saw that she had a tattoo over one breast and a nipple ring in the other. When she came closer, he realized she was shaved all over. She had a flat belly and lean thighs, and her pubic mound was prominent. Every detail was visible, not just to Kit but to her father, if he cared to look. Kit felt weird.

Harry did not seem to notice. 'Kit wants us to wait for our money, Daisy.' He stood up and tightened the belt of his robe. 'Explain to him how we feel about that – I'm too tired.' He put the newspaper under his arm and walked away.

Daisy grabbed Kit by the lapels of his best suit. 'Look,'

he pleaded. 'I just want to make sure this doesn't end in disaster for all of us.' Then Daisy jerked him sideways. He lost his balance and would have fallen to the ground, but she took his weight; then she threw him into the pool.

It was a shock but, if the worst thing she did was ruin his suit, he would count himself lucky. Then, as he got his head above the surface, she jumped on him, her knees smashing into his back painfully, so that he cried out and swallowed water as his head went under.

They were at the shallow end. When his feet touched the bottom he struggled to stand upright, but his head was clamped by Daisy's arm, and he was pulled off balance again. She held him face down under the water.

He held his breath, expecting her to punch him, or something, but she remained still. Needing to breathe, he began to struggle, trying to break her hold, but she was too strong. He became angry, and lashed out feebly with his arms and legs. He felt like a child in a tantrum, flailing helplessly in the grip of its mother.

His need for air became desperate, and he fought down panic as he resisted the urge to open his mouth and gasp. He realized that Daisy had his head under her left arm and was down on one knee with her own head just above the surface. He made himself still, so that his feet floated down. Perhaps she would think he had lost consciousness. His feet touched the bottom. Her grip did not slacken. He got a firm footing then put all his strength into a sudden upward jerk of his body, to dislodge Daisy's hold. She hardly moved, just tightening her grip on his head. It was like having his skull squeezed by steel pincers.

He opened his eyes underwater. His cheek was pressed

against her bony ribs. He twisted his head an inch, opened his mouth, and bit her. He felt her flinch, and her grip weakened a little. He clamped his jaws together, trying to bite all the way through the fold of skin. Then he felt her gloved hand on his face and her fingers pushing into his eyes. Reflexively, he tried to pull away, and involuntarily relaxed his jaws and let her flesh slip from his bite.

Panic overcame him. He could not hold his breath any longer. His body, starved of oxygen, forced him to gasp for air, and water rushed into his lungs. He found himself coughing and vomiting at the same time. After each spasm more water poured down his throat. He realized he would soon die if this went on.

Then she seemed to relent. She jerked his head out of the water. He opened his mouth wide and sucked in blessed pure air. He coughed a jet of water out of his lungs. Then, before he could take a second breath, she shoved his head under again, and instead of air he inhaled water.

Panic turned to something worse. Mad with fear, he thrashed about. Terror gave him strength, and Daisy struggled to hold him, but he could not get his head up. He no longer tried to keep his mouth shut, but let the water flood into him. The sooner he drowned, the sooner the agony would be over.

Daisy pulled his head out again.

He spewed water and drew in a precious gasp of air. Then his head was submerged yet again.

He screamed, but no sound came out. His struggles weakened. He knew Harry had not intended for Daisy to kill him, for then there would be no robbery – but Daisy was not very sane, and it seemed she was going to go too far. He decided he was going to die. His eyes were open, showing him only a green blur; then his vision began to darken, as if night were falling.

At last he passed out.

10 a.m.

Ned could not drive, so Miranda took the wheel of the Toyota Previa. Her son, Tom, sat behind with his Game Boy. The back row of seats had been folded away to make room for a stack of presents wrapped in red and gold paper and tied with green ribbon.

As they pulled away from the Georgian terrace off the Great Western Road where Miranda had her flat, a light snowfall began. There was a blizzard over the sea to the north, but the weather forecasters said it was going to bypass Scotland.

She felt content, driving with the two men in her life, heading for Christmas with her family at her father's house. She was reminded of driving back from university for the holidays, looking forward to home cooking, clean bathrooms, ironed sheets, and that feeling of being loved and cared for.

She headed first for the suburb where Ned's ex-wife lived. They were to pick up his daughter, Sophie, before driving to Steepfall.

Tom's toy played a descending melody, probably indicating that he had crashed his spaceship, or been beheaded by a gladiator. He sighed and said: 'I saw an advertisement in a car magazine for these really cool screens that go in the back of the headrests, so the people in the back seat can watch movies and stuff.'

'A must-have accessory,' said Ned with a smile.

'Sounds expensive,' said Miranda.

'They don't cost that much,' Tom said.

Miranda looked at him in the driving mirror. 'Well, how much?'

'I don't know, just, but they didn't *look* expensive, d'you know what I mean?'

'Why don't you find out the price, and we'll see if we can afford one.'

'Okay, great! And if it's too dear for you, I'll ask Grandpa.'

Miranda smiled. Catch Grandpa in the right mood and he would give you anything.

Miranda had always hoped Tom would be the one to inherit his grandfather's scientific genius. The jury was still out. His school work was excellent, but not astonishingly so. However, she was not sure what, exactly, her father's talent was. Of course he was a brilliant microbiologist, but he had something more. It was partly the imagination to see the direction in which progress lay, and partly the leadership to inspire a team of scientists to pull together. How could you tell whether an eleven-year-old had that kind of ability? Meanwhile, nothing captured Tom's imagination half as much as a new computer game.

She turned on the radio. A choir was singing a Christmas carol. Ned said: 'If I hear "Away in a Manger" one more time, I may have to commit suicide by impaling myself on a Christmas tree.' Miranda changed the station and got John Lennon singing 'War is Over'. Ned groaned and said: 'Do you realize that Radio Hell plays Christmas music all the year round? It's a well-known fact.'

Miranda laughed. After a minute she found a classical station that was playing a piano trio. 'How's this?'

'Haydn – perfect.'

Ned was curmudgeonly about popular culture. It was part of his egghead act, like not knowing how to drive. Miranda did not mind: she, too, disliked pop music, soap operas, and cheap reproductions of famous paintings. But she liked carols.

She was fond of Ned's idiosyncrasies, but her conversation with Olga in the coffee bar nagged at her. Was Ned weak? She sometimes wished he were more assertive. Her husband, Jasper, had been too much so. But she sometimes hankered after the kind of sex she had had with Jasper. He had been selfish in bed, taking her roughly, thinking only of his own pleasure – and Miranda, to her shame, had felt liberated, and enjoyed it. The thrill had worn off, eventually, when she got fed up with his being selfish and inconsiderate about everything else. All the same, she wished Ned could be like that just sometimes.

Her thoughts turned to Kit. She was desperately disappointed that he had cancelled. She had worked so hard to persuade him to join the family for Christmas. At first he had refused, then he had relented, so she could hardly be surprised that he had changed his mind again. All the same, it was a painful blow, for she badly wanted them all to be together, as they had been most Christmases before Mamma died. The rift between Daddy and Kit scared her. Coming so soon after Mamma's death, it made the family seem dangerously fragile. And if the family was vulnerable, what could she be sure of?

She turned into a street of old stone-built workers' cottages and pulled up outside a larger house that might have been occupied by an overseer. Ned had lived here with Jennifer until they split up two years ago. Before that they had modernized the place at great expense, and the payments still burdened Ned. Every time Miranda drove past this street she felt angry about the amount of money Ned was paying Jennifer.

Miranda engaged the handbrake, but left the engine running. She and Tom stayed in the car while Ned walked up the path to the house. Miranda never went inside. Although Ned had left the marital home before he met Miranda, Jennifer was as hostile as if Miranda had been responsible for the break-up. She avoided meeting her, spoke curtly to her on the phone, and – according to the indiscreet Sophie – referred to her as 'that fat tart' when speaking to her women friends. Jennifer herself was as thin as a bird, with a nose like a beak.

The door was opened by Sophie, a fourteen-year-old in jeans and a skimpy sweater. Ned kissed her and went inside.

The car radio played one of Dvořák's Hungarian dances. In the back seat, Tom's Game Boy beeped irregularly. Snow blew around the car in flurries. Miranda turned the heater higher. Ned came out of the house, looking annoyed.

He came to Miranda's window. 'Jennifer's out,' he said. 'Sophie hasn't even begun to get ready. Will you come in and help her pack?'

'Oh, Ned, I don't think I should,' Miranda said unhappily. She felt uncomfortable about going inside when Jennifer was not there.

Ned looked panicked. 'To tell you the truth, I'm not sure what a girl needs.'

Miranda could believe that. Ned found it a challenge to pack a case for himself. He had never done it while he was with Jennifer. When he and Miranda had been about to take their first holiday together – a trip to the museums of Florence – she had refused, on principle, to do it for him, and he had been forced to learn. However, on subsequent trips – a weekend in London, four days in Vienna – she had checked his luggage, and each time found that he had forgotten something important. To pack for someone else was beyond him.

She sighed and killed the engine. 'Tom, you'll have to come too.'

The house was attractively decorated, Miranda thought as she stepped into the hall. Jennifer had a good eye. She had combined plain rustic furniture with colourful fabrics in the way an overseer's house-proud wife might have done a hundred years ago. There were Christmas cards on the mantelpiece, but no tree.

It seemed strange to think that Ned had lived here. He had come home every evening to this house, just as now he came home to Miranda's flat. He had listened to the news on the radio, sat down to dinner, read Russian novels, brushed his teeth automatically, and gone unthinkingly to bed to hold a different woman in his arms.

Sophie was in the living room, lying on a couch in front of the television. She had a pierced navel with a cheap jewel in it. Miranda smelled cigarette smoke. Ned said: 'Now, Sophie, Miranda's going to help you get ready, okay, poppet?' There was a pleading note in his voice that made Miranda wince.

'I'm watching a film,' Sophie said sulkily.

Miranda knew that Sophie would respond to firmness, not supplication. She picked up the remote control and turned the television off. 'Show me your bedroom, please, Sophie,' she said briskly.

Sophie looked rebellious.

'Hurry up, we're short of time.'

Sophie stood up reluctantly and walked slowly from the room. Miranda followed her upstairs to a messy bedroom decorated with posters of boys with peculiar haircuts and ludicrously baggy jeans.

'We'll be at Steepfall for five days, so you need ten pairs of knickers, for a start.'

'I haven't got ten.'

Miranda did not believe her, but she said: 'Then we'll take what you've got, and you can do laundry.'

Sophie stood in the middle of the room, a mutinous expression on her pretty face.

'Come on,' Miranda said. 'I'm not going to be your maid. Get some knickers out.' She stared at the girl.

Sophie was not able to stare her out. She dropped her eyes, turned away, and opened the top drawer of a chest. It was full of underwear.

'Pack five bras,' Miranda said.

Sophie began taking items out.

Crisis over, Miranda thought. She opened the door of a closet. 'You'll need a couple of frocks for the evenings.' She took out a red dress with spaghetti straps, much too sexy for a fourteen-year-old. 'This is nice,' she lied.

Sophie thawed a little. 'It's new.'

'We should wrap it so that it doesn't crease. Where do you keep tissue paper?'

'In the kitchen drawer, I think.'

'I'll fetch it. You find a couple of clean pairs of jeans.'

Miranda went downstairs, feeling that she was beginning to establish the right balance of friendliness and authority with Sophie. Ned and Tom were in the living room, watching TV. Miranda entered the kitchen and called out: 'Ned, do you know where tissue paper is kept?'

'I'm sorry, I don't.'

'Stupid question,' Miranda muttered, and she began opening drawers.

She eventually found some at the back of a cupboard of sewing materials. She had to kneel on the tiled floor to pull the packet from under a box of ribbons. It was an effort to reach into the cupboard, and she felt herself flush. This is ridiculous, she thought. I'm only thirty-five, I should be able to bend without effort. I must lose ten pounds. No roast potatoes with the Christmas turkey.

As she took the packet of tissue paper from the cupboard, she heard the back door of the house open, then a woman's footsteps. She looked up to see Jennifer.

'What the hell do you think you're doing?' Jennifer said. She was a small woman, but managed to look formidable, with her high forehead and arched nose. She was smartly dressed in a tailored coat and high-heeled boots.

Miranda got to her feet, panting slightly. To her

mortification, she felt perspiration break out on her throat. 'I was looking for tissue paper.'

'I can see that. I want to know why you're in my house at all.'

Ned appeared in the doorway. 'Hello, Jenny, I didn't hear you come in.'

'Obviously I didn't give you time to sound the alarm,' she said sarcastically.

'Sorry,' he said, 'but I asked Miranda to come in and—'

'Well, don't!' Jennifer interrupted. 'I don't want your women here.'

She made it sound as if Ned had a harem. In fact he had dated only two women since Jennifer. The first he had seen only once, and the second was Miranda. But it seemed childishly quarrelsome to point that out. Instead, Miranda said: 'I was just trying to help Sophie.'

'I'll take care of Sophie. Please leave my house.'

Ned said: 'I'm sorry if we startled you, Jenny, but—'

'Don't bother to apologize, just get her out of here.'

Miranda blushed hotly. No one had ever been so rude to her. 'I'd better leave,' she said.

'That's right,' Jennifer said.

Ned said: 'I'll bring Sophie out as soon as I can.'

Miranda was as angry with Ned as with Jennifer, though for the moment she was not sure why. She turned towards the hall.

'You can use the back door,' Jennifer said.

To her shame, Miranda hesitated. She looked at Jennifer and saw on her face the hint of a smirk. That gave Miranda an ounce of courage. 'I don't think so,' she said quietly. She went to the front door.

'Tom, come with me,' she called.

'Just a minute,' he shouted back.

She stepped into the living room. Tom was watching TV. She grabbed his wrist, hauled him to his feet, and dragged him out of the house.

'That hurts!' he protested.

She slammed the front door. 'Next time, come when I call.'

She felt like crying as she got into the car. Now she had to sit waiting, like a servant, while Ned was in the house with his ex-wife. Had Jennifer actually planned this whole drama as a way of humiliating Miranda? It was possible. Ned had been hopeless. She knew now why she was so cross with him. He had let Jennifer insult her without a word of protest. He just kept apologizing. And for what? If Jennifer had packed a case for her daughter, or even got the girl to do it herself, Miranda would not have had to enter the house. And then, worst of all, Miranda had taken out her anger on her son. She should have shouted at Jennifer, not Tom.

She looked at him in the driving mirror. 'Tommy, I'm sorry I hurt your wrist,' she said.

'It's okay,' he said without looking up from his Game Boy. 'I'm sorry I didn't come when you called.'

'All forgiven, then,' she said. A tear rolled down her cheek, and she quickly wiped it away.

11 a.m.

'Viruses kill thousands of people every day,' Stanley Oxenford said. 'About every ten years, an epidemic of influenza kills around twenty-five thousand people in the United Kingdom. In 1918, flu caused more deaths than the whole of World War One. In the year 2002, three million people died of Aids, which is caused by human immunodeficiency virus. And viruses are involved in ten per cent of cancers.'

Toni listened intently, sitting beside him in the Great Hall, under the varnished timbers of the mock-medieval roof. He sounded calm and controlled, but she knew him well enough to recognize the barely audible tremor of strain in his voice. He had been shocked and dismayed by Laurence Mahoney's threat, and the fear that he might lose everything was only just concealed by his unruffled facade.

She watched the faces of the assembled reporters. Would they hear what he was saying, and understand the importance of his work? She knew journalists. Some were intelligent, many stupid. A few believed in telling the truth; the majority just wrote the most sensational story they could get away with. She felt indignant that they could hold in their hands the fate of a man such as Stanley. Yet the power of the tabloids was a brutal fact of modern life. If enough of these hacks chose to portray Stanley as a mad scientist in a Frankenstein castle, the Americans might be sufficiently embarrassed to pull the finance.

That would be a tragedy – not just for Stanley, but for the world. True, someone else could finish the testing programme for the antiviral drug, but a ruined and bankrupt Stanley would invent no more miracle cures. Toni thought angrily that she would like to slap the dumb faces of the journalists and say: 'Wake up – this is about *your* future too!'

'Viruses are a fact of life, but we don't have to accept that fact passively,' Stanley went on. Toni admired the way he spoke. His voice was measured but relaxed. He used this tone when explaining things to younger colleagues. His speech sounded more like a conversation. 'Scientists can defeat viruses. Before Aids, the great killer was smallpox – until a scientist called Edward Jenner invented vaccination in 1796. Now smallpox has disappeared from human society. Similarly, polio has been eliminated in large areas of our world. In time, we will defeat influenza, and Aids, and even cancer – and it will be done by scientists like us, working in laboratories such as this.'

A woman put up a hand and called out. 'What are you working on here – exactly?'

Toni said: 'Would you mind identifying yourself?'

'Edie McAllan, science correspondent, *Scotland on Sunday*.'

Cynthia Creighton, sitting on the other side of Stanley, made a note.

Stanley said: 'We have developed an antiviral drug.

That's rare. There are plenty of antibiotic drugs, which kill bacteria, but few that attack viruses.'

A man said: 'What's the difference?' He added: 'Clive Brown, *Daily Record*.'

The *Record* was a tabloid. Toni was pleased with the direction the questions were taking. She wanted the press to concentrate on real science. The more they understood, the less likely they were to print damaging rubbish.

Stanley said: 'Bacteria, or germs, are tiny creatures that can be seen with a normal microscope. Each of us is host to billions of them. Many are useful, helping us digest food, for example, or dispose of dead skin cells. A few cause illness, and some of those can be treated with antibiotics. Viruses are smaller and simpler than bacteria. You need an electron microscope to see them. A virus cannot reproduce itself – instead, it hijacks the biochemical machinery of a living cell and forces the cell to produce copies of the virus. No known virus is useful to humans. And we have few medicines to combat them. That's why a new antiviral drug is such good news for the human race.'

Edie McAllan asked: 'What particular viruses is your drug effective against?'

It was another scientific question. Toni began to believe that this press conference would do all that she and Stanley hoped. She quelled her optimism with an effort. She knew, from her experience as a police press officer, that a journalist could ask serious and intelligent questions then go back to the office and write inflammatory garbage. Even if the writer turned in a sensible piece, it might be rewritten by someone ignorant and irresponsible.

Stanley replied: 'That's the question we're trying to

answer. We're testing the drug against a variety of viruses to determine its range.'

Clive Brown said: 'Does that include dangerous viruses?'

Stanley said: 'Yes. No one is interested in drugs for safe viruses.'

The audience laughed. It was a witty answer to a stupid question. But Brown looked annoyed, and Toni's heart sank. A humiliated journalist would stop at nothing to get revenge.

She intervened quickly. 'Thank you for that question, Clive,' she said, trying to mollify him. 'Here at Oxenford Medical we impose the highest possible standards of security in laboratories where special materials are used. In BSL4, which stands for BioSafety Level Four, the alarm system is directly connected with regional police headquarters at Inverburn. There are security guards on duty twenty-four hours a day, and this morning I have doubled the number of guards. As a further precaution, security guards cannot enter BSL4, but monitor the laboratory via closed-circuit television cameras.'

Brown was not appeased. 'If you've got perfect security, how did the hamster get out?'

Toni was ready for this. 'Let me make three points. One, it was not a hamster. You've got that from the police, and it's wrong.' She had deliberately given Frank dud information, and he had fallen into her trap, betraying himself as the source of the leaked story. 'Please rely on us for the facts about what goes on here. It was a rabbit, and it was not called Fluffy.'

They laughed at this, and even Brown smiled.

'Two, the rabbit was smuggled out of the laboratory in

a bag, and we have today instituted a compulsory bag search at the entrance to BSL4, to make sure this cannot happen again. Three, I didn't say we had perfect security. I said we set the highest possible standards. That's all human beings can do.'

'So you're admitting your laboratory is a danger to innocent members of the Scottish public.'

'No. You're safer here than you would be driving on the M8 or taking a flight from Prestwick. Viruses kill many people every day, but only one person has ever died of a virus from our lab, and he was not an innocent member of the public – he was an employee who deliberately broke the rules and knowingly put himself at risk.'

On balance it was going well, Toni thought as she looked around for the next question. The television cameras were rolling, the flashguns were popping, and Stanley was coming across as what he was, a brilliant scientist with a strong sense of responsibility. But she was afraid the TV news would throw away the undramatic footage of the press conference in favour of the crowd of youngsters at the gate chanting slogans about animal rights. She wished she could think of something more interesting for the cameramen to point their lenses at.

Frank's friend Carl Osborne spoke up for the first time. He was a good-looking man of about Toni's age with movie-star features. His hair was a shade too yellow to be natural. 'Exactly what danger did this rabbit pose to the general public?'

Stanley answered: 'The virus is not very infectious across species. In order to infect Michael, we think the rabbit must have bitten him.'

'What if the rabbit had got loose?'

Stanley looked out of the window. A light snow was falling. 'It would have frozen to death.'

'Suppose it had been eaten by another animal. Could a fox have become infected?'

'No. Viruses are adapted to a small number of species, usually one, sometimes two or three. This one does not infect foxes, or any other form of Scottish wildlife, as far as we know. Just humans, macaque monkeys, and certain types of rabbit.'

'But Michael could have given the virus to other people.'

'By sneezing, yes. This was the possibility that alarmed us most. However, Michael seems not to have seen anyone during the critical period. We have already contacted his colleagues and friends. Nonetheless, we would be grateful if you would use your newspapers and television programmes to appeal for anyone who did see him to call us immediately.'

'We aren't trying to minimize this,' Toni put in hastily. 'We are deeply concerned about the incident and, as I've explained, we have already put in stronger security measures. But at the same time we must be careful not to exaggerate.' Telling journalists not to exaggerate was a bit like telling lawyers not to be quarrelsome, she thought wryly. 'The truth is that the public have not been endangered.'

Osborne was not finished. 'Suppose Michael Ross had given it to a friend, who had given it to someone else . . . how many people might have died?'

Toni said quickly: 'We can't enter into that kind of wild speculation. The virus did not spread. One person died.

That's one too many, but it's no reason to start talking about the Four Horsemen of the Apocalypse.' She bit her tongue. That was a stupid phrase to use: someone would probably quote it, out of context, and make it seem as if she had been forecasting doomsday.

Osborne said: 'I understand your work is financed by the American army.'

'The Department of Defense, yes,' Stanley said. 'They are naturally interested in ways of combating biological warfare.'

'Isn't it true that the Americans have this work done in Scotland because they think it's too dangerous to be done in the United States?'

'On the contrary. A great deal of work of this type goes on in the States, at the Centers for Disease Control in Atlanta, Georgia, and at the US Army Medical Research Institute of Infectious Diseases at Fort Detrick.'

'So why was Scotland chosen?'

'Because the drug was invented here at Oxenford Medical.'

Toni decided to quit while she was ahead and close the press conference. 'I don't want to cut the questioning short, but I know some of you have midday deadlines,' she said. 'You should all have an information pack, and Cynthia here has extra copies.'

'One more question,' said Clive Brown of the *Record*. 'What's your reaction to the demonstration outside?'

Toni realized she still had not thought of something more interesting for the cameras.

Stanley said: 'They offer a simple answer to a complex ethical question. Like most simple answers, theirs is wrong.'

It was the right response, but sounded a little hard-hearted, so Toni added: 'And we hope they don't catch cold.'

While the audience was laughing at that, Toni stood up to indicate the conference was over. Then she was struck by inspiration. She beckoned to Cynthia Creighton. Turning her back on the audience, she spoke in a low, urgent voice. 'Go down to the canteen, quickly,' she said. 'Get two or three canteen staff to load up trays with cups of hot coffee and tea, and hand them out to the demonstrators outside the gate.'

'What a kind thought,' said Cynthia.

Toni was not being kind – in fact she was being cynical – but there was no time to explain that. 'It must be done in the next couple of minutes,' she said. 'Go, go!'

Cynthia hurried away.

Toni turned to Stanley and said: 'Well done. You handled that perfectly.'

He took a red-spotted handkerchief from his jacket pocket and discreetly mopped his face. 'I hope it's done the trick.'

'We'll know when we see the lunch-time news on television. Now you should slip away, otherwise they'll all be trying to corner you for an exclusive interview.' He was under pressure, and she wanted to protect him.

'Good thinking. I need to get home, anyway.' He lived in a farmhouse on a cliff five miles from the lab. 'I'd like to be there to welcome the family.'

That disappointed her. She had been looking forward to reviewing the press conference with him. 'Okay,' she said. 'I'll monitor the reaction.'

'At least no one asked me the worst question.'

'What was that?'

'The survival rate from Madoba-2.'

'What does that mean?'

'No matter how deadly the infection, there are usually some individuals who live through it. Survival rate is a measure of how dangerous it is.'

'And what is the survival rate for Madoba-2?'

'Zero,' said Stanley.

Toni stared at him. She was glad she had not known that before.

Stanley nodded over her shoulder. 'Here comes Osborne.'

'I'll head him off at the pass.' She moved to intercept the reporter, and Stanley left by a side door. 'Hello, Carl. I hope you got everything you needed?'

'I think so. I was wondering what Stanley's first success was.'

'He was a member of the team that developed acyclovir.'

'Which is?'

'The cream you put on when you get cold sores. The brand name is Zovirax. It's an antiviral drug.'

'Really? That's interesting.'

Toni did not think Carl was genuinely interested. She wondered what he was really after. She said: 'May we rely on you to do a judicious piece that reflects the facts, and doesn't exaggerate the danger?'

'You mean will I be talking about the Four Horsemen of the Apocalypse?'

She winced. 'Foolish of me to give an example of the kind of hyperbole I was trying to discourage.'

'Don't worry, I'm not going to quote you.'

'Thanks.'

'You shouldn't thank me. I'd use it happily, but my audience wouldn't have the slightest idea what it means.' He changed tack. 'I've hardly seen you since you split up with Frank. How long ago is it now?'

'He left me at Christmas two years ago.'

'How have you been?'

'I've had some bad times, if you want to know the truth. But things are picking up. At least, they were until today.'

'We should get together and catch up.'

She had no desire to spend time with Osborne, but she politely said: 'Sure, why not.'

He surprised her by following up quickly. 'Would you like to have dinner?'

'Dinner?' she said.

'Yes.'

'As in, go out on a date with you?'

'Yes, again.'

It was the last thing she had expected. 'No!' she said. Then she remembered how dangerous this man could be, and tried to soften her rejection. 'I'm sorry, Carl, you took me by surprise. I've known you so long that I just don't think of you that way.'

'I might change your thinking.' He looked boyishly vulnerable. 'Give me a chance.'

The answer was still no, but she hesitated for a moment. Carl was handsome, charming, well paid, a local celebrity. Most single women pushing forty would jump at the chance. But she was not even mildly attracted to him. Even if she had not given her heart to Stanley, she would not have been tempted to go out with Carl. Why?

It took her only a second to find the answer. Carl had no integrity. A man who would distort the truth for the sake of a sensational story would be equally dishonest in other areas of life. He was not a monster. There were plenty of men like him, and a few women. But Toni could not contemplate becoming intimate with someone so shallow. How could you kiss, and confess secrets, and lose your inhibitions, and open your body, with someone who could not be trusted? The thought was revolting.

'I'm flattered,' she lied. 'But no.'

He was not ready to give up. 'The truth is, I always fancied you, even when you were with Frank. You must have sensed that.'

'You used to flirt with me, but you did that with most women.'

'It wasn't the same.'

'Aren't you seeing that weather girl? I seem to remember a photo in the newspaper.'

'Marnie? That was never serious. I did it for publicity, mainly.'

He seemed irritated by the reminder, and Toni guessed that Marnie had thrown him over. 'I'm sorry to hear that,' she said sympathetically.

'Show your compassion in actions, not words. Have dinner with me tonight. I even have a table booked at La Chaumière.'

It was a swanky restaurant. He must have made the reservation some time ago – probably for Marnie. 'I'm busy tonight.'

'You're not still carrying a torch for Frank, are you?'

Toni laughed bitterly. 'I did for a while, fool that I am, but I'm over him now. Very over.'

'Someone else, then?'

'I'm not seeing anyone.'

'But you're interested in someone. It's not the old professor, is it?'

'Don't be ridiculous,' Toni said.

'You're not blushing, are you?'

'I hope not, though any woman subjected to this kind of interrogation would be entitled to blush.'

'My God, you fancy Stanley Oxenford.' Carl was not good at taking rejection, and his face became ugly with resentment. 'Of course, Stanley's a widower, isn't he? Children grown up. All that money, and just the two of you to spend it.'

'This is really offensive, Carl.'

'The truth so often is. You really like high flyers, don't you? First Frank, the fastest-rising detective in the history of the Scottish police. And now a millionaire scientific entrepreneur. You're a starfucker, Toni!'

She had to end this before she lost her temper. 'Thank you for coming to the press conference,' she said. She held out her hand, and he shook it automatically. 'Goodbye.' She turned and walked away.

She was shaking with anger. He had made her deepest emotions seem unworthy. She wanted to strangle him, not go out with him. She tried to make herself calm. She had a major professional crisis to deal with, and she could not let her feelings get in the way.

She went to the reception desk near the door and spoke

to the supervisor of the security guards, Steve Tremlett. 'Stay here until they've all left, and make sure none of them tries to take an unofficial tour.' A determined snoop might try to enter high-security areas by 'tailgating' – waiting for someone with a pass then going through the door right behind them.

'Leave it to me,' Steve said.

She began to feel calmer. She put on her coat and went outside. The snow was falling more heavily, but she could see the demonstration. She walked to the guard booth at the gate. Three canteen staff were handing out hot drinks. The protestors had temporarily stopped chanting and waving their banners, and were smiling and chatting instead.

And all the cameras were photographing them.

Everything had gone perfectly, she thought. So why did she feel depressed?

She returned to her office. She closed the door and stood still, grateful to be alone for a minute. She had controlled the press conference well, she thought. She had protected her boss from Osborne. And the idea of giving hot drinks to the demonstrators had worked like a charm. It would be unwise to celebrate before seeing the actual coverage, of course, but she felt that every decision she had made had been right.

So why did she feel so down?

Partly it was Osborne. Any encounter with him could leave a person feeling low. But mainly, she realized, it was Stanley. After all she had done for him this morning, he had slipped away with barely a word of thanks. That was what it meant to be the boss, she supposed. And she had long known how important his family was to him. She, by contrast, was just a colleague: valued, liked, respected – but not loved.

The phone rang. She looked at it for a moment, resenting its cheerful warble, not wanting to talk. Then she picked it up.

It was Stanley, calling from his car. 'Why don't you drop in at the house in an hour or so? We could watch the news, and learn our fate together.'

Her mood lifted instantly. She felt as if the sun had come out. 'Of course,' she said. 'I'd be delighted.'

'We might as well be crucified side by side,' he said.

'I would consider it an honour.'

12 noon

The snow became heavier as Miranda drove north. Big white flakes swooped on the windscreen of the Toyota Previa, to be swept aside by the long wipers. She had to slow down as visibility diminished. The snow seemed to soundproof the car, and there was no more than a background swish of tyres to compete with the classical music from the radio.

The atmosphere inside was subdued. In the back, Sophie was listening to her own music on headphones, while Tom was lost in the beeping world of Game Boy. Ned was quiet, occasionally conducting the orchestra with one waving forefinger. As he gazed into the snow and listened to Elgar's cello concerto, Miranda watched his tranquil, bearded face, and realized that he had no idea how badly he had let her down.

He sensed her discontent. 'I'm sorry about Jennifer's outburst,' he said.

Miranda looked in the rear-view mirror and saw that Sophie was nodding her head in time to the music from her iPod. Satisfied that the girl could not hear her, Miranda said: 'Jennifer was bloody rude.'

'I'm sorry,' he said again. He obviously felt no need to explain or apologize for his own role.

She had to destroy his comfortable illusion. 'It's not Jennifer's behaviour that bothers me,' she said. 'It's yours.'

'I realize it was a mistake to invite you in without warning her.'

'It's not that. We all make mistakes.'

He looked puzzled and annoyed. 'What, then?'

'Oh, Ned! You didn't defend me!'

'I thought you were well able to defend yourself.'

'That's not the point! Of course I can look after myself. I don't need mothering. But you should be my champion.'

'A knight in shining armour.'

'Yes!'

'I thought it was more important to get things calmed down.'

'Well, you thought wrong. When the world turns hostile, I don't want you to take a judicious view of the situation – I want you to be on my side.'

'I'm afraid I'm not the combative type.'

'I know,' she said, and they both fell silent.

They were on a narrow road that followed the shore of a sea loch. They passed small farms with a few horses in winter blankets cropping the grass, and drove through villages with white-painted churches and rows of houses along the waterfront. Miranda felt depressed. Even if her family embraced Ned as she had asked them to, did she want to marry such a passive man? She had longed for someone gentle and cultured and bright, but she now realized that she also wanted him to be strong. Was it too much to expect? She thought of her father. He was always kind, rarely angry, never quarrelsome – but no one had ever thought him weak.

Her mood lifted as they approached Steepfall. The house was reached by a long lane that wound through woods. Emerging from the trees, the drive swept around a headland with a sheer drop to the sea.

The garage came into view first. Standing sideways-on to the drive, it was an old cowshed that had been renovated and given three up-and-over doors. Miranda drove past it and along the front of the house.

Seeing the old farmhouse overlooking the beach, its thick stone walls with their small windows and the steep slate roof, she was overwhelmed by a sense of her childhood. She had first come here at the age of five, and every time she returned she became, for a few moments, a little girl in white socks, sitting on the granite doorstep in the sun, playing teacher to a class of three dolls, two guinea pigs in a cage, and a sleepy old dog. The sensation was intense, but fleeting: suddenly she remembered exactly how it had felt to be herself at five, but trying to hold on to the memory was like grabbing at smoke.

Her father's dark-blue Ferrari was at the front of the house, where he always left it for Luke, the handyman, to put away. The car was dangerously fast, obscenely curvaceous, and ludicrously expensive for his daily five-mile commute to the laboratory. Parked here on a bleak Scottish cliff top, it was as out of place as a high-heeled courtesan in a muddy farmyard. But he had no yacht, no wine cellar, no racehorse; he did not go skiing in Gstaad or gambling in Monte Carlo. The Ferrari was his only indulgence.

Miranda parked the Toyota. Tom rushed in. Sophie followed more slowly: she had not been here before, though she had met Stanley once, at Olga's birthday party a few months back. Miranda decided to forget about Jennifer for now. She took Ned's hand and they went in together.

They entered, as always, by the kitchen door at the side of the house. There was a lobby, where Wellington boots were kept in a cupboard, then a second door into the spacious kitchen. To Miranda this always felt like coming home. The familiar smells filled her head: roast dinners and ground coffee and apples, and a persistent trace of the French cigarettes Mamma Marta had smoked. No other house had replaced this one as the home of Miranda's soul: not the flat in Camden Town where she had sown her wild oats, nor the modern suburban house where she had been briefly married to Jasper Casson, nor the apartment in Georgian Glasgow in which she had raised Tom, at first alone and now with Ned.

A full-size black standard poodle called Nellie wagged her whole body with joy and licked everyone. Miranda greeted Luke and Lori, the Filipino couple who were preparing lunch. Lori said: 'Your father just got home, he's washing.'

Miranda told Tom and Sophie to lay the table. She did not want the children to put down roots in front of the TV and stay there all afternoon. 'Tom, you can show Sophie where everything is.' And having a job to do would help Sophie feel part of the family.

There were several bottles of Miranda's favourite white wine in the fridge. Daddy did not drink much, but Mamma had always had wine, and Daddy made sure there was plenty in the house. Miranda opened a bottle and poured a glass for Ned.

This was a good start, Miranda thought: Sophie happily helping Tom put out knives and forks, and Ned contentedly sipping Sancerre. Perhaps this, rather than the scene with Jennifer, would set the tone for the holiday.

If Ned was going to be part of Miranda's life, he had to love this house and the family that had grown up in it. He had been here before, but he had never brought Sophie and he had never stayed overnight, so this was his first major visit. She so wanted him to have a good time and get on well with everyone.

Miranda's husband, Jasper, had never liked Steepfall. At first he had gone out of his way to charm everyone, but on later visits he had been withdrawn while here and angry after they left. He seemed to dislike Stanley, and complained that he was authoritarian, which was odd, as Stanley rarely told anyone what to do – whereas Marta was so bossy they sometimes called her Mamma Mussolini. Now, with hindsight, Miranda could see that Jasper's hold over her was threatened by the presence of another man who loved her. Jasper did not feel free to bully her while her father was around.

The phone rang. Miranda picked up the extension on the wall by the big fridge. 'Hello?'

'Miranda, it's Kit.'

She was pleased. 'Hello, little brother! How are you?'

'A bit shattered, actually.'

'How come?'

'I fell in a swimming pool. Long story. How are things at Steepfall?'

'We're just sitting around drinking Daddy's wine, wishing you were with us.'

'Well, I'm coming after all.'

'Good!' She decided not to ask what had changed his mind. He would probably just say *long story* again.

'I'll be there in an hour or so. But, listen, can I still have the cottage?'

'I'm sure you can. It's up to Daddy, but I'll talk to him.'

As Miranda cradled the handset, her father came in. He wore the waistcoat and trousers of his suit, but he had rolled the cuffs of his shirt. He shook hands with Ned and kissed Miranda and the children. He was looking very trim, Miranda thought. 'Are you losing weight?' she asked.

'I've been playing squash. Who was on the phone?'

'That was Kit. He's coming, after all.' She watched her father's face, anxious to see his reaction.

'I'll believe it when I see him.'

'Oh, Daddy! You might sound more enthusiastic.'

He patted her hand. 'We all love Kit, but we know what he's like. I hope he shows up, but I'm not counting on it.' His tone was light, but Miranda could tell that he was trying to hide an inner hurt.

'He really wants to sleep in the cottage.'

'Did he say why?'

'No.'

Tom piped up: 'He's probably bringing a girl, and doesn't want us all to hear her squeals of delight.'

The kitchen went quiet. Miranda was astonished. Where had that come from? Tom was eleven, and never talked about sex. After a moment, they all burst out laughing. Tom looked bashful, and said: 'I read that in a book.' He was probably trying to seem grown-up in front of Sophie, Miranda decided. He was still a little boy, but not for much longer.

Stanley said: 'Anyway, I don't mind where anyone sleeps, you know that.' He looked at his watch distractedly. 'I have to watch the lunch-time news on television.'

Miranda said: 'I'm sorry about the technician who died. What made him do it?'

'We all get weird ideas into our heads, but a lonely person has no one to tell him not to be crazy.'

The door opened and Olga came in. As always, she entered speaking. 'This weather is a nightmare! People are skidding all over the place. Is that wine you're drinking? Let me have some before I explode. Nellie, please don't sniff me there, it's considered vulgar in human society. Hello, Daddy, how are you?'

'Nella merde,' he said.

Miranda recognized one of her mother's expressions. It meant 'in the shit'. Mamma Marta had fondly imagined that if she swore in Italian the children would not understand.

Olga said: 'I heard about the guy who died. Is it so bad for you?'

'We'll see when we watch the news.'

Olga was followed in by her husband Hugo, a small man with impish charm. When he kissed Miranda, his lips lingered on her cheek a second too long.

Olga said: 'Where shall Hugo put the bags?'

'Upstairs,' said Miranda.

'I suppose you've staked your claim to the cottage.'

'No, Kit's having it.'

'Oh, please!' Olga protested. 'That big double bed and a nice bathroom and kitchenette, all for one person, while the four of us share the poky old bathroom upstairs?'

'He particularly asked for it.'

'Well, I'm particularly asking for it.'

Miranda felt irritated with her sister. 'For God's sake, Olga, think of someone other than yourself for a change. You know Kit hasn't been here since . . . that whole mess. I just want to make sure he has a good time.'

'So he's getting the best bedroom because he stole from Daddy – is that your logic?'

'You're talking like an advocate again. Save it for your learned friends.'

'All right, you two,' their father said, sounding just as he had when they were small. 'In this case, I think Olga's right. It's selfish of Kit to demand the cottage all to himself. Miranda and Ned can sleep there.'

Olga said: 'So no one gets what they want.'

Miranda sighed. Why was Olga arguing? They all knew their father. Most of the time he would give you anything you wanted, but when he said no it was final. He might be indulgent, but he could not be bullied.

Now he said: 'It will teach you not to quarrel.'

'No, it won't. You've been imposing these judgements of Solomon for thirty years, and we still haven't learned.'

Stanley smiled. 'You're right. My approach to child-rearing has been wrong all along. Should I start again?'

'Too late.'

'Thank God for that.'

Miranda just hoped Kit would not be offended enough to turn right around and drive away. The argument was ended by the entrance of Caroline and Craig, the children of Hugo and Olga.

Caroline, seventeen, was carrying a cage containing several white rats. Nellie sniffed it excitedly. Caroline related to animals as a way of avoiding people. It was a phase many girls went through but, Miranda thought, at seventeen she should have got over it.

Craig, fifteen, carried two plastic rubbish bags crammed with wrapped gifts. He had Hugo's wicked grin, though he was tall like Olga. He put the bags down, greeted the family perfunctorily, and made a beeline for Sophie. They had met once before, Miranda recalled, at Olga's birthday party. 'You got your belly-button pierced!' Craig said to Sophie. 'Cool! Did it hurt?'

Miranda became aware that there was a stranger in the room. The newcomer, a woman, stood by the door to the hall, so must have come in by the front entrance. She was tall, with striking good looks: high cheekbones and a curved nose, lush red-blonde hair and marvellous green eyes. She wore a brown chalk-stripe suit that was a bit rumpled, and her expert make-up did not quite hide signs of tiredness under her eyes. She was gazing with amusement at the animated scene in the crowded kitchen. Miranda wondered how long she had been watching in silence.

The others began to notice her, and slowly the room fell silent. At last, Stanley turned around. 'Ah! Toni!' he said, jumping up from his seat, and Miranda was struck by how pleased he looked. 'Kind of you to drop in. Kids, this is my colleague, Antonia Gallo.'

The woman smiled as if she thought there was nothing more delightful than a big quarrelsome family. She had a wide, generous smile and full lips. This was the ex-cop who had caught Kit stealing from the company, Miranda realized. Despite that, Stanley seemed to like her.

Stanley introduced them, and Miranda noticed the pride in his tone. 'Toni, meet my daughter Olga, her husband, Hugo, and their children, Caroline with the pet rats, and Craig the tall one. My other daughter, Miranda, her boy, Tom, her fiancé, Ned, and Ned's daughter, Sophie.' Toni looked at each member of the family, nodding pleasantly, seeming keenly interested. It was hard to take in eight new names at a time, but Miranda had a feeling Toni would remember them all. 'That's Luke peeling carrots and Lori at the stove. Nellie, the lady does not want a chew of your rawhide bone, touched though she is by your generosity.'

Toni said: 'I'm very glad to meet you all.' She sounded as if she meant it, but at the same time she seemed to be under strain.

Miranda said: 'You must be having a difficult day. I'm so sorry about the technician who died.'

Stanley said: 'It was Toni who found him.'

'Oh, God!'

Toni nodded. 'We're pretty sure he didn't infect anyone else, thank Heaven. Now we're just hoping the media won't crucify us.'

Stanley looked at his watch. 'Excuse us,' he said to his family. 'We're going to watch the news in my study.' He held the door for Toni and they went out.

The children started to chatter again, and Hugo said something to Ned about the Scottish rugby team. Miranda turned to Olga. Their quarrel was forgotten. 'Attractive woman,' she said musingly.

'Yes,' Olga said. 'About, what, my age?'

'Thirty-seven, thirty-eight, yes. And Daddy's lost weight.'

'I noticed that.'

'A shared crisis brings people together.'

'Doesn't it just?'

'So what do you think?'

'I think what you think.'

Miranda drained her glass of wine. 'I thought so.'

1 p.m.

Toni was overwhelmed by the scene in the kitchen: adults and children, servants and pets, drinking wine and preparing food and quarrelling and laughing at jokes. It had been like walking into a really good party where she knew nobody. She wanted to join in, but she felt excluded. This was Stanley's life, she thought. He and his wife had created this group, this home, this warmth. She admired him for it, and envied his children. They probably had no idea how privileged they were. She had stood there for several minutes, bemused but fascinated. No wonder he was so attached to his family.

It thrilled and dismayed her. She could, if she allowed herself, entertain a fantasy about being part of it, sitting beside Stanley as his wife, loving him and his children, basking in the comfort of their togetherness. But she repressed that dream. It was impossible, and she should not torture herself. The very strength of the family bonds kept her out.

When at last they noticed her, she got a hard look from both daughters, Olga and Miranda. It was a careful scrutiny: detailed, unapologetic, hostile. She had got a similar look from Lori, the cook, though more discreet.

She understood their reaction. For thirty years Marta had ruled that kitchen. They would have felt disloyal to her had they *not* been hostile. Any woman Stanley liked could turn into a threat. She could disrupt the family. She might change their father's attitudes, turn his affections in new directions. She might bear him children, half-brothers and half-sisters who would care nothing about the history of the original family, would not be bound to them with the unbreakable chains of a shared childhood. She would take some of their inheritance, perhaps all of it. Was Stanley sensing these undercurrents? As she followed him into his study, she felt again the maddening frustration of not knowing what was in his mind.

It was a masculine room, with a Victorian pedestal desk, a bookcase full of weighty microbiology texts, and a worn leather couch in front of a log fire. The dog followed them in and stretched out by the fire like a curly black rug. On the mantelpiece was a framed photograph of a dark-haired teenage girl in tennis whites – the same girl as the bride in the picture on his office wall. Her brief shorts showed long, athletic legs. The heavy eye make-up and the hair band told Toni that the picture had been taken in the sixties. 'Was Marta a scientist, too?' Toni asked.

'No. Her degree was in English. When I met her, she was teaching A-level Italian at a high school in Cambridge.'

Toni was surprised. She had imagined that Marta must have shared Stanley's passion for his work. So, she thought, you don't need a doctorate in biology to be married to him. 'She was pretty.'

'Devastating,' Stanley replied. 'Beautiful, tall, sexy, foreign, a demon on the court, a heartbreaker off it. I was struck by lightning. Five minutes after I met her, I was in love.'

'And she with you?'

'That took longer. She was surrounded by admirers. Men fell like flies. I could never understand why she picked me in the end. She used to say she couldn't resist an egghead.'

No mystery there, Toni thought. Marta had liked what Toni liked: Stanley's strength. You knew right away that here was a man who would do what he said and be what he seemed to be, a man you could rely on. He had other attractions, too: he was warm and clever and even well dressed.

She wanted to say: *But how do you feel now? Are you still married to her memory?* But Stanley was her boss. She had no right to ask him about his deepest feelings. And there was Marta, on the mantelpiece, wielding her tennis racket like a cudgel.

Sitting on the couch beside Stanley, she tried to put her emotions aside and concentrate on the crisis at hand. 'Did you call the US Embassy?' she asked him.

'Yes. I got Mahoney calmed down, for the moment, but he'll be watching the news like us.'

A lot hung on the next few minutes, Toni thought. The company could be destroyed or saved, Stanley could be bankrupted, she could lose her job, and the world could lose the services of a great scientist. Don't panic, she told herself; be practical. She took a notebook from her shoulder bag. Cynthia Creighton was videotaping the news, back at the office, so Toni would be able to watch it again later, but she would now jot down any immediate thoughts.

The Scottish news came on before the UK bulletin.

The death of Michael Ross was still the top story, but the report was introduced by a newsreader, not Carl Osborne. That was a good sign, Toni thought hopefully. There was no more of Carl's laughably inaccurate science. The virus was correctly named as Madoba-2. The anchor was careful to point out that Michael's death would be investigated by the sheriff at an inquest.

'So far, so good,' Stanley murmured.

Toni said: 'It looks to me as if a senior news executive watched Carl Osborne's sloppy report over breakfast and came in to the office determined to sharpen up the coverage.'

The picture switched to the gates of the Kremlin. 'Animal-rights campaigners took advantage of the tragedy to stage a protest outside Oxenford Medical,' the anchor said. Toni was pleasantly surprised. That sentence was more favourable than she would have hoped. It implied the demonstrators were cynical media manipulators.

After a brief shot of the demo, the report cut to the Great Hall. Toni heard her own voice, sounding more Scots than she expected, outlining the security system at the laboratory. This was not very effective, she realized: just a voice droning on about alarms and guards. It might have been better to let the cameras film the airlock entrance to BSL4, with its fingerprint recognition system and submarine doors. Pictures were always better than words.

Then there was a shot of Carl Osborne asking: 'Exactly what danger did this rabbit pose to the general public?'

Toni leaned forward on the couch. This was the crunch.

They played the interchange between Carl and Stanley, with Carl posing disaster scenarios and Stanley saying how unlikely they were. This was bad, Toni knew. The audience would remember the idea of wildlife becoming infected, even though Stanley had said firmly that it was not possible.

On the screen, Carl said: 'But Michael could have given the virus to other people.'

Stanley replied gravely: 'By sneezing, yes.'

Unfortunately, they cut the exchange at that point.

Stanley muttered: 'Bloody hell.'

'It's not over yet,' Toni said. It could get better – or worse.

Toni hoped they would show her hasty intervention, when she had tried to counter the impression of complacency by saying that Oxenford Medical was not trying to downplay the risk. But, instead, there was a shot of Susan Mackintosh on the phone, with a voiceover explaining how the company was calling every employee to check whether they had had contact with Michael Ross. That was all right, Toni thought with relief. The danger was bluntly stated, but the company was shown taking positive action.

The final press conference shot was a close-up of Stanley, looking responsible, saying: 'In time, we will defeat influenza, and Aids, and even cancer – and it will be done by scientists like us, working in laboratories such as this.'

'That's good,' Toni said.

'Will it outweigh the dialogue with Osborne, about infecting wildlife?'

'I think so. You look so reassuring.'

Then there was a shot of the canteen staff giving out steaming hot drinks to the demonstrators in the snow. 'Great – they used it!' said Toni.

'I didn't see this,' Stanley said. 'Whose idea was it?'

'Mine.'

Carl Osborne thrust a microphone into the face of a woman employee and said: 'These people are demonstrating against your company. Why are you giving them coffee?'

'Because it's cold out here,' the woman replied.

Toni and Stanley laughed, delighted with the woman's wit and the positive way it reflected on the company.

The anchor reappeared and said: 'The First Minister of Scotland issued a statement this morning, saying: "I have today spoken to representatives of Oxenford Medical, the Inverburn police, and the Inverburn regional health authority, and I am satisfied that everything possible is being done to ensure that there is no further danger to the public." And now other news.'

Toni said: 'My God, I think we saved the day.'

'Giving out hot drinks was a great idea – when did you think of that?'

'At the last minute. Let's see what the UK news says.'

In the main bulletin, the story of Michael Ross came second, after an earthquake in Russia. The report used some of the same footage, but without Carl Osborne, who was a personality only in Scotland. There was a clip of Stanley saying: 'The virus is not very infectious across species. In order to infect Michael, we think the rabbit must have bitten him.' There was a low-key statement from the British Environment Minister in London. The report continued the same unhysterical tone of the Scottish news. Toni was hugely relieved.

Stanley said: 'It's good to know that not all journalists are like Carl Osborne.'

'He asked me to have dinner with him.' Toni wondered why she was telling him this.

Stanley looked surprised. '*Ha la faccia peggio del culo!*' he said. 'Hell of a nerve.'

She laughed. What he had actually said was: 'His face is worse than his arse,' presumably one of Marta's expressions. 'He's an attractive man,' she said.

'You don't really think so, do you?'

'He's handsome, anyway.' She realized she was trying to make him jealous. Don't play games, she told herself.

He said: 'What did you say to him?'

'I turned him down, of course.'

'I should think so, too.' Stanley looked embarrassed and added: 'Not that it's any of my business, but he's not worthy of you, not by a light-year.' He returned his attention to the television and switched to an all-news channel.

They watched footage of Russian earthquake victims and rescue teams for a couple of minutes. Toni felt foolish for having told Stanley about Osborne, but pleased by his reaction.

The Michael Ross story followed, and once again the tone was coolly factual. Stanley turned off the set. 'Well, we escaped crucifixion by TV.'

'No newspapers tomorrow, as it's Christmas Day,' Toni observed. 'By Thursday the story will be old. I think we're in the clear – barring unexpected developments.'

'Yes. If we lost another rabbit, we'd be right back in trouble.'

'There will be no more security incidents at the lab,' Toni said firmly. 'I'll make sure of that.'

Stanley nodded. 'I have to say, you've handled this whole thing extraordinarily well. I'm very grateful to you.'

Toni glowed. 'We told the truth, and they believed us,' she said.

They smiled at one another. It was a moment of happy intimacy. Then the phone rang.

Stanley reached across his desk and picked it up. 'Oxenford,' he said. 'Yes, patch him through here, please, I'm keen to speak to him.' He looked up at Toni and mouthed: 'Mahoney.'

Toni stood up nervously. She and Stanley were convinced they had controlled the publicity well – but would the US government agree? She watched Stanley's face.

He spoke into the phone. 'Hello again, Larry, did you watch the news? . . . I'm glad you think so . . . We've avoided the kind of hysterical reaction that you feared . . . You know my facilities director, Antonia Gallo – she handled the press . . . a great job, I agree . . . Absolutely right, we must keep a very tight grip on security from now on . . . yes. Good of you to call. Bye.'

Stanley hung up and grinned at Toni. 'We're in the clear.' Exuberantly, he put his arms around her and hugged her.

She pressed her face into his shoulder. The tweed of his waistcoat was surprisingly soft. She breathed in the warm, faint smell of him, and realized it was a long time since she had been this close to a man. She wrapped her arms around him and hugged him back, feeling her breasts press against his chest.

She would have stayed like that forever, but after a few seconds he gently disengaged, looking bashful. As if to restore propriety, he shook her hand. 'All credit to you,' he said.

The brief moment of physical contact had aroused her. Oh, God, she thought, I'm wet, how could it happen so quickly?

He said: 'Would you like to see the house?'

'I'd love to.' Toni was pleased. A man rarely offered to show guests around the house. It was another kind of intimacy.

The two rooms she had already seen, kitchen and study, were at the back, looking on to a yard surrounded by outbuildings. Stanley led Toni to the front of the house and into a dining room with a view of the sea. This part looked like a new extension to the old farmhouse. In a corner was a cabinet of silver cups. 'Marta's tennis trophies,' Stanley said proudly. 'She had a backhand like a rocket launcher.'

'How far did she get with her tennis?'

'She qualified for Wimbledon, but never competed because she got pregnant with Olga.'

Across the hall, also overlooking the sea, was a drawing room with a Christmas tree. The gifts under the tree spilled across the floor. There was another picture of Marta, a full-length painting of her as a woman of forty, with a fuller figure and a softness around her jawline. It was a warm, pleasant room, but nobody was in it, and Toni guessed the real heart of the house was the kitchen.

The layout was simple: drawing room and dining room

at the front, kitchen and study at the back. 'There's not much to see upstairs,' Stanley said, but he went up anyway, and Toni followed. Was she being shown around her future home, she asked herself? It was a stupid fantasy, and she pushed it aside quickly. He was just being nice.

But he had hugged her.

In the older part of the house, over the study and drawing room, were three small bedrooms and a bathroom. They still bore traces of the children who had grown up in them. There was a poster of the Clash on one wall, an old cricket bat with its grip unravelling in a corner, a complete set of *The Chronicles of Narnia* on a shelf.

In the new extension was a master bedroom suite with a dressing room and a bathroom. The king-size bed was made and the rooms were tidy. Toni felt both excited and uncomfortable to be in Stanley's bedroom. Yet another picture of Marta stood on the bedside table, this one a colour photograph taken in her fifties. Her hair was a witchy grey and her face was thin, no doubt by reason of the cancer that had killed her. It was an unflattering photo. Toni thought how much Stanley must still love her, to cherish even this unhappy memento.

She did not know what to expect next. Would he make a move, with his wife watching from the bedside table and his children downstairs? She felt it was not his style. He might be thinking of it, but he would not jump a woman so suddenly. He would feel that etiquette demanded he woo her in the normal way. To hell with dinner and a movie, she wanted to say; just grab me, for God's sake. But she kept silent, and after showing her the marble bathroom he led the way back downstairs.

The tour was a privilege, of course, and should have drawn her closer to Stanley; but in fact she felt excluded, as if she had looked in through a window at a family sitting at table, absorbed in one another and self-sufficient. She felt a sense of anticlimax.

In the hall, the big poodle nudged Stanley with her nose. 'Nellie wants to go outside,' he said. He looked out of the little window beside the door. 'The snow has stopped – shall we get a breath of air?'

'Sure.'

Toni put on her parka and Stanley picked up an old blue anorak. They stepped outside to find the world painted white. Toni's Porsche Boxster stood beside Stanley's Ferrari F50 and two other cars, each topped with snow, like iced cakes. The dog headed for the cliff, evidently taking a habitual route. Stanley and Toni followed. Toni realized that the dog bore a distinct resemblance to the late Marta, with her curly black hair.

Their feet displaced the powdery snow to reveal tough seaside grass beneath. They crossed a long lawn. A few stunted trees grew at angles, blown slantwise by the tireless wind. They met two of the children coming back from the cliff: the older boy with the attractive grin, and the sulky girl with the pierced navel. Toni remembered their names: Craig and Sophie. When Stanley had introduced everyone, in the kitchen, she had memorized every detail eagerly. Craig was working hard to charm Sophie, Toni could see, but the girl walked along with her arms crossed, looking at the ground. Toni envied the simplicity of the choices they faced. They were young and single, at the beginning of adulthood, with nothing to do but embrace the adventure of life. She wanted to tell Sophie not to play hard to get. Take love while you can, she thought; it may not always come to you so easily.

'What are your Christmas plans?' Stanley asked.

'About as different from yours as could be. I'm going to a health spa with some friends, all singles or childless couples, for a grown-up Christmas. No turkey, no crackers, no stockings, no Santa. Just gentle pampering and adult conversation.'

'It sounds wonderful. I thought you usually had your mother.'

'I have done for the past few years. But this Christmas my sister Bella is taking her – somewhat to my surprise.'

'Surprise?'

Toni made a wry face. 'Bella has three children, and she feels that excuses her from other responsibilities. I'm not sure that's fair, but I love my sister, so I accept it.'

'Do you want to have children, one day?'

She caught her breath. It was a deeply intimate question. She wondered what answer he would prefer to hear. She did not know, so she told the truth. 'Maybe. It was the one thing my sister always wanted. The desire for babies dominated her life. I'm not like that. I envy you your family – they obviously love and respect you and like being with you. But I don't necessarily want to sacrifice everything else in life in order to become a parent.'

'I'm not sure you have to sacrifice everything,' Stanley said.

You didn't, Toni thought, but what about Marta's chance at Wimbledon? But she said something else. 'And you? You could start another family.'

'Oh, no,' he said quickly. 'My children would be most put out.'

Toni felt a little disappointed that he was so decisive about that.

They reached the cliff. To the left, the headland sloped down to a beach, now carpeted with snow. To the right, the ground dropped sheer into the sea. On that side, the edge was barred by a stout wooden fence four feet high, big enough to deter small children without obstructing the view. They both leaned on the fence and looked at the waves a hundred feet below. There was a long, deep swell, rising and falling like the chest of a sleeping giant. 'What a lovely spot,' Toni said.

'Four hours ago I thought I was going to lose it.'

'Your home?'

He nodded. 'I had to pledge the place as security for my overdraft. If I go bust, the bank takes the house.'

'But your family . . .'

'They would be heartbroken. And now, since Marta went, they're all I really care about.'

'All?' she said.

He shrugged. 'In the end, yes.'

She looked at him. His expression was serious but unsentimental. Why was he telling her this? As a message, Toni assumed. It was not true that his children were all he cared about – he was profoundly involved in his work. But he wanted her to understand how important the family's unity was to him. Having seen them together in the kitchen, she could understand it. But why had he chosen this moment to say so? Perhaps he was afraid he might have given her a wrong impression.

She needed to know the truth. An awful lot had happened in the last few hours, but all of it was ambiguous. He had touched her, hugged her, shown her his house, and asked her if she wanted children. Did it mean anything, or not? She had to know. She said: 'You're telling me you'd never do anything to jeopardize what I saw in your kitchen, the togetherness of your family.'

'Yes. They all draw their strength from it, whether they realize it or not.'

She faced him and looked directly into his eyes. 'And that's so important to you that you would never start another family.'

'Yes.'

The message was clear, Toni thought. He liked her, but he was not going to take it any farther. The hug in the study had been a spontaneous expression of triumph; the tour of the house an unguarded moment of intimacy; and now he was pulling back. Reason had prevailed. She felt tears come to her eyes. Horrified that she might be showing her emotions, she turned away, saying: 'This wind . . .'

She was saved by young Tom, who came running through the snow, calling: 'Grandpa! Grandpa! Uncle Kit's here!'

They went with the boy back to the house, not speaking, both embarrassed.

A fresh double row of tyre tracks led to a black Peugeot coupé. It was not much of a car, but it looked stylish – just right for Kit, Toni thought sourly. She did not want to meet him. She would not have relished the prospect at the best of times, and right now she was too bruised to face an abrasive encounter. But her shoulder bag was in the house, so she was obliged to follow Stanley inside.

Kit was in the kitchen, being welcomed by his family – like the prodigal son, Toni thought. Miranda hugged him, Olga kissed him, Luke and Lori beamed, and Nellie barked for his attention. Toni stood at the kitchen door and watched Stanley greet his son. Kit looked wary. Stanley seemed both pleased and grieved, in the way he did when he spoke of Marta. Kit held out a hand to shake, but his father embraced him. 'I'm very glad you came, my boy,' Stanley said. 'Very glad indeed.'

Kit said: 'I'd better get my bag from the car. I'm in the cottage, yeah?'

Miranda looked nervous and said: 'No, you're upstairs.'
'But—'

Olga overrode him. 'Don't make a fuss – Daddy has decided, and it's his house.'

Toni saw a flash of pure rage in Kit's eyes, but he covered up quickly. 'Whatever,' he said. He was trying to give the impression that it was no big deal, but that flash said otherwise, and Toni wondered what secret project he had that made him so keen to sleep outside the main house tonight.

She slipped into Stanley's study. The memory of that hug came back to her in force. That was the closest she was going to get to making love to him, she thought. She wiped her eyes on her sleeve.

Her notebook and bag lay on his antique desk where she had left them. She slid the notebook into the bag, slung the bag over her shoulder, and returned to the hall.

Looking into the kitchen, she saw Stanley saying

something to the cook. She waved to him. He interrupted his conversation and came over. 'Toni, thanks for everything.'

'Happy Christmas.'

'To you, too.' She went out quickly.

Kit was outside, opening the boot of his car. Glancing into it, Toni saw a couple of grey boxes, computer equipment of some kind. Kit was an IT specialist, but what did he need to bring with him for Christmas at his father's house?

She hoped to pass him without speaking but, as she was opening her car door, he looked up and caught her eye. 'Happy Christmas, Kit,' she said politely.

He lifted a small suitcase from the boot and slammed the lid. 'Get lost, bitch,' he said, and he walked into the house.

2 p.m.

Craig was thrilled to see Sophie again. He had been captivated by her at his mother's birthday party. She was pretty in a dark-eyed, dark-haired way and, although she was small and slight, her body was softly rounded – but it was not her looks that had bewitched him, it was her attitude. She did not give a damn, and that fascinated him. Nothing impressed her: not Grandpa's Ferrari F50, nor Craig's football skills – he played for Scotland in the under-sixteens – nor the fact that his mother was a QC. Sophie wore what she liked, she ignored 'No Smoking' signs, and if someone was boring her she would walk away in mid-sentence. At the party, she had been fighting with her father about getting her navel pierced – which he flatly forbade – and here she was with a stud in it.

It made her difficult to get on with. Showing her around Steepfall, Craig found that nothing pleased her. It seemed that silence was as near as she got to praise. Otherwise, she would utter an abbreviated put-down: 'Gross,' or 'Dumb,' or 'So weird.' But she did not walk away, so he knew he was not boring her.

He took her to the barn. It was the oldest building on the property, built in the eighteenth century. Grandpa had put in heating, lighting, and plumbing, but you could still see the original timber framing. The ground floor was a playroom with a billiards table, a bar football game, and a big TV. 'This is an okay place to hang out,' he said.

'Quite cool,' she said – the most enthusiasm she had yet shown. She pointed to a raised platform. 'What's that?'

'A stage.'

'Why do you need a stage?'

'My mother and Aunt Miranda used to do plays when they were girls. They once produced *Antony and Cleopatra* with a cast of four in this barn.'

'Strange.'

Craig pointed to two camp beds. 'Tom and I are sleeping here,' he said. 'Come upstairs, I'll show you your bedroom.'

A ladder led to the hayloft. There was no wall, just a handrail for safety. Two single beds were neatly made up. The only furniture was a coat rail for hanging clothes and a cheval mirror. Caroline's suitcase was on the floor, open.

'It's not very private,' Sophie said.

Craig had noticed that. The sleeping arrangements seemed to him to be full of promise. His older sister, Caroline, and his young cousin, Tom, would be around, of course, but nevertheless he was enjoying a vague but exciting feeling that all kinds of things might happen. 'Here.' He unfolded an old concertina screen. 'You can undress behind this if you're shy.'

Her dark eyes sparked resentment. 'I'm not *shy*,' she said, as if the suggestion were insulting.

He found her flash of anger strangely thrilling. 'Just

asking,' he said. He sat on one of the beds. 'It's quite comfortable – better than our camp beds.'

She shrugged.

In his fantasy, she would now sit on the bed beside him. In one version, she pushed him backwards, pretending to fight with him, and having started out wrestling they ended up kissing. In another scenario, she would take his hand, and tell him how much his friendship meant to her, and then she would kiss him. But now, in real life, she was neither playful nor sentimental. She turned away and looked around the bare hayloft with an expression of distaste, and he knew that kissing was not on her mind. She sang quietly: 'I'm dreaming of a shite Christmas.'

'The bathroom's underneath here, at the back of the stage. There's no bath, but the shower works all right.'

'How luxurious.' She got up from the bed and went down the ladder, still singing her obscene adaptation of Bing Crosby's Christmas classic.

Well, he thought, we've only been here a couple of hours, and I've got five whole days to win her around.

He followed her down. There was one more thing that might get her excited. 'I've got something else to show you.' He led the way outside.

They stepped into a big square yard with one building on each of its four sides: the main house, the guest cottage, the barn they had just left, and the three-car garage. Craig led Sophie around the house to the front door, avoiding the kitchen where they might be given chores. When they stepped inside, he saw that there were snowflakes caught in her gleaming dark hair. He stopped and stared, transfixed.

She said: 'What?'

'Snow in your hair,' he said. 'It looks beautiful.'

She shook her head impatiently, and the flakes disappeared. 'You're bizarre,' she said.

Okay, he thought, so you don't like compliments.

He led her up the stairs. In the old part of the house were three small bedrooms and an old-fashioned bathroom. Grandpa's suite was in the new extension. Craig tapped on the door, in case Grandpa was inside. There was no reply, and he went in.

He walked quickly through the bedroom, past the big double bed, into the dressing room beyond. He opened a closet door and pushed aside a row of suits, pinstripes and tweeds and checks, mostly grey and blue. He got down on his knees, reached into the closet, and shoved at the back wall. A panel two feet square swung open on a hinge. Craig crawled through it.

Sophie followed.

Craig reached back through the gap, pulled the closet door shut, then closed the panel. Fumbling in the dark, he found a switch and turned on the light, a single unshaded bulb hanging from a roof beam.

They were in an attic. There was a big old sofa with stuffing bursting out of holes in the upholstery. Beside it a stack of mouldering photograph albums stood on the floorboards. There were several cardboard boxes and tea chests, which Craig had found, on earlier visits, to contain his mother's school reports, novels by Enid Blyton inscribed in a childish hand *This book belongs to Miranda Oxenford age 9½*, and a collection of ugly ashtrays, bowls, and vases that must have been either unwanted gifts or ill-judged purchases. Sophie ran her fingers over the strings of a dusty guitar: it was out of tune.

'You can smoke up here,' Craig said. Empty cigarette packets of forgotten brands – Woodbines, Players, Senior Service – made him think this might have been where his mother began her addiction. There were also wrappers from chocolate bars: perhaps plump Aunt Miranda was responsible for those. And he presumed Uncle Kit had amassed the collection of magazines with titles such as *Men Only*, *Panty Play*, and *Barely Legal*.

Craig hoped Sophie would not notice the magazines, but they caught her eye immediately. She picked one up. 'Wow, get this, porn!' she said, suddenly more animated than she had been all morning. She sat on the sofa and began to leaf through it.

Craig looked away. He had been through all the magazines, though he was ready to deny it. Porn was a boy thing, and strictly private. But Sophie was reading *Hustler* right in front of him, scrutinizing the pages as if she had to take an exam on it.

To distract her, he said: 'This whole part of the house used to be the dairy, when the place was a farm. Grandpa turned the dairy into the kitchen, but the roof was too high, so he just put a ceiling in and used this space for storage.'

She did not even look up from the magazine. 'Every one of these women is shaved!' she said, embarrassing him further. 'So creepy.'

'You can see into the kitchen,' he persisted. 'Over here, where the flue from the Aga comes up through the ceiling.' He lay flat and looked through a wide gap between the boards and a metal shaft. He could see the entire kitchen:

the hall door at the far end, the long scrubbed-pine table, the cupboards on both sides, the side doors into the dining room and the laundry, the cooking range at this end, and two doors on either side of the range, one leading to a big walk-in larder and the other leading to the boot lobby and the side entrance. Most of the family were around the table. Craig's sister, Caroline, was feeding her rats, Miranda was pouring wine, Ned was reading the *Guardian*, Lori was poaching a whole salmon in a long fish-kettle. 'I think Aunt Miranda's getting drunk,' Craig said.

That caught Sophie's interest. She dropped the magazine and lay beside Craig to look. 'Can't they see us?' she said quietly.

He studied her as she stared through the gap. Her hair was pushed behind her ears. The skin of her cheek looked unbearably soft. 'Have a look, next time you're in the kitchen,' he said. 'You'll see that there's a ceiling light right behind the gap which makes it difficult to make out, even when you know it's there.'

'So, like, nobody knows you're here?'

'Well, everyone knows there's an attic. And watch out for Nellie. She'll look up and cock her head, listening, as soon as you move. She knows you're here – and anyone watching her may catch on.'

'Still, this is pretty cool. Look at my father. He's pretending to read the paper, but he keeps making eyes at Miranda. Yech.' She rolled on her side, propped herself on her elbow, and fished a packet of cigarettes out of her jeans pocket. 'Want one?'

Craig shook his head. 'You can't smoke if you're serious about football.'

'How can you be serious about football? It's a game!'

'Sports are more fun if you're good at them.'

'Yeah, you're right.' She blew out smoke. He watched her lips. 'That's probably why I don't like sports. I'm such a spastic.'

Craig realized he had broken through some kind of barrier. She was talking to him at last. And what she said was quite intelligent. 'What are you good at?' he asked.

'Not much.

He hesitated, then blurted out: 'Once, at a party, a girl told me I was a good kisser.' He held his breath. He needed to break the ice with her somehow – but was this too soon?

'Oh?' She seemed interested in an academic way. 'What do you do?'

'I could show you.'

A look of panic crossed her face. 'No way!' She held up a hand, as if to ward him off, although he had not moved.

He realized he had been too impetuous. He could have kicked himself. 'Don't worry,' he said, smiling to hide his disappointment. 'I won't do anything you don't want, I promise.'

'It's just that I've got this boyfriend.'

'Oh, I see.'

'Yeah. But don't tell anyone.'

'What's he like?'

'My boyfriend? He's a student.' She looked away, screwing up her eyes against the smoke from her cigarette.

'At Glasgow University?'

'Yes. He's nineteen. He thinks I'm seventeen.'

Craig was not sure whether to believe her. 'What's he studying?'

'Who cares? Something boring. Law, I think.'

Craig looked through the gap again. Lori was sprinkling chopped parsley over a steaming bowl of potatoes. Suddenly he felt hungry. 'Lunch is ready,' he said. 'I'll show you the other way out.'

He went to the end of the attic and opened a large door. A narrow ledge overhung a drop of fifteen feet to the ground. Above the door, on the outside of the building, was a pulley: that was how the sofa and tea chests had been brought up. Sophie said: 'I can't jump from here.'

'No need.' Craig brushed snow off the ledge with his hands, then walked along it to the end and stepped two feet down onto a lean-to roof over the boot lobby. 'Easy.'

Looking anxious, Sophie followed in his footsteps. When she reached the end of the ledge, he offered her his hand. She took it, gripping unnecessarily hard. He handed her down onto the lean-to roof.

He stepped back up on the ledge to close the big door, then returned to Sophie's side. They went cautiously down the slippery roof. Craig lay on his front and slid over the edge, then dropped the short distance to the ground.

Sophie followed suit. When she was lying on the roof with her legs dangling over the edge, Craig reached up with both hands, held her by the waist, and lifted her down. She was light.

'Thanks,' she said. She looked triumphant, as if she had come successfully through a trying experience.

It wasn't that difficult, Craig thought as they went into the house for lunch. Perhaps she's not as confident as she pretends.

3 p.m.

The Kremlin looked pretty. Snow clung to its gargoyles and crotchets, doorcases and windowledges, outlining the Victorian ornamentation in white. Toni parked and went inside. The place was quiet. Most people had gone home, for fear of getting caught in the snow – not that people needed much of an excuse to leave early on Christmas Eve.

She felt hurt and sensitive. She had been in an emotional car crash. But she had to put thoughts of love firmly out of her mind. Later, perhaps, when she lay alone in bed tonight, she would brood over the things Stanley had said and done; but now she had work to do.

She had scored a triumphant success – that was why Stanley had hugged her – but all the same a worry nagged at her. Stanley's words repeated in her brain: *If we lost another rabbit, we'd be right back in trouble.* It was true. Another incident of the same kind would bring the story back to life but ten times worse. No amount of public-relations work could keep the lid on it. 'There will be no more security incidents at the lab,' she had told him. 'I'll make sure of that.' Now she had to make her words come true.

She went to her office. The only threat that she could

imagine was from the animal rights activists. The death of Michael Ross might inspire others to attempt to 'liberate' laboratory animals. Alternatively, Michael might have been working with activists who had another plan. He might even have given them the kind of inside information that could help them defeat the Kremlin's security.

She dialled regional police headquarters in Inverburn and asked for Detective Superintendent Frank Hackett, her ex. 'Got away with it, didn't you?' he said. 'Luck of the devil. You should have been crucified.'

'We told the truth, Frank. Honesty is the best policy, you know that.'

'You didn't tell me the truth. A hamster called Fluffy! You made me look a fool.'

'It was unkind, I admit. But you shouldn't have leaked the story to Carl. Shall we call it quits?'

'What do you want?'

'Do you think anyone else was involved with Michael Ross in stealing the rabbit?'

'No opinion.'

'I gave you his address book. I presume you've been checking his contacts. What about the people in Animals Are Free, for example – are they peaceful protestors, or might they do something more dangerous?'

'My investigation is not yet complete.'

'Come on, Frank, I'm just looking for a little guidance. How worried should I be about the possibility of another incident?'

'I'm afraid I can't help you.'

'Frank, we loved one another once. We were partners for eight years. Does it have to be like this?'

'Are you using our past relationship to persuade me to give you confidential information?'

'No. To hell with the information. I can get it elsewhere. I just don't want to be treated as an enemy by someone I used to love. Is there a law that says we can't be nice to one another?'

There was a click, then a dialling tone. He had hung up.

She sighed. Would he ever come around? She wished he would get another girlfriend. That might calm him down.

She dialled Odette Cressy, her friend at Scotland Yard. 'I saw you on the news,' Odette said.

'How did I look?'

'Authoritative.' Odette giggled. 'Like you would *never* go to a nightclub in a see-through dress. But I know better.'

'Just don't tell anyone the truth.'

'Anyway, your Madoba-2 incident appears to have no connections with . . . my kind of interest.'

She meant terrorism. 'Good,' Toni said. 'But tell me something – speaking purely theoretically.'

'Of course.'

'Terrorists could get samples of a virus such as Ebola relatively easily by going to a hospital somewhere in central Africa where the only security is a nineteen-year-old cop slouching in the lobby smoking cigarettes. So why would they attempt the extraordinarily difficult task of robbing a high-security laboratory?'

'Two reasons. One, they simply don't know how easy it is to get Ebola in Africa. Two, Madoba-2 is not the same as Ebola. It's worse.'

Toni remembered what Stanley had told her, and shuddered. 'Zero survival rate.'

'Exactly.'

'What about Animals Are Free? Did you check them out?'

'Of course. They're harmless. The worst they're likely to do is block a road.'

'That's great news. I just want to make sure there's not another incident of the same kind.'

'It looks unlikely from my end.'

'Thanks, Odette. You're a friend, and that's a rare thing.'

'You sound a bit low.'

'Oh, my ex is being difficult.'

'Is that all? You're used to him. Did something happen with the Professor?'

Toni could never fool Odette, even over the phone. 'He told me his family is the most important thing in the world to him, and he would never do anything to upset them.'

'Bastard.'

'When you find a man who isn't a bastard, ask him if he's got a brother.'

'What are you doing for Christmas?'

'Going to a spa. Massage, facials, manicures, long walks.'

'On your own?'

Toni smiled. 'It's nice of you to worry about me, but I'm not that sad.'

'Who are you going with?'

'A whole crowd. Bonnie Grant, an old friend – we were at university together, the only two girls in the engineering faculty. She's recently divorced. Charles and Damien, you know them. And two couples you haven't met.'

'The gay boys will cheer you up.'

'You're right.' When Charlie and Damien let their hair down, they could make Toni laugh until she cried. 'What about you?'

'Not sure. You know how I hate to plan ahead.'

'Well, enjoy spontaneity.'

'Happy Christmas.'

They hung up, and Toni summoned Steve Tremlett, the guard supervisor.

She had taken a chance with Steve. He had been a pal of Ronnie Sutherland, the former head of security who had conspired with Kit Oxenford. There was no evidence Steve had known about the fraud. But Toni had feared he might resent her for firing his friend. She had decided to give him the benefit of the doubt, and had made him supervisor. He had rewarded her trust with loyalty and efficiency.

He arrived within a minute. He was a small, neat man of thirty-five with receding fair hair cut in the brutally short style that was fashionable. He carried a cardboard folder. Toni pointed to a chair and he sat down.

'The police don't think Michael Ross was working with others,' she said.

'I had him down as a loner.'

'All the same, we have to have this place buttoned up tight tonight.'

'No problem.'

'Let's make doubly sure of that. You have the duty roster there?'

Steve handed over a sheet of paper. Normally there

were three security guards on duty overnight and on weekends and holidays. One sat in the gatehouse, one in Reception, and one in the control room, watching the monitors. In case they needed to step away from their stations, they carried phones that were cordless extensions to the house network. Every hour, the guard from reception made a tour of the main building, and the guard from the gatehouse walked around the outside. At first, Toni had thought three was too few for such a high-security operation, but the sophisticated technology was the real security, and the human beings merely backup. All the same, she had doubled the guard for this Christmas holiday, so that there would be two people at each of the three stations, and they would patrol every half-hour.

'I see you're working tonight.'

'I need the overtime.'

'All right.' Security guards regularly worked twelve-hour shifts, and it was not very unusual for them to do twenty-four hours, when staff were short or, as tonight, in an emergency. 'Let me check your emergency call list.'

Steve passed her a laminated sheet from the folder. It listed the agencies he was to phone in case of fire, flood, power cut, computer crash, phone system faults, and other problems.

Toni said: 'I want you to ring each of these in the next hour. Just ask them if the number will be operational over Christmas.'

'Very good.'

She handed back the sheet. 'Don't hesitate to call the police at Inverburn if you're the least worried about anything.'

He nodded. 'My brother-in-law Jack is on duty tonight, as it happens. My missus has taken the children over to their place for Christmas.'

'How many people will there be at headquarters tonight, do you know?'

'On the night shift? An inspector, two sergeants, and six constables. And there'll be a duty superintendent on call.'

It was a small complement, but there would be nothing much to do once the pubs had closed and the drunks had gone home. 'You don't happen to know who the duty super is?'

'Yes. It's your Frank.'

Toni did not comment. 'I'll have my mobile phone with me day and night, and I don't expect to be anywhere out of range. I want you to call me the minute anything unusual happens, regardless of the time, okay?'

'Of course.'

'I don't mind being woken up in the middle of the night.' She would be sleeping alone, but she did not say that to Steve, who might have considered it an embarrassing confidence.

'I understand,' he said, and perhaps he did.

'That's all. I'll be leaving in a few minutes.' She checked her watch; it was almost four. 'Happy Christmas, Steve.'

'To you, too.'

Steve left. Twilight was falling, and Toni could see her own reflection in the window. She looked rumpled and weary. She closed down her computer and locked her filing cabinet.

She needed to get going. She had to return home and change, then drive to the spa, which was fifty miles away.

The sooner she hit the road, the better: the forecast said the weather would not get worse, but forecasts could be wrong.

She was reluctant to leave the Kremlin. Its security was her job. She had taken every precaution she could think of, but she hated to hand over responsibility.

She forced herself to stand up. Her job was facilities director, not security guard. If she had done everything possible to safeguard the place, she could leave. If not, she was incompetent and should resign.

Besides, she knew the real reason she wanted to stay. As soon as she turned her back on the job, she would have to think about Stanley.

She shouldered her bag and left the building.

The snow was falling more heavily.

4 p.m.

Kit was furious about the sleeping arrangements.

He sat in the living room with his father, his nephew Tom, his brother-in-law Hugo, and Miranda's fiancé, Ned. Mamma Marta looked down on them from her portrait on the wall. Kit always felt she looked impatient in that picture, as if she could hardly wait to get out of her ball gown, put on an apron, and start making lasagne.

The women of the family were preparing tomorrow's Christmas dinner, and the older children were in the barn. The men were watching a movie on TV. The hero, played by John Wayne, was a narrow-minded bully, a bit like Harry Mac, Kit thought. He found it hard to follow the plot. He was too tense.

He had *specifically* told Miranda he needed to be in the cottage. She had been so sentimental about his joining the family for Christmas, she had practically gone down on her knees to plead with him to come. But, after he had agreed to do what she wanted, she had failed to fulfil the one condition he had made. Typical woman.

The old man was not sentimental, though. He was about as soft-hearted as a Glasgow policeman on a Saturday night. He had obviously overruled Miranda, with Olga's encouragement. Kit thought his sisters ought to have been called Goneril and Regan, after the predatory daughters of King Lear.

Kit had to leave Steepfall tonight and come back tomorrow morning without anyone knowing he had been away. If he had been sleeping in the cottage, it would have been easier. He could have pretended to go to bed, turned off the lights, then sneaked away quietly. He had already moved his car to the garage forecourt, away from the house, so that no one would hear the engine starting. He would be back by mid-morning, before anyone would expect him to be up, and could have slipped quietly back into the cottage and gone innocently to bed.

Now it would be much more difficult. His room was in the creaky old part of the main house, next to Olga and Hugo. He would have to wait until everyone had retired. When the house was quiet he would have to creep out of his room, tiptoe down the stairs, and leave the house in total silence. If someone should open a door – Olga, for instance, crossing the landing to go to the bathroom – what would he say? 'I'm just going to get some fresh air.' In the middle of the night, in the snow? And what would he do in the morning? It was almost certain that someone would see him coming in. He would have to say he had been for a walk, or a drive. And then, later, when the police were asking questions, would anyone remember his uncharacteristic early-morning stroll?

He tried to put that worry out of his mind. He had a more immediate problem. He had to steal the smart card his father used to enter BSL4.

He could have bought any number of such cards from

a security supplier, but smart cards came from the manufacturer embedded with a site code that ensured they would work at only one location. Cards bought from a supplier would have the wrong code for the Kremlin.

Nigel Buchanan had questioned him persistently about stealing the card. 'Where does your father keep it?'

'In his jacket pocket, usually.'

'And if it's not there?'

'In his wallet, or his briefcase, I expect.'

'How can you take it without being seen?'

'It's a big house. I'll do it when he's in the bath, or out for a walk.'

'Won't he notice it's gone?'

'Not until he needs to use it, which won't be until Friday at the earliest. By then I'll have put it back.'

'Can you be sure?'

At that point Elton had interrupted. In his broad South London accent he had said: 'Bloody hell, Nige! We're counting on Kit to get us into a heavily guarded high-security laboratory. We're in trouble if he can't nick something off his own fuckin' father.'

Stanley's card would have the right site code, but the chip in it would contain Stanley's fingerprint data, not Kit's. However, he had thought of a way around that.

The movie was building to a climax. John Wayne was about to start shooting people. This was a good moment for Kit to make a clandestine move.

He got up, grunted something about the bathroom, and went out. From the hall, he glanced into the kitchen. Olga was stuffing a huge turkey while Miranda cleaned Brussels sprouts. Along one wall were two doors, one to the laundry and the other to the dining room. As he looked, Lori came out of the laundry carrying a folded tablecloth and took it into the dining room.

Kit stepped into his father's study and closed the door.

The likeliest place for the smart card was in one of the pockets of his father's suit coat, as he had told Nigel. He had expected to find the jacket either on the hook behind the door or draped over the back of the desk chair; but he saw immediately that it was not in the room.

He decided to check some other possibilities while he was here. It was risky – anyone might come in, and what would he say? But he had to take chances. The alternative was no robbery, no three hundred thousand pounds, no ticket to Lucca – and, worst of all, the debt to Harry Mac unpaid. He remembered what Daisy had done to him this morning, and shuddered.

The old man's briefcase was on the floor beside the desk. Kit went through it quickly. It contained a file of scatter graphs, all meaningless to Kit; today's *Times* with the crossword not quite finished; half a bar of chocolate; and the small leather notebook in which his father made lists of things he had to do. Old people always had lists, Kit had noticed. Why were they so terrified of forgetting something?

The top of the pedestal desk was tidy, and Kit could not see a card or anything that might contain one: just a small stack of files, a pencil jar, and a book entitled *Seventh Report of the International Committee on Taxonomy of Viruses*.

He started opening the drawers. His breath came fast

and he felt his heartbeat speed up. But if he were caught, what would they do – call the police? He told himself he had nothing to lose, and carried on; but his hands were unsteady.

His father had been using this desk for thirty years, and the accumulation of useless objects was staggering: souvenir key rings, dried-up pens, an old-fashioned printing calculator, stationery with out-of-date phone codes, ink bottles, manuals for obsolete software – how long was it since anyone had used PlanPerfect? But there was no smart card.

Kit left the room. No one had seen him go in, and no one saw him go out.

He went quietly up the stairs. His father was not an untidy man, and rarely lost things: he would not have carelessly left his wallet in some unlikely place such as the boot cupboard. The only remaining possibility was the bedroom.

Kit went inside and closed the door.

His mother's presence was gradually disappearing. Last time he was here, her possessions were still scattered around: a leather writing-case, a silver brush set that had belonged to her mother, a photograph of Stanley in an antique frame. Those had gone. But the curtains and the upholstery were the same, done in a bold blue-and-white fabric that was typical of his mother's dramatic taste.

On either side of the bed were a pair of Victorian commode chests made of heavy mahogany, used as bedside tables. His father had always slept on the right of the big double bed. Kit opened the drawers on that side. He found a flashlight, presumably for power cuts, and a volume of

Proust, presumably for insomnia. He checked the drawers on his mother's side of the bed, but they were empty.

The suite was arranged as three rooms: first the bedroom, then the dressing room, then the bathroom. Kit went into the dressing room, a square space lined with closets, some painted white, some with mirrored doors. Outside it was twilight, but he could see well enough for what he needed to do, so he did not switch on the lights.

He opened the door of his father's suit cupboard. There on a hanger was the jacket of the suit Stanley was wearing today. Kit reached into the inside pocket and drew out a large black leather wallet, old and worn. It contained a small wad of banknotes and a row of plastic cards. One was a smart card for the Kremlin.

'Bingo,' Kit said softly.

The bedroom door opened.

Kit had not closed the door to the dressing room, and he was able to look through the doorway and see his sister Miranda step into the bedroom, carrying an orange plastic laundry basket.

Kit was in her line of sight, standing at the open door of the suit closet, but she did not immediately spot him in the twilight, and he quickly moved behind the dressing-room door. If he peeked around the side of the door, he could see her reflected in the big mirror on the bedroom wall.

She switched the lights on and began to strip the bed. She and Olga were obviously doing some of Lori's chores. Kit decided he would just have to wait.

He suffered a moment of self-dislike. Here he was, acting like an intruder in the house of his family. He was stealing from his father and hiding from his sister. How had it got like this?

He knew the answer. His father had let him down. Just when he needed help, Stanley had said no. That was the cause of everything.

Well, he would leave them all behind. He would not even tell them where he was going. He would make a new life in a different country. He would disappear into the small-town routine of Lucca, eating tomatoes and pasta, drinking Tuscan wine, playing pinochle for low stakes in the evenings. He would be like a background figure in a big painting, the passer-by who does not look at the dying martyr. He would be at peace.

Miranda began to make up the bed with fresh sheets, and at that moment Hugo came in.

He had changed into a red pullover and green corduroy trousers, and he looked like a Christmas elf. He closed the door behind him. Kit frowned. Did Hugo have secrets to discuss with his wife's sister?

Miranda said: 'Hugo, what do you want?' She sounded wary.

Hugo gave her a conspiratorial grin, but he said: 'I just thought I'd give you a hand.' He went to the opposite side of the bed and started tucking in the sheet.

Kit was standing behind the dressing-room door with his father's wallet in one hand and a smart card for the Kremlin in the other, but he could not move without risking discovery.

Miranda tossed a clean pillowcase across the bed. 'Here,' she said.

Hugo stuffed a pillow into it. Together they arranged

the bed cover. 'It seems ages since we've seen you,' Hugo said. 'I miss you.'

'Don't talk rubbish,' Miranda said coolly.

Kit was puzzled but fascinated. What was going on here?

Miranda smoothed the cover. Hugo came around the end of the bed. She picked up her laundry basket and held it in front of her like a shield. Hugo gave his impish grin and said: 'How about a kiss, for old times' sake?'

Kit was mystified. What old times was Hugo talking about? He had been married to Olga for nearly twenty years. Had he kissed Miranda when she was fourteen?

'Stop that, right now,' Miranda said firmly.

Hugo grasped the laundry basket and pushed. The backs of Miranda's legs came up against the edge of the bed. Involuntarily, she sat down. She released the basket and used her hands to balance herself. Hugo tossed the basket aside, bent over her, and pushed her back, kneeling on the bed with his legs either side of her. Kit was flabbergasted. He had guessed that Hugo might be something of a Lothario, just from his generally flirtatious manner with attractive women; but he had never imagined him with Miranda.

Hugo pushed up her loose, pleated skirt. She had heavy hips and thighs. She was wearing lacy black knickers and a garter belt, and for Kit this was the most astonishing revelation yet.

'Get off me now,' she said.

Kit did not know what to do. This was none of his business, so he was not inclined to interfere; but he could hardly stand here and watch. Even if he turned away, he could not help hearing what was going on. Could he sneak past them while they were wrestling? No, the room was too small. He remembered the panel at the back of the closet that led to the attic, but he could not get to the closet without risking being seen. In the end he just stood paralysed, looking on.

'Just a quickie,' Hugo said. 'No one will know.'

Miranda drew back her right arm and swung at Hugo's face, hitting him square on the cheek with a mighty slap. Then she lifted her knee sharply, making contact somewhere in the area of his groin. She twisted, threw him off, and jumped to her feet.

Hugo remained lying on the bed. 'That hurt!' he protested.

'Good,' she said. 'Now listen to me. Never do anything like that again.'

He zipped his fly and stood up. 'Why not? What will you do – tell Ned?'

'I ought to tell him, but I haven't got the courage. I slept with you once, when I was lonely and depressed, and I've regretted it bitterly ever since.'

So that was it, Kit thought – Miranda slept with Olga's husband. He was shocked. He was not surprised by Hugo's behaviour – shagging the wife's sister on the side was the kind of cosy set-up many men would like. But Miranda was prissily moral about such things. Kit would have said that she would not sleep with *anyone's* husband, let alone her sister's.

Miranda went on: 'It was the most shameful thing I've done in my life, and I don't want Ned to find out about it, ever.'

'So what are you threatening to do? Tell Olga?'

'She would divorce you and never speak to me again. It would explode this family.'

It might not be that bad, Kit thought; but Miranda was always anxious about keeping the family together.

'That leaves you a bit helpless, doesn't it?' Hugo said, looking pleased. 'Since we can't be enemies, why don't you just kiss me nicely and be friends?'

Miranda's voice went cold. 'Because you disgust me.'

'Ah, well.' Hugo sounded resigned, but unashamed. 'Hate me, then. I still adore you.' He gave his most charming smile and left the room, limping slightly.

As the door slammed, Miranda said: 'You fucking bastard.'

Kit had never heard her swear like that.

She picked up her laundry basket then, instead of going out as he expected, she turned towards him. She must have fresh towels for the bathroom, he realized. There was no time to move. In three steps she reached the entrance to the dressing room and turned on the lights.

Kit was just able to slip the smart card into his trousers pocket. An instant later she saw him. She gave a squeal of shock. 'Kit! What are you doing there? You gave me a fright!' She went white, and added: 'You must have heard everything.'

'Sorry.' He shrugged. 'I didn't want to.'

Her complexion changed from pale to flushed. 'You won't tell, will you?'

'Of course not.'

'I'm serious, Kit. You must never tell. It would be awful. It could ruin two marriages.'

'I know, I know.'

She saw the wallet in his hand. 'What are you up to?'

He hesitated, then he was inspired. 'I needed cash.' He showed her the banknotes in the wallet.

'Oh, Kit!' She was distressed, not judgemental. 'Why do you always want easy money?'

He bit back an indignant retort. She believed his cover story, that was the main thing. He said nothing and tried to look ashamed.

She went on: 'Olga always says you'd rather steal a shilling than earn an honest pound.'

'All right, don't rub it in.'

'You mustn't pilfer from Daddy's wallet – it's awful!'

'I'm a bit desperate.'

'I'll give you money!' She put down the laundry basket. There were two pockets in the front of her skirt. She reached into one and pulled out a crumple of notes. She extracted two fifties, smoothed them out, and gave them to Kit. 'Just ask me – I'll never turn you down.'

'Thanks, Mandy,' he said, using her childhood name.

'But you must never steal from Daddy.'

'Okay.'

'And, for pity's sake, don't ever tell anyone about me and Hugo.'

'I promise,' he said.

5 p.m.

Toni had been sleeping heavily for an hour when her alarm clock woke her.

She found that she was lying on the bed fully dressed. She had been too tired even to take off her jacket and shoes. But the nap had refreshed her. She was used to odd hours, from working night shifts in the police force, and she could fall asleep anywhere and wake up instantly.

She lived on one floor of a subdivided Victorian house. She had a bedroom, a living room, a small kitchen and a bathroom. Inverburn was a ferry port, but she could not see the sea. She was not very fond of her home: it was the place to which she had fled when she broke up with Frank, and it had no happy memories. She had been here two years, but she still regarded it as temporary.

She got up. She stripped off the business suit she had been wearing for two days and a night, and dumped it in the dry-cleaning basket. With a robe on over her underwear she moved rapidly around the flat, packing a case for five nights at a health spa. She had planned to pack last night and leave at midday today, so she had some catching up to do.

She could hardly wait to get to the spa. It was just what

she needed. Her woes would be massaged away; she would sweat out toxins in the sauna; she would have her nails painted and her hair cut and her eyelashes curled. Best of all, she would play games and tell stories with a group of old friends, and forget her troubles.

Her mother should be at Bella's place by now. Mother was an intelligent woman who was losing her mind. She had been a high-school maths teacher, and had always been able to help Toni with her studies, even when Toni was in the final year of her engineering degree. Now she could not check her change in a shop. Toni loved her intensely, and was deeply saddened by her decline.

Bella was a bit slapdash. She cleaned the house when the mood took her, cooked when she felt hungry, and sometimes forgot to send her children to school. Her husband, Bernie, was a hairdresser, but worked infrequently because of some vague chest ailment. 'The doctor's signed me off for another four weeks,' he would usually say in response to the routine enquiry, 'How are you?'

Toni hoped Mother would be all right at Bella's place. Bella was an amiable slattern, and Mother never seemed to mind her ways. Mother had always been happy to visit the windy Glasgow council estate and eat undercooked chips with her grandchildren. But she was now in the early stages of senility. Would she be as philosophical as ever about Bella's haphazard housekeeping? Would Bella be able to cope with Mother's increasing waywardness?

Once when Toni had let slip an irritated remark about Bella, Mother had said crisply: 'She doesn't try as hard as you, that's why she's happier.' Mother's conversation had become tactless, but her remarks could be painfully accurate.

After Toni had packed, she washed her hair then took a bath to soak away two days of tension. She fell asleep in the tub. She woke with a start, but only a minute or so had passed – the water was still hot. She got out and dried herself vigorously.

Looking in the full-length mirror, she thought: I've got everything I had twenty years ago – it's all just three inches lower. One of the good things about Frank, at least in the early days, had been the pleasure he took in her body. 'You've got great tits,' he would say. She thought they were too large for her frame, but he worshipped them. 'I've never seen a pussy this colour,' he once told her as he lay between her legs. 'It's like a ginger biscuit.' She wondered how long it would be before someone else marvelled at the colour of her pubic hair.

She dressed in tan jeans and a dark-green sweater. As she was closing her suitcase, the phone rang. It was her sister. 'Hi, Bella,' said Toni. 'How's Mother?'

'She's not here.'

'What? You were supposed to pick her up at one o'clock!'

'I know, but Bernie had the car and I couldn't get away.'

'And you still haven't left?' Toni looked at her watch. It was half-past five. She pictured Mother at the home, sitting in the lobby in her coat and hat, with her suitcase beside the chair, hour after hour, and she felt cross. 'What are you thinking of?'

'The thing is, the weather's turned bad.'

'It's snowing all over Scotland, but not heavily.'

'Well, Bernie doesn't want me to drive sixty miles in the dark.'

'You wouldn't have had to drive in the dark if you'd picked her up when you promised!'

'Oh, dear, you're getting angry, I knew this would happen.'

'I'm not angry . . .' Toni paused. Her sister had caught her before with this trick. In a moment they would be talking about Toni managing her anger, instead of Bella breaking a promise. 'Never mind how I feel,' Toni said. 'What about Mother? Don't you think she must be disappointed?'

'Of course, but I can't help the weather.'

'What are you going to do?'

'There isn't anything I can do.'

'So you're going to leave her in the home over Christmas?'

'Unless you have her. You're only ten miles away.'

'Bella, I'm booked into a spa! Seven friends are expecting me to join them for five days. I've paid four hundred pounds deposit and I'm looking forward to a rest.'

'That sounds a bit selfish.'

'Just a minute. I've had Mother the last three Christmases, but I'm selfish?'

'You don't know how hard it is with three children and a husband too ill to work. You've got plenty of money and only yourself to worry about.'

And I'm not stupid enough to marry a layabout and have three children by him, Toni thought, but she did not say it. There was no point in arguing with Bella. Her way of life was its own punishment. 'So you're asking me to cancel my holiday, drive to the home, pick up Mother, and look after her over Christmas.'

'It's up to you,' Bella said in a tone of elevated piety. 'You must do what your conscience tells you.'

'Thanks for that helpful advice.' Toni's conscience said she should be with their mother, and Bella knew that. Toni could not let Mother spend Christmas in an institution, alone in her room, or eating tasteless turkey and lukewarm sprouts in the canteen, or receiving a cheap present in gaudy wrapping from the home's caretaker dressed as Santa Claus. Toni did not even need to think about it. 'All right, I'll go and fetch her now.'

'I'm just sorry you couldn't do it more graciously,' said her sister.

'Oh, fuck off, Bella,' said Toni, and she hung up the phone.

Feeling depressed, she called the spa and cancelled her reservation. Then she asked to speak to one of her party. After a delay, it was Charlie who came to the phone. He had a Lancashire accent. 'Where are you?' he said. 'We're all in the jacuzzi – you're missing the fun!'

'I can't come,' she said miserably, and she explained.

Charlie was outraged. 'It's not fair on you,' he said. 'You need a break.'

'I know, but I can't bear to think of her on her own in that place when others are with their families.'

'Plus you've had a few problems at work today.'

'Yes. It's very sad, but I think Oxenford Medical has come through it all right – provided nothing else happens.'

'I saw you on the telly.'

'How did I look?'

'Gorgeous – but I fancied your boss.'

'Me, too, but he's got three grown-up children he doesn't want to upset, so I think he's a lost cause.'

'By heck, you have had a bad day.'

'I'm sorry to let you all down.'

'It won't be the same without you.'

'I'll have to hang up, Charlie – I'd better fetch Mother as soon as possible. Happy Christmas.' She cradled the handset and sat staring at the phone. 'What a miserable life,' she said aloud. 'What a miserable bloody life.'

6 p.m.

Craig's relationship with Sophie was advancing very slowly.

He had spent all afternoon with her. He had beaten her at table tennis and lost at pool. They had agreed about music – they both liked guitar bands better than drum-and-bass. They both read horror fiction, though she loved Stephen King and he preferred Anne Rice. He told her about his parents' marriage, which was stormy but passionate, and she told him about Ned and Jennifer's divorce, which was rancorous.

But she gave him no encouragement. She did not casually touch his arm, or look intently at his face when he talked to her, or bring into the conversation romantic topics such as dating and snogging. Instead, she talked of a world that excluded him, a world of nightclubs – how did she get in, at fourteen? – and friends who took drugs and boys who had motorcycles.

As dinner approached, he began to feel desperate. He did not want to spend five days pursuing her for the sake of one kiss at the end. His idea was to win her over on the first day, and spend the holiday *really* getting to know her. Clearly this was not her timetable. He needed a short cut to her heart.

She seemed to consider him beneath her romantic notice. All this talk of older people implied that he was just a kid, even though he was older than Sophie by a year and seven months. He had to find some way to prove he was as mature and sophisticated as she.

Sophie would not be the first girl he had kissed. He had dated Caroline Stratton from Year 10 at his school for six weeks, but although she was pretty he had been bored. Lindy Riley, the plump sister of a footballing friend, had been more exciting, and had let him do several things he had never done before, but then she had switched her affections to the keyboard player in a Glasgow rock band. And there were several other girls he had kissed once or twice.

But this felt different. After meeting Sophie at his mother's birthday party, he had thought about her every day for four months. He had downloaded one of the photographs his father had taken at the party, showing Craig gesturing with his hands and Sophie laughing. He used it as the wallpaper on his computer. He still looked at other girls, but always comparing them with Sophie, thinking that by comparison this one was too pale, that one too fat, another simply plain-looking, and all of them tediously conventional. He did not mind that she was difficult – he was used to difficult women, his mother was one. There was just something about Sophie that stabbed him in the heart.

At six o'clock, slumped on the couch in the barn, he decided he had watched as much MTV as he needed for one day. 'Want to go over to the house?' he asked her.

'What for?'

'They'll all be sitting around the kitchen table.'

'So?'

Well, Craig thought, it's sort of nice. The kitchen is warm, and you can smell dinner cooking, and my dad tells funny stories, and Aunt Miranda pours wine, and it just feels good. But he knew that would not impress Sophie, so he said: 'There might be drinks.'

She stood up. 'Good. I want a cocktail.'

Dream on, Craig thought. Grandpa was not going to serve hard liquor to a fourteen-year-old. If they were having champagne, she might get half a glass. But Craig did not disillusion her. They put on coats and went out.

It was now fully dark, but the yard was brightly lit by lamps mounted on the walls of the surrounding buildings. Snow swirled thickly in the air, and the ground was slippery underfoot. They crossed to the main house and approached the back door. Just before they went in, Craig glanced around the corner of the house and saw Grandpa's Ferrari, still parked at the front, the snow now two inches thick on the sweeping arc of its rear spoiler. Luke must have been too busy to put it away.

Craig said: 'Last time I was here, Grandpa let me drive his car into the garage.'

'You can't drive,' Sophie said sceptically.

'I haven't got a licence, but that doesn't mean I can't handle a car.' He was exaggerating. He had driven his father's Mercedes estate a couple of times, once on a beach and once on a disused airstrip, but never on a regular road.

'All right, then, park it now,' Sophie said.

Craig knew he should ask permission. But if he said so, it would sound as if he were trying to back out. Anyway,

Grandpa might say no, then Craig would have lost the chance to prove his point to Sophie. So he said: 'All right, then.'

The car was unlocked, and the key was in the ignition.

Sophie leaned against the wall of the house by the back door, arms folded, her stance saying: Okay, show me. Craig was not going to let her get away with that. 'Why don't you come with me?' he said. 'Or are you scared?'

They both got into the car.

It was not easy. The seats were low-slung, almost on a level with the door sills, and Craig had to put one leg in then slide his backside across the flat armrest. He slammed the door.

The gearstick was severely utilitarian, just an upright aluminium rod with a knob on the end. Craig checked that it was in neutral, then turned the ignition key. The car started with a roar like a 747.

Craig half hoped the noise would bring Luke running out of the house, arms raised in protest. However, the Ferrari was at the front door, and the family were in the kitchen at the back of the house, overlooking the yard. The thunder of the car did not penetrate the thick stone walls of the old farmhouse.

The whole car seemed to tremble, as if in an earthquake, as the big engine turned over with lazy potency. Craig's body felt the vibrations through the black leather seat. 'This is cool!' Sophie said excitedly.

Craig switched on the headlamps. Two cones of light reached out from the front of the car, stretching across the garden, filled with snowflakes. He rested his hand on the knob of the gearstick, touched the clutch pedal with his foot, then looked behind. The driveway went back in a straight line to the garage before turning to curve around the cliff top.

'Come on, then,' said Sophie. 'Drive it.'

Craig put on a casual air to conceal his reluctance. 'Relax,' he said. He released the handbrake. 'Enjoy the ride.' He depressed the clutch, then moved the stick through the open-gate Ferrari gearshift into reverse. He touched the accelerator pedal as gently as he could. The engine snarled menacingly. He released the clutch a millimetre at a time. The car began to creep backwards.

He held the steering wheel lightly, not moving it to either side, and the car went in a straight line. With the clutch fully out, he touched the throttle again. The car shot backwards, passing the garage. Sophie let out a scream of fear. Craig transferred his foot from the accelerator to the brake. The car skidded on the snow but, to Craig's relief, it did not waver from its straight line. As it came to a halt he remembered, at the last minute, to engage the clutch and prevent a stall.

He felt pleased with himself. He had kept control, just. Better yet, Sophie had been scared, while he appeared calm. Maybe she would stop acting so superior.

The garage stood at a right angle to the house, and now its doors were ahead and to the left of the Ferrari. Kit's car, a black Peugeot coupé, was parked in front of the garage block at its far end. Craig found a remote control under the Ferrari's dashboard and clicked. The farthermost of three garage doors swung up and over.

The concrete apron in front of the garage was covered with a smooth layer of snow. There was a clump of bushes at the near corner of the building, and a large tree on the far side of the apron. Craig simply had to avoid those and slot the car into its bay.

More confident now, he moved the gear stick into the notch for first gear, touched the accelerator, then released the clutch. The car moved forward. He turned the steering wheel, which was heavy at low speed, not being power-assisted. The car obediently turned left. He depressed the throttle another millimetre, and it picked up speed, just enough to feel exciting. He swung right, aiming for the open door, but he was going too fast. He touched the brake.

That was his mistake.

The car was moving quickly on snow with its front wheels turning right. As soon as the brakes bit, the rear wheels lost traction. Instead of continuing to turn right into the open garage door, the car slid sideways across the snow. Craig knew what was happening, but had no idea what to do about it. He spun the steering wheel farther to the right, but that made the skid worse, and the car drifted inexorably over the slippery surface, like a boat blown by a gale. Craig stamped on the brake and the clutch at the same time, but it made no difference.

The garage building slid away to the right of the windscreen. Craig thought he would crash into Kit's Peugeot, but to his blissful relief the Ferrari missed the other car by several inches. Losing momentum, it slowed down. For a moment he thought he had got away with it. But, just before the car came to a complete stop, its front nearside wing touched the big tree.

'That was great!' Sophie said.

'No, it bloody was not.' Craig put the stick in neutral and released the clutch, then sprang out of the car. He walked around to the front. The impact had felt gentle but, to his dismay, he saw by the light of the lamps on the garage wall a large, unmistakable dimple in the gleaming blue wing. 'Shit,' he said miserably.

Sophie got out and looked. 'It's not a very big dent,' she said.

'Don't talk bollocks.' The size did not matter. The bodywork was damaged and Craig was responsible. He felt a sensation of nausea deep in his stomach. What a Christmas present for Grandpa.

'They might not notice it,' Sophie said.

'Of course they'll bloody notice it,' he said angrily. 'Grandpa will see it as soon as he looks at the car.'

'Well, that might not be for a while. He's not likely to go out in this weather.'

'What difference does that make?' Craig said impatiently. He knew he was sounding petulant, but he hardly cared. 'I'll have to own up.'

'Better if you're not here when the shit hits the fan.'

'I don't see . . .' He paused. He did see. If he confessed now, Christmas would be blighted. Mamma Marta would have said: 'There will be a bordello,' by which she meant uproar. If he said nothing, but confessed later, perhaps there would be less fuss. Anyway, the prospect of postponing discovery for a few days was tempting.

'I'll have to put it in the garage,' he said, thinking aloud.

'Park it with the dented side right up against the wall,' Sophie suggested. 'That way, it won't be noticed by anyone just walking past.'

Sophie's idea was beginning to make sense, Craig thought. There were two other cars in the garage: a massive Toyota Land Cruiser Amazon off-road car with four-wheel drive, which Grandpa used in weather like this, and Luke's old Ford Mondeo, in which he drove himself and Lori between this house and their cottage a mile away. Luke would certainly enter the garage this evening to get his car and drive home. If the weather got worse, he might borrow the big Land Cruiser and leave his Ford here. Either way, he had to enter the garage. But if the Ferrari were hard up against the wall the dent would not be visible.

The engine was still running. Craig sat in the driver's seat. He engaged first gear and drove slowly forward. Sophie ran into the garage and stood in the car's headlights. As it entered the garage, she used her hands to show Craig how close he was to the wall.

On his first attempt he was no closer than eighteen inches from the wall. That was not good enough. He had to try again. He looked nervously in the rear-view mirror, but no one else was around. He was grateful for the cold weather that kept everyone indoors in the warm.

On his third attempt he managed to position the car four or five inches off the wall. He got out and looked. It was impossible to see the dent from any angle.

He closed the door, then he and Sophie headed for the kitchen. Craig felt jangled and guilty, but Sophie was in high spirits. 'That was awesome,' she said.

Craig realized he had impressed her at last.

7 p.m.

Kit set up his computer in the box room, a small space that could be reached only by going through his bedroom. He plugged in his laptop, a fingerprint scanner, and a smartcard reader-writer he had bought second-hand for £270 on eBay.

This room had always been his lair. When he was small, they had had only the three bedrooms: Mamma and Daddy in the main room, Olga and Miranda in the second room, and Kit in a cot in this box room off the girls' room. After the extension was built, and Olga went off to university, Kit had the bedroom as well as the box room, but this had remained his den.

It was still furnished as a schoolboy's study, with a cheap desk, a bookshelf, a small TV set, and a seat known as the sleepchair, which unfolded into a small single bed, and had often been used by school friends coming to stay. Sitting at the desk, he thought wistfully of the tedious hours of homework he had done here, geography and biology, medieval kings and irregular verbs, *Hail, Caesar!* He had learned so much, and forgotten it all.

He took the pass he had stolen from his father and slid it into the reader-writer. Its top stuck out of the slot, clearly showing the printed word: 'Oxenford Medical'. He hoped no one would come into the room. They were all in the kitchen. Lori was making osso bucco according to Mamma Marta's famous recipe – Kit could smell the oregano. Daddy had opened a bottle of champagne. By now they would be telling stories that began: 'Do you remember when . . . ?'

The chip in the card contained details of his father's fingerprint. It was not a simple image, for that was too easy to fake – a photograph of the finger could fool a normal scanner. Rather, Kit had built a device that measured twenty-five points of the fingerprint, using minute electrical differences between ridges and valleys. He had also written a program that stored these details in code. At his apartment he had several prototypes of the fingerprint scanner and he had, naturally, kept a copy of the software he had created.

Now he set his laptop to read the smart card. The only danger was that someone at Oxenford Medical – Toni Gallo, perhaps – might have modified the software so that Kit's program would no longer work; for example, by requiring an access code before the card could be read. It was unlikely that anyone would have gone to such trouble and expense to guard against a possibility that must have seemed fanciful – but it was conceivable. And he had not told Nigel about this potential snag.

He waited a few anxious seconds, watching the screen.

At last it shimmered and displayed a page of code: Stanley's fingerprint details. Kit sighed with relief and saved the file.

His niece Caroline walked in, carrying a rat.

She was dressed younger than her age, in a flower-patterned dress and white stockings. The rat had white fur and pink eyes. Caroline sat on the sleepchair, stroking her pet.

Kit suppressed a curse. He could hardly tell her that he was doing something secret and would prefer to be alone. But he could not continue while she sat there.

She had always been a nuisance. From an early age she had hero-worshipped her young Uncle Kit. As a boy he had quickly wearied of this and become fed up with the way she followed him around. But she was hard to shake off.

He tried to be nice. 'How's the rat?' he said.

'His name is Leonard,' she replied in a tone of mild reproof.

'Leonard. Where did you get him?'

'Paradise Pets in Sauchiehall Street.' She let the rat go, and it ran up her arm and perched on her shoulder.

Kit thought the girl was insane, carrying a rat around as if it were a baby. Caroline looked like her mother, Olga, with long dark hair and heavy black eyebrows, but where Olga was drily severe, Caroline was as wet as a rainy February. She was only seventeen, she might grow out of it.

He hoped she was too wrapped up in herself and her pet to notice the card sticking up out of the reader and the words 'Oxenford Medical' printed along its top. Even she would realize he was not supposed to have a pass for the Kremlin nine months after he was fired.

'What are you doing?' she asked him.

'Work. I need to finish this today.' He longed to snatch

the tell-tale card out of the reader, but he feared that would only call her attention to it.

'I won't bother you, just carry on.'

'Nothing happening downstairs?'

'Mummy and Aunt Miranda are stuffing the stockings in the drawing room, so I've been chucked out.'

'Ah.' He turned back to the computer and switched the software into Read mode. His next step should be to scan his own fingerprint, but he could not let her see that. She might not grasp the significance herself, but she could easily mention it to someone who would. He pretended to study the screen, racking his brains for a way to get rid of her. After a minute he was inspired. He faked a sneeze.

'Bless you,' she said.

'Thanks.' He sneezed again. 'You know, I think poor dear Leonard is doing this to me.'

'How could he?' she said indignantly.

'I'm slightly allergic, and this room is so small.'

She stood up. 'We don't want to make people sneeze, do we, Lennie?' She went out.

Kit closed the door gratefully behind her, then sat down and pressed the forefinger of the right hand to the glass of the scanner. The program scrutinized his fingerprint and encoded the details. Kit saved the file.

Finally, he uploaded his own fingerprint details to the smart card, overwriting his father's. No one else could have done this, unless they had copies of Kit's own software, plus a stolen smart card with the correct site code. If he were devising the system anew he still would not bother to make the cards non-rewritable. Nevertheless, Toni Gallo might have. He looked anxiously at the screen, half-expecting an error message saying YOU DO NOT HAVE ACCESS.

No such message appeared. Toni had not outsmarted him this time. He re-read the data from the chip, to make sure the procedure had been successful. It had: the card now carried Kit's fingerprint details, not Stanley's. 'Yes!' he said aloud, mutedly triumphant.

He removed the card from the machine and put it in his pocket. It would now give him access to BSL4. When he waved the card at the reader, and pressed his finger to the touch screen, the computer would read the data on the card and compare it with the fingerprint, find they matched, and unlock the door.

After he returned from the lab he would reverse the process, erasing his own fingerprint data from the chip and reinstating Stanley's, before he replaced the card in his father's wallet some time tomorrow. The computer at the Kremlin would record that Stanley Oxenford had entered BSL4 in the early hours of 25 December. Stanley would protest that he had been at home in bed, and Toni Gallo would tell the police that no one else could have used Stanley's card because of the fingerprint check. 'Sweet,' he said aloud. It pleased him to think how baffled they would all be.

Some biometric security systems matched the fingerprint with data stored on a central computer. If the Kremlin had used that configuration, Kit would have needed access to the database. But employees had an irrational aversion to the thought of their personal details being stored on company computers. Scientists in particular often read the *Guardian* and became finicky about their civil rights. Kit had chosen to store the fingerprint record on the smart card, rather than the central database, to make the new security set-up more acceptable to the staff. He had not anticipated that one day he would be trying to defeat his own scheme.

He felt satisfied. Stage One was complete. He had a working pass for BSL4. But, before he could use it, he had to get inside the Kremlin.

He took his phone from his pocket. The number he dialled was the phone of Hamish McKinnon, one of the security guards on duty at the Kremlin tonight. Hamish was the company dope dealer, supplying marijuana to the younger scientists and Ecstasy to the secretaries for their weekends. He did not deal in heroin or crack, knowing that a serious addict was sure to betray him sooner or later. Kit had asked Hamish to be his inside man tonight, confident that Hamish would not dare to spill the beans, having his own secrets to conceal.

'It's me,' Kit said when Hamish answered. 'Can you talk?'

'And a happy Christmas to you too, Ian, you old bugger,' Hamish said cheerily. 'Just a tick, I'm going to step outside . . . that's better.'

'Everything all right?'

Hamish's voice became serious. 'Aye, but she's doubled the guard, so I've got Willie Crawford with me.'

'Where are you stationed?'

'In the gatehouse.'

'Perfect. Is everything quiet?'

'Like a graveyard.'

'How many guards in total?'

'Six. Two here, two at Reception, and two in the Control Room.'

'Okay. We can cope with that. Let me know if anything unusual happens.'

'Okay.'

Kit ended the call and dialled a number that gave him access to the telephone system computer at the Kremlin. The number was used by Hibernian Telecom, the company that had installed the phones, for remote diagnosis of faults. Kit had worked closely with Hibernian, because the alarms he had installed used phone lines. He knew the number and the access code. Once again, he had a moment of tension, worrying that the number or the code might have been changed in the nine months since he had left. But they had not.

His mobile phone was linked to his laptop by a wireless connection that worked over distances of fifty feet or so – even through walls, which might be useful later. Now he used the laptop to access the central processing unit of the Kremlin's phone system. The system had tamper detectors – but they did not register an alarm if the company's own phone line and code were used.

First he closed down every phone on the site except the one on the desk in Reception.

Next, he diverted all calls into and out of the Kremlin to his mobile. He had already programmed his laptop to recognize the numbers likeliest to come up, such as Toni Gallo's. He would be able to answer the calls himself, or play recorded messages to the callers, or even redirect calls and eavesdrop on the conversations.

Finally, he caused every phone in the building to ring

for five seconds. That was just to get the attention of the security guards.

Then he disconnected and sat on the edge of his chair, waiting.

He was fairly sure what would happen next. The guards had a list of people to call in the event of different emergencies. Their first action now should be to call the phone company.

He did not have to wait long. His mobile rang. He left it, watching his laptop. After a moment, a message appeared on the screen saying: 'Kremlin calls Toni.'

That was not what he had expected. They should have called Hibernian first. Nevertheless, he was prepared. Quickly, he activated a recorded message. The security guard who was trying to reach Toni Gallo heard a female voice saying that the mobile he was calling might be switched off or out of range, and advising him to try later. The guard hung up.

Kit's phone rang again almost immediately. Kit hoped the guards would now be calling the phone company, but once again he was disappointed. The screen said: 'Kremlin calls RPHQ.' The guards were ringing regional police headquarters at Inverburn. Kit was happy for the police to be informed. He redirected the call to the correct number and listened in.

'This is Steven Tremlett, security guard supervisor at Oxenford Medical, calling to report an unusual incident.'

'What's the incident, Mr Tremlett?'

'No big emergency, but we have a problem with our phone lines, and I'm not sure the alarms will work.'

'I'll log it. Can you get your phones fixed?'

'I'll call out a repair crew, but God knows when they'll get here, being Christmas Eve.'

'Do you want a patrol to call?'

'It wouldn't do any harm, if they've not much on.'

Kit hoped the police would pay a visit to the Kremlin. It would add conviction to his cover.

The policeman said: 'They'll be busy later, when the pubs chuck out, but it's quiet the noo.'

'Right. Tell them I'll give them a cup of tea.'

They hung up. Kit's mobile rang a third time and the screen said: 'Kremlin calls Hibernian.' At last, he thought with relief. This was the one he had been waiting for. He touched a button and said into his phone: 'Hibernian Telecom, can I help you?'

Steve's voice said: 'This is Oxenford Medical, we have a problem with our phone system.'

Kit exaggerated his Scots accent to disguise his voice. 'Would that be Greenmantle Road, Inverburn?'

'Aye.'

'What's the problem?'

'All the phones are out except this one. The place is empty, of course, but the thing is, the alarm system uses the phone lines, and we need to be sure that's working properly.'

At that point, Kit's father walked into the room.

Kit froze, paralysed with fear and terror, as if he were a child again. Stanley looked at the computer and the mobile phone and raised his eyebrows. Kit pulled himself together. He was no longer a kid frightened of a reprimand. Trying to make himself calm, he said into the phone: 'Let me call you back in two minutes.' He touched the keyboard of his laptop, and the screen went dark.

'Working?' his father said.

'Something I have to finish.'

'At Christmas?'

'I said I would deliver this piece of software by December the twenty-fourth.'

'By now your customer will have gone home, like all sensible folk.'

'But his computer will show that I emailed the program to him before midnight on Christmas Eve, so he won't be able to say I was late.'

Stanley smiled and nodded. 'Well, I'm glad you're being conscientious.' He stood silent for several seconds, obviously having something else to say. A typical scientist, he thought nothing of long pauses in conversation. The important thing was precision.

Kit waited, trying to hide his frantic impatience. Then his mobile rang.

'Shit,' he said. 'Sorry,' he said to his father. He checked his screen. This was not a diverted Kremlin call, but one directly to his mobile from Hamish McKinnon, the security guard. He could not ignore it. He pressed the phone hard to his ear, so that the voice of the caller would not leak out to be heard by his father. 'Yes?'

Hamish said excitedly: 'All the phones here have gone kaput!'

'Okay, that's expected, it's part of the program.'

'You said to tell you if anything unusual—'

'Yes, and you were right to ring me, but I have to hang up now. Thank you.' He ended the call.

His father spoke. 'Is our quarrel really behind us now?'

Kit resented this kind of talk. It suggested that the two

disputants must be equally guilty. But he was desperate to get back on the phone, so he said: 'I think so, yes.'

'I know you think you've been unjustly treated,' his father said, reading his mind. 'I don't see your logic, but I accept that you believe it. And I, too, feel that I was unfairly done by. But we have to try to forget that, and be friends again.'

'So says Miranda.'

'And I'm just not sure you have put it behind you. I sense you holding something back.'

Kit tried to keep his face wooden so that his guilt would not show. 'I'm doing my best,' he said. 'It's not easy.'

Stanley seemed satisfied. 'Well, I can't ask any more of you than that,' he said. He put his hand on Kit's shoulder, bent down, and kissed the top of his head. 'I came to tell you supper's almost ready.'

'I'm nearly done. I'll come down in five minutes.'

'Good.' Stanley went out.

Kit slumped in his chair. He was shaking with a mixture of shame and relief. His father was shrewd, and suffered no illusions – yet Kit had survived the interrogation. But it had been ghastly while it lasted.

When his hands were steady enough, he dialled the Kremlin again.

The phone was picked up immediately. Steve Tremlett's voice said: 'Oxenford Medical.'

'Hibernian Telecom here.' Kit remembered to change his voice. He had not known Tremlett well, and nine months had passed since he had left Oxenford Medical, so it was unlikely Steve would remember his voice; but he was not going to take the chance. 'I can't access your central processing unit.'

'I'm not surprised. That line must be down also. You'll have to send someone.'

This was what Kit wanted, but he was careful not to sound eager. 'It's going to be difficult to get a repair crew out to you at Christmas.'

'Don't give me that.' Steve's voice betrayed a touch of anger. 'You guarantee to attend to any fault within four hours, every day of the year. That's the service we pay you for. It's now seven fifty-five p.m., and I'm logging this call.'

'All right, keep your shirt on. I'll get a crew to you as soon as possible.'

'Give me a time estimate, please.'

'I'll do my best to get them to you by midnight.'

'Thank you, we'll be waiting.' Steve hung up.

Kit put down his mobile. He was perspiring. He wiped his face with his sleeve. So far, it had all gone perfectly.

8:30 p.m.

Stanley dropped his bombshell during dinner.

Miranda felt mellow. The osso bucco was hearty and satisfying, and her father had opened two bottles of Brunello di Montepulciano to go with it. Kit was restless, dashing upstairs every time his mobile rang, but everyone else was relaxed. The four kids ate quickly then retired to the barn to watch a DVD movie called *Scream 2*, leaving six adults around the table in the dining room: Miranda and Ned, Olga and Hugo, Daddy at the head and Kit at the foot. Lori served coffee while Luke loaded the dishwasher in the kitchen.

Then Stanley said: 'How would you all feel if I started dating again?'

Everyone went quiet. Even Lori reacted: she stopped pouring coffee and stood still, staring at him in shock.

Miranda had guessed, but all the same it was disquieting to hear him come right out and say it. She said: 'I suppose we're talking about Toni Gallo.'

He looked startled and said: 'No.'

Olga said: 'Oh, poo.'

Miranda did not believe him, either, but she refrained from contradicting him.

'Anyway, I'm not talking about anyone in particular, I'm discussing a general principle,' he went on. 'Mamma Marta has been dead for a year and a half, may she rest in peace. For almost four decades she was the only woman in my life. But I'm sixty, and I probably have another twenty or thirty years to live. I may not want to spend them alone.'

Lori shot him a hurt look. He was not alone, she wanted to say; he had her and Luke.

Olga said bad-temperedly: 'So why consult us? You don't need our permission to sleep with your secretary or anyone else.'

'I'm not asking permission. I want to know how you would feel *if* it happened. And it won't be my secretary, by the way. Dorothy is very happily married.'

Miranda spoke, mainly to prevent Olga saying something harsh. 'I think we'd find it hard, Daddy, to see you with another woman in this house. But we want you to be happy, and I believe we'd do our best to welcome someone you loved.'

He gave her a wry look. 'Not exactly a ringing endorsement, but thank you for trying to be positive.'

Olga said: 'You won't get that much from me. For God's sake, what are we supposed to say to you? Are you thinking of marrying this woman? Would you have more children?'

'I'm not thinking of marrying anyone,' he said tetchily. Olga was irritating him by refusing to argue on his terms. Mamma had always been able to get under his skin in exactly the same way. He added: 'But I'm not ruling anything out.'

'It's outrageous,' Olga stormed. 'When I was a child I hardly saw you. You were always at the lab. Mamma and I were at home with baby Mandy from seven thirty in the morning until nine at night. We were a one-parent family, and it was all for your career, so that you could invent narrow-spectrum antibiotics and an ulcer drug and an anti-cholesterol pill, and become famous and rich. Well, I want a reward for my sacrifice.'

'You had a very expensive education,' Stanley said.

'It's not enough. I want my children to inherit the money you made, and I don't want them to share it with a litter of brats bred by some tart who knows nothing except how to take advantage of a widower.'

Miranda let out a cry of protest.

Hugo, embarrassed, said: 'Don't beat about the bush, Olga dear, say what's on your mind.'

Stanley's expression darkened, and he said: 'I wasn't planning to date *some tart*.'

Olga saw that she had gone too far. She said: 'I didn't mean that last part.' For her, that amounted to an apology.

Kit said flippantly: 'It won't be much different. Mamma was tall, athletic, non-intellectual, and Italian. Toni Gallo is tall, athletic, non-intellectual, and Spanish. I wonder if she cooks?'

'Don't be stupid,' Olga told him. 'The difference is that for the last forty years Toni hasn't been part of this family, so she's not one of us, she's an outsider.'

Kit bridled. 'Don't call me stupid, Olga. At least I can see what's under my nose.'

Miranda's heart missed a beat. What was he talking about?

The same question occurred to Olga. 'What's under my nose that I can't see?'

Miranda glanced surreptitiously at Ned. She feared that later he might ask her what Kit meant. He often picked up such subtleties.

Kit backed off. 'Oh, stop cross-examining me, you're a pain in the arse.'

'Aren't you concerned about your financial future?' Olga said to Kit. 'Your inheritance is threatened as much as mine. Have you got so much money that you don't care?'

Kit laughed humourlessly. 'Yeah, right.'

Miranda said to Olga: 'Aren't you being a bit mercenary?'

'Well, Daddy did ask.'

Stanley said: 'I thought you might feel badly about your mother's being replaced by someone new. It never occurred to me that your main concern would be my will.'

Miranda felt hurt for her father. But she was more worried about Kit and what he might say. As a child, he had never been good at keeping secrets. She and Olga had been obliged to keep everything from him. If they trusted him with a confidence, he would blurt it out to Mamma in five minutes. Now he knew Miranda's darkest secret. He was no longer a child, but on the other hand he had never really grown up. This was dangerous. Her heart beat like a tom-tom. Perhaps if she took part in the conversation she had a chance of controlling it. She addressed Olga. 'The important thing is to keep the family together. Whatever Daddy decides, we mustn't let it break us up.'

'Don't lecture me about the family,' Olga said angrily. 'Talk to your brother.'

Kit said: 'Get off my case!'

Stanley said: 'I don't want to rake all that up again.'

Olga persisted. 'But he's the one who has come closest to destroying the family.'

'Fuck you, Olga,' Kit said.

'Easy,' Stanley said firmly. 'We can have a passionate discussion without descending to insults and obscenity.'

'Come on, Daddy,' Olga said. She was furious, because she had been called mercenary, and she needed to counter-attack. 'What could be more threatening to the family than one of us who steals from another?'

Kit was red with shame and fury. 'I'll tell you,' he said.

Miranda knew what was coming. Terrified, she stretched out her arm towards Kit with her hand upright in a 'Halt' sign. 'Kit, calm down, please,' she said frantically.

He was not listening. 'I'll tell you what could be more threatening to the family.'

Miranda shouted at him: 'Just shut up!'

Stanley realized there was a subtext of which he was ignorant, and he frowned with puzzlement. 'What are you two talking about?'

Kit said: 'I'm talking about someone—'

Miranda stood up. 'No!'

'—someone who sleeps—'

Miranda snatched up a glass of water and threw it in Kit's face.

There was a sudden hush.

Kit wiped his face with his napkin. With everyone watching him in shocked silence, he said: '. . . sleeps with her sister's husband.'

Olga was bewildered. 'This makes no sense. I never slept with Jasper – or Ned.'

Miranda held her head in her hands.

'I didn't mean you,' Kit said.

Olga looked at Miranda. Miranda looked away.

Lori, still standing there with the coffee pot, gave a gasp of sudden, shocked comprehension.

Stanley said: 'Good God! I never imagined that.'

Miranda looked at Ned. He was horrified. He said: 'Did you?'

She did not reply.

Olga turned to Hugo. 'You and my sister?'

He tried his bad-boy grin. Olga swung her arm and slapped his face. The blow had a solid sound, more like a punch. 'Ow!' he cried, and rocked back in his chair.

Olga said: 'You lousy, lying . . .' She searched for words. 'You worm. You pig. You bloody bastard, you rotten sod.' She turned to Miranda. 'And you!'

Miranda could not meet her eye. She looked down at the table. A small cup of coffee was in front of her. The cup was fine white china with a blue stripe, Mamma's favourite set.

'How could you?' Olga said to her. 'How could you?'

Miranda would try to explain, one day; but anything she said now would sound like an excuse. So she just shook her head.

Olga stood up and walked out of the room.

Hugo looked sheepish. 'I'd better . . .' He followed her.

Stanley suddenly realized that Lori was standing there listening to every word. Belatedly, he said: 'Lori, you'd better help Luke in the kitchen.'

She started as if awakened. 'Yes, Professor Oxenford.'

Stanley looked at Kit. 'That was brutal.' Anger made his voice shake.

'Oh, that's right, blame me,' Kit said petulantly. 'I didn't sleep with Hugo, did I?' He threw down his napkin and left.

Ned was mortified. 'Um, excuse me,' he said, and he went out.

Only Miranda and her father were left in the room. Stanley got up and came to her side. He put his hand on her shoulder. 'They'll all calm down about it, eventually,' he said. 'This is bad, but it will pass.'

She turned to him and pressed her face into the soft tweed of his waistcoat. 'Oh, Daddy, I'm sorry,' she said, and she began to cry.

9:30 p.m.

The weather was getting worse. Toni's drive to the old folks' home had been protracted, but the return journey was even slower. There was a thin layer of snow on the road, beaten hard by car tyres, frozen too solid to turn into slush. Nervous drivers went at a crawl, delaying everyone else. Toni's red Porsche Boxster was the perfect car for overtaking sluggards, but it was not at its best in slippery conditions, and there was little she could do to shorten her journey.

Mother sat contentedly beside her, wearing a green wool coat and a felt hat. She was not in the least angry with Bella. Toni was disappointed by this, and was ashamed of feeling so. Deep inside, she wanted Mother to be furious with Bella, as Toni herself had been. It would have vindicated her. But Mother seemed to think it was Toni's fault she had been kept waiting so long. Toni had said irritably: 'You do realize that Bella was supposed to pick you up hours ago.'

'Yes, dear, but your sister's got a family to take care of.'

'And I've got a responsible job.'

'I know, it's your substitute for children.'

'So it's okay for Bella to let you down, but not for me.'

'That's right, dear.'

Toni tried to follow Mother's example, and be magnanimous. But she kept thinking of her friends at the spa, sitting in the jacuzzi, or acting charades, or drinking coffee by a big log fire. Charles and Damien would become more hilariously camp as the evening progressed and they relaxed. Michael would tell stories about his Irish mother, a legendary spitfire in her home town of Liverpool. Bonnie would reminisce about college days, the scrapes she and Toni had got into as the only two females in an engineering department of three hundred students. They would all be having so much fun, while Toni drove through the snow with her mother.

She told herself to stop being pathetic. I'm a grown-up, she thought, and grown-ups have responsibilities. Besides, Mother might not be alive for many more years, so I should enjoy having her with me while I can.

She found it harder to look on the bright side when she thought about Stanley. She had felt so close to him this morning, and now the gulf between them was bigger than the Grand Canyon. She asked herself constantly whether she had pushed him too hard. Had she made him choose between his family and her? Perhaps if she had backed off he would not have felt forced into a decision. But she had not exactly thrown herself at him, and a woman had to give a man a little encouragement, otherwise he might never speak at all.

There was no point in regrets, she told herself. She had lost him, and that was that.

Up ahead she saw the lights of a petrol station. 'Do you need the toilet, Mother?' she said.

'Yes, please.'

Toni slowed down and pulled on to the forecourt. She topped up her tank, then took her mother inside. Mother went to the ladies' room while Toni paid. As Toni returned to the car, her mobile phone rang. Thinking it might be the Kremlin calling, she snatched the phone up hurriedly. 'Toni Gallo.'

'This is Stanley Oxenford.'

'Oh.' She was taken aback. She had not been expecting this.

'Perhaps I'm phoning at an inconvenient time,' he said politely.

'No, no, no,' she said quickly, sliding behind the wheel. 'I imagined the call was from the Kremlin, and I was worried that something might have gone wrong there.' She closed the car door.

'Everything's fine, as far as I know. How's your spa?'

'I'm not there.' She told him what had happened.

'How terribly disappointing,' he said.

Her heart was beating faster, for no very good reason. 'What about you – is everything all right?' She was wondering why he had phoned. At the same time, she watched the brightly lit pay booth. It would be a while before her mother emerged.

'Family dinner ended in an upset. It's not exactly unknown – we do have rows sometimes.'

'What was it about?'

'I probably shouldn't tell you.'

Then why have you phoned me? she thought. It was extraordinary for Stanley to make a pointless call. He was usually so focused that she sensed he had in front of him a list of topics he needed to cover.

'In brief, Kit revealed that Miranda had slept with Hugo – her sister's husband.'

'Good God!' Toni pictured each of them: handsome, malicious Kit; plump, pretty Miranda; Hugo, a pint-sized charmer; and the formidable Olga. It was a ripe tale, but what was more surprising was that Stanley should repeat it to her, Toni. Once again, he was treating her as if they were intimate friends. But she mistrusted that impression. If she allowed her hopes to rise he would crush her again. All the same, she did not want to end the conversation. 'How do you feel about it?' she said.

'Well, Hugo was always a bit flaky. Olga knows him by now, after almost twenty years of marriage. She's humiliated, and mad as hell – in fact I can hear her yelling at this very moment – but I think she'll forgive him. Miranda explained the circumstances to me. She didn't have an affair with Hugo, just slept with him once, when she was depressed after the break-up of her marriage; and she's been feeling ashamed of herself ever since. I think eventually Olga will forgive her, too. It's Kit who bothers me.' His voice became sad. 'I always wanted my son to be courageous and principled, and grow into an upright man who could be respected by everyone; but he's sly and weak.'

Toni realized, in a flash of revelation, that Stanley was talking to her as he would have talked to Marta. After a row such as this the two of them would have gone to bed and discussed the role of each of their children. He was missing his wife and making Toni a substitute. But this thought no longer enthralled her. Quite the reverse: she was resentful. He had no right to use her in this way. She felt exploited. And she really ought to make sure her mother was all right in the petrol-station toilet.

She was about to tell him so when he said: 'But I shouldn't burden you with all this. I called to say something else.'

That was more like Stanley, she thought. And Mother would be okay for a few minutes more.

He went on: 'After Christmas, will you have dinner with me one evening?'

What now? she thought. She said: 'Of course.' What did this mean?

'You know how I disapprove of men who make romantic advances towards their employees. It puts the employee in such a difficult position – she's bound to feel that if she refuses, she may suffer in her career.'

'I have no such fears,' she said, a bit stiffly. Was he saying that this invitation was not a romantic advance, so she did not need to worry? She found herself short of breath, and strove to sound normal. 'I'd be delighted to have dinner with you.'

'I've been thinking about our conversation this morning, on the cliff.'

So have I, she thought.

He went on: 'I said something to you then that I've been regretting ever since.'

'What . . .' She could hardly breathe. 'What was that?'

'That I could never start another family.'

'You didn't mean it?'

'I said it because I had become . . . frightened. Strange, isn't it? At my time of life, to be scared.'

'Scared of what?'

There was a long pause, then he said: 'Of my feelings.'

Toni almost dropped the phone. She felt a flush spread from her throat to her face. 'Feelings,' she repeated.

'If this conversation is embarrassing you dreadfully, you just have to say so, and I'll never refer to it again.'

'Go on.'

'When you told me that Osborne had asked you out, I realized you wouldn't be single for ever, probably not much longer. If I'm making a complete fool of myself, please tell me right away, and put me out of my misery.'

'No—' Toni swallowed. He was finding this extraordinarily difficult, she realized. It must be forty years since he had spoken this way to a woman. She ought to help him. She should make it clear that she was not offended. 'No, you're not making a fool of yourself, not at all.'

'I thought this morning that perhaps you might feel warmly towards me, and that's what scared me. Am I right to tell you all this? I wish I could see your face.'

'I'm very glad,' she said in a low voice. 'I'm very happy.'

'Really?'

'Yes.'

'When can I see you? I want to talk some more.'

'I'm with my mother. We're at a petrol station. She's just coming out of the toilet. I can see her now.' Toni got out of the car, still holding the phone to her ear. 'Let's talk tomorrow morning.'

'Don't hang up yet. There's so much to say.'

Toni waved at her mother and called: 'Over here!' Mother saw her and turned. Toni opened the passenger door and helped her in, saying: 'I'm just finishing off this phone call.'

Stanley said: 'Where are you?'

She closed the door on Mother. 'Only about ten miles from Inverburn, but progress is painfully slow.'

'I want us to meet tomorrow. We've both got family obligations, but we're entitled to some time to ourselves.'

'We'll work something out.' She opened the driver's door. 'I must go – Mother's getting cold.'

'Goodbye,' he said. 'Call me any time you feel like it. Any time.'

'Goodbye.' She flipped the phone shut and got into the car.

'That's a big smile,' Mother said. 'You've cheered up. Who was on the phone – someone nice?'

'Yes,' Toni said. 'Someone very nice indeed.'

Kit waited in his room, impatient for everyone to settle down for the night. He needed to get away as soon as possible, but everything would be ruined if someone heard him leave, so he forced himself to linger.

He sat at the old desk in the box room. His laptop was still plugged in, to conserve the battery: he would need it later tonight. His mobile phone was in his pocket.

He had dealt with three calls to and from the Kremlin. Two had been harmless personal calls to guards, and he had let them through. The third had been a call from the Kremlin to Steepfall. Kit guessed that Steve Tremlett, having failed to reach Toni Gallo, might have wanted to let Stanley know about the problem with the phones. He had played a recorded message saying there was a fault on the line.

While he waited, he listened restlessly to the sounds of the house. He could hear Olga and Hugo having a row in the next bedroom to his, Olga firing questions and assertions like a pistol, Hugo by turns abject, pleading, persuading, bantering, and abject again. Downstairs, Luke and Lori clattered pots and crockery in the kitchen for half an hour, then the front door slammed as they left to go to their house a mile away. The children were in the barn, and Miranda and Ned had presumably gone to the guest cottage. Stanley was the last to bed. He had gone into his study, closed the door, and made a phone call – you could tell when someone was on the phone elsewhere in the house, because a 'busy' light appeared on all the extensions. After a while Kit had heard him climb the stairs and close his bedroom door. Olga and Hugo both went to the bathroom, and afterwards they were quiet; either reconciled or exhausted. The dog, Nellie, would be in the kitchen, lying next to the Aga, the warmest place in the house.

Kit waited a little longer, giving them all a chance to go to sleep.

He felt vindicated by the family squabble earlier. Miranda's peccadillo proved that he was not the only sinner in the family. They blamed him for revealing a secret, but it was better to have these things out in the open. Why should his transgressions be blown up out of all proportion and hers discreetly hidden away? Let them be angry. He had enjoyed seeing Olga smack Hugo. My old sister packs a punch, he thought with amusement.

He wondered if he dared leave yet. He was ready. He had taken off his distinctive signet ring, and had replaced his stylish Armani wristwatch with a nondescript Swatch. He was dressed in jeans and a warm black sweater; he would carry his boots and put them on downstairs.

He stood up – then heard the back door slam. He cursed with frustration. Someone had come in – one or two of the kids, probably, raiding the fridge. He waited to hear the door again, indicating that they had left; but instead footsteps mounted the stairs.

A moment later he heard his bedroom door open, the footsteps crossed the outer room, and Miranda came into the box room. She wore Wellington boots and a Barbour over her nightdress, and she was carrying a sheet and a duvet. Without speaking, she went to the sleepchair and unfolded it.

Kit was irate. 'For God's sake, what do you want?'

'I'm sleeping here,' she replied calmly.

'You can't!' he said, panicking.

'I don't see why not.'

'You're supposed to be in the cottage.'

'I've had a row with Ned, thanks to your dinnertime revelation, you sneaking little shit.'

'I don't want you here!'

'I don't give a damn what you want.'

Kit tried to stay calm. He watched with dismay as Miranda made up a bed on the sleepchair. How was he going to steal out of his bedroom, with her in here where she could hear everything? She was upset, she might not go to sleep for hours. And then, in the morning, she was sure to get up before he returned, and notice his absence. His alibi was collapsing.

He had to go now. He would pretend to be even angrier than he really was. 'Fuck you,' he said. He unplugged his laptop and closed the lid. 'I'm not staying here with you.' He stepped into the bedroom.

'Where are you going?'

Out of her sight, he picked up his boots. 'I'm going to watch TV in the drawing room.'

'Keep the volume low.' She slammed the door between the two rooms.

Kit went out.

He tiptoed across the dark landing and down the stairs. The woodwork creaked, but this house shifted constantly, and no one took any notice of odd noises. A faint light from the porch lamp came through a small window beside the front door and made haloes around the hat stand, the newel post at the foot of the stairs, and the stack of directories on the telephone table. Nellie came out of the kitchen and stood by the door, wagging her tail, hoping with irrepressible canine optimism to be taken for a walk.

Kit sat on the stairs and put his boots on, listening for the sound of a door opening above him. This was a dangerous moment, and he felt a shiver of fear as he fumbled with his laces. People were always walking around in the middle of the night: Olga might want a drink of water, Caroline could come over from the barn looking for a headache pill, Stanley might be struck by scientific inspiration and go to his computer.

He tied his bootlaces and put on his black Puffa jacket. He was almost out.

If someone saw him now, he would simply go. No one would stop him. The problem would arise tomorrow. Knowing he had left, they might guess where he had gone, and his whole plan was that no one should understand what had happened.

He shoved Nellie away from the door and opened it. The house was never locked: Stanley believed that intruders were unlikely in this lonely spot, and anyway the dog was the best burglar alarm.

He stepped outside. It was bitterly cold, and the snow

was falling heavily. He pushed Nellie's nose back inside and closed the door behind him with a soft click.

The lights around the house were left on all night, but despite them he could hardly see the garage. The snow was several inches thick on the ground. In a minute his socks and the cuffs of his jeans were soaked. He wished he had worn Wellingtons.

His car was on the far side of the garage, a duvet of snow on its roof. He hoped it would start. He got in, putting his laptop on the passenger seat beside him, so that he could deal quickly with calls to the Kremlin. He turned the key in the ignition. The car coughed and spluttered but, after a few seconds, the engine turned over.

Kit hoped no one had heard it.

The snow was so heavy it was blinding. He was obliged to switch on his headlights, and pray that no one was looking out of a window.

He pulled away. The car slid alarmingly on the thick snow. He crept forward, careful not to turn the steering wheel suddenly. He coaxed the car onto the drive, manoeuvred cautiously around the headland and into the woods, and followed the lane all the way to the main road.

Here the snow was not virgin. There were tyre tracks in both directions. He turned north, heading away from the Kremlin, and drove in the tracks. After ten minutes he turned onto a side road that wound over hills. There were no tyre tracks here, and he slowed even more, wishing he had four-wheel drive.

At last he saw a sign that read 'Inverburn School of Flying'. He turned into an entry. Double wire gates stood open. He drove in. His headlights picked out a hangar and a control tower.

The place appeared deserted. For a moment, Kit half-hoped the others would not show up, and he could call off the whole thing. The thought of suddenly ending this terrible tension was so appealing that his spirits sank and he began to feel depressed. Pull yourself together, he thought. Tonight will be the end of all your troubles.

The hangar door stood partly open. Kit drove slowly in. There were no planes inside – the airfield operated only in the summer months – but he immediately saw a light-coloured Bentley Continental that he recognized as Nigel Buchanan's. Beside it stood a van marked 'Hibernian Telecom'.

The others were not in sight, but a faint light came from the stairwell. Carrying his laptop, Kit followed the stairs up to the control tower.

Nigel sat at the desk, wearing a pink roll-neck sweater and a sports jacket, looking calm, holding a mobile phone to his ear. Elton leaned against the wall, dressed in a tan trench coat with the collar turned up. He had a big canvas bag at his feet. Daisy slumped on a chair, heavy boots on the windowsill. She wore tight-fitting gloves of light-tan suede that looked incongruously ladylike.

Nigel spoke into the phone in his soft London voice. 'It's snowing quite heavily here, but the forecast says the worst of the storm will pass us by . . . yeah, you will be able to fly tomorrow morning, no problem . . . we'll be here well before ten . . . I'll be in the control tower, I'll talk to you as you come in . . . there won't be any trouble, so long as you've got the money, all of it, in fifties, as agreed.'

The talk of money gave Kit a shiver of excitement. Three hundred thousand pounds, in his hands, in twelve hours and a few minutes. True, he would have to give most of it to Daisy immediately, but he would keep fifty thousand. He wondered how much room fifty grand in fifty-pound notes would take up. Could he keep it in his pockets? He should have brought a briefcase . . .

'Thank *you*,' Nigel was saying. 'Goodbye.' He turned around. 'What-ho, Kit. You're bang on time.'

Kit said: 'Who was on the phone – our buyer?'

'His pilot. He'll be arriving by helicopter.'

Kit frowned. 'What will his flight plan say?'

'That he's taking off from Aberdeen and landing in London. No one will know that he made an unscheduled stop at the Inverburn Flying School.'

'Good.'

'I'm glad you approve,' Nigel said with a touch of sarcasm. Kit constantly questioned him about his areas of responsibility, worried that Nigel, though experienced, was not as educated nor as intelligent as he. Nigel answered his questions with an affectation of amusement, obviously feeling that Kit, as an amateur, ought to trust him.

Elton said: 'Let's get dragged up, shall we?' He took from his bag four sets of overalls with 'Hibernian Telecom' printed on the back. They all climbed into them.

Kit said to Daisy: 'The gloves look odd with the overalls.'

'Too bad,' she said.

Kit stared at her for a few moments, then dropped his gaze. She was trouble, and he wished she were not coming tonight. He was scared of her, but he also hated her, and he was determined to put her down, both to establish his authority and by way of revenge for what she had done to him that morning. There was going to be a clash before long, and he both feared it and longed for it.

Next, Elton handed out faked identity cards that said 'Hibernian Telecom Field Maintenance Team'. Kit's card bore a photograph of an older man who looked nothing like him. The man in the picture had black hair that grew halfway over his ears in a style that had never been fashionable in Kit's lifetime, plus a heavy Zapata moustache and glasses.

Elton reached into his bag yet again and handed Kit a black wig, a black moustache, and a pair of heavy-framed glasses with tinted lenses. He also gave him a hand mirror and a small tube of glue. Kit glued the moustache to his upper lip and put on the wig. His own hair was mid-brown, and cut fashionably short. Looking in the mirror, he was satisfied that the disguise altered his appearance radically. Elton had done a good job.

Kit trusted Elton. His humour covered a ruthless efficiency. He would do whatever was necessary to finish the job, Kit thought.

Tonight Kit planned to avoid anyone among the guards who had been employed at the Kremlin when he had been there. However, if he had to speak to them, he felt confident they would not recognize him. He had taken off his distinctive jewellery, and he would change his voice.

Elton also had disguises for Nigel, Daisy, and himself. They were not known to anyone at the Kremlin, so they were in no danger of being recognized immediately; but later the security guards would describe the intruders to the police, and the disguises would ensure that those descriptions bore no relation to their actual faces.

Nigel also had a wig, Kit saw. Nigel's own hair was sandy-coloured and short, but his wig was mid-grey and chin-length, making the casually elegant Londoner look like an ageing Beatle. He also had glasses with unfashionably large frames.

Daisy had a long blonde wig over her shaved head. Tinted contact lenses turned her eyes from brown to bright blue. She was even more hideous than usual. Kit had often wondered about her sex life. He had once met someone who claimed to have slept with her, but all the man would say about it was: 'I've still got the bruises.' As Kit looked, she removed the steel rings that pierced her eyebrow, her nose, and her lower lip. She looked only a little less weird.

Elton's own disguise was the most subtle. All he had was a set of false teeth that gave him an overbite – but he looked completely different. The handsome dude had gone, and in his place was a nerd.

Finally, he gave them all baseball caps with 'Hibernian Telecom' printed on them. 'Most of those security cameras are placed high,' he explained. 'A cap with a long peak will make sure they don't get a good shot of your face.'

They were ready. There was a moment of silence while they looked at one another. Then Nigel said: 'Showtime.'

They left the control tower and went down the stairs to the hangar. Elton got into the driving seat of the van. Daisy jumped in next to him. Nigel took the third seat. There was no more room in the front: Kit would have to sit on the floor in the back with the tools.

As he stared at them, wondering what to do, Daisy

edged close to Elton and put a hand on his knee. 'Do you fancy blondes?' she said.

He stared ahead expressionlessly. 'I'm married.'

She moved her hand up his thigh. 'I bet you fancy a white girl, for a change, though, don't you?'

'I'm married to a white girl.' He took hold of her wrist and moved her hand off his leg.

Kit decided this was the moment to deal with her. With his heart in his mouth, he said: 'Daisy, get in the back of the van.'

'Fuck off,' she replied.

'I'm not asking you, I'm telling you. Get in the back.'

'Try and make me.'

'Okay, I will.'

'Go ahead,' she said with a grin. 'I'm looking forward to this.'

'The operation is off,' Kit said. He was breathing hard, out of fear, but he made his voice calm. 'Sorry, Nigel. Goodnight, all.' He walked away from the van on shaky legs.

He got into his own car, started the engine, turned on the headlights, and waited.

He could see into the front of the van. They were arguing. Daisy was waving her arms. After a minute, Nigel got out of the van and held the door. Still Daisy argued. He went around to the back and opened the rear doors, then returned to the front.

At last, Daisy got out. She stood staring malevolently at Kit. Nigel spoke to her again. Finally she got in the back of the van and slammed the doors.

Kit returned to the van and got into the front. Elton

pulled away. drove out of the garage and stopped. Nigel closed the big hangar door and got into the van. Elton muttered: 'I hope they're right about the weather forecast. Look at this fucking snow.' They headed out through the gate.

Kit's mobile rang. He lifted the lid of his laptop. On the screen he read: 'Toni calling Kremlin.'

11:30 p.m.

Toni's mother had fallen asleep the moment they pulled out of the petrol station. Toni had stopped the car, reclined the seat, and made a pillow with a scarf. Mother slept like a baby. Toni found it odd, to be looking after her mother the way she would take care of a child. It made her feel old.

But nothing could depress her spirits after her conversation with Stanley. In his characteristic restrained style, he had declared his feelings. She hugged the knowledge to herself as she drove through the snow, mile after slow mile, to Inverburn.

Mother was fast asleep when they reached the outskirts of the town. There were still revellers about. The traffic kept the town roads clear of snow, and Toni was able to drive without feeling that at any moment the car might slide out of control. She took the opportunity to call the Kremlin, just to check in.

The call was answered by Steve Tremlett. 'Oxenford Medical.'

'This is Toni. How are things?'

'Hi, Toni. We have a slight problem, but we're dealing with it.'

Toni felt a chill. 'What problem?'

'Most of the phones are out. Only this one works, at Reception.'

'How did that happen?'

'No idea. The snow, probably.'

Toni shook her head, perplexed. 'That phone system cost hundreds of thousands of pounds. It shouldn't break down because of bad weather. Can we get it fixed?'

'Yes. I've called out a crew from Hibernian Telecom. They should be here in the next few minutes.'

'What about the alarms?'

'I don't know whether they're functional or not.'

'Damn. Have you told the police?'

'Yes. A patrol car dropped in earlier. The officers had a bit of a look around, didn't see anything untoward. They've left now, gone to arrest Yuletide drunks in town.'

A man staggered into the road in front of Toni's car, and she swerved to avoid him. 'I can see why,' she said.

There was a pause. 'Where are you?'

'Inverburn.'

'I thought you were going to a health farm.'

'I was, but a family problem cropped up. Let me know what the repairmen find, okay? Call me on the mobile number.'

'Sure.'

Toni hung up. 'Hell,' she said to herself. First Mother, now this.

She wound her way through the web of residential streets that climbed the hillside overlooking the harbour. When she reached her building she parked, but did not get out.

She had to go to the Kremlin.

If she had been at the spa, there would have been no question of her coming back – it was too far away. But she was here in Inverburn. The journey would take a while, in this weather – an hour, at least, instead of the usual ten or fifteen minutes – but it was perfectly possible. The only problem was Mother.

Toni closed her eyes. Was it really necessary for her to go? Even if Michael Ross had been working with Animals Are Free, it seemed unlikely that they could be behind the failure of the phone system. It could not easily be sabotaged. On the other hand, she would have said yesterday that it was impossible to smuggle a rabbit out of BSL4.

She sighed. There was only one decision she could make. Bottom line, the security of the laboratories was her responsibility, and she could not stay at home and go to bed while something strange was going on at Oxenford Medical.

Mother could not be left alone, and Toni could not ask neighbours to look after her at this hour. Mother would just have to come along to the Kremlin.

As she put the gearshift into first, a man got out of a light-coloured Jaguar saloon parked a few cars farther along the kerb. There was something familiar about him, she thought, and she hesitated to pull away. He walked along the pavement towards her. By his gait she judged that he was slightly tipsy, but in control. He came to her window and she recognized Carl Osborne, the television presenter. He was carrying a small bundle.

She put the gearshift back into neutral and wound

down the window. 'Hello, Carl,' she said. 'What are you doing here?'

'Waiting for you. I was ready to give up.'

Mother woke up and said: 'Hello, is this your boyfriend?'

'This is Carl Osborne, and he's not my boyfriend.'

With her usual tactless accuracy, Mother said: 'Perhaps he'd like to be.'

Toni turned to Carl, who was grinning. 'This is my mother, Kathleen Gallo.'

'A privilege to meet you, Mrs Gallo.'

'Why were you waiting for me?' Toni asked him.

'I brought you a present,' he said, and he showed her what was in his hand. It was a puppy. 'Merry Christmas,' he said, and tipped it into her lap.

'Carl, for God's sake, don't be ridiculous!' She picked up the furry bundle and tried to give it back.

He stepped away and held up his hands. 'He's yours!'

The little dog was soft and warm in her hands, and part of her wanted to hold it close, but she knew she had to get rid of it. She got out of the car. 'I don't want a pet,' she said firmly. 'I'm a single woman with a demanding job and an elderly mother, and I can't give a dog the care and attention it needs.'

'You'll find a way. What are you going to call him? Carl is a nice name.'

She looked at the pup. It was an English sheepdog, white with grey patches, about eight weeks old. She could hold it in one hand, just. It licked her with a rough tongue and gave her an appealing look. She hardened her heart.

She walked to his car and put the puppy gently down

on the front seat. 'You name him,' she said. 'I've got too much on my plate.'

'Well, think about it,' he said, looking disappointed. 'I'll keep him tonight, and call you tomorrow.'

She got back into her car. 'Don't call me, please.' She put the stick into first.

'You're a hard woman,' he said as she pulled away.

For some reason, that jibe got to her. I'm not hard, she thought. Unexpected tears came to her eyes. I've had to deal with the death of Michael Ross, and a rabid pack of reporters, and I've been called a bitch by Kit Oxenford, and my sister has let me down, and I've cancelled the holiday I was looking forward to. I take responsibility for myself and for Mother and for the Kremlin, and I can't manage a puppy as well, and that's flat.

Then she remembered Stanley, and she realized she did not care a hoot what Carl Osborne said.

She rubbed her eyes with the back of her hand and peered ahead into the swirling snowflakes. Turning out of her Victorian street, she headed for the main road out of town.

Mother said: 'Carl seems nice.'

'He's not very nice, actually, Mother. In fact he's shallow and dishonest.'

'Nobody's perfect. There can't be many eligible men of your age.'

'Almost none.'

'You don't want to end up alone.'

Toni smiled to herself. 'Somehow I don't think I will.'

The traffic thinned out as she left the town centre, and the snow lay thick on the road. Manoeuvring carefully through a series of roundabouts, she noticed a car close on her tail. Looking in the rear-view mirror, she identified it as a light-coloured Jaguar saloon.

Carl Osborne was following her.

She pulled over, and he stopped right behind her.

She got out and went to his window. 'What now?'

'I'm a reporter, Toni,' he said. 'It's almost midnight on Christmas Eve, and you're looking after your elderly mother, yet you're in your car and you seem to be heading for the Kremlin. This has to be a story.'

'Oh, shit,' said Toni.

CHRISTMAS DAY

Midnight

The Kremlin looked like something from a fairy tale, with snow falling thickly around its floodlit roofs and towers. As the van with 'Hibernian Telecom' on its side approached the main gate, Kit had a momentary fancy that he was the Black Knight riding up to besiege the place.

He felt relieved to get here. The storm was turning into a full-scale blizzard, contrary to the forecast, and the journey from the airfield had taken longer than expected. The delay made him fearful. Every minute that passed made it more likely that snags would threaten his elaborate plan.

The phone call from Toni Gallo worried him. He had put her through to Steve Tremlett, fearing that if he played her a fault message she might drive to the Kremlin to find out what was going on. But having listened in to the conversation, Kit thought she might do that anyway. It was lousy bad luck that she was in Inverburn, instead of at a spa fifty miles away.

The first of the two barriers lifted, and Elton moved the van forward and drew level with the gatehouse. There were two guards in the booth, as Kit expected. Elton wound down the window. A guard leaned out and said: 'We're glad to see you laddies.'

Kit did not know the man but, recalling his conversation with Hamish, he realized it must be Willie Crawford. Looking past him, Kit saw Hamish himself.

Willie said: 'It's good of you to come out at Christmas.'

'All part of the job,' Elton said.

'Three of you, is it?'

'Plus Goldilocks in the back.'

A low snarl came from behind. 'Watch your mouth, shitface.'

Kit suppressed a groan. How could they squabble at such a crucial moment?

Nigel murmured: 'Knock it off, you two.'

Willie did not appear to have heard the exchange. He said: 'I need to see identification for everyone, please.'

They all took out their fake cards. Elton had based them on Kit's recollection of what the Hibernian Telecom pass looked like. The phone system rarely broke down, so Kit had figured no guard was likely to remember what a genuine pass looked like. Now, with a security guard scrutinizing the cards as if they were dubious fifty-pound notes, Kit held his breath.

Willie wrote down the names from each card. Then he handed them back without comment. Kit looked away and allowed himself to breathe again.

'Drive to the main entrance,' Willie said. 'You'll be all right if you stay between the lampposts.' The road ahead was invisible, covered with snow. 'At Reception you'll find a Mr Tremlett who can tell you where to go.'

The second barrier lifted, and Elton pulled forward.

They were inside.

Kit felt sick with fear. He had broken the law before,

with the scam that got him fired, but that had not felt like crime, it was more like cheating at cards, something he had done since he was eleven years old. This was a straightforward burglary, and he could go to jail. He swallowed hard and tried to concentrate. He thought of the enormous sum he owed Harry Mac. He remembered the blind terror he had felt this morning, when Daisy held his head under water and he thought he was dying. He had to go through with this.

Nigel said quietly to Elton: 'Try not to aggravate Daisy.'

'It was just a joke,' Elton said defensively.

'She's got no sense of humour.'

If Daisy heard, she did not respond.

Elton parked at the main entrance and they got out. Kit carried his laptop. Nigel and Daisy took toolboxes from the back of the van. Elton had an expensive-looking burgundy leather briefcase, very slim with a brass catch – typical of his taste, but a bit odd for a telephone repairman, Kit thought.

They passed between the stone lions of the porch and entered the Great Hall. Low security lights intensified the church-like look of the Victorian architecture: the mullioned windows, the pointed arches, and the serried timbers of the roof. The dimness made no difference to the security cameras, which – Kit knew – worked by infrared light.

At the modern reception desk in the middle of the hall were two more guards. One was an attractive young woman Kit did not recognize, and the other was Steve Tremlett. Kit hung back, not wanting Steve to look at him too closely. 'You'll want to access the central processing unit,' Steve said.

Nigel answered. 'That's the place to start.'

Steve raised his eyebrows at the London accent, but made no comment. 'Susan will show you the way – I need to stay by the phone.'

Susan had short hair and a pierced eyebrow. She wore a shirt with epaulettes, a tie, dark serge uniform trousers, and black lace-up shoes. She gave them a friendly smile and led them along a corridor panelled in dark wood.

A weird calm seemed to descend on Kit. He was inside, being escorted by a security guard, about to rob the place. He felt fatalistic. The cards had been dealt, he had placed his bet, there was nothing to do now but play out his hand, win or lose.

They entered the control room.

The place was cleaner and tidier than Kit remembered, with all cables neatly stowed, and log books in a row on a shelf. He presumed that was Toni's influence. Here also there were two guards instead of one. They sat at the long desk, watching the monitors. Susan introduced them as Don and Stu. Don was a dark-skinned south Indian with a thick Glasgow accent, and Stu was a freckled redhead. Kit did not recognize either one. An extra guard was no big deal, Kit told himself: just another pair of eyes to shield things from, another brain to be distracted, another person to be lulled into apathy.

Susan opened the door to the equipment room. 'The CPU is in there.'

A moment later Kit was inside the inner sanctum. Just like that! he thought, although it had taken weeks of preparation. Here were the computers and other devices that ran not just the phone system but also the lighting, the security cameras, and the alarms. Even to get this far was a triumph.

He said to Susan: 'Thanks very much – we'll take it from here.'

'If there's anything you need, come to Reception,' she said, and she left.

Kit put his laptop on a shelf and connected it to the security computer. He pulled over a chair and turned his laptop so that the screen could not be seen by someone standing in the doorway. He felt Daisy's eyes on him, suspicious and malevolent. 'Go into the next room,' he said to her. 'Keep an eye on the guards.'

She glared resentfully at him for a moment, then did as he said.

Kit took a deep breath. He knew exactly what he had to do. He needed to work fast, but carefully.

First, he accessed the program that controlled the video feed from thirty-seven closed-circuit television cameras. He looked at the entrance to BSL4, which appeared normal. He checked the reception desk and saw Steve there, but not Susan. Scanning the input from other cameras, he located Susan patrolling elsewhere in the building. He noted the time.

The computer's massive memory stored the camera images for four weeks before overwriting them. Kit knew his way around the program, for he had installed it. He located the video from the cameras in BSL4 this time last night. He checked the feed, random-sampling footage, to make sure no crazy scientist had been working in the lab in the middle of the night; but all the images showed empty rooms. Good.

Nigel and Elton watched him in tense silence.

He then fed last night's images into the monitors the guards were currently watching.

Now someone could walk around BSL4 doing anything he liked without their knowing.

The monitors were fitted with biased switches that would detect equipment substitution, for example if the feed came from a separate videotape deck. However, this footage was not coming from an outside source, but direct from the computer's memory – so it did not trigger the alarm.

Kit stepped into the main control room. Daisy was slumped in a chair, wearing her leather jacket over the Hibernian Telecom overalls. Kit studied the bank of screens. All appeared normal. The dark-skinned guard, Don, looked at him with an enquiring expression. As a cover, Kit said: 'Are any of the phones in here working?'

'None,' said Don.

Along the bottom edge of each screen was a line of text giving the time and date. The time was the same on the screens that showed yesterday's footage – Kit had made sure of that. But yesterday's footage showed yesterday's date.

Kit was betting that no one ever looked at that date. The guards scanned the screens for activity; they did not read text that told them what they already knew.

He hoped he was right.

Don was wondering why the telephone repairman was so interested in the television monitors. 'Something we can do for you?' he said in a challenging tone.

Daisy grunted and stirred in her chair, like a dog sensing tension among the humans.

Kit's mobile phone rang.

He stepped back into the equipment room. The message on the screen of his laptop said: 'Kremlin calling Toni.' He guessed that Steve wanted to let Toni know that the repair team had arrived. He decided to put the call through: it might reassure Toni and discourage her from coming here. He touched a key, then listened in on his mobile.

'This is Toni Gallo.' She was in her car: Kit could hear the engine.

'Steve here, at the Kremlin. The maintenance team from Hibernian Telecom have arrived.'

'Have they fixed the problem?'

'They've just started work. I hope I didn't wake you.'

'No, I'm not in bed, I'm on my way to you.'

Kit cursed. It was what he had been afraid of.

'There's really no need,' Steve told Toni.

Kit thought: That's right!

'Probably not,' she replied. 'But I'll feel more comfortable.'

Kit thought: When will you get here?

Steve had the same thought. 'Where are you now?'

'I'm only a few miles away, but the roads are terrible, and I can't go faster than fifteen or twenty miles an hour.'

'Are you in your Porsche?'

'Yes.'

'This is Scotland, you should have bought a Land Rover.'

'I should have bought a bloody tank.'

Come on, Kit thought, how long?

Toni answered his question. 'It's going to take me at least half an hour, maybe an hour.'

They hung up, and Kit cursed under his breath.

He told himself that a visit by Toni would not be fatal. There would be nothing to warn her that a robbery was going on. Nothing should seem amiss for several days. It would appear only that there had been a problem with the phone system, and a repair team had fixed it. Not until the scientists returned to work would anyone realize that BSL4 had been burgled.

The main danger was that Toni might see through Kit's disguise. He looked completely different, he had removed his distinctive jewellery, and he could easily alter his voice, making it more Scots; but she was a sharp-nosed bitch and he could not afford to take any chances. If she showed up he would keep out of her way as much as possible, and let Nigel do the talking. All the same, the risk of something going wrong would increase tenfold.

But there was nothing he could do about it, except hurry.

His next task was to get Nigel into the lab without any of the guards seeing. The main problem here was the patrols. Once an hour, a guard from Reception made a tour of the building. The patrol followed a prescribed route, and took twenty minutes. Having passed the entrance to BSL4, the guard would not come back for an hour.

Kit had seen Susan patrolling a few minutes ago, when he connected his laptop to the surveillance program. Now he checked the feed from Reception and saw her sitting with Steve at the desk, her circuit done. Kit checked his watch. He had a comfortable thirty minutes before she went on patrol again.

Kit had dealt with the cameras in the high-security lab,

but there was still one outside the door, showing the entrance to BSL4. He called up yesterday's feed and ran the footage at double fast-forward. He needed a clear half-hour, with no one passing across the screen. He stopped at the point where the patrolling guard appeared. Beginning when the guard left the picture, he fed yesterday's images into the monitor in the next room. Don and Stu should see nothing but an empty corridor for the next hour, or until Kit returned the system to normal. The screen would show the wrong time as well as the wrong date, but once again Kit was gambling that the guards would not notice.

He looked at Nigel. 'Let's go.'

Elton stayed in the equipment room to make sure no one interfered with the laptop.

Passing through the control room, Kit said to Daisy: 'We're going to get the nanometer from the van. You stay here.' There was no such thing as a nanometer, but Don and Stu would not know that.

Daisy grunted and looked away. She was not much good at acting the part. Kit hoped the guards would simply assume she was bad-tempered.

Kit and Nigel walked quickly to BSL4. Kit waved his father's smart card in front of the scanner then pressed the forefinger of his left hand to the screen. He waited while the central computer compared the information from the screen with that on the card. He noticed that Nigel was carrying Elton's smart burgundy leather briefcase.

The light over the door remained stubbornly red. Nigel looked at Kit anxiously. Kit told himself this had to work. The chip contained the encoded details of his own fingerprint – he had checked. What could go wrong?

Then a woman's voice behind them said: 'I'm afraid you can't go in there.'

Kit and Nigel turned. Susan was standing behind them. She appeared friendly but anxious. She should have been at reception, Kit thought in a panic. She was not due to patrol for another thirty minutes . . .

Unless Toni Gallo had doubled the patrols as well as doubling the guard.

There was a chime like a doorbell. All three of them looked at the light over the door. It turned green, and the heavy door swung slowly open on motorized hinges.

Susan said: 'How did you open the door?' Her voice betrayed fear now.

Involuntarily, Kit looked down at the stolen card in his hand.

Susan followed his gaze. 'You're not supposed to have a pass!' she said incredulously.

Nigel moved towards her.

She turned on her heel and ran.

Nigel went after her, but he was twice her age. He'll never catch her, Kit thought. He let out a shout of rage: how could everything go so wrong, so quickly?

Then Daisy emerged from the passage leading to the control room.

Kit would not have thought he would ever be glad to see her ugly face.

She seemed unsurprised at the scene that confronted her: the guard running towards her, Nigel following, Kit frozen to the spot. Kit realized that she must have been watching the monitors in the control room. She would have seen Susan leave the reception desk and walk towards

BSL4. She had realized the danger and moved to deal with it.

Susan saw Daisy and hesitated, then ran on, apparently determined to push past.

The hint of a smile touched Daisy's lips. She drew back her arm and smashed her gloved fist into Susan's face. The blow made a sickening sound, like a melon dropped on a tiled floor. Susan collapsed as if she had run into a wall. Daisy rubbed her knuckles, looking pleased.

Susan got to her knees. Sobs bubbled through the blood covering her nose and mouth. Daisy took from the pocket of her jacket a flexible cosh about nine inches long and made, Kit guessed, of steel ballbearings in a leather case. She raised her arm.

Kit shouted: 'No!'

Daisy hit Susan over the head with the cosh. The guard collapsed soundlessly.

Kit yelled: 'Leave her!'

Daisy raised her arm to hit Susan again, but Nigel stepped forward and grabbed her wrist. 'No need to kill her,' he said.

Daisy stepped back reluctantly.

'You mad cow!' Kit cried. 'We'll all be guilty of murder!'

Daisy looked at the light-brown glove on her right hand. There was blood on the knuckles. She licked it off thoughtfully.

Kit stared at the unconscious woman on the floor. The sight of her crumpled body was sickening. 'This wasn't supposed to happen!' he said in alarm. 'Now what are we going to do with her?'

Daisy straightened her blonde wig. 'Tie her up and hide her somewhere.'

Kit's brain began to come back on line after the shock of sudden violence. 'Right,' he said. 'We'll put her inside BSL4. The guards aren't allowed in there.'

Nigel said to Daisy: 'Drag her inside. I'll find something to tie her up with.' He stepped into a side office.

Kit's mobile phone rang. He ignored it.

Kit used his card to reopen the door, which had closed automatically. Daisy picked up a red fire extinguisher and used it to prop the door open. Kit said: 'You can't do that, it will set off the alarm.' He removed the extinguisher.

Daisy looked sceptical. 'The alarm goes off if you prop a door open?'

'Yes!' Kit said impatiently. 'There are air-management systems here. I know, I put the alarms in myself. Now shut up and do as you're told!'

Daisy got her arms around Susan's chest and pulled her along the carpet. Nigel emerged from the office with a long power lead. They all passed into BSL4. The door closed behind them.

They were in a small lobby leading to the changing rooms. Daisy propped Susan against the wall underneath a pass-through autoclave that permitted sterilized items to be removed from the lab. Nigel tied her hands and feet with the electrical lead.

Kit's phone stopped ringing.

The three of them went outside. No pass was needed to exit: the door opened at the push of a green button set into the wall.

Kit was trying desperately to think ahead. His entire

plan was ruined. There was no possibility now that the theft would remain undiscovered. 'Susan will be missed quite soon,' he said, making himself keep calm. 'Don and Stuart will notice that she's disappeared off the monitors. And even if they don't, Steve will be alerted when she fails to return from her patrol. Either way, we don't have time to get into the laboratory and out again before they raise the alarm. Shit, it's all gone wrong!'

'Calm down,' Nigel said. 'We can handle this, so long as you don't panic. We just have to deal with the other guards, like we dealt with her.'

Kit's phone rang again. He could not tell who was calling without his computer. 'It's probably Toni Gallo,' he said. 'What do we do if she shows up? We can't pretend nothing's wrong if all the guards are tied up!'

'We'll just deal with her as and when she arrives.'

Kit's phone kept ringing.

0:30 a.m.

Toni was driving at ten miles an hour, leaning forward over the steering wheel to peer into the blinding snowfall, trying to see the road. Her headlights did nothing but illuminate a cloud of big, soft snowflakes that seemed to fill the universe. She had been staring so long that her eyelids hurt, as if she had got soap in her eyes.

Her mobile became a hands-free car phone when slotted into a cradle on the dashboard of the Porsche. She had dialled the Kremlin, and now she listened as it rang out unanswered.

'I don't think anyone's there,' Mother said.

The repairmen must have downed the entire system, Toni thought. Were the alarms working? What if something serious went wrong while the lines were down? Feeling troubled and frustrated, she touched a button to end the call.

'Where are we?' Mother asked.

'Good question.' Toni was familiar with this road but she could hardly see it. She seemed to have been driving for ever. She glanced to the side from time to time, looking for landmarks. She thought she recognized a stone cottage with a distinctive wrought-iron gate. It was only a couple of miles from the Kremlin, she recalled. That cheered her up. 'We'll be there in fifteen minutes, Mother,' she said.

She looked in the rear-view mirror and saw the headlights that had been with her since Inverburn: the pest Carl Osborne in his Jaguar, doggedly following her at the same sluggardly pace. On another day she would have enjoyed losing him.

Was she wasting her time? Nothing would please her more than to reach the Kremlin and find everything calm: the phones repaired, the alarms working, the guards bored and sleepy. Then she could go home and go to bed and think about seeing Stanley tomorrow.

At least she would enjoy the look on Carl Osborne's face when he realized he had driven for hours in the snow, at Christmas, in the middle of the night, to cover the story of a telephone fault.

She seemed to be on a straight stretch, and she chanced speeding up. But it was not straight for long, and almost immediately she came to a right-hand bend. She could not use the brakes, for fear of skidding, so she changed down a gear to slow the car, then held her foot steady on the throttle as she turned. The tail of the Porsche wanted to break free, she could feel it, but the wide rear tyres held their grip.

Headlights appeared coming towards her, and for a welcome change she could make out a hundred yards of road between the two cars. There was not much to see: snow eight or nine inches thick on the ground, a drystone wall on her left, a white hill on her right.

The oncoming car was travelling quite fast, she noted nervously.

She recalled this stretch of road. It was a long, wide bend that turned through ninety degrees around the foot of the hill. She held her line through the curve.

But the other car did not.

She saw it drift across the carriageway to the crown of the road, and she thought: Fool, you braked into the turn, and your back slipped away.

In the next instant, she realized with horror that the car was heading straight for her.

It crossed the middle of the road and came at her broadside. It was a hot hatch with four men in it. They were laughing and, in the split second for which she could see them, she divined that they were young merrymakers too drunk to realize the danger they were in. 'Look out!' she screamed uselessly.

The front of the Porsche was about to smash into the side of the skidding hatchback. Toni acted reflexively. Without thinking about it, she jerked her steering wheel to the left. The nose of her car turned. Almost simultaneously, she pushed down the accelerator pedal. The car leaped forward and skidded. For an instant the hatchback was alongside her, inches away.

The Porsche was angled left and sliding forward. Toni swung the wheel right to correct the skid, and applied a featherlight touch to the throttle. The car straightened up and the tyres gripped.

She thought the hatchback would hit her rear wing; then she thought it would miss by a hair; then there was a clang, loud but superficial-sounding, and she realized her bumper had been hit.

It was not much of a blow, but it destabilized the

Porsche, and the rear swung left, out of control again. Toni desperately tugged the steering wheel to the left, turning into the skid; but, before her corrective action could take effect, the car hit the drystone wall at the side of the road. There was a terrific bang, and the sound of breaking glass; then the car came to a stop.

Toni looked worriedly at her mother. She was staring ahead, mouth open, bewildered – but unharmed. Toni felt a moment of relief – then she thought of Osborne.

She looked fearfully in the rear-view mirror, thinking the hatchback must smash into Osborne's Jaguar. She could see the red rear lights of the hatch and the white headlights of the Jag. The hatchback fishtailed; the Jag swung hard over to the side of the road; the hatchback straightened up and went by.

The Jaguar came to a stop, and the car full of drunk boys went on into the night. They were probably still laughing.

Mother said in a shaky voice: 'I heard a bang – did that car hit us?'

'Yes,' Toni said. 'We had a lucky escape.'

'I think you should drive more carefully,' said Mother.

0:35 a.m.

Kit was fighting down panic. His brilliant plan had collapsed in ruins. Now there was no way the robbery would go undetected, as he had planned, until the staff returned to work after the holiday. At most, it might remain a secret until six o'clock this morning, when the next shift of security guards arrived. But if Toni Gallo was still on her way here, the time left was even shorter.

If his plan had worked, there would have been no violence. Even now, he thought with helpless frustration, it was not strictly necessary. The guard Susan could have been captured and tied up without injury. Unfortunately, Daisy could not resist an opportunity for brutality. Kit hoped desperately that the other guards could be rounded up without further nauseating scenes of bloodshed.

Now, as they ran to the control room, both Nigel and Daisy drew guns.

Kit was horrified. 'We agreed no weapons!' he protested.

'Good thing we ignored you,' Nigel replied.

They came to the door. Kit stared aghast at the guns. They were small automatic pistols with fat grips. 'This makes it armed robbery, you realize that.'

'Only if we're caught.' Nigel turned the handle and kicked the door open.

Daisy burst into the room, yelling at the top of her voice: 'On the floor! Now! Both of you!'

There was only a moment's hesitation, while the two security guards went through shock and bewilderment to fear; then they threw themselves down.

Kit felt powerless. He had intended to enter the room first, and say: 'Please stay calm and do as you're told, then you won't get hurt.' But he had lost control. There was nothing he could do, now, but string along and try to make sure nothing else went wrong.

Elton appeared in the doorway of the equipment room. He took in the scene in an instant.

Daisy screamed at the guards: 'Face down, hands behind your backs, eyes closed! Quick, quick, or I'll shoot you in the balls!'

They did as she said but, even so, she kicked Don in the face with a heavy boot. He cried out and flinched away, but remained prone.

Kit placed himself in front of Daisy. 'Enough!' he shouted.

Elton shook his head in amazement. 'She's loony fucking tunes.'

The gleeful malevolence on Daisy's face frightened Kit, but he forced himself to stare at her. He had too much at stake to let her ruin everything. 'Listen to me!' he shouted. 'You're not in the lab yet, and you won't ever get there at this rate. If you want to be empty-handed when we meet the client at ten, just carry on the way you are.' She turned away from his pointing finger, but he went after her. 'No more brutality!'

Nigel backed him. 'Ease up, Daisy,' he said. 'Do as he says. See if you can tie these two up without kicking their heads in.'

Kit said: 'We'll put them in the same place as the girl.'

Daisy tied their hands with electrical cable, then she and Nigel herded them out at gunpoint. Elton stayed behind, watching the monitors, keeping an eye on Steve in Reception. Kit followed the prisoners to BSL4 and opened the door. They put Don and Stu on the floor next to Susan and tied their feet. Don was bleeding from a nasty cut on his forehead. Susan seemed conscious but groggy.

'One left,' said Kit as they stepped outside. 'Steve, in the Great Hall. And no unnecessary violence!'

Daisy gave a grunt of disgust.

Nigel said: 'Kit, try not to say any more in front of the guards about the client and our ten o'clock rendezvous. If you tell them too much, we may have to kill them.'

Kit realized aghast what he had done. He felt a fool.

His phone rang.

'That might be Toni,' he said. 'Let me check.' He ran back to the equipment room. His laptop screen said: 'Toni calling Kremlin.' He transferred the call to the phone on the desk at Reception, and listened in.

'Hi, Steve, this is Toni. Any news?'

'The repair crew are still here.'

'Everything all right otherwise?'

With the phone to his ear, Kit stepped into the control room and stood behind Elton to watch Steve on the monitor. 'Yeah, I think so. Susan Mackintosh should have finished her patrol by now, but maybe she went to the ladies' room.'

Kit cursed.

Toni said anxiously. 'How late is she?'

On the monitor, in black-and-white, Steve checked his wristwatch. 'Five minutes.'

'Give her another five minutes, then go and look for her.'

'Okay. Where are you?'

'Not far away, but I've had an accident. A car full of drunks clipped the rear end of the Porsche.'

Kit thought: I wish they'd killed you.

Steve said: 'Are you okay?'

'Fine, but my car's damaged. Fortunately, another car was following me, and he's giving me a lift.'

And who the hell was that? 'Shit,' Kit said aloud. 'Her and some fellow.'

'When will you be here?'

'Twenty minutes, maybe thirty.'

Kit's knees went weak. He staggered and sat in one of the guard's chairs. Twenty minutes – thirty at the most! It took twenty minutes to get suited up for BSL4!

Toni said goodbye and hung up the phone.

Kit ran across the control room and out into the corridor. 'She'll be here in twenty or thirty minutes,' he said. 'And there's someone with her, I don't know who. We have to move fast.'

They ran along the corridor. Daisy, going first, burst into the Great Hall and yelled: 'On the floor – now!'

Kit and Nigel ran in after her and stopped abruptly. The room was empty. 'Shit,' said Kit.

Steve had been at the desk twenty seconds ago. He could not have gone far. Kit looked around the half-dark room, at the chairs for waiting visitors, the coffee table with science magazines, the rack of leaflets about Oxenford Medical's work, the display case with models of complex molecules. He stared up into the dimly lit skeleton of the hammer-beam roof, as if Steve might be hiding among the timber ribs.

Nigel and Daisy ran along radiating corridors, opening doors.

Kit's eye was caught by two stick figures, male and female, on a door: the toilets. He ran across the hall. There was a short corridor leading to separate men's and ladies' rooms. Kit went into the men's room.

It appeared empty. 'Mr Tremlett?' He pushed open all the cubicle doors. No one was there.

As he stepped out, he saw Steve returning to the reception desk. The guard must have been in the ladies' room – searching for Susan, Kit realized.

Steve turned around, hearing Kit. 'Looking for me?'

'Yes.' Kit realized he could not apprehend Steve without help. Kit was younger, and athletic, but Steve was a fit man in his thirties, and might not give up without a fight. 'Something I need to ask you,' Kit said, playing for time. He made his accent more Scots than was natural, to make sure Steve did not find his voice familiar.

Steve lifted the flap and entered the oval of the desk. 'And what would that be?'

'Just a minute.' Kit turned away and shouted after Nigel and Daisy. 'Hey! Back in here!'

Steve looked troubled. 'What's going on? You lot aren't supposed to be wandering around the building.'

'I'll explain in a minute.'

Steve looked hard at him and frowned. 'Have you been here before?'

Kit swallowed. 'No, never.'

'There's something familiar about you.'

Kit's mouth went dry and he found it hard to speak. 'I work with the emergency team.' Where were the others?

'I don't like this.' Steve picked up the phone on the desk.

Where were Nigel and Daisy? Kit shouted again: 'Get back in here, you two!'

Steve dialled, and the mobile in Kit's pocket rang. Steve heard it. He frowned, thinking, then a look of shocked understanding came over his face. 'You messed with the phones!'

Kit said: 'Stay calm, and you won't get hurt.' As soon as the words were out of his mouth, he realized his mistake: he had confirmed Steve's suspicions.

Steve acted quickly. He leaped nimbly over the desk and ran for the door.

Kit yelled: 'Stop!'

Steve stumbled, fell, and got up again.

Daisy came running into the hall, saw Steve, and turned toward the main door, heading him off.

Steve saw that he could not make it to the door and turned instead into the corridor leading to BSL4.

Daisy and Kit ran after him.

Steve sprinted down the long corridor. There was an exit towards the rear of the building, Kit recalled. If Steve made it outside, they might never catch him.

Daisy was well ahead of Kit, arms pumping like a sprinter, and Kit recalled her powerful shoulders in the swimming pool; but Steve was running like a hare, and pulling away from them. He was going to escape.

Then, as Steve drew level with the door leading to the control room, Elton stepped into the corridor in front of him. Steve was going too fast to take evasive action. Elton stuck out a foot and tripped Steve, who went flying.

As Steve hit the ground, face down, Elton fell on him, with both knees in the small of his back, and pushed the barrel of a pistol into his cheek. 'Don't move, and you won't get shot in the face,' he said. His voice was calm but convincing.

Steve lay still.

Elton stood, keeping the gun pointed at Steve. 'That's the way to do it,' he said to Daisy. 'No blood.'

She looked scornful.

Nigel came running up. 'What happened?'

'Never mind!' Kit shouted. 'We're out of time!'

'What about the two guards in the gatehouse?' Nigel said.

'Forget them! They don't know what's happened here, and they're not likely to find out – they stay out there all night.' He pointed at Elton. 'Get my laptop from the equipment room and wait for us in the van.' He turned to Daisy. 'Bring Steve, tie him up in BSL4, then get into the van. We have to go into the laboratory – now!'

0:45 a.m.

In the barn, Sophie had produced a bottle of vodka.

Craig's mother had ordered lights out at midnight, but she had not come back to check, so the youngsters were sitting in front of the television set, watching an old horror movie. Craig's dopey sister, Caroline, stroked a white rat and pretended she thought the film was silly. His little cousin Tom was pigging out on chocolates and trying to stay awake. Sexy Sophie smoked cigarettes and said nothing. Craig was alternately worrying about the dented Ferrari and watching for a chance to kiss Sophie. Somehow the setting was not romantic enough. But would it get any better?

The vodka surprised him. He had thought her talk of cocktails was just showing off. But she went up the ladder to the hayloft bedroom, where her bag was, and came back down with a half-bottle of Smirnoff in her hand. 'Who wants some?' she said.

They all did.

The only glasses they had were plastic tumblers decorated with pictures of Pooh and Tigger and Eeyore. There was a fridge with soft drinks and ice. Tom and Caroline mixed their vodka with Coca-Cola. Craig, not sure what to do, copied Sophie and drank it straight with ice. The taste was bitter, but he liked the warm glow as it went down his throat.

The movie was going through a dull patch. Craig said to Sophie: 'Do you know what you're getting for Christmas?'

'Two decks and a mixer, so I can deejay. You?'

'Snowboarding holiday. Some guys I know are going to Val d'Isere at Easter, but it's expensive. I've asked for the money. So you want to be a deejay?'

'I think I'd be good at it.'

'Is that, like, your career plan?'

'Dunno.' Sophie looked scornful. 'What's your *career plan*?'

'Can't make up my mind. I'd love to play football professionally. But then you're finished before you're forty. And anyway, I might not be good enough. I'd really like to be a scientist like Grandpa.'

'A bit boring.'

'No! He discovers fantastic new drugs, he's his own boss, he makes piles of money, and he drives a Ferrari F50 – what's boring?'

She shrugged. 'I wouldn't mind the car.' She giggled. 'Except for the dent.'

The thought of the damage he had done to his grandfather's car no longer depressed Craig. He was feeling pleasantly relaxed and carefree. He toyed with the idea of kissing Sophie right now, ignoring the others. What held him back was the thought that she might reject him in front of his sister, which would be humiliating.

He wished he understood girls. No one ever told you

anything. His father probably knew all there was to know. Women seemed to take to Hugo instantly, but Craig could not figure out why, and when he asked, his father just laughed. In a rare moment of intimacy with his mother, he had asked her what attracted girls to a man. 'Kindness,' she had said. That was obviously rubbish. When waitresses and shop assistants responded to his father, grinning at him, blushing, walking away with a distinct wiggle, it was not because they thought he would be kind to them, for God's sake. But what was it? All Craig's friends had sure-fire theories about sex appeal, and they were all different. One believed that girls liked a guy to be masterful and tell them what to do; another said that if you ignored them they would flock around you; others claimed girls were interested only in an athletic physique, or good looks, or money. Craig was sure they were all wrong, but he had no hypothesis of his own.

Sophie drained her glass. 'Another?'

They all had another.

Craig began to realize that the movie was, in fact, hilarious. 'That castle is so obviously made of plywood,' he said with a chuckle.

Sophie said: 'And they all have Sixties eye make-up and hairstyles, even though it's set in the Middle Ages.'

Caroline suddenly said: 'Oh, God, I'm so sleepy.' She got to her feet, climbed the ladder with some difficulty, and disappeared.

Craig thought: One down, one to go. Maybe the scene could turn romantic after all.

The old witch in the story had to bathe in the blood of a virgin to make herself young again. The bathtub scene was a hilarious combination of titillation and gross-out, and both Craig and Sophie giggled helplessly.

'I'm going to be sick,' said Tom.

'Oh, no!' Craig sprang to his feet. He felt dizzy for a second, then recovered. 'Bathroom, quick,' he said. He took Tom's arm and led him there.

Tom started to throw up a fatal second before he reached the toilet.

Craig ignored the mess on the floor and guided him to the bowl. Tom puked some more. Craig held the boy's shoulders and tried not to breathe. There goes the romantic atmosphere, he thought.

Sophie came to the door. 'Is he all right?'

'Yeah.' Craig put on the air of a snooty schoolteacher. 'An injudicious combination of chocolates, vodka, and virgin's blood.'

Sophie laughed. Then, to Craig's surprise, she grabbed a length of toilet roll, got down on her knees, and began to clean the tiled floor.

Tom straightened up.

'All done?' Craig asked him.

Tom nodded.

'Sure?'

'Sure.'

Craig flushed the toilet. 'Now clean your teeth.'

'Why?'

'So you won't smell so bad.'

Tom brushed his teeth.

Sophie threw a wad of paper into the toilet and took some more.

Craig led Tom out of the bathroom to his camp bed on

the floor. 'Get undressed,' he said. He opened Tom's small suitcase and found a pair of Spiderman pyjamas. Tom put them on and climbed into bed. Craig folded his clothes.

'I'm sorry I heaved,' Tom said.

'It happens to the best of us,' Craig said. 'Forget it.' He pulled the blanket up to Tom's chin. 'Sweet dreams.'

He returned to the bathroom. Sophie had cleaned up with surprising efficiency, and she was pouring disinfectant into the bowl. Craig washed his hands, and she stood beside him at the sink and did the same. It felt comradely.

In a low, amused voice, Sophie said: 'When you told him to brush his teeth, he asked why.'

Craig grinned at her in the mirror. 'Like, he wasn't planning to kiss anyone tonight, so why bother?'

'Right.'

She looked the most beautiful she had all day, Craig thought as she smiled at him in the mirror, her dark eyes sparkling with amusement. He took a towel and handed her one end. They both dried their hands. Craig pulled the towel, drawing her to him, and kissed her lips.

She kissed him back. He parted his lips a little, and let her feel the tip of his tongue. She seemed tentative, unsure how to respond. Could it be that, for all her talk, she had not done much kissing?

He murmured: 'Shall we go back to the couch? I never like snogging in the bog.'

She giggled and led the way out.

Craig thought: I'm not this witty when I'm sober.

He sat close to Sophie on the couch and put his arm around her. They watched the film for a minute, then he kissed her again.

0:55 a.m.

An airtight submarine door led from the changing room into the biohazard zone. Kit turned the four-spoked wheel and opened the door. He had been inside the laboratory before it was commissioned, when there were no dangerous viruses present, but he had never entered a live BSL4 facility – he was not trained. Feeling that he was taking his life in his hands, he stepped through the doorway into the shower room. Nigel followed him, carrying Elton's burgundy briefcase. Elton and Daisy were waiting outside in the van.

Kit closed the door behind them. The doors were electronically linked so that the next would not open until the last was shut. His ears popped. Air pressure was reduced in stages as you entered BSL4, so that any air leaks were inward, preventing the escape of dangerous agents.

They passed through another doorway into a room where blue plastic space suits hung from hooks. Kit took off his shoes. 'Find one your size and get into it,' he said to Nigel. 'We've got to short-cut the safety precautions.'

'I don't like the sound of that.'

Kit did not either, but they had no choice. 'The normal procedure is too long,' he said. 'You have to take off all your clothes, including underwear, even your jewellery, then put on surgical scrubs, before you suit up.' He took a suit off a hook and began to climb into it. 'Coming out takes even longer. You have to shower in your suit, first with a decontamination solution, then with water, on a predetermined cycle that takes five minutes. Then you take off the suit and your scrubs and shower naked for five minutes. You clean your nails, blow your nose, clear your throat and spit. Then you get dressed. If we do all that, half the Inverburn police could be here by the time we get out. We'll skip the showers, take off our suits and run.'

Nigel was appalled. 'How dangerous is it?'

'Like driving your car at a hundred and thirty miles an hour – it might kill you, but it probably won't, so long as you don't make a habit of it. Hurry up, get a damn suit on.' Kit closed his helmet. The plastic faceplate gave slightly distorted vision. He closed the diagonal zip across the front of the suit, then helped Nigel.

He decided they could do without the usual surgical gloves. He used a roll of duct tape to attach the suit gauntlets to the rigid circular wrists of Nigel's suit, then got Nigel to do the same for him.

From the suit room they stepped into the decontamination shower, a cubicle with spray faucets on all sides as well as above. They felt a further drop in air pressure – 25 or 50 pascals from one room to the next, Kit recalled. From the shower they entered the lab proper.

Kit suffered a moment of pure fear. There was something in the air here that could kill him. All his glib talk about shortcutting safety precautions and driving at a hundred and thirty now seemed foolhardy. I could die, he thought. I could catch a disease and suffer a haemorrhage so bad the blood would come out of my ears and eyes and my penis. *What am I doing here? How could I be so stupid?*

He breathed slowly and made himself calm. *You're not exposed to the atmosphere here in the lab, you'll be breathing pure air from outside,* he told himself. *No virus can penetrate this suit. You're a lot safer from infection than you would be in economy class on a packed 747 to Orlando. Get a grip.*

Curly yellow air hoses dangled from the ceiling. Kit grabbed one and connected it to the inlet on Nigel's belt, and saw Nigel's suit begin to inflate. He did the same for himself, and heard the inward rush of air. His terror abated.

A row of rubber boots stood by the door, but Kit ignored them. Their main purpose was to protect the feet of the suits and prevent them wearing out.

He surveyed the lab, getting his bearings, trying to forget the danger and concentrate on what he had to do. The place had a shiny look due to the epoxy paint used to make the walls airtight. Microscopes and computer work stations stood on stainless-steel benches. There was a fax machine for sending your notes out – paper could not be taken into the showers or passed through the autoclaves. Kit noted fridges for storing samples, biosafety cabinets for handling hazardous materials, and a rack of rabbit cages under a clear plastic cover. The red light over the door would flash when the phone rang, as it was difficult to hear inside the suits. The blue light would warn of an emergency. Closed-circuit television cameras covered every corner of the room.

Kit pointed to a door. 'I think the vault is through

there.' He crossed the room, his air hose extending as he moved. He opened the door on a room no bigger than a closet containing an upright refrigerator with a keypad combination lock. The LED keys were scrambled, so that the order of numbers in the squares was different every time. This made it impossible to figure out the code by watching someone's fingers. But Kit had installed the lock, so he knew the combination – unless it had been changed.

He keyed the numbers and pulled the handle.

The door opened.

Nigel looked over his shoulder.

Measured doses of the precious antiviral drug were kept in disposable syringes, ready for use. The syringes were packaged in small cardboard boxes. Kit pointed to the shelf. He raised his voice so that Nigel could hear him through the suit. 'This is the drug.'

Nigel said: 'I don't want the drug.'

Kit wondered if he had misheard. 'What?' he shouted.

'I don't want the drug.'

Kit was astounded. 'What are you talking about? Why are we here?'

Nigel did not respond.

On the second shelf were samples of various viruses ready to be used to infect laboratory animals. Nigel looked carefully at the labels, then selected a sample of Madoba-2.

Kit said: 'What the hell do you want that for?'

Without answering, Nigel took all the remaining samples of the same virus from the shelf, twelve boxes altogether.

One was enough to kill someone. Twelve could start an

epidemic. Kit would have been reluctant to touch the boxes, even wearing a biohazard suit. But what was Nigel up to?

Kit said: 'I thought you were working for one of the pharmaceutical giants.'

'I know.'

Nigel could afford to pay Kit three hundred thousand pounds for tonight's work. Kit did not know what Elton and Daisy were getting but, even if it were a smaller fee, Nigel had to be spending something like half a million. To make that worth his while, he must be getting a million from the customer, maybe two. The drug was worth that, easily. But who would pay a million pounds for a sample of a deadly virus?

As soon as Kit asked himself the question, he knew the answer.

Nigel carried the sample boxes across the laboratory and placed them in a biosafety cabinet.

A biosafety cabinet was a glass case with a slot at the front through which the scientist could put his arms in order to perform experiments. A pump ensured that the flow of air ran from outside the cabinet to inside. A perfect seal was not considered necessary when the scientist was wearing a suit.

Next, Nigel opened the burgundy leather briefcase. The top was lined with blue plastic cooler packs. Virus samples needed to be kept at low temperatures, Kit knew. The bottom half of the briefcase was filled with white polystyrene chips of the kind used to package delicate objects. Lying on the chips, like a precious jewel, was an ordinary perfume spray bottle, empty. Kit recognized the bottle. It was a brand called *Diablerie*. His sister Olga used it.

Nigel put the bottle in the cabinet. It misted over with condensation. 'They told me to turn on the air extractor,' he said. 'Where's the switch?'

'Wait!' Kit said. 'What are you doing? You have to tell me!'

Nigel found the switch and turned it on. 'The customer wants the product in deliverable form,' he said with an air of indulgent patience. 'I'm transferring the samples to the bottle here, in the cabinet, because it's dangerous to do it anywhere else.' He took the top off the perfume bottle, then opened a sample box. Inside was a clear Pyrex vial with gradation marks printed in white on its side. Working awkwardly with his gauntleted hands, Nigel unscrewed the cap of the vial and poured the liquid into the *Diablerie* bottle. He recapped the vial and picked up another one.

Kit said: 'The people you're selling this to – do you know what they want it for?'

'I can guess.'

'It will kill people – hundreds, maybe thousands!'

'I know.'

The perfume spray was the perfect delivery mechanism. It was a simple means of creating an aerosol. Filled with the colourless liquid that contained the virus, it looked completely innocent, and would pass unnoticed through all security checks. A woman could take it out of her handbag in any public place and look quite innocent as she filled the air with the vapour that would be fatal to everyone who inhaled it. She would kill herself, too – as terrorists often did. She would slaughter more people than any suicide bomber. Horrified, Kit said: 'You're talking about mass murder!'

'Yes.' Nigel turned to look at Kit. His blue eyes were intimidating even through two faceplates. 'And you're in it now, and as guilty as anyone, so shut your mouth and let me concentrate.'

Kit groaned. Nigel was right. Kit had never thought to be involved in anything more than theft. He had been horrified when Daisy coshed Susan. This was a thousand times worse – and there was nothing Kit could do. If he tried to stop the heist now, Nigel would probably kill him – and if things went wrong, and the virus was not delivered to the customer, Harry McGarry would have him killed for not paying his debt. He had to follow it through to the end and pick up his payment. Otherwise he was dead.

He also had to make sure Nigel handled the virus properly, otherwise he was dead anyway.

With his arms inside the biosafety cabinet, Nigel emptied the contents of all the sample vials into the perfume bottle, then replaced the spray-top. Kit knew that the outside of the bottle was now undoubtedly contaminated – but someone seemed to have told Nigel this, for he put the bottle into the pass-out tank, which was full of decontamination fluid, and removed it from the other side. He wiped the bottle dry then took two Ziploc food bags from the briefcase. He put the perfume bottle into one, sealed the bag, then put the bagged bottle into the second. Finally he put the double-bagged bottle back into the briefcase and closed the lid.

'We're done,' he said.

They left the lab, Nigel carrying the briefcase. They passed through the decontamination shower without using it – there was no time. In the suit room they climbed out of the cumbersome plastic space suits and put their shoes back on. Kit kept well away from Nigel's suit – the gloves were sure to be contaminated with minute traces of the virus.

They moved through the normal shower, again without using it, through the changing room and into the lobby. The four security guards were tied up and propped against the wall.

Kit checked his watch. It was thirty minutes since he had eavesdropped on Toni Gallo's conversation with Steve. 'I hope Toni isn't here.'

'If she is, we'll neutralize her.'

'She's an ex-cop – she won't be as easy to deal with as these guards. And she might recognize me, even in this disguise.'

He pressed the green button that opened the door. He and Nigel ran down the corridor and into the Great Hall. To Kit's monumental relief, it was empty: Toni Gallo had not yet arrived. We made it, he thought. But she could get here at any second.

The van was outside the main door, its engine running. Elton was at the wheel, Daisy in the back. Nigel jumped in, and Kit followed him, shouting: 'Go! Go! Go!'

Elton roared off before Kit got the door shut.

The snow lay thick on the ground. The van immediately skidded and slewed sideways, but Elton got it back under control. They stopped at the gate.

Willie Crawford leaned out. 'All fixed?' he said.

Elton wound down the window. 'Not quite,' he said. 'We need some parts. We'll be back.'

'It's going to take you a while, in this weather,' the guard said conversationally.

Kit muffled a grunt of impatience. From the back, Daisy said in a low voice: 'Shall I shoot the bastard?'

Elton said calmly: 'We'll be as quick as we can.' Then he closed the window.

After a moment the barrier lifted, and they pulled out.

As they did so, headlights flashed. A car was approaching from the south. Kit made it out to be a light-coloured Jaguar saloon.

Elton turned north and roared away from the Kremlin.

Kit looked in the mirror and watched the headlights of the car. It turned into the gates of the Kremlin.

Toni Gallo, Kit thought. A minute too late.

1:15 a.m.

Toni was in the passenger seat beside Carl Osborne when he braked to a halt alongside the gatehouse of the Kremlin. Her mother was in the back.

She handed Carl her pass and her mother's pension book. 'Give these to the guard with your press card,' she said. All visitors had to show identification.

Carl slid the window down and handed over the documents.

Looking across him, Toni saw Hamish McKinnon. 'Hi, Hamish, it's me,' she called. 'I've got two visitors with me.'

'Hello, Ms Gallo,' said the guard. 'Is that lady in the back holding a dog?'

'Don't ask,' she said.

Hamish copied the names and handed back the press card and the pension book. 'You'll find Steve in Reception.'

'Are the phones working?'

'Not yet. The repair crew just left to fetch a spare part.' He lifted the barrier, and Carl drove in.

Toni suppressed a wave of irritation at Hibernian Telecom. On a night such as this, they really should carry all the parts they might need. The weather was continuing to get worse, and the roads might soon be impassable. She doubted they would be back before morning.

This spoiled a little plan she had. She had been hoping to phone Stanley in the morning and tell him that there had been a minor problem at the Kremlin overnight but she had solved it – then make arrangements to meet him later in the day. Now it seemed her report might not be so satisfactory.

Carl pulled up at the main entrance. 'Wait here,' Toni said, and sprang out before he could argue. She did not want him in the building if she could avoid it. She ran up the steps between the stone lions and pushed through the door. She was surprised to see no one at the reception desk.

She hesitated. One of the guards might be on patrol, but they should not both have gone. They could be anywhere in the building – and the door was unguarded.

She headed for the control room. The monitors would show where the guards were.

She was astonished to find the control room empty.

Her heart seemed to go cold. This was very bad. Four guards missing – this was not just a divergence from procedure. Something was wrong.

She looked again at the monitors. They all showed empty rooms. If four guards were in the building, one of them should appear on a monitor within seconds. But there was no movement anywhere.

Then something caught her eye. She looked more closely at the feed from BSL4.

The dateline said December 24th. She checked her watch. It was after one o'clock in the morning. Today was

Christmas Day, December 25th. She was looking at old pictures. Someone had tampered with the feed.

She sat at the workstation and accessed the program. In three minutes she established that all the monitors covering BSL4 were showing yesterday's footage. She corrected them and looked at the screens.

In the lobby outside the changing rooms, four people were sitting on the floor. She stared at the monitor, horrified. Please, God, she thought, don't let them be dead.

One moved.

She looked more closely. They were guards, all in dark uniforms; and their hands were behind their backs, as if they were tied up.

'No, no!' she said aloud.

But there was no escaping the dismal conclusion that the Kremlin had been raided.

She felt doomed. First Michael Ross, now this. Where had she gone wrong? She had done all she could to make this place secure – and she had failed utterly. She had let Stanley down.

She turned for the door, her first instinct being to rush to BSL4 and untie the captives. Then her police training reasserted itself. Stop, assess the situation, plan the response. Whoever had done this could still be in the building, though her guess was that the villains were the Hibernian Telecom repairmen who had just left. What was her most important task? To make sure she was not the only person who knew about this.

She picked up the phone on the desk. It was dead, of course. The fault in the phone system was probably part of whatever was going on. She took her mobile from her pocket and called the police. 'This is Toni Gallo, in charge of security at Oxenford Medical. There's been an incident here. Four of my security guards have been attacked.'

'Are the perpetrators still on the premises?'

'I don't think so, but I can't be sure.'

'Anyone injured?'

'I don't know. As soon as I get off the phone, I'll check – but I wanted to tell you first.'

'We'll try to get a patrol car to you – though the roads are terrible.' He sounded like an unsure young constable.

Toni tried to impress him with a sense of urgency. 'This could be a biohazard incident. A young man died yesterday of a virus that escaped from here.'

'We'll do our best.'

'I believe Frank Hackett is on duty tonight. I don't suppose he's in the building?'

'He's on call.'

'I strongly recommend you phone him at home and wake him up and tell him about this.'

'I've made a note of your suggestion.'

'We have a fault on the phones here, probably caused by the intruders. Please take my mobile number.' She read it out. 'Ask Frank to call right away.'

'I've got the message.'

'May I ask your name?'

'PC David Reid.'

'Thank you, Constable Reid. We'll be waiting for your patrol car.' Toni hung up. She felt sure the constable had not grasped the importance of her call, but he would surely pass the information to a superior. Anyway, she did not have time to argue. She hurried out of the control room and ran along the corridor to BSL4. She swiped her pass through the card reader, held her fingertip to the scanner, and went in.

There were Steve, Susan, Don, and Stu, in a row against the wall, bound hand and foot. Susan looked as if she had walked into a tree: her nose was swollen and there was blood on her chin and chest. Don had a nasty abrasion on his forehead.

Toni knelt down and began to untie them. 'What the hell happened here?' she said.

1:30 a.m.

The Hibernian Telecom van was ploughing through snow a foot deep. Elton drove at ten miles an hour in high gear to keep from skidding. Thick snowflakes bombarded the vehicle. They formed two wedges at the bottom of the windscreen, and they grew steadily, so that the wipers described an ever-smaller arc, until Elton could no longer see out, and had to stop the van to clear the snow away.

Kit was distraught. He had thought himself involved in a heist that would do no real harm. His father would have lost money, but on the other hand Kit would be enabled to repay Harry Mac, a debt that his father should have paid anyway, so there was no real injustice. But the reality was different. There could be only one reason for buying Madoba-2. Someone wanted to kill large numbers of people. Kit had never thought to be guilty of this.

He wondered who Nigel's customer represented: Japanese fanatics, Muslim fundamentalists, an IRA splinter group, suicidal Palestinians, or a group of paranoid Americans with high-powered rifles living in remote mountain cabins in Montana? It hardly mattered. Whoever got the virus would use it, and crowds of people would die bleeding from their eyes.

But what could he do? If he tried to abort the heist, and take the virus samples back to the lab, Nigel would kill him, or let Daisy do it. He thought of opening the van door and jumping out. It was going slowly enough. He might disappear into the blizzard before they could catch him. But then they would still have the virus, and he would still owe Harry a quarter of a million pounds.

He had to see this through to the end. Maybe, when it was all over, he could send an anonymous message to the police, naming Nigel and Daisy, and hope that the virus could be traced before it was used. Or maybe he would be wiser to stick to his plan, and vanish. No one would want to start a plague in Lucca.

Maybe the virus would be released on his plane to Italy, and he would pay the penalty himself. There would be justice.

Peering ahead through the snowstorm, he saw an illuminated sign that read 'Motel'. Elton turned off the road. There was a light over the door, and eight or nine cars in the car park. The place was open. Kit wondered who would spend Christmas at a motel. Hindus, perhaps, and stranded businessmen, and illicit lovers.

Elton pulled up next to a Vauxhall Astra estate. 'The idea was to ditch the van here,' he said. 'It's too easily identifiable. We're supposed to go back to the airstrip in that Astra. But I don't know if we're going to make it.'

From the back, Daisy said: 'You stupid prick, why didn't you bring a Land Rover?'

'Because the Astra is one of the most popular and least noticeable cars in Britain, and the forecast said no snow, you ugly cow.'

'Knock it off, you two,' Nigel said calmly. He pulled off his wig and glasses. 'Take off your disguises. We don't know how soon those guards will be giving descriptions to the police.'

The others followed suit.

Elton said: 'We could stay here, take rooms, wait it out.'

'Dangerous,' Nigel replied. 'We're only a few miles from the lab.'

'If we can't move, the police can't either. As soon as the weather eases, we take off.'

'We have an appointment to meet our customer.'

'He's not going to fly his helicopter in this muck.'

'True.'

Kit's mobile rang. He checked his laptop. It was a regular call, not one diverted from the Kremlin system. He picked it up. 'Yeah?'

'It's me.' Kit recognized the voice of Hamish McKinnon. 'I'm on my mobile, I've got to be quick, while Willie's in the toilet.'

'What's happening?'

'She arrived just after you left.'

'I saw the car.'

'She found the other guards tied up and called the police.'

'Can they get there, in this weather?'

'They said they'd try. She just came up to the gatehouse and told us to expect them. When they'll get here— Sorry, gotta go.' He hung up.

Kit pocketed his phone. 'Toni Gallo has found the guards,' he announced. 'She's called the police, and they're on their way.'

'That settles it,' Nigel said. 'Let's get in the Astra.'

1:45 p.m.

As Craig slipped his hand under the hem of Sophie's sweater, he heard steps. He broke the clinch and looked around.

His sister was coming down from the hayloft in her nightdress. 'I feel a bit strange,' she said, and crossed the room to the bathroom.

Thwarted, Craig turned his attention to the film on TV. The old witch, transformed into a beautiful girl, was seducing a handsome knight.

Caroline emerged, saying: 'That bathroom smells of puke.' She climbed the ladder and went back to bed.

'No privacy here,' Sophie said in a low voice.

'Like trying to make love in Glasgow Central Station,' Craig said, but he kissed her again. This time, she opened her lips and her tongue met his. He was so pleased that he moaned with delight.

He put his hand all the way up inside her sweater and felt her breast. It was small and warm. She was wearing a thin cotton bra. He squeezed gently, and she gave an involuntary groan of pleasure.

Tom's voice piped: 'Will you two stop grunting? I can't sleep!'

They stopped kissing. Craig took his hand out from under her sweater. He was ready to explode with frustration. 'I'm sorry about this,' he murmured.

Sophie said: 'Why don't we go somewhere else?'

'Like, where?'

'How about that attic you showed me earlier?'

Craig was thrilled. They would be completely alone, and no one would disturb them. 'Brilliant,' he said, and he stood up.

They put on coats and boots, and Sophie pulled on a pink woolly hat with a bobble. It made her look cute and innocent. 'A bundle of joy,' Craig said.

'What is?'

'You are.'

She smiled. Earlier, she would have called him 'so boring' for saying something like that. Their relationship had changed. Maybe it was the vodka. But Craig thought the turning point had come in the bathroom, when they had dealt with Tom together. Perhaps Tom, by being a helpless child, had forced them to act like adults. After that, it was hard to revert to being sulky and cool.

Craig would never have guessed that the way to a girl's heart might be cleaning up puke.

He opened the barn door. A cold wind blew a flurry of snow over them like confetti. Craig stepped out quickly, held the door for Sophie, then closed it.

Steepfall looked impossibly romantic. Snow covered the steeply sloping roof, lay in great mounds on the windowsills, and filled the courtyard to the depth of a foot. The lanterns on the surrounding walls had haloes of golden light filled with dancing snowflakes. Snow encrusted a wheelbarrow, a stack of firewood, and a garden hose, transforming them into ice sculptures.

Sophie's eyes were wide. 'It's a Christmas card,' she said.

Craig took her hand. They crossed the courtyard with high steps, like wading birds. They rounded the corner of the house and came to the back door. Craig brushed a layer of snow off the top of a dustbin. He stood on it and heaved himself up on to the low roof of the boot lobby.

He looked back. Sophie was hesitating. 'Here!' he hissed. He held out his hand.

She grasped it and pulled herself up on to the bin. With his other hand, Craig grabbed the edge of the sloping roof, to steady himself, then helped her up beside him. For a moment they lay side by side in the snow, like lovers in bed. Then Craig got to his feet.

He stepped onto the ledge that ran below the loft door, kicked off most of the snow, and opened the big door. Then he returned to Sophie.

She got to her hands and knees but, when she tried to stand, her rubber boots slipped and she fell. She looked scared.

'Hold on to me,' Craig said, and pulled her to her feet. What they were doing was not very dangerous, and she was making more of it than she should, but he did not mind, for it gave him a chance to be strong and protective.

Still holding her hand, Craig stood on the ledge. She stepped up beside him and grabbed him around the waist. He would have liked to linger there, with her clinging to him so hard; but he went on, walking sideways along the ledge to the open door, then helped her inside.

He closed the door behind them and turned on the light. This was perfect, Craig thought excitedly. They were alone, in the middle of the night, and nobody would come in to disturb them. They could do anything they liked.

He lay down and looked through the hole in the floor into the kitchen. A single light burned over the door to the boot room. Nellie lay in front of the Aga, head up, ears cocked, listening: she knew he was there. 'Go back to sleep,' he murmured. Whether she heard him or not, the dog put her head down and closed her eyes.

Sophie was sitting on the old couch, shivering. 'My feet are freezing.'

'You've got snow in your boots.' He knelt in front of her and pulled her Wellingtons off. Her socks were soaked. He took those off, too. Her small white feet felt as if they had been in the fridge. He tried to warm them with his hands. Then, inspired, he unbuttoned his coat, lifted his sweater, and pressed the soles of her feet to his bare chest.

She said: 'Oh, my God, that feels so good.'

She had often said that to him in his fantasies, he reflected; but not in quite the same circumstances.

2:00 a.m.

Toni sat in the control room, watching the monitors.

Steve and the guards had related everything that had happened, from when the 'repair crew' entered the Great Hall up to the moment that two of them emerged from the BSL4 lab, passed through the little lobby, and vanished – one carrying a slim burgundy leather briefcase. Don had told her, while Steve gave him first aid, how one of the men had tried to stop the violence. The words he had shouted were burned into Toni's brain: *If you want to be empty-handed when we meet the client at ten, just carry on the way you are.*

Clearly, they had come here to steal something from the laboratory; and they had taken it away in that briefcase. Toni had a dreadful feeling she knew what it was.

She was running the BSL4 footage from 0:55 to 1:15. Although the monitors had not shown these images at the time, the computer had stored them. Now she was watching two men inside the lab, wearing biohazard suits.

She gasped when she saw one of them open the door to the little room that contained the vault. He tapped numbers into the keypad – he knew the code! He opened the fridge door, then the other man began to remove samples.

Toni froze the playback.

The camera was placed above the door, and looked over the man's shoulder into the refrigerator. His hands were full of small white boxes. Toni's fingers played over the keyboard, and the black-and-white picture on the monitor was enlarged. She could see the international biohazard symbol on the boxes. He was stealing virus samples. She zoomed in further, and ran the image-enhancement program. Slowly, the words on one of the boxes became clear: *Madoba-2*.

It was what she had feared, but the confirmation hit her like the cold wind of death. She sat staring at the screen, frozen with dread, her heart sounding in her chest like a funeral bell. Madoba-2 was the most deadly virus imaginable, an infectious agent so terrible that it had to be guarded by multiple layers of security, and touched only by highly trained staff in isolation clothing. And it was now in the hands of a gang of thieves who were carrying it around in a damn briefcase.

Their car might crash; they could panic and throw the briefcase away; the virus might fall into the possession of people who did not know what it was – the risks were horrendous. And even if they did not release it by accident, their 'client' would do so deliberately. Someone was planning to use the virus to murder people in hundreds and thousands, perhaps to cause a plague that might mow down entire populations.

And they had obtained the murder weapon from her.

In despair, she restarted the footage, and watched with horror while one of the intruders emptied the contents of the vials into a perfume spray marked *Diablerie*. That was obviously the delivery mechanism. The ordinary-looking perfume bottle was now a weapon of mass destruction. She watched him carefully double-bag it and place it in the briefcase, bedded in polystyrene packing chips.

She had seen enough. She knew what needed to be done. The police had to gear up for a massive operation – and fast. If they moved quickly, they could still catch the thieves before the virus was handed over to the buyer.

She returned the monitors to their default position and left the control room.

The security guards were in the Great Hall, sitting on the couches normally reserved for visitors, drinking tea, thinking the crisis was over. Toni decided to take a few seconds to regain control. 'We have important work to do,' she said briskly. 'Stu, go to the control room and resume your duties, please. Steve, get behind the desk. Don, stay where you are.' Don had a makeshift dressing over the cut on his forehead.

Susan Mackintosh, who had been coshed, was lying on a couch used by waiting visitors. The blood had been washed from her face but she was severely bruised. Toni knelt beside her and kissed her forehead. 'Poor you,' she said. 'How do you feel?'

'Pretty groggy.'

'I'm so sorry this happened.'

Susan smiled weakly. 'It was worth it for the kiss.'

Toni patted her shoulder. 'You're recovering already.'

Her mother was sitting next to Don. 'That nice boy Steven made me a cup of tea,' she said. The puppy sat on spread-out newspaper at her feet. She fed it a piece of biscuit.

'Thanks, Steve,' Toni said.

Mother said: 'He'd make a nice boyfriend for you.'

'He's married,' Toni replied.

'That doesn't seem to make much difference, nowadays.'

'It does to me.' Toni turned to Steve. 'Where's Carl Osborne?'

'Men's room.'

Toni nodded and took out her phone. It was time to call the police.

She recalled what Steve Tremlett had told her about the duty staff at Inverburn regional headquarters tonight: an inspector, two sergeants, and six constables, plus a superintendent on call. It was nowhere near enough to deal with a crisis of this magnitude. She knew what she would do, if she were in charge. She would call in twenty or thirty officers. She would commandeer snowploughs, set up roadblocks, and ready a squad of armed officers to make the arrest. And she would do it fast.

She felt invigorated. The horror of what had happened began to fade from her mind as she concentrated on what had to be done. Action always bucked her up, and police work was the best sort of action.

She got David Reid again. When she identified herself, he said: 'We sent you a car, but they turned back. The weather—'

She was horrified. She had thought a police car was on its way. 'Are you serious?' she said, raising her voice.

'Have you looked at the roads? There are abandoned cars everywhere. No point in a patrol getting stuck in the snow.'

'Christ! What kind of wimps are the police recruiting nowadays?'

'There's no need for that kind of talk, madam.'

Toni got herself under control. 'You're right, I'm sorry.' She recalled, from her training, that when the police response to a crisis went badly amiss, it was often due to wrong identification of the hazard in the first few minutes, when someone inexperienced like PC Reid was dealing with the initial report. Her first task was to make sure he had the key information to pass to his superior. 'Here's the situation. One: the thieves stole a significant quantity of a virus called Madoba-2 which is lethal to humans, so this is a biohazard emergency.'

'Biohazard,' he said, obviously writing it down.

'The perpetrators are three men – two white and one black – and a white woman. They're driving a van marked "Hibernian Telecom".'

'Can you give me fuller descriptions?'

'I'll get the guard supervisor to call you with that information in a minute – he saw them, I didn't. Three: we have two injured people here, one who has been coshed and the other kicked in the head.'

'How serious would you say the injuries are?'

She thought she had already told him that; but he seemed to be asking questions from a list. 'The guard who has been coshed should see a doctor.'

'Right.'

'Four: the intruders were armed.'

'What sort of weapons?'

Toni turned to Steve, who was a gun buff. 'Did you get a look at their firearms?'

Steve nodded. 'Nine-millimetre Browning automatic pistols, all three of them – the kind that take a thirteen-round magazine. They looked like ex-army stock to me.' Toni repeated the description to Reid.

'Armed robbery, then,' he said.

'Yes – but the important thing is that they can't be far away, and that van is easy to identify. If we move quickly, we can catch them.'

'Nobody can move quickly tonight.'

'Obviously you need snowploughs.'

'The police force doesn't have snowploughs.'

'There must be several in the area, we have to clear the roads most winters.'

'Clearing snow from roads is not a police function, it's a local-authority responsibility.'

Toni was ready to scream with frustration, but she bit her tongue. 'Is Frank Hackett there?'

'Superintendent Hackett is not available.'

She knew that Frank was on call – Steve had told her. 'If you won't wake him up, I will,' she said. She broke the connection and dialled his home number. He was a conscientious officer, he would be sleeping by the phone.

He picked it up. 'Hackett.'

'Toni. Oxenford Medical has been robbed of a quantity of Madoba-2, the virus that killed Michael Ross.'

'How did you let that happen?'

It was the question she was asking herself, but it stung when it came from him. She retorted: 'If you're so smart, figure out how to catch the thieves before they get away.'

'Didn't we send a car out to you an hour ago?'

'It never got here. Your tough coppers saw the snow and got scared.'

'Well, if we're stuck, so are our suspects.'

'You're not stuck, Frank. You can get here with a snowplough.'

'I don't have a snowplough.'

'The local council has several – phone them up.'

There was a long pause. 'I don't think so,' he said at last.

Toni could have killed him. Frank enjoyed using his authority negatively. It made him feel powerful. He especially liked defying her – she had always been too assertive for him. How had she lived with him for so long? She curbed the retort that was on the tip of her tongue and said: 'What's your thinking, Frank?'

'I can't send unarmed men chasing after a gang with guns. We'll need to assemble our firearms-trained officers, take them to the armoury, and get them kitted out with Kevlar vests, guns, and ammunition. That's going to take a couple of hours.'

'Meanwhile the thieves are getting away with a virus that could kill thousands!'

'I'll put out an alert for the van.'

'They might switch cars. They could have an off-road jeep parked somewhere.'

'They still won't get far.'

'What if they have a helicopter?'

'Toni, curb your imagination. There are no thieves with helicopters in Scotland.'

These were not local hooligans running off with jewellery or banknotes – but Frank had never really understood biohazards. 'Frank, use *your* imagination. These people want to start a plague!'

'Don't tell me how to do the job. You're not a cop any more.'

'Frank—' She stopped. He had broken the connection. 'Frank, you're a dumb bastard,' she said into the dead phone, then she hung up.

Had he always been this bad? It seemed to her that when they were living together he was more reasonable. Perhaps she had been a good influence on him. He had certainly been willing to learn from her. She recalled the case of Dick Buchan, a multiple rapist who had refused to tell Frank where the bodies were despite hours of intimidation, shouting, and threats of violence. Toni talked quietly to him about his mother, and broke him in twenty minutes. After that, Frank had asked her advice about every major interrogation. But since they split up he seemed to have regressed.

She frowned at her phone, racking her brains. How was she going to put a bomb under Frank? She had something over him – the Farmer Johnny Kirk story. If the worst came to the worst, she could use that to blackmail him. But first there was one more call she could try. She scrolled through the memory of her mobile and found the home number of Odette Cressy, her friend at Scotland Yard.

The phone was answered after a long wait. 'This is Toni,' she said. 'I'm sorry to wake you.'

Odette spoke to someone else. 'Sorry, sweetheart, it's work.'

Toni was surprised. 'I didn't expect you to be with someone.'

'It's just Santa Claus. What's new?'

Toni told her.

Odette said: 'Jesus Christ, this is what we were afraid of.'

'I can't believe I let it happen.'

'Is there anything that might give us a hint about when and how they plan to use it?'

'Two things,' Toni said. 'One: they didn't just steal the stuff – they poured it into a perfume spray. It's ready to use. The virus can be released in any crowded place – at a cinema, on a plane, in Harrods. No one would know it was happening.'

'A perfume spray?'

'*Diablerie.*'

'Well done – at least we know what we're looking for. What else?'

'A guard heard them talk about meeting the client at ten.'

'At ten. They're working fast.'

'Exactly. If they deliver the stuff to their customer by ten o'clock this morning, it could be in London tonight. They could release it in the Albert Hall tomorrow.'

'Good work, Toni. My God, I wish you'd never left the police.'

Toni began to feel more cheerful. 'Thanks.'

'Anything else?'

'They turned north when they left here – I saw their van. But there's a blizzard, and the roads are becoming impassable. So they probably aren't far from where I'm standing.'

'That means we have a chance of catching them before they deliver the goods.'

'Yes – but I haven't been able to persuade the local police of the urgency.'

'Leave that to me. Terrorism comes under the Cabinet Office. Your home-town boys are about to get a phone call from Number Ten Downing Street. What do you need – helicopters? HMS Gannet is an hour away from you.'

'Put them on standby. I don't think helicopters can fly in this blizzard, and if they could, the crew wouldn't be able to see what's on the ground. What I need is a snowplough. They should clear the road from Inverburn to here, and the police should make this their base. Then they can start looking for the fugitives.'

'I'll make sure it happens. Keep calling me, okay?'

'Thanks, Odette.' Toni hung up.

She turned around. Carl Osborne stood immediately behind her, making notes.

2:30 a.m.

Elton drove the Vauxhall Astra estate car slowly, ploughing through more than a foot of soft fresh snow. Nigel sat beside him, clutching the burgundy leather briefcase with its deadly contents. Kit was in the back with Daisy. He kept glancing over Nigel's shoulder at the briefcase, imagining a car crash in which the briefcase was crushed and the bottle smashed, and the liquid was sprayed into the air like poisoned champagne to kill them all.

He was maddened with impatience as their speed dropped to bicycle pace. He wanted to get to the airfield as fast as possible and put the briefcase in a safe place. Every minute they spent on the open road was dangerous.

But he was not sure they would get there. After leaving the car park of the Dew Drop Inn, they did not see another moving vehicle. Every mile or so they passed an abandoned car or lorry, some at the side of the road and some right in the middle. One was a police Range Rover on its side.

Suddenly a man stepped into the headlights, waving frantically. He wore a business suit and tie, and had no coat or hat. Elton glanced at Nigel, who murmured: 'Don't even dream of stopping.' Elton drove straight at the man, who dived out of the way at the last moment. As they swept by, Kit glimpsed a woman in a cocktail dress, hugging a thin shawl around her shoulders, standing beside a big Bentley, looking desperate.

They passed the turning for Steepfall, and Kit wished he was a boy again, lying in bed at his father's house, knowing nothing about viruses or computers or the odds at blackjack.

The snow became so heavy that little was visible through the windscreen but whiteness. Elton was almost blind, steering by guesswork, optimism, and glances out of the side windows. Their speed dropped to the pace of a run, then a brisk walk. Kit longed for a more suitable car. In his father's Toyota Land Cruiser Amazon, parked only a tantalizing couple of miles from where they were right now, they would have had a better chance.

On a hill, the tyres began to slip in the snow. The car gradually lost forward momentum. It came to a stop and then, to Kit's horror, began to slide back. Elton tried braking, but that only made the skid faster. He turned the steering wheel. The back swerved left. Elton spun the wheel in the opposite direction, and the car came to rest slewed at an angle across the road.

Nigel cursed.

Daisy leaned forward and said to Elton: 'What did you do that for, you pillock?'

Elton said: 'Get out and push, Daisy.'

'Screw you.'

'I mean it,' he said. 'The brow of the hill is only a few yards away. I could make it, if someone would give the car a push.'

Nigel said: 'We'll all push.'

Nigel, Daisy, and Kit got out. The cold was bitter, and the snowflakes stung Kit's eyes. They got behind the car and leaned on it. Only Daisy had gloves. The metal was bitingly cold on Kit's bare hands. Elton let the clutch out slowly, and they took the strain. Kit's feet were soaking wet in seconds. But the tyres bit. Elton pulled away from them and drove to the top of the hill.

They trudged up the slope, slipping in the snow, panting with the effort, shivering. Were they going to do this on every hill for the next ten miles?

The same thought had occurred to Nigel. When they got back into the car he said to Elton: 'Is this car going to get us there?'

'We might be all right on this road,' Elton said. 'But there's three or four miles of country lane before you get to the airfield.'

Kit made up his mind. He said: 'I know where there's a sport-utility vehicle with four-wheel drive – a Toyota Land Cruiser.'

Daisy said: 'We could get stuck in that – remember the police Range Rover we passed?'

Nigel said: 'It has to be better than an Astra. Where is this car?'

'At my father's house. To be exact, it's in his garage, the door to which is not quite visible from the house.'

'How far?'

'A mile back along this road, then another mile down a side turning.'

'What are you suggesting?'

'We park in the woods near the house, borrow the Land

Cruiser, and drive to the airfield. Afterwards, Elton brings the Land Cruiser back and takes the Astra.'

'By then it will be daylight. What if someone sees him putting the car back in your father's garage?'

'I don't know, I'll have to make up a story, but it can't be worse than getting stuck here.'

Nigel said: 'Has anyone got a better idea?'

No one did.

Elton turned the car around and went back down the hill in low gear. After a few minutes, Kit said: 'Take that side road.'

Elton pulled up. 'No way,' he said. 'Look at the snow down that lane – it's eighteen inches thick, and there's been no traffic on it for hours. We won't get fifty yards.'

Kit had the panicky feeling he got when losing at blackjack, that a higher power was dealing him all the wrong cards.

Nigel said: 'How far are we from your father's house?'

'A bit—' Kit swallowed. 'A bit less than a mile.'

Daisy said: 'It's a long way in this fucking weather.'

'The alternative,' Nigel said, 'is to wait here until a vehicle comes along then hijack it.'

'We'll wait a bloody long time,' Elton said. 'We haven't seen a moving car on this road since we left the laboratory.'

Kit said: 'You three could wait here while I go and get the Land Cruiser.'

Nigel shook his head. 'Something might happen to you. You could get stuck in the snow, and we wouldn't be able to find you. Better to stay together.'

There was another reason, Kit guessed: Nigel did not trust Kit alone. He probably feared that Kit might have second thoughts and call the police. Nothing was further from Kit's mind – but Nigel might not feel sure of that.

There was a long silence. They sat still, reluctant to leave the warmth that blasted from the car's heater. Then Elton turned off the engine and they got out.

Nigel held on tightly to the briefcase. That was the reason they were all going through this. Kit was carrying his laptop. He might still need to intercept calls to and from the Kremlin. Elton found a torch on the glove box and gave it to Kit. 'You're leading the way,' he said.

Without further discussion Kit headed off, ploughing through snow up to his knees. He heard grunts and curses from the others, but he did not look back. They would keep up with him or get left behind.

It was painfully cold. None of them was dressed for this. They had expected to be indoors or in cars. Nigel had a sports jacket, Elton a raincoat, and Daisy a leather jacket. Kit was the most warmly dressed, in his Puffa jacket. Kit wore Timberlands and Daisy had motorcycle boots, but Nigel and Elton wore ordinary shoes.

Soon Kit was shivering. His hands hurt, though he tried to keep them stuffed in his coat pockets. The snow soaked his jeans up to the knees and melted into his boots. His ears and his nose seemed frozen.

The familiar lane, along which he had walked and bicycled a thousand times in his boyhood, was buried out of sight, and he quickly began to feel confused about where he was. This was Scottish moorland, and no hedge or wall marked the edge of the road, as it would have in other parts of Britain. The land on either side was uncultivated, and no one had ever seen any reason to fence it off.

He felt he might have veered from the road. He stopped, and with his bare hands dug down into the snow.

'What now?' Nigel said bad-temperedly.

'Just a minute.' Kit found frozen turf. That meant he had strayed from the paved road. But which way? He blew on his icy hands, trying to warm them. The land to his right seemed to slope up. He guessed the road was that way. He trudged a few yards in that direction, then dug down again. This time he found tarmac. 'This way,' he said with more confidence than he felt.

In time, the melted snow that had soaked his jeans and socks began to freeze again, so that he had ice next to his skin. When they had been walking for half an hour, he had a feeling he was going around in a circle. His sense of direction failed. On a normal night, the lights outside the house should have been visible in the distance, but tonight nothing shone through the snowfall to give him a beacon. There was no sound or smell of the sea: it might have been fifty miles away. He realized that if they got lost they would die of exposure. He felt truly frightened.

The others followed him in exhausted silence. Even Daisy stopped bitching. They were breathless and shivering, and had no energy to complain.

At last Kit sensed a deeper darkness around him. The snow seemed to fall less heavily. He almost bumped into the thick trunk of a big tree. He had reached the woods near the house. He felt so relieved that he wanted to kneel down and give thanks. From this point on, he could find the way.

As he followed the winding track through the trees, he could hear someone's teeth chattering like a drum roll. He hoped it was Daisy.

He had lost all feeling in his fingers and toes, but he could still move his legs. The snow was not quite so thick on the ground, here in the shelter of the trees, and he was able to walk faster. A faint glow ahead told him he was approaching the lights of the house. At last he emerged from the woods. He headed for the light and came to the garage.

The big doors were closed, but there was a side door that was never locked. Kit found it and went inside. The other three followed. 'Thank God,' Elton said grimly. 'I thought I was going to die in sodding Scotland.'

Kit shone his torch. Here was his father's blue Ferrari, voluptuously curved, parked very close to the wall. Next to it was Luke's dirty white Ford Mondeo. That was surprising: Luke normally drove himself and Lori home in it at the end of the evening. Had they stayed the night, or . . . ?

He shone his torch at the far end of the garage, where the Toyota Land Cruiser Amazon was usually parked.

The bay was empty.

Kit felt like crying.

He realized immediately what had happened. Luke and Lori lived in a cottage at the end of a rough road more than a mile away. Because of the weather, Stanley had let them take the four-wheel-drive car. They had left behind the Ford, which was no better in the snow than the Astra.

'Oh, shit,' said Kit.

Nigel said: 'Where's the Toyota?'

'It's not here,' Kit said. 'Jesus Christ, now we're in trouble.'

3:30 a.m.

Carl Osborne was speaking into his mobile phone. 'Is anyone on the newsdesk yet? Good – put me through.'

Toni crossed the Great Hall to where Carl sat. 'Wait, please.'

He put his hand over the phone. 'What?'

'Please hang up and listen to me. Just for a moment.'

He said into the phone: 'Get ready to do a voice-record – I'll get back to you in a couple of minutes.' He pressed the hang-up button and looked expectantly at Toni.

She felt desperate. Carl could do untold damage with a scaremongering report. She hated to plead, but she had to try to stop him. 'This could finish me,' she said. 'I let Michael Ross steal a rabbit, and now I've allowed a gang to get away with samples of the virus itself.'

'Sorry, Toni, but it's a tough old world.'

'This could ruin the company, too,' she persisted. She was being more candid than she liked, but she had to do it. 'Bad publicity might frighten our . . . investors.'

Carl did not miss a trick. 'You mean the Americans.'

'It doesn't matter who. The point is that the company could be destroyed.' And so could Stanley, she thought, but she did not say it. She was trying to sound reasonable and unemotional, but her voice was close to cracking. 'They don't deserve it!'

'You mean your beloved Professor Oxenford doesn't deserve it.'

'All he's doing is trying to find cures for human illnesses, for Christ's sake!'

'And make money at the same time.'

'As you do, when you bring the truth to the Scottish television audience.'

He stared at her, not sure if she was being sarcastic. Then he shook his head. 'A story is a story. Besides, it's sure to come out. If I don't do it, someone else will.'

'I know.' She looked out of the windows of the Great Hall. The weather showed no sign of easing. At best, there might be some improvement with daylight. 'Just give me three hours,' she said. 'File at seven.'

'What difference will that make?'

Possibly none at all, she thought, but it was her only chance. 'Maybe by then we'll be able to say that the police have caught the gang, or at least that they're on the trail and expect to arrest them at any moment.' Perhaps the company, and Stanley, could survive the crisis if it were resolved quickly.

'No deal. Someone else could get the story in the meantime. As soon as the police know, it's out there. I can't take that risk.' He dialled.

Toni stared at him. The truth was bad enough. Seen through the distorting lens of tabloid television, the story would be catastrophic.

'Record this,' Carl said into his mobile. 'You can run it with a still photo of me holding a phone. Ready?'

Toni wanted to kill him.

'I'm speaking from the premises of Oxenford Medical, where the second biosecurity incident in two days has hit this Scottish pharmaceutical company.'

Could she stop him? She had to try. She looked around. Steve was behind the desk. Susan was lying down, looking pale, but Don was upright. Her mother was asleep. So was the puppy. She had two men to help her.

'Excuse me,' she said to Carl.

He tried to ignore her. 'Samples of a deadly virus, Madoba-2—'

Toni put her hand over his phone. 'I'm sorry, you can't use that here.'

He turned away and tried to continue. 'Samples of a deadly—'

She crowded him and again put her hand between his phone and his mouth. 'Steve! Don! Over here, now!'

Carl said into the phone: 'They're trying to stop me filing a report, are you recording this?'

Toni spoke loud enough for the phone to pick up her words. 'Mobile phones may interfere with delicate electronic equipment operating in the laboratories, so they may not be used here.' It was untrue, but it would serve as a pretext. 'Please turn it off.'

He held it away from her and said loudly: 'Get off me!'

Toni nodded at Steve, who snatched the phone from Carl's hand and turned it off.

'You can't do this!' Carl said.

'Of course I can. You're a visitor here, and I'm in charge of security.'

'Bullshit – security has nothing to do with it.'

'Say what you like, I make the rules.'

'Then I'll go outside.'

'You'll freeze to death.'

'You can't stop me leaving.'

Toni shrugged. 'True. But I'm not giving you back your phone.'

'You're stealing it.'

'Confiscating it for security reasons. We'll mail it to you.'

'I'll find a phone box.'

'Good luck.' There was not a public phone within five miles.

Carl pulled on his coat and went out. Toni and Steve watched him through the windows. He got into his car and started the engine. He got out again and scraped several inches of snow off the windscreen. The wipers began to operate. Carl got in and pulled away.

Steve said: 'He left the dog behind.'

The snowfall had eased a little. Toni cursed under her breath. Surely the weather was not going to improve just at the wrong moment?

A mound of snow grew in front of the Jaguar as it climbed the rise. A hundred yards from the gate, it stopped.

Steve smiled. 'I didn't think he'd get far.'

The car's interior light came on. Toni frowned, worried.

Steve said: 'Maybe he's going to sulk out there, engine turning over, heater on full blast, until he runs out of petrol.'

Toni peered through the snowstorm, trying to see better.

'What's he doing?' Steve said. 'Looks like he's talking to himself.'

Toni realized what was happening, and her heart sank. 'Shit,' she said. 'He is talking – but not to himself.'

'What?'

'He has another phone in the car. He's a reporter, he has back-up equipment. Hell, I never thought of that.'

'Shall I run out there and stop him?'

'Too late now. By the time you get there, he'll have said enough. Damn.' Nothing was going right. She felt like giving up, walking away and finding a darkened room and lying down and closing her eyes. But instead she pulled herself together. 'When he comes back in, just sneak outside and see whether he's left the keys in the ignition. If he has, take them – then at least he won't be able to phone again.'

'Okay.'

Her mobile rang and she picked up. 'Toni Gallo.'

'This is Odette.' She sounded shaken.

'What's happened?'

'Fresh intelligence. A terrorist group called Scimitar has been actively shopping for Madoba-2.'

'Scimitar? An Arab group?'

'Sounds like it, though we're not sure – the name might be intentionally misleading. But we think your thieves are working for them.'

'My God. Do you know anything else?'

'They aim to release it tomorrow, Boxing Day, at a major public location somewhere in Britain.'

Toni gasped. She and Odette had speculated that this might be so, but the confirmation was shocking. People stayed at home on Christmas Day then went out on Boxing Day. All over Britain, families would go to soccer matches, horserace meetings, cinemas and theatres and bowling alleys. Many would catch flights to ski resorts and Caribbean beaches. The opportunities were endless. 'But where?' Toni said. 'What event?'

'We don't know. So we have to stop these thieves. The local police are on their way to you with a snowplough.'

'That's great!' Toni's spirits lifted. If the thieves could be caught, everything would change. Not only would the virus be recaptured and the danger averted, but Oxenford Medical would not look so bad in the press, and Stanley would be saved.

Odette went on: 'I've also alerted your neighbouring police forces, plus Glasgow; but Inverburn is where the action will be, I think. The guy in charge there is called Frank Hackett. The name rang a bell – he's not your ex, is he?'

'Yes. That was part of the problem. He likes to say no to me.'

'Well, you'll find him a chastened man. He's had a phone call from the Chancellor of the Duchy of Lancaster. Sounds comical, doesn't it, but he's in charge of the Cabinet Office Briefing Room, which we call COBRA. In other words, he's the anti-terrorism supremo. Your ex must have jumped out of his bed as if it was on fire.'

'Don't waste your sympathy, he doesn't deserve it.'

'Since then, he's heard from my boss, another life-enhancing experience. The poor sod is on his way to you with a snowplough.'

'I'd rather have the snowplough without Frank.'

'He's had a hard time, be nice to him.'

'Yeah, right,' said Toni.

3:45 a.m.

Daisy was shivering so much she could hardly hold the ladder. Elton climbed the rungs, grasping a pair of garden shears in one frozen hand. The exterior lamps shone through the filter of falling snow. Kit watched from the garage door, his teeth chattering. Nigel was in the garage, arms wrapped around the burgundy leather briefcase.

The ladder was propped up against the side of Steepfall. Telephone wires emerged at the corner of the house and ran at roof height to the garage. From there, Kit knew, they connected with an underground pipe that ran to the main road. Severing the cables here would cut off the entire property from telephone contact. It was just a precaution, but Nigel had insisted, and Kit had found ladder and shears in the garage.

Kit felt as if he were in a nightmare. He had known that tonight's work would be dangerous, but in his worst moments he had never anticipated that he would be standing outside his family home while a gangster cut the phone lines and a master thief clutched a case containing a virus that could kill them all.

Elton took his left hand off the ladder, balancing cautiously, and held the shears in both hands. He leaned forward, caught a cable between the blades, pressed the handles together, and dropped the shears.

They landed points-down in the snow six inches from Daisy, who let out a yell of shock.

'Hush!' Kit said in a stage whisper.

'He could have killed me!' Daisy protested.

'You'll wake everyone!'

Elton came down the ladder, retrieved the shears, and climbed up again.

They had to go to Luke and Lori's cottage and take the Toyota Land Cruiser, but Kit knew they could not go immediately. They were nearly falling down with exhaustion. Worse, Kit was not sure he could find Luke's place. He had almost lost his way looking for Steepfall. The snow was falling as hard as ever. If they tried to go on now, they would get lost or die of exposure or both. They had to wait until the blizzard eased, or until daylight gave them a better chance of finding their way. And, to make absolutely sure no one could find out that they were here, they were cutting off the phones.

This time, Elton succeeded in snipping the lines. As he came down the ladder, Kit picked up the loose cable ends, twisted them into a bundle, and draped them against the garage wall where they were less conspicuous.

Elton carried the ladder into the garage and dropped it. It clanged on the concrete floor. 'Try not to make so much noise!' Kit said.

Nigel looked around the bare stone walls of the converted stable. 'We can't stay here.'

Kit said: 'Better in here than out there.'

'We're cold and wet and there's no heat. We could die.'

Elton said: 'Bloody right.'

'We'll run the engines of the cars,' Kit said. 'That will warm the place.'

'Don't be stupid,' Elton said. 'The fumes will kill us long before the heat warms us.'

'We could drive the Ford outside and sit in it.'

Daisy said: 'Fuck that. I want a cup of tea and hot food and a dram. I'm going in the house.'

'No!' The thought of these three in his family home filled Kit with horror. It would be like taking mad dogs home. And what about the briefcase with its virulent contents? How could he let them carry that into the kitchen?

Elton said: 'I'm with her. Let's go into the house.'

Kit wished bitterly that he had not told them how to cut off the phones. 'But how would I explain you?'

'They'll all be asleep.'

'And if it's still snowing when they get up?'

Nigel said: 'Here's what you say. You don't know us. You met us on the road. Our car is stuck in a snowdrift a couple of miles away. You took pity on us and brought us back here.'

'They aren't supposed to know I've left the house!'

'Say you went out for a drink.'

Elton said: 'Or to meet a girl.'

Daisy said: 'How old are you, anyway? You need to ask Daddy before you can go out at night?'

It infuriated Kit to be condescended to by a thug like Daisy. 'It's a question of what they'll believe, you brain-dead gorgon. Who would be daft enough to go out in a snowstorm and drive miles for a drink, when there's plenty of booze in the house anyway?'

She retorted: 'Someone daft enough to lose a quarter of a million pounds at blackjack.'

'You'll think of a plausible story, Kit,' said Nigel. 'Let's get inside, before our fucking feet drop off.'

'You left your disguises in the van. My family will see your real faces.'

'It doesn't matter. We're just unfortunate stranded motorists. There'll be hundreds like us, it will be on the news. Your family won't connect us with the people who robbed the laboratory.'

'I don't like it,' Kit said. He was scared of defying these three criminals, but desperate enough to do it. 'I'm not taking you into the house.'

'We're not asking your permission,' Nigel said contemptuously. 'If you don't show us the way, we'll find it ourselves.'

What they did not understand, Kit thought despairingly, was that his family were all very smart. Nigel, Elton, and Daisy would have difficulty fooling them. 'You don't *look* like a group of innocent people who got stranded.'

'What do you mean?' Nigel said.

'You're not the average Scots family,' Kit told him. 'You're a Londoner, Elton's black, and Daisy's a bloody psychopath. My sisters may notice that.'

'We'll just be polite and not say much.'

'Say nothing at all would be the best plan. Any rough stuff and the game will be up.'

'Of course. We want them to think we're harmless.'

'Especially Daisy.' Kit turned to her. 'You keep your hands to yourself.'

Nigel backed Kit. 'Yeah, Daisy, try not to give the bloody game away. Act like a girl, just for a couple of hours, okay?'

She said: 'Yeah, yeah,' and turned away.

Kit realized that at some point in the argument he had given in. 'Shit,' he said. 'Just remember that you need me to show you where the Land Cruiser is. If any harm comes to my family, you can forget it.'

With a fatalistic feeling that he was helpless to stop himself hurtling towards disaster, he led them around the house to the back door. It was unlocked, as always. As he opened it, he said: 'All right, Nellie, it's me,' so that the dog would not bark.

When he entered the boot lobby, warm air washed over him like a blessing. Behind him, he heard Elton say: 'Oh, God, that's better.'

Kit turned and hissed: 'Keep your voices down, please!' He felt like a schoolteacher trying to quiet heedless children in a museum. 'The longer they stay asleep, the easier it will be for us, don't you see that?' He led them through the lobby and into the kitchen. 'Be nice, Nellie,' he said quietly. 'These are friends.'

Nigel patted Nellie, and the dog wagged her tail. They took off their wet coats. Nigel stood the briefcase on the kitchen table and said: 'Put the kettle on, Kit.'

Kit put down his laptop and turned on the small TV set on the kitchen counter. He found a news channel, then filled the kettle.

A pretty newsreader said: 'An unexpected change in the prevailing wind has brought a surprise blizzard to most of Scotland.'

Daisy said: 'You can say that again.'

The newsreader spoke in a seductive voice, as if inviting the viewer back to her place for a nightcap. 'In some parts, more than twelve inches of snow fell in as many hours.'

'I'll give you twelve inches in some parts,' said Elton.

They were relaxing, Kit saw with trepidation. He felt even more tense than before.

The newsreader told of car accidents, blocked roads, and abandoned vehicles. 'To hell with all that,' Kit said irately. 'When's it going to stop?'

'Make the tea, Kit,' said Nigel.

Kit put out mugs, a sugar bowl, and a jug of milk. Nigel, Daisy, and Elton sat around the scrubbed-pine table, just like family. The kettle boiled. Kit made a pot of tea and a cafetière of coffee.

The television picture changed, and a weather forecaster appeared in front of a chart. They all went quiet. 'Tomorrow morning the blizzard will die away as quickly as it came,' he said.

'Yes!' Nigel said triumphantly.

'The thaw will follow before midday.'

'Be precise!' Nigel said in exasperation. 'What time before midday?'

'We can still make it,' Elton said. He poured tea and added milk and sugar.

Kit shared his optimism. 'We should leave at first light,' he said. Seeing the way ahead cheered him up.

'I hope we can,' Nigel said.

Elton sipped his tea. 'By the cringe, that's better. Lazarus must have felt like this when he was raised from the dead.'

Daisy stood up. She opened the door to the dining room and peered into the gloom. 'What room is this?'

Kit said: 'Where do you think you're going?'

'I need a shot of booze in this tea.' She turned on the light and went in. A moment later, she made a triumphant noise, and Kit heard her opening the cocktail cabinet.

Kit's father walked into the kitchen from the hall, wearing grey pyjamas and a black cashmere dressing-gown. 'Good morning,' he said. 'What's all this?'

'Hello, Daddy,' Kit said. 'Let me explain.'

Daisy came in from the dining room holding a full bottle of Glenmorangie in her gloved hand.

Stanley raised his eyebrows at her. 'Do you want a glass of whisky?' he said.

'No, thanks,' she replied. 'I've got a whole bottle here.'

4:15 a.m.

Toni called Stanley at home as soon as she had a spare moment. There was nothing he could do, but he would want to know what was happening. And she did not want him to learn about the break-in from the news.

It was a conversation she dreaded. She had to tell him that she was responsible for a catastrophe that could ruin his life. How would he feel about her after that?

She dialled his number and got the 'disconnected' tone. His phone must be out of order. Perhaps the snow had brought down the lines. She was relieved not to have to give him the dreadful news.

He did not carry a mobile, but there was a phone in his Ferrari. She dialled that and left a message. 'Stanley, this is Toni. Bad news – a break-in at the lab. Please call my mobile as soon as you can.' He might not get the message until it was too late, but at least she had tried.

She stared impatiently out of the windows of the Great Hall. Where were the police with their snowplough? They would be coming from the south, from Inverburn, on the main road. She guessed that the plough travelled at about fifteen miles per hour, depending on the depth of snow it had to clear. The trip should take twenty or thirty minutes. It should be here by now. Come on, come on!

She hoped it would leave here almost immediately, and get on the northward track of the Hibernian Telecom van. The van would be easy to spot, with the name in large white letters on a dark background.

But the thieves might have thought of that, she realized suddenly. They had probably planned to switch vehicles soon after leaving the Kremlin. That was how she would have done it. She would have picked a nondescript car, something like a Ford Fiesta that looked like a dozen other models, and left it in a car park, outside a supermarket or a railway station. The thieves would drive straight to the car park and be in a completely different vehicle a few minutes after leaving the scene of the crime.

The thought dismayed her. How then would the police identify the thieves? They would have to check every car and see whether the occupants were three men and a woman.

She wondered agitatedly whether there was anything she could do to hurry the process. Assuming the gang had switched vehicles somewhere near here, what were the possibilities? They needed a location where a vehicle might be parked for several hours without attracting attention. There were no railway stations or supermarkets in the vicinity. What was there? She went to the reception desk and got a notepad and ballpoint pen. She made a list:

— *Inverburn Golf Club*

— *Dew Drop Inn*

— *Happy Eater*

— *Greenfingers Garden Centre*

— *Scottish Smoked Fish Products*

— *Williams Press (Printing & Publishing)*

She did not want Carl Osborne to know what she was doing. Carl had returned from his car to the warmth of the hall, and was listening to everything. Unknown to him, he could no longer phone from the car – Steve had sneaked out and taken the keys from the ignition – but all the same, Toni was taking no chances.

She spoke quietly to Steve. 'We're going to do some detective work.' She tore her sheet of paper into two and gave half to Steve. 'Ring these places. Everything's closed, of course, but you should find a caretaker or security guard. Tell them we've had a robbery, but don't say what's missing. Say the getaway vehicle may have been abandoned on their premises. Ask if they can see a Hibernian Telecom van outside.'

Steve nodded. 'Smart thinking – maybe we can get on their trail and give the police a head start.'

'Exactly. But don't use the desk phone, I don't want Carl to hear. Go to the far end of the hall, where he can't eavesdrop. Use the mobile you took from him.'

Toni moved well away from Carl and took out her mobile. She called inquiries and got the number for the golf club. She dialled and waited. The phone rang for more than a minute, then a sleepy voice answered: 'Yes? Golf club. Hello?'

Toni introduced herself and told the story. 'I'm trying to locate a van with "Hibernian Telecom" on its side. Is it in your car park?'

'Oh, I get you, the getaway vehicle, aye.'

Her heart missed a beat. 'It's there?'

'No, at least it wasn't when I came on duty. There's a couple of cars here, mind you, left by gentlemen who found themselves reluctant to drive by the end of lunch yesterday, do you know what I mean?'

'When did you come on duty?'

'Seven o'clock in the evening.'

'Could a van have parked there since then? Perhaps at about two o'clock this morning?'

'Well, maybe . . . I've no way of telling.'

'Could you have a look?'

'Aye, I could look!' He spoke as if it were an idea of startling originality. 'Hold the line, I'll just be a minute.' There was a knock as he put the phone down.

Toni waited. Footsteps receded and returned.

'No, I don't think there's a van out there.'

'Okay.'

'The cars are all covered in snow, mind you, so you can't see them properly. I'm not even sure which is mine!'

'Yes, thank you.'

'But a van, you see, would be higher than the rest, wouldn't it? So it would stand out. No, there's no van there.'

'You've been very helpful. I appreciate it.'

'What did they steal?'

Toni pretended not to hear the question, and hung up. Steve was talking and clearly had not yet struck gold. She dialled the Dew Drop Inn.

The phone was answered by a cheerful young man. 'Vincent speaking, how may I help you?'

Toni thought he sounded like the kind of hotel employee who seems eager to please until you actually ask for something. She went through her routine again.

'There are lots of vehicles in our car park – we're open over Christmas,' Vincent told her. 'I'm looking at the closed-circuit television monitor, but I don't see a van. Unfortunately, the camera doesn't cover the entire car park.'

'Would you mind going to the window and having a good look? It's really important.'

'I'm quite busy, actually.'

At this time of night? Toni did not voice the thought. She adopted a sweetly considerate tone and said: 'It will save the police making a trip to interview you, you see.'

That worked. He did not want his quiet night shift disrupted by squad cars and detectives. 'Just hold on.' He went away and came back.

'Yes, it's here,' he said.

'Really?' Toni was incredulous. It seemed a long time since she had enjoyed a piece of luck.

'Ford Transit van, blue, with "Hibernian Telecom" in large white letters on the side. It can't have been there long, because it's not under as much snow as the rest of the cars – that's how come I can see the lettering.'

'That's tremendously helpful, thank you. I don't suppose you noticed whether another car is missing – possibly the car they left in?'

'No, sorry.'

'Okay – thanks again!' She hung up and looked across at Steve. 'I've found the getaway vehicle!'

He nodded towards the window. 'And the snowplough's here.'

4:30 a.m.

Daisy drained her cup of tea and filled it up again with whisky.

Kit felt unbearably tense. Nigel and Elton might be able to keep up the pretence of being innocent travellers accidentally stranded, but Daisy was hopeless. She looked like a gangster and acted like a hooligan.

When she put the bottle down on the kitchen table, Stanley picked it up. 'Don't get drunk, there's a good girl,' he said mildly. He stoppered the bottle.

Daisy was not used to people telling her what to do. Mostly they were too frightened. She looked at Stanley as if she was ready to kill him. He was elegantly vulnerable in his grey pyjamas and black robe. Kit waited for the explosion.

'A little whisky makes you feel better, but a lot makes you feel worse,' Stanley said. He put the bottle in a cupboard. 'My father used to say that, and he was fond of whisky.'

Daisy was suppressing her rage. The effort was visible to Kit. He feared what might happen if she should lose it. Then the tension was broken by his sister Miranda, who came in wearing a pink nightgown with a flower pattern.

Stanley said: 'Hello, my dear, you're up early.'

'I couldn't sleep. I've been on the sleepchair in Kit's old study. Don't ask why.' She looked at the strangers. 'It's early for Christmas visitors.'

'This is my daughter Miranda,' Stanley said. 'Mandy, meet Nigel, Elton, and Daisy.'

A few minutes ago, Kit had introduced them to his father and, before he realized his mistake, he gave their real names.

Miranda nodded to them. 'Did Santa bring you?' she said brightly.

Kit explained. 'Their car died on the main road near our turn-off. I picked them up, then my car gave out too, and we walked the rest of the way here.' Would she believe it? And would she ask about the burgundy leather briefcase that stood on the kitchen table like a bomb?

She questioned a different aspect of the story. 'I didn't know you'd left the house – where on earth did you go, in the middle of the night, in this weather?'

'Oh, you know.' Kit had thought about how he would respond to this question, and now he put on a sheepish grin. 'Couldn't sleep, felt lonely, went to look up an old girlfriend in Inverburn.'

'Which one? Most of the young women in Inverburn are old girlfriends of yours.'

'I don't think you know her.' He thought of a name quickly. 'Lisa Fremont.' He almost bit his tongue. She was a character in a Hitchcock movie.

Miranda did not react to the name. 'Was she pleased to see you?'

'She wasn't in.'

Miranda turned away and picked up the coffee pot.

Kit wondered whether she believed him. The story he had made up was not really good enough. However, Miranda could not possibly guess *why* he was lying. She would assume he was involved with a woman he didn't want people to know about – probably someone's wife.

While Miranda was pouring coffee, Stanley addressed Nigel. 'Where are you from? You don't sound Scots.' It seemed like small-talk, but Kit knew his father was probing.

Nigel answered in the same relaxed tone. 'I live in Surrey, work in London. My office is in Canary Wharf.'

'You're in the financial world.'

'I source high-tech systems for Third World countries, mainly the Middle East. A young oil sheik wants his own discotheque and doesn't know where to buy the gear, so he comes to me and I solve his problem.' It sounded pat.

Miranda brought her coffee to the table and sat opposite Daisy. 'What nice gloves,' she said. Daisy was wearing expensive-looking light-brown suede gloves that were soaking wet. 'Why don't you dry them?'

Kit tensed. Any conversation with Daisy was hazardous.

Daisy gave a hostile look, but Miranda did not see it, and persisted. 'You need to stuff them, so they'll keep their shape,' she said. She took a roll of kitchen paper from the counter. 'Here, use this.'

'I'm fine,' Daisy muttered angrily.

Miranda raised her eyebrows in surprise. 'Have I said something to offend you?'

Kit thought: Oh, God, here it comes.

Nigel stepped in. 'Don't be daft, Daisy, you don't want to spoil your gloves.' There was an edge of insistence in his voice, making the words sound more like an order than a suggestion. He was as worried as Kit. 'Do what the lady says, she's being nice to you.'

Once again, Kit waited for the explosion. But, to his surprise, Daisy took off her gloves. Kit was astonished to see that she had small, neat hands. He had never noticed that. The rest of her was brutish: the black eye make-up, the broken nose, the zippered jacket, the boots. But her hands were beautiful, and she obviously knew it, for they were well manicured, with clean nails and a pale-pink nail varnish. Kit was bemused. Somewhere inside that monster there was an ordinary girl, he realized. What had happened to her? She had been brought up by Harry Mac, that was what.

Miranda helped her stuff the wet gloves with kitchen paper. 'How are you three connected?' she asked Daisy. Her tone was conventionally polite, as if she were making conversation at a dinner party, but she was probing. Like Stanley, she had no idea how dangerous it was.

Daisy looked panicked. She made Kit think of a schoolgirl being questioned on homework she has forgotten to do. Kit wanted to fill the awkward silence, but it would look odd if he answered for her. After a moment, Nigel spoke. 'Daisy's father is an old friend of mine.'

That was fine, Kit thought, though Miranda would wonder why Daisy could not have said it herself.

Nigel added: 'And Elton works for me.'

Miranda smiled at Elton. 'Right-hand man?'

'Driver,' he replied brusquely. Kit reflected that it was a good thing Nigel was personable – he had to supply enough charm for the three of them.

Stanley said: 'Well, I'm sorry the weather has turned out so poorly for your Christmas in Scotland.'

Nigel smiled. 'If I'd wanted to sunbathe, I would have gone to Barbados.'

'You and Daisy's father must be good friends, to spend Christmas together.'

Nigel nodded. 'We go way back.'

It seemed obvious to Kit that Nigel was lying. Was that because he knew the truth? Or was it apparent to Stanley and Miranda too? Kit could not sit still any longer: the strain was unbearable. He jumped up. 'I'm hungry,' he said. 'Dad, is it okay if I scramble some eggs for everyone?'

'Of course.'

'I'll give you a hand,' Miranda said. She put sliced bread in the toaster.

Stanley said: 'Anyway, I hope the weather improves soon. When were you planning to return to London?'

Kit got a pack of bacon out of the fridge. Was his father suspicious, or merely curious?

'Heading back on Boxing Day,' Nigel said.

'A short Christmas visit,' Stanley commented, still gently challenging the story.

Nigel shrugged. 'Work to do, you know.'

'You may have to stay longer than you anticipated. I can't see them clearing the roads by tomorrow.'

The thought seemed to make Nigel anxious. He pushed up the sleeve of his pink sweater and looked at his watch.

Kit realized he needed to do something to show he was not in league with Nigel and the other two. As he began to make breakfast he resolved not to defend or excuse the strangers. On the contrary, he should question Nigel sceptically, as if he mistrusted the story. He might deflect suspicion from himself by pretending that he, too, was dubious about the strangers.

But, before he could put his resolution into practice, Elton suddenly became talkative. 'How about your Christmas, Professor?' he said. Kit had introduced his father as Professor Oxenford. 'Got your family all around you, it seems. What, two children?'

'Three.'

'With husbands and wives, of course.'

'My daughters have partners. Kit's single.'

'And grandchildren?'

'Yes.'

'How many? If you don't mind me asking.'

'I don't mind in the least. I have four grandchildren.'

'Are all the grandkids here?'

'Yes.'

'That's nice for you and Mrs Oxenford.'

'My wife died eighteen months ago, sadly.'

'Sorry to hear that.'

'Thank you.'

What was this interrogation about, Kit asked himself? Elton was smiling and leaning forward, as if his questions were motivated by nothing more than friendly curiosity, but Kit could see that it was a charade, and he wondered anxiously whether that was just as obvious to his father.

Elton had not finished. 'This must be a big house, to sleep, what, ten of you?'

'We have some outbuildings.'

'Oh, handy.' He looked out of the window, although

the snow made it difficult to see anything. 'Guest cottages, like.'

'There's a cottage and a barn.'

'Very useful. And staff quarters, I presume.'

'Our staff have a cottage a mile or so away. I doubt if we'll see them today.'

'Oh. Shame.' Elton lapsed into silence again – having carefully established exactly how many people were on the property.

Kit wondered if anyone else had noticed that.

5 a.m.

The snowplough was a Mercedes lorry with a blade hooked to its front attachment plate. It had 'Inverburn Plant Hire' on its side and flashing orange lights on its roof, but to Toni it looked like a winged chariot from heaven.

The blade was angled to push the snow to the side of the road. The plough quickly cleared the drive from the gatehouse to the main entrance of the Kremlin, its blade lifting automatically to clear speed bumps. By the time it stopped at the main entrance, Toni had her coat on, ready to go. It was four hours since the thieves had left – but if they had got stuck in the snow they could still be caught.

The plough was followed by three police cars and an ambulance. The ambulance crew came in first. They took Susan out on a stretcher, though she said she could walk. Don refused to go. 'If a Scotsman went to hospital every time he got a kick in the head, the doctors could never cope,' he said.

Frank came in wearing a dark suit with a white shirt and a tie. He had even found time to shave, probably in the car. Toni saw the grim expression on his face and realized with dismay that he was spoiling for a fight. No doubt he resented being forced by his superiors to do what Toni wanted. She told herself to be patient and avoid a showdown.

Toni's mother looked up from petting the puppy and said: 'Hello, Frank! This is a surprise. Are you and Toni getting back together?'

'Not today,' he muttered.

'Shame.'

Frank was followed by two detectives carrying large briefcases – a crime-scene team, Toni presumed. Frank nodded to Toni and shook hands with Carl Osborne, but spoke to Steve. 'You're the guard supervisor?'

'Aye. Steve Tremlett. You're Frank Hackett, I've met you before.'

'I gather four guards were assaulted.'

'Me and three others, aye.'

'Did all the assaults take place in the same location?'

What was Frank doing, Toni wondered impatiently? Why was he asking trivial questions when they needed to get going right away?

Steve answered: 'Susan was attacked in the corridor. I was tripped up in about the same place. Don and Stu were held at gunpoint and tied up in the control room.'

'Show me both places, please.'

Toni was astonished. 'We need to go after these people, Frank. Why don't you leave this to your team?'

'Don't tell me how to do the job,' he replied. He looked pleased that she had given him an opportunity to put her down. She groaned inwardly. This was not the time to rerun their marital conflicts. He turned back to Steve and said: 'Lead the way.'

Toni suppressed a curse and followed along. So did Carl Osborne.

The detectives put crime-scene tape across the corridor where Steve had been tripped up and Susan had been coshed. Then they went to the control room, where Stu was watching the monitors. Frank taped the doorway.

Steve said: 'All four of us were tied up and taken inside the BSL4 facility. Not the laboratory itself, just the lobby.'

'Which is where I found them,' Toni added. 'But that was four hours ago – and the perpetrators are getting farther away every minute.'

'We'll take a look at that location.'

'No, you won't,' Toni said. 'It's a restricted area. You can see it on monitor nineteen.'

'If it's not the actual laboratory, I presume there's no danger.'

He was right, but Toni was not going to let him waste more time. 'No one is allowed past the door without biohazard training. That's the protocol.'

'Hell with your protocol, I'm in charge here.'

Toni realized she had inadvertently done what she had vowed to avoid: gone head to head with Frank. She tried to sidestep the issue. 'I'll take you to the door.'

They went to the entrance. Frank looked at the card reader, then said to Steve: 'I'm ordering you to give me your pass.'

Steve said: 'I don't have a pass. Security guards aren't allowed in.'

Frank turned to Toni. 'Do you have a pass?'

'I've done biohazard training.'

'Give me your pass.'

She handed it over. Frank waved it at the scanner then pushed the door. It remained locked. He pointed at the small screen on the wall. 'What's that?'

'A fingerprint reader. The pass won't work without the correct fingerprint. It's a system we installed to prevent foolish people getting in with stolen cards.'

'It didn't stop the thieves tonight, did it?' Having scored a point, Frank turned on his heel.

Toni followed him. Back in the Great Hall there were two men in yellow high-visibility jackets and rubber boots, smoking. Toni thought at first that they were snowplough operators, but when Frank began to brief them she realized they were police officers. 'You check every vehicle you pass,' he said. 'Radio in the registration number, and we'll find out whether it's stolen or rented. Tell us if there's anyone in the cars. You know what we're looking for – three men and a woman. Whatever you do, don't approach the occupants. These laddies have guns, and you don't, so you're strictly reconnaissance. There's an armed-response unit on its way. If we can locate the perpetrators, we'll send them in. Is that clear?'

The two men nodded.

'Go north and take the first turn-off. I think they headed east.'

Toni knew that was wrong. She was reluctant to confront Frank again, but she could not let the reconnaissance team go the wrong way. He would be furious, but she had to do it. She said: 'The thieves didn't head east.'

Frank ignored her. 'That takes you to the main road for Glasgow.'

Toni said again: 'The perpetrators didn't go that way.'

The two constables watched the exchange with interest, looking from Frank to Toni and back like spectators at a tennis match.

Frank reddened. 'No one asked your opinion, Toni.'

'They didn't take that route,' she persisted. 'They continued north.'

'I suppose you reached that conclusion by feminine intuition?'

One of the constables laughed.

Why do you lead with your chin? Toni thought. She said calmly: 'The getaway vehicle is in the car park of the Dew Drop Inn, on this road five miles north.'

Frank turned redder, embarrassed because she knew something he did not. 'And how did you acquire this information?'

'Detective work.' I was a better cop than you, and I still am, she thought; but she kept the thought to herself. 'I phoned around. Better than intuition.' You asked for that, you bastard.

The constable laughed again, then smothered it when Frank glared at him.

Toni added: 'The thieves might be at the motel, but more likely they switched cars there and drove on.'

Frank suppressed his fury. 'Go to the motel,' he said to the two constables. 'I'll give you further orders when you're on the road. On your way.'

They hurried out. At last, Toni thought.

Frank summoned a plain-clothes detective from one of the cars and told him to follow the snowplough to the motel, check out the van, and find out whether anyone there had seen anything.

Toni turned her mind to the next step. She wanted to stay in close touch with the police operation. But she had no car. And Mother was still here.

She saw Carl Osborne talking quietly to Frank. Carl pointed at his Jaguar, still stuck halfway up the drive. Frank nodded, and said something to a uniformed officer, who went outside and spoke to the snowplough driver. They were going to free Carl's car, Toni guessed.

Toni addressed Carl. 'You're going with the snowplough.'

He looked smug. 'It's a free country.'

'Don't forget to take the puppy.'

'I was planning to leave him with you.'

'I'm coming with you.'

'You're out of your mind.'

'I need to get to Stanley's house. It's on this road, five miles beyond the Dew Drop Inn. You can leave me and Mother there.' After she had briefed Stanley she could borrow a car from him, leave Mother at Steepfall, and follow the snowplough.

'You want me to take your mother too?' Carl said incredulously.

'Yes.'

'Forget it.'

Toni nodded. 'Let me know if you change your mind.'

He frowned, suspicious of her ready acceptance of his refusal; but he said no more, and put on his coat.

Steve Tremlett opened his mouth to speak, but Toni discreetly flapped her hand at him in a 'Keep quiet' gesture.

Carl went to the door.

Toni said: 'Don't forget the puppy.'

He picked up the dog and went out to his car.

Toni watched through the windows as the convoy moved off. The snowplough cleared the pile in front of Carl's Jaguar, then climbed the slope to the gatehouse. One police car followed. Carl sat in his car for a moment, then got out again and returned to the Great Hall.

'Where are my keys?' he said angrily.

Toni smiled sweetly. 'Have you changed your mind about taking me?'

Steve jingled the bunch of keys in his pocket.

Carl made a sour face. 'Get in the damn car,' he said.

5:30 a.m.

Miranda felt uneasy about the weird threesome of Nigel, Elton, and Daisy. Were they what they claimed to be? Something about them made her wish she were not wearing her nightdress.

She had had a bad night. Lying uncomfortably on the sleepchair in Kit's old study, she had drifted in and out of consciousness, dreaming of her stupid, shameful affair with Hugo, and waking to feel resentful of Ned for failing to stand up for her once again. He should have been angry with Kit for betraying the secret, but instead he just said that secrets always come out sooner or later. They had acted out a rerun of the quarrel in the car early that day. Miranda had hoped this holiday would be the occasion for her family to accept Ned, but she was beginning to think it might be the moment when she rejected him. He was just too weak.

When she heard voices downstairs she had been relieved, for it meant she could get up. Now she felt perturbed. Did Nigel have no wife, family, or even girlfriend who wanted to see him at Christmas? What about Elton? She was pretty sure Nigel and Elton were not a gay couple: Nigel had looked at her nightdress with the speculative eyes of a man who would like to see underneath it.

Daisy would seem weird in any company. She was the right age to be Elton's girlfriend, but they seemed to dislike one another. So what was she doing with Nigel and his driver?

Nigel was not a friend of Daisy's family, Miranda decided. There was no warmth between them. They were more like people who had to work together even though they did not get on very well. But if they were colleagues, why lie about it?

Her father looked strained, too. She wondered if he was also having suspicious thoughts.

The kitchen filled with delicious smells: frying bacon, fresh coffee, and toast. Cooking was one of the things Kit did well, Miranda mused: his food was always attractively presented. He could make a dish of spaghetti look like a royal feast. Appearances were important to her brother. He could not hold down a job or keep his bank account in credit, but he was always well dressed and drove a cool car, no matter how hard up he was. In his father's eyes, he combined frivolous achievements with grave weaknesses.

Now Kit handed each of them a plate with crisp bacon, slices of fresh tomato, scrambled eggs sprinkled with chopped herbs, and triangles of hot buttered toast. The tension in the room eased a little. Perhaps, Miranda thought, that was what Kit had been aiming at. She was not really hungry, but she took a forkful of eggs. He had flavoured them with a little Parmesan cheese, and they tasted delightfully tangy.

Kit made conversation. 'So, Daisy, what do you do for

a living?' He gave her his winning smile. Miranda knew he was only being polite. Kit liked pretty girls, and Daisy was anything but that.

She took a long time to reply. 'I work with my father,' she said.

'And what's his line?'

'His line?'

'I mean, what type of business does he do?'

She seemed baffled by the question.

Nigel laughed and said: 'My old friend Harry has so many things going, it's hard to say what he does.'

Kit surprised Miranda by being insistent. In a challenging tone he said to Daisy: 'Well, give us an example of one of the things he does, then.'

She brightened and, as if struck by inspiration, said: 'He's into property.' She seemed to be repeating something she had heard.

'Sounds as if he likes owning things.'

'Property development.'

'I'm never sure what that means, "property development".'

It was not like Kit to question people aggressively, Miranda thought. Perhaps he, too, found the guests' account of themselves hard to believe. She felt relieved. This proved that they were strangers. Miranda had feared in the back of her mind that Kit was involved in some kind of shady business with them. You never knew, with him.

There was impatience in Nigel's voice as he said: 'Harry buys an old tobacco warehouse, applies for planning permission to turn it into luxury flats, then sells it to a builder at a profit.'

Once again, Miranda realized, Nigel was answering for Daisy. Kit seemed to have the same thought, for he said: 'And how exactly do you help your father with this work, Daisy? I should think you'd be a good saleswoman.'

Daisy looked as if she would be better at evicting sitting tenants.

She gave Kit a hostile glare. 'I do different things,' she said, then tilted up her chin, as if defying him to find fault with her answer.

'And I'm sure you do them with charm and efficiency,' Kit said.

Kit's flattery was becoming sarcastic, Miranda thought anxiously. Daisy was not subtle, but she might know when she was being insulted.

The tension spoiled Miranda's breakfast. She had to talk to her father about this. She swallowed, coughed, and pretended to have something stuck in her throat. Coughing, she got up from the table. 'Sorry,' she spluttered.

Her father snatched up a glass and filled it at the tap.

Still coughing, Miranda left the room. As she intended, her father followed her into the hall. She closed the kitchen door and motioned him into his study. She coughed again, for effect, as they went in.

He offered her the glass, and she waved it away. 'I was pretending,' she said. 'I wanted to talk to you. What do you think about our guests?'

He put the glass down on the green leather top of his desk. 'A weird bunch. I wondered if they were shady friends of Kit's, until he started questioning the girl.'

'Me, too. They're lying about something, though.'

'But what? If they're planning to rob us, they're getting off to a slow start.'

'I don't know, but I feel threatened.'

'Do you want me to call the police?'

'That might be an overreaction. But I wish *someone* knew these people were in our house.'

'Well, let's think – who can we phone?'

'How about Uncle Norman?' Her father's brother, a university librarian, lived in Edinburgh. They loved one another in a distant way, content to meet about once a year.

'Yes. Norman will understand. I'll tell him what's happened, and ask him to phone me in an hour and make sure we're all right.'

'Perfect.'

Stanley picked up the phone on his desk and put it to his ear. He frowned, replaced the handset, and picked it up again. 'No dialling tone,' he said.

Miranda felt a stab of fear. 'Now I *really* want us to call someone.'

He tapped the keyboard of his computer. 'No email, either. It's probably the weather. Heavy snow sometimes brings down the lines.'

'All the same . . .'

'Where's your mobile phone?'

'In the cottage. Don't you have one?'

'Only in the Ferrari.'

'Olga must have one.'

'No need to wake her.' Stanley glanced out of the window. 'I'll just throw on a coat over my pyjamas and go to the garage.'

'Where are the keys?'

'Key cupboard.'

The key cupboard was on the wall in the boot lobby. 'I'll fetch them for you.'

They stepped into the hall. Stanley went to the front door and found his boots. Miranda put her hand on the knob of the kitchen door, then hesitated. She could hear Olga's voice coming from the kitchen. Miranda had not spoken to her sister since the moment last night when Kit had treacherously blurted out the secret. What would she say to Olga, or Olga to her?

She opened the door. Olga was leaning against the kitchen counter, wearing a black silk wrap that reminded Miranda of an advocate's gown. Nigel, Elton, and Daisy sat at the table like a panel. Kit stood behind them, hovering anxiously. Olga was in full courtroom mode, interrogating the strangers across the table. She said to Nigel: 'What on earth were you doing out so late?' He might have been a delinquent teenager.

Miranda noticed a rectangular bulge in the pocket of the silk robe: Olga never went anywhere without her phone. Miranda was going to turn and tell her father not to bother to put his boots on, but she was arrested by Olga's performance.

Nigel frowned with disapproval, but answered all the same. 'We were on our way to Glasgow.'

'Where had you been? There's not much north of here.'

'A big country house.'

'We probably know the owners. Who are they?'

'Name of Robinson.'

Miranda watched, waiting for an opportunity to quietly borrow Olga's phone.

'Robinson doesn't ring a bell. Almost as common as Smith and Brown. What was the occasion?'

'A party.'

Olga raised her dark eyebrows. 'You come to Scotland to spend Christmas with your old friend, then you and his daughter go off to a party and leave the poor man alone?'

'He wasn't feeling too well.'

Olga turned the spotlight on Daisy. 'What sort of a daughter are you, to leave your sick father at home on Christmas Eve?'

Daisy stared back in mute anger. Miranda suddenly feared that Daisy could be violent. Kit seemed to have the same thought, for he said: 'Take it easy, Olga.'

Olga ignored him. 'Well?' she said to Daisy. 'Haven't you got anything to say for yourself?'

Daisy picked up her gloves. For some reason, Miranda found that ominous. Daisy put the gloves on then said: 'I don't have to answer your questions.'

'I think you do.' Olga looked back at Nigel. 'You're three complete strangers, sitting in my father's kitchen filling yourselves with his food, and the story you tell is highly implausible. I think you need to explain yourselves.'

Kit said anxiously: 'Olga, is this really necessary? They're just people who got stranded—'

'Are you sure?' she said. She turned her gaze back to Nigel.

Nigel had seemed relaxed, but now anger showed as he said: 'I don't like being interrogated.'

'If you don't like it, you can leave,' Olga said. 'But if you want to stay in my father's house, you need to tell a better story than this farrago.'

'We can't leave,' Elton said indignantly. 'Look out the window, it's a fucking blizzard.'

'Please don't use that word in this house. My mother always forbade obscenities, except in foreign languages, and we've kept her rule since her death.' Olga reached for the coffee pot, then pointed to the burgundy briefcase on the table. 'What's this?'

'It's mine,' Nigel said.

'Well, we don't keep luggage on the table.' She reached out and picked it up. 'Not much in it – ow!' She yelled because Nigel had grabbed her arm. 'That hurts!' she cried.

Nigel's mask of urbanity had gone. He spoke quietly but distinctly. 'Put the case down. Now.'

Stanley appeared beside Miranda in a coat, gloves, and boots. 'What the hell do you think you're doing?' he said to Nigel. 'Take your hands off my daughter!'

Nellie barked loudly. With a quick movement, Elton reached down and grabbed the dog's collar.

Olga stubbornly kept hold of the briefcase.

Kit said: 'Put the case down, Olga.'

Daisy grabbed the case. Olga tried to keep hold of it, and somehow the case flew open. Polystyrene packing chips scattered all over the kitchen table. Kit gave a shout of fear, and Miranda wondered momentarily what he was so frightened of. Out of the case fell a perfume bottle in a polythene bag.

With her free hand, Olga slapped Nigel's face.

Nigel slapped her back. Everyone shouted at once. Stanley gave a grunt of rage, pushed past Miranda and strode towards Nigel. Miranda shouted: 'No—'

Daisy stood in Stanley's way. He tried to push her aside.

There was a blur of movement, and Stanley cried out and fell back, bleeding from his mouth.

Then, suddenly, both Nigel and Daisy were holding guns.

Everyone went quiet except Nellie, who was barking frantically. Elton twisted her collar, throttling her, until she shut up. The room was silent.

Olga said: 'Who the hell are you people?'

Stanley looked at the perfume spray on the table and said fearfully: 'Why is that bottle double-bagged?'

Miranda slipped out through the door.

5:45 a.m.

Kit stared in fear at the *Diablerie* bottle on the kitchen table. But the glass did not smash; the top did not fall off; the double plastic bags stayed intact. The lethal fluid remained safely inside its fragile container.

But now that Nigel and Daisy had pulled guns, they could no longer pretend to be innocent victims of the storm. As soon as the news from the laboratory got out, they would be connected with the theft of the virus.

Nigel, Daisy, and Elton might escape, but Kit was in a different position. There was no doubt who he was. Even if he escaped today, he would be a fugitive from justice for the rest of his life.

He thought furiously, trying to devise a way out.

Then, as everyone stood frozen, staring at the vicious little dark-grey pistols, Nigel moved his gun a fraction of an inch, mistrustfully pointing it at Kit, and Kit was seized by inspiration.

There was still no reason why the family should suspect *him*, he realized. He might have been deceived by the three fugitives. His story that they were total strangers still stood up.

But how could he make that clear?

Slowly, he raised his hands in the traditional gesture of surrender.

Everyone looked at him. There was a moment when he thought the gang themselves would betray him. A frown passed over Nigel's brow. Elton looked openly startled. Daisy sneered.

Kit said: 'Dad, I'm so sorry I brought these people into the house. I had no idea . . .'

His father gave him a long look, then nodded. 'Not your fault,' he said. 'You can't turn strangers away in a blizzard. There was no way you could have known . . .' He turned and gave Nigel a look of scorching contempt. '. . . just what *kind* of people they are.'

Nigel got it immediately, and jumped in to back up Kit's pretence. 'I'm sorry to return your hospitality this way . . . Kit, is it? Yes . . . You saved our lives in the snow, now we're pointing guns at you. This old world never was fair.'

Elton's expression cleared as he grasped the deception.

Nigel went on: 'If your bossy sister hadn't poked her nose in, we might have left peacefully, and you would never have found out what bad people we are. But she would insist.'

Daisy finally understood, and turned away with a scornful expression.

It occurred to Kit that Nigel and the gang might just kill his family. They were willing to steal a virus that would slaughter thousands, why would they hesitate to gun down the Oxenfords? It was different, of course: the notion of killing thousands with a virus was a bit abstract, whereas shooting adults and children in cold blood would be more difficult. But they might do it if they had to. They might kill him, too, he realized with a shudder. Fortunately, they still needed him. He knew the way to Luke's cottage and the Toyota Land Cruiser. They would never find it without him. He resolved to remind Nigel of that at the first opportunity.

'What's in that bottle is worth a lot of money, you see,' Nigel finished.

To reinforce the simulation, Kit said: 'What is it?'

'Never you mind,' said Nigel.

Kit's mobile phone rang.

He did not know what to do. The caller was probably Hamish. There must have been some development at the Kremlin that the inside man thought Kit needed to know about. But how could he speak to Hamish without betraying himself to his family? He stood paralysed, while everyone listened to his ring tone playing Beethoven's ninth symphony.

Nigel solved the problem. 'Give me that,' he said.

Kit handed over his phone, and Nigel answered it. 'Yes, this is Kit,' he said, in a fair imitation of a Scots accent.

The person at the other end seemed to believe him, for there was a silence while Nigel listened.

'Got it,' he said. 'Thanks.' He hung up and pocketed the phone. 'Someone wanting to warn you about three dangerous desperadoes in the neighbourhood,' he said. 'Apparently the police are coming after them with a snowplough.'

*　　　　　*　　　　　*

Craig could not figure Sophie out. One minute she was painfully shy, the next bold to the point of embarrassment.

She let him put his hands inside her sweater, and even unfastened her bra when he fumbled with the hooks; and he thought he would die of pleasure when he held both her breasts in his hands – but then she refused to let him look at them in the candlelight. He got even more excited when she unbuttoned his jeans, as if she had been doing this sort of thing for years; but she did not seem to know what to do next. Craig wondered whether there was some code of behaviour that he did not know about. Or was she just as inexperienced as he? She was getting better at kissing, anyway. At first she had been hesitant, as if not really sure whether she really wanted to do it; but after a couple of hours' practice she was enthusiastic.

Craig felt like a sailor in a storm. All night he had ridden waves of hope and despair, desire and disappointment, anxiety and delight. At one moment she had whispered: 'You're so nice. I'm not nice. I'm vile.' And then, when he kissed her again, her face was wet with tears. What are you supposed to do, he wondered, when a girl starts crying while you've got your hand inside her knickers? He had started to withdraw his hand, feeling that must be what she wanted, but she had grabbed his wrist and held him there. 'I think you're nice,' he had said, but that sounded feeble, so he added: 'I think you're wonderful.'

Although he felt bewildered, he was also intensely happy. He had never felt so close to a girl. He was bursting with love and tenderness and joy. When he heard the noise from the kitchen, they were talking about how far to go.

She had said: 'Do you want to go the whole way?'

'Do you?'

'I do if you do.'

Craig nodded. 'I really want to.'

'Have you got condoms?'

'Yes.' He fumbled in his jeans pocket and took out the little packet.

'So you planned this?'

'I didn't have a plan.' It was half true: he hadn't had much of a plan. 'I was hoping, though. Ever since I met you I've been thinking about, well, seeing you again, and so on. And all day today . . .'

'You were so persistent.'

'I just wanted to be with you like this.'

It was not very eloquent, but it seemed to be what she wanted to hear. 'All right, then. Let's do it.'

'Are you sure?'

'Yes. Now. Quickly.'

'Good.'

'Oh, my God, what's that?'

Craig had been aware of people in the kitchen below. He had vaguely heard the murmur of voices, then someone had clattered a saucepan, and he had smelled bacon. He was not sure what the time was, but it seemed early for breakfast. However, he had taken no notice, confident that no one would interrupt them here in the attic. Now the sounds could not be ignored. First he heard Grandpa shout – an unusual event in itself. Nellie started barking like a fiend; there was a scream that sounded remarkably like Craig's mother; then several male voices yelled at once.

Sophie said in a frightened voice: 'Is this normal?'

'No,' he replied. 'They have arguments, but not shouting matches.'

'What's going on?'

He hesitated. Part of him wanted to forget the noise and act as if he and Sophie were in a universe of their own, lying on the old sofa under their coats. He could have ignored an earthquake to concentrate on her soft skin and hot breath and moist lips. But another part of him felt that the interruption was not entirely unwelcome. They had done almost everything: it might even be nice to postpone the ultimate, so that there was something else to look forward to, a further delight to anticipate.

Below them, the kitchen went quiet as suddenly as it had burst into sound.

'Strange,' he said.

'It's spooky.'

Sophie sounded frightened, and that made up Craig's mind. He kissed her lips once more, then stood up. He pulled up his jeans and stepped across the attic to the hole in the floor. He lay down and looked through the gap in the floorboards.

He saw his mother, standing up with her mouth open, looking shocked and frightened. Grandpa was wiping blood off his chin. Uncle Kit had his hands in the air. Three strangers were in the room. At first he thought they were all men, then he realized one was an ugly girl with a shaved head. The young black man was holding Nellie's collar, twisting it hard. The older man and the girl held guns.

Craig murmured: 'Bloody hell, what's happening down there?'

Sophie lay beside him. After a moment she gasped. 'Are those things guns?' she whispered.

'Yes.'

'Oh, my God, we're in trouble.'

Craig thought. 'We have to call the police. Where's your phone?'

'I left it in the barn.'

'Damn.'

'Oh, God, what can we do?'

'Think. Think. A phone. We need a phone.' Craig hesitated.

He was frightened. He really wanted to lie still and shut his eyes tightly. He might have done that, had it not been for the girl beside him. He did not know all the rules, but he knew that a man was supposed to show courage when a girl was frightened, especially when they were lovers, or nearly. And if he was not feeling brave, he had to pretend.

Where was the nearest phone? 'There's an extension beside Grandpa's bed.'

Sophie said: 'I can't do anything, I'm too scared.'

'You'd better stay here.'

'Okay.'

Craig stood up. He buttoned his jeans and buckled the belt, then went to the low door. He took a breath, then opened it. He crawled into Grandpa's suit cupboard, pushed at the door, and emerged into the dressing room.

The lights were on. Grandpa's dark-brown brogue-style shoes were side by side on the carpet, and the blue shirt he had been wearing yesterday lay on top of a pile of clothes in the linen basket. Craig stepped into the bedroom. The bed was unmade, as if Grandpa had just got out of it. On the bedside table was a copy of *Scientific American* magazine, open – and the phone.

Craig had never dialled 999 in his life. What were

you supposed to say? He had seen people do it on television. You had to give your name and location, he thought. Then what? 'There are men with guns in our kitchen.' It sounded melodramatic – but probably all 999 calls were dramatic.

He picked up the phone. There was no dialling tone.

He put his finger on the cradle and jiggled it, then listened again. Nothing.

He replaced the handset. Why were the phones out? Was it just a fault – or had the strangers cut the wires?

Did Grandpa have a mobile? Craig pulled open the bedside drawer. Inside he saw a torch and a book, but no phone. Then he remembered: Grandpa had a phone in his car, but did not carry a mobile.

He heard a sound from the dressing room. Sophie poked her head out of the suit cupboard, looking frightened. 'Someone's coming!' she hissed. A moment later, Craig heard a heavy footstep on the landing.

He darted into the dressing room. Sophie ducked back into the attic. Craig fell on his knees and crawled through the suit cupboard just as he heard the bedroom door open. He had no time to close the cupboard door. He wriggled through the low door, then quickly turned and closed it softly behind him.

Sophie whispered: 'The older man told the girl to search the house. He called her Daisy.'

'I heard her boots on the landing.'

'Did you get through to the police?'

He shook his head. 'The phone's dead.'

'No!'

He heard Daisy's heavy tread in the dressing room. She

would see the open cupboard door. Would she spot the low door behind the suits? Only if she looked carefully.

Craig listened. Was she staring into the open cupboard at this minute? He felt shaky. Daisy was not big – an inch or two shorter than he was, he guessed – but she looked absolutely terrifying.

The silence dragged out. He thought he heard her step into the bathroom. After a shorter pause, her boots crossed the dressing room and faded away. The bedroom door slammed.

'Oh, God, I'm so scared,' Sophie said.

'Me, too,' said Craig.

*　　　　*　　　　*

Miranda was in Olga's bedroom with Hugo.

When she left the kitchen she had not known what to do. She could not go outside – she was in her nightdress and bare feet. She had raced up the stairs with the thought of locking herself in the bathroom, but realized almost at once that that would be useless. She stood on the landing, dithering. She was so frightened that she wanted to vomit. She had to call the police, that was the priority.

Olga had her mobile in the pocket of her silk robe – but Hugo probably had his own.

Frightened though she was, Miranda had hesitated for a split second outside the door. The last thing she wanted was to be in a bedroom with Hugo. Then she heard someone step out of the kitchen into the hall. Quickly, she opened Hugo's door, slid inside, and closed it quietly.

Hugo was standing at the window, looking out. He was naked, and had his back to the door. 'Would you look at this bloody weather?' he said, obviously thinking his wife had come back.

Miranda was momentarily arrested by his casual tone. Obviously Olga and Hugo had made up their quarrel, after yelling at one another half the night. Had Olga already forgiven her husband for having sex with her sister? It seemed quick – but perhaps they had had this row before, about other women. Miranda had often wondered about Olga's deal with her flirtatious husband, but Olga had never spoken of it. Maybe they had a script: infidelity, discovery, quarrel, reconciliation, then back to infidelity.

'It's me,' Miranda said.

He spun around, startled, then smiled. 'And in déshabillé – what a lovely surprise! Let's get into bed, quick.'

She heard heavy footsteps on the stairs, and at the same time noticed that Hugo's belly was much bigger than when she had gone to bed with him – he looked like a little round gnome – and she wondered how she could have found him attractive. 'You have to phone the police right now,' she said. 'Where's your mobile?'

'Just here,' he said, pointing to the bedside table. 'What on earth is wrong?'

'People with guns in the kitchen – dial 999, quickly!'

'Who are they?'

'Never bloody mind!' She heard heavy footsteps on the landing. She stood frozen, terrified that the door would burst open, but the steps went by. Her voice became a kind of low scream. 'They're probably looking for me, get on with it!'

Hugo came out of shock. He snatched up his phone,

dropped it on the floor, picked it up, and jabbed at the On button. 'Damn thing takes for ever!' he said in frustration. 'Did you say *guns*?'

'Yes!'

'How did the people get in?'

'Said they were stranded – what is the matter with that phone?'

'Searching,' he said. 'Come on, come on!'

Miranda heard the footsteps outside again. This time she was ready. She flung herself on the floor and slid sideways under the double bed just as the door flew open.

She closed her eyes and tried to make herself small. Feeling foolish, she opened her eyes again. She saw Hugo's bare feet, with hairy ankles, and a pair of black motorcycle boots with steel-tipped toes. She heard Hugo say: 'Hello, gorgeous, who are you?'

His charm did not work on Daisy. She said: 'Give me that phone.'

'I was just—'

'Now, you fat fool.'

'Here, take it.'

'Now come with me.'

'Let me put something on.'

'Don't worry, I'm not going to bite your little cock off.'

Miranda saw Hugo's feet step away from Daisy. She moved quickly towards him, then there was the sound of a blow, and he let out a cry. Both pairs of feet moved towards the door together. They passed out of Miranda's sight, and a moment later she heard them going down the stairs.

Miranda said to herself: 'Oh, God, what do I do now?'

6 a.m.

Craig and Sophie lay side by side on the floorboards of the attic, looking down through the hole into the kitchen, as Craig's father was dragged naked into the room by Daisy.

Craig was shocked and disturbed. It was a scene from a nightmare, or an old painting of sinners being dragged down into hell. He could hardly grasp that this humiliated, helpless figure was his *father*, the master of the house, the only person with the nerve to stand up to his domineering mother, the man who had ruled Craig for all fifteen years of his life. He felt disoriented and weightless, as if gravity had been switched off and he did not know which way was down.

Sophie began to cry softly. 'This is awful,' she whispered. 'We're all going to be murdered.'

The need to comfort her gave Craig strength. He put his arm around her narrow shoulders. She was trembling. 'It is awful, but we're not dead yet,' he said. 'We can get help.'

'How?'

'Where is your phone, exactly?'

'I left it in the barn, upstairs by the bed. I think I dropped it into my suitcase when I changed.'

'We have to go there and use it to call the police.'

'What if those terrible people see us?'

'We'll stay away from the kitchen windows.'

'We can't – the barn door is right opposite!'

She was right, Craig knew, but they had to take the risk. 'They probably won't look out.'

'But what if they do?'

'You can hardly see across the back yard anyway, in this snow.'

'They're bound to spot us!'

He did not know what else to tell her. 'We have to try.'

'I can't do it. Let's just stay here.'

It was tempting, but Craig knew that if he hid himself and did nothing to help his family, he would feel ashamed. 'You can stay, if you like, while I go to the barn.'

'No – don't leave me alone!'

He had guessed she might say that. 'Then you'll have to come with me.'

'I don't want to.'

He squeezed her shoulders and kissed her cheek. 'Come on. Be brave.'

She wiped her nose on her sleeve. 'I'll try.'

He stood up and put on his boots and coat. Sophie sat motionless, watching him in the candlelight. Trying to walk softly, for fear of being heard below, he found her rubber boots, then knelt down and put them on her small feet. She cooperated passively, stunned by shock. He gently pulled her upright and helped her on with her anorak. He zipped it up at the front, pulled the hood over her head, then brushed her hair back with his hand. The hood gave her a gamine look, and for a fleeting moment he thought how pretty she was.

He opened the big loft door. A freezing wind blew a dense flurry of snow into the attic. The lamp over the back door spread a small half-circle of light, showing the snow lying thicker than ever on the ground. The dustbin lid looked like Ali Baba's hat.

There were two windows at this end of the house, one from the pantry and the other from the boot lobby. The sinister strangers were in the kitchen. If he was very unlucky, one of them might step into the pantry or the boot lobby at just the wrong moment, and spot him – but he thought the odds were in his favour.

'Come on,' he said.

Sophie stood beside him and looked down. 'You go first.'

He leaned out. There was a light in the boot lobby, but not in the pantry. Would anyone see him? On his own he might have been terrified, but Sophie's fear made him braver. He swept the snow off the ledge with his hand, then walked along it to the lean-to roof of the boot lobby. He swept a section of the roof clear, then stood upright and reached out to her. He held her hand as she inched along the edge. 'You're doing fine,' he said softly. It was not difficult – the ledge was a foot wide – but she was shaky. At last she stepped down to the lean-to roof. 'Well done,' Craig said.

Then she slipped.

Her feet skidded from under her. Craig still had hold of her hand, but he could not keep her upright, and she sat down with a thud that must have reverberated below. She landed awkwardly and tipped over backwards, sliding down the icy slates on her bottom.

Craig grabbed at her and grasped a handful of anorak. He tugged, trying to arrest her slide, but his feet were on the same slippery surface, and all that happened was that she drew him along with her. He skated down the roof after her, struggling to remain upright and trying to slow her down.

When her feet hit the gutter at the lip of the roof, she came to a halt; but her bottom was half off the sloping side edge. She tilted sideways. Craig tightened his grip on her coat and pulled, drawing her towards him and safety – then he slipped again. He let go of her coat, waving his arms to stay upright.

Sophie screamed and fell off the roof.

She dropped ten feet and landed in soft new snow behind the dustbin.

Craig leaned over the edge. Little light fell in that dark corner, and he could hardly see her. 'Are you all right?' he said. There was no reply. Had she been knocked unconscious? 'Sophie!'

'I'm okay,' she said miserably.

The back door opened.

Quickly, Craig lowered himself to a sitting position.

A man stepped out. Craig could just see a head of short dark hair. He glanced over the side. The extra light spilling from the open door made Sophie just visible. Her pink anorak disappeared into the snow, but her dark jeans showed. She lay still. He could not see her face.

A voice from inside called: 'Elton! Who's out there?'

Elton waved a torch from side to side, but the beam showed nothing but snowflakes. Craig flattened himself on the roof.

Elton turned to the right, away from Sophie, and walked a few steps into the storm, shining his torch in front of him.

Craig pressed himself to the roof, hoping Elton would not glance up. Then he realized that the loft door was still wide open. If Elton happened to shine his torch that way, he could not fail to see it and investigate – which would be disastrous. Moving slowly, Craig crawled up the lean-to roof. As soon as he could reach, he got hold of the lower edge of the door and gently pushed it. It swung slowly through an arc. Craig gave it a final shove and released it, then quickly lay down again. The door closed with an audible click.

Elton turned. Craig lay still. He saw the beam of the torch play over the gable end of the house and the loft door.

The voice came from inside again. 'Elton?'

The torch beam moved off. 'I can't see nothing,' Elton shouted back irritably.

Craig risked moving his head to look. Elton was walking the other way, towards Sophie. He stopped at the dustbin. If he peeked around the angle of the lobby and shone his torch into the corner, he would see her. When that happened, Craig decided, he would dive off the roof onto Elton's head. He would probably get beaten up, but Sophie might escape.

After a long moment, Elton turned away. 'Nothing out here but fucking snow,' he called out, and he stepped back inside the house and slammed the door.

Craig groaned with relief. He found he was shaking. He tried to make himself calm. Thinking about Sophie helped.

He jumped off the roof and landed beside her. Bending down, he said: 'Did you hurt yourself?'

She sat up. 'No, but I'm so scared.'

'Okay. Can you stand up?'

'Are you sure he's gone?'

'I saw him go in and close the door. They must have heard your scream, or maybe the bump as you slipped on the roof – but in this storm they probably aren't sure it was anything.'

'Oh, God, I hope so.' She struggled to her feet.

Craig frowned, thinking. The gang were obviously alert. If he and Sophie went directly across the yard to the barn, they could be seen by someone looking out of the kitchen windows. They would do better to strike out into the garden, circle around the guest cottage, and approach the barn from behind. They would still risk being seen going in through the door, but the roundabout route would minimize their exposure. 'This way,' he said. He took her hand, and she followed him willingly enough.

They felt the wind blowing more fiercely. The storm was coming in off the sea. Away from the shelter of the house, the snow no longer fell in swirling flurries, but pelted down in hard straight lines at an angle, stinging their faces and getting into their eyes.

When Craig could no longer see the house, he turned at a right angle. Their progress was slow. The snow lay two feet deep, making it tiring to walk. He could not see the cottage. Measuring his steps, Craig walked what he guessed was the width of the yard. Now completely blind, he figured he must have drawn level with the barn, and he turned again. He counted the paces until he should have bumped up against its wooden end wall.

But there was nothing.

He felt sure he could not have gone wrong. He had been meticulous. He walked another five paces. He feared they might be lost, but he did not want Sophie to know that. Suppressing a feeling of panic, he turned again, heading back towards the main house. The complete darkness meant that Sophie could not see his face so, fortunately, she did not know how scared he was.

They had been outside less than five minutes, but already his feet and hands were agonizingly cold. Craig realized they were in serious danger. If they could not find shelter, they would freeze to death.

Sophie was not stupid. 'Where are we?'

Craig made himself sound more confident than he felt. 'Just coming up to the barn. A few steps more.'

He should not have made such a rash prediction. After ten more steps they were still in blackness.

He figured he must have walked farther away from the buildings than he had at first reckoned. Therefore his return leg had been too short. He swung right again. Now he had turned so many times that he was no longer sure of his angles. He trudged ten more strides and stopped.

'Are we lost?' Sophie said in a small voice.

'We can't be far from the barn!' Craig said angrily. 'We only went a few steps into the garden.'

She put her arms around him and hugged him. 'It's not your fault.'

He knew it was, but he was grateful to her anyway.

'We could shout,' she suggested. 'Caroline and Tom might hear us and shout back.'

'Those people in the kitchen might hear us too.'

'That would be better than freezing.'

She was right, but Craig did not want to admit it. How was it possible to get lost in just a few yards? He refused to believe it.

He hugged her, but felt despair. He had thought himself superior to Sophie, because she was more frightened than he, and he had felt very manly for a few moments, protecting her; but now he had got them both lost. Some man, he thought; some protector. Her boyfriend the law student would have done better, if he existed.

From the corner of his eye, he saw a light.

He turned in that direction, and it was gone. His eyes registered nothing but blackness. Wishful thinking?

Sophie sensed his tension. 'What?'

'I thought I saw a light.' When he turned his face to her, the light seemed to reappear in the corner of his eye. But when he looked up again it was gone.

He vaguely remembered something from Biology about peripheral vision registering things invisible to direct sight. There was a reason for it that had to do with the blind spot on the retina. He turned to Sophie again. The light reappeared. This time he did not turn towards it, but concentrated on what he could make out without moving his eyes. The light flickered, but it was there.

He turned towards it, and it was gone again; but he knew its direction. 'This way.'

They ploughed through the snow. The light did not immediately reappear, and Craig wondered if he had suffered a hallucination, like the mirage of an oasis seen in the desert. Then it flickered into sight and immediately disappeared again.

'I saw it!' Sophie cried.

They trudged on. Two seconds later, it came back into view, and this time it stayed. Craig felt a rush of relief, and realized that for a few moments back there he really had thought he was going to die and take Sophie with him.

When they came closer to the light, he saw that it was the one over the back door. They had walked around in a circle, and now they were back where they had started.

6:15 a.m.

Miranda lay still for a long time. She was terrified that Daisy would return, but unable to do anything about it. In her mind, Daisy came stomping into the room in her motorcycle boots, knelt on the floor, and looked under the bed. Miranda could see Daisy's brutish face, the shaved skull and the broken nose and the dark eyes that looked bruised by the black eyeliner. The vision of that face was so scary that sometimes Miranda just squeezed her eyes shut as tightly as she could, until she saw fireworks on the back of her eyelids.

In the end it was the thought of Tom that made her move. Somehow she had to protect her eleven-year-old son. But how? There was nothing she could do alone. She would be willing to put her body between the gang and the children, but it would be pointless: she would be thrown aside like a sack of potatoes. Civilized people were no good at violence, that was what made them civilized.

The answer was the same as before. She had to find a phone and get help.

That meant she had to go to the guest cottage. She had to crawl out from under the bed, leave the bedroom, and creep downstairs, hoping she would not be heard by the gang in the kitchen, praying that one of them would not step into the hall and see her. She needed to grab a coat and boots, for she was barefoot and naked but for a cotton nightdress, and she knew she could not go three yards, dressed as she was, in a blizzard with the snow two feet deep. Then she had to make her way around the house, staying well away from the windows, to the cottage, and get the phone she had left in her handbag on the floor by the door.

She tried to summon her nerve. What was she frightened of? The tension, she thought: the strain was petrifying. But it would not be for long. Half a minute to go down the stairs; a minute to put on coat and boots; two minutes, perhaps three, to tramp through the snow to the cottage. Less than five minutes, that was all.

She began to feel resentful. How dare they make her scared to walk around her own father's house? Indignation gave her courage.

Shaking, she slid out from under the bed. The bedroom door was open. She peeped out, saw that all was clear, and stepped onto the landing. She could hear voices from the kitchen. She looked down.

There was a hat stand at the foot of the stairs. Most of the family's coats and boots were kept in a walk-in closet in the boot lobby by the back door, but Daddy always left his in the hall, and she could see his old blue anorak hanging from the stand, and below it the leather-lined rubber boots that kept his feet warm while he walked Nellie. They should be enough to keep her from freezing to death while she ploughed through the snow to the cottage. It would take her only a few seconds to slip them on and sneak out through the front door.

If she had the guts.

She started to tiptoe down the stairs.

The voices from the kitchen became louder. There was an argument going on. She heard Nigel say: 'Well, bloody well look again, then!' Did that mean someone was going to search the house? She turned and ran back, going up the stairs two at a time. As she reached the landing, she heard heavy boots in the hall – Daisy.

It was no good hiding under the bed again. If Daisy was being sent back for a second search, she was bound to look harder this time. Miranda stepped into her father's bedroom. There was one place she could hide: the attic. When she was ten years old, she had made it her den. All the children had, at different times.

The door of the suit cupboard stood open.

She heard Daisy's steps on the landing.

She fell to her knees, crawled inside, and opened the low door that led to the attic. Then she turned and closed the cupboard door behind her. She backed into the attic and closed the low door.

She realized immediately that she had made an error that might be fatal. Daisy had searched the house a quarter of an hour or so ago. She must have seen the door of the suit cupboard standing open. Would she now remember that, and realize that someone must have closed it subsequently? And would she be smart enough to guess why?

Miranda heard footsteps in the dressing room. She held her breath as Daisy walked to the bathroom and back. She heard the sound of cupboard doors being flung open. She bit her thumb to keep from screaming with fear. There was a brushing sound as Daisy rummaged among suits and shirts. The low door was hard to see, unless you got down on your knees and looked under the hanging clothes. Would Daisy be so thorough?

There was a long moment of quiet.

Then Daisy's footsteps receded through the bedroom.

Miranda felt so relieved that she wanted to cry. She stopped herself: she had to be brave. What was happening in the kitchen? She remembered the hole in the floor. She crawled slowly across to take a look.

*　　　　　*　　　　　*

Hugo looked so pathetic that Kit almost felt sorry for him. He was a short man, and podgy. He had fatty breasts with hairy nipples and a belly that hung over his genitals. The thin legs below his round body made him look like an ill-designed doll. He seemed all the more tragic by contrast with his usual self. He was normally poised and self-assured, dressed in natty suits that flattered his figure, and he flirted with the confidence of a matinee idol. Now he looked foolish and mortified.

The family were crowded together at one end of the kitchen, by the pantry door, away from any exits: Kit himself, his sister Olga in her black silk wrap, their father with swollen lips where Daisy had punched him, and Olga's husband, the naked Hugo. Stanley was sitting down, holding Nellie, stroking her to keep her calm, afraid she would be shot if she attacked the strangers. Nigel and Elton stood on the other side of the table, and Daisy was searching the upstairs.

Hugo stepped forward. 'There are towels and things in

the laundry,' he said. The laundry was off the kitchen, on the same side as the dining room. 'Let me get something to wrap around me.'

Daisy heard this as she returned from her search. She picked up a tea towel. 'Try this,' she said, and flicked it at his crotch. Kit remembered, from school shower-room horseplay, how that could sting. Hugo let out an involuntary yelp. He turned around, and she flicked it again, catching him on the backside. He skipped away, into the corner, and Daisy laughed. Hugo was completely humiliated.

It was unpleasant to see, and Kit felt slightly sick.

'Stop playing around,' Nigel said angrily. 'I want to know where the other sister is – Miranda. She must have slipped out. Where did she go?'

Daisy said: 'I've looked all over the house twice. She's not in the building.'

'She could be hiding.'

'And she could be the invisible fucking woman, but I can't find her.'

Kit knew where she was. A minute ago he had seen Nellie cock her head and lift one black ear. Someone had entered the attic, and it had to be Miranda. Kit wondered if his father had noticed Nellie's reaction. Miranda was no great threat, up there with no phone, wearing only a nightdress. Still Kit wondered if there was a way he could warn Nigel about her.

Elton said: 'Maybe she went outside. That noise we heard was probably her.'

Nigel's reply betrayed exasperation. 'So how come you didn't see her when you went to look?'

'Because it's bloody dark!' Elton was becoming irritated by Nigel's hectoring tone.

Kit guessed the noise outside had been some of the kids, fooling around. There had been a thud, then a scream, as if a person or animal had hit the back door. A deer might have bumped into the door, but deer did not scream, they made a mooing sound like cattle. A large bird could conceivably have been blown against the door by the storm, and might have made a noise like a scream. However, Kit thought the likeliest culprit was Miranda's son, young Tom. He was eleven, just the right age for creeping around at night, playing commandos.

If Tom had looked through the window and seen the guns, what would he do? First he would search for his mother, but he would not find her. Then he would wake his sister, perhaps, or Ned. Either way, Nigel had little time to spare. He needed to capture the rest of the family before anyone made a phone call. But there was nothing Kit could do without blowing his cover, so he sat tight and kept his mouth shut.

'She was only wearing a nightdress,' Nigel said. 'She can't have gone far.'

Elton said: 'Well, I'll go and check the outbuildings, shall I?'

'Wait a minute.' Nigel frowned, thinking. 'We've searched every room in the house, yeah?'

Daisy said: 'Aye, like I told you.'

'We've taken mobile phones from three of them – Kit, the naked gnome, and the snotty sister. And we're sure there are no others in the house.'

'Aye.' Daisy had checked for phones when she was searching.

'Then we'd better check the other buildings.'

'Right,' Elton said. 'There's a cottage, a barn, and a garage, the old man said.'

'Check the garage first – there will be phones in the cars. Then the cottage and the barn. Round up the rest of the family and bring them here. Make sure you get all their phones. We'll just keep them all under guard here for an hour or two, then we'll scarper.'

It was not a bad plan, Kit thought. When all the family was in one place, with no phones, there would be nothing they could do. No one was going to come to the door on Christmas morning – no milkman, no postman, no delivery van from Tesco or Majestic Wine – so there was no danger of any outsider becoming suspicious. The gang could sit tight and wait for daylight.

Elton put on his jacket and looked out of the window, peering into the snow. Following his gaze, Kit noticed that the cottage and barn across the courtyard were barely visible through the snow by the light of the outside lamps. There was still no let-up.

Daisy said: 'I'll check the garage if Elton goes to the cottage.'

Elton said: 'We'd better get on with it, someone might be dialling 999 right now.'

Daisy pocketed her gun and zipped up her leather jacket.

Nigel said: 'Before you go, let's shut this lot up someplace where they can't cause trouble.'

That was when Hugo jumped Nigel.

Everyone was taken totally by surprise. Kit had written Hugo off, as had the gang. But he leaped forward with furious energy, punching Nigel in the face again and again with both fists. He had chosen his moment well, for Daisy had put her weapon away, and Elton had never drawn his, so Nigel was the only one with a gun in his hand, and he was so busy trying to dodge blows that he could not use it.

Nigel staggered back, bumping against the kitchen counter. Hugo went at him like a fiend, thumping his face and body, screaming something incomprehensible. In a few seconds he landed a lot of blows, but Nigel did not drop the gun.

Elton was the quickest to react. He grabbed Hugo and tried to pull him off. Being naked, Hugo was hard to grasp and, for a moment, Elton could not get a grip, his hands sliding off Hugo's moving shoulders.

Stanley released Nellie, who was barking furiously, and the dog flung herself on Elton, biting his legs. She was an old dog, and had a soft mouth, but she was a distraction.

Daisy reached for her gun. The barrel seemed to catch on her pocket lining as she tried to draw it out. Then Olga picked up a plate and threw it across the room at her. Daisy dodged, and the plate hit her glancingly on the shoulder.

Kit stepped forward to grab Hugo, then stopped himself.

The last thing he wanted was for the family to overwhelm the gang. Although he was shocked by the true purpose of the theft he had organized, his own survival was uppermost in his mind. It was less than twenty-four hours since Daisy had almost killed him in the swimming pool, and he knew that, if he failed to repay her father, he faced an end every bit as painful as death from the virus in the perfume bottle. He would intervene on Nigel's side, against his own family, if he had to – but did he have to? He still wanted to maintain the fiction that he had never seen Nigel before tonight. So he stood helplessly looking on as contrary impulses clashed within him.

Elton put both arms around Hugo in a powerful bear hug. Hugo struggled gamely, but he was smaller and less fit, and could not shake Elton off. Elton lifted Hugo's feet off the ground and stepped back, pulling him away from Nigel.

Daisy kicked Nellie accurately in the ribs with a heavy boot, and the dog whimpered and fled to the corner of the room.

Nigel was bleeding from his nose and mouth, and there were angry red marks around his eyes. He glared malevolently at Hugo and raised his right hand, which still grasped the gun.

Olga took a step forward, shouting: 'No!'

Instantly, Nigel swung his arm and pointed the gun at her.

Stanley grabbed her and held her back, saying at the same time: 'Don't shoot, please don't shoot.'

Nigel kept the gun pointed at Olga and said: 'Daisy, have you still got that sap?' Looking pleased, Daisy took out her cosh. Nigel nodded towards Hugo. 'Hurt this bastard.'

Seeing what was coming, Hugo began to struggle, but Elton tightened his hold.

Daisy drew back her right arm and smashed the cosh into Hugo's face. It hit his cheekbone with a sickening crunch. He made a noise between a shout and a scream. Daisy hit him again, and blood spurted from his mouth and ran down his bare chest. With a spiteful grin, Daisy eyed his genitals, then kicked him in the groin. She hit him with the cosh again, this time on the top of his head, and he fell unconscious. But that made no difference to Daisy. She hit him full on the nose, then kicked him again.

Olga let out a wail of grief and rage, broke free of her father's grasp, and threw herself at Daisy.

Daisy swung the cosh at her, but Olga was too close, and the blow whistled behind her head.

Elton dropped Hugo, who slumped on the tiled floor, and made a grab for Olga.

Olga got her hands on Daisy's face and scratched.

Nigel had his gun pointed at Olga but he hesitated to shoot, no doubt fearing that he would hit Elton or Daisy, both of whom were struggling with Olga.

Stanley turned to the stovetop and picked up the heavy frying pan in which Kit had scrambled a dozen eggs. He raised it high in the air then brought it down on Nigel, aiming at the man's head. At the last instant Nigel saw it coming, and dodged. The pan hit his right shoulder. He cried out in pain, and the gun flew from his hand.

Stanley tried to catch the gun, but missed. It landed on the kitchen table an inch from the perfume bottle. It bounced onto the seat of a pine chair, rolled over, and dropped to the floor at Kit's feet.

Kit bent down and picked it up.

Nigel and Stanley looked at him. Sensing the dramatic change, Olga, Daisy, and Elton stopped fighting and turned to look at Kit holding the gun.

Kit hesitated, torn in half by the agony of the decision. They all stared at him for a long moment of stillness.

At last he turned the gun around, holding it by the barrel, and gave it back to Nigel.

6:30 a.m.

Craig and Sophie found the barn at last.

They had waited a few minutes by the back door, hesitating, then realized they would freeze to death if they stayed there indefinitely. Screwing up their courage, they crossed the yard directly, heads bent, praying that no one would look out of the kitchen windows. The twenty paces from one side to the other seemed to take forever through the thick snow. Then they followed the front wall of the barn, always in full view from the kitchen. Craig did not dare to look in that direction: he was too frightened of what he might see. When at last they reached the door, he took one swift glance. In the dark he could not see the building itself, just the lighted windows. The snow further obscured his view, and he could see only vague figures moving in the kitchen. There was no sign that anyone had glanced out at the wrong moment.

He pulled the big door open. They stepped inside, and he closed it gratefully. Warm air washed over him. He was shivering, and Sophie's teeth were chattering like castanets. She threw off her snow-covered anorak and sat on one of the big hospital-style radiators. Craig would have liked to take a minute to warm himself, but there was no time for that – he had to get help fast.

The place was dimly lit by a night light next to the camp bed where Tom lay. Craig looked closely at the boy, wondering whether to wake him. He seemed to have recovered from Sophie's vodka, and was sleeping peacefully in his Spiderman pyjamas.

Craig's eye was caught by something on the floor beside the pillow. It was a photograph. Craig picked it up and held it in the light. It appeared to have been taken at his mother's birthday party, and showed Tom with Sophie, her arm around his shoulders. Craig smiled to himself. I'm not the only one who was captivated by her that afternoon, he thought. He put the picture back, saying nothing to Sophie.

There was no point in waking Tom, he decided. There was nothing the boy could do, and he would only be terrified. He was better off asleep.

Craig went quickly up the ladder that led to the hayloft bedroom. On one of the narrow beds he could make out the heap of blankets that covered his sister Caroline. She seemed fast asleep. Like Tom, she was better off that way. If she woke up and found out what was going on she would have hysterics. He would try not to wake her.

The second bed had not been slept in. On the floor next to it he could see the shape of an open suitcase. Sophie said she had dropped her phone on top of her clothes. Craig crossed the room, moving cautiously in the near-dark. As he bent down he heard, very near to him, the soft rustle and squeak of something alive, and he grunted a startled curse, his heart hammering in his chest; then he realized it was Caroline's damn rats moving in their cage.

He pushed the cage aside and began to search Sophie's case.

Working by touch, he rummaged in the contents. On top was a plastic shopping bag containing a gift-wrapped parcel. Otherwise it was mostly clothes, neatly folded: someone had helped Sophie pack, he guessed, for he did not take her to be a tidy person. He was momentarily distracted by a silky bra, then his hand closed over the oblong shape of a mobile phone. He flipped its lid, but no lights came on. He could not see well enough to find the on–off switch.

He hurried back down the ladder with the phone in his hand. There was a standard lamp by the bookshelf. He turned it on and held Sophie's phone under the light. He found the power button and pressed it, but nothing happened. He could have cried with frustration. 'I can't get the bloody thing to come on!' he whispered.

She held out her hand, still sitting on the radiator, and he gave her the phone. She pressed the same button, frowned, pressed it again, then jabbed at it repeatedly. At last she said: 'The battery has run down.'

'Shit! Where's the charger?'

'I don't know.'

'In your suitcase?'

'I don't think so.'

Craig became exasperated. 'How can you *possibly* not know where your phone charger is?'

Sophie's voice went small. 'I think I left it at home.'

'Jesus Christ!' Craig controlled his temper with an effort. He wanted to tell her she was a stupid fool, but that would not help. He was silent for a moment. The memory of kissing her came back to him, and he could not be angry. His rage evaporated, and he put his arms around her. 'All right,' he said. 'Never mind.'

She rested her head on his chest. 'I'm sorry.'

'Let's think of something else.'

'There must be more phones, or a charger we can use.'

He shook his head. 'Caroline and I don't carry mobiles – my mother won't let us have them. She doesn't go to the toilet without hers, but she says we don't need them.'

'Tom hasn't got one. Miranda thinks he's too young.'

'Hell.'

'Wait!' She pulled away from him. 'Wasn't there one in your grandfather's car?'

Craig snapped his fingers. 'The Ferrari – right! And I left the keys in. All we have to do is get to the garage, and we can phone the police.'

'You mean we have to go outside again?'

'You can stay here.'

'No. I want to come.'

'You wouldn't be alone – Tom and Caroline are here.'

'I want to be with you.'

Craig tried not to show how pleased he was. 'You'd better get your coat on again, then.'

Sophie came off the radiator. Craig picked her coat up from the floor and helped her into it. She looked up at him, and he tried an encouraging smile. 'Ready?'

A trace of her old spirit came back. 'Yeah. Like, what can happen? We could be murdered, that's all. Let's go.'

They went outside. It was still pitch dark, and the snowfall was heavy, bursts of stinging pellets rather than clouds of butterflies. Once again, Craig looked nervously across the yard to the house, but he could see no more than before, which meant the strangers in the kitchen were unlikely to see him. He took Sophie's hand. Steering by the courtyard lights, he led her to the end of the barn, away from the house, then crossed the yard to the garage.

The side door was unlocked, as always. It was as cold inside as out. There were no windows, so Craig risked switching on the lights.

Grandpa's Ferrari was where Craig had left it, parked close to the wall to hide the dent. Like a flash, he remembered the shame and fear he had felt twelve hours ago, after he had crashed into the tree. It seemed strange, now, that he had been so anxious and afraid about something as trivial as a dent in a car. He recalled how eager he had been to impress Sophie and get her to like him. It was not long ago, but it seemed far in the past.

Also in the garage was Luke's Ford Mondeo. The Toyota Land Cruiser had gone: Luke must have borrowed it last night.

He went to the Ferrari and pulled the door handle. It would not open. He tried again, but the door was locked. 'Fuck,' he said feelingly.

'What's the matter?' Sophie said.

'The car's locked.'

'Oh, no!'

He looked inside. 'And the keys have gone.'

'How did that happen?'

Craig banged his fist on the car roof in frustration. 'Luke must have noticed that the car was unlocked last night, when he was leaving. He must have removed the keys from the ignition, locked the car, and taken the keys back to the house for Grandpa.'

'What about the other car?'

Craig opened the door of the Ford and looked inside. 'No phone.'

'Can we get the Ferrari keys back?'

Craig made a face. 'Maybe.'

'Where are they kept?'

'In the key box, on the wall of the boot lobby.'

'At the back of the kitchen?'

Craig nodded grimly. 'Just about two yards from those people with guns.'

6:45 a.m.

The snowplough moved slowly along the two-lane road in the dark. Carl Osborne's Jaguar followed it. Toni was at the wheel of the Jag, peering ahead as the wipers struggled to clear away the thickly falling snow. The view through the windscreen did not change. Straight ahead were the flashing lights of the snowplough; on her near side was the bank of snow freshly shovelled up by the blade; on the off side, virgin snow across the road and over the moors as far as the car's headlamps reached.

Mother was asleep in the back with the puppy on her lap. Beside Toni, Carl was quiet, dozing or sulking. He had told Toni that he hated other people driving his car, but she had insisted, and he had been forced to yield, as she had the keys.

'You just never give an inch, do you?' he had muttered before sinking into silence.

'That's why I was such a good cop,' she had replied.

From the back, Mother had said: 'It's why you haven't got a husband.'

That was more than an hour ago. Now Toni was struggling to stay awake, fighting the hypnotic sway of the wipers, the warmth from the heater, and the monotony of the view. She almost wished she had let Carl drive. But she needed to stay in control.

They had found the getaway vehicle at the Dew Drop Inn. It had contained wigs, false moustaches, and plain-lensed spectacles, obviously disguise materials; but no clues as to where the gang might be headed. The police car had stayed there while the officers questioned Vincent, the young hotel employee Toni had spoken to on the phone. The snowplough continued north, on Frank's instructions.

For once, Toni agreed with Frank. It made sense for the gang to switch cars at a location that was on their route, rather than delay their getaway with a diversion. Of course, there was always the possibility that they foresaw how the police would think, and deliberately chose a location that would mislead pursuers. But in Toni's experience villains were not that subtle. Once they had the swag in their hands, they wanted to get away as fast as they could.

The snowplough did not stop when it passed stationary vehicles. There were two police officers in the cab of the lorry with the driver, but they were under strict instructions to observe only, for they were not armed, and the gang were. Some of the cars were abandoned, others had one or two people inside, but so far none contained three men and a woman. Most of the occupied cars started up and fell in behind the snowplough, following the track it cleared. There was now a small convoy behind the Jaguar.

Toni was beginning to feel pessimistic. She had hoped by now to have spotted the gang. After all, by the time the thieves had left the Dew Drop Inn the roads were all but impassable. How far could they have got?

Could they have some kind of hideout nearby? It seemed

improbable. Thieves did not like to go to earth close to the scene of the crime – quite the opposite. As the convoy moved north, Toni worried more and more that her guess was wrong, and the thieves might have driven south.

She spotted a familiar direction sign saying 'Beach', and realized they must be near Steepfall. Now she had to put the second part of her plan into operation. She had to go to the house and brief Stanley.

She was dreading it. Her job was to prevent this kind of thing happening. She had done several things right: her vigilance had ensured that the theft was discovered sooner rather than later; she had forced the police to take the biohazard seriously and give chase; and Stanley had to be impressed by the way she had reached him in a blizzard. But she wanted to be able to tell him that the perpetrators had been caught and the emergency was over. Instead, she was going to report her own failure. It would not be the joyous reunion she had anticipated.

Frank was at the Kremlin. Using Osborne's car phone, Toni dialled his mobile.

Frank's voice came out of the Jaguar's speakers. 'Detective Superintendent Hackett.'

'Toni here. The snowplough is approaching the turn-off for Stanley Oxenford's house. I'd like to brief him on what's happened.'

'You don't need my permission.'

'I can't get him on the phone, but the house is only a mile down a side road—'

'Forget it. I've got an armed-response team here now, bristling with firepower and itching to go. I'm not going to delay finding the gang.'

'It will take the snowplough five or six minutes to clear the lane – and you'll get me out of your hair. And my mother.'

'Tempting though that is, I'm not willing to hold up the search for five minutes.'

'Stanley may be able to assist the investigation in some way. After all, he is the victim.'

'The answer's no,' Frank said, and he hung up.

Osborne had heard both sides of the conversation. 'This is my car,' he said. 'I'm not going to Steepfall – I want to stay with the snowplough. I might miss something.'

'You can stay with it. You'll leave me and my mother at the house and follow the plough back to the main road. When I've briefed Stanley, I'll borrow a car and catch you up.'

'Well, Frank has nixed that scheme.'

'I haven't played my ace yet.' She dialled Frank again.

This time, his answer was abrupt. 'What?'

'Remember Farmer Johnny.'

'Go to hell.'

'I'm using a hands-free phone, and Carl Osborne is beside me, listening to us both. Where did you tell me to go, again?'

'Pick up the fucking phone.'

Toni detached the handset from its cradle and put it to her ear, so that Carl could not hear Frank. 'Call the snowplough driver, Frank, please.'

'You bitch, you've always held the Farmer Johnny case over my head. You know he was guilty.'

'Everyone knows that. But only you and I know what you did to get a conviction.'

'You wouldn't tell Carl.'

'He's listening to everything I say.'

Frank's voice took on a sanctimonious note. 'I suppose there's no point in talking to you about loyalty.'

'Not since the moment you told Carl about Fluffy the hamster.'

That shot went home. Frank began to sound defensive. 'Carl wouldn't do the Farmer Johnny story. He's a mate.'

'Your trust is deeply touching – him being a journalist, and all.'

There was a long silence.

Toni said: 'Make up your mind, Frank – the turning is just ahead. Either the snowplough diverts, or I spend the next hour briefing Carl on Farmer Johnny.'

There was a click and a hum as Frank hung up.

Toni cradled the phone.

Carl said: 'What was that all about?'

'If we drive past the next left turn, I'll tell you.'

A few moments later, the snowplough turned on to the side road leading to Steepfall.

7 a.m.

Hugo lay bleeding on the tiled floor, unconscious but breathing.

Olga was weeping. Her chest heaved as she was racked with uncontrollable sobbing. She was close to hysterics.

Stanley Oxenford was grey with shock. He looked like a man who has been told he is dying. He stared at Kit, his face showing despair and bewilderment and suppressed anger. His expression said: *How could you do this to us?* Kit tried not to look at him.

Kit was in a rage. Everything was going wrong. His family now knew he was in league with the thieves, and there was no way they would lie about it, which meant the police would eventually know the whole story. He was doomed to a life on the run from the law. He could hardly contain his wrath.

He was also afraid. The virus sample in its perfume bottle lay on the kitchen table, protected only by two transparent plastic bags. Kit's fear heated his fury.

Nigel ordered Stanley and Olga to lie face down beside Hugo, threatening them with his gun. He was so angry at the beating he had taken from Hugo that he might have welcomed an excuse to pull the trigger. Kit would not have tried to stop him. The way he felt, he could have killed someone himself.

Elton searched out improvised ropes – appliance leads, a length of clothesline, and a ball of stout cord.

Daisy tied up Olga, the unconscious Hugo, and Stanley, binding their feet together and their hands behind their backs. She pulled the cords tight, so that they cut into the flesh, and yanked at the knots to make sure there was no looseness. Her face wore the ugly little smile she showed when she was hurting people.

Kit said to Nigel: 'I need my phone.'

Nigel said: 'Why?'

Kit said: 'In case there's a call to the Kremlin that I need to intercept.'

Nigel hesitated.

Kit said: 'For Christ's sake, I gave you your gun!'

Nigel shrugged and handed over the phone.

'How can you do this, Kit?' Olga said, as Daisy knelt on their father's back. 'How can you watch your family being treated this way?'

'It's not my fault!' he rejoined angrily. 'If you'd behaved decently to me, none of this would have happened.'

'Not your fault?' his father said in bewilderment.

'First you fired me, then you refused to help me financially, so I ended up owing money to gangsters.'

'I fired you because you stole!'

'I'm your son – you should have forgiven me!'

'I *did* forgive you.'

'Too late.'

'Oh, God.'

'I was forced into this!'

Stanley spoke in a voice of authoritative contempt that was familiar to Kit from childhood. 'No one is forced into something like this.'

Kit hated that tone: it used to be a sign that he had done something particularly stupid. 'You don't understand.'

'I fear I understand all too well.'

That was just typical of him, Kit thought. He always thought he knew best. Well, he looked pretty stupid now, with Daisy tying his hands behind his back.

'What is this about, anyway?' Stanley said.

'Shut your gob,' Daisy said.

He ignored her. 'What in God's name are you up to with these people, Kit? And what's in the perfume bottle?'

'I said shut up!' Daisy kicked Stanley in the face.

He grunted with pain, and blood came out of his mouth.

That will teach you, Kit thought with savage satisfaction.

Nigel said: 'Turn on the TV, Kit. Let's see when this bloody snow is going to stop.'

They watched advertisements: January sales, summer holidays, cheap loans. Elton took Nellie by the collar and shut her in the dining room. Hugo stirred and appeared to be coming round, and Olga spoke to him in a low voice. A newscaster appeared wearing a Santa hat. Kit thought bitterly of other families waking up to normal Christmas celebrations. 'A freak blizzard hit Scotland last night, bringing a surprise white Christmas to most of the country this morning,' the newscaster said.

'Shit,' Nigel said with feeling. 'How long are we going to be stuck here?'

'The storm, which left dozens of drivers stranded overnight, is expected to ease around daybreak, and the thaw should set in by mid-morning.'

Kit was cheered. They could still make it to the rendezvous.

Nigel had the same thought. 'How far away is that four-wheel-drive, Kit?'

'A mile.'

'We'll leave here at first light. Have you got yesterday's paper?'

'There must be one somewhere – why?'

'Check what time sunrise is.'

Kit went into his father's study and found the *Scotsman* in a canterbury. He brought it into the kitchen. 'Four minutes past eight,' he said.

Nigel checked his watch. 'Less than an hour.' He looked worried. 'But then we have to walk a mile in the snow, and drive another ten. We're going to be cutting it fine.' He took a phone out of his pocket. He began to dial, then stopped. 'Dead battery,' he said. 'Elton, give me your phone.' He took Elton's phone and dialled. 'Yeah, it's me, what about this weather, then?' Kit guessed he was speaking to the customer's pilot. 'Yeah, should ease up in an hour or so . . . I can get there, but can you?' Nigel was pretending to be more confident than he really felt. Once the snow stopped, a helicopter could take off and go anywhere, but it was not so easy for the gang, travelling by road. 'Good. So I'll see you at the appointed time.' He pocketed the phone.

The newscaster said: 'At the height of the blizzard, thieves raided the laboratories of Oxenford Medical, near Inverburn.'

The kitchen went silent. That's it, Kit thought; the truth is out.

'They got away with samples of a dangerous virus.'

Stanley spoke through smashed lips. 'So that's what's in the perfume bottle . . . Are you people mad?'

'Carl Osborne reports from the scene.'

The screen showed a photo of Osborne with a phone to his ear, and his voice was heard over a phone line. 'The deadly virus that killed laboratory technician Michael Ross only yesterday is now in the hands of gangsters.'

Stanley was incredulous. 'But why? Do you imagine you can sell the stuff?'

Nigel said: 'I know I can.'

On television, Osborne was saying: 'In a meticulously planned Christmas caper, three men and a woman defeated the laboratory's state-of-the-art security and penetrated to Biosafety Level Four, where the company keeps stocks of incurable viruses in a locked refrigerator.'

Stanley said: 'But, Kit, you didn't help them do this, did you?'

Olga spoke up. 'Of course he did,' she said disgustedly.

'The armed gang overcame security guards, injuring two, one seriously. But many more will die if the Madoba-2 virus is released into the population.'

Stanley rolled over with an effort and sat upright. His face was bruised, one eye was closing, and there was blood down the front of his pyjamas; yet he still seemed the most authoritative person in the room. 'Listen to that fellow on TV,' he said.

Daisy moved towards Stanley, but Nigel stopped her with a raised hand.

'You're going to kill yourselves,' Stanley said. 'If you really have Madoba-2 in that bottle on the table, there's no antidote. If you drop it and the bottle smashes and the fluid leaks out, you're dead. Even if you sell it to someone else and they release it after you've left, it spreads so fast that you could easily catch it and die.'

On the screen, Osborne said: 'Madoba-2 is believed to be more dangerous than the Black Death that devastated Britain in . . . ancient times.'

Stanley raised his voice over the commentary. 'He's right, even if he doesn't know what century he's talking about. In Britain in the thirteen hundreds, the Black Death killed one person in three. This could be worse. Surely no amount of money is worth that risk?'

Nigel said: 'I won't be in Britain when it's released.'

Kit was shocked. Nigel had not previously mentioned this. Had Elton also made plans to go abroad? What about Daisy and Harry Mac? Kit himself intended to be in Italy – but now he wondered if that was far enough away.

Stanley turned to Kit. 'You can't possibly think this makes sense.'

He was right, Kit thought. The whole thing bordered on insane. But then, the world was crazy. 'I'm going to be dead anyway if I don't pay my debts.'

'Come on, they're not going to kill you for a debt.'

Daisy said: 'Oh, yes we are.'

'How much do you owe?'

'A quarter of a million pounds.'

'Good God!'

'I told you I was desperate, three months ago, but you wouldn't listen, you bastard.'

'How the hell did you manage to run up a debt – no, never mind, forget I asked.'

'Gambling on credit. My system is good – I just had a very long run of bad luck.'

Olga spoke up. 'Luck? Kit, wake up – you've been had! These people lent you the money then made sure you lost, because they needed you to help them rob the laboratory!'

Kit did not believe that. He said scornfully: 'How would you know a thing like that?'

'I'm a lawyer, I meet these people, I hear their pathetic excuses when they're caught. I know more about them than I care to.'

Stanley spoke again. 'Look, Kit, surely we can find a way out of this without killing innocent people?'

'Too late, now. I made my decision, and I've got to see this through.'

'But think about it, lad. How many people are you going to kill? Dozens? Thousands? Millions?'

'I see you're willing for me to be killed. You'd protect a crowd of strangers, but you wouldn't rescue me.'

Stanley groaned. 'God knows I love you, and I don't want you to die, but are you sure you want to save your own life at that price?'

As Kit opened his mouth to reply, his phone rang.

Taking it out of his pocket, he wondered whether Nigel would trust him to answer it. But no one moved, and he held the phone to his ear. He heard the voice of Hamish

McKinnon. 'Toni's following the snowplough, and she's persuaded them to divert to your place. She'll be there any minute. And there are two police officers in the lorry.'

Kit ended the call and looked at Nigel. 'The police are coming here, now.'

7:15 a.m.

Craig opened the side door of the garage and peeped out. Three windows were lit in the gable end of the house, but the curtains were drawn, so no casual observer could see him.

He glanced back to where Sophie sat. He had turned out the lights in the garage, but he knew she was in the front passenger seat of Luke's Ford, her pink anorak pulled close around her against the cold. He waved in her direction, then stepped outside.

Moving as quickly as he could, lifting his feet high as he stepped in the deep snow, he went along the blind wall of the garage until he came level with the front of the house.

He was going to get the Ferrari keys. He would have to sneak into the lobby at the back of the kitchen and take them from the key box. Sophie had wanted to go with him, but he had persuaded her that it was more dangerous for two people than for one.

He was more frightened without her. For her sake, he had to pretend to be brave, and that made him braver. But now he had a bad attack of nerves. As he hesitated at the corner of the house, his hands were shaking and his legs felt strangely weak. He could easily be caught by the strangers, and then he did not know what he would do. He had never been in a real fight, not since he was about eight years old. He knew boys of his own age who fought – outside a pub, usually, on a Saturday night – and all of them, without exception, were stupid. The three strangers in the kitchen were none of them much bigger than Craig, but all the same he was frightened of them. It seemed to him that they would know what to do in a fight, and he had no idea. Anyway, they had guns. They might shoot him. How much would that hurt?

He looked along the front of the house. He was going to have to pass the windows of the living room and the dining room, where the curtains were not drawn. The snowfall was not as thick as before, and he could easily be seen by someone glancing out.

He forced himself to move forward.

He stopped at the first window and looked into the living room. Fairy lights flashed on the Christmas tree, dimly outlining the familiar couches and tables, the television set, and four oversize children's stockings on the floor in front of the fireplace, stuffed with boxes and packages.

There was no one in the room.

He walked on. The snow seemed deeper here, blown into a drift by the wind off the sea. Wading through it was surprisingly tiring. He almost felt like lying down. He realized he had been without sleep for twenty-four hours. He shook himself and pressed on. Passing the front door, he half expected that it would suddenly fly open, and the Londoner in the pink sweater would leap out and grab him. But nothing happened.

As he drew level with the dark dining-room windows,

he was startled by a soft bark. For a moment his heart seemed to bang against his chest, then he realized it was only Nellie. They must have shut her in there. The dog recognized Craig's silhouette, and gave a low let-me-out-of-here whine. 'Quiet, Nellie, for God's sake,' he murmured. He doubted whether the dog could hear him, but she fell silent anyway.

He passed the parked cars, Miranda's Toyota Previa and Hugo's Mercedes-Benz estate. Their sides as well as their tops were all white, so that they looked as if they might be snow all the way through, snow cars for snowmen. He rounded the corner of the house. There was a light in the window of the boot lobby. Cautiously, he peeped around the edge of the window frame. He could see the big walk-in cupboard where anoraks and boots were kept. There was a watercolour of Steepfall that must have been painted by Aunt Miranda, a yard brush leaning in a corner – and the steel key box, screwed to the wall.

The door from the lobby to the kitchen was closed. That was lucky.

He listened, but he could not hear anything from inside the house.

What happened when you punched someone? In the cinema they just fell down, but he was pretty sure that would not happen in real life. More important, what happened when someone punched you? How much did it hurt? What if they did it again and again? And what was it like to be shot? He had heard somewhere that the most painful thing in the world was a bullet in the stomach. He was absolutely terrified, but he forced himself to move.

He grasped the handle of the back door, turned it as

gently as he could, and pushed. The door swung open and he stepped inside. The lobby was a small room, six feet long, narrowed by the brickwork of the massive old chimney and the deep cupboard beside it. The key box hung on the chimney wall. Craig reached to open it. There were twenty numbered hooks, some with single keys and some with bunches, but he instantly recognized the Ferrari keys. He grasped them and lifted, but the fob snagged on the hook. He jiggled it, fighting down panic. Then someone rattled the handle of the kitchen door.

Craig's heart leaped in his chest. The person was trying to open the door between the kitchen and the lobby. He or she had turned the handle, but was obviously unfamiliar with the house, and was pushing instead of pulling. In the moment of delay, Craig stepped into the coat cupboard and closed the door behind him.

He had done it without thought, abandoning the keys. As soon as he was inside, he realized it would have been almost as quick to go out of the back door into the garden. He tried to remember whether he had closed the back door. He thought not. And had fresh snow fallen from his boots onto the floor? That would reveal that someone had been there in the last minute or so, for otherwise it would have melted. And he had left the key box open.

An observant person would see the clues and guess the truth in an instant.

He held his breath and listened.

* * *

Nigel rattled the handle until he realized that the door opened inwards, not out. He pulled it wide and looked into the boot lobby. 'No good,' he said. 'Door and a window.' He crossed the kitchen and flung open the door to the pantry. 'This will do. No other doors and only one window, overlooking the courtyard. Elton, put them in here.'

'It's cold in there,' Olga protested. There was an air-conditioning unit in the pantry.

'Oh, stop it, you'll make me cry,' Nigel said sarcastically.

'My husband needs a doctor.'

'After punching me, he's lucky he doesn't need a fucking undertaker.' Nigel turned back to Elton. 'Stuff something in their mouths so they can't make a noise. Quick, we may not have much time!'

Elton found a drawer full of clean tea towels. He gagged Stanley, Olga, and Hugo, who was now conscious, though dazed. Then he got the bound prisoners to their feet and pushed them into the pantry.

'Listen to me,' Nigel said to Kit. Nigel was superficially calm, planning ahead and giving orders, but he was pale, and the expression on his narrow, cynical face was grim. Beneath the surface, Kit saw, he was wound as tight as a guitar string. 'When the police get here, you're going to the door,' Nigel went on. 'Speak to them nicely, look relaxed, the law-abiding citizen. Say that nothing's wrong here, and everyone in the house is still asleep except you.'

Kit did not know how he was going to appear relaxed when he felt as if he were facing a firing squad. He gripped the back of a kitchen chair to stop himself shaking. 'What if they want to come in?'

'Discourage them. If they insist, bring them into the kitchen. We'll be in that little back room.' He pointed to the boot lobby. 'Just get rid of them as fast as you can.'

'Toni Gallo is coming along with the police,' Kit said. 'She's head of security at the lab.'

'Well, tell her to go away.'

'She'll want to see my father.'

'Say she can't.'

'She may not take no for an answer—'

Nigel raised his voice. 'For crying out loud, what is she going to do – knock you down and walk in over your unconscious body? Just tell her to fuck off.'

'All right,' Kit said. 'But we need to keep my sister Miranda quiet. She's hiding in the attic.'

'Attic? Where?'

'Directly above this room. Look inside the first cupboard in the dressing room. Behind the suits is a low door leading into the roof space.'

Nigel did not ask how Kit knew Miranda was there. He looked at Daisy. 'Take care of it.'

*   *   *

Miranda saw her brother speaking to Nigel and heard his words as he betrayed her.

She crossed the attic in a moment and crawled through the door into Daddy's suit cupboard. She was panting hard, her heart was racing, and she felt flushed, but she was not in a panic, not yet. She jumped out of the cupboard into the dressing room.

She had heard Kit say the police were coming and, for a joyful moment, she had thought they were saved. All she had to do was sit tight until men in blue uniforms walked in through the front door and arrested the thieves. Then she had listened with horror as Nigel rapidly devised a way of getting rid of the police. What was she to do if the police seemed about to leave without arresting anyone? She had decided she would open a bedroom window and start screaming.

Now Kit had spoiled that plan.

She was terrified of meeting Daisy again, but she held on to her reason, just.

She could hide in Kit's bedroom, on the other side of the landing, while Daisy searched the attic. That would not fool Daisy for more than a few seconds, but it might give Miranda just long enough to open a window and yell for help.

She ran through the bedroom. As she put her hand on the door knob, she heard heavy boots on the stairs. She was too late.

The door flew open. Miranda hid behind it. Daisy stormed through the bedroom and into the dressing room without looking back.

Miranda slipped out of the door. She crossed the landing and stepped into Kit's room. She ran to the window and pulled back the curtains, hoping to see police cars with flashing lights.

There was no one outside.

She peered in the direction of the lane. It was getting light, and she could see the trees laden with snow at the edge of the wood, but no cars. She almost despaired. Daisy would take only a few seconds to look around the attic and make sure no one was there. Then she would check the rest of the upstairs rooms. Miranda needed more time. How far away could the police be?

Was there any way she could shut Daisy in the attic?

She did not give herself a second to worry about risks. She ran back to her father's room. She could see the door of the suit cupboard standing open. Daisy must be in the attic right now, staring around with those bruised-looking eyes, wondering if there were any hiding places big enough to conceal a grown woman, somewhat overweight.

Without forethought, Miranda closed the cupboard door.

There was no lock, but it was made of solid wood. If she could jam it shut, Daisy would have trouble busting it open, especially as she would have little room to manoeuvre inside the cupboard.

There was a narrow gap at the bottom of the door. If she could wedge something into it the door would stick, at least for a few seconds. What could she use? She needed a piece of wood, or cardboard, or even a sheaf of paper. She pulled open her father's bedside drawer and found a volume of Proust.

She started ripping pages out.

*   *   *

Kit heard the dog bark in the next room.

It was a loud, aggressive bark, the kind she gave when a stranger was at the door. Someone was coming. Kit pushed through the swing door that led to the dining room. The dog was standing with her forepaws on the windowsill.

Kit went to the window. The snow had eased to a light scatter of flakes. He looked towards the wood and saw, emerging from the trees, a big truck with a flashing orange light on top and a snowplough blade in front.

'They're here!' he called out.

Nigel came in. The dog growled, and Kit said: 'Shut up.' Nellie retreated to a corner. Nigel flattened himself against the wall beside the window and peered out.

The snowplough cleared a path eight or ten feet wide. It passed the front door and came as close as it could to the parked cars. At the last moment it turned, sweeping away the snow in front of Hugo's Mercedes and Miranda's Previa. Then it reversed to the garage block, turned off the drive and cleared a swathe of the concrete apron in front of the garage doors. As it did so, a light-coloured Jaguar S-type came past it, using the track it had made in the snow, and pulled up at the front door.

A figure got out of the car; a tall, slim woman with bobbed hair, wearing a leather flying jacket with a sheepskin lining. In the reflected light from the headlamps, Kit recognized Toni Gallo.

'Get rid of her,' said Nigel.

'What's happened to Daisy? She's taking a long time—'

'She'll deal with your sister.'

'She'd better.'

'I trust Daisy more than I trust you. Now go to the door.' Nigel retreated into the boot lobby with Elton.

Kit went to the front door and opened it.

Toni was helping someone out of the back of the car. Kit frowned. It was an old lady in a long wool coat and a fur hat. He said aloud: 'What the hell . . . ?'

Toni took the old lady's arm and they turned around. Toni's face darkened with disappointment when she saw who had come to the door. 'Hello, Kit,' she said. She walked the old woman towards the house.

Kit said: 'What do you want?'

'I've come to see your father. There's an emergency at the laboratory.'

'Daddy's asleep.'

'He'll want to wake up for this, trust me.'

'Who's the old woman?'

'This *lady* is my mother, Mrs Kathleen Gallo.'

'And I'm not an old woman,' said the old woman. 'I'm seventy-one, and as fit as a butcher's dog, so mind your manners.'

'All right, Mother, he didn't mean to be rude.'

Kit ignored that. 'What's she doing here?'

'I'll explain to your father.'

The snowplough had turned around in front of the garage, and now it returned along the track it had cleared, heading back through the woods towards the main road. The Jaguar followed.

Kit felt panicked. What should he do? The cars were leaving, but Toni was still here.

The Jaguar stopped suddenly. Kit hoped the driver had not seen something suspicious. The car reversed back to the house. The driver's door opened, and a small bundle fell out into the snow. It looked, Kit thought, almost like a puppy.

The door slammed, and the car pulled away.

Toni went back and picked up the bundle. It was a puppy, a black-and-white English sheepdog about eight weeks old.

Kit was bewildered, but he decided not to ask questions. 'You can't come in,' he said to Toni.

'Don't be stupid,' she replied. 'This is not your house, it's your father's, and he'll want to see me.' She continued walking slowly towards him with her mother on one arm and the puppy cradled in the other.

Kit was stymied. He had expected Toni to be in her own car, and his plan had been to tell her she should come back later. For a moment, he considered running after the Jaguar and telling the driver to come back. But the driver would surely ask why. And the police in the snowplough might ask what the fuss was about. It was too dangerous. Kit did nothing.

Toni stood in front of Kit, who was blocking the doorway. 'Is something wrong?' she said.

He was stuck, he realized. If he persisted in trying to obey Nigel's orders, he might bring the police back. Toni on her own was more manageable. 'You'd better come in,' he said.

'Thanks. By the way, the puppy's name is Osborne.' Toni and her mother stepped into the hall. 'Do you need the bathroom, Mother?' Toni asked. 'It's just here.'

Kit watched the lights of the snowplough and the Jaguar disappear into the woods. He relaxed slightly. He was saddled with Toni, but he had got rid of the police. He closed the front door.

There was a loud bang from upstairs, like a hammer hitting a wall.

'What the heck was that?' said Toni.

*　　　　*　　　　*

Miranda had taken a thick sheaf of pages from the book and folded them into a wedge which she had shoved into the gap under the cupboard door. That would not hold Daisy for long. She needed a more solid barrier. Beside the bed was an antique commode chest used as a bedside table. With a huge effort, she dragged the heavy mahogany chest across the carpet, tilted it at a forty-five-degree angle, and jammed it against the door. Almost immediately, she heard Daisy pushing at the other side of the door. When pushing failed, she banged.

Miranda guessed Daisy was lying with her head in the attic and her feet in the cupboard, kicking the door with the soles of her boots. The door shuddered but did not fly open. However, Daisy was tough, and she would find a way. Nevertheless, Miranda had won a few precious seconds.

She flew to the window. To her dismay, she saw two vehicles – a lorry and a saloon car – driving *away* from the house. 'Oh, no!' she said aloud. The vehicles were already too far for the people inside them to hear her scream. Was she too late? She ran out of the bedroom.

She stopped at the top of the stairs. Down in the hall, there was an old woman she had never seen before, going into the cloakroom.

What was happening?

Next she recognized Toni Gallo, taking off a flying jacket and hanging it on the hat stand.

A small black-and-white puppy was sniffing the umbrellas.

Kit came into view. There was another bang from the dressing room, and Kit said to Toni: 'The children must be awake.'

Miranda was bewildered. How could this be? Kit was acting as if there was nothing wrong . . .

He must be fooling Toni, Miranda realized. He was

hoping to make her think that all was well. Then he would either persuade her to leave, or overpower her and tie her up with the others.

Meanwhile, the police were driving away.

Toni closed the cloakroom door on her mother. No one had yet noticed Miranda.

Kit said to Toni: 'You'd better come into the kitchen.'

That was where they would jump her, Miranda guessed. Nigel and Elton would be waiting, and they would take her by surprise.

There was a crash from within the bedroom: Daisy had broken out of the cupboard.

Miranda acted without thinking. 'Toni!' she screamed.

Toni looked up the stairs and saw her.

Kit said: 'Shit, no—'

Miranda yelled: 'The thieves, they're here, they've tied Daddy up, they've got guns—'

Daisy burst out of the bedroom and crashed into Miranda, sending her tumbling down the stairs.

7.30 a.m.

For an instant, Toni froze.

Kit stood beside her, an expression of rage on his face, looking up the stairs. With a twisted mouth he said: 'Get her, Daisy!'

Miranda was falling down the stairs, her pink nightdress billowing up to reveal plump white thighs.

Running after her was an ugly young woman with a shaved head and Gothic eye make-up, dressed in leather.

And Mother was in the cloakroom.

In a flash of comprehension, Toni understood what was happening. Thieves with guns were here, Miranda had said. There could not be two such gangs operating in this remote area on the same night. These must be the people who had robbed the Kremlin. The bald woman at the top of the stairs would be the blonde Toni had seen on the security video – her wig had been found in the getaway van. Toni's mind raced ahead: Kit seemed to be in league with them – which would explain how they had defeated the security system—

As that thought struck her, Kit hooked his arm around her neck and pulled, trying to yank her off her feet. At the same time, he yelled: 'Nigel!'

She elbowed him forcefully in the ribs, and had the satisfaction of hearing him grunt with pain. His grip on her neck eased, and she was able to turn and hit him again, this time a punch in the midriff with her left fist. He lashed out at her, but she easily dodged the blow.

She drew back her right arm for a real knockout punch but, before she could strike, Miranda reached the foot of the stairs and crashed into the back of Toni's legs. Because Toni was leaning back, ready to hit Kit, she fell backwards. A moment later, the woman in leather tripped over Miranda and Toni and collided with Kit, and all four of them ended up in a heap on the flagstone floor.

Toni realized she could not win this fight. She was up against Kit and the woman he had called Daisy, and soon she might have others to contend with. She had to get away from these people, catch her breath, and figure out what to do.

She wriggled out of the scrum and rolled over.

Kit was flat on his back. Miranda was curled up in a ball, appearing bruised and winded but not seriously injured. As Toni looked, Daisy got to her knees and, apparently in a fury, punched Miranda, striking her on the arm with a fist encased, peculiarly, in ladylike tan suede gloves.

Toni leaped to her feet. She jumped over Kit, reached the front door, and threw it open. Kit grabbed her ankle with one hand, holding her back. She twisted, and kicked at his arm with the other foot. She connected with his elbow. He cried out in pain and released his grip. Toni jumped out through the doorway and slammed the door behind her.

She turned right and dashed along the track made by the snowplough. She heard a gunshot, and a crash as a pane of glass shattered in a window near her. Someone was shooting at her from inside the house. But the bullet missed.

She ran to the garage and turned onto the concrete apron in front of the doors, where the snowplough had cleared a space. Now the garage block was between her and the person with the gun.

The snowplough, with its two police officers in the cab, had departed at normal speed along the cleared road with its blade raised. That meant that by now the truck was too far away for her to catch it on foot. What was she going to do? While she was on the cleared path, she could easily be followed by someone from the house. But where could she hide? She glanced over to the woods. Plenty of cover there, but she had no coat – she had taken off her flying jacket just before Miranda yelled her warning – so she would not last long in the open. The garage itself would be almost as cold.

She ran to the other end of the building and looked around the corner. A few yards away, she could see the door to the barn. Did she dare to risk crossing the courtyard, in view of the house? She had no other choice.

As she was about to set off, the barn door opened.

She hesitated. What now?

A small boy emerged wearing a coat over Spiderman pyjamas and a pair of rubber boots too big for his feet. Toni recognized Tom, the son of Miranda. He did not look around, but turned left and trudged through the deep snow. Toni assumed he was heading for the house, and asked herself whether she should stop him; but after a moment she realized that her assumption was wrong. Instead of crossing the courtyard to the main house, he went to the guest cottage. Toni willed him to hurry, to get out of the way before trouble started. She imagined he was looking for his mother to ask if he could open his presents. In fact, his mother was in the main house, being punched by a woman gangster in tan suede gloves. But perhaps the stepfather was in the cottage. Toni thought it wiser to leave the boy to find out. The cottage door was not locked, and Tom disappeared inside.

Still Toni hesitated. Was there someone behind one of the house windows, covering the courtyard with a nine-millimetre Browning automatic pistol? She was about to find out.

She set off at a run but, as soon as she hit the deep snow, she fell. She lay there for a second, waiting for a gunshot, but none came. She struggled to her feet, cold snow chilling her through her jeans and sweater, and pressed on, walking more carefully but more slowly. She looked fearfully at the house. She could see no one at any of the windows. It could not take more than a minute to cross the courtyard, but each big step took painfully long. At last she reached the barn, stepped inside, and swung the door closed behind her, shaking with relief that she was still alive.

A small lamp revealed a billiard table, an assortment of elderly couches, a large-screen television set, and two camp beds, both empty. There appeared to be no one else in the room, though a ladder led to a loft. Toni made herself stop shaking and climbed the ladder. When she was halfway up, she peeped over the top. She was startled by several pairs of small red eyes staring at her: Caroline's rats. She climbed the rest of the way. There were two more beds here. The somnolent lump in one was Caroline. The other had not been slept in.

It would not be long before the gang in the house came looking for Toni. She had to get help fast. She reached for her mobile phone.

Then she realized she did not have it.

She shook her clenched fists at the ceiling in frustration. Her phone was in the pocket of the flying jacket, which she had hung up in the hall.

What was she going to do now?

*   *   *

'We've got to get after her,' Nigel said. 'She could be on the phone to the police already.'

'Wait,' Kit said. He stepped across the hall to the hat stand. He was rubbing his left elbow where Toni had kicked him, but he stopped in order to search her jacket. Triumphantly, he produced a phone from one of her pockets. 'She can't call the police.'

'Thank God for that.' Nigel looked around the hall. Daisy had Miranda face down on the floor with her arm bent behind her back. Elton stood in the kitchen doorway. Nigel said: 'Elton, get some more rope so Daisy can tie up this fat cow.' He turned back to Kit. 'Your sisters are a right bloody pair.'

'Never mind that,' Kit said. 'We can get away now, can't we? We don't have to wait for daylight or fetch the four-wheel-drive. We can use any car, and take the path cleared by the snow-plough.'

'Your man said there were coppers in that snowplough.'

'The one place they won't look for us is right behind them.'

Nigel nodded. 'Clever. But the snowplough's not going all the way to . . . where we need to be. What do we do when it turns off our route?'

Kit suppressed his impatience. They had to get away from Steepfall at any cost, but Nigel had not yet figured that out. 'Look out of the window,' he said. 'The snow has stopped. It will start to thaw soon, the forecast said.'

'We could still get stuck.'

'We're in worse danger here, now that the road has been cleared. Toni Gallo might not be the only visitor to show up.'

Elton returned with a length of electric cable. 'Kit's right,' he said. 'We can easily get there by ten o'clock, barring accidents.' He handed the cable to Daisy, who tied Miranda's hands behind her back.

'Okay,' Nigel said. 'But first we have to round everyone up, including kids, and make sure they can't call for help for the next few hours.'

Daisy dragged Miranda through the kitchen and shoved her into the pantry.

Kit said: 'Miranda's phone must be in the cottage, otherwise she would have used it by now. Her boyfriend, Ned, is there.'

Nigel said: 'Elton, go to the cottage.'

Kit went on: 'There's a phone in the Ferrari. I suggest Daisy goes to the garage to make sure no one is trying to use it.'

'What about the barn?'

'Leave it till last. Caroline, Craig, and Tom don't have phones. I'm not sure about Sophie, but she's only fourteen.'

'All right,' Nigel said. 'Let's get it done as fast as possible.'

The cloakroom door opened and Toni Gallo's mother came out, still wearing her hat.

Kit and Nigel stared at her for a moment. Kit had forgotten she was in there.

Then Nigel said: 'Stick her in the pantry with the others.'

'Oh, no,' the old woman said. 'I think I'd rather sit by the Christmas tree.' She crossed the hall and went into the living room.

Kit looked at Nigel, who shrugged.

*   *   *

Craig opened the door of the boot cupboard a crack. Peeping out, he saw that the lobby was empty. He was about to step out when one of the gangsters, Elton, came in from the kitchen. Craig pulled the door an inch towards himself and held his breath.

It had been like this for a quarter of an hour.

One of the gang was always in view. The cupboard smelled mustily of damp anoraks and old boots. He worried about Sophie, sitting in Luke's Ford in the garage, getting cold. He tried to wait patiently. His chance would surely come soon.

A few minutes ago Nellie had barked, which must mean someone at the door. Craig's heart had lifted in hope; but Nigel and Elton had stood inches away from Craig, talking in whispers that he could not quite make out. They must be hiding from the visitor, Craig decided. He wanted to burst out of the cupboard and run to the door yelling for help, but he knew he would be seized and silenced the instant he revealed himself. It was maddeningly frustrating.

There was a banging from upstairs, as if someone was trying to bash a door down. Then there was a different bang, more like a firework – or a gun going off. It was followed instantly by the sound of breaking glass. Craig was dismayed and frightened. Until this moment, the gang had used guns only to threaten. Now that they had started shooting, where would it end? The family was in terrible danger.

At the gunshot Nigel and Elton went, but left the door open, and Elton remained in sight at the far end of the kitchen, talking urgently to someone in the hall. Then he returned, but went out the back way, leaving the door wide open.

At last Craig could move without being seen. The others were in the hall. This was his chance. He stepped out of the cupboard.

He flipped open the key box and snatched the Ferrari keys. This time they came off the hook without snagging.

In two strides he was out of the door.

The snow had stopped. Somewhere beyond the clouds dawn was breaking, and he could see in black-and-white. To his left was Elton, trudging through the snow, heading for the guest cottage. Elton's back was turned and he did not see Craig. Craig went the other way and turned the corner, so that the house hid him from Elton.

He was shocked to see Daisy only yards away.

Fortunately she, too, had her back to him. She had

obviously come out of the front door, and was walking away from him. There was a cleared path, and he realized that a snowplough had been here while he was hiding in the boot cupboard. Daisy was heading for the garage – and Sophie.

He ducked behind his father's Mercedes. Peeping around the wing, he saw Daisy reach the end of the building, leave the cleared path, and turn the corner of the house, disappearing from view.

He went after her. Moving as fast as he could, he went along the front of the house. He passed the dining room, where Nellie stood with her forepaws on the windowsill; then the front door, which was shut; then the living room with its flashing Christmas tree. He was astonished to see an old lady sitting by the tree with a puppy in her lap. He did not pause to wonder who she was.

He reached the corner and looked around. Daisy was heading straight for the side door of the garage. If she went in there, she would find Sophie sitting in Luke's Ford.

She reached into the pocket of her black leather jacket and took out her gun.

Craig watched, helpless, as she opened the door.

7:45 a.m.

The pantry was cold.

The Christmas turkey, too large to fit into the kitchen refrigerator, stood in a baking tray on a marble shelf, stuffed and seasoned by Olga, ready for roasting. Miranda wondered dismally if she would live to eat it.

She stood with her father, her sister, and Hugo, the four of them trussed like the turkey and crammed into a space three feet square, surrounded by food: vegetables in racks, a shelf of pasta in jars, boxes of breakfast cereals, cans of tuna and plum tomatoes and baked beans.

Hugo was in the worst state. He seemed to be drifting in and out of consciousness. He was leaning against the wall and Olga was pressing herself to his naked body, trying to keep him warm. Stanley's face looked as if he had been hit by a truck, but he was standing erect and his expression was alert.

Miranda felt helpless and miserable. It was heartbreaking to see her father, such a strong character, wounded and tied up. Hugo was a rotter but he hardly deserved this: he looked as if he might have suffered permanent damage. And Olga was a hero, trying so hard to comfort the husband who had betrayed her.

The others had tea towels stuffed into their mouths, but Daisy had not bothered to gag Miranda, presumably because there was no point in anyone shouting now that the police had gone. Miranda realized, with a spurt of hope, that she might be able to remove the gags. 'Daddy, lean down,' she said. He bent his tall figure over her obediently, the end of the gag trailing from his mouth. She tilted her head as if to kiss him. She was able to catch a corner of the tea towel between her teeth. She tugged, pulling part of it out; then, frustratingly, it slipped.

Miranda let out an exclamation of exasperation. Her father bent down, encouraging her to try again. They repeated the process, and this time the whole thing came out and fell to the floor.

'Thank you,' he said. 'By God, that was ghastly.'

Miranda did the same for Olga, who said: 'I kept wanting to puke, but I was afraid I would choke myself.'

Olga removed Hugo's gag by the same method. 'Try to stay awake, Hugo,' she said urgently. 'Come on, keep your eyes open.'

Stanley asked Miranda: 'What's going on out there?'

'Toni Gallo came here with a snowplough and some policemen,' she explained. 'Kit went to the door as if everything was all right, and the police left, but Toni insisted on staying.'

'That woman is incredible.'

'I was hiding in the attic. I managed to warn Toni.'

'Well done!'

'That frightful Daisy pushed me down the stairs, but Toni got away. I don't know where she is now.'

'She can phone the police.'

Miranda shook her head. 'She left her phone in her coat pocket, and Kit's got it.'

'She'll think of something – she's remarkably resourceful. Anyway, she's our only hope. No one else is free, except the children, and Ned, of course.'

'I'm afraid Ned won't be much use,' Miranda said gloomily. 'In a situation like this, the last thing you need is a Shakespeare scholar.' She was thinking how feeble he had been yesterday with his ex, Jennifer, when she threw Miranda out of the house. What hope was there that such a man would stand up to three professional thugs?

She looked out of the pantry window. Dawn had broken and the snow had stopped, so she could see the cottage where Ned lay sleeping and the barn where the children were. She was horrified to see Elton crossing the courtyard. 'Oh, God,' she said. 'He's heading for the cottage.'

Her father looked out. 'They're rounding people up,' he said. 'They'll tie everyone before they leave. We can't let them get away with that virus – but how can we stop them?'

Elton went into the cottage.

'I hope Ned's all right.' Miranda was suddenly glad Ned was not the belligerent type. Elton was tough, ruthless, and armed. Ned's only hope was to come quietly.

'It could be worse,' Stanley said. 'That lad's a villain, but he's not a complete psychopath. The woman is.'

'She makes mistakes because she's insane,' Miranda said. 'In the hall, a few minutes ago, she was punching me when she should have been catching Toni. That's why Toni got away.'

'Why did Daisy want to punch you?'

'I locked her in the attic.'

'You locked her in the attic?'

'She went there looking for me, and I closed the cupboard door behind her and jammed it shut. That's what made her so angry.'

Her father seemed choked up. 'Brave girl,' he whispered.

'I'm not brave,' Miranda said. The idea was absurd. 'I was just so terrified that I was willing to do anything.'

'I think you're brave.' Tears came to his eyes, and he turned away.

Ned emerged from the cottage. Elton was close behind, holding a gun to the back of Ned's head. With his left hand, Elton held Tom by the arm.

Miranda gasped with shock. She had thought Tom was in the barn. He must have woken up and gone looking for his mother. He was wearing his Spiderman pyjamas. Miranda fought back tears.

The three of them were heading for the house, but then there was a shout, and they stopped. A moment later Daisy came into view, dragging Sophie by the hair. Sophie was bent double, stumbling in the snow, crying with pain.

Daisy said something to Elton that Miranda could not hear. Then Tom screamed at Daisy: 'Leave her alone! You're hurting her!' His voice was a childish treble, made more high pitched by fear and rage.

Miranda recalled that Tom had a pre-adolescent passion for Sophie. 'Be quiet, Tommy,' she murmured fearfully, although he could not hear her. 'It doesn't matter if she gets her hair pulled.'

Elton laughed. Daisy grinned and yanked more viciously at Sophie's hair.

It was probably being laughed at that drove Tom over the edge. He suddenly went berserk. He jerked his arm out of Elton's grasp and threw himself at Daisy.

Miranda shouted: 'No!'

Daisy was so surprised that when Tom crashed into her she fell backwards, letting go of Sophie's hair, and sat down in the snow. Tom dived on top of her, pummelling her with his small fists.

Miranda found herself shouting uselessly: 'Stop! Stop!'

Daisy pushed Tom away and got to her feet. Tom jumped up, but Daisy hit him with her gloved fist on the side of the head, and he fell down again. She heaved him up off the ground and, in a fury, held him upright with her left hand while she punched him with her right, hitting his face and body.

Miranda screamed.

Suddenly Ned moved.

Ignoring the gun that Elton was pointing at him, he stepped between Daisy and Tom. He said something that Miranda could not hear, and put a restraining hand on Daisy's arm.

Miranda was astonished: weak Ned standing up to thugs!

Without letting go of Tom, Daisy punched Ned in the stomach.

He doubled over, his face screwed up in a grimace of agony. But, when Daisy drew back her arm to punch Tom again, Ned straightened up and stood in her way. Changing her mind at the last instant, she punched Ned instead of

Tom, hitting him in the mouth. Ned cried out, and his hands flew to his face, but he did not move.

Miranda was profoundly grateful that Ned had distracted Daisy from Tom – but how long could he stand this beating?

He continued to remonstrate with Daisy. When he took his hands away from his face, blood poured out of his mouth. As Miranda watched, Daisy punched him a third time.

Miranda was awestruck. Ned was like a wall. He simply stood there and took the blows. And he was doing it, not for his own child, but for Tom. Miranda felt ashamed of thinking he was weak.

At that moment Ned's own child, Sophie, acted. She had been standing still, watching in a stunned way, since Daisy let go of her hair. Now she turned around and moved away.

Elton made a grab for her, but she slipped through his grasp. For a moment, he lost balance, and Sophie broke into a run, crossing the deep snow with balletic leaps.

Hastily, Elton righted himself; but Sophie had disappeared.

Elton grabbed Tom and shouted at Daisy: 'Don't let that girl get away!' Daisy looked disposed to argue. Elton yelled: 'I've got these two. Go, go!'

With a malevolent look at Ned and Tom, Daisy turned and went after Sophie.

8 a.m.

Craig turned the key in the ignition of the Ferrari. Behind him, the huge rear-mounted V12 engine started, then died.

Craig closed his eyes. 'Not now,' he said aloud. 'Don't let me down now.'

He turned the key again. The engine fired, faltered, then roared like an angry bull. Craig pumped the throttle, just to be sure, and the roar turned into a howl.

He looked at the phone. It said: 'Searching . . .' He jabbed at the number pad, dialling 999, even though he knew it was useless before the phone had connected to the network. 'Come on,' he urged. 'I don't have much time—'

The side door of the garage flew open, and Sophie stumbled in.

Craig was taken by surprise. He thought Sophie was in the hands of the dreadful Daisy. He had watched as Daisy dragged her out of the garage. He had wanted desperately to rescue her, but he did not think he could beat Daisy in a fight even if she had not got a gun. He had struggled to remain calm as he watched Daisy maliciously dragging Sophie along by the hair. He kept telling himself that the best thing he could do for Sophie was to stay free and phone the police.

Now she seemed to have escaped unaided. She was sobbing and panicky, and he guessed that Daisy must be on her tail.

The passenger side of the car was so close to the wall that the door could not be opened. Craig threw open the driver's door and said: 'Get in quick – climb over me!'

She staggered over to the car and fell in.

Craig slammed the door.

He did not know how to lock it, and he was too rushed to find out. Daisy could not be more than a few seconds away, he figured as Sophie scrambled over him. There was no time to phone – they had to get out of there. As Sophie collapsed into the passenger seat, he fumbled under the dashboard and found the remote-control device that opened the garage door. He pressed it, and heard behind him a squeak of unlubricated metal as the mechanism operated. He looked in the rear-view mirror and saw the up-and-over door begin to move slowly.

Then Daisy came in.

Her face was red with exertion and her eyes were wide with rage. There was snow in the creases of her black leather clothes. She hesitated in the doorway, peering into the gloom of the garage; then her staring eyes locked on to Craig in the driving seat of the car.

He depressed the clutch and shoved the gearshift into reverse. It was never easy, with the Ferrari's six-speed box. The stick resisted his push, and there was a grinding of cogs; then something slipped into place.

Daisy ran across the front of the car and came to the driver's side. Her tan glove closed on the door handle.

The garage door was not yet fully open, but Craig could

wait no longer. Just as Daisy opened the car door, he released the clutch and trod on the accelerator pedal.

The car leaped backwards as if fired from a catapult. Its roof struck the lower edge of the aluminium garage door with a clang. Sophie gave a yell of fear.

The car flew out of the garage like a champagne cork. Craig stamped on the brake. The snowplough had cleared the thick overnight layer of snow from in front of the garage, but more had fallen since, and the concrete apron was slippery. The Ferrari went into a backwards skid and stopped with a bump against a bank of snow.

Daisy came out of the garage. Craig could see her clearly in the grey dawn light. She hesitated.

The car phone suddenly spoke in a female voice. 'You have one new message.'

Craig pushed the gearshift into what he hoped was first. He eased the clutch out and, to his relief, the tyres found purchase and the car moved forward. He turned the wheel, heading for the way out. If only he could make it onto the drive, he could get away from there with Sophie and summon help.

Daisy must have had the same thought, for she fumbled in the pocket of her jacket and brought out a gun.

'Get down!' Craig yelled at Sophie. 'She's going to shoot!'

As Daisy levelled the gun, he stamped on the accelerator and swung the steering wheel, desperate to get away.

The car went into a skid, slipping across the icy concrete. Alongside his fear and panic, Craig had the feeling of déjà vu: he had skidded this car, in this place, only yesterday, a lifetime ago. Now he struggled to control the vehicle, but the ground was even more slippery after a night of steady snow and freezing temperatures.

He turned into the skid, and for a moment the tyres gripped again, but he overdid it, and the car skidded in the opposite direction and spun around in a half-circle. Sophie was flung from side to side in the passenger seat. He kept waiting for the bang of a gunshot, but none came yet. The only good thing, a part of Craig's terrified mind told him, was that it was impossible for Daisy to take steady aim at a vehicle that was being driven so erratically.

The car stopped, with great good luck, in the middle of the drive, facing directly away from the house and towards the lane. The path in front of Craig had obviously been swept by the snowplough. He had a clear road to freedom.

He pressed on the accelerator pedal, but nothing happened. The engine had stalled.

Out of the corner of his eye, he saw Daisy raise the gun and take careful aim at him.

He turned the key, and the car jerked forward: he had forgotten to take it out of gear. The mistake saved his life for, in the same instant, he heard the unmistakable firecracker bang of a gun, only slightly deadened by the soft snow covering everything; then the side window of the car shattered. Sophie screamed.

Craig knocked the stick into neutral and turned the key again. The throaty roar filled his ears. He could see Daisy taking aim again as he pressed the clutch and found first gear. He ducked involuntarily as he pulled away, and it was lucky that he did, for this time his side window smashed.

The bullet also went through the windscreen, making a small round hole and causing the entire screen to craze over. Now he could see nothing ahead but blurred shapes of darkness and light. Nevertheless he kept the accelerator depressed, doing his best to stay on the driveway, knowing he would die if he did not get away from Daisy and her gun. Beside him, Sophie was curled up in a ball on the passenger seat, hands covering her head.

On the periphery of his vision, he saw Daisy running after the car. Another shot banged. The car phone said: 'Stanley, this is Toni. Bad news – a break-in at the lab. Please call my mobile as soon as you can.'

Craig guessed that the people with guns must be connected to the break-in, but he could not think about that now. He tried to steer by what he could see out of the smashed side window, but it was no good. After a few seconds, the car went off the cleared path, and he felt the sudden drag as it slowed. The shape of a tree appeared in the crazed glass of the windscreen, and Craig slammed on the brakes, but he was too late, and the car hit the tree with a terrific crash.

Craig was thrown forward. His head hit the broken windscreen, knocking out shards of glass, cutting the skin of his forehead. The steering wheel bruised his chest. Sophie was flung against the dashboard and fell with her bottom on the floor and her feet up on the seat, but she swore and tried to right herself, so he knew she was all right.

The engine had stalled again.

Craig looked in the rear-view mirror. Daisy was ten yards behind him, walking steadily across the snow towards the car, holding the gun in her suede-gloved hand. He knew instinctively that she was coming closer just to get a clear shot. She was going to kill him and Sophie.

He had only one chance left. He had to kill her.

He started the engine again. Daisy, five yards away now and directly behind the car, raised her gun arm. Craig put the gearshift into reverse and closed his eyes.

He heard a bang just as he stamped on the throttle. The rear window shattered. The car leaped backwards, straight at Daisy. There was a heavy thump, as though someone had dropped a sack of potatoes on the boot.

Craig took his foot off the throttle and the car rolled to a stop. Where was Daisy? He pushed broken glass out of the windscreen and saw her. She had been thrown sideways by the impact, and was lying on the ground with one leg at an odd angle. He stared, horrified at what he had done.

Then she moved.

'Oh, no!' he cried. 'Why won't you die?'

She reached out with one arm and picked up her gun, lying on the snow nearby.

Craig put the car into first gear.

The car phone said: 'To erase this message, press three.'

Daisy looked into his eyes and pointed the gun at him.

He let out the clutch and stamped on the throttle.

He heard the bang of the gun over the bellow of the Ferrari engine, but the shot went wild. He kept his foot down. Daisy tried to drag herself out of the way, and Craig deliberately turned the wheel in her direction. An instant before the impact he saw her face, staring in terror, her mouth open in an inaudible scream. Then the car hit her with a thud. She disappeared beneath its curved front. The low-slung chassis scraped over something lumpy. Craig saw that he was headed straight for the tree he had hit before.

He braked, but too late. Once again, the car crashed into the tree.

The car phone, which had been telling him how to save messages, stopped in mid-sentence. He tried to start the engine, but nothing happened. There was not even the click of a broken starter motor. He saw that none of the dials was working, and there were no lights on the dashboard. The electrical system had failed. It was hardly surprising, after the number of times he had crashed the car.

But that meant he could not use the phone.

And where was Daisy?

He got out of the car.

In the driveway behind him was a pile of ripped black leather, white flesh and gleaming red blood.

She was not moving.

Sophie got out and stood beside him. 'Oh, God, is that her?'

Craig felt sick. He could not speak, so he nodded.

Sophie whispered: 'Do you think she's dead?'

Craig nodded again, then nausea overwhelmed him. He turned aside and vomited into the snow.

8:15 a.m.

Kit had a terrifying feeling that everything was coming unglued.

It should have been a simple thing for three tough crims such as Nigel, Elton, and Daisy to round up stray members of a law-abiding family. Yet things kept going wrong. Little Tom had made a suicide attack on Daisy; Ned had stunned everyone by protecting Tom from Daisy's revenge; and Sophie had escaped in the confusion. And Toni Gallo was nowhere to be seen.

Elton brought Ned and Tom into the kitchen at gunpoint. Ned was bleeding from several places on his face, and Tom was bruised and crying, but they were walking steadily, Ned holding Tom's hand.

Kit reckoned up who was still at large. Sophie had run away, and Craig would not be far from her. Caroline was probably still asleep in the barn. Then there was Toni Gallo. Four people, three of them children – surely it could not take long to capture them? But time was running out. Kit and the gang had less than two hours to get to the airfield with the virus. Their customer would not wait very long, Kit guessed. If something seemed wrong he would fear a trap and leave.

Elton threw Miranda's phone onto the kitchen table. 'Found it in a handbag in the cottage,' he said. 'The guy doesn't seem to have one.' The phone landed beside the perfume spray. Kit longed for the moment when the bottle would be handed over, never to be seen again, and he would get his money.

He was hoping that the major roads would be cleared of snow by the end of today. He planned to drive to London and check into a small hotel, paying cash. He would lie low for a couple of weeks, then catch a train to Paris with fifty thousand pounds in his pocket. From there he would make his leisurely way across Europe, changing small amounts of money as he needed it, and end up in Lucca.

But first, they had to account for everyone here at Steepfall, in order to delay pursuit. And it was proving absurdly difficult.

Elton made Ned lie on the floor, then tied him up. Ned was quiet but watchful. Nigel tied Tom, who was still snivelling. When Elton opened the pantry door to put them inside, Kit saw to his surprise that the prisoners had managed to remove their gags.

Olga spoke first. 'Please, let Hugo out of here,' she said. 'He's badly injured and he's so cold. I'm afraid he'll die. Just let him lie on the floor in the kitchen, where it's warm.'

Kit shook his head in amazement. Olga's loyalty to her unfaithful husband was incomprehensible.

Nigel said: 'He shouldn't have punched me in the face.'

Elton pushed Ned and Tom into the pantry with the others.

Olga said: 'Please, I'm begging you!'

Elton closed the door.

Kit put Hugo out of his mind. 'We've got to find Toni Gallo, she's the dangerous one.'

Nigel said: 'Where do you think she is?'

'Well, she's not in the house, not in the cottage because Elton's just searched it, and not in the garage because Daisy's just been there. So either she's out of doors, where she won't last long without a coat, or she's in the barn.'

'All right,' Elton said. 'I'll go to the barn.'

*　　　　　*　　　　　*

Toni was looking out of the barn window.

She had now identified three of the four people who had raided the Kremlin. One was Kit, of course. He would have been the planner, the one who told them how to defeat the security system. There was the woman whom Kit had called Daisy – an ironic nickname, presumably, for someone whose appearance would give a vampire a fright. A few minutes ago, in the prelude to the fracas in the courtyard, Daisy had addressed the young black man as Elton, which might be a first name or a surname. Toni had not yet seen the fourth, but she knew that his name was Nigel, for Kit had shouted to him in the hall.

She was half scared and half thrilled. Scared, because they were clearly tough professional criminals who would kill her if necessary, and because they had the virus. Thrilled, because she was tough, too, and she had a chance to redeem herself by catching them.

But how? The best plan would be to get help, but she had no phone and no car. The house phones had been cut off, presumably by the gang. No doubt they had also grabbed any mobile phones lying around. What about cars?

Toni had seen two parked in front of the house, and there must be at least one more in the garage, but she had no idea where the keys were.

That meant she had to capture the thieves on her own.

She thought about the scene she had witnessed in the courtyard. Daisy and Elton were rounding up the family. But Sophie, the tarty kid, had escaped, and Daisy had gone after her. Toni had heard distant noises from beyond the garage – a car engine, breaking glass, and gunfire – but she could not see what was going on, and she hesitated to expose herself by going to investigate. If she let herself get captured, all hope was lost.

She wondered if anyone else was at liberty. The gang must be in a hurry to get going, for their rendezvous was at ten o'clock, but they would want to account for everyone before leaving, so that no one could call the police. Perhaps they would begin to panic and make mistakes.

Toni fervently hoped so. The odds against her were fearsome. She could not cope with all four villains at once. Three of them were armed – with thirteen-shot Browning automatic pistols, according to Steve. Her only chance would be to pick them off one by one.

Where should she start? At some point she had to enter the main house. At least she knew the layout – fortuitously, she had been shown around yesterday. But she did not know where in the house everyone was, and she was reluctant to jump into the dark. She was desperate for more information.

As she was racking her brains, she lost the initiative. Elton emerged from the house and came across the courtyard towards the barn.

He was younger than Toni, probably twenty-five. He was tall and looked fit. In his right hand he carried a pistol, pointed down at the ground. Although Toni was trained in combat, she knew he would be a formidable adversary even without the gun. If possible, she had to avoid getting into a hand-to-hand fight with him.

She wondered fearfully if she could hide. She looked around the barn. No hiding place suggested itself. Besides, there was no point. She had to confront the gang, she thought grimly, and the sooner the better. This one was coming for her on his own, apparently confident he would not need help dealing with a mere woman. Perhaps that would turn out to be his crucial mistake.

Unfortunately, Toni had no weapons.

She had a few seconds to find some. She looked hurriedly at the things around her. She considered a billiard cue, but it was too light. A blow from one would hurt like hell, but would not render a man unconscious, or even knock him down.

Billiard balls were much more dangerous: heavy, solid and hard. She stuffed two into her jeans pockets.

She wished she had a gun.

She glanced up at the hayloft. Height was always an advantage. She scrambled up the ladder. Caroline was fast asleep. On the floor between the two beds was an open suitcase. On top of the clothes was a plastic shopping bag. Next to the case was a cage of white rats.

The barn door opened, and Toni dropped to the floor and lay flat. There was a fumbling sound, then the main lights came on. Toni could not see the ground floor from her prone position, so she did not know exactly where

Elton was; but he could not see her, either, and she had the advantage of knowing he was there.

She listened hard, trying to hear his footsteps over the thunder of her heart. There was an odd noise that she interpreted, after a few moments' puzzlement, as Elton overturning the camp beds in case a child was hiding underneath. Then he opened the bathroom door. There was no one inside – Toni had already checked.

There was nowhere left to look but the hayloft. He would be coming up the ladder any second now. What could she do?

Toni heard the unpleasant squeak of rats, and was struck by inspiration. Still lying flat, she took the shopping bag from the open suitcase and removed its contents, a gift-wrapped package labelled 'To Daddy, Happy Xmas from Sophie with love'. She dropped the package back in the suitcase. Then she opened the rats' cage.

Gently, she picked the rats up one by one and put them in the plastic bag. There were five.

She felt an ominous vibration in the floor that told her Elton had started to climb the ladder.

It was now or never. She reached forward with both arms and emptied the bag of rats over the top of the ladder.

She heard Elton give a roar of shock and disgust as five live rats dropped on his head.

His shout woke Caroline, who let out a squeal and sat upright.

There was a crash as Elton lost his footing on the ladder and fell to the floor.

Toni sprang to her feet and looked down. Elton had fallen on his back. He did not seem seriously hurt, but he was yelling in panic and frantically trying to brush rats off his clothing. They were as frightened as he, and trying desperately to cling to something.

Toni could not see his gun.

She hesitated only a fraction of a second, then jumped off the loft.

She came down with both feet on Elton's chest. He gave an agonized grunt as the air was knocked out of him. Toni landed like a gymnast, rolling forward, but still the impact hurt her legs.

From above, she heard a scream: 'My babies!' Looking up, she saw Caroline at the top of the ladder, wearing lavender pyjamas with a pattern of yellow teddy bears. Toni felt sure she must have squashed one or two of Caroline's pets as she landed, but the rats scattered, apparently unhurt.

Desperate to keep the upper hand, Toni struggled to her feet. One ankle gave her a stab of pain, but she ignored it.

Where was the gun? He must have dropped it.

Elton was hurt, but perhaps not immobilized. She fumbled in her jeans for a billiard ball, but it slipped through her fingers as she tried to pull it out of her pocket. She suffered a moment of pure terror, a feeling that her body would not obey her brain and she was completely helpless. Then she used both hands, one to push from outside her pocket and the other to grasp the ball as it emerged.

But the momentary delay had allowed Elton to recover from the shock of the rats. As Toni raised her right hand above her head, he rolled away from her. Instead of bringing the heavy ball down on his head in the hope of knocking him senseless, she was forced to change her mind at the last instant and throw it at him.

It was not a forceful throw, and in some part of her brain she heard her ex, Frank, say scornfully: 'You couldn't throw a ball if your life depended on it.' Now her life did depend on it, and Frank was right – the throw was too weak. She hit the target, and there was an audible thud as the billiard ball connected with Elton's skull, causing him to roar in pain; but he did not slump unconscious. Instead he got to his knees, holding his bruised head with one hand, then struggled to his feet.

Toni took out the second ball.

Elton looked at the floor all around him, searching in a dazed way for his gun.

Caroline had climbed halfway down the ladder, and now she leaped to the floor. She stooped and grabbed one of the rats that was hiding behind a leg of the billiard table. Turning to pick up another, she collided with Elton. He mistook her for his adversary, and punched her. It was a powerful blow that connected with the side of her head, and she fell to the floor. But it hurt him, too, for Toni saw him grimace in agony and wrap his arms around his chest, and she guessed she had broken some ribs when she jumped on him.

Something had caught Toni's eye as Caroline had reached under the billiard table for a rat. Toni looked again and saw the gun, dull grey against the dark wood of the floor.

Elton saw it at the same time. He dropped to his knees.

As Elton reached under the table, Toni raised her arm high above her head and brought the ball down with all her might, squarely on the back of his head. He slumped unconscious.

Toni fell to her knees, physically exhausted and emotionally drained. She closed her eyes for a moment; but there was too much to do for her to rest long. She picked up the gun. Steve had been right, it was a Browning automatic pistol of the kind issued by the British army to 'special' forces for clandestine work. The safety catch was on the left side, behind the grip. She turned it to the locked position, then stuffed the gun in the waist of her jeans.

She unplugged the television and ripped the cable out of the back of the set, then used it to tie Elton's hands behind his back.

Then she searched him, looking for a phone; but, to her intense disappointment, he did not have one.

8:30 a.m.

It took Craig a long time to work up the courage to look again at the motionless form of Daisy.

The sight of her mangled body, even viewed from a distance, had made him throw up. When there was nothing left in him to come out, he had tried to clean his mouth with handfuls of fresh snow. Then Sophie came to him and put her arms around his waist, and he hugged her, keeping his back to Daisy. They had stood like that until at last the nausea passed, and he felt able to turn and see what he had done.

Sophie said: 'What are we going to do now?'

Craig swallowed. It was not over yet. Daisy was only one of three thugs – and then there was Uncle Kit. 'We'd better take her gun,' he said.

Her expression told him she hated that idea. She said: 'Do you know how to use it?'

'How hard can it be?'

She looked unhappy, but just said: 'Whatever.'

Craig hesitated a moment longer; then he took her hand and they walked towards the body.

Daisy was lying face down, her arms beneath her. Although she had tried to kill Craig, he still found it horrible to look at a human being so mangled. The legs were the worst. Her leather trousers had been ripped to shreds. One leg was twisted unnaturally and the other was gashed and bloody. The leather jacket seemed to have protected her arms and body, but her shaved head was covered with blood. Her face was hidden, buried in the snow.

They stopped six feet away. 'I can't see the gun,' Craig said. 'It must be underneath her.'

They stepped closer. Sophie said: 'I've never seen a dead person.'

'I saw Mamma Marta in the funeral parlour.'

'I want to see her face.' Letting go of Craig's hand, Sophie went down on one knee and reached out to the bloodstained body.

Quick as a snake Daisy lifted her head, grabbed Sophie's wrist, and brought her right hand out from under her with the gun in it.

Sophie screamed in terror.

Craig felt as if he had been struck by lightning. He shouted: 'Christ!' and jumped back.

Daisy jammed the snout of the little grey pistol into the soft skin of Sophie's throat. 'Stand still, laddie!' she yelled.

Craig froze.

Daisy wore a cap of blood. One ear was almost completely ripped from her head, and hung grotesquely by a narrow strip of skin. But her face was unmarked, and now showed an expression of pure hatred. 'For what you've done to me, I should shoot her in the belly, and let you watch her bleed to death, screaming in agony.'

Craig shook with horror.

'But I need your help,' Daisy went on. 'If you want to

save your little girlfriend's life, just do everything I tell you, instantly. Hesitate, and she dies.'

Craig felt she really meant it.

'Get over here,' she said.

He had no choice. He stepped closer.

'Kneel down.'

Craig knelt beside her.

She turned her hateful eyes on Sophie. 'Now, you little whore, I'm going to let go of your arm, but don't you try to move away, or I'll shoot you, and enjoy it.' She took her left hand off Sophie's arm, but kept the gun pushed into the flesh of Sophie's neck. Then she put her left arm around Craig's shoulders. 'Hold my wrist, lad,' she said.

Craig grasped Daisy's wrist as it dangled over his shoulder.

'You, lassie, get under my right arm.'

Sophie changed her position slowly, and Daisy put her right arm over Sophie's shoulders, managing all the time to keep the gun pointed at Sophie's head.

'Now, you're going to lift me up and carry me to the house. But do it gently. I think I've got a broken leg. If you jog me it might hurt, and if I flinch I might accidentally pull the trigger. So, easy does it . . . and lift.'

Craig tightened his grip on Daisy's wrist and raised himself from the kneeling position. To ease the burden on Sophie, he put his right arm around Daisy's waist and took some of her weight. The three of them slowly stood upright.

Daisy was gasping with pain, and as pale as the snow on the ground all around them; but, when Craig looked sideways and caught her eye, he saw that she was watching him intently.

When they were upright, Daisy said: 'Forward, slowly.'

They walked forward, Daisy dragging her legs

'I bet you two were hidden away somewhere all night,' she said. 'What were you up to, eh?'

Craig said nothing. He could hardly believe that she had enough breath and malice left to rail at them.

'Tell me, laddie,' she jeered. 'Did you put your finger in her little pussy, eh? You dirty little bastard, I bet you did.'

Craig *felt* dirty when she talked like that. She was able to sully an experience that had been carefree. He hated her for spoiling his memory. He longed to drop her on the ground, but he felt sure she would pull the trigger.

'Wait,' she said. 'Stop.' They halted, and she put some of her weight on her left leg, the one that was not twisted.

Craig looked at her terrible face. Her black-lined eyes were closed in pain. She said: 'We'll just rest here for a minute, then we'll go on.'

*   *   *

Toni stepped out of the barn. Now she could be seen. By her calculations, there were two of the gang in the house – Nigel and Kit – and either of them might look out of a window at any moment. But she had to take the risk. Listening for the shot that would kill her, she walked as fast as she could, pushing through the snow, to the guest cottage. She reached it without incident and dodged around the corner of the building out of sight.

She had left Caroline searching tearfully for her pet rats. Elton was trussed up under the billiard table, blindfolded and gagged to make sure that when he came round he could not talk dopey Caroline into untying him.

Toni circled the cottage and approached the main house from the side. The back door stood open, but she did not go in. She needed to reconnoitre. She crept along the back of the building and peeped in at the first window.

She was looking into the pantry. Six people were crammed in there, bound hand and foot but standing: Olga; Hugo, who seemed to be naked; Miranda; her son Tom; Ned; and Stanley. A wave of happiness washed over Toni when she saw Stanley. She realized she had feared, in the back of her mind, that he might be dead. She caught her breath when she saw his bruised and bloody face. Then he spotted her, and his eyes widened with surprise and pleasure. He did not appear to be seriously wounded, she saw with relief. He opened his mouth to speak. Quickly, Toni raised a finger to her lips for silence. Stanley closed his mouth and nodded understanding.

Toni moved to the next window and looked into the kitchen. Two men sat with their backs to the window. One was Kit. Toni felt a surge of pity for Stanley, having a son who would do something like this to his family. The other man wore a pink sweater. He must be the one Kit had called Nigel. They were looking at a small television set, watching the news. The screen showed a snowplough clearing a motorway in the light of early morning.

Toni chewed her lip, thinking. She had a gun now but, even so, it could be difficult to control the two of them. But she had no choice.

As she hesitated, Kit stood up, and she quickly ducked back out of sight.

8:45 a.m.

Nigel said: 'That's it. They're clearing the roads. We have to go *now*.'

'I'm worried about Toni Gallo,' Kit said.

'Too bad. If we wait any longer, we'll miss the rendezvous.'

Kit looked at his watch. Nigel was right. 'Shit,' he said

'We'll take that Mercedes outside. Go and find the keys.'

Kit left the kitchen and ran upstairs. In Olga's bedroom, he pulled out the drawers of both bedside tables without finding any keys. He picked up Hugo's suitcase and emptied the contents onto the floor, but nothing jingled. Breathing hard, he did the same with Olga's case. Then he spotted Hugo's blazer draped over the back of a chair. He found the Mercedes keys in the pocket.

He ran down to the kitchen. Nigel was looking out of the window. 'Why is Elton taking so long?' Kit said. He could hear a note of hysteria in his own voice.

'I don't know,' said Nigel. 'Try to stay calm.'

'And what the hell's happened to Daisy?'

'Go and start the engine,' Nigel said. 'Brush the snow off the windscreen.'

'Right.'

As Kit turned away, his eye was caught by the perfume spray, in its double bag, lying on the kitchen table. On impulse, he picked it up and stuffed it into his jacket pocket.

Then he went out.

*   *   *

Toni peeped around the corner of the house and saw Kit emerge from the back door. He went in the opposite direction, to the front of the building. She followed him and saw him unlock the green Mercedes estate car.

This was her chance.

She took Elton's pistol from the waist of her jeans and moved the safety catch to the unlocked position. There was a full magazine in the grip – she had checked. She held the gun pointing skywards, in accordance with her training.

She breathed slowly and calmly. She knew how to do this kind of thing. Her heart was pounding like a bass drum, but her hands were steady. She ran into the house.

The back door gave on to a small lobby. A second door led to the kitchen proper. She threw it open and ran in. Nigel was at the window, looking out. 'Freeze!' she screamed.

He spun around.

She levelled the gun at him. 'Hands in the air!'

He hesitated.

His pistol was in the pocket of his trousers – she could see the lumpy bulge it made, the right size and shape for an automatic just like the one she was holding. 'Don't even think about reaching for your gun,' she said.

Slowly, he raised his hands.

'On the floor! Face down! Now!'

He went down on his knees, hands still held high. Then he lay down, his arms spread.

Toni had to get his gun. She stood over him, transferred her pistol to her left hand, and thrust its nose into the back of his neck. 'The safety catch is off, and I'm feeling jumpy,' she said. She went down on one knee and reached into his trousers pocket.

He moved very fast.

He rolled over, swinging his right arm at her. For a split second she hesitated to pull the trigger, then it was too late. He knocked her off balance and she fell sideways. To break her fall, she put her left hand flat on the floor – dropping her gun.

He kicked out at her wildly, his shoe connecting with her hip. She regained her balance and scrambled to her feet, coming upright before he did. As he got to his knees, she kicked him in the face. He fell back, his hand flying to his cheek, but he recovered fast. He looked at her with an expression of fury and hatred, as if outraged that she should fight back.

She snatched up the gun and pointed it at him, and he froze.

'Let's try again,' she said. 'This time, *you* take the gun out. Slowly.'

He reached into his pocket.

Toni stretched her arm out in front of her. 'And please – give me an excuse to blow your head off.'

He took the gun out.

'Drop it on the floor.'

He smiled. 'Have you ever actually shot a man?'

'Drop it – now.'

'I don't think you have.'

He had guessed right. She had been trained to use firearms, and she had carried a gun on operations, but she had never shot at anything other than a target. The idea of actually making a hole in another human being revolted her.

'You're not going to shoot me,' he said.

'You're a second away from finding out.'

Her mother walked in, carrying the puppy. She said: 'This poor dog hasn't had any breakfast.'

Nigel raised his gun.

Toni shot him in the right shoulder.

She was only six feet away, and she was a good shot, so it was not difficult to wound him in exactly the right place. She pulled the trigger twice, as she had been taught. The double bang was deafening in the kitchen. Two round holes appeared in the pink sweater, side by side where the arm met the shoulder. The gun fell from Nigel's hand. He cried out in pain and staggered back against the refrigerator.

Toni felt shocked. She had not really believed she could do it. The act was repellent. She was a monster. She felt sick.

Nigel screamed: 'You fucking bitch!'

Like magic, his words restored her nerve. 'Be glad I didn't shoot you in the belly,' she said. 'Now lie down.'

He slumped to the floor and rolled over on his face, still clutching his wound.

Mother said: 'I'll put the kettle on.'

Toni picked up his dropped gun and locked the safety catch. She stuffed both guns into her jeans and opened the pantry door.

Stanley said: 'What happened? Was someone shot?'

'Nigel,' she said calmly. She took a pair of kitchen scissors from the knife block and cut the washing line that bound Stanley's hands and feet. When he was free, he put his arms around her and squeezed her hard. 'Thank you,' he murmured in her ear.

She closed her eyes. The nightmare of the last few hours had not changed his feelings. She hugged him hard for a precious second, wishing the moment could last longer; then she broke the clinch. Handing him the scissors, she said: 'You free the rest.' She drew one of the pistols from her waistband. 'Kit's not far away. He must have heard the shots. Does he have a gun?'

'I don't think so,' Stanley replied.

Toni was relieved. That would make it easier.

Olga said: 'Get us out of this cold room, please!'

Stanley turned to cut her bonds.

Kit's voice rang out: 'Nobody move!'

Toni spun around, levelling the gun. Kit stood in the doorway. He had no gun, but he was holding a simple glass perfume spray in his hand as if it were a weapon. Toni recognized the bottle that she had seen, on the security video, being filled with Madoba-2.

Kit said: 'This contains the virus. One squirt will kill you.'

Everyone stood still.

*   *   *

Kit stared at Toni. She was pointing the gun at him, and he was pointing the spray at her. He said: 'If you shoot me, I'll drop the bottle, and the glass will break on these tiles.'

She said: 'If you spray us with that stuff, you'll kill yourself as well.'

'I'll die, then,' he said. 'I don't care. I've put everything into this. I made the plan, I betrayed my family, and I became a party to a conspiracy to murder hundreds of people, maybe thousands. After all that, how can I fail? I'd rather die.' As he said it, he realized it was true. Even the money had diminished in importance now. All he really wanted was to win.

Stanley said: 'How did we come to this, Kit?'

Kit met his father's gaze. He saw anger there, as he expected, but also grief. Stanley looked the way he had when Mamma Marta died. Too bad, Kit thought angrily; he brought this on himself. 'Too late now for apologies,' he said harshly.

'I wasn't going to apologize,' Stanley said sadly.

Kit looked at Nigel, sitting on the floor, holding his bleeding right shoulder with his left hand. That explained the two gunshots that had caused Kit to arm himself with the spray before coming back into the kitchen.

Nigel struggled to his feet. 'Ah, bollocks, it hurts,' he said.

Kit said: 'Hand over the guns, Toni. Quick, or I'll press this nozzle.'

Toni hesitated.

Stanley said: 'I think Kit means what he says.'

'On the table,' Kit said.

She put the guns on the kitchen table, beside the briefcase that had contained the perfume bottle.

Kit said: 'Nigel, pick them up.'

With his left hand, Nigel picked up a gun and stuffed it into his pocket. He took the second, hefted it, then, with sudden speed, smashed it across Toni's face. She cried out and fell back.

Kit was furious with him. 'What do you think you're doing?' he cried. 'There's no time for that! We have to get going.'

'Don't you give me orders,' Nigel said harshly. 'This cow shot me.'

Kit could tell from Toni's face that she thought she was about to die. But there was no time to enjoy revenge. 'That cow ruined my life, but I'm not hanging around to punish her,' Kit said. 'Knock it off!'

Nigel hesitated, staring malevolently at Toni.

Kit said: 'Let's go!'

At last Nigel turned away from Toni. 'What about Elton and Daisy?'

'To hell with them.'

'We should tie up your old man and his tart.'

'You stupid fool, don't you realize we're out of time?'

The stare Nigel gave Kit was sulphuric. 'What did you call me?' Nigel wanted to kill someone, Kit realized, and right now he was thinking of shooting Kit. It was a terrifying moment. Kit raised the perfume spray high in the air and stared back, waiting for his life to end.

Then Nigel looked away and said: 'All right, let's get out of here.'

9 a.m.

Kit ran outside. The engine of the Mercedes was throbbing low, and the snow on its bonnet was already melting from the heat. The windscreen and side windows were partly clear where he had hastily swept them with his hands. He jumped in, stuffing the perfume spray into his jacket pocket. Nigel clambered into the passenger seat, grunting with the pain of his gunshot wound.

Kit put the automatic gearshift into Drive and touched the accelerator pedal. The car seemed to strain forward, but did not move. The plough had stopped a couple of feet away, and snow was piled two feet high in front of the bumper. Kit increased pressure on the pedal as the car laboured to move the snow out of the way. 'Come on!' Kit said. 'This is a Mercedes, it ought to be able to shift a few pounds of snow! How big is the damn engine, anyway?' He pressed a little harder, but he did not want the wheels to lose traction and begin to spin. The car eased forward a few inches, and the piled-up snow seemed to crack and shift. Kit looked back. His father and Toni stood outside the house, watching. They would come no closer, Kit guessed, because they knew Nigel had the guns.

The car suddenly sprang forward as the snow gave way.

Kit felt a soaring elation as he accelerated along the cleared driveway. Steepfall had seemed like a jail from which he would never escape – but he had. He passed the garage – and saw Daisy.

He braked reflexively.

Nigel said: 'What the hell?'

Daisy was walking towards them, supported by Craig on one side and by Ned's sulky daughter, Sophie, on the other. Daisy's legs dragged uselessly behind her, and her head was a mass of blood. Beyond them was Stanley's Ferrari, its sensuous curves battered and deformed, its gleaming blue paintwork scraped and scratched. What the hell had happened there?

'Stop and pick her up!' Nigel said.

Kit remembered how Daisy had humiliated him and almost drowned him in her father's pool only yesterday. 'Fuck her,' he said. He was at the wheel, and he was not going to delay his escape for her. He put his foot down.

*   *   *

The long green bonnet of the Mercedes seemed to lift like the head of an eager horse, and it leaped forward. Craig had only a second to act. He grabbed the hood of Sophie's anorak with his right hand and pulled her to the side of the drive, moving the same way himself. Because they were tangled up with Daisy, she moved with them, and all three fell into the soft snow beside the track, Daisy screaming in pain and rage.

The car shot past, missing them by inches, and Craig glimpsed his Uncle Kit at the wheel. He was flabbergasted. Kit had nearly killed him. Was it intentional, or had Kit known that Craig had time to get out of the way?

'You bastard!' Daisy screamed after the car, and she levelled her pistol.

Kit accelerated past the crashed Ferrari and along the curving driveway that ran beside the cliff top. Craig watched, frozen, as Daisy took aim. Her hand was steady, despite the pain she was in. She squeezed off a shot, and Craig saw a rear side window shatter.

Daisy tracked the speeding car with her arm and fired repeatedly, cartridge cases spewing from the ejection slot of the gun. A line of bullet holes appeared in the car's side, then there was a different kind of bang. A front tyre blew out, and a strip of rubber flew through the air.

The car continued in a straight line for a second. Then it slewed sideways, its bonnet ploughing into the piled snow at the side of the drive, sending up a fantail of white. The back swung out and crashed into the low wall that ran along the cliff edge. Craig heard the metallic scream of tortured steel.

The car skidded sideways. Daisy kept firing, and the windscreen shattered. The car went into a slow roll, tilting sideways, seeming to hesitate, then toppling over onto its roof. It slid a few feet upside-down then came to a stop.

Daisy stopped shooting and fell backwards, her eyes closed.

Craig stared at her. The gun fell from her hand. Sophie started to cry.

Craig reached across Daisy. He watched her eyes, terrified that they would open at any moment. His hand closed over the warm gun. He picked it up.

He held it in his right hand and put his finger into the trigger guard. He pointed it at a spot exactly between

Daisy's eyes. All he cared about was that this monster should never threaten him and Sophie and their family ever again. Slowly, he squeezed the trigger.

The gun clicked on an empty magazine.

*   *   *

Kit was lying flat on the inside roof of the overturned car. He felt bruised all over, and his neck hurt as if he had twisted it, but he could move all his limbs. He managed to right himself. Nigel lay beside him, unconscious, possibly dead.

Kit tried to get out. He pulled the handle and pushed at the door, but it would not move. Something had jammed in the crash. He hammered madly at it with his fists, with no result. He jabbed at the button of the electric window, but nothing happened. He thought frantically that he might be imprisoned until the fire brigade arrived to cut him out, and he suffered a moment of panic and despair. Then he saw that the windscreen was crazed. He shoved at it with his hand and easily pushed out a big section of broken glass.

He crawled through the windscreen. He was careless of the broken glass, and a shard cut the palm of his hand painfully. He cried out and sucked the wound, but he could not pause. He slithered out from under the bonnet of the car and scrambled to his feet. The wind off the sea blew madly in his face. He looked around.

His father and Toni Gallo were running along the drive towards him.

*   *   *

Toni stopped to look at Daisy. She seemed to be out cold. Craig and Sophie appeared scared but unhurt. 'What happened?' Toni said.

'She was shooting at us,' Craig replied. 'I ran over her.'

Toni followed Craig's gaze and saw Stanley's Ferrari, dented at both ends and with all its windows smashed.

Stanley said: 'Good God!'

Toni felt for a pulse in Daisy's neck. It was there, but weak. 'She's still alive – just.'

Craig said: 'I've got her gun. It's empty, anyway.'

They were all right, Toni decided. She looked ahead to the crashed Mercedes. Kit had climbed out. She ran towards him. Stanley followed close behind.

Kit started to run away, along the drive, heading for the woods; but he was battered and shaken by the crash, and he ran erratically. He was never going to make it, Toni could see. After a few paces he staggered and fell.

He seemed to realize that he could not escape that way. Scrambling to his feet, he changed direction, and turned towards the cliff.

Toni glanced into the Mercedes as she passed it. Nigel lay in a crumpled heap, eyes open with the blank stare of the dead. That accounted for the three thugs, Toni thought: one tied up, one unconscious, and one dead. Only Kit was left.

Kit slipped on the icy drive, staggered, regained his balance, and turned around. He took the perfume spray from his pocket and held it out like a gun. 'Stop, or I'll kill us all,' he said.

Toni and Stanley stopped.

Kit's face was all pain and rage. Toni saw a man who

had lost his soul. He might do anything: kill his family, kill himself, destroy the world.

Stanley said: 'It won't work out here, Kit.'

Toni wondered if that was true. Kit had the same thought, and said: 'Why not?'

'Feel this wind,' Stanley said. 'The droplets will disperse before they can do any harm.'

'To hell with it all,' Kit said, and he threw the bottle high in the air. Then he turned around, jumped over the low wall, and ran full tilt at the cliff edge a few feet away.

Stanley jumped after him.

Toni caught the perfume bottle before it hit the ground.

Stanley leaped through the air, hands stretched out in front of him. He almost got Kit by the shoulders, but his hands slipped. He hit the ground, but managed to grab one leg and grip it tight. Kit fell to the ground with his head and shoulders jutting out over the edge of the cliff. Stanley jumped on top of him, holding him down with his weight.

Toni looked over the edge, down a hundred-foot drop to where the sea boiled among jagged rocks.

Kit struggled, but his father held him down, and eventually he became still.

Stanley got slowly to his feet and pulled Kit up. Kit's eyes were shut. He was shaking with emotion, like someone in a fit. 'It's over,' Stanley said. He put his arms around his son and held him. 'It's all over now.' They stood like that on the edge, with the wind blowing their hair, until Kit stopped shaking. Then, gently, Stanley turned him around and led him back towards the house.

*   *   *

The family were in the living room, stunned and silent, still not sure that the nightmare was over. Stanley was talking to the Inverburn ambulance service on Kit's mobile phone while Nellie tried to lick his hands. Hugo lay on the couch, covered in blankets, while Olga bathed his wounds. Miranda was doing the same for Tom and Ned. Kit lay on his back on the floor, eyes closed. Craig and Sophie talked in low voices in a corner. Caroline had found all her rats and sat with their cage on her knees. Toni's mother sat next to Caroline with the puppy in her lap. The Christmas tree twinkled in the corner.

Toni called Odette. 'How far away did you say those helicopters were?'

'An hour,' Odette replied. 'But that was then. As soon as the snow stopped I moved them. Now they're at Inverburn, waiting for instructions. Why?'

'I've caught the gang and I've got the virus back, but—'

'What, on your own?' Odette was amazed.

'Never mind that. The important man is the customer, the one who's trying to buy this stuff and use it to kill people. We need to find him.'

'I wish we could.'

'I think we can, if we act fast. Could you send a helicopter to me?'

'Where are you?'

'At Stanley Oxenford's house, Steepfall. It's right on the cliff exactly fifteen miles north of Inverburn. There are four buildings in a square, and the pilot will see two crashed cars in the garden.'

'My God, you have been busy.'

'I need the chopper to bring me a bug, a miniature radio beacon, the kind you plant on someone you need to follow. It has to be small enough to fit into a bottle cap.'

'How long does the transmitter need to operate?'

'Forty-eight hours.'

'No problem. They should have that at police headquarters in Inverburn.'

'One more thing. I need a bottle of perfume – *Diablerie*.'

'They won't have *that* at police headquarters. They'll have to break into Boots in the High Street.'

'We don't have much time— Wait.' Olga was saying something. Toni looked at her and said: 'What is it?'

'I can give you a bottle of *Diablerie*, just like the one that was on the table. It's the perfume I use.'

'Thanks.' Toni spoke into the phone. 'Forget the perfume, I've got a bottle. How soon can you get the chopper here?'

'Ten minutes.'

Toni looked at her watch. 'That might not be fast enough.'

'Where's the helicopter going after it picks you up?'

'I'll get back to you on that,' Toni said, and she ended the call.

She knelt on the floor beside Kit. He was pale. His eyes were closed, but he was not asleep: his breathing was shallow and he trembled intermittently. 'Kit,' she said. He did not respond. 'Kit, I need to ask you a question. It's very important.'

He opened his eyes.

'You were going to meet the customer at ten o'clock, weren't you?'

A tense hush fell on the room as the others turned and listened.

Kit looked at Toni but said nothing.

She said: 'I need to know where you were going to meet them.'

He looked away.

'Kit, please.'

His lips parted. Toni leaned closer. He whispered: 'No.'

'Think about it,' she urged. 'You might earn forgiveness, in time.'

'Never.'

'On the contrary. Little harm has been done, though much was intended. The virus has been recovered.'

His eyes moved from side to side as he looked from one family member to the next.

Reading his mind, Toni said: 'You've done a great wrong to them, but they don't yet seem ready to abandon you. They're all around you.'

He closed his eyes.

Toni leaned closer. 'You could begin to redeem yourself right now.'

Stanley opened his mouth to speak, but Miranda stopped him with a raised hand. She spoke instead. 'Kit, please,' she said. 'Do one good thing, after all this rottenness. Do it for yourself, so that you'll know you're not all bad. Tell her what she needs to know.'

Kit closed his eyelids tight, and tears appeared. At last he said: 'Inverburn Flying School.'

'Thank you,' Toni whispered.

10 a.m.

Toni sat in the control tower at the flying school. With her in the little room were Frank Hackett, Kit Oxenford, and a local police detective. In the hangar, parked out of sight, was the military helicopter that had brought them here. It had been close, but they had made it with a minute to spare.

Kit clutched the burgundy briefcase. He was pale, his face expressionless. He obeyed instructions like an automaton.

They all watched through the big windows. The clouds were breaking up, and the sun shone over the snow-covered airstrip. There was no sign of a helicopter.

Toni held Nigel Buchanan's mobile phone, waiting for it to ring. The batteries had run out at some point during the night, but it was the same kind as Hugo's, so she had borrowed his charger, which was now plugged into the wall.

'The pilot should have called by now,' she said anxiously.

Frank said: 'He may be a few minutes late.'

She pressed buttons and discovered the last number Nigel had dialled. It looked like a mobile number, and it was timed at 11:45 p.m. yesterday. 'Kit,' she said. 'Did Nigel call the customer just before midnight?'

'His pilot.'

She turned to Frank. 'This will be the number. I think we should call it.'

'Okay.'

She pressed Send, and handed the mobile to the local police detective. He put it to his ear. After a few moments, he said: 'Yeah, this is me, where are you?' He spoke with a London accent similar to Nigel's, which was why Frank had brought him along. 'That close?' he said, looking through the window up at the sky. 'We can't see you—'

As he spoke, a helicopter came down through the clouds.

Toni tensed.

The police officer hung up. Toni took out her own mobile and called Odette, who was now in the operations room at Scotland Yard. 'Customer in sight.'

Odette could not repress the excitement in her voice. 'Give me the tail number.'

'Just a minute . . .' Toni peered at the helicopter until she could make out the registration mark, then read the letters and numbers to Odette. Odette read them back then hung up.

The helicopter descended. Its rotors blew the snow on the ground into a storm. It landed a hundred yards from the control tower.

Frank looked at Kit and nodded. 'Off you go.'

Kit hesitated.

Toni said: 'Just do everything as planned. Say: "We had

some problems with the weather, but everything worked out okay in the end." You'll be fine.'

Kit went down the stairs, carrying the briefcase.

Toni had no idea whether he would perform as instructed. He had been up for more than twenty-four hours, he had been in a car crash, and he was emotionally wrecked. He might do anything.

There were two men in the front seats of the helicopter. One of them, presumably the co-pilot, opened a door and got out, carrying a large suitcase. He was a stocky man of medium height, wearing sunglasses. Ducking his head, he moved away from the aircraft.

A moment later, Kit appeared outside the tower and walked across the snow towards the helicopter.

'Stay calm, Kit,' Toni said aloud. Frank grunted.

The two men met halfway. There was some conversation. Was the co-pilot asking where Nigel was? Kit pointed to the control tower. What was he saying? *Nigel sent me to make the delivery*, perhaps. But it could just as easily be *The police are up there in the control tower*. There were more questions, and Kit shrugged.

Toni's mobile rang. It was Odette. 'The helicopter is registered to Adam Hallan, a London banker,' she said. 'But he's not on board.'

'Shame.'

'Don't worry, I wasn't expecting him. The pilot and co-pilot are employees of his. They filed a flight plan to Battersea Heliport – just across the river from Mr Hallan's house in Cheyne Walk.'

'He's Mister Big, then?'

'Trust me. We've been after him for a long time.'

The co-pilot pointed at the burgundy briefcase. Kit opened it and showed him a *Diablerie* bottle in a nest of polystyrene packing chips. The co-pilot put his suitcase on the ground and opened it to reveal stacks of banded fifty-pound notes, closely packed together; at least a million pounds, Toni thought, perhaps two million. As he had been instructed, Kit took out one of the stacks and riffled it.

Toni told Odette: 'They've made the exchange. Kit's checking the money.'

The two men on the airfield looked at one another, nodded, and shook hands. Kit handed over the burgundy briefcase, then picked up the suitcase. It seemed heavy. The co-pilot walked back to the helicopter, and Kit returned to the control tower.

As soon as the co-pilot got back into the aircraft, it took off.

Toni was still on the line to Odette. 'Are you picking up the signal from the transmitter in the bottle?'

'Loud and clear,' Odette said. 'We've got the bastards.'

BOXING DAY

7 p.m.

London was cold. No snow had fallen here, but a freezing wind whipped the ancient buildings and the curled streets, and people hunched their shoulders and tightened the scarves around their necks as they hurried to the warmth of pubs and restaurants, hotels and cinemas.

Toni Gallo sat in the back of a plain grey Audi beside Odette Cressy. Odette was a blonde woman Toni's age, wearing a dark business suit over a scarlet shirt. Two detectives sat in the front, one driving, one studying a direction-finding radio receiver and telling the driver where to go.

The police had been tracking the perfume bottle for thirty-three hours. The helicopter had landed, as expected, in south-west London. The pilot had got into a waiting car and driven across Battersea Bridge to the riverside home of Adam Hallan. All last night the radio transmitter had remained stationary, beeping steadily from somewhere in the elegant eighteenth-century house. Odette did not want to arrest Hallan yet. She wanted to catch the maximum number of terrorists in her net.

Toni had spent most of that time asleep. When she lay down in her flat just before noon on Christmas Day, she felt too tense to sleep. Her thoughts were with the helicopter as it flew the length of Britain, and she worried that the tiny radio beacon would fail. Despite her anxieties, she had dropped off in seconds.

In the evening, she had driven to Steepfall to see Stanley. They had held hands and talked for an hour in his study, then she flew to London. She slept heavily all night at Odette's flat in Camden Town.

As well as following the radio signal, the Metropolitan Police had Adam Hallan and his pilot and co-pilot under surveillance. In the morning Toni and Odette joined the team watching Adam Hallan's house.

Toni had achieved her main objective. The deadly virus samples were back in the BSL4 laboratory at the Kremlin. But she also hoped to catch the people responsible for the nightmare she had lived through. She wanted justice.

Today Hallan had given a lunch party, and fifty people of assorted nationalities and ages, all wearing expensive casual clothes, had visited the house. One of the guests had left with the perfume bottle. Toni and Odette and the team tracked the radio beacon to Bayswater, and kept watch over a student rooming house all afternoon.

At seven o'clock in the evening, the signal moved again.

A young woman came out of the house. In the light of the street lamps, Toni could see that she had beautiful dark hair, heavy and lustrous. She carried a shoulder bag. She turned up the collar of her coat and walked along the pavement. A detective in jeans and an anorak got out of a tan Rover and followed her.

'I think this is it,' Toni said. 'She's going to release the spray.'

'I want to see it,' Odette said. 'For the prosecution, I need witnesses to the attempted murder.'

Toni and Odette lost sight of the young woman as she turned into a Tube station. The radio signal weakened worryingly as the woman went underground. It remained steady for a while, then the beacon moved, presumably because the woman was on a train. They followed the feeble signal, fearing it would fade out and she would shake off the detective in the anorak. But she emerged at Piccadilly Circus, the detective still tailing her. They lost visual contact for a minute when she turned into a one-way street, then the detective called Odette on his mobile phone and reported that the woman had entered a theatre.

Toni said: 'That's where she'll release the spray.'

The unmarked police cars drew up outside the theatre. Odette and Toni went in, followed by two men from the second car. The show, a ghost story with songs, was popular with visiting Americans. The girl with beautiful hair was standing in the queue for collection of prepaid tickets.

While she waited, she took from her shoulder bag a perfume bottle. With a quick gesture that looked entirely natural, she sprayed her head and shoulders. The theatregoers around her paid no attention. Doubtless she wanted to be fragrant for the man she was meeting, they would imagine, if they thought about it at all. Such beautiful hair ought to smell good. The spray was curiously odourless, but no one seemed to notice.

'That's good,' said Odette. 'But we'll let her do it again.'

The bottle contained plain water, but all the same Toni shivered with dread as she breathed in. Had she not made the switch, the spray would have contained live Madoba-2, and that breath would have killed her.

The woman collected her ticket and went inside. Odette spoke to the usher and showed him her police card, then the detectives followed the woman. She went to the bar, where she sprayed herself again. She did the same in the ladies' room. At last she took her seat in the stalls and sprayed herself yet again. Her plan, Toni guessed, was to use the spray several times more in the interval, and finally in the crowded passages while the audience was leaving the building. By the end of the evening, almost everyone in the theatre would have breathed the droplets from her bottle.

Watching from the back of the auditorium, Toni listened to the accents around her: a woman from the American south who had bought the most beautiful cashmere scarf; someone from Boston talking about where he pahked his cah; a New Yorker who had paid five *dollars* for a cup of cawfee. If the perfume bottle had contained the virus as planned, these people would by now be infected with Madoba-2. They would have flown home to embrace their families and greet their neighbours and go back to work, telling everyone about their holiday in Europe.

Ten or twelve days later, they would have fallen ill. 'I picked up a lousy cold in London,' they would have said. Sneezing, they would have infected their relations and friends and colleagues. The symptoms would have got worse, and their doctors would have diagnosed flu. When they started to die, the doctors would have realized that this was something much worse than flu. As the deadly infection spread rapidly from street to street and city to city, the medical profession would have begun to understand what they were dealing with; but by then it would be too late.

Now none of that would happen – but Toni shuddered as she thought how close it had been.

A nervous man in a tuxedo approached them. 'I'm the theatre manager,' he said. 'What's happening?'

'We're about to make an arrest,' Odette told him. 'You may want to delay the curtain for a minute.'

'I hope there won't be a fracas.'

'Believe me, so do I.' The audience was seated. 'All right,' Odette said to the other detectives. 'We've seen enough. Pick her up, and gently does it.'

The two men from the second car walked down the aisles and stood at either end of the row. The woman with beautiful hair looked at one, then the other. 'Come with me, please, miss,' said the nearer of the two detectives. The theatre went quiet as the waiting audience watched. Was this part of the show? they wondered.

The woman remained seated, but took out her perfume bottle and sprayed herself again. The detective, a young man in a short Crombie coat, pushed his way along the row to where she sat. 'Please come immediately,' he said. She stood up, raised the bottle, and sprayed it into the air. 'Don't bother,' he said. 'It's only water.' Then he took her by the arm and led her along the row and up the aisle to the back of the theatre.

Toni stared at the prisoner. She was young and attractive. She had been ready to commit suicide. Toni wondered why.

Odette took the perfume bottle from her and dropped

it into an evidence bag. '*Diablerie*,' she said. 'French word. Do you know what it means?'

The woman shook her head.

'The work of the devil.' Odette turned to the detective. 'Put her in handcuffs and take her away.'

CHRISTMAS DAY
a year later

5:50 p.m.

Toni came out of the bathroom naked and walked across the hotel room to answer the phone.

From the bed, Stanley said: 'My God, you look good.'

She grinned at her husband. He was wearing a blue towelling bathrobe that was too small for him, and it showed his long, muscular legs. 'You're not so bad yourself,' she said, and she picked up the phone. It was her mother. 'Happy Christmas,' she said.

'Your old boyfriend is on the television,' Mother said.

'What's he doing, singing carols in the police choir?'

'He's being interviewed by that Carl Osborne. He's telling how he caught those terrorists last Christmas.'

'*He* caught them?' Toni was momentarily indignant, then she thought: What the hell. 'Well, he needs the publicity – he's after a promotion. How's my sister?'

'She's just getting the supper ready.'

Toni looked at her watch. On this Caribbean island it was a few minutes before six o'clock in the evening. For Mother, in England, it was coming up to ten o'clock at night. But meals were always late at Bella's. 'What did she give you for Christmas?'

'We're going to get something in the January sales, it's cheaper.'

'Did you like my present?' Toni had given Mother a cashmere cardigan in salmon pink.

'Lovely, thank you, dear.'

'Is Osborne okay?' Mother had taken the puppy to live with her, and he was now full grown, a big shaggy black-and-white dog with hair that covered his eyes.

'He's behaving very well and hasn't had any accidents since yesterday.'

'And the grandchildren?'

'Running around breaking their presents. I must go now, the Queen's on the telly.'

'Bye, Mother. Thank you for calling.'

Stanley said: 'I don't suppose there's time for a bit of, you know, before dinner.'

She pretended to be shocked. 'We just had a bit of *you know*!'

'That was hours ago! But if you're tired . . . I realize that when a woman gets to a certain age—'

'A certain age?' She leaped onto the bed and knelt astride him. 'A certain age?' She picked up the pillow and beat him with it.

He laughed helplessly and begged for mercy, and she relented and kissed him.

She had expected Stanley to be fairly good in bed, but it had come as a surprise to her that he was such a pistol. She would never forget their first holiday together. In a suite at the Ritz in Paris, he had blindfolded her and tied her hands to the bedhead. As she lay there, naked and helpless, he had stroked her lips with a feather, then with a silver teaspoon, then with a strawberry. She had never before concentrated so intensely on her bodily sensations. He caressed her breasts with a silk handkerchief, with a cashmere scarf, and with leather gloves. She had felt as if she were floating in the sea, rocked gently by waves of pleasure. He kissed the backs of her knees, the insides of her thighs, the soft undersides of her upper arms, and her throat. He did everything slowly and lingeringly, until she was bursting with desire. He touched her nipples with ice cubes, and put warm oil inside her. He carried on until she begged him to enter her, then he made her wait a little longer. Afterwards, she had said: 'I didn't know this, but all my life I've wanted a man to do that.'

'I know,' he had said.

Now he was in a playful mood. 'Come on, just a quickie,' he said. 'I'll let you be on top.'

'Oh, all right.' She sighed, pretending to feel put-upon, as she adjusted her position over him. 'The things a girl has to do nowadays—'

There was a knock at the door.

Stanley called out: 'Who is it?'

'Olga. Toni was going to lend me a necklace.'

Toni could see that Stanley was about to tell his daughter to go away, but she put a hand on his mouth. 'Just a minute, Olga,' she called.

She detached herself from Stanley. Olga and Miranda were coping well with having a stepmother their own age, but Toni did not want to push her luck. Best if they were not reminded that their father was having hot sex.

Stanley got off the bed and went into the bathroom. Toni pulled on a green silk robe and opened the door.

Olga strode in, dressed for dinner in a black cotton dress with a low neckline. 'You said you'd lend me that jet necklace.'

'Of course. Let me dig it out.'

In the bathroom, the shower ran.

Olga lowered her voice, an unusual event. 'I wanted to ask you – has he seen Kit?'

'Yes. He visited the prison the day before we flew out here.'

'How is my brother?'

'Uncomfortable, frustrated and bored, as you would expect, but he hasn't been beaten up or raped, and he isn't using heroin.' Toni found the necklace and put it around Olga's neck. 'It looks better on you than me – black really isn't my colour. Why don't you ask your father directly about Kit?'

'He's so happy, I don't want to spoil his mood. You don't mind, do you?'

'Not in the least.' On the contrary, Toni was flattered. Olga was using her the way a daughter would use a mother, to check on her father without bothering him with the kind of questions men did not like. Toni said: 'Did you realize that Elton and Hamish are in the same jail?'

'No – how awful!'

'Not really. Kit's helping Elton learn to read.'

'Elton can't read?'

'Barely. He knows a few words from road signs – motorway, London, town centre, airport. Kit is teaching him *The cat sat on the mat.*'

'My God, how things work out. Did you hear about Daisy?'

'No.'

'She killed another inmate of the women's prison, and she was tried for murder. A young colleague of mine defended her, but she was convicted. She got a life sentence added to her existing term. She'll be in jail until she's seventy. I wish we still had the death penalty.'

Toni understood Olga's hatred. Hugo had never completely recovered from the beating Daisy gave him with the cosh. He had lost the sight in one eye. Worse, he had never regained his old ebullience. He was quieter, and less of a rake, but he was not so funny, and the wicked grin was rarely seen.

'A pity her father is still at large,' Toni said. Harry Mac had been prosecuted as an accomplice, but Kit's testimony had not been enough to convict him, and the jury had found him not guilty. He had gone straight back to his life of crime.

Olga said: 'There's news of him, too. He's got cancer. Started in his lungs, but now it's everywhere. He's been given three months to live.'

'Well, well,' said Toni. 'There is justice, after all.'

*   *   *

Miranda put out Ned's clothes for the evening, black linen trousers and a check shirt. He did not expect her to do it but, if she did not, he might absent-mindedly go down to dinner in shorts and a T-shirt. He was not helpless, just careless. She had accepted that.

She had accepted a lot about him. She understood that he would never be quick to enter a conflict, even to protect her; but, to compensate for that, she knew that in a real crisis he was a rock. The way he had taken punch after punch from Daisy to protect Tom proved that.

She was dressed already, in a pink cotton frock with a pleated skirt. It made her look a bit wide across the hips, but then she was a bit wide across the hips. Ned said he liked her that way.

She went into the bathroom. He was sitting in the tub, reading a biography of Molière in French. She took the book from him. 'The butler did it.'

'Now you've spoiled the suspense.' He stood up.

She handed him a towel. 'I'm going to check on the kids.' Before she left the room, she took a small package from her bedside table and tucked it into her evening bag.

The hotel rooms were individual huts along a beach. A warm breeze stroked Miranda's bare arms as she walked to the cabin her son Tom was sharing with Craig.

Craig was putting gel in his hair while Tom tied his shoelaces. 'Are you boys okay?' Miranda asked. The question was superfluous. They were both tanned and happy after a day spent windsurfing and waterskiing.

Tom was not really a little boy any more. He had grown two inches in the last six months, and he had stopped telling his mother everything. It made her sad. For twelve years she had been all in all to him. He would continue to be dependent on her for a few more years, but the separation was beginning.

She left the boys and went to the next hut. Sophie was sharing with Caroline, but Caroline had already left and Sophie was alone. She stood at her wardrobe in her underwear, choosing a dress. Miranda saw with disapproval that she was wearing a sexy black half-bra and matching thong panties. 'Has your mother seen that outfit?' Miranda said.

'She lets me wear what I like,' Sophie said sulkily.

Miranda sat on a chair. 'Come here, I want to talk to you.'

Reluctantly, Sophie sat on the bed. She crossed her legs and looked away.

'I'd really prefer your mother to say this but, as she's not here, I'll have to.'

'Say what?'

'I think you're too young to have sexual intercourse. You're fifteen. Craig is only sixteen.'

'He's nearly seventeen.'

'Nevertheless, what you're doing is actually illegal.'

'Not in this country.'

Miranda had forgotten they were not in the UK. 'Well, anyway, you're too young.'

Sophie made a disgusted face and rolled up her eyes. 'Oh, God.'

'I knew you'd be ungracious, but it had to be said,' Miranda persisted.

'Well, now you've said it,' Sophie rejoined rudely.

'However, I also know that I can't force you to do what I say.'

Sophie looked surprised. She had not been expecting concessions.

Miranda took the package out of her evening bag. 'So, if you decide to disobey me, I want you to use these condoms.' She handed them over.

Sophie took them wordlessly. Her face was a picture of astonishment.

Miranda stood up. 'I don't want you getting pregnant when you're in my care.' She went to the door.

As she went out, she heard Sophie say: 'Thanks.'

       *   *   *

Grandpa had reserved a private room in the hotel restaurant for the ten members of the Oxenford family. A waiter went around pouring champagne. Sophie was late. They waited a while for her, then Grandpa stood up, and they all went quiet. 'There's steak for dinner,' he said. 'I ordered a turkey, but apparently it escaped.'

They all laughed.

He went on in a more sombre tone. 'We didn't really have a Christmas last year, so I thought this one should be special.'

Miranda said: 'And thank you for bringing us, Daddy.'

'The last twelve months have been the worst year of my life, and the best,' he went on. 'None of us will ever completely get over what happened at Steepfall one year ago today.'

Craig looked at his father. He certainly would never recover. One eye was permanently half-closed, and the expression on his face was amiably blank. He often seemed just to tune out, nowadays.

Grandpa went on: 'Had it not been for Toni, God alone knows how it would have ended.'

Craig glanced at Toni. She looked terrific, wearing a chestnut-brown silk dress that showed off her red hair. Grandpa was nuts about her. He must feel almost the same way I do about Sophie, Craig thought.

'Then we had to relive the nightmare twice more,'

Grandpa said. 'First with the police. By the way, Olga, why do they take statements that way? They ask you questions, and take down your answers; then they write out something that isn't what you said, and is full of mistakes, and doesn't sound like a human being at all, and they call it your statement.'

Olga said: 'The prosecution likes things phrased a certain way.'

'I was proceeding in a westerly direction, and so on?'

'Yes.'

Grandpa shrugged. 'Well, then we had to live it all over *again* during the trial, and we had to sit and listen to suggestions that somehow *we* were at fault for injuring people who had come into our house and attacked us and tied us up. Then we had to read the same stupid innuendoes in the newspapers.'

Craig would never forget it. Daisy's advocate had tried to say that Craig had attempted to murder her, because he had run over her while she was shooting at him. It was ludicrous, but for a few moments in court it had sounded almost plausible.

Grandpa went on: 'The whole nightmare reminded me that life is short, and I realized that I should tell you all how I felt about Toni and waste no more time. I need hardly say how happy we are. Then my new drug was passed for testing on humans, the future of the company was secured, and I was able to buy another Ferrari – and driving lessons for Craig.'

They laughed, and Craig flushed. He had never told anyone about the *first* time he had dented the car. Only Sophie knew. He was still embarrassed and guilty about it.

He thought he might confess when he was really old, like thirty or something.

'Enough of the past,' said Grandpa. 'Let's drink a toast. Merry Christmas, everybody.'

They all said: 'Merry Christmas.'

Sophie came in as the first course was being served. She looked wonderful. She had put her hair up and wore small dangling earrings. She looked so mature, at least twenty. Craig's mouth went dry at the thought that she was his girl.

As she passed his chair, she stooped and whispered in his ear: 'Miranda gave me some condoms.'

He was so surprised that he spilled his champagne. 'What?'

'You heard,' she said, and she took her seat.

He smiled at her. He had his own supply, of course. Funny old Aunt Miranda.

Grandpa said: 'What are you grinning at, Craig?'

'Just happy, Grandpa,' he said. 'That's all.'

Acknowledgements

I was privileged to visit two laboratories with BSL4 facilities. At the Canadian Science Center for Animal and Human Health in Winnipeg, Manitoba, I was helped by Stefan Wagener, Laura Douglas, and Kelly Keith; and at the Health Protection Agency in Colindale, London, by David Brown and Emily Collins. Further advice on BSL4 laboratories and procedures came from Sandy Ellis and George Korch.

On security and biosecurity I was advised by Keith Crowdy, Mike Bluestone, and Neil McDonald. For insight into possible police responses to biohazards, I talked to Assistant Chief Constable Norma Graham, Superintendent Andy Barker and Inspector Fiona Barker, all of the Central Scotland Police in Stirling.

On gambling I spoke to Anthony Holden and Daniel Meinertzhagen, and I was permitted to read the typescript of David Anton's book *Stacking the Deck: Beating America's Casinos at their own Game*.

Many of the above experts were located for me by Daniel Starer of Research for Writers in New York City.

For comments on drafts of the book I'm grateful to my editors Leslie Gelbman, Phyllis Grann, Neil Nyren, and Imogen Taylor; to my agents Al Zuckerman and Amy Berkower; to Karen Studsrud; and to my family, especially Barbara Follett, Emanuele Follett, Greig Stewart, Jann Turner, and Kim Turner.

www.panmacmillan.com